The

Collected Stories of

Jack Schaefer

Books by
J<small>ACK</small> S<small>CHAEFER</small>

Shane

First Blood

The Big Range

The Canyon

The Pioneers

Company of Cowards

The Kean Land and Other Stories

Old Ramon (*for children*)

Monte Walsh

The Great Endurance Horse Race

Stubby Pringle's Christmas (*for children*)

Heroes Without Glory: Some Goodmen of the Old West

The Collected Stories of Jack Schaefer

The
Collected Stories of
Jack Schaefer

With an introduction by Winfield Townley Scott

Houghton Mifflin Company Boston
The Riverside Press Cambridge
1966

Contents

Contents

Introduction by Winfield Townley Scott

J ACK SCHAEFER is a story-teller, as Sherwood Anderson liked to describe himself. Sometimes his narrator says right out that he is telling a story, and over and over again we get narrative as drama projected through character. This is an older fashion than the evocation of delicate mood so prevalent in recent American short stories. And so Schaefer has not been generally recognized for what he is: a master of a particular genre.

Misapprehension about his work has been aggravated by the fact that the locale which repeatedly lures him is the American West, the West in its final, late-nineteenth-century vigor, or just fading out of that vigor and represented by a single sturdy but ancient survivor of the good old days. Thus Jack Schaefer may be thought of as a "writer of westerns," but in the usual sense of the phrase this is a misnomer. The serious intention of his writing—and that is its intention even when he writes, as he sometimes does, hilarious humor—has nothing whatsoever to do with the "shoot-'em-ups" so dear to minor movies and television melodrama. Such trash is false to the history of the American West. Schaefer, on the other hand, is a researcher, a scholar of that history, and his talents are intensely focused to dramatize its truth in fiction, to tell stories about it.

He himself has put it clearly: "I like to write," he says, "about the wide open spaces when they were still open and their wideness could enter into the people, some of the people, who left life's footprints on them." He declares that throughout his stories "the essential purpose is the same . . . to establish a distinct and individual major character and pit him against a specific human problem and show how he rose to meet it." Realism and romance, he admits, "run hand-in-hand," but many of his stories evolve from "an actual incident of recorded fact." In short, his bases are solid.

Is there a literary tradition behind Schaefer? I am sure so. His work has been compared, with some justification, to that of the author of *The Virginian,* Owen Wister. But a closer ancestor is Stephen Crane. Certainly Schaefer flourishes in a line that can be traced from "The Bride Comes to Yellow Sky," that story so especially admired by Willa Cather and Ford Madox Ford. Crane's method looks simple, though of course it is not. The reporting is straight and sensitive and careful; detail upon detail is set forth; the feel, the atmosphere, of a train, a place, and an era are built up as though it were casually done; there is no prettiness; each sentence is laid on with a craftsman's ingenuity for building character and incident. This is Jack Schaefer's method.

As Carl Van Vechten said of Crane: "He was not primarily a novelist. His gifts were his intense perception and realization of what he had briefly seen or imagined, his bright freedom from dragging illusions, his insistence on writing about what really happened or must have happened, his mastery of lightning images. He was a story-teller without nonsense, a kind of poet among story-tellers."

Much of that praise is descriptive of Jack Schaefer's style, which also merits it. Incidentally, isn't his famous *Shane* Schaefer's *Red Badge of Courage?* I do not imply derivation, only an indigenous tradition renewed in his way by Schaefer. I was not surprised, on asking him, that he admires Stephen Crane: but then, who that loves American literature does not?

The ambition of the stories here collected, therefore, is literature, and the achievement of it is frequent enough to warrant Schaefer a distinctive place among writers of the contemporary American short story; possibly a unique place.

Once in a while he may bring a last bleeding drop of sentiment out of a situation which may not quite carry *that* much. Once in a while, as in "Stubby Pringle's Christmas," his usually excellent gift for writing in the human voice stalls in a self-conscious stylization, a mistaken hunch (so at least it seems to me) as to how to clothe the story. Perhaps once in a while, too, we may feel a shade unconvinced by an overplay of the insistence that there were giants in the earth: the urge to believe, as someone says of Jeremy Rodock, "They don't grow men like that around here any more." And once in a while, of course, Schaefer draws a very long bow; but there we cannot fault him, for the tradition is the American tall story. "Cooter James" and "Cat Nipped" and "Nate Bartlett's Store" are samples of wonderful comedy in just that droll fashion of yarn-spinning.

Most of the time in reading these stories we are the happy recipients of clear, functional writing, authentic dialogue, and a speed of narrative enclosed within a thoughtfulness of tone.

Given the era which fascinates Schaefer, there is often in his stories an elegiac music. The mood is of the end of an era.

In "The Old Man," young Jerry Linton:

> Walking to school he saw the other houses in their neat rectangles of yards, the squared corners of the streets laid out in regular blocks, and he knew that almost everywhere out beyond the town were the neat sectioned farms with their neat cultivated fields and pastures, almost everything here and out there neat and decent and respectable. It was not always like that. Indians once roamed even this tamed land at will. And buffalo. Men had made it the way it was, men like his father, steady and dependable, careful with figures, planning ahead. And suddenly he knew, knew in real knowing not just as an idea taught in class, that other men had come first, men who didn't stick to roads and who knew Indians and fought them and sometimes even lived with them and could bring in eleven hundred buffalo hides in a single season. The wind drifting in from the west was not just the wind any more. Maybe that blowing against his cheek came from way off, beyond this Minnesota, from beyond the far Black Hills near the Devil's Tower where the old man had killed a mountain lion once or even up in the real mountains themselves where Boone Helm lay buried with a rope-broken neck.

Some of the stories present the twilight aftermath; others, the immediacy of those tough but fragrant days. In both worlds there is always the delineation of character. In "Old Anse" and "Salt of the Earth" we get—a favorite theme of Schaefer's—an apotheosis of brave independence, of stubborn hardihood, of a kind of passionate loyalty and integrity. In the stories called by their names, "Kittura Remsberg" and "Hugo Kertchak, Builder," two who might well have belonged to Willa Cather, we have a sturdiness of indomitable personality that survives illness or age or diminished fortune. And sometimes the individual—determined, solitary, unvanquished—is set within haunting atmospherics of desert exile, as in "The Fifth Man."

The narrator of "Enos Carr" puts it this way:

> I'm writing about this Enos Carr character. Not a story, not anything like that, because it doesn't have any form and hasn't any action and doesn't get anywhere. Just an account of what we saw of him and learned about him. I'm writing it because I collect odd characters, like to get them down on paper. They're quaint, interesting. They're not important because a world made up of odd characters would be a weird one to live in and probably couldn't even function at all. Matter of fact, studying odd characters can help you appreciate the normal everyday capable people who keep the world wagging on a fairly even keel, a place where most of us can earn a decent living and get some enjoyment out of life.

The passage illustrates some of the beguilements of Jack Schaefer's carefully informal way with words, and how by a turn of irony he begins to sketch in his narrator.

Given the locale, we have men set against a vast landscape, men close to animals—most often horses, but sometimes a bear, and men and women set against their own kind, for better or for worse. The stage is primitive. Because Schaefer seeks his drama of a lost world through typical or exceptional human beings, his stories legitimately are rich with moral values. These are within the situation (not preached about), and they are solved. Who can forget Sergeant Houck's decision as to what to do about the white woman and her Indian child? Or, to cite only one other example, who could not be moved in "Jacob" by the tenderness of recognition between the boy and the Indians?

I return, finally, not to the material *per se* but to the admirable craftsmanship. To Schaefer's sense for what a place looks, feels, smells like, and the descriptive evocation which is an important part of the distinction of his prose. The reader feels the silence of a town on a hot afternoon, inhales the shadowy stillness of a barroom, watches the three or four customers drowsing—now and then taking a shot of whiskey, and hears the clomp of boots approaching on the boardwalk outside. Because all this has been skillfully brought to us, we are there. A world has been preserved, has been summoned alive again, and it becomes a part of our knowing and not just an idea taught in class. This is the magic of story-telling. And here is a book filled with it.

WINFIELD TOWNLEY SCOTT

The

Collected Stories of

Jack Schaefer

Major Burl

"YOU CALL this a town?" says the man from Horner's Crossing. "Why, a thirsty jackass that knew its way around wouldn't stop off here to sniff a rain-barrel." He stomps out so heavy the whole shack shakes.

The five men left there look at the floor. "Hell 'n' Marier," says Pumper Pete. "One of us ought of called him on that."

Big Joe squirms in his chair and takes to pushing his bottle with a finger on the table in front of him.

"Yep," says Jim Farrango. "Burl's Gulch is more a town already than the Crossing'll ever be."

"Certain is," says Pumper Pete. "An' that galoot talks thataway an' nary one of us pips a squeak. What's wrong with us?"

"I'll tell you what's wrong," says Major Burl, puffing slow behind his bar. "I can speak free about the Gulch because it's more my place than anyone else's. Bears my name. Tagged after my emporium here. I'll stretch up and be counted in it any time the trumpet blows. But it ain't a town."

"Easy, Major," says Pumper Pete. "Maybe you have got more sense than the rest of us boggled together. Leastways you can stitch words in a string so they sound mighty important. But you're stumblin' now. The Gulch has everything a town needs. There's your place here an' there's Murray's store. There's a stage stoppin' in an' gold goin' out. There's eleven claims staked close and maybe a dozen more up the creek. Must be more'n forty head of us when the tally's full."

"And a couple women," says Jim Farrango.

"Certain are," says Pumper Pete. "My old woman an' Big Joe's squaw."

"We've got all that," says the Major. "We're even marked as a post stop. Burl's Gulch is on the map. But it ain't a town."

"So," says Storekeeper Murray. "So what is a town, Major?"

"A town," says the Major, "is more than a batch of buildings. It's more than a place where people live. It's a place where they live together. It's a place where things happen. Things that count."

"Plenty things happen here," says Pumper Pete. "You know that, Major. Most of 'em happen here in this shack."

"Those things don't count," says the Major. "They ain't permanent and abiding. A town is a place where things happen that make folks know they're partners in this ornery business of living and all wear the same brand of the human race."

"Good stitchin'," says Pumper Pete. "But too fancy for my mind. Try it simple. Name off a thing or two."

The Major tugs at his chins. "What we need," he says, "is something to pull us together. Might be a parade could do it."

He heaves to his feet behind his bar. "Dogdamn it, men," he says, "we'll do it! A week come Wednesday will be the Fourth! We'll unfurl Old Glory over Burl's Gulch with a parade they'll hear all the way to the Crossing!"

Inside the week the plans are pushing a finish. The Major gives the orders and the Committee of Three sees that the roster is complete. Pumper Pete does the talking. Jim Farrango and Big Joe supply the backing. They line up every man in the Gulch and along the creek to the main bend. They are plenty persuasive, Pumper Pete talking fast with Jim on one side smiling quiet and rubbing the handle of the gun in his belt and Big Joe on the other side scowling straight ahead and cracking his big knuckles like his hands are itching to be doing something mean.

But once the idea gets around and across, not much persuading is needed. Seems as if the Gulchers have just been aching for the feel of being a town. The only catch that develops is when Woolhead Sam, handyman at Murray's store, offers his own ante. He wants to ride his mule in the procession and Jim Farrango balks.

"For myself," says Jim, "I wouldn't pay no mind. But my pappy home in Tennessee would rise out of his grave was I to ride in the same parade with a black man."

Sam looks sorrowful at Jim. He always likes to be near Jim ever since Jim puts a bullet through the whip arm of a teamster who is ragging him for being slow with a store order. Sam is little and bent and older than anyone knows. But he is a big man inside.

"Don't go afrettin', Jim," he says. "I'll just stand by an' watch. Somebody's got to do the yellin'."

Jim clamps teeth on his cigar and glares at the Major. "Damn it," he says, "Sam's a Gulcher too. Guess I can talk back to a spirit even if it's my pappy. Sam's in."

"He's in," says the Major. "He's riding that mule and carrying the colors. He's tipped us a notion too. Who ever heard of a parade that nobody watched? Pete, there's the spot for the womenfolk. We'll use my front steps for the reviewing stand. You get the ladies primed to cheer when we step right smart."

They step right smart all right when the time arrives. They form up the creek in the cedar woods. Smack on noon by Storekeeper Murray's stemwinder they come along the wagon tracks.

The Major is in the lead, sitting his sorrel in his best show at military posting, his belly bumping the saddle horn but his shoulders square and his face stern and dignified.

Woolhead Sam is next, bareback on his mule with the butt end of the flag stick poked in his left boot-top and the cloth folds waving over his head. Behind him is the Committee of Three, straight in their saddles and trying to make their horses step dainty and high.

Then comes Storekeeper Murray perched on the seat of his flatbed wagon, clucking to his team and holding with one hand to the silk topper he has dug somewhere out of his stock. He has trimmed the wagon in red and white cloth and has a blue-covered pedestal in the middle of it on which is fastened the stuffed eagle that usually sits on the top shelf behind his main counter.

The rest of the Gulchers follow, three abreast, scrubbed and brushed and greased till they almost shine in the sun. They are keeping fair time to the rhythm young Mel Osborn is beating out on a whiskey keg he has hung around his neck and bumping against his stomach as he walks.

The Major leads them to the lower ford and doubles them back to the reviewing stand. He eases off his horse and hoists himself to the top step beside the women. The men gather by the bottom step and he soars into fancy oratory. He starts with the thirteen colonies and the Declaration of Independence. He sweeps from the rock-ribbed coasts of Maine to the sun-swept slopes of California. He wraps himself and the Gulchers in the flag and makes even the stuffed eagle scream. When his breath is gone, he wipes his brow and drops to an ordinary pitch. "Well, boys," he says, "I've done my derndest. You take over."

Then all of them, forty-two by Pumper Pete's tally, unloose the huzzas. Guns pop out of pockets and belts and boot-tops and begin to pepper the tree branches. For a pair of minutes Burl's Gulch is one big echoing noise. The silence after is deep and impressive.

Everyone is still savoring it when the delegation arrives. The man from Horner's Crossing paces in front of his crew. He is a tall, well-stacked gent with a scratchy chuckle.

"We heard you peeping over here," he says. "Thought you might be celebrating the day. Thought you might be pleased to step over our way and find out what real celebrating is."

"Thank you, sir," says the Major. "I calculate you're just trying to be neighborly. But we're doing all right ourselves."

"Doing all right?" says the man from Horner's Crossing. "With this ragtag outfit and in this place? Why, I wonder," he says. "I wonder the flag wouldn't be ashamed to be flying around here."

A muttering grumble runs through the crowd of Gulchers. Jim Farrango straightens from a slouch against a tree. That quiet smile begins to play around his lips. Big Joe looms up from a squat on the steps. His big hands begin to curl into big knobby fists.

The man from Horner's Crossing teeters on his boot-soles, rocking from heel to toe and back. His chuckle scratches the air. He is prospecting for tumble-trouble and expects he has found it, and the thought is pleasing to him.

But Jim Farrango slumps against his tree again, the smile fading. Big Joe falls to studying the ground at his feet, letting his hands uncurl loose and limp.

Disappointment shows plain in the man from Horner's Crossing. "Creeping catfish," he says to his crew. "This place beats me. It ain't even got gumption." He stomps off with his crew trailing.

The Gulchers all look at the Major. He is puffing hard and pulling at his chins.

"Well, boys," he says at last, "our parade helped. Sort of put us under the flag, set us down as part of the U.S.A. But we ain't a real town yet."

"Are we licked, Major?" says Storekeeper Murray.

"Certain not," says Pumper Pete. "Name off another thing or two, Major."

"Maybe I can pan out a few more," says the Major. "But they won't assay much. Trouble is the Gulch ain't equipped yet for the things they do in real towns."

"Like what?" says Pumper Pete.

"Like——" says the Major. "Well, like a wedding."

"Hell 'n' Marier," says Pumper Pete. "You got to have a woman for that. One that ain't got a rope on her yet. Reckon we are licked."

"Reckon not," comes a voice from the gathering, piping high with embarrassment but proud too. "Reckon I can take care of that."

Everyone looks at Red Ed Storey. His face is grinning foolish under the rusty beard that scraggles around his chin and up to his ears.

"I got a woman coming to marry me," he says. "Coming on the next stage. A widow lady. Name of Hulda Munson."

Red Ed has never packed much weight in the Gulch before, being a mild man who has arrived late and keeps to himself most of the time. Now he is heavy in the public eye. His shack is rocking every evening with Gulchers offering advice. The Major himself rides all the way to the county seat to be sworn as a justice of the peace so he can perform the ceremony. The Gulch is more excited even than for the parade. The entire tally is determined Red Ed is tied tight and right.

Not a one is missing from the space in front of the Major's emporium when the stage rolls to a stop. Red Ed, uneasy in a starched collar, stands dignified as possible on the steps. Jim Farrango opens the stage door and this woman backs out and to the ground. She turns around. She is short and dumpy with a face like a batch of biscuit dough someone has been working on careless for quite a spell. There is a commotion on the steps and then Red Ed is tearing along the road as fast as he can go.

The woman watches bewildered while Jim Farrango takes her box from the driver and the stage starts off. She picks the Major as the most ample man in view.

"Can you tell me," she says, "where I will find Mr. Storey?"

"Madam," says the Major, bowing as far as his waist will let him, "Madam, that is Mr. Storey hightailing it up the road there."

She stares at the Major and then at the dust whirl that is Red Ed and then she lets a howl and is pounding in the other direction after the stage as fast as plump legs and a hobble skirt will allow. She sees she is losing and stops puffing in the wagon ruts.

She is so golplumed comical standing there, with her hat hanging lopsided over the bun on her head and her shoulders heaving, that chuckles are sprouting into guffaws, when sudden everyone realizes she is crying. The quick silence is so complete the sobs can be heard clear.

No one seems to know what to do. It is the Major shows what kind of a man he is.

"Jim," he says, "Jim, fetch her into my emporium here. Pete," he says, "you and Big Joe go corral that gallivanting galoot."

Red Ed is still struggling when they bring him in. The shack is full to bulging except for a small space in front of the Major, who has set a chair on a couple of boxes and heaved himself up into it. The woman is at one side of the space, flanked by Mrs. Pumper Pete and Big Joe's squaw. The men hustle Red Ed to the other side facing her. He shudders and pins his eyes to the floor.

"Mr. Storey," says the Major, slow and deliberate, "Mr. Storey, hereinafter to be referred to as Red Ed. Did you or did you not, in the run of epistolary communications with this woman, promise to make her your lawful wedded wife?"

Red Ed scratches busy behind one ear. "I 'fess it straight, Major," he says. "I give my word as per pen and paper right enough. To a woman, yes. But, by cracky, not to this woman."

"No?" says the Major, frowning firm. "Can you stake that? She's shown me the letter."

"Sure can," says Red Ed. He fishes in a hip pocket and hooks out a dog-eared picture card. "I been hiding this so as to surprise you boys. This here is my woman."

The men crowd around and whistles rise free. The woman on the card, smiling sweetly under a stylish bonnet, is the kind that any man, howsomever choosy, would be proud to let leave her slippers alongside his bed.

"Hand that here," says the Major. He studies it for a moment. "Red Ed," he says, owl solemn, "Red Ed Storey. Are you atrying to josh us?"

"Nary an ounce," says Red Ed. "I'm true talking. That there is my woman. Name of Hulda Munson."

"No," says the Major. "Hulda Munson is this woman standing here. That picture card is the light and glory of the American theeayter. Name of Miss Lillie Langtry."

"Certain is," says Pumper Pete, peering close. "Ed, you been took. Skedaddled up a tree."

"Madam," says the Major, turning to the woman, "we been prepared to use a little persuasion on Red Ed here to behave as a man should when he has spoke pretty to a woman. But it appears you tripped him with crooked dice."

The woman stares steady at the Major, but the blob of dough that is her chin is quivering.

"I never had a picture of my own," she says. "And he's no right to complain. Anyways, I wouldn't marry him iffen he scrooged down in the dirt. Here's what he sent me."

She fumbles in her handbag. She pulls out another picture card. The Major takes it and scowls terrific.

"I'll be broke to the ranks," he says, "if this ain't more of the same. It's the prime player of this whole age. Maurice Barrymore."

"Two of a kind," says Jim Farrango. "A pair of jokers. That's a poor play in any game."

"Maybe not," says the Major. "This is one time two jokers make a pat hand. She tries to fool Red Ed and he tries to fool her, and that stacks it even. Under the circumstances I calculate we can insist they meet the terms agreed and give us our wedding."

"No!" howls Red Ed. "Feed me pizen! But keep her away!"

They can scarce hear him because the woman is wailing her own tune. "No! Not that raggety brier patch. It don't even look like a man."

The Gulchers begin to mutter about feathers and a rail. They have been sighting ahead to a wedding. They take no enjoyment having it scratched. Things are shaping ugly when the Major takes hold again.

"Quiet, boys," he says. "This calls for tactics. Pete," he says, "you and Joe tote Ed here over to your place." He whispers brief in Pumper Pete's ear. "Madam," he says, "you step into my back room. Better do as I say. I'm the law hereabouts. Now the rest of you," he says, "you take care of yourselves outside for the next hour. Sashay back in here then and we'll proceed with the proceedings."

Punctual on the hour the shack is crowded again. The buzzing is loud, then fades as Pumper Pete and Big Joe show in the doorway. They are pulling a man between them. The other Gulchers look sharp and make out it is Red Ed. The bristles have been shaved away and the top thatch trimmed. There are nicks and red spots around his chin. But he looks younger, plenty cleaner, and almost presentable at a picnic.

The Major comes from the back room, the woman with him. She has shed her hat and her hair is blowing around her head kind of feminine and appealing. The Major climbs to his chair.

"Hulda Munson," he says, "rest your eyes on this man that was hiding behind the whiskers. He ain't one to make the ladies' hearts flutter special fast. But he's a man fair enough. He works reasonable steady. He don't drink more than a man ought. He has a good-paying claim upcreek and he ships dust regular."

The woman looks at Red Ed. You can see she is thinking new thoughts and not shying from them.

"Now," says the Major, waving at her. "Go bring in a piece of that culinary concoction you're keeping warm in my oven."

She promenades to the back room. In she comes again carrying on a plate a man-size slice of pie.

"Red Ed," says the Major, "take that pie. It's peach. Lucky I had a can for the filling. Eat it. Eat it slow and tasting. She rassled that pie together in a way to bug your eyes."

Red Ed picks the spoon from the plate and tries a bite. He chews it serious and reaches for another. He finishes the whole piece and scrapes for the crust crumbs.

"Red Ed," says the Major, dropping his voice deep, "do you figure you could eat pie like that for the rest of your natural life?"

"I could try," says Red Ed. He flicks his tongue to snag the last crumb from the corner of his mouth. "Yes, by cracky, I could."

"Hulda Munson," says the Major, "do you figure you could stand having this man cluttering your house and caring for your needs the rest of your natural life?"

"Well," she says, coy in her dumpy way, "well, now. If I pushed myself, maybe I might."

"Tactics wins!" shouts Pumper Pete. "Now for our wedding!"

They have their wedding right enough, the best the Major can boss. He decorates the ceremony with all the fancy words he can remember out of years of fancy talking. Storekeeper Murray dusts his fiddle and the men take turns twirling the women till the three of them beg out from worn feet. The toasts are often and hearty, more than sufficient to put a rosy tinge on the lamplight.

They keep it going pretty late. When the whole crowd has walked Red Ed and his new Mrs. home and helped bed them for the night, the regulars reassemble with the Major for a final round.

"Are we a town yet, Major?" says Storekeeper Murray.

The Major is sobering and has his thinking feet under him again.

"I feel better about the Gulch," he says. "A heap better. But I ain't positive." He snaps a finger sudden at Big Joe. "Joe, remember that ornery jumper from the Crossing. If he was here now and blame-talking the Gulch, what would you do?"

Big Joe tries to look fierce. He fails to make it.

"I know how he feels," says Jim Farrango. "Plant the critter here and set him to bragging and I'd be plumb irritated. I'd wish him a deck full of trouble. But I wouldn't feel any compelling call to deal it to him."

The Major wipes a hand across his face. "So we still miss," he says.

"After all that aimin'," says Pumper Pete. " 'Tain't fair."

"Not fair," says the Major. "But a fact. Must be we been trying to make something you just can't make. I reckon it's got to come natural, sort of grow out of things that happen of themselves."

The regulars meander home, quiet and heavy thinking. They go to bunk feeling mean and crawl out in the morning still tasting the bitter. The Gulch always takes its cue from them and the whole place slows to a dull pace. Three more claims are pegged and a barrel-built man arrives to set up a blacksmith and harness shop and this boosting of the tally hardly helps at all. Not even the news getting about that Mrs. Pumper Pete is expecting to do her share thataway too can whip up much interest.

The Gulch is a glum place these days when a man can walk the full stretch up the creek and never see any but sour faces. Arguments, the slipping into nasty kind, get to be frequent. The days are just days, one tagging another, none standing out special, and they drag past like that until the week of the big rain.

Monday afternoon it starts, a thin drizzle in the Gulch backed by a darkness up in the hills that must mean heavy rain where the thunderheads are hugging the high rocks. Tuesday it is going steady and most of the diggings are too mucky to be worked. By evening the Gulchers notice the creek has crept up a few feet and is throwing an ugly snarl where the current roils over the shallow spots.

Wednesday morning Storekeeper Murray, whose story-and-a-half hugs the bank, starts moving his stock to the loft as the first trickles creep through his floor boards. Jim Farrango sloshes along and comes in to lend a hand, remarking casual that his shack must be almost to the Missouri by now.

"Rocked me out of bed when she pulled loose," he says. "Just had time to jump clear before she took off. Sailed out of the hollow and headed downstream like Noah's Ark, half under and half showing."

He and Murray with Woolhead Sam helping stow the stuff dry. When they finish, the water is a foot deep around the counters, so they wade out and go upslope to the Major's emporium.

Quite a crowd is collected there. Two other shacks have departed cruising and the talk tells that more will be pulling anchor unless the creek falls mighty soon. The Major is busy chalking his bar for bunk space. The moment he sights Jim and Storekeeper Murray, he begins barking orders.

"Murray," he says, "take a squad here and scurry back to your place. Swim if you have to, but bring me a pile of blankets and a pack of victuals. Jim," he says, "organize a scouting party and work your way upstream. Some of the folks may——"

He stops short, caught by a screech outside coming faint through the drizzle and moving closer. There is a frantic clumping on the steps and Mrs. Red Ed stumbles through the doorway. She looks like a damp dishrag. She has been screeching so long her voice is almost gone, but she is unable to choke it to let real words out. Jim Farrango has to shake her by the shoulders to bring her out of it.

Red Ed, she makes plain at last, is trapped in the tunnel shaft he has driven into the gulch side behind their shack following a good vein into the rock. He has been worried about the rain weakening the side walls and gone in to shore them up and a slide has blocked the entrance. She is sure Red Ed has cashed his chips.

"Nonsense," says the Major. "No rock slide can squelch a Burl's Gulcher, 'specially an onery maverick as tough as Ed. We'll have him out in a jiffy. Forward, men. On the double."

He is wasting words. The others, Jim Farrango in the lead, are already trooping out the door at a fast trot. The Major is left to do the tagging, which is all a man of his girth can do when hurrying is required. By time he reaches Red Ed's place, puffing noisy but being gallant to the Mrs. by the arm, the rest of the tally is already assembled. They are gathered by the big blob of silt and broken stone that covers the entrance to the tunnel. Pumper Pete is on his knees, scrooging in the dirt with a little pickaxe. The others are standing around watching. Plenty of shovels are in sight, but the men are just leaning on them. The Major explodes.

"This ain't a teaparty!" he shouts. "Swing those shovels and start digging!"

Pumper Pete looks up. "Major," he says mild, "you don't know a tinker about this kind of work. Stand clear and close your yap." He pivots again to the dirt. In another moment he has uncovered the end of a wooden rail, part of the track Red Ed has been using to bring ore out of the tunnel. He taps it several times with the flat of the pickaxe. He bends to put his ear to the wood. He pulls up and shakes his head and taps again. He bends down. Everyone waits, so quiet only the steady drizzle on the tree leaves can be heard.

Sudden and sharp Pumper Pete jumps up. "Ed's alive!" he says. "Alive and atappin' in there! Hop it, boys! This hill's a bad one an' we'll have to work fast. Three at a time can ditch it to the shaft mouth. The rest of you clear that loose stuff above and drive a row of stakes to hold back any more that has a mind to start movin'."

They fall to, quiet and earnest. The first shift, Big Joe with a pick pacing a pair of husky shovelmen, hits the main digging through the slide.

The Major watches in a moody silence. He tries comforting Mrs. Red Ed and hovering protective by Mrs. Pumper Pete, who ought not be out in such weather in her interesting condition. He shoos them along with Big Joe's squaw into Red Ed's shack and gets them to steaming a wash boiler full of coffee. That kind of piddling doing fails to satisfy. He scours around till he finds a stray shovel and he joins the crew working on the loose slide above the tunnel. He can scarce bend enough to scoop the dirt, but he wheezes game at it.

Pumper Pete sights him fighting the shovel. "Major," he says, "quit that foolishness. You're blocking good diggers."

The Major knows the true when he hears it. He teeters down. "Dogdamn it, Pete," he says, "at a time like now a man's got to do something."

"Certain does," says Pumper Pete. "But no diggin' for you. There's too blame much of you an' all of it gets in the way. Chase on down the line and see how many buckets you can find. Soon as we ditch in deeper we'll have trouble haulin' the stuff out. Too mucky for barrows. A bucket brigade'll do it."

The Major puffs red. "Me!" he says. "You'd make me an errand boy!" He subsides in a slow dwindle. "Yes," he says, "yes. Was I you I'd do the same." He marches off, head up and blinking at the drizzle.

By time he comes back, the upper slide is staked tight. The ditching is close to the shaft mouth, which is uncovered enough to show it is caved part way in.

He can be heard a long ways acoming. He has buckets on ropes bouncing on his back and hanging from his arms and a stack of them upside down on his head. He shakes them in a clatter to the ground in front of Pumper Pete. "Buckets you have," he says. "And I've another little contribution to contribute." He peels his pockets and they pan four bottles of his best rum.

The smell that drifts through the drizzle as the rum joins the coffee in the boiler is enough to make muscles feel big. The mixture itself is positive power in a man. The Gulchers need the lift. They are into the long pull, the period when it's plug along without much progress showing at any particular time and a slump can set in all too easy. Now they settle to the work in a straight earnest, the buckets swinging down the line full from the digging shift and up empty in steady rhythm.

The hours creep past and the morning is gone and the hours creep past and the tunnel is clear maybe a dozen feet in. The opening is twice what it was before from the cave-in, but the rock formation roofing it seems to be holding. All the same, Pumper Pete keeps looking up anxious and bending his head close to the walls like he is listening for whisperings in the rock.

Big Joe is pacing the digging shift again, swinging his pick to loosen the small stuff and using it to pry the big rock chunks. He straightens sudden and lets out a whoop. The point has crashed through to open space beyond. Pumper Pete leaps to the spot. He scraggles a hole with his hands and shouts into it. Faint and a stretch farther a voice answers. The words are muffled in the inner blackness. Pumper Pete listens close. He swings around.

"Ed's pinned by a couple shoring posts," he says. "We'll have to go in and get him. An' fast. The whole hill back there is ready to slip."

He grabs the pick and chokes it short to tear at the hole. He has it about big enough for a man to crawl through when he jumps back, looking up. There is a shivering in the rock. Little cracks fan out from what must be bigger ones farther under out of sight.

He looks quick from one man to another. This is a volunteer job if it is to be done at all. He shakes his shoulders and turns to go himself. He is too late. Jim Farrango is brushing past him.

Jim disappears into the tunnel darkness and before any one of the others thinks to move another man is scrambling after him. It is Woolhead Sam, so frantic in a hurry that he slips back and makes it through the hole only on a second try.

Waiting is a hard doing while the rumbling swells far and deep through the inner rock and the dull sound of chunks falling comes through the hole. Then Jim Farrango's voice is heard, clipped and plain inside.

"We've got him," he is saying. "But he's fainted out cold. Grab aholt."

Red Ed's head and shoulders appear in the hole, limp and bobbing on the dirt. Big Joe hauls him through in one big heave.

The rumbling is becoming a thunder now, and Jim's voice is small over it. "Get going, Sam. Hop into that hole afore I kick you into it."

"No, sir, Jim," they can hear Sam say. "You got to go first. This here rock ain't waitin' for——"

The thunder cuts the rest. Then Jim Farrango's head pops into sight in the hole. He looks surprised and mad and is trying to pull back when Big Joe gets his shoulders and yanks him through.

The thunder is a sustained roar now. The hill seems to shake and settle on itself far inside. The sound drops and dies away in pieces and silence creeps to take and hold the whole world.

It breaks with Jim Farrango cursing soft to himself. "Trumped my ace," he says. "The damned black monkey. Pushed me."

Not much digging is needed this time. They find Sam just beyond the first barrier. He is caught between two big rocks, twisted in a way that tells the full story at once. They carry him to the clear and lay him on the pine needles. His eyes open once and roll till they sight Jim Farrango standing stern to one side. "You all right, Jim?" he says, and his head drops sideways in the last stillness.

They are a wet and dirty crew slogging the mud down creek. Jim Farrango hoists Sam's body to a shoulder and steps off deliberate, and though he has heavy going no one is fool enough to offer help. The Major sends young Mel Osborn ahead to rassle together a blaze in his fireplace. The emporium is beginning to warm when they get there. They crowd in till the entire tally is pressing the walls.

The Major mounts his chair and tunes his vocal cords. He is just getting under way when he stops short. Mrs. Pumper Pete has let out a gasp and clutched Pumper Pete so sudden he has squawked in surprise.

From his high point the Major takes in the situation. "Ladies," he says, "my emporium is at your disposal. The stove, properly coaxed, will heat water as fast as required. Clean flour sacking I use for towels will be found on the shelves." He beams on his brother Gulchers. "There are times," he says, "when words and men are alike useless. This is one."

He shoos them out and follows, dragging Pumper Pete with him. They hunch on the porch and steps, walking careful to avoid Wool-head Sam's body where Jim has laid it out of the wet. The Major pauses by it.

"Might be we'd be rushing things," he says. "But there's no reason we can't give Sam a good funeral right now."

He likes the notion and starts organizing at once and everyone enlists willing. They lay Sam away in a packing case floated from

Murray's store. They lower it in a grave dug in the pine grove where Sam liked to smoke a pipe of a lazy evening after chores. They are too busy to notice that the drizzle has dried out of the sky and the afternoon air is brightening clear.

When the case hits bottom, the Major makes to unwind some of his prize oratory. Jim Farrango halts him with a hand on his arm. Jim plants his feet at the grave head.

"Fancy words don't go with Sam," he says. "Might be these will do." He puts his head back and looks up through the tree branches. "There wasn't much of Sam even when he stood tall. But he was man all through. Fate dealt him a mighty poor hand. But he played what cards he had right." Jim reaches in a pocket and brings out a deck. He riffles it and picks out the ace of spades. He steps around the grave and to a pine about twenty paces away and wedges the card in the bark cracks. He steps back to his spot. His hand moves and his gun shows in it and all in almost the same flash five shots shatter the air.

Everyone stares at the card. A jagged hole has blotted the center spade. Jim looks down at the long box. "Sam always did admire my shooting," he says. He reloads the gun slow and silent. He picks up a shovel and starts throwing dirt into the grave. Sunlight comes filtering through the trees and plays on him working there and others join him to give Sam a final covering.

The Major has been still long enough. His voice rolls like a ferry foghorn. "From dust we come. To dust we return. And so man——"

"Shush," says Storekeeper Murray. "Something's doing with the womenfolk."

The Major turns to look at his place off through the trees. Mrs. Red Ed is on the porch waving vigorous. Pumper Pete is leading the stampede in her direction.

The men gather at the foot of the steps, staring up. They wait for Pumper Pete to do the talking. He tries and gulps frantic and tries again, but his throat is cramped tight. Mrs. Red Ed smiles hearty at him. Just as she points inside, they all hear it, a thin and new-sounding wail, kind of astonished and angry at the world, that starts small and grows and then ends in a satisfied gurgle. Pumper Pete makes a terrible effort. "What's the brand?" he says.

Mrs. Red Ed smiles again. "It's a girl," she says. "You can see her soon as we get things ready." She disappears inside.

Pumper Pete's legs are wobbling. He grins foolish and sits down on the steps. The others are joshing him when the delegation arrives.

The man from Horner's Crossing advances ahead of his crew and takes a stand, hands on hips.

"Halloo," he says. "What's the to-doing over here? From the look of things you're in bad shape. Sort of rained out."

"Rained in," says the Major. "I'd say we're rained in to good shape."

The man from Horner's Crossing stares around at the whole soggy scene. His scratchy chuckle claws along the Gulchers' nerves.

"Why," he says, "you'd shove a man to laugh wasn't he sorry for you. You never had much here worth a brag. Now you've got just about nothing at all."

Big Joe busts out of the crowd of Gulchers. He is moving steady and purposeful and he looms bigger than he ever has before. His eyes are shining and his mouth is twisting and everyone can see that at last he has something to say. He stops, hard on his heels, and works troubled at it and then he has it. "We got a baby," he says.

He moves again, straight for the man from Horner's Crossing. That man grins delighted and waits, rocking on his feet with arms ready. They tangle like a brace of bulls, heaving to throw each other till the sweat streams from them both, then breaking to hammer each other till they have to drag out for breath. Sudden the man drops his head and rams it bitter into Big Joe's midriff, sending him back and down on his buttocks. Immediate the man dives at him, but Big Joe rolls aside and the man lands sprawling. Big Joe is up first and as the man scrambles for footing, Big Joe smashes a fist to the side of his head and puts him down complete.

The Gulchers cheer. The Crossing delegation mutters mad. Hard words are passing when the man pushes to his feet, shaking his head to clear the cobwebs.

"Stop the fussing," he tells his crew. "I was spoiling for a fight and this overgrown elk gave it to me. He licked me square and he's the first ever did and I ain't ashamed of it. A tussle like that can knock the grouch out of me for a long spell. It's time we made tracks for home."

He points a friend-like look at Big Joe. "You've got a baby," he says. "Maybe you've even got the makings of a town."

He stomps off, leading his crew, a man who can take a licking and not lose in the taking.

The Gulchers watch him out of sight. "Give him time," says the Major, "and that man will turn out a good neighbor. But he's wrong on that last."

The Major gathers them all in one warm glance. "We've got more than the makings," he says. "I feel it in my marrow the way Big Joe did a few moments ago. Today did it. Life ending and life beginning and all of us pulling together on a tough job. We're a town, boys. Now let's sashay in and have a peek at Miss Pumper Pete."

Miley Bennett

IN THE morning I saddled the gray and rode into town, not hurrying because I didn't like what I was going to do. But I had thought this all out after the trial was over, and I couldn't see any other answer that would let me sleep at night.

There was a chill in the air and that was good because I could be wearing my blue denim work jacket and no one would think that strange. As a matter of fact, few people were stirring on the street and not a one paid attention to me at all.

I stepped on the low porch of the solid frame building that served as marshal's office and jail. I opened the door and went through and to the railing that sliced the front room in half. Marshal Eakins sat at his rolltop desk behind it, finishing a cup of coffee from the pot topping the one-burner oil stove on a table in the right corner.

"Morning, John," he said. "Think I'll have another cup. Join me?"

I shook my head.

"Don't take to drinking alone," he said. "Not even coffee. Company tangs it better."

I shook my head again.

"First time in here for you, John," he said. "Bringing me business?"

"No," I said. "I just want to go in there and talk to him."

Eakins seemed surprised. "Funny company for you to be keeping," he said.

"It's a free country," I said.

"Damned if it ain't," he said. "You can have five minutes. So the rules say."

I swung the little gate and went through.

"Before you go in," he said, "I'll have to relieve you of this." He lifted the jacket on my right side and slipped the gun out of the holster and laid it on his desk. "No weapons inside," he said, unlocking the door to the back part of the building. "Except on me or a sworn deputy."

He led to the middle one of the three barred cubicles and unlocked this and let me in and locked it again after me.

"Not too particular about time," he said. "A little hazy on how long is five minutes. Whistle if you want out sooner."

I stood with my back to the bars until he was out in the front room again. Miley Bennett sat on a stool below the lone high little window of the back wall. He was staring at the floor and he needed a shave, looking smaller and more meager and burnt-eyed than the day before at the trial, and he was staring at the floor.

I sat on the bunk slung by straps from the right side bars. He was staring at the floor, his eyes following a split in one of the planks, along and back, along and back.

"There's a new man out on the range, Miley," I said. "He's rounding up what's left of them, going to drive them over to the Association's spread near Meeteetsee where they'll be safe. He's treating them right."

He wouldn't say a word to me. You couldn't tell he even knew I was there. I lifted the straw-stuffed burlap pillow and put the gun under it, the one I had hanging on a cord around my shoulder and under my left arm beneath the blue denim jacket. I patted the pillow and I saw his eyes flick over quickly at my hands and go back to the crack in the thick plank.

I went to the front bars and whistled. Eakins came and let me out and led to the front room, locking the door again behind us. He handed me the gun from the desk and I slipped it into the holster.

"Changed your mind about the coffee?" he said.

"No," I said. I went outside and swung up on the gray and started home. The sun was a little higher up the sky and the air was warming. I took off the jacket and folded it and tucked it under the front of the saddle.

Yes, I gave Miley Bennett the gun.

But, then, I knew what he would do with it.

I guess you'll have to let me tell this in my own way. There's no one else can tell it, not so it comes out right. I guess I'll just have to hope you understand what I mean. And how I felt.

The first time I saw Miley Bennett he was jogging steadily along my inner fence line on his burro. Small as he was, he was oversize on the tiny beast. I had just finished washing the supper dishes, plate and cup, and stepped out on the porch of my two-room frame ranchhouse and I saw him, legs almost dragging, head bouncing.

He came right up to the house, slid off the burro, stepped on the porch, straightened the whole five-foot—well, maybe five-foot two or three—of him and grinned at me.

"The name is Bennett," he said. "Miley Bennett. Have you got any tobacco about the place?"

I had. And I had enough politeness or plain curiosity to ask this pint-size package of queer humanity in to smoke a pipeful with me. Things got mighty lonesome when your nearest neighbor was some two miles away and you were working hard to get a place in shape so you could have it ready and stock it before winter came down out of the mountains.

He was a talker, the first and only of his kind I ever knew to be. In half an hour I had a good handful of facts.

He was a sheepherder. He was herding sheep for one of the Association outfits with headquarters at Thermopolis. They had outfitted him and sent him off with a flock of eight hundred to graze them all spring and summer on government range. He was new at it then, so new that he took the job. It was four months later now, and he had worked his way, as near as I could judge from his talk, to a valley five miles above my place. The supply wagon that was supposed to stop by every six weeks or so was overdue. He had run out of tobacco two days ago and stood it as long as he could. He had left the sheep bedded for the night with the dogs and poked the burro into taking him in search of some he could borrow and someone who might bring him a supply from a next trip to the nearest town.

Some queer instinct must have headed him in my direction, kept him from the other places he might have hit. He certainly was an innocent one.

Half an hour seemed to be all he would allow himself. Call it one good pipeful. With a pokebag packed from my canister in his pocket and a promise I would have a supply soon in his mind, he became fidgety and stopped looking straight at me when he talked.

"Got to be going," he blurted suddenly. "Got to be getting back quick as I can."

"It'll be full dark before you get there," I said. "Are you sure you can find the way?"

He was at the door. "I'll find it. Or Beulah will. She can always find her way back to camp." He looked at me quickly and away. "You see, I've got to. The sheep are depending on me. I told them I'd be back early."

I listened to the soft little hoofbeats dropping away in the dusk and I thought of that funny frog-faced little man riding his burro through strange country in the darkness. And I began to realize just how innocent he was.

He probably thought he had a good job, was getting good pay. The pay part at least would be right. Members of the Sheepmen's Association were paying good wages for herders—when they could get them. They had to. Few men who knew what was what would take on the work at any price. Not in this section of the newly organized State where the cattlemen had been running beef stock, mostly on wide open range, for plenty of years and had dominant influence all along the line. Most cattlemen hated sheep and any-one who had anything to do with them, claimed they ruined the range. Sheep ate the grass, crown and all, right down to the roots, not just cropping the way cattle did, and they bunched together so closely and worked over the ground so thoroughly that when they moved on it was mighty bare, knocked out for the rest of the season. Some ranchers said they left a bad smell in the ground so that cattle would never go back where they had grazed. I think that was exag-gerated, but it shows how far some men would go in their thinking.

Sheep didn't bother me. I was a newcomer to this Territory with some fairly new ideas. I knew the open range wouldn't last, would be taken over by homesteaders and carved up by the creeping fence lines. I had seen it all happen before back in the Dakotas before I moved on to this new State of Wyoming. I knew you would make out better in the long run with a small herd held by fences, with your own pastures you could improve. You could control your breeding and feed right in the winter, get better grade stuff with hardly any losses. I had my land and my first fences. A consignment of low-slung Herefords would be along in about a month. The only thing I'd want from the open range would be some hay to add to that I'd clip from my own pasture. Sheep didn't worry me any.

They did worry the old-style ranchers. Worried them and made them mad. They had been running cattle in their own way a long time and didn't see any reason why they shouldn't keep right on as they always had. These men and their kind controlled the State Government. It didn't mean a thing to them that the free grass belonged to the Federal Government and that the Federal laws made no distinction between cattle and sheep. They did, and they intended to enforce it, and they had been finding ways. Sheep had been killed and flocks stampeded. I knew of two herders found dead back in the hills and several more beaten badly. Miley Bennett's was the only flock I had heard about anywhere around that year.

A week went past and he didn't appear. There was a three-pound can of tobacco waiting for him in the kitchen. It represented a cash outlay to me and I wanted to collect. Maybe that was why or maybe I was just plain curious again. Anyway, I saddled the gray late one afternoon, tied the can in a bag behind the saddle, tucked the Winchester in the worn scabbard, and rode out looking for him. I found him about where I figured. He was warming a can of beans over a wood fire and they smelled good and tasted the same.

The sheep were a hundred yards away where the ground was packed like they had been spending the night there for quite a while. They were in a tight bunch with two dogs patrolling, one old and knowing and taking this easy, the other a youngster wasting energy and acting excited despite a noticeable limp. Miley was haggard like a man needing sleep. He seemed pleased to see me and not just for the tobacco.

"What's wrong with the dog?" I said when the coffee was in the tin cup he handed me.

"Murderers," he said. "Damn sneaking murderers. Wolves. They got three of my sheep the other night and damn near killed the one dog. The other one's a coward, must have stayed out of reach."

"He's not a coward," I said. "He's sensible. A wolf can kill a dog in about one slice. Have you seen them?"

"You bet I've seen them," he said. "Three of them. They came sneaking back the next night, last night. Not close enough for a shot, though. They won't get any more of my sheep. I won't let them. But I thought they weren't ever around this time of year."

"They come down out of the timber sometimes," I said. "There's a bounty on them. You want me to stay and see if we can scare them back tonight? Two guns are better than one." I was thinking of my own cattle coming. Wolves had a taste for calves. I was thinking he wouldn't be much good at this kind of thing and of the small shotgun leaning against a nearby rock. A wolf would just laugh at a nuisance like that. He must have known what I was thinking.

"Hey, would you?" he said. "But let me show you something. I use that shotgun for snakes." He threw the empty bean can as far as he could out on the sod. He crawled into his little pup tent and came out with an old Army Hotchkiss. "I've been practicing ever since I started this job," he said.

He hit that can, a jagged chunk of tin bouncing farther away each time, four shots out of the five.

"You'll do," I said. "If you can do the same when your sights are down on a wolf."

He could all right. And he could lie absolutely quiet on his belly behind a boulder, patient as you had to be often in this country, for more than two hours on the windward side of the flock, which was the way the wolves would come. He drilled his clean, just behind the shoulder, and it dropped in its tracks. Mine stumbled with a broken leg and scrambled up and I had to pump in another shot quickly or it would have gotten away. The third one was off so fast, belly low and over a knoll, that we didn't have a chance at it.

"You won't have any trouble with that last one," I said when we had the ears and were back where the dogs were tied. "It'll head for the timber now."

Miley was so excited he could hardly settle down. He had to go over to his sheep and tell them all about it before he could sit by the fire I had got going again. Then he talked like he had a lot of words dammed inside him that had to break loose. I filled in behind the facts I already knew.

He was born and grew up back East in the factory badlands of

New Jersey across the Hudson from the human beehives of Man-
hattan. His father was a factory hand and he was one of nine kids,
and they rarely had full meals, and they lived on the streets as much
as they did in the old tenement. He was the runt of the family. I
guess he was slapped around plenty by his brothers as well as the
neighborhood gang because he pulled out when he was sixteen and
went on his own, setting pins in a bowling alley and living in a loft
room the operator let him use.

After that he must have had a couple of dozen different jobs in
nearly as many years, none of them amounting to much. He was
just a little guy lost among the thousands of others, puttering
through life and getting slapped around always by the bigger guys.
The best job he ever had, he seemed to think, was as second bartender in a Newark saloon. His size didn't matter there. The other
man was a husky brute who took a liking for him and could handle
any trouble in the place without any help. Miley was working
there when the coughing started and the doctor told him he'd not
last long if he didn't head for a high dry climate.

The doctor meant some sanitarium. Miley had no money for
anything like that, never had and never expected to have. It was
the big bartender gave him the push. Fired him and handed him
an extra week's pay and told him to keep going West till he reached
the mountains, real mountains past the Mississippi and the prairie
States.

He had reached Cheyenne the spring before, panhandling and
picking up odd work on the way. A haying job nearly killed him,
but carried him through the summer. Dishwashing in a scrubby
hotel took him through the winter—and started the coughing again.
The herding offer, spotted in a weekly paper, struck him like a
miracle out of the blue. As near as I could gather, he had some silly
notions about the noble life of the shepherd out in the great open
spaces, all tied in somehow with some pictures he remembered from
an early schoolbook. He still had them and he was proud that he
hadn't lost a lamb all through the spring season.

He sat there by the fire talking and finally he talked himself out.
The moon, a clear three-quarters moon, climbed over the far horizon
and silvered the land, making pools of shadow between the rolls of
the valley floor and shifting patterns of light and dark on the hills

in front of the solid black of the soaring mountains beyond. The fire was only a few embers and I was trying to decide whether to saddle the gray or borrow one of his blankets for the night when he spoke.

"It's big, ain't it?" he said.

That was what it was. Big. You could use a lot of fancy words and never get anywhere as close as with that one little word.

"Makes a man feel big too," he said.

I stood up and started to walk around. Here was a funny frog-faced little runt from the worrying squirrel-cages of the eastern seaboard telling me for the first time, making me realize for the first time, why I was out in this Territory myself, why I had kept moving on out of the flat States till I found this Big Horn country.

I came back by the fire and I made my try. I tried to tell him what he was up against bringing sheep into this cow country and grazing them on the open range. I tried to tell him how the cowmen felt.

"That's all kind of silly," he said. "Look." He crawled into his pup tent again and scrooged around and came out with a paper pamphlet in his hand. "That's from the Government," he said. "You can't read it now, but I'll tell you about it. It's all about sheep raising. It says sheep eat things close down to the ground all right. But it says if you don't let them eat too long any one place, the grass comes back better than ever the next spring. That's the way I'm doing with them. It says that country like this up here is better for sheep than cows, anyway, because they'll eat stuff the cows won't and get more from every acre. It says they're more productive on rough range because they're two-crop animals, wool as well as lambs. Why, these cowmen you talk about would be better off if they took to sheep themselves."

"I won't argue that," I said. "I don't know enough. I just happen to like cows. They smell cleaner and they've got more sense."

"Oh, that's where you're wrong," he said. "Sheep don't smell bad after you get used to it. It's kind of a warm nice smell on a chilly night. They've got lots of sense. They pick a leader and follow him. They get to know you and depend on you and do what you say. They'll listen to you and sometimes you get to understanding what they're saying back."

"Sounds crazy to me," I said. "But that's outside the argument. If you've got any sense yourself, you'll pack that burro and start moving yourself and your talking sheep far away."

"That's what the other fellow told me," he said. "Only he told me meaner."

"What other fellow?" I said.

"A big fellow on a black horse," he said. "They stopped by here two days ago."

"Must be Jeff Clayton," I said. "He has a lot of cattle on the range. He's not one to play games with. Are you taking his advice?"

"No," he said. "The man who hired me told me to come up this way and stay till September. My sheep aren't hurting anybody. I don't believe all that you've been telling me. People can't really act that way up here where it's so big. There's plenty of room for us all."

I was so peeved at the thick-headed little fool that I saddled the gray in the dark and rode home even though it was past midnight when I got there.

A couple of days later I took the ears into town and collected the bounty and for some reason on the way back Miley's share was burning a hole in my pocket, so I kept right on going. About noon when I headed into the valley I was surprised to see sheep scattered in little bunches in every direction.

The gray didn't like it much, and the sheep were slow and stupid, running in little spurts everywhere but where you wanted them to go, but I began herding them up the valley toward his camp. About half a mile coming over a knoll I saw him. He and the dogs were gathering them in, herding them into a single flock again. He was plodding along on foot and the dogs were racing after strays. He waved at me, grim-faced, and plodded on, and I kept my side closing in till the flock was about complete.

"What happened this time?" I said, dismounting to rest the gray.

"Horses," he said. "Lots of them. Wild ones. Worse murderers than those wolves. Before I got up this morning they came tearing. Ran right through my sheep. They trampled nine of them."

I pointed to one sheep whose left foreleg was dangling. "Better shoot that one," I said. "It won't be able to travel."

He looked at me like he thought I was out of my mind. "Shoot her? Shoot one of my sheep? I'll fix that leg with a splint. What do you mean travel?"

"If you've got a grain of sense," I said, "you'll be heading out of here now. There are no wild horses around here. Half-wild, maybe, but you'll find every one has a brand. And not even wild ones would stampede through a herd of sheep by themselves. Come on, I'll show you."

We followed the trail of the hooves back up the valley a ways and at last off to one side a bit I found what I was looking for.

"See, Miley," I said, "that horse had shoes. It's being worked. Someone was riding it. Hunt around some more and probably we'd find more tracks."

He didn't say a word all the way back to his camp. He dug through his stuff and pulled out a small short miner's shovel.

"What's that for?" I said.

"I'm going to bury my sheep like I did the others," he said.

"You're the worst kind of a fool," I said. "You don't have to bury things out here. The buzzards take care of that. With that toy in this ground it would take you two whole days."

"No buzzards are getting my sheep," he said. He looked up at me, the whole little length of him shaking. "We're not getting out of here neither. I was pushed around enough back home. I'm not going to be pushed around here. We're going into that canyon on up there where there's good grass for a couple of weeks at least and I'm camping at the way in and nothing's going to get in to bother my sheep. Not with me there. I'll stay awake every night if I have to."

I quit trying then. I gave him his share of the bounty and I rode home, and I felt I had to call him plenty of hard names to myself all the way.

What happened after that isn't easy to tell. I can put it together fairly well because I knew Miley Bennett and had heard him talk. The few words they got out of him at the trial helped some. What one of Jeff Clayton's men told, talking slow because of the bullet-hole in his shoulder, didn't mean much because he had to cover himself, but parts of it fitted the rest. Add all this to what I figured when I went over the ground the morning after it happened and you can fill in the whole thing. As I said before, I'll have to tell it in my own way. Small parts may be wrong, but the substance has to be right.

Miley Bennett buried his sheep and it took him at least the two days. He buried each in a separate grave and he lugged stones quite a distance to mark them. He got three buzzards with the shotgun while he was doing it. He herded the flock into the canyon, came back and packed everything tight on the burro and led her there too, and put his new camp in the neat order he liked. Two more days and nights went by and he slept only in snatches, watching the bigness of the dark land from his spy perch on a flat rock. Along about the middle of the morning of the third day there, he saw a man in the distance riding up the valley toward him. He climbed down from the rock and stepped behind, peering over the top with the shotgun ready in his right hand. He was watching the rider approach when a voice behind him told him to drop the gun and reach for a piece of sky. He whirled and another man had come slipping quietly down the rocks and was there with a handkerchief tied over his face up to the eyes and a gun in his hand pointing straight at Miley's belt buckle. Miley was so startled that he couldn't make a move of his own while this one yanked the shotgun out of his grasp and sent him around the rock and into the open with a hard slap on the side of the head.

The rider came close and he too now had a handkerchief over his face. Then another man, a big man on a black horse with his handkerchief over his face, rode into sight down and around from the high rocks of the canyon top leading another horse.

The three of them were quiet and businesslike. The big man rode his horse right over the little pup tent, crushing it flat and trampling it. He dismounted and the other rider with him. They tied Miley Bennett to a tree facing up the canyon toward his grazing flock. Methodically they smashed everything in sight, the shotgun and the food bags and the cans of beans, even the can of tobacco. The big man stepped close to Miley Bennett. "Watch this," he said. "Then crawl back where you came from and tell every smelly sheep-owner what happens to them in cattle country."

All three of them pulled high-powered rifles from their saddle scabbards and started toward the sheep. The first shots took the dogs. Then the bullets began plowing into the flock, tearing through two and three bodies at a time. The sheep screamed their terror and scattered, running their short spurts and huddling in groups, and the bullets followed and plowed into them. The rifle barrels were hot when the last shells were used and the men came for their horses and rode after the scattered remnants, trampling them as they could, chasing the terrified sheep in among the rocks and scrub growth of the canyon edges.

And all this while Miley Bennett, tight to torture against the tree, saw what he could not avoid seeing.

The men rode back and one dismounted to loosen the rope slightly and mounted again and they rode out of the canyon and down the valley and away.

Miley Bennett's mind climbed slowly back to consciousness out of a deep red darkness. It kept on climbing far above his surroundings, cool and detached from awareness of the immediate scene, unconcerned about his struggling body. He was alone with his dead and his wounded and his far-scattered living. The rope galls were deep in his arms and ankles and across his chest and he did not know it. Hours might have passed. It had really been perhaps twenty minutes.

His mind settled in a far niche and was quiet and a cold, clear logic flowed from it. He stopped struggling. He began to move in precise calculated lunges sidewise under the rope, edging around the tree trunk, oblivious of the rasping pull of the hemp along his body. When his fingers found the knot, his wrists bent at a grotesque upward angle, he picked slowly and steadily at it. When the rope loosened, his shoulders surged outward and the ends flipped free and he fell forward, wrenching his ankles on the lower coil that still held. When his feet were free, he crawled straight to the wrinkled, stomped canvas of the crushed pup tent.

Beneath the canvas in the sorry mess of the two blankets lay the old Hotchkiss. The stock was split with jagged splinters showing. The barrel and breach were intact. The last cartridge box was crumpled and broken, the cartridges pressed into the ground. He gathered as many as he could and cleaned them carefully and put them in his pockets. Standing up stiffly, he looked all around and whistled gently and then more loudly and saw a stirring in some far bushes. He limped there and made the snapped tether rope into a halter rein for the little burro. He pulled himself on her back and headed her out of the canyon and down the valley, holding the rope-rein in his left hand, the old Hotchkiss in his right hand.

He was no tracker and this was difficult for him. He found at last where the riders had swung off the main trace through the valley and gone left through the rolling ridges and climbing foothills. The little burro plodded patiently and waited, head hanging, when he lost the trail and had to search in a circle for it. The sun was posting past noon when he topped the last rise and saw Clem Murphy's ranchhouse in its flat hollow and the three horses ground-reined in the shade of a tree by the corral.

He turned back below the top of the rise and slid off the little burro and tied her to a scrub tree. Back at the top, he lay on his belly and peered over and crawled carefully from bush to bush down the slope to a stack of weathering fence posts about a hundred yards from the house. He rubbed dirt on the barrel of the old Hotchkiss to remove any lingering metal glint and lay again on his belly behind the stack, peering through the opening between two leaning posts that gave a clear view of the porch and the three horses and the ground between. He pushed the barrel of the old Hotchkiss through the opening and settled flat to the earth and waited. The sun beat on his back and the stinging buffalo flies came and he did not move and patiently waited.

Inside the house the three men finished a final round of coffee with Clem Murphy and told him to remember they had been there most of the morning. They rinsed off their dishes in the tin dishpan and in straggling order started out the door.

Miley Bennett waited until they were past the porch in the open space going toward the horses. I do not know whether he saw them as wolves or as men or as anything at all except as evil moving scars on the decent bigness of the broad land. His first bullet smashed through the side of Jeff Clayton's head. The second tore a hole in the shoulder of one of the other two, going in clean and taking a piece of collarbone out with it and flattening him unconscious on the ground. The third kicked up dust beside the last of the three as he ducked behind the watering trough by the iron pump. The fourth crashed full into the breastbone of Clem Murphy as he ran through the doorway and onto the porch to see what was happening.

Silence dropped over the scene and the dust settled. Time passed and the sun beat down and the flies found the bodies. The man behind the watering trough saw a crack beneath it and through this studied every foot of the ground opposite him. The only cover was the stack of fence posts. At last he made out the dull deadliness of the gun barrel poking through. He waited and there was no movement. Revolver in hand, he peered cautiously over the top of the trough and fired four shots in quick aim at the small opening between the posts. He crouched low again and reloaded the revolver and waited and there was no movement and no sound.

His nerves became jumpy and he could no longer remain still. He leaped up and ran toward the horses, firing rapidly as he ran. He was on one and pulling it in a pawing semicircle when the bullet drilled into his back, snapping the bone and knocking him sidewise out of the saddle to hit a corral post and bounce in a broken heap to the ground.

Marshal Eakins found Miley Bennett late that afternoon. He found him in the little canyon. He was working doggedly with his small shovel, burying his sheep and marking the graves. He didn't seem surprised when Eakins rode up after ordering the posse to stay behind a ways. Only he couldn't seem to focus on anyone directly. He kept staring into space, and even while he was working he wasn't really focusing on it. He had nothing to say except to ask Eakins whether he could finish burying the sheep. When Eakins said no, there would have to be a trial before anything else could be done, he came along quietly, pulling back just long enough to tell the burro to take care of things while he was gone and keep the buzzards away and then letting them tie him on a horse and going along without any fuss, just staring at the bigness all around.

There was talk of a lynching in town, but not very strong because everyone respected Eakins and Federal Judge Stillwell was there on temporary circuit. I don't know what would have happened if the case had been in a State court. But Eakins said it was a Federal case because at bottom it was a controversy over Federal range and Judge Stillwell took jurisdiction.

No jury was needed because the plea was plain guilty. The trial took a little more than an hour, and Miley Bennett sat through it staring always out the window and hardly noticing what went on around him. All they got out of him beyond a few nods to direct questions was a single burst, after a question about Clem Murphy,

that he didn't mean to shoot that one and just couldn't stop shooting and please couldn't they understand he didn't mean to shoot
that one. The lawyer assigned to his defense argued extenuating circumstances fairly well, though his heart was not in it. Judge Stillwell
cut the thing short by stating that the real extenuating circumstance
was that the man had obviously lost his sanity. The Judge knew his
audience and added that it was commonly known anyone who took
to sheepherding was half-crazy to begin with and this made them all
chuckle and held the grumbling down when he made the sentence
life imprisonment. And Miley Bennett was staring out the window
when they led him away to the jail where he would stay till they took
him to the new Federal prison, and I knew it would take time but
not too long before the whole meaning would sink home in him.

I guess that's all. Except perhaps the visit Marshal Eakins paid
me the afternoon of the day they buried Miley Bennett with a
powder-burned mouth and a mass of clotted blood where the back
of his head had been. Eakins rode up to where I was stringing
barbed wire. He didn't dismount. He simply reached down and
handed me the gun.

"I reckon this is yours," he said.

"Yes," I said.

"Can't think of a charge," he said. "After all, you saved the Government the expense of feeding him for maybe a passel of years."

"I wasn't thinking of that," I said.

He nodded at me and reined the horse around and started back
toward town. I watched him go, a man riding straight and steady
across the big land.

Emmet Dutrow

THREE DAYS he was there on the rock ledge. I don't think he left it once. I couldn't be sure. I had things to do. But I could see him from my place and each time I looked he was there, a small dark-clad figure, immeasurably small against the cliff wall rising behind him.

Sometimes he was standing, head back and face up. Sometimes he was kneeling, head down and sunk into his shoulders. Sometimes he was sitting on one of the smaller stones.

Three days it was. And maybe the nights too. He was there when I went in at dusk and he was there when I came out in early morning. Once or twice I thought of going to him. But that would have accomplished nothing. I doubt whether he would even have noticed me. He was lost in an aloneness no one could penetrate. He was waiting for his God to get around to considering his case.

I guess this is another you'll have to let me tell in my own way. And the only way I know to tell it is in pieces, the way I saw it.

Emmet Dutrow was his name. He was of Dutch blood, at least predominantly so; the hard-shell deep-burning kind. He came from Pennsylvania, all the way to our new State of Wyoming with his heavy wide-bed wagon and slow, swinging yoke of oxen. He must have been months on the road, making his twelve to twenty miles a day when the weather was good and little or none when it was bad. The wagon carried food and farm tools and a few sparse pieces of stiff furniture beneath an old canvas. He walked and must have walked the whole way close by the heads of his oxen, guiding them with a leather thong fastened to the yoke. And behind about ten paces and to the side came his woman and his son Jess.

They camped that first night across the creek from my place. I saw him picketing the oxen for grazing and the son building a fire and the woman getting her pans from where they hung under the wagon's rear axle, and when my own chores were done and I was ready to go in for supper, I went to the creek and across on the stones in the shallows and toward their fire. He stepped out from it to confront me, blocking my way forward. He was a big man, big and broad and bulky, made more so by the queer clothes he wore. They were plain black of some rough thick material, plain black loose-fitting pants and plain black jacket like a frock-coat without any tails, and a plain black hat, shallow-crowned and stiff-brimmed. He had a square trimmed beard that covered most of his face, hiding the features, and eyes sunk far back so that you felt like peering close to see what might be in them.

Behind him the other two kept by the fire, the woman shapeless in a dark linsey-woolsey dress and pulled-forward shielding bonnet, the son dressed like his father except that he wore no hat.

I stopped. I couldn't have gone farther without walking right into him.

"Evening, stranger," I said.

"Good evening," he said. His voice was deep and rumbled in his throat with the self-conscious roll some preachers have in the pulpit. "Have you business with me?"

"There's a quarter of beef hanging in my springhouse," I said. "I thought maybe you'd appreciate some fresh meat."

"And the price?" he said.

"No price," I said. "I'm offering you some."

He stared at me. At least the shadow-holes where his eyes hid were aimed at me. "I'll be bounden to no man," he said.

The son had edged out from the fire to look at me. He waved an arm at my place across the creek. "Say mister," he said. "Are those cattle of yours——"

"Jess!" The father's voice rolled at him like a whip uncoiling. The son flinched at the sound and stepped back by the fire. The father turned his head again to me. "Have you any further business?"

"No," I said. I swung about and went back across the creek on the stones and up the easy slope to my little frame ranchhouse.

The next day he pegged his claim, about a third of a mile farther up the valley where it narrowed and the spring floods of centuries ago had swept around the curve above and washed the rock formation bare, leaving a high cliff to mark where they had turned. His quarter section spanned the space from the cliff to the present-day creek. It was a fair choice on first appearances; good bottom land, well-watered with a tributary stream wandering through, and there was a stand of cottonwoods back by the cliff. I had passed it up because I knew how the drifts would pile in below the cliff in winter. I was snug with the bend in the valley and the hills behind protecting me. It was plain he didn't know this kind of country. He was right where the winds down the valley would hit him when the cold came dropping out of the mountains.

He was a hard worker and his son too. They were started on a cabin before the first morning was over, cutting and trimming logs and hauling them with the oxen. In two days they had the framework up and the walls shoulder high, and then the rain started and the wind, one of our late spring storms that carried a lingering chill and drenched everything open with a steady lashing beat. I thought of them there, up and across the creek, with no roof yet and unable to keep a fire going in such weather, and I pulled on boots and a slicker and an old hat and went out and waded across and went up to their place. It was nearly dark, but he and the son were still at work setting another log in place. They had taken pieces of the old canvas and cut holes for their heads and pulled the pieces down over their shoulders with their heads poking through. This made using their arms slow and awkward, but they were still working. He had run the wagon along one wall of the cabin, and with this covering one side and the rest of the old canvas fastened to hang down the other, it formed a low cavelike shelter. The woman was in there, sitting on branches for a floor, her head nearly bumping the bed of the wagon above. I could hear the inside drippings, different from the outside patter, as the rain beat through the cracks of the wagon planks and the chinks of the log wall.

He stepped forward again to confront me and stop me, a big bulgy shape in his piece of canvas topped by the beard and hat with the shadow-holes of the eyes between.

"It's a little wet," I said. "I thought maybe you'd like to come over to my place where it's warm and dry till this storm wears itself out. I can rig enough bunks."

"No," he said, rolling his tone with the organ stops out. "We shall do with what is ours."

I started to turn away and I saw the woman peering out at me from her pathetic shelter, her face pinched and damp under the bonnet, and I turned back.

"Man alive," I said, "forget your pride or whatever's eating you and think of your wife and the boy."

"I am thinking of them," he said. "And I am the shield that shall protect them."

I swung about and started away, and when I had taken a few steps his voice rolled after me. "Perhaps you should be thanked, neighbor. Perhaps you mean well."

"Yes," I said, "I did."

I kept on going and I did not look back and I waded across the creek and went up to my house and in and turned the lamp up bright and tossed a couple more logs into the fireplace.

I tried once more, about two weeks later. He had his cabin finished then, roofed with bark slabs over close-set poles and the walls chinked tight with mud from the creek bottom. He had begun breaking ground. His oxen were handy for that. They could do what no team of horses could do, could lean into the yoke and dig their split hooves into the sod and pull a heavy plowshare ripping through the roots of our tough buffalo grass.

That seemed to me foolish, tearing up sod that was perfect for good cattle, getting ready for dirt farming way out there far from any markets. But he was doing it right. With the ground plowed deep and the sod turned over, the roots would be exposed and would rot all through the summer and fall and by the next spring the ground would be ready to be worked and planted. And meanwhile he could string his fences and build whatever sheds he would need and get his whole place in shape.

We ought to be getting really acquainted, I thought, being the only neighbors there in the valley and more than that, for the nearest other place was two miles away toward town. It was up to me to make the moves. I was the first in the valley. He was the second, the newcomer.

As I said, I tried once more. It was a Saturday afternoon and I was getting ready to ride to town and see if there was any mail and pick up a few things and rub elbows with other folks a bit and I thought of them there across the creek, always working and penned close with only a yoke of oxen that couldn't make the eight miles in less than half a day each way. I harnessed the team to the buckboard and drove bouncing across the creek and to their place. The woman appeared in the cabin doorway, shading her eyes and staring at me. The son stopped plowing off to the right and let go of the plow handles and started toward me. The father came around the side of the cabin and waved him back and came close to my wagon and stopped and planted his feet firmly and looked at me.

"I'm heading toward town," I said. "I thought maybe you'd like a ride in and back. You can look the place over and meet some of the folks around here."

"No, neighbor," he said. He looked at me and then let his voice out a notch. "Sin and temptation abide in towns. When we came past I saw two saloons and a painted woman."

"Hell, man," I said, "you find those things everywhere. They don't bite if you let them alone."

"Ah, yes," he said. "Everywhere. All along the long way I saw them. They are everywhere. That is why I stopped moving at last. There is no escaping them in towns. Wherever people congregate, there is sin. I shall keep myself and mine apart."

"All right," I said. "So you don't like people. But how about your wife and the boy? Maybe they'd like a change once in a while."

His voice rolled out another notch. "They are in my keeping." He looked at me and the light was right and for the first time I saw his eyes, bright and hot in their shadow-holes. "Neighbor," he said, all stops out, "have I trespassed on your property?"

I swung the team in an arc and drove back across the creek. I unharnessed the team and sent them out in the side pasture with slaps on their rumps. I whistled the gray in and saddled him and headed for town at a good clip.

That was the last time. After that I simply watched what was happening up the valley. You could sum most of it with the one word—

work. And the rest of it centered on the rock ledge at the base of the cliff where a hard layer jutted out about ten feet above the valley floor, flat on top like a big table. I saw him working there, swinging some tool, and after several days I saw what he was doing. He was cutting steps in the stone, chipping out steps to the ledge top. Then he took his son away from the plowing for a day to help him heave and pry the fallen rocks off the ledge, all except three, a big squarish one and two smaller ones. Up against the big one he raised a cross made of two lengths of small log. Every day after that, if I was out early enough in the morning and late enough when the dusk was creeping in, I could see him and his woman and the son, all three of them on the ledge, kneeling, and I could imagine his voice rolling around them and echoing from the cliff behind them. And on Sundays, when there would be nothing else doing about their place at all, not even cooking-smoke rising from the cabin chimney, they would be there hours on end, the woman and the son sometimes sitting on the two smaller stones, and the father, from his position leaning over the big stone, apparently reading from a book spread open before him.

It was on a Sunday, in the afternoon, that the son trespassed on my place. He came toward the house slow and hesitating like he was afraid something might jump and snap at him. I was sitting on the porch, the Winchester across my knees, enjoying the sunshine and waiting to see if the gopher that had been making holes in my side pasture would show its head. I watched him come, a healthy young figure in his dark pants and homespun shirt. When he was close, I raised my voice.

"Whoa, Jess," I said. "Aren't you afraid some evil might scrape off me and maybe get on you?"

He grinned kind of foolish and scrubbed one shoe-toe in the dirt. "Don't make fun of me," he said. "I don't hold with that stuff the way father does. He said I could come over anyway. He's decided perhaps you're all right."

"Thanks," I said. "Since I've passed the test, why not step up here and sit a spell."

He did, and he looked all around very curious and after a while he said: "Father thought perhaps you could tell him what to do to complete the claim and get the papers on it."

I told him, and we sat awhile, and then he said: "What kind of a gun is that?"

"It's a Winchester," I said. "A repeater. A right handy weapon."

"Could I hold it once?" he said.

I slipped on the safety and passed it to him. He set it to his shoulder and squinted along the barrel, awkward and self-conscious.

"Ever had a gun of your own?" I said.

"No," he said. He handed the gun back quickly and stared at the porch floor. "I never had anything of my own. Everything belongs to father. He hasn't a gun anyway. Only an old shotgun and he won't let me touch it." And after a minute: "I never had even a nickel of my own to buy a thing with." And after a couple of minutes more: "Why does he have to be praying all the time, can you tell me that? That's all he ever does, working and praying. Asking forgiveness for sins. For my sins and Ma's sins too. What kind of sins have we ever had a chance to do? Can you tell me that?"

"No," I said. "No, I can't."

We sat awhile longer, and he was looking out at the pasture. "Say, are those cattle——"

"Yes," I said. "They're Herefords. Purebreds. Some of the first in these parts. That's why they're fenced tight."

"How'd you ever get them?" he said. "I mean them and everything you've got here."

"Well," I said, "I was a fool youngster blowing my money fast as I found it. Then one day I decided I didn't like riding herd on another man's cattle and bony longhorns at that when I knew there were better breeds. So I started saving my pay."

"How long did it take?" he said.

"It was eleven years last month," I said, "that I started a bank account."

"That's a long time," he said. "That's an awful long time."

"How old are you, Jess?" I said.

"Nineteen," he said. "Nineteen four months back."

"When you're older," I said, "it won't seem like such a long time. When you're getting along some, time goes mighty fast."

"But I'm not older," he said.

"No," I said. "No. I guess you're not."

We sat awhile longer and then I got foolish. "Jess," I said, "the plowing's done. That was the big job. The pressure ought to be letting up a bit now. Why don't you drop over here an afternoon or two and help me with my haying. I'll pay fair wages. Twenty-five cents an hour."

His face lit like a match striking. "Hey, mister!" Then: "But Father——"

"Jess," I said, "I never yet heard of work being sinful."

I wondered whether he would make it and Wednesday he did, coming early in the afternoon and sticking right with me till quitting hour. He was a good worker. He had to be to make up for the time he wasted asking me questions about the country and people roundabout, and my place and my stock and the years I'd spent in the saddle. He was back again on Friday. When I called quits and we went across the pasture to the house, the father was standing by the porch waiting.

"Good evening, neighbor," he said. "According to my son you mentioned several afternoons. They are done. I have come for the money."

"Dutrow," I said, "Jess did the work. Jess gets the money."

"You do not understand," he said, the tone beginning to roll. "My son is not yet of man's estate. Until he is I am responsible for him and the fruit of his labor is mine. I am sworn to guard him against evil. Money in an untried boy's pocket is a sore temptation to sin."

I went into the house and took three dollars from the purse in my jacket pocket and went out and to Jess and put them in his hand. He stood there with the hand in front of him, staring down at it.

"Jess! Come here!"

He came, flinching and unwilling, the hand still stiff in front of him, and the father took the money from it.

"I'm sorry, Jess," I said. "Looks like there'd be no point in your working here again."

He swung his eyes at me the way a whipped colt does and turned and went away, trying to hold to a steady walk and yet stumbling forward in his hurry.

"Dutrow," I said, "I hope that money burns your hand. You have already sinned with it."

"Neighbor," he said, "you take too much on yourself. My God alone shall judge my actions."

I went into the house and closed the door.

It was about a month later, in the middle of the week, that the father himself came to see me, alone and in midmorning and wearing his black coat and strange black hat under the hot sun as he came to find me.

"Neighbor," he said, "have you seen my son this morning?"

"No," I said.

"Strange," he said. "He was not on his pallet when I rose. He missed morning prayers completely. He has not appeared at all."

He stood silent a moment. Then he raised an arm and pointed a thick forefinger at me. His voice rolled at its deepest. "Neighbor," he said, "if you have contrived with my son to go forth into the world, I shall call down the wrath of my God upon you."

"Neighbor Dutrow," I said, "I don't know what your son's doing. But I know what you're going to do. You're going to shut your yap and get the hell off my place."

I don't think he heard me. He wiped a hand across his face and down over his beard. "You must pardon me," he said. "I am sore overwrought with worry."

He strode away, down to the creek and left along it out of the valley toward town. The coat flapped over his hips as he walked and he grew smaller in the distance till he rounded the first hill and disappeared.

He returned in late afternoon, still alone and dusty and tired, walking slowly and staring at the ground ahead of him. He went past on the other side of the creek and to his place and stopped at the door of the cabin and the woman emerged and they went to the rock ledge and they were still kneeling there when the dark shut them out of my sight.

The next day, well into the afternoon, I heard a horse coming along the trace that was the beginning of the road into the valley and Marshal Eakins rode up to me by the barn and swung down awkward and stiff. He was tired and worn and his left shoulder was bandaged with some of the cloth showing through the open shirt collar.

"Afternoon, John," he said. "Any coffee in the pot you could warm over?"

In the house I stirred the stove and put the pot on to heat. I pointed at his shoulder.

"One of our tough friends?" I said.

"Hell, no," he said. "I can handle them. This was an amateur. A crazy youngster."

When he had his cup, he took a first sip and leaned back in his chair.

"That the Dutrow place up the creek?" he said.

"Yes," I said.

"Must be nice neighbors," he said. "It was their boy drilled me." He tried the cup again and finished it in four gulps and reached for the pot. "His father was in town yesterday. Claimed the boy had run away. Right he was. The kid must have hid out during the day. Had himself a time at night. Pried a window at Walton's store. Packed himself a bag of food. Took a rifle and box of shells. Slipped over to the livery stable. Saddled a horse and lit out."

"He couldn't ride," I said.

"Reckon not," Eakins said. "Made a mess of the gear finding a bridle and getting it on. Left an easy track too. Didn't know how to make time on a horse. I took Patton and went after him. Must have had hours start, but we were tailing him before ten. Got off or fell off, don't know which, and scrambled into some rocks. I told him we had the horse and if he'd throw out the gun and come out himself there wouldn't be too much fuss about it. But he went crazy wild. Shouted something about sin catching up with him and started blazing away."

"He couldn't shoot," I said.

"Maybe not," Eakins said. "But he was pumping the gun as fast as he could and he got Patton dead center. We hadn't fired a shot."

Eakins started on the second cup.

"Well?" I said.

"So I went in and yanked him out," Eakins said. "Reckon I was a little rough. Patton was a good man."

He finished the second cup and set it down. "Got to tell his folks. Thought maybe you'd go along. Women give me the fidgets." He pushed at the cup with a finger. "Not much time. The town's a little hot. Trial will be tomorrow."

We walked down to the creek and across and up to their place. The woman appeared in the cabin doorway and stared at us. The father came from somewhere around the side of the cabin. He planted his feet firmly and confronted us. His head tilted high and his eyes were bright and hot in their shadow-holes. His voice rolled at us.

"You have found my son."

"Yes," Eakins said, "we've found him." He looked at me and back at the father and stiffened a little, and he told them, straight, factual. "The trial will be at ten tomorrow," he said. "They'll have a lawyer for him. It's out of my hands. It's up to the judge now."

And while he was talking, the father shrank right there before us. His head dropped and he seemed to dwindle inside his rough black clothes. His voice was scarcely more than a whisper.

"The sins of the fathers," he said, and was silent.

It was the woman who was speaking, out from the doorway and stretching up tall and pointing at him, the first and only words I ever heard her speak.

"You did it," she said. "You put the thoughts of sin in his head, always praying about it. And keeping him cooped in with never a thing he could call his own. On your head it is in the eyes of God. You drove him to it."

She stopped and stood still, looking at him, and her eyes were bright and hot and accusing in the pinched whiteness of her face, and she stood still looking at him.

They had forgotten we were there. Eakins started to speak again and thought better of it. He turned to me and I nodded and we went back along the creek and across and to the barn and he climbed stiffly on his horse and started toward town.

In the morning I saddled the gray and rode to the Dutrow's place. I was thinking of offering him the loan of the team and the buck-board. There was no sign of any activity at all. The place looked deserted. The cabin door was open and I poked my head in. The woman was sitting on a straight chair by the dead fireplace. Her hands were folded in her lap and her head was bowed over them. She was sitting still. There's no other way to describe what she was doing. She was just sitting.

"Where is he?" I said.

Her head moved in my direction and she looked vaguely at me and there was no expression on her face.

"Is he anywhere around?" I said.

Her head shook only enough for me to catch the slight movement and swung slowly back to its original position. I stepped back and took one more look around and mounted the gray and rode toward town, looking for him along the way, and did not see him.

I had no reason to hurry and when I reached the converted store building we used for a courthouse, it was fairly well crowded. Judge Cutler was on the bench. We had our own judge now for local cases. Cutler was a tall, spare man, full of experience and firm opinions, honest and independent in all his dealings with other people. That was why he was our judge. Marshal Eakins was acting as our sheriff until we would be better organized and have an office established. That was why he had taken charge the day before.

They brought in Jess Dutrow and put him in a chair at one side of the bench and set another at the other side for a witness stand. There was no jury because the plea was guilty. The lawyer they had assigned for Jess could do nothing except plead the youth of his client and the hard circumstances of his life. It did not take long, the brief series of witnesses to establish the facts. They called me to identify him and tell what I knew about him. They called Walton and the livery stable man to testify to the thefts. They called Eakins and had him repeat his story to put it in the court records. The defense lawyer was finishing his plea for a softening of sentence when there was a stirring in the room and one by one heads turned to stare at the outer doorway.

The father was there, filling the doorframe with his broad bulk in its black clothes. Dirt marks were on them as if he had literally wrestled with something on the ground. His hat was gone and his long hair flowed back unkempt. His beard was ragged and tangled and the cheeks above it were drawn as if he had not slept. But his voice rolled magnificently, searching into every corner of the room.

"Stop!" he said. "You are trying the wrong man!"

He came forward and stood in front of the bench, the wooden pedestal we used for a trial bench. He looked up at Judge Cutler on the small raised platform behind it.

"Mine is the guilt," he said. "On my head let the punishment fall. My son has not yet attained his twenty and first birthday. He is still of me and to me and I am responsible for aught that he does. He was put into my keeping by God, to protect him and guard him from temptation and bring him safely to man's estate. My will was not strong enough to control him. The fault therefore is in me, in his father that gave him the sins of the flesh and then failed him. On me the judgment. I am here for it. I call upon you to let him depart and sin no more."

Judge Cutler leaned forward. "Mr. Dutrow," he said in his precise, careful manner, "there is not a one of us here today does not feel for you. But the law is the law. We cannot go into the intangibles of human responsibilities you mention. Hereabout we hold that when a man reaches his eighteenth birthday he is a capable person, responsible for his own actions. Legally your son is not a minor. He must stand up to his own judgment."

The father towered in his dirty black coat. He raised an arm and swept it up full length. His voice fairly thundered.

"Beware, agent of man!" he said. "You would usurp the right of God Himself!"

Judge Cutler leaned forward a bit farther. His tone did not change. "Mr. Dutrow. You will watch quietly or I will have you removed from this room."

The father stood in the silence and dwindled again within his dark clothes. He turned slowly and looked over the whole room and everyone in it. Someone in the front row moved and left a vacant seat and he went to it and sat down, and his head dropped forward until his beard was spread over his chest.

"Jess Dutrow," Judge Cutler said, "stand up and take this straight. Have you anything to say for yourself?"

He stood up, shaky on his feet, then steadying. The whipped-colt look was a permanent part of him now. His voice cracked and climbed.

"Yes," he said. "I did it and he can't take that away from me! Everything's true and I don't give a damn! Why don't you get this over with?"

"Very well," Judge Cutler said. "There is no dispute as to the pertinent facts. Their logic is plain. You put yourself outside the law when you committed the thefts. While you were still outside the law you shot and killed a peace officer in the performance of his duty and wounded another. You did not do this by accident or in defense of your life. Insofar as the law can recognize, you did this by deliberate intent. By the authority vested in me as a legally sworn judge of the people of this State I sentence you to be hanged tomorrow morning at ten by this courthouse clock."

Most of us were not looking at Jess Dutrow. We were looking at the father. He sat motionless for a few seconds after Judge Cutler finished speaking. Then he roused in the chair and rose to his feet and walked steadily to the doorway and out, his head still low with the beard fanwise on his chest and his eyes lost and unseeable in their deep shadow-holes. I passed near him on the way home about an hour later and he was the same, walking steadily along, not slow, not fast, just steady and stubborn in his face. I called to him and he did not answer, did not even raise or turn his head.

The next morning I woke early. I lay quiet a moment trying to focus on what had wakened me. Then I heard it plain, the creaking of wagon wheels. I went to the door and looked out. In the brightening pinkish light of dawn I saw him going by on the other side of the creek. He had yoked the oxen to the big wagon and was pushing steadily along, leading them with the leather thong. I watched him going into the distance until I shivered in the chill morning air and I went back into the house and closed the door.

It was the middle of the afternoon when he returned, leading the oxen, and behind them on the wagon was the long rectangular box. I did not watch him. I simply looked toward his place every now and then. I had things to do and I was glad I had things to do.

I saw him stop the oxen by the cabin and go inside. Later I saw him standing outside the door, both arms thrust upward. I could not be sure, but I thought his head was moving and he was shouting at the sky. And later I saw him back in the shadow of the rock ledge digging the grave. And still later I saw him there digging the second grave.

That brought me up short. I stared across the distance and there was no mistaking what he was doing. I set the pitchfork against the barn and went down to the creek and across on the stones and straight to him. I had to shout twice, close beside him, before he heard me.

He turned his head toward me and at last he saw me. His face above and beneath the beard was drawn, the flesh collapsed on the bones. He looked like a man driven by some terrible torment. But his voice was low. There was no roll in it. It was low and mild.

"Yes, neighbor?" he said.

"Damn it, man," I said, "what are you doing?"

"This is for my wife," he said. His voice did not change, mild and matter-of-fact. "She killed herself." He drew a long breath and added gently, very gently. "With my butchering knife."

I stared at him and there was nothing I could say. At last: "I'll do what I can. I'll go into town and report it. You won't have to bother with that."

"If you wish," he said. "But that is all a foolishness. Man's justice is a mockery. But God's will prevail. He will give me time to finish this work. Then He will deal with me in His might."

He withdrew within himself and turned back to his digging. I tried to speak to him again and he did not hear me. I went to the cabin and looked through the doorway and went away quickly and to my place and saddled the gray and rode toward town. When I returned, the last shadows were merging into the dusk and the two graves were filled with two small wooden crosses by them and I saw him there on the ledge.

Three days he was there. And late in the night of the third day the rain began and the lightning streaked and the thunder rolled through the valley, and in the last hour before dawn I heard the deeper rolling rumble I had heard once before on a hunting trip when the whole face of a mountain moved and crashed irresistibly into a canyon below.

Standing on the porch in the first light of dawn, I saw the new broken outline of the cliff up and across the valley and the great slant jagged pile of stone and rubble below where the rock ledge had been.

We found him under the stones, lying crumpled and twisted near the big squarish rock with the wooden cross cracked and smashed beside him. What I remember is his face. The deep-sunk, sightless eyes were open and they and the whole face were peaceful. His God had not failed him. Out of the high heaven arching above had come the blast that gave him his judgment and his release.

Sergeant Houck

SERGEANT HOUCK stopped his horse just below the top of the ridge ahead. The upper part of his body was silhouetted against the skyline as he rose in his stirrups to peer over the crest. He urged the horse on up and the two of them, the man and the horse, were sharp and distinct against the copper sky. After a moment he turned and rode down to the small troop waiting. He reined beside Lieutenant Imler.

"It's there, sir. Alongside a creek in the next hollow. Maybe a third of a mile."

Lieutenant Imler regarded him coldly. "You took your time, Sergeant. Smack on the top too."

"Couldn't see plain, sir. Sun was in my eyes."

"Wanted them to spot you, eh, Sergeant?"

"No, sir. Sun was bothering me. I don't think——"

"Forget it, Sergeant. I don't like this either."

Lieutenant Imler was in no hurry. He led the troop slowly up the hill. He waited until the men were spread in a reasonably straight line just below the ridge top. He sighed softly to himself. The real fuss was fifty-some miles away. Captain McKay was hogging the honors there. Here he was tied to this disgusting sideline detail. Twenty men. Ten would have been enough. Ten, and an old hand like Sergeant Houck with no officer to curb his style. Thank the War Department for sergeants, the pickled-in-salt variety. They could do what no commissioned officer could do. They could forget orders and follow their own thoughts and show themselves on the top of a hill.

Lieutenant Imler sighed again. Even Sergeant Houck must think this had been time enough. He lifted his drawn saber. "All right, men. If we had a bugler, he'd be snorting air into it right now."

Saber pointing forward, Lieutenant Imler led the charge up and over the crest and down the long slope to the Indian village. There were some scattered shots from bushes by the creek, ragged pops indicating poor powder and poorer weapons, probably fired by the last of the old men left behind when the young braves departed in war-paint ten days before. A few of the squaws and children, their dogs tagging, could still be seen running into the brush. They reached cover and faded from sight, disappeared into the surrounding emptiness. The village was silent and deserted and dust settled in the afternoon sun.

Lieutenant Imler surveyed the ground taken. "Spectacular achievement," he muttered to himself. He beckoned Sergeant Houck to him.

"Your redskin friend was right, Sergeant. This is it."

"Knew he could be trusted, sir."

"Our orders are to destroy the village. Send a squad out to round up any stock. There might be some horses around. We're to take them in." Lieutenant Imler waved an arm at the thirty-odd skin-and-pole huts. "Set the others to pulling those down. Burn what you can and smash everything else."

"Right, sir."

Lieutenant Imler rode into the slight shade of the cottonwoods along the creek. He wiped the dust from his face and set his campaign hat at a fresh angle to ease the crease made by the band on his forehead. Here he was, hot and tired and way out at the end of nowhere with another long ride ahead, while Captain McKay was having it out at last with Gray Otter and his renegade warriors somewhere between the Turkey Foot and the Washakie. He relaxed to wait in the saddle, beginning to frame his report in his mind.

"Pardon, sir."

Lieutenant Imler swung in the saddle to look around. Sergeant Houck was afoot, was standing near with something in his arms, something that squirmed and seemed to have dozens of legs and arms.

"What the devil is that, Sergeant?"

"A baby, sir. Or rather, a boy. Two years old, sir."

"How the devil do you know? By his teeth?"

"His mother told me, sir."

"His mother?"

"Certainly, sir. She's right here."

Lieutenant Imler saw her then, close to a neighboring tree, partially behind the trunk, shrinking into the shadow and staring at Sergeant Houck and his squirming burden. He leaned to look closer. She was not young. She might have been any age in the middle years. She was shapeless in the sacklike skin covering with slit-holes for her arms and head. She was sun- and windburned dark, yet not as dark as he expected. And there was no mistaking her hair. It was light brown and long and braided, and the braid was coiled around on her head.

"Sergeant! It's a white woman!"

"Right, sir. Her name's Cora Sutliff. The wagon train she was with was wiped out by a raiding party. She and another woman were taken along. The other woman died. She didn't. The village here bought her. She's been in Gray Otter's lodge." Sergeant Houck smacked the squirming boy briskly and tucked him under one arm. He looked straight at Lieutenant Imler. "That was three years ago, sir."

"Three years? Then that boy——"

"That's right, sir."

Captain McKay looked up from his desk to see Sergeant Houck stiff at attention before him. It always gave him a feeling of satisfaction to see this big slab of cross-grained granite that Nature had hewed into the shape of a man. The replacements they were sending these days, raw and unseasoned, were enough to shake his faith in the Service. But as long as there remained a sprinkling of these case-hardened oldtime regulars, the Army would still be the Army.

"At ease, Sergeant."

"Thank you, sir."

Captain McKay drummed his fingers on the desk. This was a ridiculous proposition. There was something incongruous about it and the solid, impassive bulk of Sergeant Houck made it seem even more so.

"That woman, Sergeant. She's married. The husband's alive, wasn't with the train when it was attacked. He's been located, has a place about twenty miles out of Laramie. The name's right and everything checks. You're to take her there and turn her over with the troop's compliments."

"Me, sir?"

"She asked for you. The big man who found her. Lieutenant Imler says that's you."

Sergeant Houck considered this behind the rock mask of his weather-carved face. "And about the boy, sir?"

"He goes with her." Captain McKay drummed on the desk again. "Speaking frankly, Sergeant, I think she's making a mistake. I suggested she let us see the boy got back to the tribe. Gray Otter's dead, and after that affair two weeks ago there's not many of the men left. But they'll be on the reservation now and he'd be taken care of. She wouldn't hear of it, said if he had to go she would too." Captain McKay felt his former indignation rising again. "I say she's playing the fool. You agree with me, of course."

"No, sir. I don't."

"And why the devil not?"

"He's her son, sir."

"But he's—— Well, that's neither here nor there, Sergeant. It's not our affair. We deliver her and there's an end to it. You'll draw expense money and start within the hour. If you push along, you can make the stage at the settlement. Two days going and two coming. That makes four. If you stretch it another coming back, I'll be too busy to notice. If you stretch it past that, I'll have your stripes. That's all."

"Right, sir." Sergeant Houck straightened and swung about and started for the door.

"Houck."

"Yes, sir."

"Take good care of her—and that damn kid."

"Right, sir."

Captain McKay stood by the window and watched the small cavalcade go past toward the post gateway. Lucky that his wife had come with him, even on this last assignment to this Godforsaken station lost in the prairie wasteland. Without her they would have been in a fix with the woman. As it was, the woman looked like a woman now. And why shouldn't she, wearing his wife's third-best crinoline dress? It was a bit large, but it gave her a proper feminine appearance. His wife had enjoyed fitting her, from the skin out, everything except shoes. Those were too small. The woman seemed to prefer her worn moccasins anyway. And she was uncomfortable in the clothes. But she was decently grateful for them, insisting she would have them returned or would pay for them somehow. She was riding past the window, side-saddle on his wife's horse, still with that strange shrinking air about her, not so much frightened as remote, as if she could not quite connect with what was happening to her, what was going on around her.

Behind her was Private Lakin, neat and spruce in his uniform, with the boy in front of him on the horse. The boy's legs stuck out on each side of the small improvised pillow tied to the forward arch of the saddle to give him a better seat. He looked like a weird, black-haired doll bobbing with the movements of the horse.

And there beside the woman, shadowing her in the mid-morning sun, was that extra incongruous touch, the great granite hulk of Sergeant Houck, straight in his saddle with the military erectness that was so much a part of him that it would never leave him, solid, impassive, taking this as he took everything, with no excitement and no show of any emotion, a job to be done.

They went past, and Captain McKay watched them ride out through the gateway. It was not quite so incongruous after all. As he had discovered on many a tight occasion, there was something comforting in the presence of that big, angular slab of a man. Nothing ever shook him. He had a knack of knowing what needed to be done whatever the shifting circumstances. You might never know exactly what went on inside his close-cropped, hardpan skull, but you could be certain that what needed to be done he would do.

Captain McKay turned back to his desk. He would wait for the report, terse and almost illegible in crabbed handwriting, but he could write off this detail as of this moment. Sergeant Houck had it in hand.

They were scarcely out of sight of the post when the boy began his squirming. Private Lakin clamped him to the pillow with a capable right hand. The squirming persisted. The boy seemed determined to escape from what he regarded as an alien captor. Silent, intent, he writhed on the pillow. Private Lakin's hand and arm grew weary. He tickled his horse forward with his heels until he was close behind the others.

"Beg pardon."

Sergeant Houck shifted in his saddle and looked around. "Yes?"

"He's trying to get away. It'd be easier if I tied him down. Could I use my belt?"

Sergeant Houck held in his horse to drop back alongside Private Lakin. "Kids don't need tying," he said. He reached out and plucked the boy from in front of Private Lakin and laid him, face down, across the withers of his own horse and smacked him sharply. He picked the boy up again and reached out and set him again on the pillow. The boy sat still, very still, making no movement except that caused by the sliding motion of the horse's foreshoulders. Sergeant Houck pushed his left hand into his left side pocket and it came forth with a fistful of small hard biscuits. He passed these to Private Lakin. "Stick one of these in his mouth when he gets restless."

Sergeant Houck urged his horse forward until he was beside the woman once more. She had turned her head to watch, and she stared sidewise at him for a long moment, then looked straight forward again along the wagon trace before them.

They came to the settlement in the same order, the woman and Sergeant Houck side by side in the lead, Private Lakin and the boy tagging at a respectful distance. Sergeant Houck dismounted and helped the woman down and plucked the boy from the pillow and handed him to the woman. He unfastened one rein from his horse's bridle and knotted it to the other, making them into a lead strap. He did the same to the reins of the woman's horse. He noted Private Lakin looking wistfully at the painted front of the settlement's one saloon and tapped him on one knee and handed him the ends of the two straps. "Scat," he said, and watched Private Lakin turn his horse and ride off leading the other two horses. He took the boy from the woman and tucked him under one arm and led the way into the squat frame building that served as general store and post-office and stage stop. He settled the woman on a preserved-goods box and set the boy in her lap and went to the counter to arrange for their fares. When he returned to sit on another box near her, the entire permanent male population of the settlement had assembled just inside the door, all eleven of them staring at the woman.

". . . that's the one . . ."

". . . an Indian had her . . ."

". . . shows in the kid . . ."

Sergeant Houck looked at the woman. She was staring at the floor. The blood was retreating from beneath the skin of her face, making it appear old and leathery. He started to rise and felt her hand on his arm. She had leaned over quickly and clutched his sleeve.

"Please," she said. "Don't make trouble account of me."

"Trouble?" said Sergeant Houck. "No trouble." He rose and confronted the fidgeting men by the door. "I've seen kids around this place. Some of them small. This one now needs decent clothes and the store here doesn't stock them."

The men stared at him, startled, and then at the wide-eyed boy in his clean but patched skimpy cloth covering. Five or six of them went out through the door and disappeared in various directions. The others scattered through the store, finding little businesses to excuse their presence. Sergeant Houck stood sentinel, relaxed and quiet, by his box, and those who had gone out straggled back, several embarrassed and empty-handed, the rest proud with their offerings.

Sergeant Houck took the boy from the woman's lap and stood him on his box. He measured the offerings against the small body and chose a small red flannel shirt and a small pair of faded overalls. He peeled the boy with one quick motion, ripping away the old cloth, and put the shirt and overalls on him. He set the one pair of small scuffed shoes aside. "Kids don't need shoes," he said. "Only in winter." He heard the sound of hooves and stepped to the door to watch the stage approach and creak to a stop, the wheels sliding in the dust. He looked back to see the men inspecting the boy to that small individual's evident satisfaction and urging their other offerings upon the woman. He strode among them and scooped the boy under one arm and beckoned the woman to follow and went out the door to the waiting old Concord coach. He deposited the boy on the rear seat inside and turned to watch the woman come out of the store escorted by the male population of the settlement. He

helped her into the coach and nodded up at the driver on his high
box seat and swung himself in. The rear seat groaned and sagged
as he sank into it beside the woman with the boy between them. The
woman peered out the window by her, and suddenly, in a shrinking,
experimental gesture, she waved at the men outside. The driver's
whip cracked and the horses lunged into the harness and the coach
rolled forward, and a faint suggestion of warm color showed through
the tan of the woman's cheeks.

They had the coach to themselves for the first hours. Dust drifted
steadily through the windows and the silence inside was a persistent
thing. The woman did not want to talk. She had lost all liking for
it and would speak only when necessary, and there was no need.
And Sergeant Houck used words with a natural and unswerving
economy, for the sole simple purpose of conveying or obtaining
information that he regarded as pertinent to the business immediately in hand. Only once did he speak during these hours and
then only to set a fact straight in his mind. He kept his eyes fixed
on the dusty scenery outside as he spoke.

"Did he treat you all right?"

The woman made no pretense of misunderstanding him. Her
thoughts leaped back and came forward through three years and
she pushed straight to the point with the single word. "Yes," she
said.

The coach rolled on and the dust drifted. "He beat me once,"
she said, and the coach rolled on, and four full minutes passed
before she finished this in her own mind-and in the words: "Maybe
it was right. I wouldn't work."

Sergeant Houck nodded. He put his right hand in his right
pocket and fumbled there to find one of the short straight straws
and bring it forth. He put one end of this in his mouth and chewed
slowly on it and watched the dust whirls drift past.

They stopped for a quick meal at a lonely ranchhouse and ate
in silence while the man there helped the driver change horses.
Then the coach rolled forward and the sun began to drop overhead. It was two mail stops later, at the next change, that another
passenger climbed in and plopped his battered suitcase and himself
on the front seat opposite them. He was of medium height and
plump. He wore city clothes and had quick eyes and features small

in the plumpness of his face. He took out a handkerchief and wiped his face and removed his hat to wipe all the way up his forehead. He laid the hat on top of the suitcase and moved restlessly on the seat, trying to find a comfortable position. His movements were quick and nervous. There was no quietness in him.

"You three together?"

"Yes," said Sergeant Houck.

"Your wife, then?"

"No," said Sergeant Houck. He looked out the window on his side and studied the far horizon. The coach rolled on, and the man's quick eyes examined the three of them and came to brief rest on the woman's feet.

"Begging your pardon, lady, but why do you wear those things? Moccasins, aren't they? They more comfortable?"

She looked at him and down again at the floor and shrank back farther in the seat and the blood began to retreat from her face.

"No offense, lady," said the man. "I just wondered——" He stopped. Sergeant Houck was looking at him.

"Dust's bad," said Sergeant Houck. "And the flies this time of year. Best to keep your mouth closed."

He looked again out the window and the coach rolled on, and the only sounds were the running beat of the hooves and the creakings of the old coach.

A front wheel struck a stone and the coach jolted up at an angle and lurched sideways and the boy gave a small whimper. The woman pulled him to her and onto her lap.

"Say," said the man, "where'd you ever pick up that kid? Looks like——" He stopped.

Sergeant Houck was reaching up and rapping a rock fist against the top of the coach. The driver's voice could be heard shouting at the horses and the coach slowed and the brakes bit on the wheels and the coach stopped. One of the doors opened and the driver peered in. Instinctively he picked Sergeant Houck.

"What's the trouble, soldier?"

"No trouble," said Sergeant Houck. "Our friend here wants to ride up on the box with you." He looked at the plump man. "Less dust up there. It's healthy and gives a good view."

"Now, wait a minute," said the man. "Where'd you get the idea——"

"Healthy," said Sergeant Houck.

The driver looked at the bleak, impassive hardness of Sergeant Houck and at the twitching softness of the plump man. "Reckon it would be," he said. "Come along. I'll boost you up."

The coach rolled forward and the dust drifted and the miles went under the wheels. They rolled along the false-fronted one street of a mushroom town and stopped before a frame building tagged "Hotel." One of the coach doors opened and the plump man retrieved his hat and suitcase and scuttled away and across the porch and into the building. The driver appeared at the coach door. "Last meal here before the night run," he said, and wandered off around the building. Sergeant Houck stepped to the ground and helped the woman out and reached back in and scooped up the boy, tucked him under an arm, and led the way into the building.

When they came out, the shadows were long and fresh horses had been harnessed and a bent, footsore old man was applying grease to the axles. When they were settled again on the rear seat, two men emerged from the building lugging a small but heavy chest and hoisted it into the compartment under the high driving seat. Another man, wearing a close-buttoned suitcoat and curled-brim hat and carrying a shotgun in the crook of one elbow, ambled into sight around the corner of the building and climbed to the high seat. A moment later a new driver, whip in hand, followed and joined him on the seat and gathered the reins into his left hand. The whip cracked and the coach lurched forward and a young man ran out of the low building across the street carrying a saddle by the two stirrup straps swinging and bouncing against his thigh. He ran alongside and heaved the saddle up to fall thumping on the roof inside the guard-rail. He pulled at the door and managed to scramble in as the coach picked up speed. He dropped onto the front seat, puffing deeply.

"Evening, ma'am," he said between puffs. "And you, General." He leaned forward to slap the boy gently along the jaw. "And you too, bub."

Sergeant Houck looked at the lean length of the young man, at the faded levis tucked into short high-heeled boots, the plaid shirt, the brown handkerchief knotted around the tanned neck, the amiable, competent young face. He grunted a greeting, unintelligible but a pleasant sound.

"A man's legs ain't made for running," said the young man. "Just to fork a horse. That last drink was near too long."

"The Army'd put some starch in those legs," said Sergeant Houck.

"Maybe. Maybe that's why I ain't in the Army." The young man sat quietly, relaxed to the jolting of the coach. "Is there some other topic of genteel conversation you folks'd want to worry some?"

"No," said Sergeant Houck.

"Then maybe you'll pardon me," said the young man. "I hoofed it a lot of miles today." He worked hard at his boots and at last got them off and tucked them out of the way on the floor. He hitched himself up and over on the seat until he was resting on one hip. He put an arm on the window sill and cradled his head on it. His eyes closed. They opened and his head rose a few inches. "If I start sliding, just raise a foot and give me a shove." His head dropped down and the dust whirls outside melted into the dusk and he was asleep.

Sergeant Houck felt a small bump on his left side. The boy had toppled against him and was struggling back to sitting position, fighting silently to defeat the drowsiness overcoming him. Sergeant Houck scooped him up and set the small body across his lap with the head nestled into the crook of his right arm. He leaned his head down and heard the soft little last sigh as the drowsiness won. The coach rolled on, and he looked out into the dropping darkness and saw the deeper black of hills far off on the horizon. He looked sidewise at the woman and dimly made out the outline of her head falling forward and jerking back up, and he reached his left arm along the top of the seat until the hand touched her far shoulder. Faintly he saw her eyes staring at him and felt her shoulder stiffen and then relax as she moved closer and leaned toward him. He slipped down lower in the seat so that her head could reach his shoulder and he felt the gentle touch of the topmost strands of the braided coil of brown hair on his neck above his shirt collar. He waited patiently, and at last he could tell by her steady deep breathing that all fright had left her and all her thoughts were stilled.

The coach rolled on and reached a rutted stretch and began to sway and the young man stirred and began to slide on the smooth leather of his seat. Sergeant Houck put up a foot and braced it against the seat edge and the young man's body came to rest against it and was still. Sergeant Houck leaned his head back on the top of the seat and against the wall of the coach. The stars emerged in the clear sky and the coach rolled on, and the running beat of the hooves had the rhythm of a cavalry squad at a steady trot and gradually the great granite slab of Sergeant Houck softened slightly into sleep.

Sergent Houck awoke as always all at once and aware. The coach had stopped. From the sounds outside fresh horses were being buckled into the traces. The first light of dawn was creeping into the coach. He raised his head and the bones of his neck cracked and he realized that he was stiff in various places, not only his neck but his right arm where the sleeping boy still nestled and his leg stretched out with the foot braced against the opposite seat.

The young man there was awake. He was still sprawled along the hard leather cushion, but he was pulled back from the braced foot and his eyes were open. He was inspecting the vast leather sole of Sergeant Houck's boot. His eyes flicked up and met Sergeant Houck's eyes, and he grinned.

"That's impressive footwear," he whispered. "You'd need starch in the legs with hooves like that." He sat up and stretched, long and reaching, like a lazy young animal. "Hell," he whispered again, "you must be stiff as a branding iron."

He took hold of Sergeant Houck's leg at the knee and hoisted it slightly so that Sergeant Houck could bend it and ease the foot down to the floor without disturbing the sleeping woman leaning against him. He stretched out both hands and gently lifted the sleeping boy from Sergeant Houck's lap and sat back with the boy in his arms.

Sergeant Houck began closing and unclosing his right hand to stimulate the blood circulation in the arm. The coach rolled forward and the first copper streak of sunlight found it and followed it.

The young man studied the boy's face. "Can't be yours," he whispered.

"No," whispered Sergeant Houck.

"Must have some Indian strain."

"Yes."

The young man whispered down at the sleeping boy. "You can't help that, can you, bub?"

"No," said Sergeant Houck suddenly, full voice, "he can't."

The woman jerked upright and pulled over to the window on her side, rubbing at her eyes. The boy awoke, wide awake on the instant, and saw the unfamiliar face above him and began to squirm violently.

The young man clamped his arms tighter. "Morning, ma'am," he said. "Looks like I ain't such a good nursemaid."

Sergeant Houck reached one hand and plucked up the boy by a grip on the small overalls and deposited him in sitting position on the seat beside the young man. The boy stared at Sergeant Houck and sat still, very still.

The sun climbed into plain view and the coach rolled on. It was stirring the dust of a well-worn road now. It stopped where another crossed and the driver jumped down to deposit a little packet of mail in a box on a short post.

The young man inside pulled on his boots. He bobbed his head in the direction of a group of low buildings up the side road. "Think I'll try it there. They'll be peeling broncs about now and the foreman knows I can sit a saddle." He opened a door and jumped to the ground and whirled to poke his head in. "Hope you make it right," he said, "wherever you're heading."

The door closed and he could be heard scrambling up the back of the coach to get his saddle. There was a thump as he and the saddle hit the ground and then voices began outside, rising in tone.

Sergeant Houck pushed his head through the window beside him. The young man and the driver were facing each other over the saddle. The young man was pulling the pockets of his levis inside out.

"Lookahere, Will," he said, "you can see they're empty. You know I'll kick in soon as I have some cash. Hell, I've hooked rides with you before."

"Not now no more," said the driver. "The company's sore. They hear of this they'd have my job. I'll have to hold the saddle."

The young man's voice had a sudden bite. "You touch that saddle and they'll pick you up in pieces from here to breakfast."

Sergeant Houck fumbled for his inside jacket pocket. This was difficult with his head through the window, but he succeeded in finding it. He whistled sharply. The two men swung to see him. His eyes drilled the young man. "There's something on the seat in here. Must have slipped out of your pocket." He saw the young man stare, puzzled, and start toward the door. He pulled his head back and was sitting quietly in place when the door opened.

The young man leaned in and saw the two silver dollars on the hard seat and swiveled his head to look up at Sergeant Houck. Anger blazed in his eyes and he looked at the impassive rock of Sergeant Houck's face and the anger faded.

"You've been in spots yourself," he said.

"Yes," said Sergeant Houck.

"And maybe were helped out of them."

"When I was a young squirt with more energy than brains," said Sergeant Houck. "Yes."

The young man grinned. He picked up the two coins in one hand and swung the other to slap Sergeant Houck's leg, sharp and stinging and grateful. "Age ain't hurting you any, General," he said, and closed the door.

The coach rolled on, and the woman looked at Sergeant Houck and the minutes passed and still she looked at him. He stirred on the seat.

"If I'd had brains enough to get married," he said, "might be I'd have had a son. Might have been one like that."

The woman looked away, out her window. She reached up to pat at her hair and the firm line of her lips softened in the tiny imperceptible beginnings of a smile. The dust drifted and the minutes passed and Sergeant Houck stirred again.

"It's the upbringing that counts," he said, and settled into silent immobility, watching the miles go by.

Fifteen minutes for breakfast at a change stop and the coach rolled on. It was near noon when they stopped in Laramie and Sergeant Houck handed the woman out and tucked the boy under one arm and led the way to the waiting room. He stationed the woman and the boy in two chairs and strode away. He was back in five minutes with sandwiches and a pitcher of milk and two cups. He strode away again and was gone longer and returned driving a light buckboard wagon drawn by a pair of deep-barreled bays. The front part of the wagon bed was well padded with layers of empty burlap bags. He went into the waiting room and scooped up the boy and beckoned to the woman to follow. He deposited the boy on the burlap bags and helped the woman up on the driving seat.

"Straight out the road, they tell me," he said. "About fifteen miles. Then right along the creek. Can't miss it."

He stood by the wagon, staring along the length of the street and the road leading on beyond. The woman leaned from the seat and clutched at his shoulder. Her voice broke and climbed. "You're going with me?" Her fingers clung to the cloth of his service jacket. "Please! You've got to!"

Sergeant Houck put a hand over hers on his shoulder and released her fingers. "Yes, I'm going."

He walked around the wagon and stepped to the seat and took the reins and clucked to the team. The wagon moved forward and curious people along the street stopped to watch, and neither Sergeant Houck nor the woman was aware of them. The wheels rolled silently in the thick dust, and on the open road there was no sound except the small creakings of the wagon body and the muffled rhythm of the horses' hooves. A road-runner appeared from nowhere and raced ahead of them, its feet spatting little spurts of dust, and Sergeant Houck watched it running, effortlessly, always the same distance ahead.

"You're afraid," he said.

The wheels rolled silently in the thick dust and the road-runner swung contemptuously aside in a big arc and disappeared in the low bushes.

"They haven't told him," she said, "about the boy."

Sergeant Houck's hands tightened on the reins and the horses slowed to a walk. He clucked sharply to them and slapped the reins on their backs and they quickened again into a trot, and the wheels unwound their thin tracks endlessly into the dust and the high bright sun overhead crept over and down the sky on the left. The wagon topped a slight rise and the road ahead sloped downward for a long stretch to where the green of trees and tall bushes showed in the distance. A jackrabbit started from the scrub growth by the roadside and leaped high in a spy-hop and leveled out, a gray-brown streak. The horses shied and broke rhythm and quieted to a walk under the firm pressure of the reins. Sergeant Houck kept them at a walk, easing the heat out of their muscles down the long slope to the trees. He let them step into the creek up to their knees and dip muzzles in the clear running water. The front wheels of the wagon were into the current and he reached behind him to find a tin dipper tucked among the burlap bags and leaned far out and down to dip up water for the woman and the boy and himself. He backed the team out of the creek and swung them into the wagon cuts leading along the bank to the right.

The creek was on their left and the sun was behind them, warm on their backs, and the shadows of the horses pushed ahead, grotesque moving patterns always ahead, and Sergeant Houck watched them and looked beside him once and saw that the woman was watching them too. The shadows were longer, stretching farther ahead, when they rounded a bend along the creek and the buildings came in sight, the two-room cabin and the several lean-to sheds and the rickety pole corral.

A man was standing by one of the sheds, and when Sergeant Houck stopped the team, he came toward them and halted about twenty feet away. He was not young, perhaps in his middle thirties, but with the young look of a man on whom the years have made no mark except that of the simple passing of time. He was tall, soft, and loose-jointed in build, and indecisive in manner and movement. His eyes wavered and would not steady as he looked at the woman and the fingers of his hands hanging limp at his sides twitched as he waited for her to speak.

She climbed down her side of the wagon and faced him. She stood straight and the sun behind her shone on and through the escaping wisps of the coiled braid of her hair.

"Well, Fred," she said, "I'm here."

"Cora," he said. "It's been a long time, Cora. I didn't know you'd come so soon."

"Why didn't you come get me? Why didn't you, Fred?"

"I didn't rightly know what to do, Cora. It was all so mixed up. Thinking you were dead. Then hearing about you. And what happened. I had to think about things. And I couldn't get away easy. I was going to try maybe next week."

"I hoped you'd come. Right away when you heard."

His body twisted uneasily, a strange movement that stirred his whole length while his feet remained flat and motionless on the ground. "Your hair's still pretty," he said. "The way it used to be."

Something like a sob caught in her throat and she started toward

him. Sergeant Houck stepped down on the other side of the wagon
and strode off to the creek and kneeled to bend and wash the dust
from his face. He stood, shaking the drops from his hands and
drying his face with a handkerchief and watching the little eddies
of the current around several stones in the creek. He heard the
voices behind him and by the wagon.

"Wait, Fred. There's something you have to know——"

"That kid? What's it doing here with you?"

"It's mine, Fred."

"Yours? Where'd you get it?"

"It's my child. Mine."

Silence, and then the man's voice, bewildered, hurt. "So it's really
true what they said. About that Indian."

"Yes. He bought me. By their rules I belonged to him."

Silence, and then the woman's voice again. "I wouldn't be alive
and here now, any other way. I didn't have any say about it."

Silence, and then the man's voice with the faint beginning of
self-pity creeping into the tone. "I didn't count on anything like
this."

Sergeant Houck turned and strode back by the wagon. The
woman seemed relieved at the interruption.

"This is Sergeant Houck," she said. "He brought me all the way."

The man nodded his head and raised a hand to shove back the
sandy hair that kept falling forward on his forehead. "I suppose I
ought to thank you, soldier. All that trouble."

"No trouble," said Sergeant Houck. "Unusual duty. But no
trouble."

The man pushed at the ground in front of him with one shoe,
poking the toe into the dirt and studying it. "It's silly, just standing around here. I suppose we ought to go inside. It's near suppertime. I guess you'll be taking a meal here, soldier. Before you start
back to town."

"Right," said Sergeant Houck. "And I'm tired. I'll stay the night
too. Start in the morning. Sleep in one of those sheds."

The man pushed at the ground more vigorously. The little dirt
pile in front of his shoe seemed to interest him greatly. "All right,
soldier. Sorry there're no quarters inside." He swung quickly and
started for the cabin. The woman took the boy from the wagon and

followed him. Sergeant Houck unharnessed the horses and led them to the creek for a drink and to the corral and led them through the gate. He walked quietly to the cabin doorway and stopped just outside. He could see the man sitting on a straight-backed chair by the table, turned away from him. The woman and the boy were out of sight to one side.

"For God's sake, Cora," the man was saying, "I don't see why you had to bring that kid with you. You could have told me about it. I didn't have to see him."

Her voice was sharp, startled. "What do you mean?"

"Why, now we've got the problem of how to get rid of him. Have to find a mission or some place that'll take him. Why didn't you leave him where he came from?"

"No! He's mine!"

"Good God, Cora! Are you crazy? Think you can foist off a thing like that on me?"

Sergeant Houck stepped through the doorway. "It's been a time since last eating," he said. "Thought I heard something about supper." He looked around the small room and brought his gaze to bear upon the man. "I see the makings on those shelves. Come along, Mr. Sutliff. She can do without our help. A woman doesn't want men cluttering about when getting a meal. Show me your place before it gets dark."

He stood, waiting, and the man scraped at the floor with one foot and slowly rose and went with him.

They were well beyond earshot of the cabin when Sergeant Houck spoke again. "How long were you married? Before it happened?"

"Six years," said the man. "No, seven. It was seven when we lost the last place and headed this way with the train."

"Seven years," said Sergeant Houck. "And no child."

"It just didn't happen. I don't know why." The man stopped and looked sharply at Sergeant Houck. "Oh! So that's the way you're looking at it."

"Yes," said Sergeant Houck. "Now you've got one. A son."

"Not mine," said the man. "You can talk. It's not your wife. It's bad enough thinking of taking an Indian's leavings." He wiped his lips on his sleeve and spat in disgust. "I'll be damned if I'll take his kid."

"Not his any more. He's dead."

"Look, man. Look how it'd be. A damned little half-breed. Around all the time to make me remember what she did."

"Could be a reminder that she had some mighty hard going. And maybe came through the better for it."

"She had hard going! What about me? Thinking she was dead. Getting used to that. Maybe thinking of another woman. Then she comes back—and an Indian kid with her. What does that make me?"

"Could make you a man," said Sergeant Houck. "Think it over."

He swung away and went to the corral and leaned on the rail, watching the horses roll the sweat-itches out on the dry sod. The man went slowly down by the creek and stood on the bank, pushing at the dirt with one shoe and kicking small pebbles into the water. The sun, holding to the horizon rim, dropped suddenly out of sight and dusk swept swiftly to blur the outlines of the buildings. A lamp was lit in the cabin, and the rectangle of light through the doorway made the dusk become darkness. The woman appeared in the doorway and called and the men came their ways and converged there and went in. There was simple food on the table and the woman stood beside it. "I've already fed him," she said, and moved her head toward the door to the inner room. She sat down and they did and the three of them were intent on the plates.

Sergeant Houck ate steadily and reached to refill his plate. The man picked briefly at the food before him and stopped and the woman ate nothing at all. The man put his hands on the table edge and pushed back and rose and went to a side shelf and took a bottle and two thick cups and returned to set these by his plate. He filled the cups a third full from the bottle and shoved one along the table boards toward Sergeant Houck. He lifted the other chin-high. His voice was bitter. "Happy home-coming," he said. He waited and Sergeant Houck took the other cup and they drank. The man lifted the bottle and poured himself another cup-third.

The woman moved her chair and looked quickly at him and away.

"Please, Fred."

The man paid no attention to the words. He reached with the bottle toward the other cup.

"No," said Sergeant Houck.

The man shrugged. "You can think better on whiskey. Sharpens the mind." He set the bottle down and took his cup and drained it. He coughed and put it carefully on the table in front of him and pushed at it with one forefinger. Sergeant Houck fumbled in his right side pocket and found one of the short straight straws there and pulled it out and put one end in his mouth and chewed slowly on it. The man and the woman sat still, opposite each other at the table, and seemed to forget his quiet presence. They stared at the table, at the floor, at the cabin walls, everywhere except at each other. Yet their attention was plainly concentrated on each other across the table top. The man spoke first. His voice was restrained, carrying conscious patience.

"Look, Cora. You wouldn't want to do that to me. You can't mean what you said before."

Her voice was low, determined. "He's mine."

"Now, Cora. You don't want to push it too far. A man can take just so much. I didn't know what to do after I heard about you. But I remembered you had been a good wife, I was all ready to forgive you. And now you——"

"Forgive me!" She knocked against her chair rising to her feet. Hurt and bewilderment made her voice ragged as she repeated the words. "Forgive me?" She turned and fairly ran into the inner room. The handleless door banged shut and bounced open again inward a few inches and she leaned against it inside to close it tightly.

The man stared after her and shook his head a little and reached again for the bottle.

"Enough's enough," said Sergeant Houck.

The man became aware of him and shrugged in quick irritation. "For you, maybe," he said, and poured himself another cup-third. He thrust his head a little forward at Sergeant Houck. "Is there any reason you should be noseying in on this?"

"My orders," said Sergeant Houck, "were to deliver them safely. Both of them. Safely."

"You've done that," said the man. He lifted the cup and drained it and set it down carefully. "They're here."

"Yes," said Sergeant Houck, "they're here." He rose and stepped to the outside door and looked into the night. He waited a moment until his eyes were accustomed to the darkness and could distinguish objects faintly in the starlight. He stepped on out and went to the strawpile behind one of the sheds and took an armload and carried it back by the cabin and dropped it at the foot of a tree by one corner. He lowered his bulk to the straw and sat there, legs stretched out, shoulders against the tree, and broke off a straw stem and chewed slowly on it. After a while his jaws stopped their slow, slight movement and his head sank forward and his eyes closed.

Sergeant Houck awoke, completely, in the instant, and aware. The stars had swung perhaps an hour overhead. He was on his feet in the swift reflex, and listening. The straw rustled under his shoes and was still. He heard the faint sound of voices in the cabin, indistinct but rising as tension rose in them. He went toward the doorway and stopped just short of the rectangle of light from the still burning lamp.

"You're not going to have anything to do with me!" The woman's voice was harsh with stubborn anger. "Not until this has been settled right!"

"Aw, come on, Cora." The man's voice was fuzzy, slow-paced. "We'll talk about that in the morning."

"No!"

"All right!" Sudden fury shook the man's voice. "You want it settled now! Well, it's settled! We're getting rid of that damn kid first thing tomorrow!"

"No!"

"What gave you the idea you've got any say around here after what you did? I'm the one to say what's to be done. You don't be careful, maybe I won't take you back."

"Maybe I don't want you to take me back!"

"So damn finicky all of a sudden! After being with that Indian and maybe a lot more!"

Sergeant Houck stepped through the doorway. The man's back was to him and he put out his left hand and took hold of the man's shoulder and spun him around, and his right hand smacked against the side of the man's face and sent him staggering against the wall.

"Forgetting your manners won't help," said Sergeant Houck. He looked around and the woman had disappeared into the inner room. The man leaned against the wall rubbing his cheek, and she emerged, the boy in her arms, and ran toward the outer door.

"Cora!" the man shouted. "Cora!"

She stopped, a brief hesitation in flight. "I don't belong to you," she said, and was gone through the doorway. The man pushed out from the wall and started after her and the great bulk of Sergeant Houck blocked the way.

"You heard her," said Sergeant Houck. "She doesn't belong to anybody now. But that boy."

The man stared at him and some of the fury went out of the man's eyes and he stumbled to his chair at the table and reached for the nearly empty bottle. Sergeant Houck watched him a moment, then turned and quietly went outside. He walked toward the corral and as he passed the second shed she came out of the darker shadows and her voice, low and intense, whispered at him.

"I've got to go. I can't stay here."

Sergeant Houck nodded and went on to the corral and opened the gate and, stepping softly and chirruping a wordless little tune, approached the horses. They stirred uneasily and moved away and stopped and waited for him. He led them through the gate to the wagon and harnessed them quickly and with a minimum of sound. He finished buckling the traces and stood straight and looked toward the cabin. He walked steadily to the lighted rectangle of the doorway and stepped inside and over by the table. The man was leaning forward in his chair, elbows on the table, staring at the empty bottle.

"It's finished," said Sergeant Houck. "She's leaving now."

The man shook his head and pushed at the bottle with one forefinger. "She can't do that." He swung his head to look up at Sergeant Houck and the sudden fury began to heat his eyes. "She can't do that! She's my wife!"

"Not any more," said Sergeant Houck. "Best forget she ever came back." He started toward the door and heard the sharp sound of the chair scraping on the floor behind him. The man's voice rose, shrilling up almost into a shriek.

"Stop!" The man rushed to the wall rack and grabbed the rifle there and swung it at his hip, bringing the muzzle to bear on Sergeant Houck. "Stop!" He was breathing deeply and he fought for control of his voice. "You're not going to take her away!"

Sergeant Houck turned slowly. He stood still, a motionless granite shape in the lamplight.

"Threatening an Army man," said Sergeant Houck. "And with an empty gun."

The man wavered and his eyes flicked down at the rifle, and in the second of indecision Sergeant Houck plunged toward him and one huge hand grasped the gun barrel and pushed it aside and the shot thudded harmlessly into the cabin wall. He wrenched the gun from the man's grasp and his other hand took the man by the shirt front and shook him forward and back and pushed him over and down into the chair.

"No more of that," said Sergeant Houck. "Best sit quiet." His eyes swept the room and found the box of cartridges on a shelf and he took this with the rifle and went to the door. "Look around in the morning and you'll find these." He went outside and tossed the gun up on the roof of one of the sheds and dropped the little box by the strawpile and kicked straw over it. He went to the wagon and stood by it and the woman came out of the darkness of the trees by the creek, carrying the boy.

The wagon wheels rolled silently and the small creakings of the wagon body and the thudding rhythm of the horses' hooves were distinct, isolated sounds in the night. The creek was on their right and they followed the tracking of the road back the way they had come. The woman moved on the seat, shifting the boy's weight from one arm to the other, and Sergeant Houck took him by the overalls and lifted him and reached behind to lay him on the burlap bags.

"A good boy," he said. "Has the Indian way of taking things without yapping. A good way."

The thin new tracks in the dust unwound endlessly under the wheels and the late waning moon climbed out of the horizon and its light shone in pale, barely noticeable patches through the scattered bushes and trees along the creek.

"I have relatives in Missouri," said the woman. "I could go there."

Sergeant Houck fumbled in his side pocket and found a straw and put this in his mouth and chewed slowly on it. "Is that what you want?"

"No."

They came to the main road crossing and swung left and the dust thickened under the horses' hooves. The lean dark shape of a coyote slipped from the brush on one side and bounded along the road and disappeared on the other side.

"I'm forty-seven," said Sergeant Houck. "Nearly thirty of that in the Army. Makes a man rough."

The woman looked straight ahead at the far dwindling ribbon of the road and a small smile curled the corners of her mouth.

"Four months," said Sergeant Houck, "and this last hitch is done. I'm thinking of homesteading on out in the Territory." He chewed on the straw and took it between a thumb and forefinger and flipped it away. "You could get a room at the settlement."

"I could," said the woman. The horses slowed to a walk, breathing deeply, and he let them hold the steady, plodding pace. Far off a coyote howled and others caught the signal and the sounds echoed back and forth in the distance and died away into the night silence.

"Four months," said Sergeant Houck. "That's not so long."

"No," said the woman. "Not too long."

A breeze stirred across the brush and took the dust from the slow hooves in small whorls and the wheels rolled slowly and she put out a hand and touched his shoulder. The fingers moved down along his upper arm and curved over the big muscles there and the warmth of them sank through the cloth of his worn service jacket. She dropped the hand again in her lap and looked ahead along the ribbon of the road. He clucked to the horses and urged them again into a trot, and the small creakings of the wagon body and the dulled rhythm of the hooves were gentle sounds in the night.

The wheels rolled and the late moon climbed, and its pale light shone slantwise down on the moving wagon, on the sleeping boy, and on the woman looking straight ahead and the great granite slab of Sergeant Houck.

Jeremy Rodock

JEREMY RODOCK was a hanging man when it came to horse thieves. He hanged them quick and efficient, and told what law there was about it afterwards. He was a big man in many ways and not just in shadow-making size. People knew him. He had a big ranch—a horse ranch—about the biggest in the Territory, and he loved horses, and no one, not even a one of his own hands—and they were careful picked—could match him at breaking and gentling his big geldings for any kind of road work. Tall they were, those horses, and rawboned, out of Western mares by some hackney stallions he'd had brought from the East, and after you'd been working with cowponies they'd set you back on your heels when you first saw them. But they were stout in harness with a fast, swinging trot that could take the miles and a heavy coach better than anything else on hooves. He was proud of those horses, and he had a right to be. I know. I was one of his hands for a time. I was with him once when he hanged a pair of rustlers. And I was with him the one time he didn't.

That was a long ways back. I was young then with a stretch in my legs, about topping twenty, and Jeremy Rodock was already an old man. Maybe not so old, maybe just about into his fifties, but he seemed old to me—old the way a pine gets when it's through growing, standing tall and straight and spreading strong, but with the graying grimness around the edges that shows it's settling to the long last stand against the winds and the storms. I remember I was surprised to find he could still outwork any of his men and be up before them in the morning. He was tough fiber clear through, and he took me on because I had a feeling for horses and they'd handle for me without much fuss, and that was what he wanted.

"You'll earn your pay," he said, "and not act your age more than you can help, and if your sap breaks out in sass, I'll slap you against a gatepost and larrup the hide off your back." And he would, and I knew it. And he taught me plenty about horses and men, and I worked for him the way I've never worked for another man.

That was the kind of work I liked. We always paired for it, and Rodock was letting me side him. The same men, working as a team, always handled the same horses from the time they were brought in off the range until they were ready and delivered. They were plenty wild at first, four- and five-year-olds with free-roaming strong in their legs, not having had any experience with men and ropes from the time they were foaled except for the few days they were halter-broken and bangtailed as coming two-year-olds. They had their growth and life was running in them, and it was a pleasure working with them.

Rodock's system was quick and thorough; you could tell a Rodock horse by the way he'd stand when you wanted him to stand and give all he had when you wanted him to move, and respond to the reins like he knew what you wanted almost before you were certain yourself. We didn't do much with saddle stock except as needed for our personal use. Rodock horses were stage horses. That's what they were bred and broke for. They were all right for riding, maybe better than all right if you could stick their paces, because they sure could cover ground, but they were best for stage work.

We'd rope a horse out of the corral and take him into a square stall and tie a hind leg up to his belly so he couldn't even try to kick without falling flat, and then start to get acquainted. We'd talk to him till he was used to voices, and slap him and push him around till he knew we weren't going to hurt him. Then we'd throw old harness on him and yank it off and throw it on again, and keep at this till he'd stand without flicking an inch of hide no matter how hard the harness hit. We'd take him out and let the leg down and lead him around with the old harness flapping till that wouldn't mean any more to him than a breeze blowing. We'd fit him with reins and one man would walk in front with the lead-rope and the other behind holding the reins and ease him into knowing what they meant. And all the time we'd speak sharp when he acted up and speak soft and give him a piece of carrot or a fistful of corn when he behaved right.

Hitching was a different proposition. No horse that'll work for you because he wants to, and not just because he's beat into it, takes kindly to hitching. He's bound to throw his weight about the first time or two and seem to forget a lot he's learned. We'd take our horse and match him with a well-broke trainer, and harness the two of them with good leather to a stout wagon. We'd have half-hobbles on his front feet fastened to the spliced ends of a rope that ran up through a ring on the underside of his girth and through another ring on the wagon tongue and up to the driving seat. Then the two of us would get on the seat and I'd hold the rope and Rodock'd take the reins. The moment we'd start to move, the trainer heaving into the traces, things would begin to happen. The new horse would be mighty surprised. He'd likely start rearing or plunging. I'd pull on the rope and his front legs would come out from under him and down he'd go on his nose. After trying that a few times, he'd learn he wasn't getting anywhere and begin to steady and remember some of the things he'd learned before. He'd find he had to step along when the wagon moved, and after a while he'd find that stepping was smoothest and easiest if he did his share of the pulling. Whenever he'd misbehave or wouldn't stop when he should, I'd yank on the rope and his nose would hit the soft dirt. It was surprising how quick he'd learn to put his weight into the harness and pay attention to the boss riding behind him. Sometimes, in a matter of three weeks, we'd have one ready to take his place in a four-horse pull of the old coach we had for practice runs. That would be a good horse.

Well, we were readying twenty-some teams for a new stage line when this happened. Maybe it wouldn't have happened, not the way it did, if one of the horses hadn't sprung a tendon and we needed a replacement. I don't blame myself for it, and I don't think Rodock did either, even though the leg went bad when I pulled the horse down on his nose. He was something of a hollow-head anyway, and wasn't learning as he should and had kept on trying to smash loose every time the wagon moved.

As I say, this horse pulled a tendon, not bad, but enough to mean a limp, and Rodock wouldn't send a limping horse along even to a man he might otherwise be willing to trim on a close deal. Shoo him out on the range, he told me, and let time and rest and our good grass put him in shape for another try next year. "And saddle my bay," he said, "and take any horse you'd care to sit, son. We'll ramble out to the lower basin and bring in another and maybe a spare in case something else happens."

That was why we were riding out a little before noon on a hot day, leaving the others busy about the buildings, just the two of us loafing along toward the first of the series of small natural valleys on Rodock's range where he kept the geldings and young studs. We were almost there, riding the ridge, when he stopped and swung in the saddle toward me. "Let's make a day of it, son. Let's mosey on to the next basin and have a look-see at the mares there and this year's crop of foals. I like to see the little critters run."

That's what I mean. If we hadn't been out already, he never would have taken time to go there. We'd checked the mares a few weeks before and tallied the foals and seen that everything was all right. If that horse hadn't gone lame, it might have been weeks, maybe months, before any of us would have gone up that way again.

We moseyed on, not pushing our horses because we'd be using them hard on the way back, cutting out a couple of geldings and hustling them home. We came over the last rise and looked down into that second small valley, and there wasn't a single thing in sight. Where there ought to have been better than forty mares and their foals, there wasn't a moving object, only the grass shading to deeper green down the slope to the trees along the stream and fading out again up the other side of the valley.

Jeremy Rodock sat still in his saddle. "I didn't think anyone would have the nerve," he said, quiet and slow. He put his horse into a trot around the edge of the valley, leaning over and looking at the ground, and I followed. He stopped at the head of the valley where it narrowed and the stream came through, and he dismounted and went over the ground carefully. He came back to his horse and leaned his chest against the saddle, looking over it and up at me.

"Here's where they were driven out," he said, still quiet and slow. "At least three men. Their horses were shod. Not more than a few days ago. A couple of weeks and there wouldn't have been any trail left to follow." He looked over his saddle and studied me. "You've been with me long enough, son," he said, "for me to know what you can do with horses. But I don't know what you can do with that gun you're carrying. I wish I'd brought one of the older men. You better head back and give the word. I'm following this trail."

"Mister Rodock," I said, "I wish you wouldn't make so many remarks about my age. One thing a man can't help is his age. But
anywhere you and that bay can go, me and this roan can follow.
And as for this gun I'm carrying, I can hit anything with it you
can and maybe a few things you'd miss."

He looked at me over his saddle and his eyebrows twitched a
little upwards.

"Careful, son," he said. "That comes close to being sass." His
jawline tightened, and he had that old-pine look, gray and grim and
enduring. "You'll have hard riding," he said, and swung into his
saddle and put his horse into a steady trot along the trail, and that
was all he said for the next four-five hours.

Hard riding it was. Trotting gets to a man even if he's used to
being on a horse. It's a jolting pace, and after a time your muscles
grow plain tired of easing the jolts and the calluses on your rump
warm up and remind you they're there. But trotting is the way to
make time if you really intend to travel. Some people think the best
way is to keep to a steady lope. That works on the back of your neck
after a while and takes too much out of the horse after the first couple of hours. Others like to run the horse, then give him a breather,
then run him again, and keep that up. You take it all out of him the
first day doing that. Trotting is the best way. A good horse can trot
along steady, his shoulders and legs relaxed and his hooves slapping
down almost by their own weight, do it hour after hour and cover
his fifty-to-sixty miles with no more than a nice even sweat and be
ready to do the same the next day and the next after that, and a lot
longer than any man riding him can hope to take it.

Rodock was trotting, and his long-legged bay was swinging out the
miles, and far as I could tell the old man was made of iron and didn't
even know he was taking a beating. I knew I was, and that roan I'd
picked because he looked like a cowpony I'd had once, was working
with his shorter legs to hold the pace, and I was shifting my weight
from one side to the other about every fifteen minutes so I'd burn
only half of my rump at a time.

It was dark night when Rodock stopped by water and swung down
and hobbled his horse and unsaddled, and I did the same.

"Might miss the trail in the dark," he said. "Anyways, they're moving slow on account of the colts. I figure we've gained at least a day
on them already. Maybe more. Better get some sleep. We'll be

traveling with the first light." He settled down with his saddle for a pillow and I did the same, and after a few minutes his voice drifted out of the darkness. "You came along right well, son. Do the same tomorrow and I'll shut up about your age."

Next thing I knew he was shaking me awake and the advance glow of the sun was climbing the sky, and he was squatting beside me with a hatful of berries from the bushes near the water. I ate my share and we saddled and started on, and after I shook the stiffness I felt fresh and almost chipper. The trail was snaking in wide curves southwest, following the low places, but rising, as the whole country was, gradually up through the foothills toward the first tier of mountains.

About regular breakfast time, when the sun was a couple of hours over the horizon behind us, Rodock waved to me to come alongside close.

"None of this makes sense," he said, without slacking pace. "A queer kind of rustling run-off. Mares and foals. I've tangled with a lot of thievery in my time, but all of it was with stock could be moved fast and disposed of quick. Can't do that with mares and sucking colts. How do you figure it, son?"

I studied that awhile. "Mister Rodock," I said, "there's only one advantage I see. Colts that young haven't felt a branding iron yet. Get away with them and you can slap on any brand you want."

"You're ageing fast, son," he said. "That's a right good thought. But these foals couldn't be weaned for three months yet. Say two months if you were the kind could be mean and not worry about getting them started right. What good would they be, even with your brand on them, still nursing mares that have got my J-tailed-R brand?"

"I'd be mighty embarrassed," I said, "every time anybody had a look at a one of them. Guess I'd have to keep them out of sight till they could be weaned."

"For two-three months, son?" he said. "You'd ride herd on them two-three months to keep them from heading back to their home range? Or coop them some place where you'd have to feed them? And be worrying all the time that maybe Jeremy Rodock would jump you with a hanging rope in his hand?"

"No," I said, "I wouldn't. I don't know what I'd do. Guess I just don't have a thieving mind."

"But somebody's doing it," he said. "Damned if I know what."

And we moved along at that steady fast trot, and my roan dropped back where he liked to stay, about twenty feet behind where he could set his own rhythm without being bothered trying to match the strides of the longer-legged bay. We moved along, and I began to feel empty clear down into my shanks and I began to hunch forward to ease the calluses on my rump. The only break all morning was a short stop for brief watering. We moved along and into the afternoon, and I could tell the roan felt exactly as I did. He and I were concentrating on just one thing, putting all we had into following twenty feet after an old iron ramrod of a man on one of the long-legged, tireless horses of his own shrewd breeding.

The trail was still stale, several days at least, and we were not watching sharp ahead, so we came on them suddenly. Rodock, being ahead and going up a rise, saw them first and was swinging to the ground and grabbing his horse's nose when I came beside him and saw the herd, bunched, well ahead and into a small canyon that cut off to the right. I swung down and caught the roan's nose in time to stop the nicker starting, and we hurried to lead both horses back down the rise and a good ways more and over to a clump of trees. We tied them there and went ahead again on foot, crawling the last stretch up the rise and dropping on our bellies to peer over the top. They were there all right, the whole herd, the mares grazing quietly, some of the foals lying down, the others skittering around the way they do, daring each other to flip their heels.

We studied that scene a long time, checking every square yard of it as far as we could see. There was not a man or a saddled horse in sight. Rodock plucked a blade of grass and stuck it in his mouth and chewed on it.

"All right, son," he said. "Seems we'll have to smoke them out. They must be holed up somewhere handy waiting to see if anyone's following. You scout around the left side of that canyon and I'll take the right. Watch for tracks and keep an eye cocked behind you. We'll meet way up there beyond the herd where the trees and bushes give good cover. If you're jumped, get off a shot and I'll be on my way over ahumping."

"Mister Rodock," I said, "you do the same and so will I."

We separated, slipping off our different ways and moving slow behind any cover that showed. I went along the left rim of the canyon, crouching by rocks and checking the ground carefully each time before moving on and peering down into the canyon along the way. I came on a snake and circled it and flushed a rabbit out of some bushes, and those were the only living things or signs of them I saw except for the horses below there in the canyon. Well up beyond them, where the rock wall slanted out into a passable slope, I worked my way down and to where we were to meet. I waited, and after a while Rodock appeared, walking toward me without even trying to stay under cover.

"See anything, son?" he said.

"No," I said.

"It's crazier than ever," he said. "I found their tracks where they left. Three shod horses moving straight out. Now what made them chuck and run like that? Tracks at least a day old too."

"Somebody scared them," I said.

"It would take a lot," he said, "to scare men with nerve enough to make off with a bunch of my horses. Who'd be roaming around up here anyway? If it was anyone living within a hundred miles, they'd know my brand and be taking the horses in." He stood there straight, hands on his hips, and stared down the canyon at the herd. "What's holding them?" he said.

"Holding who?" I said.

"Those horses," he said. "Those mares. Why haven't they headed for home? Why aren't they working along as they graze?"

He was right. They weren't acting natural. They were bunched too close and hardly moving, and when any of them did move there was something wrong. We stared at them, and suddenly Rodock began to run toward them and I had trouble staying close behind him. They heard us and turned to face us and they had trouble turning, and Rodock stopped and stared at them and there was a funny moaning sound in his throat.

"My God!" he said. "Look at their front feet!"

I looked, and I could see right away what he meant. They had been roped and thrown and their front hooves rasped almost to the quick, so that they could barely put their weight on them. Each step hurt, and they couldn't have traveled at all off the canyon grass out on the rocky ground beyond. It hurt me seeing them hurt each time they tried to move, and if it did that to me I could imagine what it did to Jeremy Rodock.

They knew him, and some of them nickered at him, and the old mare that was their leader, and was standing with head drooping, raised her head and started forward and dropped her head again and limped to us with it hanging almost to the ground. There was a heavy iron bolt tied to her forelock and hanging down between her eyes. You know how a horse moves its head as it walks. This bolt would have bobbed against her forehead with each step she took, and already it had broken through the skin and worn a big sore that was beginning to fester.

Rodock stood still and stared at her and that moaning sound clung in his throat. I had to do something. I pulled out my pocketknife and cut through the tied hairs and tossed the bolt far as I could. I kicked up a piece of sod and reached down and took a handful of clean dirt and rubbed it over the sore on her forehead and then wiped it and the oozing stuff away with my neckerchief, and she stood for me and only shivered as I rubbed. I looked at Rodock and he was someone I had never seen before. He was a gaunt figure of a man, with eyes pulled back deep in their sockets and burning, and the bones of his face showing plain under the flesh.

"Mister Rodock," I said, "are we riding out on that three-horse trail?"

I don't think he even heard me.

"Not a thing," he said. "Not a single solitary goddamned thing I can do. They're traveling light and fast now. Too much of a start and too far up in the rocks for trailing. They've probably separated and could be heading clean out of the Territory. They're devilish smart and they've done it, and there's not a goddamned thing I can do."

"We've got the mares," I said. "And the foals."

He noticed me, a flick of his eyes at me. "We've got them way up here and they can't be moved. Not till those hooves grow out." He turned toward me and threw words at me, and I wasn't anyone he knew, just someone to be a target for his bitterness. "They're devils! Three devils! Nothing worth the name of man would treat horses like that. See the devilishness of it? They run my horses way up here and cripple them. They don't have to stay around. The horses can't get away. They know the chances are we won't miss the mares for weeks, and by then the trail will be overgrown and we won't know which way they went and waste time combing the whole damn coun-

try in every direction, and maybe never get up in here. Even if someone follows them soon, like we did, they're gone and can't be caught.
One of them can slip back every week or two to see what's doing, and
if he's nabbed, what can tie him to the run-off? He's just a fiddlefoot
riding through. By weaning-time, if nothing has happened, they can
hurry in and take the colts and get off clean with a lot of unbranded
horseflesh. And there's not a thing we can do."

"We can watch the mares," I said, "till they're able to travel some,
then push them home by easy stages. And meantime be mighty
rough on anyone comes noseying around."

"We've got the mares," he said. "They're as well off here as anywhere now. What I want is those devils. All three of them. Together
and roped and in my hands." He put out his hands, the fingers
clawed, and shook them at me. "I've got to get them! Do you see
that? I've got to!" He dropped his hands limp at his sides, and his
voice dropped too, dry and quiet with a coldness in it. "There's one
thing we can do. We can leave everything as it is and go home and
keep our mouths shut and wait and be here when they come for the
colts." He took hold of me by the shoulders and his fingers hurt my
muscles. "You see what they did to my horses. Can you keep your
mouth shut?"

He didn't wait for me to answer. He let go of my shoulders and
turned and went straight through the herd of crippled mares without looking at them and on down the canyon and out and over the
rise where we first sighted them and on to the clump of trees where
we had tied our horses.

I followed him and he was mounted and already starting off when
I reached the roan and I mounted and set out after him. He was in
no hurry now and let the bay walk part of the time, and the roan and
I were glad of that. He never turned to look at me or seemed to notice whether I followed or not. A rabbit jumped out of the brush
and I knocked it over on the second shot and picked it up and laid
it on the saddle in front of me, and he paid no attention to me, not
even to the shots, just steadying the bay when it started at the sharp
sounds and holding it firm on the back trail.

He stopped by a stream while there was still light and dismounted,
and I did the same. After we had hobbled and unsaddled the horses,
he sat on the ground with his back to a rock and stared into space.
I couldn't think of anything to say, so I gathered some wood and

made a fire. I took my knife and gutted the rabbit and cut off the head. I found some fairly good clay and moistened it and rolled the rabbit in a ball of it and dropped this in the fire. When I thought it would be about done, I poked it out of the hot ashes and let it cool a bit. Then I pried off the baked clay and the skin came with it and the meat showed juicy and smelled fine. It was still a little raw, but anything would have tasted good then. I passed Rodock some pieces and he took them and ate the meat off the bones mechanically like his mind was far away some place. I still couldn't think of anything to say, so I stretched out with my head on my saddle, and then it was morning and I was chilled and stiff and staring up at clear sky, and he was coming toward me leading both horses and his already saddled.

It was getting toward noon, and we were edging onto our home range when we met two of the regular hands out looking for us. They came galloping with a lot of questions and Rodock put up a palm to stop them.

"Nothing's wrong," he said. "I took a sudden mind to circle around and look over some of the stock that's strayed a bit and show the boy here parts of my range he hadn't seen before. Went farther'n I intended to and we're some tuckered. You two cut over to the lower basin and take in a pair of four-year-olds. Hightail it straight and don't dawdle. We've got that stage order to meet."

They were maybe a mite puzzled as they rode off, but it was plain they hadn't hit the second basin and seen the mares were missing. Rodock and I started on, and I thought of something to say and urged the roan close.

"Mister Rodock," I said, "I don't like that word 'boy.' "

"That's too damn bad," he said, and went steadily on and I followed, and he paid no more attention to me all the rest of the way to the ranch buildings.

Things were different after that around the place. He didn't work with the horses himself any more. Most of the time he stayed in his sturdy frame house where he had a Mexican to cook for him and fight the summer dust, and I don't know what he did in there. Once in a while he'd be on the porch, and he'd sit there hours staring off where the foothills started their climb toward the mountains. With him shut away like that, I was paired with Hugh Claggett. This Claggett was a good enough man, I guess. Rodock thought some of him. They had knocked around together years back, and when he had showed up needing a job sometime before I was around the place, Rodock gave him one, and he was a sort of acting foreman when Rodock was away for any reason. He knew horses, maybe as much as Rodock himself in terms of the things you could put down as fact in a book. But he didn't have the real feel, the deep inside feel, of them that means you can sense what's going on inside a horse's head; walk up to a rolled-eye maverick that's pawing the sky at the end of a rope the way Rodock could, and talk the nonsense out of him and have him standing there quivering to quiet under your hand in a matter of minutes. Claggett was a precise, practical sort of a man, and working with him was just that, working, and I took no real pleasure in it.

When Rodock did come down by the stables and working corral, he was different. He didn't come often, and it would have been better if he hadn't come at all. First thing I noticed was his walk There was no bounce to it. Always before, no matter how tired he was, he walked rolling on the soles of his feet from heels to toes and coming off the toes each step with a little bouncy spring. Now he was walking flatfooted, plodding, like he was carrying more weight than just his body. And he was hard and driving in a new way, a nasty and irritable way. He'd always been one to find fault, but that had been because he was better at his business than any of us and he wanted to set us straight. He'd shrivel us down to size with a good clean tongue-whipping, then pitch in himself and show us how to do whatever it was and we'd be the better for it. Now he was plain cussed all through. He'd snap at us about anything and everything. Nothing we did was right. He'd not do a lick of work himself, just stand by and find fault, and his voice was brittle and nasty, and he'd get personal in his remarks. And he was mighty touchy about how we treated the horses. We did the way he had taught us and the way I knew was right by how the horses handled, still he would blow red and mad and tear into us with bitter words, saying we were slapping on leather too hard or fitting bridles too snug, little things, but they added to a nagging tally as the days passed and made our work tiring and troublesome. There was a lot of grumbling going on in the bunkhouse in the evenings.

Time and again I wanted to tell the others about the mares so maybe they would understand. But I'd remember his hands stretching toward me and shaking and then biting into my shoulders and I'd keep what had happened blocked inside me. I knew what was festering in him. I'd wake at night thinking about those mares, thinking about them way up there in the hills pegged to a small space of thinning grass by hooves that hurt when weight came on them and sent stabs of pain up their legs when they hit anything hard. A good horse is a fine-looking animal. But it isn't the appearance that gets into you and makes something in you reach out and respond to him. It's the way he moves, the sense of movement in him even when he's standing still, the clean-stepping speed and competence of him that's born in him and is what he is and is his reason for being. Take that away and he's a pitiful thing. And somewhere there were three men who had done that to those mares. I'd jump awake at night and think about them and maybe have some notion of what it cost Jeremy Rodock to stay set there at his ranch and leave his mares alone with their misery far off up in the hills.

When the stage horses were ready to be shod for the last real road tests, he nearly drove our blacksmith crazy cursing every time a hoof was trimmed or one of them flinched under the hammer. We finished them off with hard runs in squads hitched to the old coach and delivered them, and then there was nothing much to do. Not another order was waiting. Several times agents had been to see Rodock and had gone into the house and come out again and departed, looking downright peeved. I don't know whether he simply refused any more orders or acted so mean that they wouldn't do business with him. Anyway, it was bad all around. There was too much loafing time. Except for a small crew making hay close in, no one was sent out on the range at all. The men were dissatisfied and they had reason to be, and they took to quarreling with each other. Some of them quit in disgust and others after arguing words with Rodock, and finally the last bunch demanded their time together and left, and Claggett and I were the only ones still there. That's not counting the Mexican, but he was housebroke and not worth counting. Claggett and I could handle the chores for the few horses kept regularly around the place and still have time to waste. We played euchre, but I never could beat him and then got tired of trying. And Rodock sat on his porch and stared into the distance. I didn't think he even noticed me when I figured that his bay would be getting soft and started saddling him and taking him out for exercise the same as I did the roan. One day I rode him right past the porch. Rodock fooled me on that, though. I was almost past, pretending not to see him, when his voice flicked at me. "Easy on those reins, boy. They're just extra trimming. That horse knows what you want by the feel of your legs around him. I don't want him spoiled." He was right too. I found you could put that bay through a figure eight or drop him between two close-set posts just by thinking it down through your legs.

The slow days went by, and I couldn't stand it any longer. I went to the house.

"Mister Rodock," I said, "it's near two months now. Isn't it time we made a move?"

"Don't be so damn young," he said. "I'll move when I know it's right."

I stood on one foot and then on the other and I couldn't think of anything to say except what I'd said before about my age, so I went back to the bunkhouse and made Claggett teach me all the games of solitaire he knew.

Then one morning I was oiling harness to keep it limber when I looked up and Rodock was in the stable doorway.

"Saddle my bay," he said, "and Hugh's sorrel. I reckon that roan'll do for you again. Pick out a good packhorse and bring them all around to the storehouse soon as you can."

I jumped to do what he said, and when I had the horses there he and Claggett had packs filled. We loaded the extra horse, and the last thing Rodock did was hand out Henrys and we tucked these in our saddle scabbards and started out. He led the way, and from the direction he took it was plain we were not heading straight into the hills, but were going to swing around and come in from the south.

I led the packhorse and we rode in a compact bunch, not pushing for speed. It was in the afternoon that we ran into the other riders, out from the settlement and heading our way, Ben Kern, who was federal marshal for that part of the Territory, and three of the men he usually swore in as deputies when he had a need for any. We stopped and they stopped, looking us over.

"You've saved me some miles," Kern said. "I was heading for your place."

Rodock raised his eyebrows and looked at him and was silent. I kept my mouth shut. Claggett, who probably knew as much about the mares as I did by now, did the same. This was Rodock's game. "Not saying much, are you?" Kern said. He saw the Henrys. "Got your warpaint on too. I thought something would be doing from what I've been hearing about things at your place. What's on your mind this time?"

"My mind's my own," Rodock said. "But it could be we're off on a little camping trip."

"And again it couldn't," Kern said. "Only camping you ever do is on the tail of a horse thief. That's the trouble. Twice now you've ridden in to tell me where to find them swinging. Evidence was clear enough, so there wasn't much I could do. But you're too damn free with your rope. How we going to get decent law around here with you oldtimers crossing things up? This time, if it is a this time, you're dong it right and turn them over to me. We'll just ride along to see that you do it."

Rodock turned to me. He had that grim and enduring look and the lines by his mouth were taut. "Break out those packs, boy. We're camping right here." I saw what he was figuring and I dismounted and began unfastening the packs. I had them on the ground and was fussing with the knots when Kern spoke.

"You're a stubborn old bastard," he said. "You'd stay right here and outwait us."

"I would," Rodock said.

"All right," Kern said. "We'll fade. But I've warned you. If it's rustlers you're after, bring them to me."

Rodock didn't say a thing and I heaved the packs on the horse again, and by time I had them fastened tight, Kern and his men were a distance away and throwing dust. We started on, and by dark we had gone a good piece. By dark the next day we had made a big half-circle and were well into the hills. About noon of the next, we were close enough to the canyon where we had found the mares, say two miles if you could have hopped it straight. Claggett and I waited while Rodock scouted around. He came back and led us up a twisting rocky draw to a small park hemmed in part way by a fifteen-foot rock shelf and the rest of the way by a close stand of pine. It was about a half-acre in size, and you'd never know it was there unless you came along the draw and stumbled into it. We picketed the horses there and headed for the canyon on foot, moving slow and cautious as we came close. When we peered over the rim, the herd was there all right, the foals beginning to get some growth and the mares stepping a lot easier than before. They were used to the place now and not interested in leaving. They had taken to ranging pretty far up the canyon, but we managed to sight the whole count after a few minutes watching.

We searched along the rim for the right spot and found it, a crack in the rim wide enough for a man to ease into comfortably and be off the skyline for anyone looking from below, yet able to see the whole stretch where the herd was. To make it even better, we hauled a few rocks to the edge of the opening and piled brush with them, leaving a careful spy-hole. We brought a flat-topped rock for a seat behind the hole. The idea was that one of us could sit there watching while the other two holed in a natural hiding-place some fifty feet back under an over-hanging ledge with a good screen of brush. The signal, if anything happened, was to be a pebble chucked back toward the hiding-place.

I thought we'd take turns watching, but Rodock settled on that flat-top stone and froze there. Claggett and I kept each other company under the ledge, if you could call it keeping company when one person spent most of the time with his mouth shut whittling endless shavings off chunks of old wood or taking naps. That man Claggett had no nerves. He could keep his knife going for an hour at a time without missing a stroke or stretch out and drop off into a nap like we were just lazing around at the ranch. He didn't seem to have much personal interest in what might develop. He was just doing a job and tagging along with an oldtime partner. As I said before, he didn't have a real feel for horses. I guess to be fair to him I ought to remember that he hadn't seen those mares with their hooves rasped to the quick and flinching and shuddering with every step they took. Me, I was strung like a too-tight fiddle. I'd have cracked sure if I hadn't had the sense to bring a deck in my pocket for solitaire. I nearly wore out those cards and even took to cheating to win, and it seemed to me we were cooped there for weeks when it was only five days. And all the time, every day, Rodock sat on that stone as if he was a piece of it, getting older and grayer and grimmer.

Nights we spent back with the horses. We'd be moving before dawn each morning, eating a heavy breakfast cooked over a small quick fire, then slipping out to our places with the first streaks of light carrying a cold snack in our pockets. We'd return after dark for another quick meal and roll right afterwards into our blankets. You'd think we hardly knew each other the way we behaved, only speaking when that was necessary. Claggett was never much of a talker, and Rodock was tied so tight in himself now he didn't have a word to spare. I kept quiet because I didn't want him smacking my age at me again. If he could chew his lips and wear out the hours waiting, I could too, and I did.

We were well into the fifth day and I was about convinced nothing would ever happen again, any time ever anywhere in the whole wide world, when a pebble came snicking through the brush and Rodock came hard after it, ducking low and hurrying.

"They're here," he said. "All three." And I noticed the fierce little specks of light beginning to burn in his eyes. "They're stringing rope to trees for a corral. Probably planning to brand here, then run." He looked at me and I could see him assessing me and dismissing me, and he turned to Claggett. "Hugh," he started to say, "I want you to——"

I guess it was the way he had looked at me and the things he had said about my age. Anyway, I was mad. I didn't know what he was going to say, but I knew he had passed me by. I grabbed him by the arm.

"Mister Rodock," I said, "I'm the one rode with you after those mares."

He stared at me and shook his head a little as if to clear it.

"All right, boy," he said. "You do this and, by God, you do it right. Hurry back and get your horse and swing around and come riding into the canyon. Far as I can tell at the distance, these men are strangers, so there's not much chance they'd know you worked for me. You're just a drifter riding through. Keep them talking so Hugh and I can get down behind them. If they start something, keep them occupied long as you can." He grabbed me by the shoulders the way he had when we found the mares. "Any shooting you do, shoot to miss. I want them alive." He let go of me. "Now scat."

I scatted. I never went so fast over rough country on my own feet in my life. When I reached the roan, I had to hang onto his neck to get some breath and my strength back. I slapped my saddle on and took him at a good clip out of the draw and in a sharp circle for the canyon mouth, a good clip, but not too much to put him in a lather. I was heading into the canyon, pulling him to an easy trot, when it hit me, what a damn fool thing I was doing. There were three of them in there, three mighty smart men with a lot of nerve, and they had put a lot of time and waiting into this job and wouldn't likely be wanting to take chances on its going wrong. I was scared, so scared I could hardly sit the roan, and I came near swinging him around and putting my heels to him. Maybe I would have. Maybe I would have run out on those mares. But then I saw that one of the men had spotted me and there was nothing much to do but keep going toward them.

The one that had spotted me was out a ways from the others as a lookout. He had a rifle and he swung it to cover me as I came near and I stopped the roan. He was a hardcase specimen if ever I saw one and I didn't like the way he looked at me.

"Hold it now, sonny," he said. "Throw down your guns."

I was glad he said that, said "sonny," I mean, because it sort of stiffened me and I wasn't quite so scared, being taken up some with being mad. I tried to act surprised and hold my voice easy.

"Lookahere," I said, "that's an unfriendly way to talk to a stranger riding through. I wouldn't think of using these guns unless somebody pushed me into it, but I'd feel kind of naked without them. Let's just leave them alone, and if you're not the boss, suppose you let me talk to him that is."

I figured he wouldn't shoot because they'd want to know was I alone and what was I doing around there, and I was right. He jerked his head toward the other two.

"Move along, sonny," he said. "But slow. And keep your hands high in sight. I'll blast you out of that saddle if you wiggle a finger."

I walked the roan close to the other two and he followed behind me and circled around me to stand with them. They had been starting a fire and had stopped to stare at me coming. One was a short, stocky man, almost bald, with a fringe of grizzled beard down his cheeks and around his chin. The other was about medium height and slender, with clean chiseled features and a pair of the hardest, shrewdest, bluest eyes I ever saw. It was plain he was the boss by the way he took over. He set those eyes on me and I started shivering inside again.

"I've no time to waste on you," he said. "Make it quick. What's your story?"

"Story?" I said. "Why, simple enough. I'm footloose and roaming for some months and I get up this way with my pockets about played out. I'm riding by and I see something happening in here and I drop in to ask a few questions."

"Questions?" he said, pushing his head forward at me. "What kind of questions?"

"Why," I said, "I'm wondering maybe you can tell me, if I push on through these hills do I come to a town or some place where maybe I can get a job?"

The three of them stood there staring at me, chewing on this, and I sat my saddle staring back, when the bearded man suddenly spoke. "I ain't sure," he said, looking at the roan. "But maybe that's a Rodock horse."

I saw them start to move and I dove sideways off the roan, planning to streak for the brush, and a bullet from the rifle went whipping over the saddle where I'd been, and I hadn't more than bounced the first time when a voice like a chill wind struck the three of them still. "Hold it, and don't move!"

I scrambled up and saw them stiff and frozen, slowly swiveling their necks to look behind them at Rodock and Hugh Claggett and the wicked ready muzzles of their two Henrys.

"Reach," Rodock said, and they reached. "All right, boy," he said. "Strip them down."

I cleaned them thoroughly and got, in addition to the rifle and the usual revolvers, two knives from the bearded man and a small but deadly derringer from an inside pocket of the slender man's jacket.

"Got everything?" Rodock said. "Then hobble them good."

I did this just as thoroughly, tying their ankles with about a two-foot stretch between so they could walk short-stepped, but not run, and tying their wrists together behind their backs with a loop up and around their necks and down again so that if they tried yanking or pulling they'd be rough on their own Adam's apples.

They didn't like any of this. The slender man didn't say a word, just clamped his mouth and talked hate with his eyes, but the other two started cursing.

"Shut up," Rodock said, "or we'll ram gags down your throats." They shut up, and Rodock motioned to me to set them in a row on the ground leaning against a fallen tree and he hunkered down himself facing them with his Henry across his lap. "Hugh," he said, without looking away from them, "take down those ropes they've been running and bring their horses and any of their stuff you find over here. Ought to be some interesting branding irons about." He took off his hat and set it on the ground beside him. "Hop your horse, boy," he said; "get over to our hide-out and bring everything back here."

When I returned leading our other horses, the three of them were still right in a row leaning against the log and Rodock was still squatted on the ground looking at them. Maybe words had been passing. I wouldn't know. Anyway, they were all quiet then. The hardcase was staring at his own feet. The bearded man's eyes were roaming around and he had a sick look on his face. The slender man was staring right back at Rodock and his mouth was only a thin line in his face. Claggett was standing to one side fussing with a rope. I saw he was fixing a hangman's knot on it and had two others already finished and coiled at his feet. When I saw them I had a funny empty feeling under my belt and I didn't know why. I had seen a hanging before and never felt like that. I guess I had some kind of a queer notion that just hanging those three wouldn't finish the whole thing right. It wouldn't stop me waking at night and thinking about those mares and their crippled hooves.

My coming seemed to break the silence that had a grip on the whole place. The slender man drew back his lips and spit words at Rodock.

"Quit playing games," he said. "Get this over with. We know your reputation."

"Do you?" Rodock said. He stood up and waggled each foot in turn to get the kinks out of his legs. He turned and saw what Claggett was doing and a strange little mirthless chuckle sounded in his throat. "You're wasting your time, Hugh," he said. "We won't be using those. I'm taking these three in."

Claggett's jaw dropped and his mouth showed open. I guess he was seeing an old familiar pattern broken and he didn't know how to take it. I wasn't and I had caught something in Rodock's tone. I couldn't have said what it was, but it was sending tingles through my hair roots.

"Don't argue with me, Hugh," Rodock said. "My mind's set. You take some of the food and start hazing the herd toward home. They can do it now if you take them by easy stages. The boy and I'll take these three in."

I helped Claggett get ready and watched him go up the canyon to bunch the herd and get it moving. I turned to Rodock and he was staring down the back trail.

"Think you could handle four horses on lead ropes, boy?" he said. "The packhorse and their three?"

"Expect I could, strung out," I said. "But why not split them? You take two and I take two."

"I'll be doing something else," he said, and that same little cold chuckle sounded in his throat. "How far do you make it, boy, to the settlement and Kern's office?"

"Straight to it," I said, "I make it close to fifty mile."

"About right," he said. "Kind of a long hike for those used to having horses under them. Hop over and take the hobbles off their feet."

I hopped, but not very fast. I was feeling some disappointed. I was feeling that he was letting me and those mares down. A fifty-mile hike for those three would worry them plenty, and they'd be worrying, too, about what would come at the end of it. Still it was a disappointment to think about.

"While you're there," Rodock said, "pull their boots off too."

I swung to look at him. He was a big man, as I said before, but I'd run across others that stood taller and filled a doorway more, but right then he was the biggest man I ever saw anywhere any time in my whole life.

I didn't bother to take off the hobbles. I left them tied so they'd hold the boots together in pairs and I could hang them flapping over the back of the packhorse. I pulled the boots off, not trying to be gentle, just yanking, and I had a little trouble with the hardcase. He tried to kick me, so I heaved on the rope between his ankles and he came sliding out from the log flat on his back and roughing his bound hands under him, and after that he didn't try anything more. But what I remember best about the three of them then is the yellow of the socks the slender man wore. Those on the others were the usual dark gray, but his were bright yellow. I've thought about them lots of times and never been able to figure why and where he ever got them.

Rodock was rummaging in their stuff that Claggett had collected.

He tossed a couple of branding irons toward me. "Bring these along," he said. "Maybe Kern will be interested in them." He picked up a whip, an old but serviceable one with a ten-foot lash, and tested it with a sharp crack. "Get up," he said to the three, and they got up. "I'll be right behind you with this. You'll stay bunched and step right along. Start walking."

They started, and he tucked his Henry in his saddle scabbard and swung up on the bay.

By time I had the other horses pegged in a line with the packhorse as an anchor at the end and was ready to follow, they were heading out of the canyon and I hurried to catch up. I had to get out of the way, too, because Claggett had the herd gathered and was beginning to push the mares along with the foals skittering around through the bushes. Anyone standing on the canyon edge looking down would have seen a queer sight, maybe the damndest procession that ever paraded through that lonesome country. Those three were out in front, walking and putting their feet down careful even in the grass to avoid pebbles and bits of deadwood, with Rodock big and straight on his bay behind them, then me with my string of three saddled but riderless horses and the packhorse, and behind us all the mares and the skittering foals with Claggett weaving on his sorrel to keep the stragglers on the move.

Once out of the canyon we had to separate. Rodock and I and our charges turned southeast to head for the settlement. Claggett had to swing the herd toward the northeast to head for the home range. He had his trouble with the mares because they wanted to follow me and my string. But he and his sorrel knew their business and by hard work made the break and held it. I guess he was a bit huffy about the whole thing because I waved when the distance was getting long between us, and he saw me wave and didn't even raise an arm. I don't know as I blame him for that.

This was mid-afternoon and by camping time we had gone maybe ten miles and had shaken down to a steady grind. My horses had bothered the roan some by holding back on the rope and had bothered themselves a few times by spreadeagling and trying to go in different directions, but by now the idea had soaked in and they were plugging along single-file and holding their places. The three men out in front had learned to keep moving or feel the whip. The slender man stepped along without paying attention to the other two and never looked back at Rodock and never said a word. The bearded man had found that shouting and cursing simply wore out his throat and had no effect on the grim figure pacing behind them. The hardcase had tried a break, ducking quick to one side and running fast as he could, but Rodock had jumped the bay and headed him the same as you do a steer, and being awkward with his hands tied he had taken a nasty tumble. Not a one of them was going to try that again. Their feet were too tender for hard running, anyway, especially out there in the open where the grass was bunchy with bare spaces aplenty, and there were stretches with a kind of coarse gravel underfoot. When Rodock called a halt by water, they were ready to flop on the ground immediately and hitch around and dabble their feet in the stream, and I noticed that the bottoms of their socks were about gone and the soles of their feet were red where they showed in splotches through the dirt ground in. I enjoyed those ten miles, not with a feeling of fun, but with a sort of slow, steady satisfaction.

I prepared food and Rodock and I ate, and then we fed them, one at a time. Rodock sat watch with his Henry on his lap while I untied them and let them eat and wash up a bit and tied them again. We pegged each of them to a tree for the night, sitting on the ground with his back to the trunk and a rope around so he wouldn't topple when he slept. I was asleep almost as soon as I stretched out, and I slept good, and I think Rodock did too.

The next day was more of the same except that we were at it a lot longer, morning and afternoon, and our pace slowed considerably as the day wore on. They were hard to get started again after a noon stop and the last hours before we stopped, they were beginning to limp badly. They weren't thinking any more of how to make a break. They were concentrating on finding the easiest spots on which to set each step. I figured we covered twenty miles, and I got satisfaction out of every one of them. But the best were in the morning because along late in the afternoon I began to feel tired, not tired in my muscles but tired and somehow kind of shrinking inside. When we stopped, I saw that their socks were just shredded yarn around their ankles and their feet were swelling and angry red and blistery through the dirt. With them sullen and silent and Rodock gray and grim and never wasting a word, I began to feel lonesome, and I couldn't go to sleep right away and found myself checking and re-checking in my mind how far we had come and how many miles we still had to go.

The day after that we started late because there was rain during the night and we waited till the morning mists cleared. The dampness in the ground must have felt better to their feet for a while because they went along fairly good the first of the morning after we got under way. They were really hard to get started, though, after the noon stop. During the afternoon they went slower and slower, and Rodock had to get mean with the whip around the heels of the hardcase and the bearded man. Not the slender one. That one kept his head high and marched along and you could tell he was fighting not to wince with every step. After a while, watching him, I began to get the feel of him. He was determined not to give us the satisfaction of seeing this get to him in any serious way. I found myself watching him too much, too closely, so I dropped behind a little more, tagging along in the rear with my string, and before Rodock called the halt by another stream, I began to see the occasional small red splotches in the footprints on dusty stretches that showed the blisters on their feet were breaking. The best I could figure we had come maybe another ten miles during the day, the last few mighty slow. That made about forty all together, and when I went over it in my mind I had to call it twelve more to go because we had curved off the most direct route some to avoid passing near a couple of line cabins of the only other ranch in that general neighborhood north of the settlement.

There weren't many words in any of us as we went through the eating routine. I didn't know men's faces were capable of such intense hatred as showed plain on the hardcase and the bearded man. They gobbled their food and glared at Rodock from their night-posts against trees, and for all I know glared without stopping all night because they had the same look the next morning. It was the slender man who suddenly took to talking. The hatred he'd had at the start seemed to have burned away. What was left was a kind of hard pride that kept his eyes alive. He looked up from his food at Rodock.

"It was a good try," he said.

"It was," Rodock said. "But not good enough. Your mistake was hurting my horses."

"I had to," the man said. "That was part of it. I saw some of your horses on a stage line once. I had to have a few."

"If you wanted some of my horses," Rodock said, "why didn't you come and buy them?"

"I was broke," the man said.

"You were greedy," Rodock said. "You had to take all in that basin. If you'd cut out a few and kept on going, you might have made it."

"Maybe," the man said. "Neither of us will ever know now. You planning to keep this up all the way in?"

"I am," Rodock said.

"Then turn us over?" the man said.

"Yes," Rodock said.

"You're the one that's greedy," the man said.

He shut up and finished his food and crawled to his tree and refused to look at Rodock again. I fixed his rope and then I had trouble getting to sleep. I lay a long time before I dozed and what sleep I got wasn't much good.

In the morning Rodock was grayer and grimmer than ever before. Maybe he hadn't slept much either. He stood off by himself and let me do everything alone. I couldn't make the hardcase and the bearded man get on their feet, and I found my temper mighty short and was working up a real mad when the slender man, who was up and ready, stepped over and kicked them, kicked them with his own swollen feet that had the remains of his yellow socks flapping around the ankles.

"Get up!" he said. "Damn you, get up! We're going through with this right!"

They seemed a lot more afraid of him than of me. They staggered up and they stepped along with him as Rodock came close with the whip in his hand and we got our pathetic parade started again. We couldn't have been moving much more than a mile an hour, and even that pace slowed, dropping to about a crawl when we hit rough stretches, and more and more red began to show in the footprints. And still that slender man marched along, slow but dogged, the muscles in his neck taut as he tried to stay straight without wincing.

Rodock was mean and nasty, crowding close behind them, using the whip to raise the dust around the lagging two. I didn't like the look of him. The skin of his face was stretched too tight and his eyes were too deep-sunk. I tried riding near him and making a few remarks to calm him, but he snapped at me like I might be a horse thief myself, so I dropped behind and stayed there.

He didn't stop at noontime, but kept them creeping along, maybe because he was afraid he'd never get them started again. It was only a short while after that the bearded man fell down, just crumpled and went over sideways and lay still. It wasn't exactly a faint or anything quite like that. I think he had cracked inside, had run out his score and quit trying, even trying to stay conscious. He was breathing all right, but it was plain he wouldn't do any more walking for a spell.

Rodock sat on his horse and looked down at him. "All right, boy," he said. "Hoist him on one of your string and tie him so he'll stay put." I heaved him on the first of the horses behind me and slipped a rope around the horse's barrel to hold him. Rodock sat on his bay and looked at the other two men, not quite sure what to do, and the slender one stared back at him, contempt sharp on his face, and Rodock shook out the whip. "Get moving, you two!" he said, and we started creeping along again.

It was about another hour and maybe another mile when the hardcase began screaming. He threw himself on the ground and rolled and thrashed and kept screaming, then stretched out taut and suddenly went limp all over, wide awake and conscious, but staring up as if he couldn't focus on anything around him.

Rodock had to stop again, chewing his lower lip and frowning. "All right, boy," he said. "Hoist that one too." I did, the same as the other one, and when I looked around, damned if that slender man wasn't walking on quite a distance ahead with Rodock right behind him.

I didn't want to watch, but I couldn't help watching that man stagger on. I think he had almost forgotten us. He was intent on the terrible task of putting one foot forward after the other and easing his weight onto it. Rodock, bunched on his bay and staring at him, was the one who cracked first. The sun was still up the sky, but he shouted a halt and when the man kept going he had to jump down and run ahead and grab him. It was a grim business making camp. The other two had straightened out some, but they had no more spirit in them than a pair of limp rabbits. I had to lift them down, and it wasn't until they had some food in them that they began to perk up at all. They seemed grateful when I hiked a ways and brought water in a folding canvas bucket from one of the packs and let them take turns soaking their swollen bloody feet in it. Then I took a saddle blanket and ripped it in pieces and wrapped some of them around their feet. I think I did that so I wouldn't find myself always sneaking looks at their feet. I did the same for the slender man, and all the time I was doing it he looked at me with that contempt on his face and I didn't give a damn. I did this even though I thought Rodock might not like it, but he didn't say a word. I noticed he wouldn't look at me and I found I didn't want to look at him either. I tried to keep my mind busy figuring how far we had come and made it six miles with six more still to go, and I was wishing those six would fade away and the whole thing would be over. The sleep I got that night wasn't worth anything to me.

In the morning I didn't want any breakfast and I wasn't going to prepare any unless Rodock kicked me into it. He was up ahead of me, standing quiet and chewing his lower lip and looking very old and very tired, and he didn't say a word to me. I saddled the horses the way I had been every morning because that was the easiest way to tote the saddles along and tied them in the usual string. The slender man was awake, watching me, and by time I finished the other two were too. They were thoroughly beaten. They couldn't have walked a quarter of a mile with the devil himself herding them. I thought to hell with Rodock and led the horses up close and hoisted the two, with them quick to help, into their saddles. They couldn't put their feet in the stirrups, but they could sit the saddles and let their feet dangle. I went over to the slender man and started to take hold of him, and he glared at me and shook himself free of my hands and twisted around and strained till he was up on his feet. I stood there gaping at him and he hobbled away, heading straight for the settlement. I couldn't move. I was sort of frozen inside watching him. He made about fifty yards and his legs buckled under him. The pain in his feet must have been stabbing up with every step and he simply couldn't stand any longer. And then while I stared at him he started crawling on his hands and knees.

"God damn it, boy!" Rodock's voice behind me made me jump. "Grab that man! Haul him back here!"

I ran and grabbed him and after the first grab, he didn't fight and I hauled him back. "Hoist him on his horse," Rodock said, and I did that. And then Rodock started cursing. He cursed that man and he cursed me and then he worked back over us both again. He wasn't a cursing man and he didn't know many words and he didn't have much imagination at it, but what he did know he used over and over again and after a while he ran down and stopped and chewed his lower lip. He turned and stalked to the packhorse and took the pairs of tied boots and came along the line tossing each pair over the withers of the right horse. He went back to the packs and pulled out the weapons I'd found on the three and checked to see that the guns were empty and shook the last of the flour out of its bag and put the weapons in it with the rifle barrel sticking out the top. He tied the bag to the pommel of the slender man's saddle.

"All right, boy," he said. "Take off those lead ropes and untie their hands."

When I had done this and they were rubbing their wrists, he stepped close to the slender man's horse and spoke up at the man.

"Back to the last creek we passed yesterday," he said, "and left along it a few miles you come to Shirttail Fussel's shack. From what I hear for a price he'll hide out anything and keep his mouth shut. A man with sense would fix his feet there and then keep traveling and stay away from this range the rest of his days."

The slender man didn't say a word. He pulled his horse around and started in the direction of the creek and the other two tagged him, and what I remember is that look of hard pride still in his eyes, plain and sharp against the pinched and strained bleakness of his face.

We watched them go and I turned to Rodock. He was old, older even than I thought he was when I first saw him, and tired with heavy circles under his eyes. At that moment I didn't like him at all, not because he had let them go, but because of what he had put me through, and it was my turn to curse him. I did it right. I did a better job than he had done before and he never even wagged a muscle. "Shut up," he said finally. "I need a drink." He went to his bay and mounted and headed for the settlement. I watched him, hunched forward and old in the saddle, and I was ashamed. I took the lead rope of the packhorse and climbed on the roan and followed him. I was glad when he put the bay into a fast trot because I was fed up with sittting on a walking horse.

He bobbed along ahead of me, a tired old man who seemed too

small for that big bay, and then a strange thing began to happen. He began to sit straighter in the saddle and stretch up and look younger by the minute, and when we reached the road and headed into the settlement he was Jeremy Rodock riding straight and true on a Rodock horse and riding it like it was the part of him that in a way it really was. He hit a good clip the last stretch and my roan and the packhorse were seesawing on the lead rope trying to keep up when we reached the buildings and pulled in by a tie-rail. I swung down right after him and stepped up beside him and we went toward the saloon. We passed the front window of Kern's office and he was inside and came popping out.

"Hey, you two," he said. "Anything to report?"

We stopped and faced him and he looked at us kind of funny. I guess we did look queer, dirty and unshaved and worn in spots.

"Not a thing," Rodock said. "I told you we could be taking a camp trip and that's all I'll say. Except that I'm not missing any stock and haven't stretched any rope."

We went into the saloon and to the bar and downed a stiff one apiece.

"Mister Rodock," I said, "when you think about it, that man beat us."

"Damned if he didn't," Rodock said. He didn't seem to be bothered by it and I know I wasn't. "Listen to me, son," he said. "I expect I haven't been too easy to get along with for quite a few weeks lately. I want you to know I've noticed how you and that roan have stuck to my heels over some mighty rough trail. Now we've got to get home and get a horse ranch moving again. We'll be needing some hands. Come along with me, son, and we'll look around. I'd like your opinion on them before hiring any."

That was Jeremy Rodock. They don't grow men like that around here any more.

Cooter James

Cooter James rode in from the line camp blowing flakes of the first snow off his mustache and feeling sorry for himself. He was in no mood for light talk when he pulled up by the ranchhouse porch and found Jess Winslow standing there watching him approach.

"Jess," he said, "stock's all right and camp's tight. But you'd best send another man out. Can't winter it again."

"Trouble," said Jess Winslow. "I ought to know trouble's riding with you the way your mustache sags. What is it? Age getting you soft?"

Cooter James was too low to flare much at that. "Only turned forty last year," he said. "Just when a man's got his growth and a bit of sense in him. Three years running I've rode that line. Not doing it again."

"Money," said Jess. "That's what it is. You're hitting me for more money."

Cooter James sighed. "Not a matter of money. Matter of principle. Way back doing line work got worried being alone. Promised myself when I took to spooking easy and talking to myself I'd take fair warning. Last night an owl woke me shivering. This morning caught myself talking to the coffeepot. Saddled up and came straight in."

"Letting me down," said Jess. "That's what you're doing. Just when I need that line rode right you're letting me down."

"Sorry, Jess," said Cooter. "Man that can't keep a promise to himself's a peaked kind of mangy packrat."

"That's how you look to me this minute now," said Jess Winslow. "Jumping at owls and scared of your own voice. Packrat's too nice a word."

Cooter James sighed again. He wasn't much to look at and he knew it. Short and thickening around the middle with a limp from a bronc-thrown broken bone that never healed right. Scrambled features burnt and weathered with always-squinting, muddy-blue eyes and a hooked nose over a handlebar mustache that drooped to hide a short upper lip. But he was a good hand on any man's ranch and he knew that too.

"Easy, Jess," he said. "I'm quitting. Just made myself another promise. Going to winter warm and lazy in town. Thank you for my time quick as convenient."

Cooter James rode into town sighing soft into the drooping ends of his mustache. "Change," he said. "That's what I need. Easy living for a spell." He had money to spend and he spent it, on thorough barbering and town clothes and genteel living quarters, a room at Mrs. Pearson's boardinghouse. Four days and he had his fill of that. The food was solid and staying, but he had an uneasy feeling that Mrs. Pearson disapproved of his table manners. The bed was too bouncy and the floor was too smooth, and he had difficulty navigating among the fussy scatter rugs that gave treacherous footing for a man used to unfinished planks. He was uncomfortable in his town clothes, and he felt shorter than ever in shoes lacking the high heels of his worn old boots. And he never could remember to scrape his feet on the mat before coming in the front door.

On the evening of the fourth day, Cooter took a long look at Mr. Pearson, who clerked ten hours at a stretch at the railroad freight office and came home to scrape his feet careful on the mat. Cooter sighed into what was left of his mustache and went upstairs to bed, mighty thoughtful. In the morning he rolled his town clothes into a neat bundle. He put on his old blue jeans and flannel shirt and work jacket. He struggled to get his feet again into his boots and jammed his faded Stetson on his head. He left an extra five-dollar bill on the bed and went downstairs and out the front door.

Two hours' walking found him what he wanted, a sagging shed at the edge of town abandoned when the railroad section gang moved

on. Three days later he was snug and settled; the shed braced and
tight, a bunk rigged, a cracked stove brought from the blacksmith
shop and food on shelves along one wall. He could sleep late and
putter around the place with not a thing pressing. He could wander
around town and toss the time of day with plenty of folks and stop
at the livery stable to visit his horse. He could spend as many hours
as he wanted sitting by his stove reading through the stack of old
newspapers he had found in a corner of the shed. Then late one
night a board squeaked and he woke shivering and got up and made
a pot of coffee and started talking to it.

"What's wrong with me?" said Cooter. "Took fair warning.
Warm and lazy in town. Still there's an itch inside I can't get at.
Might be I need something new to be doing."

That was why Cooter James went to working in Silas John Unger's
general store and got himself involved with a barrel of flour.

Silas John Unger knew Cooter from the time they were Circle Bar
hands together. He was lean with a lantern jaw and hair lightened
with streaks of gray. He was maybe ten years older, and fatherly in
his feeling for Cooter James. "Cooter boy," he said, "it pleases me to
have you acquiring some smattering of sense at last. I'm doing well
and putting money in the bank. You should be doing the same.
When the sun's shining, get ready for a rainy day."

"Rain don't bother me," said Cooter. "And storekeeping's not my
style. Want only to wear out the winter with it. If there's work
enough to warrant."

"There's work enough," said Silas John. "During the selling times
at least. When things are slack, we can play checkers like in the old
days."

Several weeks went by, and Cooter was twenty-nine games ahead
on the chart they kept, when Silas John read a letter in one morning's mail. He chewed a pencil and made tracks on a piece of paper
and came out of the cubbyhole he called his office.

"Cooter boy," he said, "the country hereabouts is getting thick
with homesteaders and I'm thinking of adding a line of farm machinery. I'll have to go East to Chicago to tie the deal. Do you
reckon you can handle things while I'm gone?"

"Reckon so," said Cooter.

Silas John tapped his nose with the pencil. "One thing worries me. You never had much head for figures. I like my books kept straight and neat."

Cooter blew air through the ends of his mustache that was growing out again the way he liked. "Set me on a corral rail," he said. "Drive steers past all day. Come night I'll have you the tally right with the swaybacks and bigjaws marked. Reckon I can keep figures on a cramped little store like this."

"Steers are one thing," said Silas John. "Store goods another."

"Take your trip," said Cooter. "Take your time. If my figures don't tot up exact, I'll teach you how to beat that checker game of mine."

Cooter James kept his figures clean and straight in the two books, one for cash and one for credit, and he lined down the pages neater than Silas John ever did. One day he tallied out fifteen cents ahead on the cash account. That bothered him till he undercharged a homesteader's wife fifteen cents on her winter dress goods and decided that balanced the account. Then reports came of a blizzard in the hills, and people began crowding into town by wagon to lay in quantity supplies for the hard months. He was busy as he had ever been at branding time, making up orders, packing goods into the wagons, and keeping the books posted. He was a tired man but a triumphant man when Silas John strolled in and sat down on a nail keg and set his satchel on the floor and looked around.

"You've been doing business," said Silas John. "My shelves look like people been buying."

"Been putting money in the bank for you," said Cooter. "Been protecting any checker game too."

Silas John went into his cubbyhole and bent over the books. After a while he came out and looked at Cooter perched on the rear counter and shook his head and went back in and chewed a pencil. Then he began coming out and counting articles and going back in to check the books. He kept at this till Cooter was blowing his mustache with chuckles.

"Enjoying yourself?" said Cooter. "Remind me of a chipmunk laying up nuts in a hollow tree." He slid off the counter and went up front to tend to a customer. When that was done he found Silas

John occupying the perch on the rear counter and jutting his jaw at a high angle.

"Cooter boy," said Silas John, "you've lost me a barrel of flour."

"Crazy as a cracked teapot," said Cooter. "Couldn't lose anything that big."

"You could," said Silas John. "There were nineteen barrels out back when I left. There's four now. That means you sold fifteen. But there's only fourteen marked in the books, three cash and eleven credit."

Cooter's mustache sagged. His jawline stiffened. "Certain of those figures?"

Silas John slid off the counter and straightened tall. "That I am," he said.

"Right," said Cooter. His jawline stiffened even more and his muddy-blue eyes tightened at the corners in a serious squint. "Take the price out of my pay."

"That I'll not," said Silas John. "What's a little matter of a barrel of flour between you and me?"

"Not a little matter," said Cooter. "Matter of principle."

"Pay for it, then," said Silas John. "I know better than to try to stop you. But I'm giving you a bonus for taking care of my store while I was gone. I make it the price of a barrel of flour. You know better than to try to stop me."

Cooter sighed into the drooping ends of his mustache and his lips relaxed in a small smile behind it. "Reminds me of the old days," he said. He reached behind the counter and pulled out the battered checkerboard. "Got another debt to pay," he said, and began setting the checkers in place.

Two weeks went by, and Cooter James was only seven games ahead on the chart and fighting to hold his lead. That gave a mild tingle to the days, and it was pleasant wagging away the time with Silas John. It was pleasant too at his shed where he could be his own boss yet close to other folks within a nice neighborly reach. Then early one morning a train tooted faint and far off down the track, and he woke shivering and crawled out of bed in his undershirt and made a pot of coffee and started talking to it.

"Can't get to the bottom of this," said Cooter. "Doing something new and enjoying myself. Still there's that itch I can't scratch. Might be I need something to occupy my mind." That was why, in the middle of a game during the noon slack, he leaned back and looked at Silas John.

"Barrel of flour," he said.

"Gone and forgotten," said Silas John. "Get on with the game."

"Not forgotten," said Cooter. "Going to find what happened to it."

It was Silas John's turn to lean back and look interested.

"Cooter boy," he said, "how're you planning to do that?"

"Simple," said Cooter. "Add a barrel of flour to every bill. Man that got it will pay. Won't know we don't know. Other'll scratch it off or complain when they stop in."

"Sounds simple," said Silas John. "But simple-sounding things often ain't so."

"This one is," said Cooter. "Just keep out of my way and let me make out the bills."

Cooter James burned his kerosene lamp late over the bills and in the morning took them to the postoffice. "Only a matter of time now," he said, and went on to the store where there was plenty of work waiting. The next three days, while Silas John handled the inside business, he was busy building an open-face shed by the store for the farm machinery that was coming. The day after that he was busy uncrating the sample machinery that had arrived. He was so busy he all but forgot that barrel of flour. And Silas John said never a word about it. During the afternoon of the second day, he stepped outside and looked at Cooter wrassling shed timbers and shook his head mournful and went back inside. Twice on the third day he did the same. Late in the fourth day he stood in the doorway and called. When they were settled on the rear counter, he tapped his nose with the pencil in his hand.

"Cooter boy," he said, "I have kept my mouth from yapping so as not to disturb your muscular enthusiasm with that shed. And I wanted to give your little lost-barrel scheme plenty of play. But already it's had too much."

"What now?" said Cooter. "Not working?"

"It's working," said Silas John. "It's working too well. Thirty-seven people have paid their bills. Twenty have complained about a barrel of flour."

"Told you they would," said Cooter. "Supposed to work that way."

"Cooter boy," said Silas John, "you never were much good at figures. Twenty from thirty-seven leaves seventeen. Up to and as of now seventeen people have paid for that one barrel of flour."

Cooter's mustache sagged and he blew air through it. He sucked in the drooping ends and chewed them slow. His jawline stiffened and a serious squint formed at the corners of his muddy-blue eyes.

"Need the names and the money," he said. "Reckon to be riding around evenings paying it back."

Three weeks went by, and Cooter James was nine games behind on the checker chart. The flour-barrel score stood at seventy with forty-two complaints and twenty-eight payments. These last had all been returned, and he was tired of crisscrossing the countryside in the evenings. But that worry was ended. He had sent out new bills to cancel the old and no more payments were coming in. He wasn't even bothered by the fact that his evening trips had let the town and most of the territory around know about the missing barrel and easy-tongued folk were beginning to rib him about it. He strolled along the plank sidewalks after store-closing and took the joshing and enjoyed the feel of being part of a community. He built a fire in his stove and had a lazy meal and sat warm and unworrying with his old newspapers waiting for the night freight to go past and tell him to go to bed. Then one morning about sunup a cat scrambled across his tin roof and he woke shivering and sat up in the bunk and stared at the coffeepot across the shed and began talking to it.

"Clean licked on this," he said. "Can't even locate that itch. Might be I need to settle this barrel business to settle my mind."

He was early at the store and busy with a can of paint, a small brush, and the cardboard bottom of an overall carton. He needed two cardboards before he was finished with his sign. He tacked them one under the other on the inside wall by the front door.

On or about the first week of December last one barrel of flour departed these premises leaving no record in S. J. Unger's account books. Person or persons giving information of aforesaid barrel's whereabouts will receive five dollars ($5) reward and the undying gratitude of—

C. James

Cooter James's sign provided plenty of amusement for Silas John and folks coming in, and it gave the ribbing a fresh boost. But it brought no news about the barrel. Cooter worried over that and was low in his mind. He began to think he would wear out the winter without tracing that barrel. Then one afternoon, when the sun was warming toward spring, a scrawny red-haired boy came in for a piece of patching cloth and stopped by the sign and kept staring at it.

Cooter eased alongside. "Like it, son?" he said.

"We got a barrel of flour this winter," said the boy.

"Know anything about that particular barrel?" said Cooter.

The boy shied away and started edging toward the door.

"G'wan," he said. "Suppose I did, I wouldn't tell you."

"Easy, now," said Cooter. "No way to talk to your elders."

"Go fry an egg," said the boy, and skipped out the door.

It was maybe an hour later that the boy came back and with him a little waist-high girl with the same red hair in pigtails, and both of them tagging a woman in a faded gingham dress with a man's coat on over it. This woman was plump and solid inside the coat and she had a lot of red hair pulled up with old celluloid hairpins haphazard on top of her head. Her plain round face would have been pleasant with the permanent smile crinkles around the eyes except that her mouth was pursed tight right now, so tight that it pulled her plump chin into little bumps. She swung around by the door and read the sign and she turned about and started toward Silas John in the rear of the store.

"Mr. Unger," she said, trying to hold her voice firm, "just what is the meaning of that thing on the wall?"

"Afternoon, Mrs. Moser," said Silas John. "Any questions pertaining to that peculiar piece of writing should be addressed to Mr. Cooter James here."

She turned to look at Cooter, and for some reason he began to feel fidgety and troubled in his mind.

"So that's C. James," she said. "I remember him. I did business with him last time I was in here." She glared at Cooter and the bumps on her chin started quivering. "Well, Mr. C. James," she said, "you open your mouth and explain that sign to me."

"Easy, now," said Cooter. "Ain't much. Was missing a barrel of flour and trying to find what happened to it."

"Well, it makes me do some wondering," she said. "I got a barrel of flour that week and I didn't pay for it or charge it either. You gave it to me."

Cooter's mustache sagged, and his voice came through it feeble and fumbling. "Did I now?" he said.

"That's right," said the boy. "We ain't ever eat so good."

The woman was talking straight along so fast the words were pushing each other out of the way.

"I came in here for my winter goods and I knew exactly what I had money for and you made out the list and I paid you and I asked for a bag of flour and when you brought it out to the wagon it was a barrel and ever since my man died last fall everybody's been so kind and I've been a good customer here because I can't afford much but what I buy I get here and I thought you were being kind and I thanked you for it and you said that was all right you were pleased to do it."

"Did I now?" said Cooter again. "Reckon I did. But I thought —" He shut off his talk and chewed the ends of his mustache slow and thoughtful.

"And what did you think?" said the woman. "It surprises me you can think at all. Making a woman feel maybe she's got something she wasn't supposed to have."

"Mrs. Moser, ma'am," said Cooter, "all my mistake. You were supposed to have it. So busy back then slipped my mind."

"Humph," said the woman. "Things like that don't slip minds easy. You stop squirming and tell me what you thought."

"No," said Cooter. "Won't."

The woman waggled her head at Cooter so hard the celluloid pins started loosening and he was afraid they might fall.

"It's not my fault I'm not a man," she said. "You treat me like one. You speak honest to me. You tell me what you thought."

Cooter was caught when she talked like that and he knew it.

"Thought you were thanking me for stowing things in the wagon," he said. He saw her chin quivering again, and he pushed his mind scurrying for words. "Easy, now, ma'am. So maybe I didn't mean to give it you then. Do now. Didn't know about your man passing on. Glad about it now. About the mistake, I mean. Wish it had been two. Two barrels. Give you the other one now." He started past her toward the rear of the store.

The woman's chin was quivering, but quivering mad.

"Mr. C. for Cooter James," she said, and stopped him in stride. She stared at him accusing, and the boy and the girl lined beside her and looked the same, and her words pushed each other out of the way in their hurry. "Mr. Mind-slipping James," she said, "I wouldn't take the tiniest speck of flour there ever was from you if me and mine were starving and you the last man on the whole earth. Doing a thing like that to a woman that's always paid her bills hard as it might be and making her find out the food she's been putting in the mouths of her babes ought to've been paid for and wasn't."

"Don't look like babes to me," said Cooter, beginning to be a bit peeved himself. "Got some size on them. Want to be treated like a man you do, so I will. Stop yammering at me and wobbling your chin. Barrel's been paid for. Know what I wanted to know and there's nothing more to it."

"Nothing more you think," said the woman. "I want to know who paid for it."

"I did," said Cooter. "In a way I did."

"Humph," said the woman. "So it's you I owe the price and just when I haven't got any cash money and don't know when I'll ever see any again with thinking the pig and the garden that isn't plowed yet will take us through the summer till I get some kind of a crop in and sold and money's always been scarce with us anyways and no extras for barrels that oughtn't to have to be paid for but do because a fool man doesn't know a person and lets his mind slip."

"Mrs. Moser, ma'am," said Cooter, getting a firm hold on himself, "you don't owe me the least little bit of nothing. Try to pay me a solitary single cent and I head howling for the next county."

"Be good riddance," said the woman. "Howsomever, I don't have a single cent. But I'm going to pay you. I won't have a thing like that hanging on my mind, letting a man do for me what he didn't mean to. A barrel of flour costs fourteen dollars. Well, you owe me five dollars reward money as that sign there says and I make it nine dollars still owing and I'm going to pay it not knowing how right now but that I'm going to." She waggled her head emphatic at Cooter and two of the celluloid pins fell bouncing to the floor. She stooped and grabbed them and stuck them into the pile of red hair and glared at Cooter and marched out the door. The boy and the girl took turns according to size doing the same, the glaring and the marching, and a silence settled in the store.

Then the voice of Silas John came purring from the rear. "Cooter boy," he said, "that woman's got a rope on you."

"No rope," said Cooter. "How's she going to pay me when I won't take it?"

"I wouldn't know," said Silas John. "But there's one item I do know. I know the color of her hair."

Cooter James went home to his shed feeling sorry for himself. "Town life's mighty strenuous," he said. He burned his beans chewing his mustache and forgetting them on the stove. And he couldn't stay put in his chair with his newspapers. He pulled on his jacket and took a long hike along the tracks and return to weary his muscles and worried away some hours before he fell asleep. In the morning a metal-bumping sound woke him shivering, and he lay still listening to strange noises in his shed. The tasty smell of bacon grease tickled his nose and he raised his head to peer over the blanket. The woman was there by his stove, her back to him, bustling about in a knowing manner.

Cooter lay quiet for two minutes, maybe three. He held the blanket up under his chin and raised himself to a sitting position. He had trouble finding his voice.

"Mrs. Moser, ma'am," he said, "what in tarnation you doing here?"

"Fixing your breakfast," said the woman. "I figured I'd charge you a quarter each time till I was paid up. I've changed my mind and made it fifty. I'm a good cook and you keep your things dirty just like a man."

Cooter lay back down and tried to untangle his mind and was still trying when she snapped at him.

"It's ready," she said.

"It," said Cooter. "Not me. Can't get out of my bunk with you standing there."

"Humph," said the woman. "Wouldn't be the first time I saw a man in his drawers. If you're so delicate about yourself, I'll look the other way."

She did, and Cooter slipped out of the bunk and whipped on his old blue jeans and flannel shirt. With them on he felt better and able to work up the beginnings of a good mad.

"Blamed if I'm hungry," he said.

"Eat it or don't eat it," said the woman. "Anyways, I've fixed it, and a man that was a man 'stead of a mindslipper that'd take the taste out of the food a woman that pays her bills puts in the mouth of her babes would eat it hungry or not hungry and I never knew a man that wasn't hungry in the mornings anyways."

Cooter was caught again and he knew it. He sat down and started to eat and the woman watching bothered him.

"Fixed it," he said. "Time to get out, and let me be."

"Where I come from," said the woman, "fixing a meal means cleaning up after."

Cooter sighed, and then his mad was boiling strong. He looked at the food, bacon and biscuits and coffee.

"Woman," he said, "where's my eggs?"

She jumped, and one of the hairpins fell and she stooped to pick it up and put it in place. "Didn't know you had any," she said.

"In that tobacco can," said Cooter. "Four I want. Fried and flipped."

He ate right through every snitch of bacon, every biscuit in the pan, the four eggs, and finished with a third cup of coffee. He pulled on his boots and jacket and jammed on his hat and slammed the door behind him.

Cooter James was upset and touchy all day. He kept busy by himself in the machinery shed and hurried home before closing time. He was worrying about what he might find and his worrying was justified. The place had a different feel the moment he entered. Everything was scrubbed and polished and so neat and orderly that he shuddered when he looked around. A flour bag had been ripped apart at the seams and the halves trimmed and put up at the side windows for curtains. A bunch of winter-ivy leaves from out by the tracks was in water in a coffee cup on the table. Beside it was a note written on the edge of a piece of newspaper.

Mr. C. James—50 cents for fixing breakfast. 1 dollar for scrubbing out dirt. 50 cents for fixing curtains and such. 7 dollars owing.—Mrs. A. (Agnes) Moser.

Cooter stared at the note a long time. "Agnes," he said. "Was sweet on a girl named Agnes once. Didn't have red hair." He smiled into his mustache, remembering, and started to get his supper, and each thing he wanted was in a new place. "Women," he said. "Interfering things. Can't leave a man be." By time he was ready to eat, he had a good grip on his mad again. "Find a way to fix her," he said, and went to bunk early, determined to be up before she arrived, and slept only in cat naps worrying over the time. He was dressed and fed and had the place slicked, and he was by the window watching when she came in sight. He waited till she was near the door, then opened it, and came out and shut it behind him.

"Morning, Mrs. Moser, ma'am," he said. "Had breakfast. Everything's clean."

He went off toward the store, leaving her staring at him, and felt fine for almost the whole morning.

Along about noon worry began creeping back into his mind. Silas John beat him two more games and the afternoon seemed unusual long. He hurried home early with the worry big inside him and the woman was there in his shed by the stove preparing his supper. He pulled off his hat and leaned against the wall and sighed into his mustache.

"Stop making that silly noise," said the woman. "Thought you were cute didn't you sneaking up early to get breakfast ahead of me leaving a woman that's determined to pay her bills feeling that she's owing to you and why don't you act like a man that's got more sense than a fieldmouse and take off that jacket where it's warm in here so you won't catch cold if you go out again."

Cooter James was licked and he knew it. He took off his jacket and hung it on a nail and the hat over it.

"Determined to pay the whole price?" he said.

"I am," said the woman.

"Do it friendly, then," said Cooter. "Sit down and eat with me each time. Can't chew right with you just watching."

"Maybe I might," said the woman. "But you mind to think

straight and not go notioning that I don't get enough to eat at home because maybe we do only have bread and homily grits most of the time with the other winter things about gone but that's filling and we'll have a garden soon—and, oh, I just thought you being the kind of mind-slipping man you are you'll likely expect me to pay for what I eat."

"Woman," said Cooter, blowing his mustache out straight, "man can provide food for a woman in his own house without her having to pay for it. Stop yammering and get supper ready." He sat on the bunk and watched her bustling by the stove. He forgot the worry and began remembering yesterday's breakfast. "Woman," he said, "might be we could have some of those biscuits you make?"

Two days more, and it was the end of the week and the woman didn't come on Sunday. Three days into the next week and by her figuring, two meals a day at fifty cents each, she owed Cooter only one dollar and fifty cents more.

The following morning Cooter looked across the table at her.

"Time's getting short," he said. "Want to know how you make those biscuits."

"The way anyone does," she said. "Flour and water and shortening and a pinch of this and a pinch of that till it feels right."

"Been making biscuits many a year," said Cooter. "Never taste like yours."

"A man can't make decent biscuits," she said. "But about any woman could on that stove of yours."

"That stove?" said Cooter. "Just a fall-apart that was lying around at the blacksmith shop."

"It's a better stove than I've had for years and years," she said. "And I don't mean to tell you it's not hard cooking on a stove that's got to be patched all the time and puts smoke in your face and gets you all sooty so you have to scrub all the time to be fitten for seeing."

Cooter saw the little bumps forming on her chin and the whole chin starting to quiver. He was embarrassed and looked out the window.

"Might be," he said, "you'd let me get you a stove."

She pushed up from the table and waggled her head at him so hard some of the red hair fell down by her face.

"I will not," she said. "I wouldn't let you give me anything. Not you. Not ever." She sat down again sudden, and several of the hair-pins bounced on the floor and she stooped to get them. When her head came up again, her eyes were snapping and hard. "Get on off to that store," she said. "And right away quick so I can clean this mess and get away from this place that minds me of you every time I see it."

Cooter took his hat and jacket off the wall and slipped out the door. He walked slow to the store. He was sharp-tongued to customers all morning, and during the afternoon he managed to work up a quarrel with Silas John. When he realized what he was doing, he clamped down on his tongue and stomped out. He wandered over by the town saloon and looked in. "Snapped me out of meanness when I was younger," he said. "Not now." He wandered on and far out of town along some road, and about suppertime he wandered back toward his shed. He waited and worried a moment about opening the door, and when he did the place was empty. It was scrubbed and polished again and empty except for another note on the table.

50 cents for fixing breakfast. 1 dollar for scrubbing out a week's dirt. Makes 9 dollars now. Not a cent owing.

Cooter stared at the note. "Fooled with that scrubbing," he said. "Thought a couple more meals coming." He had been afraid at the door that maybe her chin would be quivering inside to meet him, but now he was disappointed. "That's done, anyways," he said. "Done. Finished. Over with. No more of it." He started to prepare his own supper and burned the beans, and his biscuits, even with a pinch of this and of that, were lumpy in his mouth and heavy in his stomach. He fussed around the shed and out and in a half-dozen times and started to hike along the tracks and came back as many times more till he began to think that he could call it spring and the winter over and be heading for the range again. "Where I belong," he said. "In the open where figures ain't so important."

He pulled off his outer clothes feeling better and planning an early start in the morning. He lay on the bunk and closed his eyes counting steers and checking the bigjaws and swaybacks and drifted off, counting, into sleep. A light rain began to fall tapping on his tin roof and thunder talked in the distance, and the night freight went by and he didn't hear it. Then along about sunup a mouse skittled across a shelf and a cup made a small jangle, and he sat up in the bunk shivering and stared across the shed at the coffeepot. He stared a long time and the light grew stronger. He shook his head and sighed into his mustache. "No sense fighting it," he said. "Know about that itch. Time comes to every man. Mine's now." He sat still, thinking, and after a while a chuckle waggled the ends of his mustache. "Not so bad at figures after all," he said, and slipped out of the bunk and dressed himself in his town clothes. He looked down at himself and snorted and pulled the town clothes off and made himself neat as he could in his old jeans and flannel shirt.

He stopped by the door to pick up his axe, changed his mind and took the hand whetstone instead. He started toward the center of the town and then swung along the road the woman had walked each way morning and evening coming to his place, and after a while he saw it, the unpainted two-room shack with rips showing in the tar-papered roof. A sagging small barn was at one side and two gaunt draft horses were in a makeshift corral behind it.

Cooter studied the place in the early morning light. He sniffed the air. "Spring all right," he said. "Plowing time for them's got a mind for farming." He went to the sagging barn and around it to a pile of old wood. There was a rusty axe on the ground still wet from the night rain. He picked it up and felt the blade. "Just like a woman," he said, and went to work with his whetstone till he had an edge that could slice a hair of his mustache. He pulled wood off the pile and began cutting it into stove lengths. He was swinging the axe steady when he noticed the woman standing by the corner of the barn and staring at him. He stopped chopping and leaned on the axe.

"Morning, Mrs. Moser, ma'am," he said. "Nice morning."

"Maybe it's a nice morning," she said, "and maybe it isn't and I don't care what it is because I don't mean to tell you I'll not have you snooping around here and trying to make me owing to you."

"Me that's owing," said Cooter, taking a deep breath. "Forgot back there you paid for a bag of flour when you got the barrel. Two dollars you paid. Means two dollars you're overpaid now. Figure to pay that back cutting wood. Twenty-five cents each morning for cutting a day's supply. Stubborn as you on things like that."

The woman stared at him, and then the bumps were forming on

her chin. "Just like the man you are," she said, "to be finding ways to make fun of a woman that pays her bills and tries to get along best she can, and even so if maybe it's you that's owing it's silly with charging things back and forth all the time we might never be out straight and somebody'd always be owing somebody."

Cooter's head came up straight and his mustache sat out stiff. "That be so bad?" he said. "Always doing things for each other, I mean."

She stared at him and her chin began to quiver, and she tried to speak, but the words would not come, and Cooter swung the axe solid into a chunk of wood and left it there and faced her square on.

"Agnes," he said, "through talking about barrels and owing and getting things paid. Talking now like a man that's found his woman and aims to know will she have him."

He looked at her, and she looked at him, and her voice when it came was so low he could scarce hear it. "Babes," she said. "I've got two babes."

"What's wrong with babes?" said Cooter. "Grow up to be people, don't they?"

She looked at him a long moment and her chin stopped quivering and the pleasant wrinkles by her eyes showed plain. "Cooter," she said, "that's no christened name. What's it really?"

Cooter James sighed into his mustache. "Courtney," he said.

The woman looked at him, and she smiled just a little, and her voice was as soft and tender as one of her biscuits. "I think I'll call you Cooter," she said. "I like Cooter best."

Kittura Remsberg

KITTURA REMSBERG was my grandmother. My mother's mother. I knew her only the few weeks I spent at the ranch near Kalispell one summer, and then only as little more than a presence, dark eyes and still dark hair above the prominent cheekbones of a permanent invalid held to her bed within the walls of the room that compassed all that remained of her life. It was a big room, big and quiet and cool even when the summer sun burned the wide reaches of the range outside. I was in it only the few times she asked for me. I never went in voluntarily because I was afraid of her. She was not a storybook grandmother. She was an impatient, sharp-tongued personality with no softness for me in her. Yet I remember that room with a clarity and a feeling that spring unfailing across the years. I remember it because she was there and she filled it with a bigness and a quietness and a strange cool strength of spirit. There was peace in that room.

I would not have spent those weeks at the ranch if my parents had not been hard-pressed and unable to hire a nurse when my sister had rheumatic fever. They felt I should be sent away for a while and there was no place else to send me. They worried for days before they did send me because my mother disapproved of Ben Remsberg, her father, my grandfather. She had married early to get away and into town and not be dependent on him. She said that he drank too much and that he had a violent temper. She said that no decent person who could get away would live long in the same house with him. From her point of view perhaps she was right. I saw him drunk more than once during those few weeks and heard him shout in frequent fury at the fat old Mexican woman who did the housework and at the one old cowhand who had stayed with him. But he was kind to me and let me tag him about asking endless questions. And he told me about the woman, his wife, my grandmother, lying quietly in the big cool room.

There was nothing peculiar about his telling me, though my mother always said he was difficult to talk to. He told me because I asked him. I asked him because I noticed he was different when he went into that room. He was loud and angry much of the time outside of it. But when he passed through that doorway he was different. He usually closed the door after him, and then for a while after he came out he would be soft-spoken and absent-minded as if he were out of focus with things immediately around him. Once he left the door partly open and I peered in. He was sitting on a chair by the bed with one of his blunt hands resting on the counterpane beside her and she was sitting in the bed with her back to a pillow and one of her thin hands was on his hand and they were just sitting there together. When he came out I asked him about her and he told me. He told me about her and about the mirror, and I saw it once in the loft of the storage barn, the heavy gilt paint of the ornate frame chipping off and only a few pieces of jagged glass left in one corner.

The whole story has come clear in my mind through the years. Some of the details and spoken words may not be true to absolute exact fact. But the whole of it means truth to me. Kittura Remsberg was my grandmother and I want to tell you about her.

Kittura Perkins was her maiden name. She was the third daughter of a prosperous landowner in Pennsylvania about thirty miles out of Philadelphia. He was a man of real substance in his part of the State. They lived in the main farmhouse on the property where he could hold sharp watch on his crops and see that the hired men earned their keep. He also owned a share in a shipping business in the city and he had filled the farmhouse with fine furniture brought from Europe at bargain intervals by his company's ships. His wife, Kittura's mother, had died when she was small, and the two older sisters had done their futile best to raise her as a proper young lady.

Kitt Perkins everyone called her during those years just after the Civil War, and she knew everyone in the neighborhood and everyone knew her as a strong-willed girl whose vital coloring and manner contrasted sharply with the pallid gentility of her sisters and whose habits of going her own way and speaking her own mind annoyed her careful father. The young men knew her and wanted to know her better. She herself was constantly disappointed in them. She knew what she wanted and one day she saw it.

What she saw was a deep-bodied young man lifting an anvil out of a wagon and setting it on the ground and kneeling to hammer horseshoes into shape on it with slow deliberate strokes. He was the son of a Belgian immigrant who had come into the neighborhood some years before and set up a blacksmith shop. She had seen him often helping his father, but now she really saw him for the first time. She liked the shape of him, solid and thick through. She liked the way he looked at her, measuring her without offense as a healthy human animal whose vitality might match his own. She did not like the way he kept silent, withdrawing as if he realized a gap between them.

She went straight to him. "Why won't you speak to me?"

He laid the hammer on the anvil and looked up at her. "That wouldn't do anybody any good. I'm not your kind."

"That's ridiculous."

"Yes? Your father wouldn't like it."

"Ben Remsberg," she said, "I am not my father."

That was the beginning. They were together each evening after that for nearly two weeks. They walked the fields long miles that seemed short, often talking eagerly and as often being silent and content to be. Then one evening she stopped and looked straight at him. "I want you to call on me tomorrow night. At home."

He came, and he was awkward in his dress-up clothes. He was uncomfortable talking to her in the fine parlor. He was more uncomfortable when her sisters stepped in to be introduced and made a point of departing quickly upstairs. He stood stiffly at attention when her father entered and greeted him coldly, and in the midst of a tight silence he turned and walked steadily out and down the flat stone path toward the road.

She sat silent, hurt anger rising, and then there was no anger and she ran after him. She called from the front stoop and he went steadily on and she caught him by the picket gate and swung him around. "Ben, don't be a fool."

He took her by the arms and shook her fiercely and her head rose defiantly and he pulled her to him. She came reaching for him, and as she felt the hard crushing strength of his body, she knew that she was right.

She stepped back, chewing on her lower lip. "Ben, be honest with me. Are you afraid of my father?"

"No, but he doesn't want me in his house so I'll never set foot in it again."

"Then I won't either."

He stared at her, startled. "Where will you go?"

"Wherever you go."

"But—but I oughtn't to marry you."

"Why not?"

"No money, that's why. I haven't got anything."

"Ben," she said, "you'll have me."

They were married that night. They sent word to her father and went home to the little house behind the blacksmith shop and his father blessed them in his flowing French and moved into the room over the shop and they were alone in the little house together. In the morning he was tall with the arrogance of possession and she was certain that she was right. She was so certain of many things.

"Ben, we'll have to set foot in father's house again, after all. To get my clothes. And of course my mirror."

They drove a wagon to the big farmhouse and her sisters watched in disapproving silence while they carried out the contents of her old mahogany wardrobe. He was surprised when he saw the mirror. It was full-length, tall enough for the tallest man, cased in a heavy frame, hand-carved and gilt-painted. He had to rest often lugging it down the stairs and to the wagon. And all the while she talked, telling him about it. "I've had it ever since I was a little girl. Father had it brought from England, some old place there, and I made such a fuss he said I could have it. I like to sit with it. Fixing myself and thinking. That's how I first knew you were the man I'd marry. Oh, not you, of course, then. Someone like you."

And when he carried it into their little house, the ceiling of their bedroom was too low for it to stand upright and he had to rig a way to fasten it sideways on the wall where it looked strange and grotesque until she covered the heavy carving of the top and bottom, now the sides, with cloth like curtains, and it was a part of the room, giving depth like a seeing into and beyond the confining walls.

They lived quietly to themselves and for the first months being together was enough. But the blacksmith shop was small. Most of its meager business came from the poorer farmers who lived nearby. They would barely have scraped along except for the small income she had from her mother's estate. Then one morning he and his father were repairing the cracked axle of a loaded grain cart and suddenly the cart crumpled and overturned, sending him sprawling and pinning his father under the weight of the piled bags. Three days his father lay in the bedroom watching the mirror catch the sun through the one window and on the third day died, apologetic to his last breath over the trouble he had caused. And money was a bit easier for them after the funeral expenses because all that came into the shop was theirs.

Easier. Not easy enough. Ben Remsberg was no businessman, not in the cautious penny-watching way of the people with whom he had to deal. He used better materials and did better work than most of his customers paid for. He could not refuse a call on his time even from a man already behind in paying for past work. At the end of the month he would be short on the rent for the shop and the house and it would be her money that matched the amount. For the next days he would be irritable and too harsh demanding payment and his mouth would be tight in a straight line.

Then one evening she looked at him over the supper dishes and chewed on her lower lip. "Ben, you don't want to be a blacksmith all your life, do you?"

He stared down at his empty plate, searching his own mind for her. "No. And not here. When I was a kid, I used to think some of striking out somewhere for myself."

"Why didn't you?"

"Oh, I don't know. First there was papa. Now there's you."

She looked at him, serious and perhaps a bit frightened. "Ben, be honest with me. What do you want to do with your life?"

"I guess I want to be some place where it's new. Where a man can start with nothing and show what he is. I've thought some of going West."

She chewed on her lip a long moment. She remembered many

things out of the passing days, little things like his sullen naming
of a price for a poor farmer when his impulse was to give freely of
himself in open fellowship. She remembered the wideness of him,
the stretching bigness that was not of his body alone that seemed to
be shrinking at each month's end. She remembered and spoke
quickly to have it said.

"You ought to do it, Ben. Go West or wherever you want."

He stared at her, startled. "You mean just do it? Just like that?"

"Yes. That's the way to do things. Or else you might never do
them."

"But—but you don't mean go and leave you?"

"I mean go find where you want to be and come back and get me."

"But—but a man can't——"

"Ben, don't ever let me be in your way."

He left her in the morning, swinging down the road to Philadelphia and a start on the first train west with an extra shirt and
several pairs of socks in a neat bundle under his arm. She watched
him go and turned back into the house and closed the door, and
with it closed a period in her life and began another, the years of
being alone.

Four years. Four years and some months. She sold the equipment
in the shop and rented the building to an elderly farmer for a small
grocery store. With that and her own income she was independent.
She waited and sat hours in front of the mirror and steadied her
mind against the waiting with thoughts of the fine big home they
would build, somewhere, sometime. And she saved what she could
of the money available and bought things they would need for that
home. Bedclothes and linens and dishes, and on rare occasions pieces
of silver. She took wooden boxes from the store and packaged the
things in these, snugly packed and repacked for the journey to wherever they would be together.

With Ben gone, she began to see her family again. Once a month
her sisters came to call in the family carriage. They came with a
sense of duty and did not disguise the fact that they were sorry for
her, and they never stayed long because she never let them see that
she might be sorry for herself. Once a week her father came. He
would knock on the door, and when she opened it he would take
off his hat and say: "Well, Kittura, are you ready to come home

now?" And when she would shake her head, he would turn and walk away in stubborn wonderment.

A few weeks after Ben left, a card came from Cincinnati. He was working his way on a river boat and moving west. Later there was another from St. Louis. He was moving on by rail tending a carload of herd bulls and thought there might be a ranch job at the end of the line. That was all. And the months stretched into years, and the note came, the hurried scrawl: "Forget about me. I'm not your kind."

She sat by the mirror and read the note again and again. She took a piece of paper and a pencil and wrote on the paper and chewed on her lower lip and wrote again. She tore the paper across and dropped it on the floor and took another piece and wrote a single line on it. "Ben," she wrote, "don't be a fool." She tucked this piece in an envelope and saw the Fort Laramie postmark on his note and addressed her envelope to him care of General Delivery there and walked to the postoffice and mailed it. The months passed and she sat by the mirror and saw the straightness growing in her lips, and she cut expenses more to buy more things for the boxes beginning to fill the front room of the little house. And after four years and some months he was there, suddenly and completely and travel-worn in the doorway with her paper in his hand.

"Kitt, I came damn near being a fool. This caught up with me and I pulled in sharp. Got me a stake and found a place."

"A place, Ben? Is it what you want?"

"Yes. A nice piece of range off near the mountains where nobody's spoiled it. I've got a few mavericks on it already."

"Mavericks, Ben?"

"Sure. Calves. Orphans. No one to claim them. I scoured them out of the brush and slapped my brand on them. Our brand. A straight big K."

He was sunburned and rugged with the hard fitness of tough cordwood. He stood in the doorway, a man who owned the earth in company with all men who were men. She felt the wideness spreading out from him. She dropped into a chair and her shoulders shook as the sobs fought in her throat. He leaped to kneel beside her and put out his arms and she gripped him with fingers that dug into his welcome hardness.

"Ben," she kept saying, "Ben. I was right after all, wasn't I, Ben?"

She let him sleep late in the morning while she cooked a good breakfast and she waited until he had eaten. Then she could wait no longer and hurried to show him her boxes. He followed from one to the next and on to them all, and amazement grew in him till it burst out in a shout that shook the house.

"Good God, Kitt! All that stuff! It's wonderful! But do you realize where you're going? Way out to the end of nowhere. It's four hundred miles from the nearest railhead. All I've got anyway is a two-room shack. We're starting small, Kitt."

"Suppose we are. We won't always be small. We'll be building a decent place."

"Sure. That'll come. But we've got no use for stuff like this now. What we need is good breeding cows and a couple of the right kind of range bulls."

"I just don't care, Ben. These things are going with us. We'll keep them till we can use them. I'll get mother's money from the bank and we'll send them by train and buy wagons for the rest of the way."

"Why, I bet you'd even try to take that mirror."

"Of course. Especially my mirror."

They waited five weeks for the shipment at the railhead out of Corinne in Utah Territory. She had time after the excitement of the long train trip to become accustomed to the change in all that had been familiar. She learned to endure the dust and the heat that swirled by day through the one street of the crowded town and the nighttime noise that penetrated the room over a saloon that was the only one they could find. She was even proud of Ben in his worn Western clothes with a gun at his side and meeting and mingling with strange kinds of men in an easy equality. But it was then that the fear began to creep into her, not a physical fear but a far-back shrinking from the newness and rawness and sprawling bigness of the land. She clung in her mind to the thought of her boxes coming and with them the wide flat crate that held the mirror, the tangible evidences of the life she had known that she would be taking with her. She was reassured when the things came and were stowed with their supplies in two heavy wagons and they headed north, she and Ben and her boxes and the two teams pulling the wagons and the lank silent prospector who was driving one to pay his way northward to the mining country. They moved along rapidly the first days and crossed into Idaho and pushed steadily north until the ground began to drop into the valley of the Snake River and they reached the south bank and followed upsteam to cross at Fort Hall.

They had to wait two more weeks there because reports of Indian raids were drifting down country and military orders were that no wagons could travel except in companies of ten or more. When they started again, part of a long various procession of vehicles, their driver disappeared the first night out, disappeared into the darkness, and why and what happened to him they never knew, and she had to drive their second wagon after that, wincing at the grind of the hard leather until the calluses formed on her hands.

The season was far advanced by now. Grass for the horses was sparse and burned and water was often more than a full day's drive ahead. Day merged into day as the motley procession climbed the long rolling rise out of the valley and struck across the high plateau toward the mountains and the Montana line and the safety of Bannack City. Twice the company's lone point rider reported Indian signs and once they saw smoke signals rising far off in the horizon haze. The men drove for all possible distance each daylight hour and grew ever more grim in the circle of wagons at night. The nameless fear of the new land crept into her again, and she might have begged Ben to turn back if turning back would not have been worse than going forward. Their horses, straining long days into the tugs of the heavy wagons, wasted down to a weakening thinness and slowed in pace until she and Ben dropped back place by place in the procession and were among the last stragglers to reach camp at night. And then, in the forenoon of one day so relentlessly like the others, the fear took her.

They had reached a rocky dry gulch where they had expected to find at least a trickle of water still running. There were only dust and caked mud and the bare stones baking in the sun. The other wagons had crossed the dry ford and were pushing on. She had seen Ben, showing her the way for their own wagons as he always did, swing his team to hit the crossing at an angle and avoid the biggest stones. She followed and tried to do the same, and as the horses settled to the pull up the other side a rear wheel struck a rock and the wagon stopped. She urged the team sideways and forward and heard the wheel grind on the rock and drop back immovable. She saw the other wagons moving on, the distance growing, and the fear rushed through her. Frantically she slapped at the horses with the reins and they lunged forward and one of them floundered in the loose gravel of the slope and went down. She saw the horse fight upward and stand with one leg hanging useless and her scream brought men upright and pulling in their teams all along the line ahead.

She sat on the seat silent and unable to move. She saw Ben standing beside the wagon and staring at her and at the horse and then walking to meet the other men coming and stand with them in hurried talk. She saw them scatter toward their own wagons and Ben coming toward her. He looked up and managed a small tight smile for her. "This does it, Kitt. We tried anyway. Wait for me at the other wagon."

At the sound of his voice she could move and she climbed down and went forward and pulled herself up to the other driving seat. She did not dare look around until after the shot, and when she did turn he was leading the other horse unharnessed and tying it by the bridle to the tailboard behind her. She looked back at the wagon in the gulch piled with her boxes beneath the dusty canvas.

She spoke softly in simple wonder. "I don't understand, Ben. What are we going to do? Will we tow it?"

"Good God, Kitt! We're going to leave it. Damn near everything else too."

The words hit her mind, but she did not grasp them until he began to pull boxes out of the wagonbed behind her and heave them to one side. Then the fear raced through her again, and she jumped to the ground and ran headlong at him and beat him with her hands. "You can't, Ben! You can't!"

He held her from him, shaking her by the arms. "Listen, Kitt. We're miles from anywhere. No water. Horses about played out. Indians maybe near. We have to travel light and might not make it even then."

"No! You can't!" She broke from him and blocked him from the wagon. "I won't have anything left! Not anything!" Her voice rose wailing and he snapped at her in contempt. "If they can, we can." She looked and saw the other men stripping down their wagons and some of the women helping, and she was suddenly ashamed and stepped aside. She stood quietly while he stripped the wagon to the sparse necessities—food and a few tools and the two rifles and several blankets—and she drove away the fear that was not a physical fear, and the conviction came. He was throwing away her defenses against the brutal indifference of this raw land, and if she let this happen she would be alone in a strange nakedness and she would lose contact with a way of life she could never recapture.

When he finished, she spoke quietly. "All right, Ben. I won't make any more fuss. But you've forgotten my mirror." When he stared at her, she spoke again quietly, "I'll leave everything else, but I won't leave that. If we can't take it I'll stay here too." When he still stared at her, she spoke again just as quietly, "Ben, I mean it."

When they moved on, more rapidly now and the last in the long line driving for distance, he sat beside her grim and refusing to look at her as he had been getting the wide flat crate from the abandoned wagon and struggling with it end over end up the slope. She sat huddled on the seat beside him in her own taut silence, and the hours crawled by and she watched the barren burned miles passing under the horses' hooves, and for the first time when they were together they were not together and they lay apart in separate blankets that night, not sleeping and perhaps not hearing the lonely night sounds.

It was the same in the morning. She watched the dust rising under the hooves and moving backwards under the wagon, and with each passing hour the effort to speak became more difficult. Then her head began to rise and a faint suggestion of freshness touched the air, and far ahead almost beyond vision the haze began to shift and take shapes and was no longer haze, but the remote challenging solidity of the mountains. And when speaking no longer seemed possible she spoke: "I was wrong, Ben. I have you."

He swung his head to look at her and some of the grimness left his face. Speaking was easier now and her voice gained strength.

"I was wrong too about bringing all those things. I should have saved the money and we'd have some now for you to buy your cattle."

He sat up straighter on the seat and clucked to the horses. "Just as well, Kitt. Now we're starting right."

She nodded and watched the mountains emerging in sharper out-

line. "I guess, Ben, I just couldn't accept all this new way of doing things. This—this land. It's so big, and it doesn't seem to know that we're even here. But you don't need to worry about me any more."
"I'm not worrying," he said. "Not about you." And they were together on the seat, gaunt and tired and dusty in a creaking wagon at the tag end of a motley worn procession, but together. He stirred on the seat and licked his dry lips and grinned a little. "That mirror. I guess we've got to take it through somehow if I have to carry the damned thing."

They took it through. Flat in the wagonbed, the wide crate was a seat for two families whose own wagons had broken past repair during the last days before they rolled into Bannack City. It was there, firm ballast in the bottom, when they struck on north through the mountains to Butte and on past Deer Lodge and Gold Creek to Fort Missoula. It was there, almost the only thing left to unload, when they reached the Flathead Lake country and stopped at last by the shack that was their home for the next years.

Nothing, no trick of curtains, could make that mirror be anything but grotesque in that shack. It was out of place, out of keeping, an unbelievable burst of elegance out of another world. Yet there was a rightness in its very wrongness. It was a symbol and a signpost. A reminder and a beckoning. And certainly it was a mark of distinction. It made them quickly known through the Territory, the "looking-glass people," and the word ran and far neighbors came miles to see it. Hung sideways again, it nearly filled one end of the main room of the shack, eye-holding and impressive, and it hung there during the years they put themselves and everything possible into the ranch, reaching out, buying land and cattle, taking long chances on slim credit and always somehow pulling through, the two of them together, seen and known by everyone and always together. And then things were easy for them. He had what he wanted, miles of good range and hundreds of cattle on it, and she could have what she wanted, a house to match the mirror.

Building that house must have been an event in that growing Territory. While she was still planning it, word came that her father had died and she could draw on a third of his estate and they tossed discretion aside and built the house big, rambling and roomy with wide walls and deep-set windows and high-ceilinged with huge beams freighted down from the mountain forests. And she bought and bought things for it, sending as far as Denver and even all the way to New York for them, feeling that at last in a sense she had again and was unpacking her wooden boxes. Together they had defeated the land that had almost defeated her, and her house was her victory banner, what she had once had and known remade for her. She filled it with fine things as her father had his house, and when she was finished the mirror stood upright in their bedroom and merged into the over-all magnificence.

Her one child was born in that bedroom. One. There were no others. Perhaps that bothered her as sometimes it bothered Ben, but it did not mar the running rightness of their being together. They kept open house for all the surrounding country and lived smack up to the edge of their income and beyond and never worried because they had put that behind them years and miles before on the hard board seat of a dust-covered wagon. With heads high and eyes forward they lived straight into the bitter winter of '86.

Summer came early that year, dry and warm. As it progressed, hot winds swept through the valleys and the grass was stunted and shriveled back on its roots. Droughts far down in the Southwest sent extra numbers of cattle north and Ben jumped at the low prices and rented more range and bought till this too was crowded. As fall came he held his herds late, hoping for a rise in the market, and then it was too late. Winter dropped out of the mountains six weeks earlier than usual and gripped the land with a blizzard that blocked all movement. Deadly cold settled and stayed, and as the weeks passed blizzard after blizzard buried even the level stretches under four or five feet of dry packing snow. When the first thaw broke in mid-March, the overflowing streams were choked with the emaciated bodies of dead cattle. When the snow had gone down enough for an attempt at a spring round-up, there were only a few pitiful survivors where thousands had grazed.

Days passed and their men were paid off somehow and drifted away, and Ben Remsberg sat and looked out over the ruined land and Kitt Remsberg wandered through her big house and sat by the mirror chewing on her lower lip.

She went to him and sat beside him. "How bad is it, Ben?"

"We're wiped out. Not enough left to pay taxes. And we still owe on cattle lying dead out there. We'll be lucky to hold on to your house." He tried a grin for her and it was worn and thin like the feeling coming from him. "I guess I can always be a blacksmith again."

"Ben, what would it take to lick winters like that?"

"Only one way, Kitt. Wind shelters. Plenty of hay for the rough times when the grass is covered. That would take money. For lumber and equipment and barn space. We haven't got it."

"We've got a lot of things in this house that cost a lot of money."

He stared at her, startled. "You—you'd—you mean——"

"I mean we can strip down this house the way you did a wagon once. We can tear down part of it, too, and use the lumber. We'll sell everything in it and start small again."

He stared at her and he grinned again, and she felt the wideness beginning to spread again beside her. "Everything, Kitt?"

"Well, no. Of course not. Not my mirror."

Together they did it, went back to the beginning and began again. They sold everything for what they could get, everything except the mirror and beds for themselves and the little girl, and they paid most of their debts and he made what other furniture they needed out of old boards, rough and crude but adequate. They ripped down more than half of the house and built their first hay barn and the first of their wind shelters. They sold part of their range and bought the small first of their new herds and a used mower and a dump-rake. They worked together and progress was slow now, but they moved ahead, and the mirror stood lonely against the wall of their bedroom, but not grotesque in the emptiness of the bare room because it was still the beginning that could always be made again. And then, when they were solidly on their feet again, came the one blow that could break them.

She was riding out to find Ben across the vast stretch of level ground they kept for hay. Life sang in her and she urged the horse into full gallop and it stumbled in a small gully hidden in the tall grass and went to its knees and she pitched forward over its head and rolled with the momentum to crumple unconscious against a rock. Hours later he found the riderless horse by the home corral gate. Still later he found her, struggling toward him, clutching at the tough grasses to drag herself along in limp agony. There was little any doctor could do except ease her pain. She had fractured the base of her spine and she endured the hard cast for months, and when the pain left and the bone knit, the paralysis came, freezing the lower half of her body in a wasting immobility.

She lay in their big bedroom and drove out the despair and hopelessness. She learned to order her household through the two Mexican women Ben hired to do for her. She held to their ranch through the hours Ben spent with her telling her about it. The months moved inevitably, and she lay in the bedroom and watched the slow changes creep into Ben and herself and their house. She saw them and she refused to see them. She shut them away in her mind and willed herself to believe that nothing of importance was changed. She lay there at night with Ben beside her and waited until he breathed with the long slow regularity of sleep and she could force herself to believe that everything was as it had been because they were there together. But the morning was always bad, the time when he left her, when she watched him disappear through the doorway. And then she discovered what the mirror could do.

Lying there, looking over the foot of the bed, she had been able to see the top of it against the far wall, the carved gilt top of the frame and a small part of the glass. Now she found that when she was raised up to sit against the pillows, she could see almost all of it and it reflected for her the view through the wide window of the side wall. It was thus itself a window, a vista for her vision into the outside world showing part of the broad porch across the front of the house and the curving lane, and beyond that a corner of the barn and the corral beside it, and farther beyond that the stretching reaches of grassland. It carried her out through the confining walls into the world Ben entered when he left the room. She could be out there with him in her thoughts. And looking out through the mirror she could watch when he moved unknowing into the frame of her vision. She could try to determine, from his appearance or actions or something carried, what he was doing, what was happening about the place. Then she could surprise him with what she knew when he came into this other world, their room, to be with her. This was her secret, her solace, her defense. The mirror was her shield until it betrayed her.

She sat in the bed and watched Ben standing on the porch and the other figure appear from somewhere on some errand, the younger of the Mexican women, and stop by him, close and conscious of the closeness. She saw but could not hear them talking and the woman turned away and tossed her head in a quick provocative sidewise glance and he took her by the shoulders and swung her around and pulled her to him. She saw the two figures molded as one in the single intensity and they separated slightly and moved away together out of the mirror, out of the rigid limits of her vision.

Kittura Remsberg lay limp against the pillows of the bed and stared across the room at the mirror. Faithfully it held open its vista into the world outside, but she did not see that. She saw there the slow changes that had been creeping into them, into Ben and herself, and that she had refused to see. She saw the lines deepening about his mouth and his temper thinning to snap ever more easily. She saw his pity for her changing, unaware, to pity for himself and the bitterness taking him. She saw herself becoming irritable, sharp-tongued, wanting and demanding to know what he did every moment he was out of the room. She saw herself slipping into resentment of him, of his untouched vitality, his ability to stand erect and move about and go through the doorway away from her. She saw these things happening and it had taken the mirror-caught sight of two figures fusing into one in a simple elemental hunger to tell her why. She lay against the pillows and her hands beat at the cover over the thin immobility of her hips and she chewed on her lower lip till it was raw with the blood showing. Yet she was still and her voice was quiet when at last he was there by the bed looking down at her.

"I want to tell you something, Ben. My mirror. You've never noticed, but from here it lets me see right out that window. Almost the same as if I could be out there."

"That's fine, Kitt. But I've been thinking maybe I could rig some kind of a special wheelchair. Then you could——"

"No, Ben. I'll never leave this room." And while he stared at her she spoke quickly to have it said. "I saw you. In that mirror. With that woman."

Deeper color climbed behind the burned brown of his face, but his voice was as steady as hers. "I'm sorry, Kitt."

"That I saw you? No. That had to be." He started to speak and she stopped him with a shake of her head. "Ben, give me your gun."

He looked down at her for a long moment.

"Ben, my life is my own. Give me your gun."

He looked down at her, and he knew the quality of her and he was man enough for her to lift the gun from the holster by his side and lean to place it in her hands.

She lay against the pillows with the gun in her lap. "Ben, be honest with me. Would it be better for you if I were out of the way?"

Time moved past them and small drops of sweat stood out on his forehead as he pushed deep into his own mind.

"No, Kitt. I need you. I need to know that you are. Without that there'd be no meaning in my life."

A small sigh came from her and she looked at him and felt the wideness reaching out, wavering and twisted perhaps from the beating of the years, but a wideness for her to feel.

"All right, Ben," she said. "This is our room and all I can have. I don't want ever to see anything that you do outside of this room. I don't even want to know what you do, except about our ranch and what you want to tell me."

She did not falter as she raised the big gun and it bucked in her hand. The roar of the shot echoed from the walls and the mirror shattered in its ornate carved frame and when the last piece fell tinkling to the floor there was an abiding quietness in the room.

Kittura Remsberg was my grandmother. She is buried under a stone of mountain granite on the slight rise of ground behind the corral of the ranch that belongs to someone else now. There is another stone beside hers. I believe that Ben Remsberg, her husband, my grandfather, told her the truth when he looked down at her as she lay in the bed with the big gun in her lap. When I saw him at the simple funeral, he still seemed broad and strong, rugged as an oak that sheds the years like water. Yet within a year after he raised the stone on her grave, he lay down in their bed to sleep and slipped quietly away without waking in the now empty peace of that room.

General Pingley

THE PINGLEYS came into our section of Wyoming to take over the claim of a cousin who made the mistake of trying to drive a buckboard over a mountain trail while tipping a bottle of whiskey. This cousin had proved up on the claim and the title was clear, and the Pingleys were the closest of kin. They were ready to leave their place in Nebraska for a middling good reason. From what I heard they had left other times from other places for the same reason, one that walked on two legs, an old man, Bert Pingley's father, old J. Clayburn Pingley.

They were a mixed lot, these Pingleys. Bert was a big mild middle-aged man, about the hardest-working and easiest-natured I've ever known. His wife was some years younger, a pretty woman, fluttery in her actions, and so shy that sometimes you might think she was silly in the head. There were two children, a little girl just beginning to walk and trying to hide in her mother's skirts when strangers were near, and a boy, coming seven or eight, I'd say, fair-sized for his age and easy-natured like his father. And, of course, there was the old man, stiff-backed as a ramrod, still fighting the Civil War thirty years after the last shot had been fired.

The first time I saw him he was wearing his old gray uniform coat and campaign hat. It was a Saturday afternoon, and I was in town to pick up any mail and rub elbows with other folks a bit. I saw him in Eiler's general store. He was ordering some tobacco and complaining about the price. He had a fringe of white chin whiskers that stood out straight when he talked.

"Double damn Yankees," he said. "Robbers. Every last one of you."

Eiler was surprised. He leaned forward on his counter. "Easy now, pop," he said. "I was born back in Georgia myself."

"A renegade, eh? Lived so long among these thieving Yankees you're the same."

I saw this big man, Bert, hurrying over, a smile busting his face wide open.

"Don't mind my father," he said. "It's one of his bad days. Can't seem to learn the war's over and forgotten." He smiled at Eiler and shrugged his shoulders a little. "You see, Father hasn't surrendered yet."

"You're double damned right I haven't. I'll just keep on telling every yellow-bellied bluecoat I find just what——"

Bert's smile stayed the same, but his hand on the old man's arm stopped the words. "Father, wait for me at the wagon. I'll bring your tobacco."

I saw him later the same afternoon in front of the old stage post where folks liked to meet and swap neighborhood news and wait for the mail coach. The three or four other men there with him must have been working on him because he was hopping mad when I came along. The chin whiskers were sticking out stiff as hog bristles.

"——never was a time," he was saying, "any Federal troops could stand to one of our charges. I mind me once when General Pick-ett——"

"Choke it, whiskers," said one of the men. "You rebs were licked before you started, only you didn't know it. Too many crazy old goats like you."

The old man pulled himself up even straighter. "Bert," he shouted, looking around. Right enough, Bert was hurrying over again, smiling again at the whole world. "Bert, you heard it. You going to——"

"Shucks," said Bert. "You'd want I should smack him just be-cause you riled him into calling names?"

"My own son! A coward in my own family!"

Bert's smile didn't change. That was when I began to like him. As I say, he was a big man. He could have taken any two of us there and my money would have been on him.

"Shucks, Father," he said. "You forget when we're needing sup-plies we come in under a truce flag."

The old man subsided like a sudden thunderstorm ending. "You're right, son. So we do." He took off his ancient campaign hat and bowed to the rest of us. "I'm sorry, gentlemen. I forgot myself. But perhaps some other time——" He marched off erect toward their wagon, and I saw it there, a white cotton handkerchief tied to a buggy whip whose butt was stuck between the sideboards.

Someone was standing close beside me. That was our marshal, Clyde Eakins. He was watching the old man.

"Stubborn old coot," I said.

"Yes," Eakins said. "But his kind of fun ain't exactly enjoyable after a while. Beginning already to get some folks' nerves ruffled."

He was not really so bad, not at first, anyway. You find some touchy ones anywhere you go. We had our share. But most of us were willing to let him talk his war. We couldn't be peeved at anyone who belonged to a man like Bert. I guess the old man had a right to a grudge at that. His other son, Bert's brother, had died at Shiloh, and the shock of that, together with Federal troop occupation of the family place in Virginia, had killed his wife, Bert's mother. Then he lost everything he owned in the early carpetbag days. There was not much left for him except to tag along when Bert struck out into the new Territories.

For quite a while people in town tolerated his talk. They liked to stir him a little and watch the chin whiskers wag. They could count on Bert to step in smiling before real sparks flew. And they had a kind of admiration for the old man's unwavering belligerence. They began calling him the General, and he liked that. Bert didn't. "Shucks," Bert would say, "he wasn't a general. He was only a sort of reserve captain. Managed a supply depot down in North Carolina and didn't even hear a gun go off." Bert himself had. He had fought through the four years, starting as a green kid of seventeen and coming out a man. But he never talked about that. It was a job he had to do, and when it was done it was finished. Maybe he felt that the old man did enough talking for the whole Pingley tribe.

It was in July that the town's temper turned. July Fourth. We always celebrated the day. A town committee would make the arrangements, and those like me who lived out a ways would be on hand to make a respectable crowd for the doings. There would be

shooting matches, rifle and revolver, and things like that, and about
midmorning we would raise the flag on the town flagpole in the park
space opposite the hotel and salute it with a lot of cheers and gun-
powder. Then we would jam into the former storeroom we used
for a courthouse and listen to the speechmaking and work up an
appetite for the hot lunch some of the ladies always sold for the
benefit of the volunteer fire department.

Judge Cutler usually made the main speech. He was dry and
short with words on the bench, but his special orations were something to hear. This time he never got to finish. He was not much
more than well unlimbered in the throat when someone standing by
the door gave a shout and people turned to look where he was pointing, and there was a stampede through the doorway and across to
the park space. Old J. Clayburn Pingley was standing stiff-backed
by the pole. He had pulled down the flag and tossed it aside and
run up an old Confederate flag instead.

People stopped in a half-circle around him and the pole gawking
up at his faded old flag. And then things happened fast. Young
Pard Wheeler, who had considerable celebrating under his belt,
pulled his gun and aimed upward and started shooting. I think he
was only trying to cut the rope, but the bullets ripped through the
flag and the rents showed plain. The old man screamed and started
toward Wheeler, reaching in his side pocket and his hand came out
with an old-fashioned little derringer. Marshal Eakins scrambled
quick and caught him and wrenched the arm, and the little weapon
fell to the ground, and he broke loose from Eakins and went at
Wheeler beating with his hands. Wheeler backed away trying to
fend off the blows and stopped and gave the old man a push that
sent him sprawling. And Bert Pingley burst out of the crowd and
crashed a big fist to the side of Wheeler's head and Wheeler went
down like a steer when you poleaxe it.

Two things stick in my mind when I remember that. One is the
look of the old man lying on the ground. He wasn't making any
effort to get up. He was lying there, quiet now, leaning on one
elbow and watching Bert, and mighty pleased about something. The
other is the look of Bert Pingley standing there, big as the side of a
mountain, not smiling, and disgusted with himself and ashamed.

Maybe I ought to add a third thing. Young Pard Wheeler, somehow acting for all of us, staggering a little when he got to his feet and trying to make Bert see that he understood what had happened.

The General wasn't amusing after that, not to most of the people around. I guess they remembered his scream and the little derringer coming out of his pocket. And there were some who were shocked at his hauling down the American flag. He wasn't a joke, a neighborhood character any more. He was a nuisance that might cause trouble. But there wasn't any trouble because he was hardly ever in town again. That must have been Bert's doing. Bert was easy-natured. But he probably could be firm when he felt that he had to be.

The next I heard the old man was being sighted around the country, keeping out of people's way and getting about in a little buggy pulled by an old horse Bert let him use. Sometimes the boy would be with him and might wave a friendly arm, but the old man would drive right along, straight on the seat, not turning his head. He drove that buggy in the damndest places, where there were no roads and not even trails, smack across open range land and up into the mountains where you wouldn't think anything on wheels could go. When people spoke to Bert about it, Bert would just smile and shrug his shoulders. "Shucks," Bert would say, "he ain't worrying anybody, is he? Likes to camp out a few days at a time. Takes good care of the boy too." Then nobody was seeing much of him at all, and nobody seemed to know what he was doing, and Bert wasn't saying, even if he knew, and I was the first to find out what it was.

When the weather was right and no work pressing, I liked to saddle the gray and ride on up my valley and into the hills. After a few miles I'd be in the high country where the rock formations climbed and the bigness took you into itself in a comfortable quiet. Riding up there kept the horse in condition and my own mind too.

Sometime in late summer I was drifting along and came out on the wide chunk of tableland that was the far edge part of Sam Piegan's range. During dry periods when grass was sparse near his home spread, Piegan ran some of his cattle on those high plateaus. One year he had tried wintering some there and had built a line camp on this stretch of tableland. By spring he knew better, and was lucky to have enough of the cattle still alive to pay his man's wages. The only mark left was the abandoned log cabin. I had passed it a few times and noticed that the door was gone and the walls sagging and holes beginning to show in the roof.

When I saw it in the distance this time, it had a different look. Smoke was rising out of the stone chimney. I rode closer, and saw it had a makeshift door with pieces of old harness nailed for hinges and the walls were being chinked and new slabs of bark were on the roof. There was a pole sticking up from one corner, and flapping out from this was an old Confederate flag.

The door opened and the old man stood in the doorway. He had a battered Sharps carbine in his hands. "Ought to blast you out of that saddle," he said. "Yankee spy. Nosing around my fort."

"Easy, General," I said, "you're no bushwhacker. I didn't know you were here."

"You know it now. So keep moving and don't come back." The chin whiskers stood out straight at me. "This is Confederate territory. By right of conquest." He waved the gunbarrel to point at the cabin wall beside the door and I saw stretched there by its paws the skin of a good-sized black bear.

I sat on the gray chuckling. I couldn't help it. But I wasn't chuckling after a warning bullet from his carbine sang uncomfortably close by my right ear. I swung the gray and went into retreat, about as scared as mad. I never had any fondness for bullets moving in my direction. But halfway home, I was chuckling again. When I told Sam Piegan about it, he chuckled too. "The old boy can use the place all he wants. Maybe it'll keep him out of trouble. We'll pass the word around so nobody'll bother him."

I didn't ride out much the next months. Haying knocked off the rest of the summer and fattening my three-year steers for market on special rations took the fall. But I saw him a few times driving past my place in his little buggy. The best route to that rebel roost of his was up my valley and left along the trail that climbed through the notch to the tablelands. Even that must have been a hard pull for his old horse. I didn't know how often he made the trip because sometimes I'd miss seeing him and only know he had gone past by chancing on his fresh wheel tracks in the mud where the road forded the valley stream not far from my house. Then the cold edge of late fall began to creep into the air and I didn't see him or his tracks at all.

Winter hit us early that year. It hit us weeks ahead of the usual first snow with a surprise storm that whipped over the near line of mountains and caught plenty of us unprepared. I know because it caught me and shook me for a nice loss. I liked to keep my market-age steers as long as possible, putting on the last possible pounds with good grain, and move them out just before the winter snows when the price was at a peak. I hadn't even begun thinking about moving them that year when the storm hit. I had checked my fences and filled the trays in the feedlot again and come in and gone to bed early, and along before midnight I woke startled and heard the wind shrieking in the chimney. I crawled out of the bunk and went to the door and opened it and the snow struck me in a sheet and stung my face. It was the worst kind, dry and fine and driving. I was plenty worried, not about the cattle themselves because I had stout shelters, but about what a real blizzard could mean. Not many hours of that kind of snow could choke the trails and even the traveled roads. If the cold held and later snows kept building the drifts, I might have to feed my steers all winter and sell in a dropping spring market.

I pulled on clothes and went out to take care of the horses. They were bunched under the roof-shelter out from the barn. I propped open the door to the stretch of stalls and didn't have to use any coaxing to get them in. There were knee-high drifts already by the time I pushed against the wind back to the house.

By morning I was snowed in tight, and the wind was still piling it down. I fought and floundered my way to the barn and saw the little path I made filling in fast again. I got one of the heavy work horses and climbed on him bareback and sent him plowing back and forth from the barn to the house and return till I had a real path showing. But this kept on filling in, too, so I took fence posts from my stock pile and stuck them in the snow on the wind side of the path about six feet apart and found enough planks in the barn to set against them for the beginnings of a barrier. The snow packed against the planks and held them firm and the drifts started this way protected the path quite a bit. Snow kept blowing over the top and into the path, of course, but not so bad that I couldn't clear it away every few hours without too much trouble. I was set then for as long a siege as that storm wanted to give me. There was fodder in the barn and food in the house, and my woodpile would last a whole winter.

Along in the afternoon of that first day, the snow slackened and almost stopped, but the wind kept at its battering, and sometime during the night it whipped in reinforcements from far up in the mountains and began piling down the snow again. When it finally eased during the third day, my path was almost a tunnel, shoulder high on one side and a foot above my head on the other. If there had been a strong crust on the snow, I could have walked right onto the roof of the barn from the big drift along one side. I settled into a nice routine, catching up on my sleep, fussing around the barn and adjoining feedlot morning and evening, walking the horses along the path to take the stall-kinks out of their legs, and the rest of the time loafing snug and warm in the house. When I didn't remember about missing the market, I even enjoyed the quiet laziness.

It was late in the morning of the fifth or sixth day, I'm not sure now which, that I heard faint shouts outside. I went out on the porch, and there were two men bucking the drifts toward my house from where the road was under the snow. They were leading and almost dragging their horses by the reins. They were wrapped right for the weather with only a little of their faces showing, and I couldn't recognize them at first. They came closer, and I saw the big man in front was Bert Pingley and the one plodding behind was Marshal Eakins. They were beat, and no wonder. It was eight miles out from town to my place. They dropped the reins by the porch and nodded at me and went past me into the house and collapsed on the nearest chairs. I set a bottle on the table by Eakins and put the coffeepot to warming on the stove and went out again to their horses. I never knew two more grateful animals than those were when I led them to the barn and worked over them quick and pulled down some hay. They had plugged through drifts so long that their legs were quivering and could scarcely hold them up.

Back in the house I poured coffee around and waited for the others to talk. Bert gulped his cup and sat still, staring at the floor. Eakins finished his and poured himself another.

"Thanks, John," he said. "Nothing like coffee ever." He let the warmth work through him. He lifted an arm and pointed it on up the valley toward the hills, and let it drop. "The old man's up there," he said.

"Is he?" I said. "What the devil's he doing there?"

Bert raised his head briefly and let it drop again. "He had to get his flag."

"Yes," Eakins said. "Bert finally made it to town this morning for help and found me. The old fool left his flag up there and got to worrying about it. Started for it day before the storm. Must have been caught and couldn't get back."

I thought around that. "Well," I said, "I'd let the old coot hibernate there all winter. He's got shelter and firewood's handy."

"No," Eakins said. He shook his head and gulped his second cup of coffee and looked at me. "The boy's up there with him."

Bert raised his head again and almost shouted. "He had to get his flag, don't you see? His flag. And I couldn't go. Who knew about this storm anyway? It was his flag. Do you think I could say no?"

Eakins didn't pay any attention to him. Eakins just looked at me. "The boy's up there. They didn't take any supplies. Maybe a meal or two. Were coming back in the morning."

Eakins looked at me and I fidgeted on my chair. I felt the way you feel when there's something you know you have to do and don't want to do it.

"Hell, man," I said, "it can't be done. The notch will be plugged with drifts higher than this house."

Eakins just looked at me. "John," he said, "the old man's had his time. But the boy's up there. You know this country out here better'n about anyone else. Thought maybe you could figure a way through. An hour's rest and we'll start."

I left them in the house and went to the barn and put out plenty of feed for the cattle and hay for the horses. I fastened the door open so the horses could go out all right if I was a while getting home again. I passed by the gray and the big buckskin and the mare. She was with foal anyway. I looked over the work team and decided they were the ones. I didn't want speed or quickness or know-how. I wanted power and pull. I gave them a couple of quarts of grain each, and when they had eaten put on them the bridles with the long driving reins. I led them out by the porch and went in the house and wrapped myself good. I dropped the bottle in a side pocket and shook Eakins awake in his chair. I didn't need to shake Bert. He was up and had found my saddle-bags and was packing them with food. He strapped them together and went out and slung them over the back of one of the horses and Eakins and I followed him.

"We'll use the horses to break trail as far as we can," I said. "We'll alternate them in the lead. Then we'll be on our own."

I took the reins of one horse and started him down the track already broken toward the road and Bert followed with the other horse and Eakins tagged us. When we reached the road, I swung toward town, keeping to the track they had made coming out. I heard Bert shouting behind me and he sounded angry, and I kept straight on and I heard Eakins's voice. "Shut up and follow him." I held to the track till we cleared the entrance to my valley, and then swung sharp right across the open land and the untouched whiteness of the snow.

I had it all clear in my mind, the one way we might have a chance. I kept the lead, trying to stay out of the hollows where the snow was too deep for movement and to follow the rolling rises that the wind had swept fairly clear and work my way through the foothills to the right place in the rimrock where the mountains soared into their high climb. It was hard going almost every yard of the way. The snow was dry and loose and gave no real foothold, and there were times when there was nothing to do except plow ahead and try to smash through. More than once the horse fought forward till he was helpless, unable to strike down through the snow to the ground, and I had trouble getting him back out for a swing around to try another spot. After the first twenty minutes, he was dripping sweat and in about an hour he had enough.

I stopped and called back to Bert it was his turn and gave him the general direction and he took the lead with the other horse. He made a faster pace than I had, I guess because it was his boy and his father up there and not his horse fighting the drifts, and he was harsh urging it ahead. I thought of calling him on that, then thought better of it and kept my mouth shut. But I shouted time on him quicker than I had on myself. If we were going to kill my horses, we were going to do it the right way and conserve their strength and get the most out of them. We had a long way to go.

I don't know how many turns I called and alternated the horses. Time got to be hazy as we plugged along. Walking in that snow even with the trail broken by those big hooves wasn't easy. And for the last couple of hours we were moving uphill most of the time. I know the horses were done, completely exhausted, with the strength out of them, when we hit the steep rocky slope, almost a cliff, I was looking for. I didn't dare tell Bert where we would head next or he would have started right on. I let him stew while I scraped the thick sweat out of the horses' matted hair and tied them under the shelter of an overhanging ledge and yanked down some pine branches for them. "All right," I said when I was ready. "It's not far now. If we can scramble up here, we'll come out on those flat stretches. They're like steps up the mountain. Third one up's the place."

I was right that this was where we could make it. That rocky slope was almost bare of snow except where outcropping ledges had caught it. We could zigzag up where the footholds were best and pull ourselves along by grabbing at the big rocks. Climbing took the breath out of us, but the flat stretches themselves were the really hard going. They had their own drifts and we had to break our own trail. I doubt whether Eakins and I could have crossed them without Bert smashing ahead of us. We were at the bottom of the last slope when we heard a shot somewhere above us. We shouted, but our voices would not carry, and then we couldn't shout because we needed all our breath for the final scramble to the top.

I wonder sometimes what exactly we expected to see when we reached the top. Not the peaceful scene we found. Everything was quiet and lovely in the late afternoon light. For some reason the quietness and the loveliness remain in my mind. All the long way we had been too busy fighting the snow to appreciate what was around us. Now it hit me suddenly. The cabin off in the distance, small and alone against the mountain wall behind it, was serene and untroubled in the midst of the white wonder and smoke was rising from its chimney. Close to us, where the wagon trail swung in an arc, was the little buggy, the wheels buried in a drift, and we could see the track it had made from the cabin and the spread snow where the horse had floundered and been caught and had been unharnessed and led back toward the cabin. And perched on the buggy seat was the boy, alive and alert and staring at us with the battered Sharps carbine across his knees.

Eakins was the first to speak. "What was that shot?" he said.

The boy gulped and found his voice. "Grandpa told me to shoot every so often, so somebody might hear. You took an awful long time. I've only got two bullets left." He stared at us, and suddenly he dropped the gun clattering on the buggy floorboards and jumped down and struggled through the snow toward us, and Bert leaped with long strides to meet him and gather him up, and the boy was crying and laughing in his arms and saying, "I knew you'd come." And after a moment he quieted and looked at Eakins and me. "Grandpa said some of you'd come too. He said even if you are Yankees, you'd worry about us and come get us."

Bert jerked his head toward the cabin. "Is he all right?"

"Oh, sure he is. I've kept the fire going like he said." Suddenly the boy was very serious. "He's broke his leg, though. But he says that isn't bad. He chopped and chopped an awful lot of wood and then he fell on something and his leg broke. But he says that'll get all right. He says he has good bones."

We started toward the cabin, Bert carrying the boy, and when we were almost there the boy was serious again.

"Please be quiet," he said. "Grandpa's awful tired and sleeps a lot. He hasn't waked up at all yet today."

We went in quietly, and when we saw the stillness of the thin old figure on the bunk, we knew that he would never waken. I saw Bert's face set in stern lines, and he put the boy down gently and went over and stood staring at the still figure. Eakins took the boy by an arm and led him outside, and I followed.

"Is daddy going to wake him?" the boy said.

"No," Eakins said. "Not right now." He looked off into the distance and then at the boy again. "You hungry?"

"No," the boy said. "I don't think so. My stomach feels kind of puffy. We've only had a bag of dried apples that was here, and I only eat a little bowlful at a time and only twice a day the way grandpa says. But dried apples make your stomach feel puffy."

Eakins looked off into the distance again, into the wide vast openness where the slope dropped away as if it were the edge of the world. "Your grandfather," he said, "has he been eating them too?"

"Oh, no," the boy said. "He doesn't want any. He says dried apples are bad for anyone with a broken leg."

I saw Bert in the doorway and Eakins did too and spoke quickly to him. "Take the boy, Bert, and backtrack to where we left the horses. Get a fire going and rustle out some food. Start him in easy on it. John and I'll take care of things here."

We stood by the bunk and looked down at the wasted figure, at the thin old face with its sunken cheeks and pathetic fringe of chin whiskers.

"He was a stubborn old coot," I said.

"Yes," Eakins said, "he was."

I pulled the blanket up over the face, and together we made the best temporary grave we could to hold him till spring and proper burial in town. We scraped away snow and used the axe to dig into the hard ground. We yanked down part of the chimney to pile rocks over the grave so no animal could get at him. And just before we left, Eakins went inside again and came out with the torn flag and tied it to the pole from the corner of the cabin and stuck the pole firmly in among the rocks.

The last thing I saw in the fading light, as we went over the edge of the tableland and started down the steep slope, was that old flag whipping out straight and stiff in the mountain wind.

Elvie Burdette

I'VE BEEN deputy sheriff ever since we had a sheriff at Cubb's Crossing, and that's close to thirty years. We haven't had many sheriffs because we don't go in much for change out here, not in our politics. Get a good man and keep him is our way. We kept Sheriff Godbee till he died, and Sheriff Lantz till he retired, and I expect we'll keep Sheriff Virts till he does one or the other. And all of them have kept me because I've known how to handle the fussy little cases and the office routine without bothering them and never have minded tending the jail. That's my specialty, tending the jail. I'm proud of the nice tight comfortable jail I've fixed with the little money available off and on.

Nearly thirty years it's been, and in all that time I've had only one woman in my jail and only two jail breaks. You may not believe me, but that one woman staged those two breaks.

Elvie Burdette was her name. Well, no, I can't swear to that. Elvie was for Elvira and probably was right. But none of us ever knew whether she really was married to Hebb Burdette. They never referred to each other as husband and wife. They just came to the Crossing together and lived together, and in those days when the Territory was new nobody pushed much into anybody else's past. We spoke of her as Mrs. Burdette till we got to speaking of her as Elvie, and that was good enough for us.

She was a big buxom woman when they first came, big-featured and pleasant-looking. She had yellow hair, and maybe did something to it to make it that bright yellow, and she had a lot of it. She always wore the same dress when she was out where people could see her. I expect it was the only dress she had, and it was red and had spangles around the bottom, and up top there were marks that looked like places where spangles had been and been cut off. She filled that dress in a way that was satisfying to see, and she could handle men all right, which was what some of the boys learned when they tried a bit of experimenting and she set them back on their heels in a hurry.

Hebb was different. He was little and mean-faced and dark-complected, and not much any way you wanted to look at him. He would have faded away into any crowd without being noticed. He couldn't do anything worth while and he didn't want to do anything worth while, and you wouldn't think any woman with meat on her bones would know he even existed. But he certainly was boss in his own house. He could snap his fingers and make Elvie jump to do what he said. He was cantankerous and rough with her, and out in public too, and he let her do all the taking care for both of them as if she owed that to him and couldn't ever do enough or do it right.

They took a claim, a poor one other people had passed by but close in to town, probably so he could walk in easy for liquor and a card game whenever she found money for him. My guess is he figured taking up that claim was a chance to make something without working. Under the homestead law, if you filed on a quarter section and lived on it three years and made some pretense of improving it, you'd get clear title. He had to live somewhere, so he figured he might as well live on a piece of land that would be his for just living on it. Elvie would see that they had food and that he had pocket money.

She did. She did in the damndest ways. She baked bread and a kind of coffee cake with nuts or berries of whatever she could get hold of for filling and trundled the stuff into the Crossing on a push-cart-like contraption. It was good stuff, and she soon had regular customers—the stage post where you could get meals and Rickey's saloon with its free-lunch counter. She trundled that pushcart around and picked up washing from some of our bachelors and scrubbed it out cleaner than they ever could, and delivered it again. And she talked Clem Rickey into letting her have the job of giving his place its weekly clean-out and scrubbing on Sunday mornings after the usual Saturday night fracas.

She had to get up mighty early Sunday mornings for that because she had to be finished in time to scrub herself some and get to church. Why she did that I've never been able to figure. We had only one church, and it wasn't really a church except for the cemetery beside it, because it was our schoolhouse just being used for church services and the minister was one of the homesteaders who felt he had a call, which couldn't have been very strong because he was as dull a preacher as they come. Hardly anybody went except the womenfolk and the few husbands that could be argued or dragged into it. But Elvie was there every Sunday. The only one she missed, till the real trouble started and she was too busy to go, was when Hebb had pneumonia and she was afraid to leave him alone. She couldn't have enjoyed it. Not that preacher. And the other women sniffed and looked away when she came in and wouldn't sit on the same bench with her. But still she would be there, alone on her bench with a quarter hidden from Hebb ready for the collection, and her red dress, getting faded from so many washings, as neat as she could make it.

And Hebb? Well, the thought of Hebb inside a church would have given most of us a heartier kick than a shot of Rickey's strongest. Hebb would be home sleeping on their bed where she had put him when she took him home from the saloon a few hours before she started her Sunday morning scrubbing. He was one of the regulars at Rickey's, there so often he was almost a fixture, and always there on Saturday night because she collected on Saturday mornings and he'd have money that night. He'd sit in on a card game and always lose and sometimes be nasty about it, and during the early part of the evening he would drink by the clock, one an hour. He was a small man with a small stomach and couldn't take much. Along about midnight he would lose count and start forgetting the clock, and then it would be a matter of just when he'd begin to wag his head in that peculiar way and stand up and turn completely around once or twice and collapse on the floor. That would be Elvie's signal. She would have been waiting outside, watching through a window, and she would come in and help him to his feet and support him out the door and home. It wasn't long, of course, before we all knew that schedule and tried to make it easier for her. We'd watch too, and when the head-wagging started, several of us would grab him and tote him to the door and turn him over to her. We never did that earlier than the head-wagging because then he would still be aware enough to be mean and make trouble for her probably all the way home. She never forgot to thank us when we brought him out.

"Funny woman, Elvie," Clem Rickey said one night after she had taken him away. "Won't let anyone really do a thing for her. Heard her humming once when scrubbing, and had an idea. She's a good-looking woman still. There's a lot of her and it's well placed. Offered her a job working here. Made it nice. None of the extras like the other girls. Just singing a little and helping keep you boys amused. She jumped down my throat like I'd insulted her. So I asked if she wanted me to put a limit on Hebb or keep him out of here. She got even madder. Told me to let him be and do whatever he wants."

I expect I got to know Elvie about as well as anyone around. Hebb spent a lot of time in my jail, and she used to bring him warm meals in a big kettle with a top to hold in the heat. That was after they moved into town, after they had proved up on the claim and sold it right away and moved into a shack in town and Hebb had some real money to spend. He bought her a nice church-going dress and a hat. I have to give him credit for that. He togged himself in some fancy clothes and began to have big ideas about himself as a gambling man. He'd cut into bigger games at the saloon and try to look tough and stone-faced when the big bets were running. As long as his roll lasted, he put up a fair bluff. When it was gone and he was back where he'd been before with only what Elvie could get for him to spend, he began to go to pieces. The meanness in him got to be too much to be used on her alone. He was mean to everyone, nasty talking and quarrelsome. If he'd been a bigger man, he might have been a real troublemaker. Being small and afraid to use a gun, he was just a nuisance. Sheriff Godbee was still alive then, and when he'd feel he had to pull Hebb in for disturbing the peace, Judge Cutler would only give Hebb a couple of days' cooling off at a time. Fines wouldn't do any good. Elvie would have to pay them. Maybe a couple of days in my jail wouldn't do any good either. Do him any good, I mean. But at least it would make things quieter around town for a while.

As I say, I got to know Elvie pretty well, which was as much as anyone did. She wasn't a talker, and when she did talk, trying to be pleasant because she knew I made Hebb comfortable as I could in my jail, it was about the weather and little happenings about town—things like that. She wouldn't say a word about herself. And she wouldn't let me or anyone say a word about Hebb to her. Him being the kind of man he was, you couldn't talk about him without blaming, and she wasn't going to let anybody blame him about anything.

"Elvie," I said one time she came in with her covered kettle, "you aren't getting any younger." She wasn't. She was ageing fast. Her yellow hair was beginning to show streaks and she was skimpier than she used to be, and her hands were red and rough from so much scrubbing and she was getting to be sort of shapeless in her new dress. "Elvie," I said, "you ought to cut loose from Hebb while there's time. Find yourself a real man that'll treat you better."

She looked at me like I was speaking some strange language she couldn't understand. Then she began to laugh in a peculiar way, low in her throat, and she looked at me like I was something small and crawly that ought to be stepped on quick. "A real man?" she said. "Better'n Hebb?" She kept on laughing in that way that wasn't nice to hear and went over by the inner door and waited for me to unlock it. And let me be cussed out proper if she didn't stop on her way back out to smile at me and be pleasant and thank me for letting her take the food in.

I simply couldn't figure her at all. Sometimes I'd open the inner door a crack and peer through at Hebb over behind the bars playing solitaire with the cards and listening to the old gramophone I kept there for whoever might be locked up. I knew he'd be hoping I'd come in so he would have somebody to argue with and talk mean to, and I couldn't see what it was about him that she saw. He was such an insignificant little piece of meanness and laziness. He didn't seem the least bit big even about being a bad one. Then he pulled the trick that proved we all had underestimated him in one way at least.

There was a mining camp, placer mining, up in the hills about twenty miles from the Crossing. Not a big strike, just a fair return for the men who worked the silt banks of a dry stream bed there. A syndicate had been formed to pool their takings, and once a month this syndicate shipped the dust out by the stage that stopped at the

Crossing. I checked the papers each time and the usual payload ran around ten to eleven thousand. It would be in care of our office until it reached the next town about sixty miles away, and Sheriff Godbee used to ride guard himself on the stage. He wasn't taking any extra chances because the commission we were paid helped cover our office expenses.

This time the syndicate agent with his own guards had brought the tin box in and I'd weighed the dust and marked it down in the book—ten thousand four hundred sixty-three dollars I remember it was—and I had locked the box and handed it to Sheriff Godbee, and he had stowed it in the boot and was ready to climb up with the driver when Hebb Burdette came hurrying along. They didn't think about it then, of course, but he had picked this time because there weren't any passengers and the stage was empty.

"Wait a minute," he said. "I'm going along."

Sheriff Godbee was surprised. "Never knew you to go any place," he said, short and irritated the way he always was with Hebb, "except to Rickey's."

"I've got business to tend to up the line," Hebb said. "Thinking of making a move. I'm sick of this town."

"It's sick of you," Sheriff Godbee said. "If you're going, pay your fare, hurry it." So Hebb paid the driver and climbed inside and they started off, and that was that.

You know how it is. You see a man around a lot and get to know him as a worthless little runt that's just a nuisance and that nobody can take seriously, and wouldn't even tolerate if it wasn't for his woman, and he comes along when you have an important job to do and you don't tie the two things together in your mind at all, and you just see him and forget about him being there. That was the way it was with Sheriff Godbee and the driver. They knew Hebb was in the coach, but they didn't really know it.

They rolled along at a good clip and changed horses at Burr's ranch and were some miles beyond on the flat sandy stretch when they remembered Hebb because he began pounding on the inside of the coach roof. Sheriff Godbee leaned over the side and shouted at him, and Hebb kept shouting back, "Stop! I'm sick, I tell you! Sick!" Sheriff Godbee was mad. He had a rule that they should never stop the coach between stations no matter who hailed from along the road, but this was different. There was nobody in sight for miles around and the flat land gave good vision and it was only Hebb inside the coach yelling. Sheriff Godbee told the driver to stop, and Hebb opened the door and almost fell out. He looked sick all right, and they didn't know that was because he had had a time nerving himself to what he was doing. He looked like he might keel over any minute, and they jumped down to see what they could do for him, and they were two mighty surprised men when he pulled a gun out of his belt under his coat and held it on them.

"Don't make me shoot," he kept saying. "I don't want to, so don't make me."

And they were a lot more scared than surprised when they saw how his hand twitched with the gun and how staring his eyes were and how he trembled all over with a kind of desperate excitement. "Turn around," he said, and when they did, he took their guns out of the holsters. "Start walking," he said, and they did, expecting maybe to feel bullets smack into their backs any time, and then they heard noises behind them, and when they turned Hebb was scrambling up on the driver's seat and grabbing the reins and whipping the horses into a run. They stood staring after the coach as it pulled away fast, and Sheriff Godbee was cursing himself for not keeping the shotgun in his hand when he jumped down.

Well, they hiked back to Burr's ranch and got guns and horses there and started out right away with a couple of Burr's men to side them. They found where Hebb had swung the coach off the main trace and cut over into the hills and stopped it on a slope and pegged the wheels with stones and had taken the box out of the boot and unhitched the horses and kicked away the stones so the coach would go careening down the slope and smash out of sight in a thick woods. They could tell by the tracks that he had sent three of the horses off with slaps on the rump or something to make them go and had climbed on the fourth and headed away through the rockiest stretch he could find to try to hide his trail. They could follow it, though, because he wasn't much good at that, and when they'd lose it they'd spread out and search around in a circle, and when one of them would spot it again, he'd fire a shot and they would gather and start on. They came to a place where the horse stumbled and Hebb fell off, probably because he didn't have a saddle to hold on to and the horse got away from him. It was all plain in the tracks. There was even a dent in the ground where a corner of the box hit. And then it wasn't so easy to follow him because he was a little man and even with the weight of the box he didn't make clear tracks except over the soft spots.

Night was sneaking in on them, so Sheriff Godbee called a halt and took his bearings and led the way to one of Burr's line camps that was handy, planning to start again with first light in the morning. It was round-up time, so no one was staying there, but they'd find food and maybe some blankets for the night chill. The cabin was small and the ceiling was made low by the bark-slab floor of the little storage loft, and the four of them made it seem mighty full. The chimney was a poor job and the fireplace smoked, and they were thinking they would have to throw water on the fire or sleep outside when they heard a sudden burst of sneezing and coughing up above in the loft.

Sheriff Godbee pulled his gun. "Come down out of there," he said, "before I start blasting through the roof."

"Don't shoot," said this voice between coughs. "Please don't shoot." And it was Hebb came scrambling down through the hole in the ceiling and the four of them couldn't help laughing at the ridiculous scared littleness of him.

So Hebb was back in jail. Only this time he wasn't there to cool off for a couple of days. He was waiting trial, which would be when Judge Cutler returned from swinging around the circuit of settlements he served every few months. There was a lot of interest in it because everyone knew it might be a humming dinger of a trial, with so many charges against Hebb that no one could tell just who would get him and with what charge. Sheriff Godbee was after him for robbery with a dangerous weapon and stern about it, because that was the first time anybody ever put him on the wrong end of a gun while his own was buckled to his belt. The stage company was after him for stealing and smashing their coach and hot about it, because the coach had been the new one they had paid to have delivered all the way from the East a week or two before. And the syndicate was after Hebb for their box and the dust in it. The cabin had been searched and his back trail followed, but no trace of the box had been found. All he would say was that he had hidden it and nobody else would ever get it. That's about all he would say about anything except to curse when anybody tried to question him.

So Hebb was in my jail. Not in the cooling-off quarters with the barred door and barred window and the gramophone, but in the waiting-for-trial quarters with bars all around. He slept a lot and prowled in a circle a lot and mumbled to himself and pounded the floor some. I had to make new rules about visitors because people kept wanting to come in and look at him and try to see what they hadn't seen before, and that made him angry and start shouting at them.

And every evening Elvie brought him a warm meal in her covered kettle.

She was suddenly older and her hair more streaked, and she was wearing the old red dress again with the tarnished spangles around the bottom. She went right on working, because she was saving her money for a lawyer, and when she thought she had enough for a showing she went to Rudy Ferebee, the only lawyer we had, who was really a storekeeper, but a lawyer too. Rudy told her he didn't want any money but would be glad to do what he could, but that wouldn't be much except maybe hold down the sentence. He told her it was an open-shut case and no doubt about it. He told her Hebb would be lucky to get by with ten years and then only if he tipped where he hid the box. She didn't have much faith in lawyers, so after that she asked me what I thought and what could I do but tell her the same?

"Ten years?" she said. "Lock up Hebb ten years just for doing that?" She couldn't seem to realize he had stepped way over the line at last. "Not Hebb," she said. "Nobody would do that to Hebb." She couldn't seem to see him for the miserable little thing he was. I could. But I couldn't see her for what she really was or she never would have put it over me the way she did.

She was late bringing her kettle on the evening I mean. She didn't come till Sheriff Godbee was out to supper and I was alone in my front office with his adjoining office empty. I should have noticed that, just as I should have noticed she set the kettle down for a moment when I had unlocked the inner door and gone with her to unlock the barred door to Hebb's quarters. A man tending a jail has to notice the small things out of the ordinary. But you know how it is. You get used to a woman bringing special food to a man who isn't convicted yet and still has some privileges, and you're sorry for her like everyone is and want to make it easy for her, and she's just Elvie whom you've known quite a time, and you've done this so often you don't pay much attention to what she's doing. That's the way it was with me. My back was to her while I was unlocking the barred door, and I heard a small rattle and turned to see her lifting the gun out of the kettle by its barrel and raising it high, and I only had time to try to fend it off with an arm before the butt crashed down on my head and the walls whirled around me and went black.

When I knew what was happening again, I was sitting on the floor slumped against the side wall of that inner room where the waiting-for-trial cell was, and I had company. Sheriff Godbee was sitting beside me, not slumped but straight-backed against the wall and looking mad. The syndicate agent was sitting beside him the same way and looking madder. They weren't moving or trying to get up, and I saw why. Elvie was standing against the front wall by the door with the gun in her hand. She looked younger, and her head was high and her eyes were blazing bright, and you could tell she was right willing to shoot. I swiveled my head to see the whole room. Hebb was gone, and I guess my gun was gone with him. It wasn't anywhere in sight. Sheriff Godbee's and the agent's were on the floor by the edge of Elvie's spangled skirt.

She had it all figured. She had pulled me over to the wall where I couldn't be seen through the door by anyone in the front room. She had waited inside by the door, and when Sheriff Godbee came in to see where I was, she had stuck the gun in his ribs and taken his and made him sit down by me. She had done the same to the syndicate agent. She would do the same to anyone else might come along. She wasn't going to let anyone find that Hebb was gone and get out to spread the news and start after him. I expect she was ready to keep us there all night.

We must have appeared foolish sitting there. I felt foolish till I worked up my own share of mad, because that was the first time anyone had gone out of my jail without me showing the way out.

The syndicate agent smacked one hand on the floor. "Our dust gone," he said. "The man too." He swung his head at me. "Fine work," he said. "Wonderful. Letting her pull this."

"Shut up," Sheriff Godbee said. "She got me, didn't she? You too."

And Elvie stood there watching us with her eyes bright and the gun in her hand.

"Say," the agent said, "do you really think she'd shoot?"

"Yes," Sheriff Godbee said.

The agent swung his head at me again.

"Sure thing," I said.

"Bats," the agent said. "I don't think so. She's just a woman."

"No," Sheriff Godbee said. "That's not just a woman. That's Elvie."

The agent grunted, and started to push himself up. Elvie stuck out her chin and leveled the gun at him. "Sit down, mister," she said.

"Hell, lady," he said, still pushing up. "Can't a man even straighten his legs? Got kinks in 'em."

He stood right up by the wall and stretched each leg out separate, pretending not to be paying attention to her at all, and she watched him with eyes big and stary. He put one hand against the wall like he wanted to steady himself and suddenly he shoved himself out from the wall and plunged at her, and she squealed high and shrill and the gun roared in her hand, and he stopped like he had run into a stone wall and he collapsed forward on the floor.

I couldn't have things like that going on in my jail. I knew I couldn't the instant he started to stand up, and I was ready and I scrambled on my hands and knees and got my toes under me and dove straight at Elvie. My head hit her in the middle, and she bounced against the wall behind her and the gun clattered on the floor, and she fell hard on top of me gasping with the breath knocked out of her.

Sheriff Godbee was scrambling on the floor too. He gathered her gun and his and the agent's. He got to his feet and watched me crawl out from under Elvie.

"Help her up," he said. When I did and kept tight hold on her

arm, he came over and put one of the guns in my holster and put
his own in his own holster and the other in his belt. "Put her
behind your bars," he said. "Do something with what's left of our
friend here. I've got to go get that fool Hebb again."

So now Elvie was in my jail, and I didn't feel mean at first about
locking her in because my head still hurt and I had a dead man
to worry over. People had heard the shot and had come running,
and I had to tell them what had happened. I sent someone for
Rudy Ferebee, who acted as an undertaker too, and he took the
agent's body away and promised to send word to the mining camp
and if folks wanted to see it was hauled there. I chased them all
away at last, and checked again to be sure Elvie was safe behind
my bars and nursed my head with cold water and tried to get some
sleep on the couch in my office.

I couldn't sleep much, and along about first light in the morning
I went back to see Elvie again. She was right where she had been.
She hadn't tried either of the two bunks. She was sitting on the one
chair proud and kind of scornful of me, and almost young-looking
in that red dress and with her eyes daring me to say anything to
her. "I'll fix some breakfast pretty soon," I said, and went out front
and sat on the steps of the building and watched the light beginning
to climb the sky. After a while I saw the horses coming along the
road into town.

Sheriff Godbee was on the first one. One of those behind him
was carrying double. Another one had something slung over the
saddle that was limp like a bag of grain, only it had arms that hung
down on one side and legs on the other. They stopped by the building. Sheriff Godbee swung down. He was stiff and tired.

"Yes," he said, "it's Hebb. He wasn't any damn good even as an
outlaw. Running was all he could do. Left a trail a boy could
follow. I swore in a few deputies and picked up more on the way.
Chased him up into the hills again. He holed in some rocks and
we had him surrounded. Tried to make him see that and come out
peaceful. All he'd do was run. Came out running and did some
shooting. One of us plugged him and I don't rightly know who.
Too many bullets flying there for a space. But it's no matter. Everybody was sworn right and it was all legal and proper." Sheriff God-

bee sighed. "Too damn many killings in one night for my liking. I'm tired. You take over and let me get some rest."

So I had to tap the till to pay the men the ten cents an hour we did in cases like that as a sort of official sign of appreciation for them helping out when there was need. And I had to get hold of Rudy Ferebee again to take care of Hebb's body. And I had to be the one to tell Elvie.

She didn't say a word when I told her. She sat on the chair and the pride went out of her along with the brightness in her eyes, and she was a shapeless growing-old woman in a funny faded red dress who wouldn't say a word. I fixed breakfast and she ate some of it because I told her to, but she didn't know what she was eating or even that she was eating at all. She was the same all morning and at lunch time. It wasn't till late afternoon when I came back from helping bury Hebb that she spoke to me.

"Where did you put him?" she said.

"We fixed a nice grave," I told her. "We fixed it out on the slope by the river near your old place."

"Out there?" she said. "That's no decent place for Hebb. Why didn't you put him in the church cemetery?"

"Well, now, Elvie," I said, "you know only regular church members are buried there." I couldn't tell her the church people had refused to have Hebb in their cemetery. I couldn't tell her about the remarks I'd been hearing that we were starting our own boothill planting ground on that slope by the river. "It's a nice place, Elvie," I said. "Real nice. Maybe I can get a writ from the judge to take you out to see it."

She wasn't listening. She was starting to cry. She didn't cry hard or sob out loud or anything like that. She just cried quiet and steady and like she was alone with no one to see or hear her. That's how she put it over on me the second time. Only in a sense she didn't really. She could have, but she didn't. Not really.

What was the matter with me was knowing that she was crying. That was the last small touch that made me soft. I'd look in at her through the doorway and it wouldn't seem right for a woman to be behind my bars. You oughtn't to need iron bars with a woman. You oughtn't to shut a woman up behind bars in a place that was built for men, because nobody ever bothered to think a woman might be kept there, and where anyone, even if only the one who tends the jail, can gawk at her at any time. That's the way I was feeling, and then knowing that she was crying made it worse.

Sheriff Godbee was up and around and in his office making out his reports about Elvie and about Hebb, and I went in and told him what I wanted to do. "It's your jail," he said. "Got enough to stew about myself here. You run it howsomever suits you."

So I took a look at the storage room we planned to keep files and records in when we had enough. It was fair-sized and had a stout door and only one window for ventilation and that was small and high up out of reach even if you stood on a chair. I moved out the old saddles and pieces of harness we had stuck in there and moved in a cot and a chair and a box for a table and a wash basin and a few other things. I found a padlock for the hasp-catch on the door. I went back and unlocked the barred door of the waiting-for-trial quarters and took Elvie around to that storage room. She came without any fuss, and I left her there and snapped the padlock shut and pulled on it several times to make sure it was fastened tight. I went to my office and flopped on the couch and was asleep before I could even think to unbutton my leather vest. I needed that sleep. I needed it specially because there was a shock waiting me early the next morning.

I woke early the way I had trained myself and stretched and washed the sand out of my eyes and made my rounds. When I came to the storage room, I unfastened the padlock and knocked on the door. I couldn't hear a sound inside. I opened the door a little and peered in, and Elvie was gone. The room was quiet and empty and Elvie wasn't in there.

I don't know how she managed to do it. She had pushed the cot under the window and then put the table-box on the cot and the chair on the box and pried the window out of its frame with something or other. That pile of things must have given unsteady footing and the window opening must have been a tight squeeze and there was a ten-foot drop outside, and the only way she could have gone through must have been head first. But she did it. She was gone.

I went to Sheriff Godbee's office and opened the side window there and reached out to ring the cowbell we kept hanging on the outside wall. He lived in the next house and I used the bell to call him when there was any important reason he should be in his office. In a few minutes he came in, muttering to himself and pulling on his jacket. He stopped muttering when I spoke to him.

"Sheriff," I said, "I think maybe I'd better resign. Elvie's gone."

He looked at me sharp. "You let her go?"

"No," I said. "She wiggled out that little window."

He sat down in his swivel chair and stared at me. "That woman beats me," he said. "But then she always has."

"All right," I said. "You want my badge?"

"Don't be a fool," he said. "That Elvie would beat anyone." He stared at me some more. "Damned if I'll go after her," he said. "Never chased a woman yet. Not that way."

He sat in his chair and stared at me, and I stood there and stared back, and I don't know what we would have done if the door hadn't opened and two people came in, and the one in front was Clem Rickey and the one behind him was Elvie.

They were tired and dirty, and Elvie was some sight with her streaked hair all tangled and her old dress torn from her squirming through that window, and only a few of the tarnished spangles were left around the bottom. She had a stubborn look on her face and wouldn't say a word. It was Clem Rickey who plumped his feet wide apart and spoke to us.

"Godbee," he said, "I want one thing understood. I didn't bring her back. She wanted to come back. Routed me out middle of the night and told what she had to do. I helped her and would again. I'd have found her a horse and money and cheered her off, but she wouldn't go. Did what she wanted and insisted on coming back here."

You can see what I mean when I say that she didn't really put it over me that time and could have but didn't. She could have gone off and given us a chase if we'd had stomachs enough to go after her. But she didn't. She just went out for a while and came back.

"Now what!" Sheriff Godbee said. "What the devil have you two been doing?"

"That?" Clem Rickey said. "Why, we been digging Hebb up and planting him in the church cemetery."

*

Well, that's what I started out to tell you, about the only woman I've ever had in my jail and the two breaks she staged. I expect I'd better go on with the trial that finished it up.

Judge Cutler got back to the Crossing the afternoon of that same day. He was a plump, good-natured man with a thorough knowledge of law and enough respect for it—enough and not too much—to make him the kind of judge we liked. He'd been hearing some tall rumors along the way and he came direct to Sheriff Godbee's office. When he had it all straight about the last day's doings, he sat quiet and bit on his knuckles.

"Godbee," he said, "we've got to be rough on Elvie. She killed a man and hanging's the usual recipe for that. Killed him to help a jail break too. But one thing we can do. You go call on our town councilmen, all three of them. Tell them they're to approve a new law I'm making as of right now. Tell them they'll approve or I'll quit this job, and they'll have to whistle all around the creek for a new judge. That'll fetch 'em. From this moment forward it's going to be a felony to move a dead body that's been lowered into the ground and earth heaped upon it. That'll keep Hebb where she wants him."

He bit on his knuckles some more. He sent me to bring Rudy Ferebee to the office.

"Ferebee," he said, "if Elvie pleads guilty, I'll have to pass judgment on her. I refuse that responsibility. We've got to make this a jury trial. Can you guarantee me she'll plead not guilty?"

Ferebee scratched his chin and looked at me, and I handed him my keys and he went back to the jail part of the building and returned after a while.

"Judge," he said, "Elvie says thank you for the new law and Hebb told her the dust box is in the chimney of that line cabin. She says she doesn't care what we do with her now."

"Good," Judge Cutler said. "I'm satisfied. You make it not guilty, and we'll get this over with. My court will convene at ten o'clock tomorrow morning."

We had the biggest crowd in our little courthouse we'd ever had. People were staking out seat claims early as nine o'clock. The only trouble we had was naming a jury. Women weren't allowed to serve, of course. And the men didn't want to. They thought of the

damndest excuses and Judge Cutler had to be firm and draft most
of the dozen. I think maybe it was because they felt mean about it
and enjoyed the eyebrow-tilting of some of the women present that
they picked Clem Rickey to be their foreman. And while this was
going on, Elvie sat in the chair where I had put her and stared at
the floor. She had fixed her hair and fussed with her old dress and
made herself neat as she could, and that was the only thing about
her that suggested she knew anything unusual was happening. She
didn't seem the least interested in what was being done. She just
sat and stared at the floor.

As a trial I expect it was pretty dull. Most of it, anyway. Everybody there knew Elvie and had known Hebb, and by now knew
about all the pertinent facts. It was simply a matter of getting these
down in the official record. Sheriff Godbee was in a peculiar spot.
He had to act as prosecutor and be the chief witness too. He put
himself on the stand and told what had happened, simple and
straightforward. He put me on the stand and had me tell it again
my way. Then he rested his case. Ferebee cross-examined us both,
but the best he could do with the facts was to emphasize that the
syndicate agent was jumping at Elvie when she shot him. He called
Elvie to the stand, and I had to take her by the arm and lead her
there, and he couldn't do anything with her. She wouldn't help herself. She wouldn't even answer questions he had thought up to win
sympathy for her. He was ready to quit when Clem Rickey stood up.

"Judge," Rickey said, "we here on this jury can ask questions,
can't we?"

"Certainly," Judge Cutler said.

Rickey leaned forward a little and looked straight at Elvie. "Well,
now, Elvie," he said, "we want to know something. Why didn't you
see what kind of a low-crawling snake Hebb was when he stole that
coach and was going to skip off and leave you?"

Elvie jerked up on the witness chair. "That's a lie!" she said. "If
he'd got away safe, he'd have sent for me. I just know he would."

A couple of the other jurors were pulling at Rickey. He turned,
and they whispered together, and he looked back at Elvie.

"All right," he said. "Maybe I put that question wrong. We want
to know why you did it. Why you put up with that—with Hebb all
these years?"

She looked at Rickey and her eyes were blazing bright. "I'll tell

you why," she said. "You men. All of you. You think I don't know
what you're like? You think I don't know how you sneak around on
back streets and in strange houses? You think I don't know what
goes on upstairs in your saloons? You're all soiled. But he wasn't.
He was different." She stood up straight in her old red dress with
a few spangles left around the bottom. "He never looked at another
woman. He was mine."

They acquitted her. They acquitted her with a verdict that Judge
Cutler had to unscramble for the official record, because the way
they put it was that the deceased was killed in self-defense and ought
to have had better sense than to jump a woman with a gun, and
why couldn't it just be set down that he died by the accidental dis-
charge of a weapon. They meant to be kind to her and maybe they
were. But I've never been sure. I saw her when she left town on
the stage later that day. Someone told me something about her having some relatives back East a ways. She was wearing the red dress,
and she had a small bundle that must have held her other dress,
the church-going one Hebb had bought her. She looked to me like
a person who might go on living, but whose life was over.

Josiah Willett

T HE TROUBLE between us Willetts and the Tavenners began way
back before I was born. It began back when my folks lived
in Missouri where some of our Willett cousins still live. My father
was a young fellow just after marrying then and his father was head
of the whole family. They lived scattered around the south base of
a scraggly mountain in the Ozarks and tried to make out farming
crops some and raising hogs. They had board houses and some with
two-three rooms. The Tavenners lived on up the mountain in mud-
chinked cabins spotted here and there through the woods. They
were a wild lot, and not a one of them had the God-given sense to
try to make things grow. That's what my father used to say. They
hunted some, and when they weren't hunting, they loafed around,
and when they needed a little cash money, they cut some timber and
hauled it down to the settlements and bought themselves some whiskey and went on up the mountain to loaf some more. They didn't
even have get-up enough to make their own moonshine. That's
what my father always said.

They did have one old milch cow. She belonged to Lige Tavenner, who was head of his family the way my grandfather was of all
us Willetts then. Lige wouldn't build a fence or put a rope on that
cow, and she used to wander down the slopes because that was the
easiest way to go and find my grandfather's corn patch. So my grandfather told Lige one time he didn't blame a cow for doing what a
man was shiftless enough to let her do, but all the same if she ate
any more of our liquor-makings he'd put a bullet in her. A few
days later she did, and my grandfather shot her and heaved the
carcass on his stone-sledge and hauled it up the mountain and

dumped it near the first Tavenner cabin he came to. A few days after that, someone winged my grandfather in the shoulder from the bushes near his corn patch, and my father and all the Willett cousins around took their guns and went up the mountain hunting Tavenners, and for about three days there was a lot of powder used in those woods. The shooting might have lasted longer, but they ran out of bullets and the Tavenners did too. All the same, there was burying enough to be done around that mountain. Two of us Willetts were dead and others in need of patching and the Tavenners were digging three graves.

After that there was trouble every so often. Let a Willett run onto a Tavenner and there was bound to be. If there wasn't any running onto for a spell, it could start in other ways. Old Lige Tavenner might get a hankering for a taste of milk and remember his cow and talk more meanness into his kin, and then a Willett pig or two would be found growing stiff and cold in the brush. And if that wasn't enough to keep the trouble going, my grandfather's shoulder might start paining him again and a couple or more of our Willett cousins would start up the mountains to see about paying off the Tavenners some more.

That went on maybe ten-twelve years. It quieted some after Lige Tavenner broke his neck scrambling down a rockslide to a deer he'd shot. Then my grandfather died too, and it might have quieted more if only he had died natural. But he died of the quick lung-sickness that he caught hiding out in the damp one night with his rifle after he'd heard that some of the young Tavenners had been talking about his pigs. He died fast with his shoulder paining and that was the Tavenners' fault. So one of our Willett cousins called a Tavenner on it and they took to arguing and then to fighting, and the Tavenner pulled a knife and our Willett cousin was cut bad. And the trouble was strong again, with only the difference that my father was head of us Willetts now, and Lige's oldest son Asa was head of the Tavenners.

It was about a year later that my father called all the cousins together. Near as he could figure, he told them, us Willetts had taught the Tavenners plenty of good lessons and were ahead any way you might want to look at it, so no one could say he was scared and running away. But he was done with trying to make things grow in that rocky, tired old ground around there. He was moving on

into the Territories to find himself some land he liked. He'd be
pleased to have any of them that felt the same go along with him.
Some of them did and some of them didn't. So my father pulled
out leading those that did and leaving Cousin Aaron to be head
of the Missouri Willetts, and he led the way wandering through
Kansas and up into Nebraska till he found some land he liked near
the Wyoming border, and he and the others spotted their claims
close to good water and now he was head of the Nebraska Willetts.

My brother Ira could remember that wandering. I couldn't because I wasn't born yet. I wasn't born till my folks had been in the
new Territory more than a year. That's why the trouble with the
Tavenners never got a real hold on me. It was just something I
heard about. My father and the cousins that came with him used
to talk about it a lot, and I guess I heard tell over and over about
every fight and almost every shot ever fired at a Tavenner. "Mean
as a Tav'nner," my father would say when he wanted to pin a man
sharp and wrong. It was the worst thing he could think to say. But
still all that trouble seemed to me something over and done and
back in Missouri. Then my brother Ira rode home from town one
day with a bruise-mottled face and one eye swollen closed and a
bad knife-cut down his left arm.

Ira was coming twenty then, and that means I was pushing eleven.
He was a good brother even if he didn't have much time for me.
All of us worked hard most of the time, and he worked extra hard
spring and summer helping father grow things in our good soil, and
come fall he'd hire out to help the ranchers over the Wyoming
border with their round-up. The last few winters he'd worked for
one of them riding line and staying in a cabin up in the hills. He'd
gone to town this time to get some supplies he'd need, and he rode
home still mad after the long riding and went straight into the
house with my father and I followed and found them in the kitchen.

"In town?" my father was saying. "Nate Tav'nner? That'd be
Asa's whelp. And doing what around here?"

"They've taken a place east of town," Ira said. "Came in a month
or so ago."

"Followed us, eh?" my father said. "That's it. Mean as can be
and getting meaner. Followed us looking for trouble."

"Could be," Ira said. "But he was surprised as I was."

"Just their way," my father said. "Sly and sneaking to fool you. What did he say, eh?"

"More'n enough," Ira said. "Claimed us Willetts ought to like it around here. Plenty of other people's cows to shoot."

"A Tav'nner sure," my father said. "Hope you fixed him."

"I tried," Ira said. "Tried hard."

"Pulled a knife on you, eh?" my father said. "Should of been packing your gun. What did you use?"

"Grabbed me a bottle," Ira said. "Broke it for good cutting. I'd of killed him if they hadn't hauled me off."

"Should have," my father said. "Killing a Tav'nner's no more 'count than killing a snake."

So the trouble was starting again, sort of picked up and brought from Missouri and starting again in this new Territory. My father and Ira and the Nebraska cousins and their older sons talked about it and emptied several jugs talking about it.

"Only one thing to do," my father said. "Tav'nners dirtied the country back in Missoury and Tav'nners will dirty the country round here too." He looked about at all us Nebraska Willetts and saw we were listening straight. "Thing to do," he said, "is rout them out afore they're dug in too deep. But Ira's leaving for line camp tomorrow. Wouldn't be fair to have him miss the doings. Winter's setting in, and you all know what the snow's like. Can't rightly do much till spring. When the snow's gone, we'll get together and run every last Tav'nner that's come here clean out of the Territory."

So Ira was gone off to the line camp up in the hills and we were doing winter chores and waiting for spring. It was a hard winter with the snow staying and piling deeper each time more came down. There was little traveling being done because the roads were drifted over. That's why it was near to March before Mr. Follin got through to see us. We were surprised when he pulled his horse in by our porch and swung down and came and knocked on the kitchen door. He was the ranch man Ira worked for, and the only time we'd ever seen him before was when he came to arrange about the job.

"Come in," my father said. "Come right in and sit a spell. Any word for us from Ira?"

Mr. Follin came in and sat on one of our chairs. He didn't say a word for maybe a minute. He looked at my father sitting on another chair facing him and at my mother standing by the stove, and he sighed.

"I don't like to do this," he said. "But it's mine to do. He was working for me."

"Speak it," my father said. "What's he done?"

"He's dead," Mr. Follin said. "I don't know what it was about, but up there by the camp he bumped into a young fellow working for the next ranch and they shot each other. My foreman was checking through and heard the shots. When he got there, the other one was dead. Your boy lived just long enough to send you a message. He said to tell you—"

"Wait," my father said. His eyes were narrowed and like little stones and his lips were tight. "What was the other one's name?"

"Tavenner," Mr. Follin said. "Nathan Tavenner. But why? He was new around here."

My father didn't try to answer him. "Now," my father said, "now give me that message."

"All right," Mr. Follin said. "Your boy said to tell you he killed a snake. He said to tell you he kept the score even."

My father didn't say a word, and after a minute Mr. Follin started talking again.

"I'll send down his things when the roads are better. He's buried up there. Both of them. There was nothing else to do. My foreman did it. Wrapped them in a wagon sheet and buried them. The ground was frozen and he had to use an axe on it, but he says they're deep enough so nothing can get at them. It was the best he could do. They couldn't be brought down in weather like that."

"Weather like that," my father said. "When was it?"

"Back before Christmas," Mr. Follin said. "Blizzard time and drifts too high. I'm sorry I couldn't get—"

Mr. Follin stopped talking. My mother was making a queer noise. She hadn't said a word yet, and now she was making that noise in her throat and finally the words came out.

"We had us a nice Christmas," she said. "And all the time he was lying up there cold in the dirt."

She stumbled over by the wall and leaned against it and sort of slipped down till she was sitting on the floor. She pulled her apron up over her head and you could hear the sobs coming through it.

My father sat on his chair and reached up with his hands and took hold of his own hair and pulled at it.

"Don't hesitate to speak out," Mr. Follin said. "If there's anything I can do—"

"No," my father said. "Any doing that's done us Willetts will do it."

Mr. Follin fidgeted on his chair and stood up, and when nobody said anything more to him, he slipped out the door and closed it soft behind him. My father sat on his chair pulling at his hair and my mother sat on the floor with the apron over her head, and I slumped on the floor too, feeling numb and like maybe I was dreaming all that.

"Josiah," my mother said through the apron, "are you going to leave my boy up there cold in the dirt?"

"Hell's afire, woman!" my father said. He jumped up from his chair. "Live with me twenty year and not know me better! He's lying up there alongside a Tav'nner!" My father began to pound around the kitchen waving his arms. "Yank that apron offen your face. Look at that snow out there. How's a man to get a wagon through till it melts?"

So we were still doing winter chores and waiting for a real spring thaw. My father had the wagon ready and the coffin made and resting in it. He had looked all over our place and picked him his spot for the grave. It was on the knoll behind our house that was our winter windbreak and where the drainage was good, and a small stand of trees stood tall, and where you could sit lazy of a summer evening and see our whole homestead all around you. He had cleared away the snow and dug the hole already, straight-sided and deep, as much for something to be doing as for anything else because the ground was still hard and the digging took him the good part of three days.

It was late in March, about the last week, when the wind swung around from the southwest and the snow began to soften. Then the rain cleared the levels and began working on the drifts, and the sun fighting through once in a while did its share. So one morning my father sent me to tell the nearest cousins to keep on eye on the place and stay some with my mother, and when I got back he had food packed in the wagon and was ready to go. He told me if I bundled thick I could go along to spell him with the horses, and I did and climbed up on the seat with him and we started off.

The snow didn't bother us any now. It was the mud that did. If the wagon had been heavy loaded, we'd of stuck many a time. And fording the streams was bad. They were big and boiling along. There was once in the middle of one the horses could scarce keep footing and the wagon was awash, and as we were about pulling through the water floated the coffin right out of the wagonbed. We had to jump to the bank and chase it downstream maybe a hundred feet and drag it back to the wagon. When we had it in again, we lashed it tight and fastened up the tailboard, and it was a good thing we'd put the bag of food on the seat with us or it would have been soaked through.

The rest of that day and all of the next and part of the third morning we took getting to Mr. Follin's ranch. My father didn't speak to me all that way, not himself starting to talk to me. He sat hunched on the seat and stared at the horses and the road ahead, and when he wanted me to drive he just handed the reins to me. The only times he spoke to me were when I asked him questions and he'd just answer and go right on staring ahead. I couldn't keep my mind away from Ira lying up there in the hills and things about him lying up there were bothering me.

"Paw," I said, "what'll he look like?"

"Like Ira," my father said.

"It's been more'n three months," I said.

"Cold months," my father said. "The cold will have kept him."

We drove on for a while, and I couldn't keep my mind away from him up there.

"Suppose there's been some warm spells," I said. "What if we can't tell which one's him?"

"Hell's afire!" my father said. "You stop talking that way. He's awearing your grandpaw's ring. We can tell him by that."

When we pulled in by the ranchhouse, Mr. Follin came out to meet us. He told us the quickest wagon way to the line camp. He asked if we wanted him to send someone along to help us.

"No," my father said. "Rightful burial is a family doing."

We were starting away when Mr. Follin called out. "There's another wagon been ahead of you. Two days ago."

My father pulled the horses to a stop and turned on the seat and looked at Mr. Follin.

"Asa Tav'nner?" he said.

"Yes," Mr. Follin said. "And a couple of boys somewheres the age of yours there."

My father didn't say another word. He turned back to the horses and clucked to them and kept them at a fast walk or a trot all the rest of the way except when he had to let them have a breather because the way was uphill most of the time now.

When we reached the cabin in mid-afternoon, no one was there. The whole country roundabout, back down the way we had come and on up farther into the climbing hills, seemed lonesome and empty. Beside the cabin you could see where someone had been digging, where dirt had been dug up and put back and smoothed over some. We took the shovel and the spade from the wagon and started digging in the loose dirt. When we reached the canvas of the wagon sheet, we moved the dirt careful and easy away from the shapeless roll till it was all uncovered. My father leaned on the shovel and looked down at the dirt-colored canvas a long time.

"All right," he said at last. "Get back a ways. Could be this ain't for a boy to see."

I walked away and turned to watch, and I was glad to go because I was feeling sick deep down in my stomach, and that wasn't just because of the wisps of strange oily smell that were spreading through the air. I saw my father pull at the canvas sheet till it unrolled some and take a corner and lift it and peer under and stand there bent over and stiff like he was unable to move and staring under the sheet. He let the corner fall, and he straightened and looked around as if he didn't know just where he was, and he saw me and came toward me. When he spoke to me his voice was soft, almost a whisper.

"There've been warm spells," my father said in that small voice. "Can't rightly make out much of anything. But there ain't a ring there at all." I stared back at him, and suddenly he grabbed ahold of his hat and threw it on the ground and his voice was big and angry.

"That damned Tav'nner's taken our Ira!"

What we did after that my father did. I was too sick to do much of anything. He rolled the canvas up the way it had been and took a piece of rope and cut it in half and tied the halves tight around the two ends of the roll. He picked the whole thing up in his arms and lugged it to the wagon and put it in beside the coffin. He gathered the shovel and the spade and put them in too and stepped up to the driving seat and called to me. I managed to climb beside him and we started back down the way we had come.

"Paw," I said, "what're we going to do?"

"Find that damned Tav'nner," my father said. "Then we'll swap them. Get our Ira back."

We were driving along at a fast clip because the way was downhill and my father was in a hurry, but still we couldn't keep ahead of the smell from what was behind us there in the wagon. I kept on being sick every little while and the horses were uncomfortable and rolled-eyed and my father was blowing like he was doing part of the pulling.

"No," my father said suddenly, "there's nothing can make me do that."

We drove along, and it was suppertime and past and we weren't hungry at all, and the smell was right there with us, moving along with us and all around us.

"I hate to do it," my father said. "But maybe Ira would understand." He stopped the horses and climbed over the seat into the wagonbed. He opened the lid of the coffin he'd made for Ira and he took up the clumsy canvas roll and pushed it into the coffin and bent the tied ends over so it would fit in and the top could come down again. He lashed the top down tight and climbed back to the driving seat. We started on again and I felt better and somehow not just because the smell was about gone. We kept on driving and right past Mr. Follin's ranch without stopping and kept on till the stars had been showing plain in the sky a long time before we stopped and unharnessed and hobbled the horses and ate a little something and lay down in our blankets.

Almost first light in the morning my father was shaking me and we hurried to be started again. We moved along fast as the horses could and still keep going for distance. The ground was drying some and we made good time, and I was so busy wondering what was going to happen when we found the Tavenners that I was startled and nearly fell off the seat when my father spoke to me.

"Decent speaking and respectful," he said. "That's how we've got to be. That's how anyone's got to be when there's doings with dead bodies and family buryings. You remember that, boy. If he riles me into sharp words, you mind me of it."

We drove along and followed the way we had come till late in the afternoon we were near the neighborhood of our town, and then we swung left to the eastward toward where my father knew Asa Tavenner had his claim. We came on the wheel tracks of his wagon and followed them, and at last we saw the place. It was mostly level ground, the first of several homesteads along a little stream, and there were deep plow furrows run to mark the boundary lines. There was a sod-roofed hutlike building that looked mighty low for people to live in till you saw it was sort of a dugout house set into the slope rising from the stream. There was a three-sided shed close by the house and the wagon and an odd-lot of tools were in it, and next to it was a small chicken coop with a few old hens scratching around, and next to that was a small poled pasture with a thin old milch cow hunting for some early spring grass. And beyond that there was a field that had last year's corn stubble showing and in the field was a man plowing the stubble under with a team of thin but willing work horses.

My father stopped our team and looked over the place and I did too, and it was just like many places I'd seen where people were making out without much to do with and were getting started in this new Territory and were working hard to do something with what they had. The man turned a corner of the field and saw us and stopped his plowing and shaded his eyes to stare at us across the distance. He dropped his reins over the plow handles and started toward us, and when he was getting closer he stopped and shaded his eyes again and stared at us some more. Suddenly he started forward again and angled toward the house and two boys about my age, maybe one a little younger, ran out of the house, and he waved them back in and followed them in and came out again carrying a rifle and came straight toward us.

I don't know just what I'd expected to see when I first saw a Tavenner. I guess I'd thought he'd be some sort of a strange creature with the meanness showing plain and maybe fearsome. This man wasn't mean-looking. He was tired-looking. He was a lot like all the men I'd always known, like my father and our Willett cousins, lean-shanked and flat-stomached and a little stoop-shouldered, and carrying his head pushed forward with the chin jutting some and blowing just a bit through a ragged mustache when he breathed. He was tired-looking and worried and maybe afraid, knowing we were Willetts and wondering what we wanted and were going to do. He stopped about twenty feet away and stared steady at us.

"Asa," my father said, decent-speaking and respectful, "you been up in the hills getting a body."

"I got my boy," Asa said. He looked sideways toward a clump of trees by the stream, and we looked too and saw the mound of fresh-turned dirt and the wide board set at the head of it with letters that had been burned on with a hot iron.

"No," my father said, "you got our Ira. Your boy's in the box on this here wagon."

Asa stared at us, and you could see the tiredness grow in him. "You sure?" he said. "That's not Willett talk sniffing for trouble?"

"Hell's afire, man!" my father said. "You think I'd cart a stinking Tav'nner all these miles and in my boy's box lessen I was sure? You get busy now and dig up my boy, so I can get out of here back with decent folk."

Asa didn't move. "I'll not dig him up," he said.

My father was about ready to bust right there on the wagon seat. His face was red and the anger was making him shake. I remembered what he had told me and took hold of his arm to remind him of it and he caught himself and quieted down.

"Trust a Tav'nner," he said, low, and like talking to himself, "to be mean even a time like this. I'll do it myself."

He jumped to the ground and took the shovel out of the wagon and swung it up on his shoulder and started toward the grave by the trees. But Asa hurried to get in front of him and blocked the way. Asa's face was getting red now too and he shifted his grip on the rifle.

"You'll not do it, either," Asa said.

My father stopped and jutted his chin farther forward. He spoke spacing the words low and bitter. "You'd try to stop me getting my own boy?"

"We've had one burying here," Asa said. "It near killed my woman. Another would finish her. I'm telling you there ain't going to be another. Not a Tavenner burying anyhow."

The two of them stood there jutting their chins at each other and Asa's hands were tight on his rifle and my father's fingers were tightening on his shovel, and all kinds of thoughts were whirling in my head. I was thinking how strange it was that the Tavenners were people just like us, only they had a different name, and how their Nate must have meant just as much to them as our Ira had to us. I could see myself listening to my father say "mean as a Tav'nner," and all at the same time I could see those boys in that sod-roofed house listening to their father say "mean as a Willett," and none of it made any sense to me. I scrambled and almost fell from the wagon seat, and I ran up close to the two of them there.

"My brother Ira and that other one," I said. "Does it make any difference to them which one's in which grave?"

My father looked at me and Asa Tavenner looked at me, and I don't think either one of them really saw me. They looked back at each other and Asa Tavenner let the rifle slide down through his hands till the stock end was resting on the ground.

"Josiah Willett," he said, "I gave your boy decent burying. Can you do the same for my boy?"

My father looked at Asa, and then he turned his head a little and looked at the grave by the trees, and then he turned his whole body and walked slow and steady over by the little stream. He stood there and watched the water running with its little ripples over the small stones and on across the land as far as you could see and into the dim distance. He stood there what seemed a long time. He turned around and came back and took me by the arm and we went to our wagon and he tossed the shovel in and we got up on the seat, and he swung the team in a big circle and we started off the way we had come. He was in no hurry now and let the horses walk most of the time. The sun went behind the far hills and the dusk began to settle into dark.

"Plowing," my father said. "A Tav'nner plowing ground. Growing things." We went almost another full mile before he spoke again. "Kind of crooked furrows," he said. And the stars were clear and bright and we were almost home before he spoke again.

"Not a word about this," he said. "Not to anyone. 'Specially your maw. Let her think it's Ira in that box. Women don't always understand things the way we men do."

So that was the last of the trouble with the Tavenners. My father made our Willett cousins stay quiet, and there wasn't any more of it. We almost forgot there were any Tavenners at all except when we might see one passing on the street in town. But I couldn't forget them really, not when I could see the stone on the knoll behind our house and my brother's name on it and know that it was not him there underneath it. And somehow, remembering that and knowing that, no matter how mad I've been able to get at any man, I've never been able to get really mad at him, not mad enough to want to kill him.

Something Lost

June

THIS WAS far up in the mountains and still the great peaks climbed, thrusting up and thinning to the bare bones of rock above the timberline. The high upland valley was lost among them, an irregular pocket caught in the soaring immensity, rimmed by the timeless rock, its glints of meadow green shading into the darker green of forest where it broke into the downward slopes. The figure of the man by the stream near the upper end of the valley, where the water slowed from its rush down the rocks, was unbelievably small in the vastness. He stood stooped by a sandbar where the riffles swung and died in a pool and the slant sunlight flashed on the worn tin in his hands and his shoulders rocked as his arms moved in a circular motion.

The motion stopped and the man bent his head farther to peer into the pan in his hands and the dull gleaming of the flakes there was reflected in the pale hazel irises of his eyes. He straightened and nodded his head in slow satisfaction. He studied the sandbar and the pool where the water slipped into apparent stillness and the silt of years had settled to the bottom. He raised his head and looked at the untouched wilderness about him. The valley lay open around him, a half-mile wide and a mile long, its level floor cut by the swinging course of the stream. At its head the mountain wall rose steeply in huge broken steps that the stream took in rushes and falls as it drove down from the endless snow in the far upper reaches of rock. Along the valley sides the slopes climbed, tree-dotted and thicket-entangled, to stop against the enduring stone, on the near side against a high sharp ridge, on the opposite side against a vast rock buttress towering out to tremendous cliff edge. Between the ridge and the buttress the valley entrance swept out to open parkland that dropped abruptly into jack pine forest covering the downward slopes and divided by the deepening gorge of the stream as it sought the lower levels. And beyond the ground rose again, rising in ridge upon ridge to the high eastward mountain barrier.

The man nodded his head again in slow satisfaction and the sun shone warm on the broad flat planes of his face beneath the wide squared brim of his hat. He took a leather pouch from a pocket and eased the flakes into it. He strode across the carpet of wild flowers bordering the stream and bent to pick up the trailing lead rope of the grazing burro. By the slope of the near valleyside, where a thickening stand of spruce and juniper fringed the valley floor, he stopped and pulled the rifle and ax and short shovel from under the tie ropes and unfastened the pack and picketed the burro on a twenty-foot rope length. He selected a fallen tree, angling up, the upper end wedged in a crotch of another tree. Using this as his ridgepole, he began building his shelter. He shed his jacket and sweat darkened the faded brown of his shirt as his short broad body swung in steady rhythm and the ax blade bit into the springy wood.

Across the meadow green, across the wild-flower carpet and the stream, half a mile across the stretching expanse of valley floor and two hundred yards up the opposite slope where bare rock jutted over a flat ledge, the great bear lay and watched the man. It lay limp on the ledge in the warm slant sun, hind legs sprawled back, front legs stretched forward with the big head, broad and dished to the muzzle, resting on the rock between them. A light breeze ruffled through the short brown fur made ragged by the remaining long still unshed hairs touched with silver on the tips. Its small farsighted eyes followed the man's every move among the distant trees.

Eighty-odd miles away, over the mountain barrier to the east, where a ragged collection of rude log cabins and tents straggled along the side of an almost dry stream bed, men worked at their wooden cradles and sluice boxes and grumbled to themselves and each other. The showings of color that had drawn them there to stake their claims were dwindling. In the oblong tarpaulin-roofed shack that served as store and bar other men spoke of the one who had left, quietly, speaking to no one, abandoning his slow half-worked claim to disappear with his burro into the high distances to the west. Their talk was tainted with envious wondering. They argued with each other in edged monotones. Unrest and disappointment crawled through the mining camp.

Far up in his valley, as the midnight stars wheeled in their slow course, the man stirred on his bed of spruce boughs and sat up, suddenly alert. The embers of the fire outside the open end of his shelter had faded to a dull glow that meant nothing to the moonless dark under the trees. He heard the burro moving restlessly on its shortened picket rope. In the following silence he felt a familiar prickling on the back of his neck as the short hairs there stiffened in response to some instinct beyond reach of the mind. His right hand moved and took the rifle and he was leaning forward to rise when he heard the burro scream and lunge to the end of the rope. He leaped to his feet and stood in the open end of the shelter, baffled by the unrelenting blackness of the night. Gradually he could make out the darker shapes of the trees. He went cautiously toward the burro and found it half choked by the taut rope. He spoke softly and it pushed against him and together they stood in a silence that lived and breathed around them. There was not a single separate discernible sound, yet the prickling persisted on his neck and the flesh of the burro quivered against him. The prickling died and the burro quieted and they stood in an empty silence. The man returned to the fire and piled wood on it and kneeled to blow until flames sprang and a circle of firelight fought back the dark. He shifted the burro closer to the circle before he lay again on his spruce bed.

In the morning the man found the tracks. Those of the forefeet were nearly seven inches wide and nine long, those of the hind feet eight inches wide and fourteen long. The claw marks of all five toes on each were plain. Apprehension crept along the man's spine. His hands tightened on the rifle. The tracks led in a circle around his camp and close in by the shelter and again by the place where the burro had first been picketed. He crawled inside his shelter to the low diminishing end where his meager supplies, depleted by weeks of wandering, were cached behind a barrier of short logs. He took a handful of cartridges and dropped them into a jacket pocket. Outside again, he strode off, steady and unhurried, following the tracks away.

They led him across the stream below the pool and across the level of the valley. He lost them on the edge of a field of slide rock near the lower end of the valley. He skirted the field and could find no further trace. He turned back and began a thorough circuit of the valley.

He found signs in many places, old tracks caked where the ground had dried and fresher tracks in soft ground. He found three rubbing trees with bark worn thin and high up, higher than he could reach, gashes where the bark had been torn open crosswise by big gripping jaws. He found the trail angling up the far slope to the ledge. It was hard-packed by years of use by generations of animals reaching back into the dim past, so packed that the imprints of the big claws were all but invisible scratches on the hard surface. Approaching the ledge, he saw the wide and narrowing crevice behind it leading back to blackness under the overhanging rock. No light could penetrate the inner dark depth. He dropped silently back down the trail fifty yards and crouched behind a big stone and shouted and there was no response except the jeering call of a jay. He shouted again and waited. At last he strode down the trail and across the valley. In a few moments he was stooped by the pool, his arms moving in circular motion as the sun glinted on the pan in his hands. But now he looked up at regular intervals and scanned the expanse all around him and the rifle lay within quick reach not more than a yard from his steady hands.

Out of the valley, eight miles around the jagged sweep of the vast rock buttress that towered above the opposite slope, out where the forest of jack pine below the edging parkland flowed unbroken down to the shore of a small lake, the great bear lay in a patch of sunlight on the soft needle carpet. Already it had forgotten the man and the burro. They were new sights, new scents, never before known, tucked away now in the reservoir of experience and would remain untouched until a fresh encounter summoned remembrance into being. They had been seen and smelled and investigated in the caution of the night and dismissed. There was no challenge in them for the bear to understand.

A marten drifted down the trunk of a nearby tree, stretching its small pointed head outward to stare intently at the bear. The scritch of the small claws in the bark was barely audible a few feet away, yet the bear's head rose. The marten scurried back up the tree. The big head dropped and the bear, full-fed and lazy, drowsed in the sunlight. The tree shadows moved slowly and crept to engulf the bear and it rose and padded softly on through the forest. It was obeying its own instinctive calendar of habit, moving on the periodic four-day feeding march that took it out of the valley on a wide swing and return through the thirty-seven miles of its mountain-bound range.

July

The man strode up the stretch of parkland that edged the forest and led to the valley entrance. The late afternoon sun was full in his face. Behind him the burro trotted obediently, weighted by the big pack, whose new canvas covering gleamed white in the sunlight. Where the parkland leveled to enter the valley he stopped and turned to look back the way he had come, down the long rolling forested slope sliced by the stream gorge and up and over the first high ridge beyond. Satisfied at last that no one followed, he turned again and led the burro up the valley and across the green carpet to his camp in the spruce and juniper fringe. Everything there was as he had left it eight days before. But in the soft ground by the pool he found the big five-toed tracks crossing the stream toward his camp and going back again. He looked across the valley and up. The steep sideslope curving to the high rock buttress was splendid in the late sunlight and the overhanging rock and the ledge two hundred yards above the valley floor shone rust-red and gray against the green around them. A hawk floated in the air above the scattered clinging trees. There was no other sign of life. He strode back to his camp and began unpacking the burro.

Far to the eastward, over the mountain barrier, where the rude cabins and tents marred the bank of the stream bed, men talked to the keeper of the tarpaulined store and bar, worrying again the worn questions of four days about the one who had returned with his burro and bought supplies and shaken bright flakes out of a leather pouch in payment and disappeared again into the western heights. Already the legend was growing. He had made a rich strike. He was

scooping dust out of rich silt pockets by the handful. He had unlimited wealth in dust and nuggets cached in his mountain hideout.
The voice of a lean man with narrow hatchet face gashed by a thin-
lipped mouth was tinged with bitterness as he told of his failure in
following the boot and hoofmark traces into the mountains. A trail
that well hidden must have been deliberately cloaked to cover its
destination. The talk warmed and eyes glittered and the storekeeper
did good business over his hewn-log bar.

Twice in the night the man woke, alert and rising to sitting position on his bed of boughs. There was no sound beyond the barrier
of logs with which he had closed the open end of his shelter except
an occasional soft movement of the burro in the narrow high-poled
enclosure he had built for it. In the morning there were no new
tracks. It was the same the next night and the next and early during
the night after that thunder echoed through the mountains and
lightning laced down through the peaks and enough rain fell in the
valley to dampen the ground and renew it for fresh writing by any
living thing that walked it. In the morning the man took the rifle
and made another thorough circuit of the valley. He found no fresh
signs, no five-toed tracks except what remained of the old after the
erasing action of the rain. But in the moist sand by the stream where
it eddied around rolled rocks well below the pool, he found other
tracks, split-hooved, deeply indented. He studied these a long moment. He followed them along the stream and when they faded
into the firm sod he kept on down the valley. His stride, long for the
length of his legs, gnawed steadily into distance.

Half an hour later he was skirting the vast rock buttress, pausing
often to scan the sweep of slope opening below him. He was well
around, out of sight of the valley entrance, when he saw the elk,
three of them, more than a mile away, on the edge of the parkland
that slipped abruptly into the jack pine forest. Patient and steady,
he began the long approach, angling down the slope to put the light
wind directly in his face.

Far ahead where the forest dipped into a deep ravine, a thin col-
umn of smoke floated upward from the inside hollow of the shattered
stump of a long dead pine. The slow fire, legacy of the lightning,
glowed faintly as it ate into the punklike wood. It edged through a

split in the old bark and little flames began to flicker along the side of the stump. It worked down and began to creep through the carpet of brown needles. It crept to the tiny outstretched dried twigs of the branch ends of a fallen tree and moved hungrily along them, reaching for the more solid wood.

The man was on his hands and knees, lifting the rifle carefully and setting it down gently with each forward movement of his right hand. He crawled to the top of a slight rise and lay flat to peer over. He was within rifle-shot of the elk. He eased the gun forward and let the sights sink down on the closest of the three. It stood quartering away from him and he aimed a bit behind and below the high foreshoulder and squeezed the trigger. He saw his elk leap a fraction of a second before the others and the three of them swirl and melt like sudden swift shifting shadows into the forest. He rose and went forward and followed. He was well in among the trees when he found the first blood drops, spattered and dark from internal bleeding. He lengthened his stride to follow the trace deeper into the forest. Forty minutes later, winded from climbing over and around down timber, he jumped the wounded elk out of a bushed hollow and his bullet, fired almost without aiming in the instant reflex of long experience, broke the animal's neck as it strove with flagging strength to leap away.

Down the slope, farther into the thick of the forest, the great bear prowled, sniffing for rotted logs among a tangle of fallen trees. It heard the second shot, faint yet distinct, a sound foreign and unknown. The big body stopped moving and the big head, unacquainted with fear in any form, rose and turned toward the sound. The bear waited, listening, then the head lowered and the long straight foreclaws sank into the outer shell of a log and, seeming without effort, ripped it open. The tongue, surprisingly small in the big mouth, licked quickly at the scurrying insects and slowed to take the sluggish wriggling white grubs.

The man worked steadily with his knife, quartering the elk carcass. He had already bled and dressed it. He lifted one of the forequarters, testing the weight, and set it aside. He began to cut poles on which to hang the remaining quarters until he could return with the burro. The small of his back ached from bending over and he straightened to rest it, and as his head came up he caught the first faint tang in the air. His body stiffened and the tiny premonitions running through him tightened into awareness. Smoke. Smoke drifting over the forest ceiling and filtering down fine tendrils that could elude the eyes but not the nose.

The man stood motionless, testing the breeze. It stirred gently, barely whispering through the branches above him. Disregarding the rest of the meat, he hoisted the one forequarter to a shoulder and steadied it with one hand and took the rifle with the other. He started at a right angle to the direction of the breeze, straight up the slope, the shortest path to the edge of the forest and the open parkland. Steadily he hammered on and the breeze freshened and talked in the branches and smoke began weaving among the tree trunks from the left. He angled toward the right, still climbing, and the smoke thickened, seeming to come from ahead as well as from the left, and at last he stopped, listening between the labored rush of his own breathing. The breeze strengthened and was a wind sighing high overhead and faint and far he could hear, not so much heard as sensed, the sullen roar of the racing fire. Around him he could fairly feel the hurrying of panic, the small life of the forest moving, unseen but known, past him down the slope. A deer bounded out of the smoke and saw him and swerved and was gone. He lowered his shoulder and the meat slid to the ground and without hesitation he turned and struck down the slope.

The smoke thickened and the light dimmed strangely and the roar rose until it was clearly audible and a high crackling breaking over it, and in a short while he was running, using his free hand to help him vault fallen logs, stumbling often and driving downward. The ground leveled and the trees ended and he broke through bushes and tripped full length into the shallow shore waters of a lake. The rifle leaped from his hand and disappeared beneath the surface and he scrambled after it. But the water deepened suddenly a few feet out and he floundered, with his chest heaving for air. He struggled back to the shallow edge and stood quietly while his lungs eased their frantic labor. Smoke rolled around him and he kneeled to keep his head close to the water and the layer of clear air just above it. Fire flared on the rim of the forest to the right and moved toward him and the heat grew until it drove him into the deeper water. He stood stretched upward with his head alone above the surface and looked out over the lake through the rolling smoke clouds. Fifty yards from shore a huge rock showed, humping out of the water like the low ridged back of some vast immobile beast. He swam slowly to it, fighting the drag of his clothes and boots, and crawled up on it and lay flat, while his tired muscles jumped and knotted and relaxed to rest.

The man lay on the rock and watched the fire work its way along the shore. He saw flames spire swiftly up one tree and leap to the next and sometimes, driven by the surge of their own tremendous draft, lunge to engulf several trees at once. The roar of the burning drowned all possible other sound. It was nothing heard, little more than a slight prickling on the back of his neck, that turned his eyes to the water past the other end of the rock. Only the broad head showed, with the muzzle cutting the water, as the great bear swam toward the rock. Quietly the man slipped into the water, stretching out in it with one hand holding to the stone while the other took the knife from its sheath on his belt. Silent in the water, he saw the bear's head rise over the rock opposite him, not more than twenty feet away, the forepaws stretch for footing, the massive shoulders emerge into view. He watched the bear turn broadside and shake and send the drops spattering clear across the rock. He watched it settle on its haunches, facing the flaming shoreline, and let its forepaws slide forward until the broad belly rested on the rock and the big head sank on them. He moved cautiously to look out over the rest of the lake. Through the clear area just over the surface he saw that it was almost ringed with fire and there was no other haven showing above water. He turned his head back to the rock and his body stiffened. The bear was looking at him. Its head was raised and swung toward him and the small eyes watched. His knees began to flex under him for a swift thrust outward from the rock but the bear remained motionless and while he waited, taut in tenseness, he saw the big mouth open and stretch in a yawn and the white of the great teeth and the lips drawing lazily back and the muzzle crinkling. The jaws closed and the head swung away and dropped on the forepaws again.

The hot air, uncomfortable but not unendurable, beat against the man's face and the chill of the water sank into his body. Cautiously he reached and put the knife between his teeth and placed both hands on the rock and began to draw himself forward and up on it. The bear's head rose and swung toward him and the small eyes watched. He waited and the bear did not move and he inched forward until at last he was on his hands and knees on the rock. Slowly he shifted position until he was sitting cross-legged, ready for an instant scrambling push striking into the water. The bear watched and when he was settled the big head swung straight again and sank down. Gradually the man's muscles softened and the instant alertness eased out of them. The hot air dried his clothes, and the fingers holding the knife now in his right hand relaxed. The smoke clouds rolled and made a strange unnatural dusk and the fire roared through it along the shore. The man's back and buttocks ached with the strain of his position on the hard rock. Slowly he shifted again until he was stretched full length on his side with his face toward the bear and his head pillowed on his left arm. The bear's ears twitched upright but the big head did not move and in a moment the ears eased limp again. The heat in the air lessened slightly and the fire roared dwindling along the shore. Far off it reached the edge of the gorge of the stream running out of the valley and sought to leap across and failed and fell back and was content with the timber it had taken, held now within the limits of the ravine where it had started behind this and the open parkland above and the gorge cutting down the long slope ahead of it and the beginnings of the open rocky climb below where the first ridge of the eastward mountain barrier thrust upward in the new ascent.

The sun, hidden behind the smoke clouds, dropped behind the westward heights and the remaining flames around the lake sent weird lights dancing in the murky dark over the water. The man's eyes closed and opened abruptly and closed again and at last remained closed. The wind died and the smoke trailed away in wisps and the high stars wheeled in the clearing sky above the two silent figures pinpointed together on their rock in the heart of the soaring immensity of the timeless mountains.

The man woke suddenly in the gray dawn of the light before sunrise. He had rolled over in his sleep on his back and the knife had slipped from his opened hand. As awareness flooded him he fought

the stiffness in his muscles to turn quickly on his side and fumble
for the knife handle. The seeking fingers halted before they found
it. The rock stretched away from him empty and open to the sky.
The bear was gone. He pushed to his feet and stooped to take the
knife and stood straight. The sound of splashing water turned his
head toward the near shore. The bear was emerging from the lake
onto a short sandy spit. Against the background of rising slope with
charred trunks above blackened floor and thin wisps of smoke still
spiraling lazily, it was a miracle of enduring life, enormous and indomitable in the half-light in defiance of the barren desolation. It
started inland and drew back with quick mincing steps. There were
hot embers under the ashes and flames ready to break forth flickering
strong in many places at the push of any breeze. It started to the
right along the shore, picking its way in the shallow water. It moved
along the shoreline three hundred yards and more and turned inland
and disappeared almost in the instant of turning.

The man slipped into the water and swam to the sandy spit.
Working from there he made systematic forays into the deeper water
until he found the rifle. He washed away the bottom muck and
broke it open to blow the barrel and firing chamber clean. Shivering
in the first rays of the sun, he moved along the shoreline as the bear
had done, stepping slowly but swinging his arms vigorously to warm
his muscles. Where the bear had turned he came on a narrow gorge
that sliced down the slope to the lake edge with rocky walls guarding
a small stream. The fire had done little damage here because there
was little to burn and it had leaped over to race on around the lake.
The man started the climb, still traveling slowly, and he nodded to
himself when he came on the big tracks in soft spots among the bottom stones.

Hidden in an aspen thicket a short way out on the parkland above
the stricken forest, the great bear stood over the carcass of a whitetail
doe that had fallen in the flight of fear into the upper gorge and
broken its neck. The bear had dragged the carcass to the open of
the parkland and into the thicket. The big head lifted and the small
eyes peered through the thicket. The man was passing, sixty yards
away. A low rumble sounded in the bear's throat, soft and deep, not
audible to the man and not meant to be. He strode on with the tire-

less stride of a man long used to the mountains. The bear watched him, its head turning slowly to follow his passing, and when his figure grew small in the distance the big head dropped to feed again.

August

In the clear light of early morning the man stood by the pool and looked at the shallow pan in his hands. The bottom of it was almost covered with the dull gleaming flakes. The pool silt had become richer as he worked deeper into it. He took the leather pouch from a pocket and shook the flakes into it. This was his third panning of the morning and already the pouch was full. He went to his camp and behind it among the trees and stopped by a flat stone. He heaved at the stone to raise one side and braced it against one leg while he set a piece of stout branch to prop it up. In a hollow underneath lay a five-pound salt bag filled to plumpness and another partly filled. He emptied the pouch into the second bag and lowered the stone into place. He went back by the pool and stood slapping the pan gently against his thigh while he looked over the valley. The air was fresh on his face and mystic cloud shadows wandered on the mountain wall at the head of the valley. He dropped the pan on the sandbar and took the rifle from the grassbank and strode off down the valley with the sun warm in his face. He was close to the valley entrance, where the big boulders of an ancient rockslide had rolled out to become bedded in the ageless sod, when he met the bear, suddenly, coming toward him around one of the rocks.

The bear stopped and the man stopped, thirty feet apart. Slowly the man swung up the rifle so that his left hand could grip the barrel and his right forefinger slipped around the trigger. The bear watched him and the low rumble, soft and deep, formed in its throat. Slowly the man stepped to the left, moving in a half-circle, always facing the bear, yielding the right of way. The bear watched him, turning its head to follow him until its neck was arched around. When he completed the half-circle the man turned, deliberately turned from the bear, and his will clamped hard on his muscles to hold them to a steady walk away. When he had traveled some forty feet he looked back. The bear had gone forward on its own way and its big, ridiculously tiny-tailed rump was toward him as it overturned scattered stones and sniffed for the scuttling insects.

Five hours later, in the early afternoon, the man returned to his camp, back-packing the dressed carcass of a small whitetail buck. Across the valley the great bear lay on the ledge and watched him. He could see it there, a dark shape on the stone, while he skinned the deer and pegged out the hide for drying. He built a big fire of dry wood and while he waited for it to burn down to glowing embers he began cutting the meat into strips. He looked across the valley and saw the bear rise and disappear into the dark recess of the crevice and he nodded to himself. He know its habits now. Always when it was in this part of its range it fed at night and in the early morning hours. By midmorning it was lying on the ledge. When the sun was high overhead, sliding into the afternoon slant, it sought the cool darkness of the rock depth.

The man raised the poles in a rack over the fire and hung the strips of meat on it. He piled green wood on the fire and retreated from the smoke and sat resting with his back against a tree looking out across the valley. The dropping sun glinted on the pan lying on the sandbar but the man remained still against his tree, rising at long intervals to replenish his fire.

The stream gathered speed as it left the valley and skipped in stony steps down past the edge of the burned-out forest where new green was beginning to rise above the blackened ground. It dropped, gaining momentum, into the deepening gorge that took it farther down and where it raced and whirled in rock pools and raced on. The man stood on the low cliff edge overlooking the gorge. Thirty-five feet below him the great bear lay beside the stream. Its new coat was lengthening and a pale silvery cast was beginning to touch the tips of the thick-grown hairs. It lay limp and relaxed on the pebble strand. Suddenly a forepaw darted and flipped a fat trout flashing through the air and the bear leaped from its lying position to seize the fish as it landed flopping a dozen feet away. Lazily the bear fed, then wandered up the stream to where a smooth rock slanted straight into the water. Standing at the top of the slant, it gave a small bounce and went forward on its belly on the rock with legs outstretched and slid splashing into the stream. The man leaned over the cliff to watch and a soundless chuckle shook him. Lazily the bear climbed again to the top of the smooth rock and rolled over on its back and slid down, tail first, thick legs waving. Its rump struck the water with a spattering smack and the chuckle in the man grew into sound. The bear whirled and rose in the water and looked up. It looked away and inspected the opposite bank in plain pretense that the man was not there. Its head dropped and it shuffled away down the gorge and out of sight around the first turn.

Farther to the eastward, far over the mountain barrier, only a few men worked by the shallow pools that were all that remained of the stream flowing there in the spring and early summer. Most of the cabins were sinking into ruins and only a few tents remained. Under the tarpaulin roof of the store and bar several men argued the failure of prospecting trips into the surrounding country. The storekeeper, short and thick with deep burnt-out eyes in a round bullet head, stood at one end of his bar listening to the low voice of the hatchet-faced man with the thin-lipped mouth. He looked about at his scantily stocked shelves and shrugged his shoulders. Greed and bitterness and discouragement crawled through the mining camp.

Quiet against the sky the man stood on the first ridge outside the valley and saw, small in the vast panorama below him, the great bear stalking an elk. It slipped upwind along a dry gulch and crept out to the shelter of a scrub thicket. The elk grazed closer and the bear broke from the thicket. The elk wheeled into flight, legs driving with the strength of terror. But the bear overtook it and was alongside and reared and a paw flashed in a blur of motion beyond vision and struck the elk's head sideways and snapped the neck like a twig breaking. There had been stillness, a flash of movement, then stillness again, the motionless body of the elk on the grass and the bear standing beside it. The man watched the bear feed slowly then drag the carcass into the gulch and scoop a hole in the soft shale and pull the carcass into this and begin covering it. A small grim smile touched his lips. He turned and started down the other side of the ridge to hunt in another part of the wilderness empire he shared with the great bear.

The chill of the night lingered, gradually giving way to the sun's warmth. The morning air was crystal in its distinct clarity. The man stood by the pool and looked at the pan in his hands. There were only a few scattered flakes in it. The pool was almost worked out. He started to walk along the stream, studying its flow and occasional silt banks. His steps slowed and at last stopped and he looked out over the valley. New color was showing on the clumps of low bushes that dotted the valley floor. Berries were ripening there and along the climbing sides of the valley. Far by the opposite slope he saw the bear rise out of the bushes, settling back on its haunches like a big sitting squirrel, stripping berries into its mouth with its long foreclaws. He strode back to his camp and tossed the pan to one side and lifted the flat stone. Three full salt bags lay there now and a fourth partly filled. He emptied the leather pouch into the fourth bag and lowered the stone in place. Rifle in hand he wandered out through his side of the valley, tasting berries along the way.

September

The green of the valley was changing, darker with a brown cast in barely discernible splotches. The thin cutting edge of fall was invading the air. Among the trees behind the man's camp the flat stone lay undisturbed with grass blades curling over it. The camp itself was neat and orderly. Firewood was stacked in a long pile. A little to one side the pan lay, no longer glinting bright, spotted with dirt and rust. Where the tree fringe abutted the open of the valley the man sat, cross-legged in the sun. Across his lap was a deerskin, tanned with lye from wood ashes and worked to fairly smooth flexibility. Carefully he sliced into the leather, cutting doubled patterns for moccasins to replace his worn boots.

Across the valley, working along the base of the slope and up a short way, the great bear was digging for ground squirrels, ripping into the soil several feet with half a dozen powerful strokes and lying flat on its belly for the final reaching, scraping thrust. The increasing richness of the fur with its silver tipping shone in the clear light. Alternately the man bent to his cutting and raised his head to watch the bear. Suddenly, with the suddenness of decision, he rose and strode back among the spruce and juniper and about, until he found a level space between the trees to his liking. Here he laid out a rough rectangle, scratching the lines with his boot heel. He marked off space inside for a bunk and another rectangle, small and against one end, for a fireplace. He studied his design and nodded to himself and looked around, estimating the standing timber close by. He strode to his shelter and crawled to the low end to inspect what remained of his staple supplies. He came out carrying a small pack and closed the open end of the shelter with its log barrier. He strode to the flat stone and filled the leather pouch from one of the bags. A few moments later he was striding eastward out of the valley with the rifle in one hand, the lead rope of the burro in the other.

A cool wind whipped down the valley, whispering of the winter still hidden far up in the soaring peaks. It moved over the changing green that was darker with the brown splotches plainer and spreading. It moved out the valley entrance and down the rolling slope where the man strode steadily forward, facing straight into it. He was leading a loaded packhorse now and the burdened burro trotted behind. At the crest of the slope he stopped and searched his back trail for long minutes. His head rose higher and his stride lengthened as he passed through the valley entrance and the horse and the burro followed.

Three miles away on the ridge overlooking the last slope, ten feet back in the timber that topped the ridge, two men stood in the tree shadows and watched the three figures entering the valley. The taller of the two, lean even in his thick mackinaw jacket, had a narrow hatchet face gashed by a thin-lipped mouth. The other, shorter but bulking thick from shoulders to hips, had burnt-out eyes in a round bullet head. The thin-lipped one snapped his fingers and nodded to the other. Together they went back deeper into the timber and mounted the two horses there and rode out and down the ridge, circling to the right toward the high shoulder of climbing rock that would give them a view out over the valley.

Restless on its rock ledge, the great bear lay on the stone and watched the empty camp across the valley. Its ears twitched and the big head rose and swung to the right. It saw the man entering the valley and the horse and burro following. It saw the man stop and look toward it and wave his arms and start forward again. The low rumbling, soft and deep, rolled out from the ledge and died away in the afternoon wind. Quietly the bear watched the man stride toward his camp and begin untying the packs. Quietly it rose and padded on the stone into the darkness of the crevice.

Vigor flowed through the man. The afternoon air of his valley flooded his muscles with strength. His ax leaped in his hands and he felled four trees of the right foundation size and lopped away the branches and cut the logs to the lengths he wanted and notched them. Using the ax handle for a measure he took three pieces of rope and used the three-four-five rule to square the corners as he fitted the logs together. As he straightened from checking the fourth joint he saw first the heavy boots, and as his eyes swept upward he saw the small wicked muzzle of the rifle bearing on his belly and the thin-lipped gash of a mouth in the narrow face.

The two men wasted no time. They asked their questions and when he did not answer they roped him to a thick tree. They searched through his camp and came back by him and built a fire and when this was blazing strong they took his rifle and emptied the magazine and laid it with the barrel reaching into the flames and waited for the metal to heat.

The man stood tight against the tree and the pale hazel of his eyes was startling against the dead bloodless brown of his broad wind-burned face. He stared out over the valley and his gaze moved upward and stopped two hundred yards up the opposite slope, and the beginning of living color crept into his face. The muscles along his jaw were ridged hard and he waited, cautious in his cunning, until the hot steel was close to his flesh before he spoke. He spoke quickly and bobbed his head toward the far slope. The two others turned. They saw the ledge and the uneven dark outline of the crevice. They spoke briefly together and the burnt-eyed one swung abruptly and started across the valley and the thin-lipped one sat hump-kneed on the ground and picked up his rifle and set it across his lap.

The man tight against the tree and the thin-lipped one hump-kneed on the ground watched the other move out and across the valley floor. They saw him stop at the base of the opposite side and look around for the trail and find it. They saw him start up, hurrying now, and reach the ledge almost running and disappear into the crevice.

Time passed and they watched, each in his own intentness, and nothing moved across the way. The ledge under its overhanging rock slept in its own quietness in the afternoon sun. The thin-lipped one rose and unloosened the rope holding the man to the tree and ordered him ahead and prodded him in the small of the back with

the rifle. The man led and the thin-lipped one followed and they
started across the valley floor.

Deep in the crevice darkness the great bear stood over the crumpled body. The big head with the small eyes, red-rimmed now,
swung slowly from side to side. The sound of running steps had
brought it from sleep into instant alertness. The forward leap out
of the inner darkness into the dimness near the crevice entrance and
the incredibly swift slashing stroke of forepaw had been instinctive
reactions to the challenging affront of invasion. Silently it had
dragged the body back into the protective darkness and stepped over
it, facing the entrance. The scent of the body, familiar yet unfamiliar, rose in its nostrils and caution at an experience never
before known held it waiting in the darkness, listening for further
sound out beyond the rock opening.

Striding steadily, the man led the way up the trail. His face was
a fixed mask and his muscles bunched in tight tension. When the
bear broke from the crevice, red-rimmed eyes blinking for swift focus
in the sunlight, the man leaped sideways off the trail and down the
steep slope, falling and rolling over the sharp rocks and hard against
the trunk of a sturdy spruce. He scrambled to his feet and jumped
for the first limb and swung his legs in to the trunk and began climbing.

Above him on the trail the thin-lipped one swung up the rifle and
fired and the bullet thudded into the bear's left shoulder and scraped
the bone and bore back along the side under the skin. In a silent
rush the great bear drove down the trail and the thin-lipped one
screamed and turned to run and a crashing forepaw crushed his spine
forward into his breastbone and raked tearing down through the
muscles of his back. The big jaws closed on the already lifeless body
and shook it and flung it twenty feet away.

Close against the trunk, the man peered through the thick
branches of the spruce. Below him the great bear quartered the
ground like a huge dog on a hunt, moving with a silent flowing
deadliness, raising its head often to test the wind. It limped slightly,
favoring its left foreleg, and the recurrent pain from the flesh wound
in the shoulder swelled the steady rage within and brightened the
reddened rims of the eyes. It worked back along the trail near the

valley floor and looked across at the man's camp. Abrutly it swung and with steady purpose went up the trail to the ledge and passed along the slopeside and faded into the tangled growth near the head of the valley.

Safe in his spruce, the man watched it go and disappear from his sight. He waited. At last he climbed to the ground and scrambled up to the trail and grabbed the rifle there. Quickly he ejected the spent cartridge shell and pumped another cartridge into the firing chamber. Quickly he checked the magazine and saw it was almost full. Cautious and alert he slipped down and started across the valley.

The packhorse and burro grazed by the camp, quiet now after the brief startling from the single shot across the way. In the fringe of trees behind them and around the camp nothing stirred except the wind whispering its endless murmur through the evergreen branches. As the man approached, downwind, he stopped often to peer forward and swing his head to scan the whole long fringe of trees, searching with his eyes every possible cover. It was the drumming of the horse's hooves as it pounded to the length of its picket rope and jerked around, strangling, that whirled him toward the sound. The great bear streaked toward him out of thicket shadow and he fired in the instant, instinctively—aiming as rapidly as he could pump the gun. The first shot bored into the junction of neck and right shoulder and shattered the bone there and the second smashed into the massive breast and ripped back through the lungs. The great bear drove ahead, uneven in bounding stride with a deep coughing tearing its throat, and the third shot struck through the mouth and back into the spine. The man leaped aside and the bear's rush took it past and it crumpled forward to the ground. The man stood by the bear's body and stared down. It was smaller with the life gone. The muscles of the man's shoulders shook a little and he swung his head slowly from one side to the other and the flat planes of his face were hard as the rock formations ringing the valley.

He stood by the rectangle of notched logs a long time. Quietly he turned and went to the flat stone and took the plump salt bags from under it and carried them over by his shelter and began to prepare his packs. Half an hour later he strode across the valley floor and the packhorse and the burro followed. The sun, dropping below the far peaks, was behind him. The chill rising wind beat against his back. Unbelievably small in the vastness he strode out of the valley, and with him went a new loneliness and a sense of something lost.

Leander Frailey

NEW CALYPSO was getting to be a real town when Baldpate Frailey settled there. It wasn't tucked away so far in a corner of Nebraska that you couldn't find it on a map if you looked hard enough. On a big map. It bumped out with a fair quota of low buildings and squared-corner roads on each side of the railroad and twice a week a freight train stopped and when the station agent sold a ticket he could set the signals and one of the two-a-day one-each-way passenger trains would squeal to a halt instead of chugging straight through. The local farmers shipped there in harvest season and the local cattlemen too and supplies came in for the whole surrounding countryside. Yes, New Calypso had grown to town-size when Baldpate Frailey stepped off the train with the tools of his trade in a black leather valise and set up shop in a squat two-room shack between a saloon and a sprawling feedstore.

Baldpate was a barber. Maybe it was peculiar for a man without a hair on his own long thin head to make a living out of other men's head-crops, but he was a fair-to-middling barber who could trim your hair without nicking your ears and scrape away your stubble leaving most of the skin intact. His shop was on the wrong side of the tracks. Well, wrong side to some people. It was on the side with most of the saloons and the stockyard and the warehouse and the basket mill and the in-and-out squatters' shacks. It wasn't on the side with the saloon that had upstairs rooms to rent and called itself a hotel and the prosperous livery stable and the good retail stores and the solid respectable houses of the solid respectable townsfolk. That side already had a barber shop that had already caught the fancy trade with its neatly painted pole out front and its big mirror behind the two chairs and its shiny brass spittoon that its proprietor called a cuspidor. Baldpate started with a makeshift chair that he could raise and lower with a wooden lever. He finally acquired a real barber chair second-hand out of Lincoln. He finally acquired a small mirror and a black-painted spittoon. But he couldn't compete with the other shop and he didn't try. He got the fringe trade, the men who worked on the same side of the tracks and an occasional cowboy nursing his nickels and trainmen stopping off and the squatters, who sometimes could pay and sometimes couldn't. He had to be content with that and he was. He didn't ask much out of life.

When Baldpate stepped off the train he wasn't alone. He had two boys with him, his sons, Leander and Greenberry. Leander was the older, already stretching long and thin in body and head with such a meager scraggly topknot of hair you could tell he wouldn't be wearing a man's pants long before he'd be bald as a bean. He took after his father. Greenberry was a pair of years younger, considerably shorter but plumper, with a waving tangle of hair that would have made a fine big floor mop. He must have taken after his mother, who had quietly checked out of the Frailey family and the whole of this world some years before.

The three of them lived in the back room of the shop. Baldpate did the barbering and Leander did the housekeeping and Greenberry did nothing. Nothing except eat hearty, wander around town with other boys, and sit lazy in the sun, which was what he liked best after the eating. Old Baldpate favored Greenberry, maybe because of that mop of hair, and was always telling Leander to take care of him and watch out for him. So naturally it was Leander not Greenberry who began to be snapping the shears at the chair in the afternoons when Baldpate grew tired and felt the arthritis creeping into his joints. And then one night along about the time the boys had their full growth Baldpate sat up on his cot in the dark and called across the little room, "Leander. You mind me now. You take care of your brother." And old Baldpate lay back down and rolled his head on the pillow and died.

You can forget about Baldpate Frailey now. He's not important to this story. He brought the family to New Calypso and started the family business and told Leander what to do and died and that's enough said about him. It's Leander and Greenberry we're interested in.

Leander first. He was a good boy, quiet and steady, so naturally he became a good man, quiet and steady still. The only thing unusual about his growing stage was the stretch he spent a lot of time drawing pictures with a thick surveyor's pencil he'd found somewhere, on any scrap of paper that came to hand. Nobody paid any attention to that. Nobody except Greenberry, who just looked and laughed and settled back to more lazing in the sun. But anyone who paid real attention might have noticed that Leander liked to draw heads, men's heads, with plenty of hair on them and sideburns and all kinds of mustaches and beards. Then he didn't have time for that because he was helping with the barbering as well as doing the housekeeping and then his father was dead and he had full-time barbering to keep him busy. He didn't need to draw heads after that. He had real ones to work with.

It wasn't long before folks on the wrong side of the tracks knew they had a prize barber there who wouldn't be worrisome about being paid on the dot as long as they brought him heavy manes of hair or thick crops of whiskers to be sheared. They gave him plenty of practice and by the time he had his techniques worked out it was a treat to be barbered by that Leander. He'd set you in that one chair and stand back and circle you slowly, studying your head from all around. Then he'd pick up the right tool and go to work. Sometimes it'd be the handclippers. He could do a whole handsome haircut with those clippers alone. Sometimes it'd be the heavy shears or again the light scissors or an alternating of them. Whatever it was, there'd be a wonderful snipping rhythm soothing about your ears. Leander had more than rhythm. He had positive melodies matching the work in hand. If your hair was coarse and strong, you'd hear a marching tune from the flying blades as the locks fell. If your hair was light and fluffy, you'd hear something like a delicate dance tune. His combing was right in time and his soft old brush with the powder on it would be dusting dainty about your neck at the exact second the cut tag ends of hair might be beginning to get itchy and threatening to slide down under your shirt. And when he'd lower the chairback and lather your face and take the right razor out of old Baldpate's box that had one marked for each day in the week, then you knew you were in the hands of a master. His razors were always so sharp the toughest whiskers surrendered without a struggle. His strokes were so deft you weren't certain you felt them. When he raised the chairback again and stepped away and circled you again, you sat still and waited for the verdict. Maybe he'd shake his head and snatch up his scissors and make a fresh attack on your hair or mustache or beard or even eyebrows and by that time you'd not even think of interfering because you knew that when he was finished you'd look better than you ever did before. Let him do it his way and Leander could make anybody look like somebody.

As good as his barbering, some people said, was the effect he had on his customers. He wasn't a talking barber and that marked him as different right away. He was usually so intent on the portrait he was making out of the raw material of features and hair and whiskers in his chair that he might not even hear you if you spoke to him. But if you listened closely you might hear him muttering to himself, not much and not often, just a few words now and then. "Interesting head to work on . . . now these are eyebrows . . . no sense hiding that chin," things like that. No matter how low and picayune you felt going into the shop, you had the feeling coming out that maybe the face you presented to the world had a point or two in its favor.

The first the folks on the right side of the tracks began to have some notion what had been developing over on the other side was when Osgood R. Buxton, proprietor of the Big Bargain Mercantile Establishment and president of the New Calypso Bank, was stranded there with a half-hour to kill. The day had started bad for him. All through breakfast his wife had complained again about the wide drooping mustache that had taken him years to cultivate into the kind of upperlip canopy he thought impressive. "Makes you look like a seasick mastiff," she said and was so delighted at her comparison that he stomped out madder than usual. Then he went down to the freight office to check the shipment he was expecting and found it wasn't in and the train would be half an hour late. He stomped up and down the dirt street kicking at the dust, and the unfairness of it all hit him so hard he decided to strike back in some drastic way. Through the open door of Leander's shop he saw the barber chair empty and stomped in and planked himself in it. He took hold of his mustache with both hands. "Shave this damn thing off," he said.

Leander didn't pay any attention to the words. Leander was padding around him in a circle studying his head from all sides. Buxton slapped both hands on the chair arms. "You hear me?" he shouted. "I said shave this damn cookie duster off me!"

Leander focused on him as someone speaking. "No," Leander said. "It belongs there."

Buxton subsided with a blowing gurgle that waggled the mustache. "Belongs there?"

"Yes," Leander said. "It just needs a little pointing so it won't fight with your forehead."

"Fight with my forehead?" Buxton said in a small voice. He relaxed in the chair and a big piece of checkered cloth covered him up to the neck and was tied behind and a clipping rhythm began about his head and something like a cheery marching tune tickled his ears. When the cloth came off he stood up and peered into the little mirror. His hair had been thinned along the sides so suddenly it seemed thicker on top. His eyebrows had acquired a faintly quizzical air. His mustache was almost the same yet remarkably different. It had a slight upward twist suggestive of jauntiness without being aggressive and the side tips somehow pointed your glance upward to notice that broad forehead. The whole effect was that of a man who could do things in the world and was of consequence in his community. When he walked out the door Buxton was snapping his knees in long strides, and though the train was another half-hour late he spent the time chatting cheerfully with the station agent and trying to catch the light right so he could see his reflection in a window.

With a beginning like that and a booster like Buxton only a few months were needed for Leander to have a steady clientele from the right side of the tracks. There were those who remained faithful to the other shop and that was sensible because even Leander couldn't have kept the entire masculine quotient of New Calypso in trim. But he had all the trade he could handle, fancy and fringe, and it was all the same to him. A customer was a customer regardless of where he lived or how full or empty his pocket. Leander would do as artistic a job on a stray tramp as on Osgood R. Buxton himself. He stayed right on in the same one-chair shop and made only the one change of buying a bigger mirror. New Calypso became real proud of him and Gus Hagelin, who ran the *New Calypsan Herald-Gazette,* printed items about his shop once in a while and kept notes on some of the stories about him to be included someday in a history of the township.

You've probably never heard the one about the haircutting contest with Polkadot City's best entry. New Calypso rarely talked about that one. Some of them got to blowing boastful over Polkadot City way about Leander's speed with the shears, which was silly because speed with Leander was just a part of his skill and not a purpose in itself. But anyway that started an argument and the upshot was that the New Calypsans bet that Leander could trim down two shaggy heads before the best barber Polkadot City could find could finish one. The bets were heavy before Leander heard about it. He didn't like it but he couldn't let any of his regulars lose money on him by default so he said he'd make the race. They thought he ought to go into training, practice finger exercises and things like that, but he just said to tell him when and went on with his regular barbering. When they came for him on the day he just picked up his clippers and a comb and dropped them in a pocket and went along. They had three men lined up on kitchen chairs and those were really shaggyheaded. The other barber had a tray ready with half a dozen pairs of scissors laid out. Leander shrugged his shoulders and took out his own old clippers and waited. At the start-off gun the two of them went at it, and it was Leander's race all the way. While the other barber clacked his shears and tangled himself in the hair and nipped his own fingers in his hurry, Leander skimmed along, swift and sure, and a fine racing-fast jigtime tune played around the two heads he was working on, first one and then the other. There wasn't any waste motion. Each cut was exact and true. He was carving out neat haircuts with his clippers like a sculptor chipping a statue.

He was going strong and about finished when the inevitable happened. He started muttering to himself. He had the two heads trimmed in a way that would have made any ordinary barber proud when he stepped back and made a circuit of his two men and shook his head. He didn't even hear the shoutings of his supporters and he stepped close again and started the final little delicate polishing strokes that would bring out the best-barbered points of those two men. While the New Calypsans groaned the other barber made a last jagged slice and claimed a finish, and considerable argument developed but the judges gave him the decision. And Leander wasn't even aware of the argument. He was quietly padding around his two subjects and nodding satisfied to himself. The New Calypsans paid their bets grumbling and in time most of them conceded that Leander couldn't have done anything else and still been Leander but they never talked much about that contest. They preferred telling the stories like the one about the time the Governor was worried over re-election and as a campaign stunt came all the way to New Calypso for some of Leander's barbering and Leander touched him up so noble and convincing that he won with a thumping majority. But you've heard that one. Everybody has.

It's Greenberry's turn now. Just as Leander kept on the way he had started, growing longer and thinner and balder and more energetic, so Greenberry kept on the way he had started too, growing plumper so that he seemed shorter, and thicker-haired and lazier. He sprouted whiskers at a remarkably early age and they weren't sparse and blond like Leander's, which had to be shaved off because they were such poor specimens. No, Greenberry's whiskers were stout and dark and close-sprouting and he showed prodigious power in producing them. By time he was old enough to vote, if he'd ever bother to do anything taking that much energy, he had the biggest, bushiest beard in New Calypso. And it kept right on growing. No razor, not even a pair of scissors, had ever touched the main body of it. The only clipping he gave it was a mere minor pruning around the mouth to keep the way clear for his frequent intake of food. It roamed around his face from ear to ear and down over his chest like a magnificent stand of underbrush and merged above into his dark waving hair crop so that his upper cheeks and eyes and forehead peeped out like someone hiding in a thicket. Maybe he clung to that wondrous beard because he realized it represented his one real accomplishment. Some backbiting folks said he did it because he was mean and worthless and was trying to shame his brother and in a figurative sense thumb his nose at the very family business that enabled him to stay so plump and well fed. That couldn't have been true. Greenberry Frailey wasn't mean. Maybe close to worthless. But not mean. He was just lazy. He was just trifling. Matter of fact, he was as proud of Leander as anyone in New Calypso and if arguing hadn't been too much trouble he'd have been ready to argue with anyone that Leander was the best brother and the best barber in the country.

All the same it was peculiar to see the most amazing crop of hair and whiskers anywhere in civilized captivity sitting day after day in the sun on the little porch of a barber shop. That was what Greenberry did every day the sun shone. Nobody ever knew whether he would have tried to do any barbering if the shop had had another chair. Probably not, because Leander hinted about getting another one once and Greenberry promptly pointed out there wasn't room enough. So Greenberry took over the chore of meals, which was somewhat to his liking, and after breakfast he'd settle on the porch till time for his midmorning snack and then settle again till time for lunch and after that settle again till time for his midafternoon jaunt all the way next door to the neighboring saloon. Just before this last he'd go into the shop and around Leander by the chair and pull open the money drawer under the scissors shelf and slip into his pocket one dollar, never any more and never any less. When that dollar was in the hands of the bartender he would come back for the evening meal. If his taste had been for the good liquor at a quarter a shot, he'd still be able to navigate among the dishes and play a fair game of backgammon with Leander after supper. If it had been for the cheap liquor at ten cents a shot, he'd likely soon be snoring on his cot and Leander would have to be the cook. Those times Leander might begin to worry he wasn't doing right by his brother and shake him awake and try telling him he ought to get a job of some kind and Greenberry would simply say, "Why? We're doing all right, aren't we?" and Leander wouldn't know what to say because they were.

There they were, Leander doing his barber's magic inside the shop and Greenberry raising whiskers on the porch and they might have continued that way indefinitely if Leander hadn't acquired an obsession that started as a small notion and grew until it was so bad it could quiver in his fingertips. He had all his regular patrons in the New Calypso territory well in hand, each fitted with the hair styles and whiskery facial adornments or lack of same that would make the emphatic most of their natural endowments. The task now was simply to keep them trimmed that way. There was no challenge left in them, no demand for fresh creative effort. He welcomed strangers who wandered in with positive delight. But they were few and long between. He began to feel frustrated and barren of inspiration. And then he stood on the little porch one afternoon and looked at Greenberry snoozing in the sun and a breeze waggled the long soft ends of Greenberry's beard and the small notion was born. By evening it was so big in him that he could hardly look at Greenberry across the supper table. During the next days it swelled to such proportions that it interfered with his barbering. He had to shake his head sharp to rid it of the image of that magnificent shock of raw material and the rhythmic melody of his cutting would break as his fingers quivered on the clippers. And then Greenberry all unknowing tripped the trigger of the trap awaiting him by taking on ten shots and coming home and falling asleep.

Leander closed the shop door at five o'clock as usual and padded into the back room and saw Greenberry gently snoring and a sudden little tremor ran through him. He rocked on his feet a moment and closed his mouth with a sudden snap. He padded into the shop and returned and laid out his tools on a chair by the cot, the clippers and the scissors, big and small, and a comb and the right razor and the brush and the soap mug. Carefully he raised Greenberry's shoulders with one arm and slipped two pillows behind them. Carefully he spread the checkered cloth over Greenberry's plump middle and raised Greenberry's beard to slide the upper edge of the cloth under it. For a long time he stood staring at the huge thatch of wondrous hair and whiskers framed against the cloth and the top pillow. He was not studying the head, because he did not need to. He knew every possible configuration hidden inside that thicket, every feature that everyone else in New Calypso had long forgotten. He was tasting the sweet tangy ecstasy of anticipation. At last he carefully set another chair by the cot side and sat down on it and leaned forward. With a soft sigh of complete contentment he picked up the clippers and went to work.

Greenberry stirred once at a slight tugging on his chin but a rich majestic melody of snipping blades was playing about his head and it soothed him even deeper into slumber. He woke late in the evening in the lamplight and was surprised that Leander had not roused him to supper. He was more surprised when he saw Leander limp on the other cot, asleep, and on his long thin bald-topped face the beatific smile of a man who has made a supreme effort and found it good. Greenberry heaved to his feet and was so befuddled he was not aware that he was a changed man. Out of sheer habit he ate five big sandwiches and did not notice the new freedom of access to his mouth and lay down again and slept once more. He was still unaware in the morning despite the secretive proud glances Leander gave him and awareness did not touch him until he went out the back door and took hold of the two-wheeled pushcart there and started off on his weekly food-shopping jaunt to Oscar Trittipoe's General Grocery Store.

He never reached the store. Not on that trip. He was accustomed to being ignored by most people passing and that pleased him because it saved the energy of a return greeting. He was accustomed to having those who did speak make humorous references to his beard. But this time neither thing happened. Everyone noticed him. Very definitely. They stared at him as if they had never seen him before and turned to watch him go by. And no one spoke about his beard. No one spoke at all. Most of them nodded to him, respectful and deferential, and some of the men involuntarily tipped their hats. It was too much for Greenberry's somnolent mind to grasp all at once. He hurried back to the shop, went in and turned to Leander, puttering at his instrument shelf, and in the turning saw himself in the big mirror.

Not himself. Someone else. A man of amazingly impressive presence. A thick shock of hair tamed and disciplined to dignity yet with the inherent vitality plain in every faultless wave. Strong eyebrows subtly arched to emphasize the width and nobility of the brow. A sturdy mustache, firm and short-cropped, speaking of confidence and self-assurance in itself and somehow also pointing out the out-thrust power of the nose above. Rugged sideburns clipped close yet with a faint flaring that suggested breadth of mind. And a beard, deep under the chin and reliable, short but not too short, wide but not too wide, a solid foundation for the face proclaiming serenity and wisdom with every sturdy hair.

Greenberry shook with the shock. He threw Leander one look of frenzied reproach and fairly ran into the back room and closed the door. He sat on the edge of his cot and leaned the superb portrait that was now his head forward into his plump hands and let the frightening knowledge that he was marked with distinction sweep over him. It was characteristic that he never once thought that a few strokes with scissors could reduce him again to a scraggly nonentity. He would have had to make those scissor strokes. He sat motionless a long time. At last his head rose and he made a few exploratory motions with his hands around his chin and cheeks. He stood up and placed himself in front of the little mirror that had once served in the shop and his mind was braced now for what he would see. He studied himself, turning his head sideways and rolling his eyes to catch the splendor from various angles. Unconsciously he stood straighter and pulled in his bulging waistline and puffed out his chest. By noontime the new Greenberry Frailey, fortified with a full lunch, was ready to face the world.

The new Greenberry Frailey. That is precisely what he was. A new man. A changed man. In all outward semblance at least. The very first day he discovered what his impressive appearance could accomplish in promoting prompt, actually scurrying service and the choicest cuts of meat from the formerly lackadaisical and almost contemptuous Oscar Trittipoe. On the third day he learned the ease with which he could obtain virtually unlimited credit at the Big Bargain Mercantile Establishment and forthwith arrayed himself in what was to be thereafter his unvarying uniform, black trousers and black frock coat and gorgeous gray vest and white shirt and celluloid collar and blackstring bow tie, unseen beneath that now disciplined matchless beard except when he thrust his chin outward and fluffed the beard up in a gesture calculated to draw attention to its perfect proportions. By the end of the first week he had even acquired a gold-headed cane and his voice had dropped several notes to a deepening resonance and he was developing a flowing almost courtly manner. By the end of the second week he was settled in his new role, rapidly becoming another New Calypsan institution, a monumental figure seen every clear day on the center bench between the town watering trough and the town flagpole across from the post office. You can assay the true measure of Leander's art when you understand that already the New Calypsans were forgetting the old Greenberry who sat in his ancient red-plaid shirt and split-seam dungarees on the porch of the little shop and were drifting so completely under the spell of the new Greenberry that they accepted his benign nods as benedictions and felt that their town was a better place because such a towering testament to the dignity and nobility of the human race dwelt among them. When he had snoozed on the shop porch he had been a shiftless disgrace to be ignored. Now, when he drowsed on the bench, serene and nodding in the sun, he was a philosopher thinking deep thoughts and pondering grave problems and giving tone to the community. Why, it's a fact there was not even a noticeable chuckle when he began calling himself J. Greenberry Frailey.

It was Osgood R. Buxton himself who launched Greenberry on his public career. The time came when Buxton was a mite worried about the New Calypso Bank. More than a mite worried. The bank had overreached itself in granting loans and the cattle market was wobbly and a lot of the loans might have to be carried over and a few rumors got to skipping about and Buxton was worried what would happen if a run started. He sat at his desk by the bank's front window worrying and stroking the mustache Leander had saved for him and out the window he noticed with a sudden idea-prompted push the never failing impressiveness of Greenberry on the bench. Five minutes and a brief talk later Buxton was on his way to Gus Hagelin with an item for the *Herald-Gazette* to the effect that J. Greenberry Frailey had kindly consented to become a director of the New Calypso Bank. The only immediate change for Greenberry was the addition of ten dollars a month to his pocket and a slight shift of sitting quarters, from the bench by the flagpole to a bench in front of the bank where the sun was even better and his presence was a steady reassurance to troubled depositors. The monthly meetings were no real chore. All he had to do was attend and sit quiet and murmur "Hmmmm" in a thoughtful tone when an important decision was posed, and the other directors would proceed exactly as they would have done without him, buttressed now with the feeling that they were being wise and judicious indeed. But this first gesture into the realm of actual activity encouraged other people to draw him into other things. He discovered the lure of speechmaking. The deep roll of his voice combined with the overpowering benignity of his appearance to produce hypnotic effect on his audiences. The words were unimportant. It was the impression that prevailed. He auctioned the box lunches at town dances and could obtain good prices for those prepared by the most unattractive unattached females. He presided at the annual Strawberry Festival and the Stockmen's Show and was the Fourth of July orator. There was no doubt about it. With little real effort on his part he had become an unofficial public functionary.

And Leander? Well, Leander was content. He had done what old Baldpate told him to do. He had taken care of Greenberry in the most important way and what remained of the taking care was merely a matter of helping to maintain Greenberry in the style to which he had become accustomed. That was simple because Greenberry was not active enough to wear out clothes rapidly and ate, if anything, less than before and his drinks were almost invariably supplied by admirers more than willing to pay for the privilege. Leander now had constantly before him the inspiration of his finest masterpiece, the one perfect portrait that he never tired of retouching and keeping in perfect trim. And Greenberry, in his way, was properly grateful. His innocent trust that Leander would take care of him had been justified in a surprising and superlative degree. He never failed, when extolling the glories of New Calypso in his occasional orations, to include some mention of the tonsorial wizardry of that far-famed prince among barbers, my brother Leander. He continued to grace the little shop building with his presence as his eating and sleeping quarters. He continued to spend his spare evenings playing backgammon with Leander. So complete was his hold on the town that many people regarded this as somewhat of a condescension on his part.

Yes, Leander had worked out a way of life for himself and Greenberry that satisfied them both and was a double-weight asset to New Calypso. Then enter the serpent, Worthington P. C. Stimmel. That was the name in Old English lettering on his calling cards and he carried his cards in a cardcase. They also stated, in smaller but no less compelling type, that he was President and Corresponding Secretary, the Amalgamated Association for the Betterment of American Communities. This Stimmel had long since made an interesting discovery. He had learned that when towns attained some size they found themselves needing such modern improvements as sewers and cobblestone pavements and those ingenious means of public transportation, horsecars. He had discovered that sometimes the people of an ambitious small town could be persuaded that the process would work in reverse, that if they would sell bonds to themselves to raise the funds and draw plans for new streets and install sewers and pavements and horsecars, then their town would automatically attract newcomers and grow swiftly and become boomingly prosperous. It was unfortunate that the promotional expenses and the cost of this Stimmel's invaluable services always approximated most if not all of the funds raised. But by time the townsfolk learned that in full eye-opening force this Stimmel would be far away planning the improvement of another community in another part of the country.

A man of Worthington P. C. Stimmel's experienced discernment could see at once the splendid future that awaited New Calypso. He could recognize with equal facility the unusual opportunity offered by J. Greenberry Frailey's bewhiskered magnificence. He had not been in New Calypso ten days before stationery was printed and bonds were being engraved and both stationery and bonds proclaimed the fact that J. Greenberry Frailey was Chairman of the New Calypso Progressive Citizens' League, the latest chapter of the A.A.B.A.C. There was some opposition led by Oscar Trittipoe, who was by nature an obstinate individual, and Gus Hagelin, who had acquired from his newspaper work a suspicious trend of mind and some knowledge of human frailties. But obstinacy and suspicion could not prevail against the majesty of the Greenberry whiskers. The N.C.P.C. League gained momentum like an avalanche moving and the date was set for the public meeting that would launch the bond sale.

All this bothered Leander not at all. He never interfered in Greenberry's doings. His own doubts about the League project were overwhelmed by Greenberry's contagious optimism. To him the thought of a bigger and more booming New Calypso was pleasant because that might mean new and unfamiliar customers. He went quietly on with his barbering. And then Worthington P. C. Stimmel made a mistake. Operating on the principle of when in Rome doing what the Romans do, he went into the little shop for a hair trim.

"Heard about you from your brother," this Stimmel said in his best patronizing manner. There was no reply. Leander was circling the chair, studying him from all sides. The first eager small smile on Leander's face was fading into a tight-lipped frown. Muttonchop whiskers. Leander had never liked muttonchop whiskers and refused to permit them on any regular customer. They were not right for any decent human head. They could have only one purpose, to hide or draw attention away from other things. Correct. These muttonchops gave a broadness and solidity to this head that was not really there. They obscured the whole sinister, greedy, calculating cast of the countenance. Leander picked up his big scissors and they hovered about Stimmel's head, and the rhythmic tune they played in their first warming-up skirmishes in the air was a stern and resolute one. But they never touched a hair or whisker. Leander stopped and laid them down. He could not do it. He picked up the small scissors and for the first time since he was a boy relieving old Baldpate in the afternoons he gave an ordinary haircut, merely trimming into neatness the original portrait presented to him.

That was all that happened then in the shop. But afterwards Leander did what he had never done before. He closed the shop during working hours and went to see Gus Hagelin and what he learned there added more worry to what he had learned in the shop and he tried to talk to several League members and they laughed and told him to stick to his barbering and he tried to talk to Greenberry that evening and Greenberry laughed too and at last grew huffy and said he'd move to a room at the hotel if Leander didn't stop harping on something he knew nothing about. So Leander kept his worry to himself and it grew till it was a new obsession in him and he kept remembering what old Baldpate had said and realizing that Greenberry was in this slick Stimmel scheme and in a sense the kingpin of it, the asset that could push it through. And so at last when he had worried himself thinner and the time was short, he did something else he had never done before. On the day before the public meeting he went to the saloon next door and bought a bottle of the cheap liquor and had it on the table when he played backgammon with Greenberry that evening. He poured more into Greenberry's glass whenever that was empty and his own slick scheme succeeded. By eleven o'clock Greenberry was snoring soundly on his cot. Leander padded forward into the shop and returned and laid out his tools on a chair and spread the checkered cloth over Greenberry's chest. For a long time he stood staring down at the finest portrait he had ever achieved. With a soft sigh of torment he picked up his clippers and a slow sad melody of snipping blades began to play around Greenberry's head.

Greenberry slept straight through the night and well into the morning. He woke slowly and then focused suddenly on the old clock on a shelf. Five minutes past ten. The meeting had begun five minutes ago and he was not there. No time even for breakfast and that was a drastic thing to happen to him. He shrugged as quickly as he could into his frock coat and grabbed his gold-headed cane and hurried out through the shop past Leander sitting mournful in his own barber chair. He hurried out the front door disregarding Leander's calling to him, and hurried up the street and across the tracks and to the crowded space behind the flagpole where a bandstand had been erected and the four-piece New Calypso band was seated and Worthington P. C. Stimmel was standing erect delivering his practiced spiel.

There on the stand this Stimmel, talking against time, saw with relief the magnificent wavy shock of Greenberry's hair moving toward him through the assembled people. He shifted smoothly into remarks introducing that almost legendary repository of wisdom and civic foresight, that peerless pillar of New Calypsan community life, J. Greenberry Frailey, and waved to the approaching pillar to ascend the stand. And Greenberry burst out of the crowd and went up the steps and took his dignified stance and thrust his head forward a bit and reached up in the strange hushed silence that had gripped the whole scene to fluff his beard.

It was that gesture that released the first of the sniggering chuckles into loud and contagious guffaws. Greenberry's hand came up in the familiar movement to fluff his beard and there was no beard for him to fluff. There was only what the New Calypsans had long ago forgotten, the ridiculous small and round little-boyish dimpled chin that the beard had hidden. As the laughter rolled around the flagpole and New Calypsans thumped each other on the back, Worthington P. C. Stimmel, that man of experienced discernment, slipped down from the stand and away and Gus Hagelin, that man aware of human frailties, leaped up on the stand and shouted at the band and raucous music began to blare. And through the midst of the over-all merriment came a long and thin and bald-headed figure, stoop-shouldered and sad and ashamed, to take care of his brother and lead him home.

All the rest of the day the little shop was closed. The next day it was open and time had gone backwards. A plump figure in a red-plaid shirt and split-seam dungarees sat on the little porch in the sun. But inside there were no more snipping melodies. There was only the plain pedestrian plodding of routine cutting. Greenberry sat in the sun and some of the time actually snoozed and Leander went on with his barbering inside, but it was an ordinary barber's barbering. He had used his art to destroy and not to create and the magic was gone from his fingers.

In midafternoon Greenberry rose and went into the shop and pulled open the money drawer and took out a dollar and reached and took another and looked at Leander patiently working his scissors in dull routine and put the second dollar back and plodded out. It was a ten-shot session for him and he returned barely able to navigate and lay down on his cot and in a few moments was sleeping, and almost anyone seeing him there would have said that was all he was doing.

But he was doing something else. All unaware he was doing the one thing that he could do better than anyone else in New Calypso. Leander saw it when he came into the back room from the shop and started to prepare some supper. He saw what he, a barber, had actually forgotten. He saw the dark stubble emerging on Green-berry's chin and remembered Greenberry's prodigious talent for raising whiskers. His eyes brightened and small rhythmic melodies began to stir again in his finger muscles. He had not failed old Baldpate. Not yet. He could try again and, if necessary, again. It would not take long, not with Greenberry so obligingly concentrating even in his sleep on that one wondrous accomplishment.

Already Leander could begin to see the next portrait. Not dignity and thoughtfulness and deep wisdom this time. No. A portrait built around a short, stubby, square-cut beard, the beard of a man steady and dependable and competent at whatever work he might have in hand.

Jacob

THOSE MOCCASINS? Mine. Though I never wore them. Had them on just once to see if they fitted. They did. A bit tight but I could get them on.

Don't touch them. The leather's old and dry and the stitching rotted. Ought to be. They've been hanging there a long time. Look close and you can see the craftsmanship. The best. They're Nez Percé moccasins. Notice the design worked into the leather. It's faint now but you can make it out. Don't know how they did that but the Nez Percé could really work leather. A professor who studied such things told me once that design means they're for a chief. For his ceremonial appearances, sort of his dress-up footwear. Said only a chief could use that design. But it's there. Right there on those moccasins.

Yes. They're small. Boy size. That's because I was a boy then. But they're a chief's moccasins all the same. Kept them down the years because I'm proud of them. And because they mind me of a man. He had a red skin. Copper would be closer the color. A muddy copper. And I only saw him once. But he was a man.

That was a long way from here. A long way. In years and in miles. I was ten then, maybe eleven, maybe twelve, in that neighborhood, I disremember exactly. Best I can do is place it in the late seventies. Funny how definite things like dates and places slip away and other stray things, like the way you felt at certain times and how your first wild strawberries tasted, can remain clear and sharp in your mind. We were living, my folks and my older brother and myself, in a little town in eastern Montana. Not much of a place.

Just a small settlement on the railroad that wouldn't have amounted to anything except that it had a stretch of double track where a train going one direction could pull off to let one going the other get past. My father was a switchman. Looked after track and handled the west-end switch. That was why we were there.

The Indian smell was still in the air in those days. People around here and nowadays wouldn't know what that means. It was a knowing and a remembering that not so far away were still real live free-footed fighting Indians that might take to raiding again. They were pegged on treaty lands and supposed to stay there. But they were always hot over one thing or another, settlers gnawing into their hunting grounds or agents pinching their rations or maybe the government forgetting to keep up treaty payments. You never knew when they might get to figuring they'd been pushed far enough and would start council fires up in the hills and come sudden and silent out of the back trails, making trouble. It was only a year or two since the Custer affair on the Little Big Horn southwest of where we were. No-one with any experience in those things expected the treaty that ended that business to hold long.

Don't take me wrong. We didn't look for Indians behind bushes and sit around shivering at night worrying about attacks. The nearest reservation was a fair jump away and if trouble started we'd know about it long before it reached us, if it ever did. Matter of fact it never did. I grew up in that territory and never once was mixed in any Indian trouble past an argument over the price of a blanket. Never even saw any fighting Indians except this once I'm telling about and then they weren't fighting any more. It was just a smell in the air, the notion there might be trouble any time. Indians were quite a topic when I was a boy and the talk of an evening chewed it plenty.

Expect I heard as much of it as any of the boys around our settlement. Maybe more. My father had been in the midst of the Sioux outbreak in Minnesota in the early sixties. He'd seen things that could harden a man. They settled his mind on the subject. "Only good Indian," he'd say, "is a dead one." Yes. That's not just a saying out of the storybooks. There were men who really said it. And believed it. My father was one. Said it and believed it and said it so often I'd not be stretching the truth past shape to figure he averaged it couple times a week and so naturally we boys believed it too, hearing it all the time. I'll not argue with anyone wants to believe it even today. I'm only telling you what happened to me.

Hearing that kind of talk we boys around the settlement had our idea what Indians were like. I can speak for myself anyway. The Indians I saw sometimes passing through on a train or loafing around a town the few times I was in one with the folks didn't count. They were tame ones. They were scrawny mostly and they hung around where white people were and traded some and begged liquor when they couldn't buy it. They weren't dangerous or even interesting. They didn't matter more'n mules or dogs or anything like that cluttering the landscape. It was the wild ones filled my mind, the fighting kind that lived the way they always had and went on the warpath, and made the government send out troops and sign treaties with them. Can't recall exactly what I thought they looked like, but they were big and fierce and dangerous and they liked to burn out homesteaders' cabins and tie people to wagon wheels and roast them alive over slow fires, and it took a brave man to go hunting them and look at them down the sights of his gun. Days I felt full of ginger I'd plan to grow up quick and be an Indian fighter. Late afternoon, before evening chores, I'd scout the countryside with the stick I used for a gun and when I'd spot a spray of red sumac poking out of a brush clump, I'd belly-it in the grass and creep to good cover and poke my gun through and draw my bead. I'd pull on the twig knob that was my trigger and watch careful, and sometimes I'd have to fire again and then I'd sit up and cut another notch on the stick. I had my private name for that. Making good Indians, I called it.

What's that got to do with those moccasins? Not much I guess. But I'm telling this my way. It's all part of what I remember when I sit back and study those moccasins a spell.

The year I'm talking about was a quiet one with the Sioux but there was some Indian trouble all right, along in the fall and a ways away, over in the Nez Percé country in Idaho. It started simple enough like those things often did. There was this band lived in a valley, maybe seven hundred of them all told, counting the squaws and young ones. Biggest safe estimate I heard was three hundred braves, fighting men I mean. Can't remember the name of the valley, though I should. My brother settled there. But I can recall the name of the chief. That sticks. Always will. Not the Indian

of it because that was a fancy mouthful. What it meant. Mountain
Elk. Not that exactly. Big-Deer-That-Walks-the-High-Places. Mountain Elk is close enough. But people didn't call him that. Most
Indians had a short name got tagged to them somehow and were
called by it. His was Jacob. Sounded funny first time I heard it
but not after I'd been hearing it a while.

As I say, this trouble started simple enough. We heard about it
from the telegraph operator at the settlement who took his meals
at our place. He picked up information relaying stuff through his
key. News of all kinds and even military reports. Seems settlers
began closing in around Jacob's valley and right soon began looking
at the land there. Had water which was important in that country.
Some of them pushed in and Jacob and his boys pushed them back
out. So complaints were being made and more people wanted to
move in, and talk went around that land like that was too good
for Indians anyway because they didn't use it right, the way white
men would, and when there was enough steam up a government
man went in to see Jacob. Suggested the band would be better off
living on some outside reservation. Get regular rations and have
an agent to look after them. No, Jacob said, he and his were doing
all right. Had been for quite a spell and expected to keep on doing
the same. Sent his thanks to the Great White Chief for thinking
about him but he wasn't needing any help. So after a while the
pressure was stronger and another government man went in. Offered
to buy the land and move the band in style to a reservation. No,
said Jacob, he and his children—he called them all his children
though he wasn't much past thirty himself—he and his children
liked their land and weren't interested in selling. Their fathers had
given up land too much in the past and been forced to keep wandering and had found this place when no one wanted it, and it was
good and they had stayed there. Most of them then living had been
born there and they wanted to die there too and that was that.

Well, the pressure went on building and there were ruckuses here
and yonder around the valley when some more settlers tried moving
in and a bunch of young braves got out of hand and killed a few.
So another government man went in, this time with a soldier escort.
He didn't bother with arguing or bargaining. He told Jacob the
Great White Chief had issued a decree and this was that the whole
tribe was to be moved by such and such a date. If they went peace-

able, transportation would be provided and good rations. If they kept on being stubborn, soldiers would come and make them move and that would be a bad business all around. Yes, said Jacob, that would be a bad business but it wouldn't be his doing. He and his children wouldn't have made the storm but they would stand up to it if it came. He had spoken and that was that.

So the days went along toward the date set which was in the fall I'm telling about. Jacob and his band hadn't made any preparations for leaving and the officer in charge of this whole operation thought Jacob was bluffing and he'd just call that bluff. He sent about four hundred soldiers under some colonel into the valley the week before the moving was supposed to happen, and Jacob and the others, the whole lot of them, just faded away from their village and off into the mountains behind the valley. The colonel sent scouting parties after them but couldn't make contact. He didn't know what to do in that situation so he set up camp there in the valley to wait and got real peeved when some of Jacob's Nez Percés slipped down out of the mountains one night and stampeded his stock. Finally he had his new orders and on the supposed moving day he carried them out. He put his men to destroying the village and they wiped it level to the ground, and the next morning early there was sharp fighting along his upper picket lines and he lost quite a few men before he could jump his troops into the field in decent force.

That was the beginning. The government wanted to open the valley for homesteading but couldn't without taking care of Jacob first. This colonel tried. He chased Jacob and his band into the mountains and thought overtaking them would be easy with the squaws and young ones slowing Jacob down, but Jacob had hidden them off somewhere and was traveling light with his braves. He led this colonel a fast run through rough country and caught him off watch a few times and whittled away at his troops every odd chance till this colonel had to turn back, not being outfitted for a real campaign. When he, that'd be this colonel, got back he found Jacob had beat him there and made things mighty unpleasant for those left holding the camp before slipping away again. About this time the government realized what it was up against and recalled the colonel and maybe whoever was his boss, and assigned a general—a brigadier—to the job and began mounting a real expedition.

We heard plenty about what happened after that, not just from the telegraph operator but from my brother who was busting the seams of his breeches those days and wanting to strike out for himself, and signed with the freighting company that got the contract carting supplies for the troops. He didn't see any of the fighting but he was close to it several times and he wrote home what was happening. Once a week he'd promised to write and did pretty well at it. He'd send his letters along to be posted whenever any of the wagons were heading back, and my mother would read them out to my father and me when they arrived. Remember best the fat one came after he reached the first camp and saw Jacob's valley. Took him two chunks of paper both sides to tell about it. Couldn't say enough about the thick green grass and the stream tumbling into a small lake and running quiet out again, and the good trees stepping up the far slopes and the mountains climbing on to the end of time all around. Made a man want to put his feet down firm on the ground and look out steady like the standing trees and stretch tall. Expect that's why my brother quit his job soon as the trouble was over and drove his own stakes there.

Yes. I know. I'm still a long way from those moccasins. I'm over in Idaho in Jacob's valley. But I get to remembering and then I get to forgetting maybe you're not interested in all the sidelines of what I started to tell you. I'll try to move it faster.

As I was saying, the government outfitted a real expedition to go after Jacob. A brigadier general and something like a thousand men. There's no point telling all that happened except that this expedition didn't accomplish much more than that first colonel and his men did. They chased Jacob farther and almost penned him a few times and killed a lot of braves and got wind of where his women and their kids were hidden, and forced him to move them farther into the mountains with them getting out just in time, not being able to carry much with them. But that wasn't catching Jacob and stopping him and his braves from carrying on their hop-skip-and-jump war against all whites in general and these troops in particular. Then a second general went in and about a thousand more soldiers with them and they had hard fighting off and on over a couple hundred miles and more, and the days drove on into deep winter and Jacob was licked. Not by the government and its soldiers and their guns. By the winter. He and his braves, what was left of them, had kept two generals and up to two thousand troops busy for four months fighting through parts of three states and then the winter licked him. He came to the second general under truce in what remained of his Chief's rig and took off his headdress and laid it on the ground and spoke. His children were scattered in the mountains, he said, and the cold bit sharp and they had few blankets and no food. Several of the small ones had been found frozen to death. From the moment the sun passed overhead that day he would fight no more. If he was given time to search for his children and bring them together he would lead them wherever the Great White Chief wished.

There. I'm closer to those moccasins now even though I'm still way over in Idaho. No. Think it was in western Montana where Jacob surrendered to that second general. Well, the government decided to ship these Nez Percés to the Dump, which was what people called the Indian Territory where they chucked all the tribes whose lands weren't just cut down but were taken away altogether. That meant Jacob and his children, all that was left of them, about three hundred counting the squaws and kids, would be loaded on a special train and sent along the railroad that ran through our settlement. These Nez Percé Indians would be passing within a stone's throw of our house and we would have a chance to see them at least through the windows and maybe, if there was need for switching, the train would stop and we would have a good look.

Wonder if you can scratch up any real notion what that meant to us boys around the settlement. To me maybe most of all. These weren't tame Indians. These were wild ones. Fighting Indians. About the fightingest Indians on record. Sure, the Sioux wiped out Custer. But there were a lot more Sioux than soldiers in that scuffle. These Nez Percés had held their own mighty well against a big chunk of the whole United States Army of those days. They were so outnumbered it had got past being even a joke. Any way you figured, it had been about one brave to six or seven soldiers and those braves hadn't been well armed at the start and had to pick up guns and ammunition as they went along from soldiers they killed. Some of them were still using arrows at the finish. I'm not being funny when I tell you they kept getting bigger and fiercer in my mind all the time I was hearing about that long running fight in the mountains. It was notches for Nez Percés I was cutting on

my stick now and the way I felt about them, even doing that took
nerve.

The day came the train was to pass through, some time late afternoon was the first report, and all of us settlement boys stayed near
the telegraph shack waiting. It was cold, though there wasn't much
snow around. We'd sneak into the shack where there was a stove,
till the operator was peeved at our chattering and shooed us out,
and I expect I did more than my share of the chattering because in
a way these were my Indians because my brother was connected with
the expedition that caught them. Don't think the other boys liked
how I strutted about that. Well, anyway, the sun went down and
we all had to scatter home for supper and the train hadn't come.
Afterwards some of us slipped back to the shack and waited some
more while the operator cussed at having to stick around waiting
for word, and one by one we were yanked away when our fathers
came looking for us, and still the train hadn't come.

It was some time past midnight and I'd finally got to sleep when
I popped up in bed at a hammering on the door. I looked into the
kitchen. Father was there in his nightshirt opening the outside door
and the operator was on the step cussing some more that he'd had
word the train was coming, would get there in half an hour, and
they'd have to switch it and hold it till the westbound night freight
went past. Father added his own cussing and pulled on his pants
and boots and heavy jacket and lit his lantern. By time he'd done
that I had my things on too. My mother was up then and objecting,
but my father thought some and shushed her. "Fool kid," he said,
"excited about Indians all the time. Do him good to see what thieving smelly things they are." So I went with him. The late moon
was up and we could see our way easy and I stayed in the shack
with the operator and my father went off to set his signal and tend
his switch. Certain enough, in about twenty minutes the train came
along and swung onto the second line of track and stopped.

The telegraph operator stepped out and started talking to a brakeman. I was scared stiff. I stood in the shack doorway and looked
at the train and I was shaking inside like I had some kind of fever.
It wasn't much of a train. Just an engine and little fuel car and four
old coaches. No caboose. Most trains had cabooses in those days
because they carried a lot of brakemen. Had to have them to wrangle the hand brakes. Expect the brakeman the operator was talking

to was the only one this train had. Expect that was why it was so late. I mean the railroad wasn't wasting any good equipment and any extra men on this train, and it was being shoved along slow when and as how between other trains.

I stood there shaking inside and the engine was wheezing some and the engineer and fireman were moving slow and tired around it, fussing with an oilcan and a tin of grease. That was the only sign of life I could see along the whole train. What light there was in the coaches, only one lantern lit in each, wasn't any stronger than the moonlight outside and that made the windows blank-like and I couldn't see through them. Except for the wheezing engine, that train was a tired and sleeping or dead thing on the track. Then I saw someone step down from the first coach and stretch and move into the moonlight. He was a soldier, a captain, and he looked tired and sleepy and disgusted with himself and the whole world. He pulled a cigar from a pocket and leaned against the side of the coach, lighting the cigar and blowing out smoke in a slow puff. Seeing him so lazy and casual, I stopped shaking and moved into the open and closer to the coach and shifted around trying to find an angle that would stop the light reflection on the windows and let me see in. Then I stopped still. The captain was looking at me. "Jee-sus," he said. "Why does everybody want to gawk at them? Even kids." He took a long drag on his cigar and blew a pair of fat smoke rings. "You must want to bad," he said. "Up so late. Go on in take a look." I stared at him, scared now two ways. I was scared to go in where those Indians were and scared not to, after he'd said I could and just about ordered I should. "Go ahead," he said. "They don't eat boys. Only girls. Only at lunchtime." And sudden I knew he was just making a tired joke, and it would be all right and I went up the steps to the front platform and peered in.

Indians. Fighting Indians. The fighting Nez Percés who had led United States soldiers a bloody chase through the mountains of three states. The big and fierce redmen who had fought many times their own number of better armed soldiers to a frequent standstill in the high passes. And they weren't big and they weren't fierce at all. They were huddled figures on the coach seats, two to a seat down the twin rows, braves and squaws and young ones alike, all dusty and tired and hunched together at the shoulders in drowsy silence or sprawled apart over the window sills and seat arms in sleep. In the dim light they looked exactly like the tame Indians I'd seen, and they seemed to shrink and shrivel even more as I looked at them and there was no room in me for any emotion but disappointment, and when I noticed the soldiers sleeping in the first seats close to me I sniffed to myself at the silly notion any guards might be needed on that train. There wasn't the slightest hint of danger anywhere around. Being on that train was no different from being off it except that it was being on a stopped train and not being outside on the ground. It didn't even take any particular nerve to do what I did when I started walking down the aisle.

The only way I know to describe it is that I was in a sort of trance of disappointment and I wanted to see everything and I went straight down the aisle looking all around me. And those Indians acted like I wasn't there at all. Those that were awake. Each of them had his eyes fixed somewhere, maybe out a window or at the floor or just at some point ahead, and didn't move them. They knew I was there. I could tell that. A feeling. A little crawling on my skin. But they wouldn't look at me. They were somehow off away in a place all their own and they weren't going to let me come near getting in there with them or let me know they even saw me outside of it. Except one. He was a young one, a boy like me only a couple of years younger, and he was scrooged down against a sleeping brave—maybe his father—and his small eyes, solid black in the dim light, looked at me, and his head turned slow to keep them on me as I went past and I could sense them on me as I went on till the back of the seat shut them off.

Still in that funny trance I went into the next coach and through it and to the third coach and on to the last. Each was the same. Soldiers slumped in sleep, and the huddled figures of the Indians in different pairings and sprawled positions but the effect the same and then at the end of the last car I saw him. He had a seat to himself and the headdress with its red-tipped feathers hung from the rack above the seat. He was asleep with an arm along the window sill, his head resting on it. I stopped and stared at him and the low light from the lantern near the end of the coach shone on the coppery texture of his face and the bare skin of his chest where it showed through the fallen-apart folds of the blanket wrapped around him. I stared at him and I felt cheated and empty inside. Even Jacob wasn't big or fierce. He wasn't as big as my father. He was short.

Maybe broad and rather thick in the body but not much, even that way. And his face was quiet and—well, the only word I can ever think of is peaceful. I stared at him and then I started a little because he wasn't sleeping. One eyelid had twitched a bit. All at once I knew he was just pretending. He was pretending to be asleep so he wouldn't have to be so aware of the stares of anyone coming aboard to gawk at him. And sudden I felt ashamed and I hurried to the back platform to leave the train, and in the shadow there I stumbled over a sleeping soldier and heard him rousing himself as I scrambled down the steps.

That started what happened afterwards. Expect I'm really to blame for it all. Mean to say it probably wouldn't have happened if I hadn't been hurrying and wakened that soldier. He didn't know I was there. He was too full of sleep at first and didn't know what had awakened him. While I stayed in the dark shadow by the coach, afraid to go out into the moonlight, he stood up and stretched and came down the steps without noticing me and went around the end of the train toward the wider shadow on the other side, and as he went I saw him pulling a bottle out of a pocket. I felt safe again and started away and turned to look back, and the light was just right for me to see some movement inside through the window by the last seat. Jacob was standing up. All kinds of wild notions poured through my mind and I couldn't move and then he was emerging through the rear door on to the platform and I wasn't exactly scared because I wasn't conscious of feeling anything at all except that I couldn't move. Time seemed to hang there motionless around me. Then I realized he wasn't doing anything and wasn't going to do anything. He wasn't even aware of me or if he was I was without meaning for him and he had seen me and dismissed me. He was standing quiet by the rear railing and his blanket was left inside and the cold night air was blowing against his bare chest above his leather breeches but he didn't appear to notice that. He was looking back along the double iron line of the track toward the tiny point of light that was my father's lantern by the west switch. He stood there, still and quiet, and I stayed where I was and watched him and he did not move and stood there looking far along the westward track and that was what we were doing, Jacob and I, when the soldier came back around the end of the train.

Thinking about it later I couldn't blame that soldier too much.

Maybe had orders to keep the Indians in their seats or not let them on the rear platform or something like that. Probably was worried about drinking on duty and not wanting to be caught letting anything slip with the tang plain on his breath. Could be too he'd taken on more than he could handle right. Anyway he was surprised and mad when he saw Jacob standing there. He reached first and pulled some object off the platform floor and when he had it I could see it was his rifle. Then he jumped up the steps and started prodding Jacob with the rifle barrel toward the door. Jacob looked at him once and away and turned slow and started to move and the soldier must have thought Jacob moved too slow because he swung the gun around to use the stock end like a club and smack Jacob on the back. I couldn't see exactly what happened then because the scuffle was too sudden and quick but there was a blur of movement and the soldier came tumbling off the platform to the ground near me and the gun landed beside him. He was so mad he tripped all over himself getting to his feet and scrabbling for the gun and he whipped it up and hip-aimed it at Jacob and tried to fire it and the breech mechanism jammed some way and he clawed at it to make it work.

And Jacob stood there on the platform, still and quiet again, looking down at the soldier with bare breast broadside to the gun. I could see his eyes bright and black in the moonlight and the shining on the coppery firmness of his face and he did not move and of a sudden I realized he was waiting. He was waiting for the bullet. He was expecting it and waiting for it and he would not move. And I jumped forward and grabbed the rifle barrel and pulled hard on it. "No," I shouted. "Not like that." And the soldier stumbled and fell against me and both of us went down and someone was yelling at us and when I managed to get to my feet I saw it was the captain and the soldier was up too, standing stiff and awkward at attention. "Bloody Indian," the soldier said. "Trying to get away." The captain looked up and saw Jacob standing there and jerked a bit with recognizing who it was. "He was not," I said. "He was just standing there." The captain looked at the soldier and shook his head slow. "Jee-sus," he said. "You'd have shot that one." The captain shook his head again like he was disgusted and tired of everything and maybe even of living. "What's the use," he said. He flipped a thumb at the soldier. "Pick up your gun and get on forward." The soldier hurried off and the captain looked at Jacob and Jacob looked down at him, still and quiet and not moving a muscle. "There's fools of every color," the captain said and Jacob's eyes brightened a little as if he understood and I expect he did because I'd heard he could speak English when he wanted to. The captain wiped a hand across his face. "Stand on that damned platform as long as you want," he said. He remembered he had a cigar in his other hand and looked at it and it was out and he threw it on the ground and swung around and went toward the front of the train again, and I wanted to follow him but I couldn't because now Jacob was looking at me.

He looked down at me what seemed a long time and then he motioned at me and I could tell he wanted me to step out further into the moonlight. I did and he leaned forward to peer at me. He reached a hand out toward me, palm flat and down, and said something in his own language and for a moment I was there with him in the world that was different and beyond my own everyday world and then he swung away and stepped to stand by the rear railing again and I knew I was outside again, outside of his mind and put away and no more to him than any other object around. He was alone there looking far down the track and it sank slow and deep in me that he was looking far past the tiny light point of my father's lantern, far on where the lone track ran straight along the slow-rising reaches of distance into the horizon that led past the longest vision at last to the great climbing mountains. He was looking back along the iron trail that was taking him and his children away from a valley that would make a man want to put his feet firm on the earth and stretch tall and was taking them to an unknown place where they would not be themselves any longer but only some among many of many tribes and tongues and all dependent on the bounty of a forgetful government. It wasn't an Indian I was seeing there any more. It was a man. It wasn't Jacob, the tamed chief that even foolish kids could gawk at. It was Mountain Elk, the Big-Deer-That-Walks-the-High-Places and he was big, really big, and he was one meant to walk the high places.

He stood there looking down the track and the westbound night freight came rumbling out of the east and strained past, and he stood there watching it go westward along the track and his train began to move, creeping eastward slow and feeling forward, and I watched it go and long as I could see him he was standing there, still and quiet, looking straight out along the back trail.

Well. I've taken you to where I was headed. It's only a hop now to those moccasins. I tried to tell the other boys about it the next day and likely boasted and strutted in the telling and they wouldn't believe me. Oh, they'd believe I saw the Indians all right. Had to. The telegraph operator backed my saying I was there. Even that I went aboard. But they wouldn't believe the rest. And because they wouldn't believe me I had to keep pounding it at them, telling it over and over. Expect I was getting to be mighty unpopular. But Jacob saved me even though I never saw him again. There was a day a bunch of us boys were playing some game or other back of the telegraph shack and sudden we realized someone had come up from somewhere and was watching us. An Indian. Seemed to be just an ordinary everyday sort of tame Indian. But he was looking us over intent and careful and he picked me and came straight to me. He put out a hand, palm flat and down, and said something to me in his Indian talk and pointed far off to the east and south and back again to me and reached inside the old blanket he had fastened around him with a belt and took out a dirty cloth-wrapped package and laid it at my feet and went away and faded out of sight around the shack. When I unrolled that package there were these moccasins.

Funny thing. I never wanted to go around telling my story to the other boys again. Didn't need to. Whether they believed or not wasn't important any more. I had those moccasins. In a way they made me one of Jacob's children. Remembering that has helped me sometimes in tough spots.

My Town

ASK PARDON, gents, but heard you talking. Seems a strange boasting. About cemeteries. The boothill brand. Now in my town. . . .

Me? Nobody much. Just a lonesome passing through, plain and peaceable. Always get to wondering when talk swings around to towns and how many folks in each catch lead poisoning awearing their outdoor boots. Always wonder why burying's cause for boasting. About a town's toughness that is. Seems silly. Take my town now. Not much of a place. But the toughest town its size this side the devil's fireplace. More shooting there than in all your towns together. But no folks being planted. All enjoying life too much.

One man's responsible. No. Two. Two men. Have to divvy it between them but one's a mite more responsible than the other. That one's Samuel J. L. Claggett. Our sheriff. Sandburr we call him. Sandburr Sam Claggett. Started calling him that a time back because when he goes after a man he sticks to the trail like a sandburr to a mule's tail. Come to think of it he hasn't done much trailing for quite a stretch now. No need to. Folks in my town behave. Behave sensible that is. No one wants Old Sandburr sticking to his trail. Now a man like that can do things with a six-gun you wouldn't believe not having seen him do them. He's long and he's lean and kind of double-jointed all over and he's about the gentlest and kindliest man you'd bump into in a month's riding. And the toughest.

Maybe not quite that last. Wilbur Morriston Burton is plenty tough too. He's the other man. Black Ace he's called. Black Ace Burton. Can see you've heard of him. Most folks have. Maybe

don't know the Wilbur Morriston part but when they hear the
Black Ace they tumble. Probably wonder why tales about him
aren't running any more. That's because he's living in my town,
plain and peaceable like the rest of us. Used to be about the fastest
gunfighter ever to hit these territories. Still is. Fast as Old Sandburr
himself. Still doing plenty shooting. But not the kind you'd hear
about. . . .

Yep. All this starts the day Black Ace rides into town. He rides
in, big and brawny on his horse with that black stubble scratching
around his chin, and looks the place over and doesn't think much
of it. He meanders into Willie Lord's saloon and soaks up a few.
Reaches in his pocket where he carries his silver and the pocket's
empty. Bottom frayed out. Cusses some and tells Willie wait a minute he'll go get some cash. Willie's heard the cussing and seen the
two big guns hanging down his flanks so Willie says forget it, the
drinks are on the house. No, Black Ace says, he's not particular
about some kind of debts but a drinking debt is one he always
honors. He meanders out and looks the place over again and meanders into the little frame bank building. Tells the clerk there he
needs some cash and his name being Black Ace he figures he won't
have much trouble getting it. The clerk hears the name and looks
around wild and sees there's no one else handy and drops quiet in
a faint on the floor. Black Ace is a mite peeved at having to go
around behind into the wire cage himself but does so and scoops
up what he wants. Meanders back to the saloon and pays Willie and
out to his horse and rides on. It's maybe twenty minutes later the
clerk has come to and run to the sheriff's office and waked Sandburr
Sam out of his early afternoon nap and Sandburr has strapped on
his own guns and hit the trail.
    Black Ace is easing along casual when he sees Sandburr's dust
back along a loop. Hell, he tells himself, being as there's only one
of them the only way he can have fun out of this is make it a race.
He larrups his horse and skitters off into the hills and Old Sandburr,
catching the scent, swings his quirt and skitters after him. They
have themselves a time for maybe two hours, tearing up the landscape, working deep into the hills, where the big rocks climb, playing hide-and-seek all over the rough ground. So busy skittering
around they don't know they're not the only two-legged critters in

the neighborhood. Black Ace can't shake Sandburr and finally gets tired chasing around. Enough's enough, he tells himself. Too bad having to knock over a man can stick after him like that but he can't play games all day. Picks a spot and drops off his horse and waits where he figures Old Sandburr'll have to come at him straight and it'll be a square scuffle. But Sandburr's an old hand at this kind of business too. He's stopping now and again to listen. Notes the other horse has quit running so he drops off his horse and slips in among the boulders on foot. Moves so quiet Black Ace can't hear him and Black Ace gets restless and slips in among the boulders himself. Same thing. He moves so quiet Old Sandburr can't hear him. Hard to believe, but those two are so eternal damned good at slipping around quiet they spend maybe half an hour in and around those boulders without once tagging each other. Both get to thinking the same. That the other's gone. Both holster their guns and start back where they left their horses. Sandburr's up higher among the boulders and tries to short cut over a big one and skids and comes coasting on his rump and bounces and lands flat on his back not ten feet behind Black Ace, who whirls quick and there are two mighty surprised men a-staring at each other in a hollow among those boulders. Old Sandburr is stretched out spread-eagle looking along his own length and over his boot toes at Black Ace and Black Ace is looking down over those same boot toes at Sandburr's lean old face. They're caught like that for a second of surprise and in another tiny tick of time those two, maybe the fastest gunfighters ever slapped leather, might be blazing at each other but in that same second there's a wapping sound and an arrow bounces off a boulder close to Black Ace and lots of whoops whistle in the air and more arrows are wapping around and in a flash of movement that's a dead heat for them those two maybe the fastest gunfighters ever wore boots are showing their skill in another kind of action. They're side by side behind boulders and they're talking back to the arrows in a right hearty gunshot tune.

It isn't really a fair fight. There's only twenty-three of the redskins. Could be why Old Sandburr and Black Ace never talk much about that scuffle. Doesn't take them long. There's a moment when a redskin pokes up quick way over to the right and Sandburr sights him out the corner of his right eye and flicks his right-hand gun around without seeming to aim and that redskin rubs a dead nose in the dirt. "Nice," Black Ace says. "Very nice." There's another moment when another redskin behind a rock gets careless and lets a foot show a fraction of a second and Black Ace nicks it and that makes the redskin jump and his head bobs up about two inches over the rock and down again and has a hole in it when it goes down. "Pretty," Old Sandburr says. "Very pretty."

They're really beginning to enjoy themselves when the four redskins left alive fade off glad to go. Black Ace turns his guns up and blows the smoke out the barrels and looks at Sandburr and Sandburr does the same and looks at him and they both grin. But Black Ace's grin dwindles. "Disappointed," he says. "Saw you miss one. When he peeked around that flat rock there. Missed by two feet. Saw that other rock beside there chip where your bullet hit." Old Sandburr just chuckles. "Certain it chipped," he says. "Meant it to hit there. Had to bounce it off that second rock to get it around behind the first one and drill him where it'd count." Black Ace grunts. "No," he says. "I'm the only man can pull a stunt like that. Maybe you tried but your angle was wrong." Old Sandburr chuckles again. "Wrong from where you're standing," he says. "Not from here. There's a dead redskin behind that rock. Shot through the left side about over the fourth rib."

He leads the way over and he's right even to the rib and Black Ace looks at him long. "So there's two of us," Black Ace says. "Too bad I've got to kill you." And Old Sandburr just chuckles again. "Try to, you mean," he says. "But that reminds me. How were we when this little interruption interrupted?" Black Ace is reloading his guns. "You were patting the ground with your backside," he says. "Well, how'll we do this? Pace it off and arrange a signal?" Old Sandburr is reloading his guns too. "No," he says. "Maybe I'm old-fashioned but want things like this done right. Get over where you were when I landed." Black Ace is puzzled but does as he's told. Sandburr finds his own spot and lays down flat on his back and spraddles out his arms. "This the way I was?" he says and Black Ace nods. "All right," Sandburr says. "See that bird on that bush? When he pops off that branch we'll both start fanning."

Black Ace isn't anywhere near grinning now. "You mean," he says, "you're agoing to lie there and give me the advantage?" Old Sandburr isn't near grinning either. "Certain I do," he snaps. "This is the way I was." Black Ace is beginning to sweat some though the weather's cool. "Maybe you don't know," he says. "I'm Black Ace Burton." Sandburr just shrugs his shoulders there on the ground and Black Ace sweats more. "You've heard of me haven't you?" he says almost plaintive. "Certain I have," Sandburr snaps. "Don't care if you're Old Nick himself." Sweat is standing out plain on Black Ace's forehead. "But I'll drill you," he says. "You won't have a chance scrabbling against the dirt." Old Sandburr shrugs again. "Maybe I won't," he says. "Again maybe I might. I'm right pert with a gun too. But if I go I'll go right. Keep your eye on that bird. It's getting restless."

Yep. There they are, Sandburr flat on his back and Black Ace standing facing him and the bird is twiddling its feathers like it might take off at any time and sweat runs down Black Ace's face and he groans and sudden he reaches both hands high up over his head. "Can't do it!" he shouts. "You hell-scorched old he-buzzard! Can't kill you! Not like that!" Old Sandburr pushes up till he is leaning on one elbow. "Son," he says, "are you surrendering to me?" Black Ace looks surprised and then thoughtful. "Reckon I am," he says. "Can't see any other way out of this, you being so damn stubborn." It's Sandburr's turn to look thoughtful. "Can't take you in," he says. "Can't lock up a man won't draw because he thinks it ain't square. Let's mosey to town and you hand back the money and we'll call it quits." Black Ace lowers his hands and hooks them in his belt. "No," he says. "Used part for a drinking debt. Need the rest for more the same till I get me another stake. Got it on the strength of my name, and not giving it up." Old Sandburr snorts. "Who's being stubborn now?" he says. Gets to his feet and scratches an ear. "Only one way out of that. You sign a note for the money and that's still using the strength of your name only a bit different way and maybe the same because you being you the bank won't dare refuse it. I'll put you on the payroll as a deputy till you've squared it off." Black Ace's jaw drops. "Me?" he says. "Me be a sheriff's man?" Sandburr snorts again. "Certain. It ain't so bad. Another thing. You'll promise me not to use those guns on any man 'less I give the word. Just till this is squared of course." Black Ace snaps his jaw tight. "No," he says. "Now you're on your feet let's shoot this out fair." But Old Sandburr flops quick again down on his back. "Shoot it," he says. "But it's got to be this way." There they are, Sandburr down and staring up and Black Ace up and staring

down, and sweat starts again on Black Ace's forehead and he can't
see any other way out, not with him being what he is and this old
he-buzzard what he is too. "All right," Black Ace Burton says and
the words are bitter on his tongue and his face is long and disgusted
under the black stubble all the while he and Sandburr find their
horses and start toward town.

They jog along and Sandburr notes that disgusted look and worries over it and after a time has an idea. He swoops down one
side his saddle and picks up a plump little pebble. He holds the
pebble so Black Ace can see it and tosses it in the air ahead. Black
Ace watches it rise in an arc and start to fall and sudden gets the
notion. There's a blur of movement maybe an eagle might catch
but nothing else could, and a gun is in his right hand and it blasts
and that pebble goes spinning crazy before it hits the ground. Black
Ace drops the gun back in its holster and looks at Sandburr and
Old Sandburr looks at him and they both begin to grin and they
both hop off their horses and gather a handful of pebbles each and
mount. Whenever Black Ace thinks Sandburr may be off guard he
tosses out a pebble and Sandburr gives that funny little wriggle of
his and a gun seems to come out of the air into his hand and the
pebble takes a beating. The same happens whenever Sandburr
tosses a pebble and the two of them jog along enjoying themselves.
First time either one has come on a man good as himself and they
get to showing off like a pair of colts. Black Ace gets tricky and
whams a pebble twice before it hits ground and whams it again
there before it stops rolling and Old Sandburr lifts his eyebrows
and worries a moment. Then he smiles and holds up two fingers
and when Black Ace tosses two pebbles at once Old Sandburr drops
his reins and wriggles and both his guns show and he hits both
pebbles simultaneous. They jog along, grinning foolish at each
other, and by time they reach town each one knows he's found a
man he'd stand back to back with against the whole eternal damned
world. . . .

Yep. That's the way it starts. Black Ace fits into town in no time
to bother over. Rest of us are a mite upset at first having him
around but get over that. Find he's a quiet soft-spoken gent a lot
like Old Sandburr long as nobody rubs him the wrong way. Only
thing that shows the toughness inside is that black stubble around

his chin. Doesn't shave it because can't shave it. Razors nick too
fast working at it. Can't keep it trimmed close even with scissors.
Carries a small pair of wire cutters and uses them once a week.
Sunday mornings.

With him there as deputy folks behave even better'n before.
Town's quiet except for an hour each afternoon right after Sandburr's nap. He'll come out his office and look up Black Ace and
the two'll go into the big old barn standing empty behind Willie
Lord's and close the doors and for about an even sixty minutes
there'll be queer noises and bursts of shooting coming out the place.
Then the two'll walk out, grinning foolish at each other, and their
holsters'll have a scorched look from having hot guns dropped back
in them. Things drift like that till the day this smoke-eating young
gun toter hits town.

He's built like a young bull and has his hair cropped close over
a hard hatless head and he wears two big guns low down along his
flanks with the holster tips tied tight. Everything about him speaks
toughness till you study him some and see he's younger than he
seems and he's worked long to get that tough look and it ain't full
natural yet. He's a maverick hankers to be a gunfighter and wants
to get a reputation quick by knocking off somebody with a big name.
That's plain soon as he struts into Willie Lord's and starts talking.
"Hear Black Ace Burton's hanging around here," he says to Willie.
"That right?" Willie nods and points where Black Ace is sitting at
a table dealing himself poker hands that always somehow give him
the ace of spades. This young maverick squints his eyes at Black
Ace and snorts and turns to the four-five rest of us there. "Name's
Poison Pete," he says. "Poison Pete Humphrey. My folks gave me
the Pete but gave myself the Poison. Know why? Because I'm poison
to any galoot whose face I don't like and I'll be dogdamned if I see
anything to like about that black-whiskered baboon over there
likely cheating himself with those cards."

Black Ace looks up, takes in this Poison Pete, looks back at his
cards. "You hear me?" says Poison Pete throwing his words direct
at Black Ace. "That face of yours makes my trigger finger itchy."
Black Ace looks up again, breathes hard, gets a hold on himself.
"Don't like it myself," he says mild. "But do the best I can with it."
Poison Pete feels he has the edge and starts crowding. "Bet even
your mother couldn't stand that face. Probably took off in a hurry

after one look." Black Ace crumbles a card in his hand then catches himself and straightens it out careful. "Matter of fact," he says, "she did." Poison Pete is pushing in hard now. "Bet she mixed with a lot of men to produce a scrambled-up phiz like that. Bet you don't even know who your father was." Black Ace stacks the whole deck together and rips it across in half and sets the torn deck on the table. "Matter of fact," he says still mild, "you're right. But never worry who my father was. Just worry who I am myself." Poison Pete throws about for what to try next. "Those guns you're awearing," he says. "Bet just for show. Bet you don't even know which end a bullet comes out."

Black Ace stiffens and stands up. He's had himself and his folks mean-talked. He's taken that. But this young maverick has talked low about his guns and that's one thing he can't take. He stalks to the swinging doors and pushes them wide. "Sandburr!" he bellows. "Sandburr you he-buzzard! Get along down here fast!" And up the street in the sheriff's office Old Sandburr stirs out of his early afternoon nap and has his guns buckled on before he's blinked the sleep out his eyes and starts dogtrotting toward the saloon. He comes in puffing and there's this Poison Pete strutting by the bar thinking he's made Black Ace Burton crawl and there's Black Ace standing by the door chewing a knuckle. "Sandburr," says Black Ace, "ain't asked you a favor yet. Asking one now. Let me off that promise just a little part one second so's I can eliminate this young nuisance that's been braying around here like an ornery jackass." Old Sandburr looks at this Poison Pete who's thinking sudden maybe now he'll have a shooting scuffle after all and is dropping into a kind of crouch with his head thrust forward and his arms out in half-circles with the hands clawed ready by his gun handles. Sandburr shakes his head like he can't quite believe what he sees and Black Ace speaks up again. "Sandburr," he says, "this jackass has been prodding me something fierce. Look at him. Ever see a self-respecting gunfighter take a position like that?" And then Black Ace says what maybe he's never said to another man. "Please," he says. "Please, Sandburr, let me kill him. Cart the carcass away myself so you won't have to bother any." And Old Sandburr looks at Poison Pete and something tickles around in his mind and he soars up somewhere to the heights of pure genius.

Yep. That's when our Sandburr does it. He prowls forward and pads soft in a circle around this Poison Pete, looking at him from every side. "Think you're good with those guns, eh?" he says and Poison Pete snarls in his throat and tries to look tougher and glares around. "All right," Sandburr says, "we'll give you a chance to prove it. Come along outside." He heads straight for the door and tips a wink at Black Ace and Black Ace begins to get him and swings to follow. Poison Pete paws the floor some and snarls in his throat again but there's nothing for him to do but follow too, which he does muttering how he'll take them both on and fill them so full of lead it'll take three men to lift them into coffins. No need to mention the rest of us follow too. Man ain't born yet wouldn't.

Sandburr leads around back to that old barn and pushes the doors wide and then we're all inside. Not much in there. Pile of old boards and a couple weird contraptions and plenty of space. Sandburr picks the broadest board he can find and sets it upright at the other end of the barn. Takes a piece of chalk out a pocket and sketches quick on the board the outline of a man. Draws a little heart in the right place and comes to join the rest of us by the open doors. Poison Pete is looking disgusted but Black Ace is grinning. He has Old Sandburr complete now and is ready to play it the way he's likely the only man could. "Ain't much of an artist," he says. "Forgot to give that thing a face." He doesn't seem to more than shrug his shoulders a little but his guns are in his hands and both aroaring and sudden two holes for eyes and two close together for a nose and four in a line for a mouth appear on the board spaced just right in the chalk-line head. There's a gulp from Poison Pete but Old Sandburr just chuckles. "Too grim for my liking," he says. He gives that little wriggle and his guns are in his hands and both blast once and two more holes appear just tipping the mouth on each end so it seems to turn up in a kind of grin. Poison Pete gulps again. But he's game and isn't going to be bluffed. He pulls a gun and he's fair fast but you can see him doing it and he blasts at the board and a hole shows in the middle of the figure there. "Belly button," he says. But Black Ace just shakes his head sorrowful. "Ain't polite," he says, "to make that chalk fellow naked like that. Reckon he needs clothes." Out of somewhere one of Black Ace's guns, reloaded, is in his right hand and his left hand fans the hammer so fast the six shots are one long blast and across the middle of the figure where the belly button was appears a line of holes making a belt.

Poison Pete seems to shrink some. He's forgetting to work at being big and tough. He chews a lip and shakes himself back to size. "If you're through playing games," he snarls, "let's get—" But Old Sandburr has fixed him with a cold eye. "Boy," Sandburr says, "me and Black Ace has a regular date each day about this time to amuse ourselves here. You'll wait and if you're still of a mind then reckon I'll have to let Black Ace take care of you." He beckons to Black Ace and the two of them take a stand with their backs to that board figure the length of the barn away. "Willie," Sandburr says, "when you feel the urge call 'shoot.'" Willie Lord bugs his eyes and sudden starts to say "shoot" and gets out the "shoo" part but hasn't finished forming the "oot" part before Old Sandburr and Black Ace have whirled and each has a gun in a hand and those guns have blasted and a hole shows dead center in that chalk heart, and if you peer sharp you can see it's a bit bigger than one bullet would make.

"Yippee!" yells Old Sandburr. "That one's aready for burying! Acey son, I've thought up a new one. Can you follow me on this?" His other gun's popped into his other hand and both start blasting and holes appear in the lower left corner of the board forming a neat letter R. Black Ace scratches his head with the barrel of the gun in his right hand and looks puzzled. Then a grin spreads through his black stubble and his other gun pops into his other hand and both start blasting and a neat letter E shows next to the R. Then the two of them are at it, reloading and firing in rapid succession and alternating on the letters. In maybe a minute they've spelled it out: R E S T I N P E A C E. And then the two of them really cut loose.

No sense telling all they do. Nobody'd believe didn't see it. They do things like setting up a couple small boards with nails started in them and racing each other driving those nails clear in. They do things like fastening calendar sheets on the wall and taking turns with one calling out numbers in crazy order and the other shooting out those numbers as called. They do things like setting up a grooved plank on a slant with a nest of pool balls in a box at the top with a little catch door on the box with a string tied to it so each time the string's pulled a ball pops out and rolls quick down the groove. Idea is for one to take the string and yank it whenever he has a mind and the other stands there guns holstered and the instant a ball shows tries to draw and smack it before it reaches the floor. Old Sandburr knocks his balls off one after the other and not a one gets past the three-foot mark down the groove. Black Ace takes his stand and grins a bit devilish. "Aiming for a record," he says and be eternal damned if he don't knock all but his last ball off ahead of the two-foot mark and that last one, which he misses, just knicking it a slice, he smacks with another bullet at about the three-and-a-half-foot mark and is just peeved enough to keep it popping all over the barn floor till he's emptied both guns.

They do things like that and others a man wouldn't dare tell less he be named a liar till their gun barrels glow red and you can smell the scorched leather of their holsters and finally Old Sandburr calls enough. He sort of shakes himself back into realizing the rest of us are still there. Poison Pete is leaning limp against a support post. All the poison's long since oozed out of him. Now he isn't trying to look and be tough, he's a likable young galoot who has been shook so far down inside him he can't stand alone. Old Sandburr fixes him with a cold eye. "Seem to recall," he says, "some unfinished business was worrying you some."

Poison Pete pushes out from his post and fights with himself till he can stand without wobbling. He stares at Old Sandburr and he stares at Black Ace and at last he gets his hanging lower jaw under control so he can close his mouth. Yep. Poison Pete makes his play then and it's a good one. He pulls out his guns slow and easy so no one can mistake what he's doing and he looks down at his hands and the guns in them and he shakes his head and bends and lays the guns on the floor and straightens and walks over till he's in front of Black Ace. "Mr. Black Ace," he says, "I know when I'm beat, and not just in shooting. Can't call that face of yours handsome but ready to admit things about it are mighty impressive. Now I've said my sorries and I'm ready to do anything you say might square my foolishness."

Black Ace looks at him and scratches at his stubble and right then Black Ace does some soaring of his own. Looks over at Old Sandburr and grins at what he's remembering and turns back to Poison Pete. "Son," he says, "there is something you can do. You can sign on as deputy with me and Sandburr here." Poison Pete jumps back

a step. "Me?" he says. "Me be a sheriff's man?" Black Ace just grins.
"It ain't so bad," he says. "Another thing. You'll promise me not
to use those guns of yours on any man 'less I say you can." Poison
Pete twists his mouth like he's tasting bitter and throws his mind at
this proposition and can't see any way out because he's give his word.
He gulps and nods his head and his face is long and disgusted. But
Old Sandburr and Black Ace note that disgusted look and close in
on him. Sandburr is on one side. "You'll do plenty of shooting,
son," he's saying. "You've got the makings. Just a kink or two in
that draw of yours. Take them out easy. Just tuck your elbows in
and glide up smooth and curl your—" And Black Ace is on the other
side. "Only thing wrong with your aiming," he's saying, "is your
hand's too tense. Hold firm without squeezing on the butt and flip
your barrel like it was—" And Poison Pete is bouncing his head
from one to the other, young and eager and with a new kind of pride
sprouting in him. . . .

That's my town. That's all you need know about it. Because it's
only a few weeks and Poison Pete is living there like the rest of us,
plain and peaceable, and giving Old Sandburr and Black Ace a run
for their money in that empty barn. Might say he leaves the student
class and graduates the day he shows those two a stunt he's worked
up all himself. Does it with empty whiskey bottles. Sets them on
their sides on a rack he's made with the necks pointing toward him.
Backs off. Gives a little combination wriggle and shrug that's his
own brand now and a gun's in his hand and he works swift down the
line of bottles sending his bullets right through the open necks without nicking the glass and blowing out the bottoms of the bottles behind. Sandburr looks at Black Ace and Black Ace looks at Sandburr
and both lift their eyebrows and both grin so foolish you'd think
they'd done it themselves. And that's the way things are going till
the day this big-jawed rustler with red hair hits town.

He's tired and dusty and full of meanness because he's had a hard
three days shaking a posse down southwest somewhere. Too many
of them for him to shoot it out so he had to scat and that's made
him edgy and looking for a scuffle to give him a feeling of being
back to size again. Climbs off his horse and loosens the two big guns
in the low-cut holsters he wears kind of high on his hips which is
his style. Stalks into Willie Lord's and rakes his throat with straight

stuff and looks around for a likely. Misses Black Ace and Old Sandburr playing casino at a side table. Sees Poison Pete inspecting pictures of tooled-leather boots in a mail order catalogue at the other
end of the bar. Spots Pete's two guns and licks his lips. "Sonny boy,"
he says, "that's a lot of fancy hadware you're packing." Pete looks
at him peeved at the sonny-boy business, catches himself, grins pleasant. "Not so fancy," he says. "Just plain ordinary everyday sort of
guns." This rustler sticks his big jaw out. "Rawhide Red, that's
me," he says. "Tough as rawhide with a liking to see red blood running. Where I come from we don't let little boys run around wearing guns like that." Pete holds tight to his temper. "Good notion,"
he says. "They might get hurt." This rustler ain't tired any more.
He's scenting what he wants. "Right," he says. "So if they don't
show they can use them, we pop our little boys over our knees and
paddle their cute little backsides." He pushes out his jaw till
it's jutting like a rock ledge. So busy thinking Pete's quietness
means he's scared he doesn't notice the sound of a couple of chairs
scraping the floor. Is some surprised when a long lean kind of
double-jointed man and a brawny black-stubbled other one prowl
up and pad around him in circles looking at him from all sides.
"Think you're good with those guns, eh?" says Black Ace Burton.
"We'll just give you a chance to prove it," says Old Sandburr Sam
Claggett. "Come along outside. You too, Petey son. While you're at
it bring along some empty whiskey bottles. . . ."

Yep. That's my town.

Old Anse

OLD ANSE BIRKITT sat on the worn log doorsill of his cabin and looked down the slope and across the creek and watched Sid Jenkins and the stringy woman Sid called his wife pile their few belongings in a rickety buckboard. The morning sun was warm on his face and he wriggled his old bare feet in the warm dust of his dooryard and watched the Jenkinses drive away without a glance back at the shack in which they had lived for better than four years. *Footloose,* he thought. *Would be the first to go. . . .*

The sun made its circuit overhead and dropped into the mountains behind the cabin and in the morning Old Anse sat in his doorway and looked down and across and watched workmen pull apart the plank building that had been Bartlett's store. He scrooged in a pocket of his faded jeans and found a remnant of tobacco quid and gnawed off a small chew. He watched John Bartlett fuss about and shout directions as the workmen loaded the planks on a part of flatbed wagons. *Greedy,* he thought. *Got a price for it and carting it away too. . . .*

The sun climbed past noon and what had been Bartlett's store building went away on the wagons along the lower valley road and darkness swept out of the mountains and Old Anse lit his lantern and prepared his evening meal. In the morning he sat on his log doorsill and looked down and across the creek at what remained of the little roadfork town and watched the people departing. The flies were bad and he slapped at them and let the sun's warmth soak into his old bones and watched the people go, family after family in wagons or buggies and the Crutchleys with their stairstep line of kids on foot and the blacksmith with his anvil and heavy tools on an

oxcart and the schoolmaster on horseback with saddlebags full of
books. The sun swung on its high arc and the afternoon rays beat
against the back of the cabin and across the creek on the almost empty
town and when darkness took it the only other light in the valley
outside the cabin was in the big frame house rising above the others
on the town side of the creek. Old Anse stood in his doorway and
studied the yellow-patch windows of the big house across and almost
level with his cabin. He blew out his lantern and shed his jeans and
lay on his bunk. *Waiting to be the last of them,* he thought. *But
he'll go like all the rest. . . .*

Light crept over the eastern valley rim behind the big house and
broke free and streaked across the sky and the sun shone warm on
the cabin doorway. Old Anse rinsed his frying pan and coffee cup
and settled on the log doorsill and watched the Peabodys strip the
big house of its furnishings and load these on their big freight wagon.
He slapped at the flies and watched Luke Peabody and his two big
sons lash the load tight and harness the big work teams in double
tandem and bring out the surrey with the tall trotter in the traces.
The womenfolk came from the house and climbed into the surrey
and the men swung up on the wagon and Old Anse sat still and
watched them go.

The wagon stopped and the surrey behind it. Luke Peabody
swung out on a wheel hub and to the ground and walked back and
stood in the road dust looking at the big house. He turned and
looked across the creek at Old Anse. He walked to the creek edge
and made a funnel of his hands at his mouth and shouted. Old Anse
caught the voice with ears that could still catch the rustle of deer
hooves in grass at more than fifty paces, but he sat quiet and waited
and watched Luke Peabody shake his head in exasperation and shout
again and at last stride across the creek through water above his
knees and come up the slope.

"Birkitt," said Luke Peabody, "seventeen years I've lived here and
not once known you be neighborly. Could be my fault some. I've
thought you an opinionated, shiftless old fool and said so many a
time. That doesn't matter much now. I'd like to leave with a
friendly word. Here's my hand on it."

Luke Peabody put out a big hand with the fingers stretched and
reaching and Old Anse sat still and looked up with eye corners
tightening. Luke Peabody let his hand drop. "So be it," he said.

"All the same I'm asking a favor." And Old Anse tightened his eye corners more. "Thought there'd be a ketch to it," he said.

"Do you think I'd ask you was there anyone else left around?" Luke Peabody raised his hand and wiped it palm flat across his face. "I want you to set fire to my place." And Old Anse's eyes opened wide and he looked down at the dooryard dust and up again sharp and quick. "Why?"

"Because I don't like to think what'll happen to it if it just stands there."

Old Anse looked down at his feet in the dust and pulled them in close under him and stood up and held out a hand. "Changed my mind." And Old Anse Birkitt and Luke Peabody shook hands, both of them slow and solemn, and Luke Peabody started away and swung his head back without stopping and spoke fast. "You'll wait till we're out of sight around the bend?"

Old Anse sat on his doorsill and slapped at the flies and watched the wagon and the surrey fade in a dust haze around the bend of the lower valley road. *Got some of a man's feelings,* he thought. *But can't do the hard things himself. . . .*

The sun arched overhead and Old Anse went inside and opened a can of beans. After he had eaten he went down to the creek and rolled up his jeans and waded across. He went along the lane by the squat stone piers on which Barlett's store had rested and on by the deserted houses and shacks to the big house. He made a slow circuit of the place, peering in at the stripped-empty rooms. He took an armload of old straw from the stable and pushed this under the jutting rear porch. When the flames were licking at the wood he went back to the creek and waded across and on up to his cabin. He sat in his doorway, legs out drying in front of him, and watched the flames leap into view over the rear roof of the house and eat their way forward on the shingles. The wood of the house was dry with the years and the season and the fire reached and ran till the whole structure was blazing. Old Anse sat quiet and watched and it was his alone. There was no one else in the whole section of the valley to see it.

The uprush of flames slackened and the charring shell of the house shuddered and collapsed backward and the flames leaped again then settled down to steady gnawing at the wreckage. Old Anse stirred and swung his head to study the wide view before him.

Shadows were long now, stretching away from him, and the deserted town and sweep of valley were hushed in the silence of their emptiness. *Breathing's easier,* he thought. *No people crowding a man's elbows. . . .*

He looked down the valley to the right where the lower road curved away and ran on beyond vision around the bend to where he knew the crews of men were at work and the heavy stone-wagons were rolling and the carloads of gravel and cement were shuttling on the railroad spur. His eye corners tightened and he looked away with a quick jerk of his head.

The shadows merged into the over-all darkening of dusk as the sun dropped into the mountains behind the cabin and he straightened and went around the corner to the left and to the near stand of trees where the tall square stone of white mountain marble still showed plain against the dark ivy on the ground. He stooped to pull away an ivy sprig starting up the stone. *Just you and me again, Marthy,* he thought. *Like it was in the beginning. . . .*

A thin sliver of moon passed low over the horizon and the stars wheeled above and an hour before dawn Old Anse rolled out of his bunk and pulled on his faded jeans and a pair of moccasins. He was restless with a renewed eager spryness oiling his old joints. He took from the wall the old Colt repeating cylinder rifle that had never failed him in almost forty years' service. When the sun broke over the eastern valley rim he was three miles up the creek and over the first side ridge, heading into the rocky highlands toward the small hidden canyon that he alone knew.

Three hours later he was headed homeward with the dressed carcass of a small whitetail buck draped over his shoulders. His knees gave him trouble now and he stopped often to rest. Several times the fingers of his left hand holding the legs locked together in front grew numb and could no longer grasp and the carcass slid from his shoulders and he had to flex the fingers till strength returned to them, then kneel and stoop to get the carcass in place again and use the rifle as a cane to lever himself to his feet. Once he fell and rolled twenty feet downslope, bruising against stone, and lay still for a while breathing in short gasps and cursing soft to himself. The sun shone on him with the remembered friendliness of long past days and warmed his old bones and he rose and retrieved the rifle and gathered up the carcass again. He made the final stretch to the cabin with a sustained stumbling rush because he was afraid that if he stopped he might not get started with his burden once more. It dropped to the dooryard with a soft thud and he sank on the log doorsill and kicked off the moccasins to wriggle his old toes in the warm dust. *Knew it,* he thought. *Knew I could still do it. . . .*

Old Anse reached inside the cabin for his ramrod and a piece of greasy rag. Quiet and serene in the sunlight he began cleaning the rifle. He was polishing the worn stock when his ears caught the sound and his head lifted and he saw the small wagon coming up the lower valley road. He rested the rifle across his knees and watched the wagon approach and turn to ford the creek below him and stop on the near side. His eye corners tightened into a squint as he watched the broad homely gray-topped figure of Sheriff Jesse Whitfield climb to the ground, followed by another man, bigger even than the sheriff, taller and wide-shouldered and handsome in his city clothes. He squirmed a bit on the doorsill and froze to stillness as they came close.

"Morning, Anse," said Sheriff Whitfield and nodded at the deer carcass. "So you can still find 'em when nobody else can." And Old Anse sat quiet. The carcass itself was his response.

Sheriff Whitfield wiped the sweat beads from his forehead and ran the hand on back through his thick gray hair. He sighed and pushed himself to his task. "Anse. You're being honored today. This is Hanson J. Powell. Engineer. Boss of the whole works. The whole blooming project. Insisted on seeing you himself."

Engineer Powell stepped forward and unleashed a rich voice, hearty and confident. "Delighted to meet you, Mr. Birkitt." And Old Anse looked at him with one quick glance and away and sat quiet.

Engineer Powell stepped back a pace and rocked on the soles of his trim new boots. "No reason for hard feelings, Mr. Birkitt. I came myself because I'm sure our agents failed to put the proposition to you in the proper light. Everyone else is co-operating. They have been paid good prices and have moved out. They are not standing in the path of progress. They know what we are doing is big. Really big. Why, when we finish the dam and this valley is filled we will have a reservoir that will irrigate fifty-seven thousand acres of that dry land out on the level. Fifty-seven thousand acres,

Mr. Birkitt. Enough to provide prosperous living for hundreds of healthy farm families. More than that. We will have shown the way for the whole territory. There will be other projects like this. We will be making the desert bloom—"

Sheriff Jesse Whitfield shifted his weight from one foot to the other. "I told you, Powell," he said. "You're wasting breath."

"No," said Engineer Powell. "I refuse to believe one man would be so stubborn as to try to block the will of many others. I refuse to believe that any man would cling so tightly to a scrubby little cabin like this and a few poor acres he doesn't even try to do anything with." Engineer Powell rocked again on his boot soles and his voice dropped to a lower, more confidential tone. "Mr. Birkitt, I will give you double the last price offered you and that is a final figure."

Old Anse rubbed one hand along the rifle barrel and back and sat quiet and Sheriff Whitfield spoke, dry and disgusted. "Get on with it, Powell. Tell him what's happened."

"Very well," said Engineer Powell. "I made that offer, Mr. Birkitt, simply to satisfy my own conscience. There was no need for it. Your property here has been condemned by court order and taken over by rule of eminent domain. You are being paid the assessed value only plus a small sum for the supposed inconvenience caused you. A check has been deposited in your name at the county bank. This property, along with all the rest, now belongs to the land development company. We drove out this morning to tell you and move your belongings, if you have any, to the county seat. What you do thereafter is no concern of mine."

Old Anse sat still but his hands moved and the rifle swung until its barrel pointed at Engineer Powell. "Get off my land," he said.

Engineer Powell put his hands on his hips and rocked on his boot soles, bringing the toes down firm. "This is no longer your land." And Old Anse pulled back the hammer on the old rifle with a little snap. "You heard me," he said. "Ain't in the habit of speaking twice." And Sheriff Whitfield spoke, his voice crisp. "Go back to the wagon, Powell. I'll handle this."

The wagon creaked as Engineer Powell climbed to the seat and silence settled up the slope over the cabin dooryard. Sheriff Whitfield stood, big and broad, and his shadow covered Old Anse on the doorsill and his voice was mild. "The gun's empty," he said. "You were cleaning it." And Old Anse shrugged his shoulders a bit. "Can't talk to that bedamned easterner," he said.

"You're up against the law now," said Sheriff Whitfield. And Old Anse looked at him, eyes wide and clear. "Remember when your father came here," said Old Anse. "Walking with his oxcart up this valley. Staking a claim over that first ridge. Remember when you were born. Remember Marthy feeding you biscuit in this cabin afore you shed your first teeth. Remember showing you how to find deer. Remember when you married. Remember when your kids were born. And their kids too. You'll not put me off."

Sheriff Whitfield drew a long breath and let it out sighing and leaned against the cabin wall. "But why? You're too old to be living off here alone. You can't have much time left. Should think you'd want to spend it where things are easier."

Old Anse stretched his legs and reached to scratch a toe with the end of the rifle barrel. "Don't want things easy. Want them like now. Better with all those newcomers gone. Was too bedamned crowded. Came here afore anyone else. The first. Now the last." He set the rifle across his knees and looked down at it and ran one hand over and over along the barrel. "Moved all around these territories way back then. Always trying it over the next hills. Marthy took it long enough. 'Always settling,' she put it, 'and never settled.' Made me promise to find a place and keep it. Found this. Kept it."

The voice of Engineer Powell rose in a shout, impatience driving it up the slope. "Doesn't that old fool know his place'll be under twenty feet of water soon as the valley is filled?"

Sheriff Whitfield gave no sign he had heard. He looked down at Old Anse. "Martha's been dead a long time," he said. And Old Anse gave a small jerk of his head toward the left corner of the cabin. "She's here," he said.

"They'll move her for you. Just say the word and they'll move her down to the cemetery at the county seat." And Old Anse whipped his head up quick and his eye corners tightened sharp. "Move her? Moved her too often when she was alive."

The voice of Engineer Powell drove up the slope. "Sheriff, are you going to bring him along?" The voice of Sheriff Whitfield drove down the slope with a sudden snap. "No. I'm an old fool too." And the voice of Engineer Powell became cold and contemptuous.

"Come along then. My time is valuable. Let him stay there and rot. He'll get out fast enough when the water starts rising."

Dust rose along the lower valley road again and Old Anse sat in his doorway and watched the wagon disappear around the bend. The flies were gathering and he rose to tend to the meat. *Always could handle Jesse,* he thought. *Being sheriff hasn't changed him any. . . .*

The sun arched overhead and dropped into the mountains and the night breeze talked in the trees and the days passed and the nights between and Old Anse endured them with slow satisfaction in his solitude. Several times on a Sunday curious people from the work camp in the lower valley came up the road, but when he sat on his doorsill with the old rifle across his knees they kept a wary distance and went away soon. At odd intervals Sheriff Jesse Whitfield appeared, ambling in from various directions on his big bunchy roan, to bring a fragrant tobacco quid and lean against the cabin and look out over the valley and speak after long moments of memories of the old days. The rest of the time Old Anse was alone and the quiet independent serenity of other years crept back and sat with him on the doorsill as he watched the weeds take the cleared places around the deserted houses across the creek or went with him as he wandered the neighbor hills, rifle in hand, and saw the small game working back into long lost territory. Sometimes, sitting still in the doorway, his old ears caught the rumbling down valley that must be dynamite blasts and rock-car unloadings where the valley narrowed and the side walls came close and the dam was rising and these were the times he pushed to his feet and went off on long tramps over almost forgotten trails.

The days passed and the nights between and haze began to fill the shortening afternoons as the edge of fall sharpened the air and he killed another deer and strained to pack the carcass home and smoked the meat and dragged fallen timber to the cabin to be cut and stacked close against the walls. Then all rumbling ceased in the distance and days passed and the silence in that direction deepened and he found himself unable or unwilling to leave the cabin and the almost unconscious expectancy gripped him and the waiting began. Day after day he sat still, bundled now in his old buffalo coat, and his head turned ever more often to the right toward the lower valley and at last he saw it, the slow widening of the creek where it followed the road around the bend.

It was no more than a gradual swelling at first, a broadening of the lazy late-fall creek where this curved around and out of sight. For hours at a time he saw no difference at the distance then with a start he realized the water had slipped sidewise into another hollow and spread its hold on the land. By evening of the third day he saw the upward-inching line clear across the valley bed and the solid sheen of water behind broken only by clumps of bushtops and the lonely boles of trees whose roots were engulfed. He sat still and was so sunk in the watching that he did not hear the horses coming down the old trail behind the cabin until they moved around the side toward him.

Sheriff Jesse Whitfield let drop the reins of the empty-saddled horse he was leading and swung down from his big roan. He leaned against the cabin wall and looked down valley at the edging sheen of water. "Winter's being hatched in the mountains," he said. "Get your things together, Anse. We've fixed a room at my place."

Old Anse pulled the buffalo coat closer around him. "Bedamned about it," he said in sudden irritation. "Why're you so all-fired keen on taking care of me?"

Sheriff Whitfield pulled a sliver of ancient bark from the cabin wall and chewed on it in slow thought. "Maybe because you mean something to me," he said. "You sort of stand for the way it was when I was a kid." And Old Anse looked at him and away and down at his moccasined feet. "Maybe that's why I won't go." He waved an arm at the water down valley. "Can't rise much during the cold. Got plenty of food and wood. Intend to see it through." The sound of one horse stamping a hoof was sharp in the long silence and Old Anse stirred on the doorsill. "One more winter," he said. "Not much for a man to want." And Sheriff Whitfield smacked a fist into the cabin wall and stepped out and scooped up the reins of the other horse and swung up on his big roan. Old Anse sat still and heard the sound of the hooves fading on the trail behind the cabin. *Still the same Jesse,* he thought. *Raised them right in those days. . . .*

The landscape browned and the now endless wind strengthened and stripped the trees till only the evergreens held their color and the water crept forward, measuring its advance by almost imperceptible degrees according to the ground confronting it. Old Anse sat and watched it every daylight hour till the cold drove him inside and then he kept a fire blazing and sat on his barrel-stool and watched through the window in the south wall. Ice formed in the creek and thickened and the flow dwindled and the first snow floated down from the mountains and the days passed and the snow came again whipping into a blizzard that packed the low places and piled the drifts. He could see only driving white through the window and when the weather cleared the valley was wrapped for winter and the edge of water was lost beneath the blanket of snow spreading unbroken from the frozen ground on over the surface of ice.

Old Anse stayed inside now and the days passed and the weeks. Daylight and dark were the same to him and he waked and dozed and ate when hunger prompted and fed the fire, with no attention to time. Outside the winter held its course rigid with repeated snowings and inside he lived through other winters in his mind. Remembrance ran back into the far years and he sat by the fire and talked to Martha and he knew she was not there but outside under the tall stone and yet he talked to her and the old cabin was filled with her quiet listening. He dozed and woke to feed the fire and dozed again and he came over the high slope behind the cabin with the tireless energy of youth in his legs and the valley reached untouched before him and he turned to call her to hurry beside him. He stirred and brought in more wood and the fire leaped again and the muscles of his back and shoulders ached with a satisfying weariness as he drove his ax deep into the trunks of stout trees and felled them and lopped away the branches and drag-rolled the logs to the cabin site and she helped him notch them and set them in place. He let the ash-choked fire go out and cleaned the fireplace and coaxed new flames into leaping action and he stood outside with the sunset behind him and the contentment of a man's full-day work upon him and she was beside him and they looked down the valley where people passed along the trail by the creek he had made packing in supplies, and the people fanned out to settle in the surrounding hills and he knew them all and was one of them and their neighborliness was a good thing with no pressure in it and they gathered to help him bury her and the stillborn child under the white stone.

The endless wind rushed with rising strength outside and beat through chinks in the cabin wall and fought with the fire and he kept this well fed and pulled his stool close and he sat on the log doorsill alone in the round of the days and one by one old neighbors over the hills faded out of knowing and the trail broadened into a road and the town grew house by house and the people were strangers who kept away from him, afraid of his long silences and sudden sharp speech, and told themselves strange tales about him and he watched them and their hurryings and let time glide past in the inevitable moving of the years.

The days grew longer and the wind slackened and rose and slackened and rose again, coming now in gusts and sighing with a new softness. The snow settled during the days to harden only at night and the ice became spongy and at last the creek broke through all covering and cleared its bed and raced with rising vigor, tumbling slush and ice chunks with it. The sun beat down and the snow settled and faded and clear spots appeared on the high slopes and Old Anse stood in his doorway and saw the water stretching in a vast sheet from the small rise at the edge of the empty town on down the valley and out of sight around the bend below.

The creek rose, shouting in spring exuberance, and poured the water from the melting snow far up its course in the mountains down into the growing lake. The level of the stretching sheet climbed by visible hourly stages and Old Anse sat on the doorsill and watched it top the rise by the town edge and run like a reaching finger along the road and spill into the cellar hole where Bartlett's store had been. Down valley the trees surrounded in the fall stayed brown and bare but up the high slopes the small buds burst and a tinge of green flushed along the boughs and he sat still and shed his old buffalo coat in the sun and watched the water take the houses, inching upward board by board.

It coiled around their lonely walls and slithered through cracks to explore the barren rooms. It swirled around their eaves and rolled up their roofs and over and they were only dark shadows fading into the over-all sameness under the smooth wet sheen of the surface. It washed over the charred remnants of Luke Peabody's place and that blackened scar on the opposite slope was gone and the lake held it a lost secret. There was no semblance of the creek now. It fed into the lake far on up the valley and the widening water crept up the slope toward the cabin. The sun shimmered on it by day and the slice of growing moon by night and Old Anse wore away the hours on his doorsill and watched it move in and across his dooryard. Eating and the little necessities were mechanical habits, and with the apparent unthinking indifference of an old rock he watched the water rise and erase all that was familiar before him. When the first ripples reached his feet he straightened and stepped up and stood in the doorway. When they lapped against the log he stepped back and closed the door. He looked all about him, studying every object in the cabin, and shook his head. Empty-handed he went to the small rear door that gave on the rising slope behind, and opened it and hesitated and returned by the fireplace to take the old rifle from its pegs. Holding it in the crook of an arm he went out the rear door and kicked this shut after him. Fifty feet up the slope he stopped on a small outcropping ledge and lowered himself to sit on the rock.

The water edged along the sides of the cabin now, feeling about the base logs. Old Anse sat still and watched it slide to the left and finger through the grass and slip under and through the ivy leaves to curl slow and relentless around the base of the white stone. The sun swung far overhead and the water crept up the stone and the sun dropped into the mountains behind him and the moon rose and silvered the lake and filtered its pale light through the trees by the cabin and the soft shimmering of the water was halfway up the stone. The night cold sank into his joints and the white shaft seemed to sway in the rippling sheen and he stared at it and toppled in a slow descent on his side in the sleep of exhaustion.

In the first light of morning Old Anse woke with a start and fought the chill stiffness of his old muscles to get back to a sitting position. He peered forward through the clearing grayness. Only the pointed tip of the white stone showed above the water and ripples raised by the freshening breeze washed over it. He watched and the water seemed to hold back from the point and then closed with a soft swish over it and the stone was a gray-white shadow under the surface. Old Anse shivered and swung his head to look at the cabin. The water surrounded it and was high up the sides, and through the top panes of the side window he saw his stool floating past inside. The water rose and gurgled under the eaves and started its climb up the low ridge of the roof. The ripples sent their small wettings ahead and the abiding edge of the water followed. Only the hump of the ridge remained and this dwindled and became no more than the line of the center peak and then this too was taken and the lake spread untroubled from slope to far slope.

Old Anse stirred and shook his head and the slow accumulating anger of the months came forward in his mind and broke and left him empty and old beyond reckoning. He pushed to his feet and staggered and caught himself and as he looked around in a strange indecision he saw the broad figure standing ten yards away.

"All right, Anse," said Sheriff Jesse Whitfield. "It's finished. Come along now. I'm taking you home with me."

Old Anse Birkitt sat on the top step of the porch of Sheriff Whitfield's house and looked out over the front hedge at the streets framing the central square of the county seat and the row of buildings beyond. The late spring sun was warm upon him and he was grateful for it. Somehow he was never warm clear through any more. Across the way the stores were busy and people passed up and down the courthouse steps and wagons moved along the street. Behind the buildings where the railroad cut through to the station, an engine whistled and its heavy breathing and the clatter of cars drifted across the square. Old Anse fidgeted on his step. *Bedamned lot of goings on,* he thought. *Makes a man tired just watching. . . .*

He pushed up and went around the house across the back yard to the stable. He took a manure fork off the rack and went in the big roan's empty stall and began pitching the dirtied straw through the window to the pile outside. There was no snap left in his muscles and he grunted with each forkful but he kept at it with grim satisfaction. Footsteps sounded in the stable and he stopped. Sheriff Whitfield's dull-witted handyman stood in the stall doorway bobbing his head in slow rhythm. "That's my work, Mr. Anse. Sheriff says you don't have to do anything around here."

Old Anse dropped the fork and let it lay though the prongs were up. He pushed past the handyman and out of the stable and swung on a circuit of the big yard just inside the hedge where his frequent tramping had already worn a path. He caught a movement of curtain at a house window and a glimpse of the sheriff's wife peering out. He stopped short. *Somebody's always checking on me,* he thought. *Seem to have the notion I'm off my rocker.* . . .

Back on the front step he opened his old knife and began whittling aimless shavings from a small piece of wood he had picked off the main stovepile. They flowed from the blade and fell around his feet cluttering the bottom step and at last he was conscious of them. He stopped whittling and stared at them a long moment. He reached and picked them up one by one till the step was clear. He looked around and there was no place along the neat house front to put them and he jammed them with the knife into the pockets of his faded jeans. He sat still and watched the people and wagons across the way. *Don't belong here,* he thought. And after a while his eye corners tightened and his old lips folded in to a firm line. *Jesse's wrong. It's not finished. Not yet.* . . .

The sunset glow bathed the house and died away into dusk and Old Anse sat at the supper table and listened in friendly attention to Sheriff Whitfield telling of the day's doings and thanked the sheriff's wife for a good meal though it still seemed strange to him to be eating food prepared by someone else, and at last was upstairs in the room they had fixed for him. He sat by the window and watched the late moon rise and waited till long after the whole house was dark and silent. With the old rifle in his hand he slipped into the hall and down the stairs. His moccasined feet made no sound as he eased out the back door. He took the ax from the block by the woodpile and an empty feed bag and a coil of rope from the stable. *Jesse won't mind,* he thought. *Won't grudge me these.* . . .

By sunup he was past the dam and working along the valley rim. Through the trees he could see the lake below him stretching broad and strange and beautiful on beyond the upper bend. He came on the faint trace of the back trail that had led down to the cabin and pushed on without stopping. A third of a mile farther he slipped down the slope to where a shoulder of land pushed out into the water. Sitting cross-legged by the water's edge he studied the whole scene. The shimmering expanse of the lake seemed to throw the whole wide view out of focus and for a time everything appeared unfamiliar to him. At last the water barrier began to fade in his mind and he grasped the valley again, complete and as it used to be. Turning his head in slow scrutiny he scanned the entire valley rim and fixed his landmarks for imaginary lines spanning the lake from side to side and lengthwise, and where they crossed was the spot he sought. He picked up a twig and tossed it into the water and watched it move away. There was a current, slight and almost imperceptible, but moving and in the right direction.

A few feet into the water nearby he found three trees of manageable size and dead, water-killed and bare. He stood in the shallow water and swung the ax and some of the former snap seemed to flow into his old muscles. He felled two of the trees without halting and rested and the third took longer then it too lay ready, partway into the water, and he trimmed away the branches and lopped off the thin upper ends. Tugging at the logs he got them farther into the water, floating with only the inner ends grounded, and with part of the rope he lashed them into a crude raft. He was panting now and soaked and had to sink on the shore to rest. As he lay full length on the ground he heard, down valley, the sound of a horse whinnying and in the following silence he listened and caught the faint far-off shouting of several voices. He pushed up from the ground, hurrying now, and took the feed bag and filled it with stones and tied the mouth shut and struggled with it until he had it on the near end of his raft. He paused to ease the breath fighting in his chest and heard the voices coming closer, and frantic in haste he laid the rifle on the raft and splashed through the water to the outer end and heaved until it was floating free. Careful not to tilt it, he crawled aboard and lay flat along the logs and paddled with his hands over the sides until his arm muscles bunched and refused to move.

Time passed and boots crashed through brush along the lake shore and voices shouted and these were meaningless sounds to him. His muscles relaxed some and his breath eased and he raised his head, straining it back on his neck like a turtle. He was well out into the lake and the slow current was drifting him down and out toward the middle. He slapped against the water with his left hand and arm in a desperate flurry and relief ran through him as the forward end of the raft swung in a gradual arc in the right direction. He turned his head back and there were figures running on the shore and one broad figure standing motionless on the shoulder of land watching him. *Don't care a bedamn about anyone else,* he thought. *But Jesse'll understand. . . .* And then he forgot them all and concentrated on steering his raft toward the crossing of his landmark lines.

The slow, almost imperceptible movement brought him closer and closer and peering ahead and down he saw shifting shadows that steadied and became the clumped branches of a stand of submerged trees. Peering down with his face almost touching the water he saw and saw not and seemed to see again a glimmering of white far down among the tree trunks and ahead the big humped shadow of the cabin roof. Inching around on the raft he sat up and reached and took the free end of the rope from the bag and looped it around his waist and knotted it tight. He held the old rifle firm in one hand and hunched along the logs until his feet touched the bag and began to push it. His weight and the weight of the bag together tilted the raft and water washed over the end and the bag slid and dropped in silent descent and the rope tightened taut to his waist and he heaved himself forward and down into the dim water. Cold engulfed him in a downward rush and his limbs thrashed and he did not know it and his fingers remained clamped around the rifle. *It's finished,* he thought, and all thinking ceased in an endless nothingness and the disturbed water rocked above and the small waves spread and died and the cool surface of the lake spread serene and untroubled from slope to slope of the valley.

That Mark Horse

Not that horse, mister. Not that big slab-sided brute. Take any or all of the rest, I'm selling the whole string. But not that one. By rights I should. He's no damn good to me. The best horse either one of us'll likely ever see and he's no damn good to me. Or me to him. But I'll not sell him. . . .

Try something, mister. Speak to him. The name's Mark. . . . There. See how his ears came up? See how he swung to check you and what you were doing? The way any horse would. Any horse that likes living and knows his name. But did you notice how he wouldn't look at me? Used to perk those ears and swing that head whenever he heard my voice. Not any more. Knows I'm talking about him right now and won't look at me. Almost ten months it is and he still won't look at me. . . .

That horse and I were five-six years younger when this all began. I was working at one of the early dude ranches and filling in at the rodeos roundabout. A little riding, a little roping. Not too good, just enough to place once in a while. I was in town one day for the mail and the postmaster poked his head out to chuckle some and say there was something for me at the station a mite too big for the box. I went down and the agent wasn't there. I scouted around and he was out by the stock corral and a bunch of other men too all leaning on the fence and looking over. I pushed up by the agent and there was that horse inside. He was alone in there and he was the damndest horse I'd ever seen. Like the rest around I'd been raised on cow ponies and this thing looked big as the side of a barn to me and awkward as all hell. He'd just been let down the chute from a boxcar on the siding. There were bits of straw clinging to him and he stood still with head up testing the air. For that first moment he looked like a kid's crazy drawing of a horse, oversize and exaggerated with legs too long and big stretched-out barrel and high-humped withers and long-reaching neck. The men were joshing and wondering was it an elephant or a giraffe and I was agreeing and then I saw that horse move. He took a few steps walking and flowed forward into a trot. That's the only way to put it. He flowed forward the way water rolls down a hill. His muscles didn't bunch and jump under his hide. They slid easy and smooth and those long legs reached for distance without seeming to try. He made a double circuit of the corral without slowing, checking everything as he went by. He wasn't trying to find a way out. He just wanted to move some and see where he was and what was doing roundabout. He saw us along the fence and we could have been posts for all the particular attention he paid us. He stopped by the far fence and stood looking over it and now I'd seen him move there wasn't anything awkward about him. He was big and he was rough-built but he wasn't awkward any more even standing there still. Nobody was saying a word. Everyone there knew horses and they'd seen what I saw. "Damn it to eternal hell," I said. "That's a horse." The agent turned and saw who it was. "Glad you think so," he said. "It's your horse. This came along too." And he stuck a note in my hand.

It had my name on it all right. It was from a New York State man who ran some sort of factory there, made shoes I think he told me once. He'd been a regular at the ranch, not for any dude doings but once a summer for a camping trip and I'd been assigned to him several years running. It wasn't long. It said the doctors had been carving him some and told him he couldn't ride again so he was closing his stable. He'd sold his other stock but thought this horse Mark ought to be out where there was more room than there was back east. Wanted me to take him and treat him right.

I shoved that note in a pocket and eased through the fence. "Mark," I called and across the corral those ears perked stiff and that big head swung my way. "Mark," I called again and that horse turned and came about halfway and stood with head high, looking me over. I picked a coil of rope off a post and shook out a loop and he watched me with ears forward and head a bit to one side. I eased close and sudden I snaked up the loop and it was open right for his head and he just wasn't there. He was thirty feet to the left and I'd have sworn he made it in one leap. Maybe a dozen times I tried and I didn't have a chance. The comments coming from the fence line weren't improving my temper any. Then I noticed he wasn't watching me, he was watching the rope, and I had an attack of common sense. He was wearing a halter. This wasn't any western range horse. This was one of those big eastern crossbreds with a lot of thoroughbred in them I'd heard about. Likely he'd never had a rope thrown at him before. I tossed the rope over by the fence and walked toward him and he stood blowing his nostrils a bit and looking at me. I stopped a few feet away and didn't even try to reach for the halter. He looked at me and he was really seeing me the way a horse can and I was somebody who knew his name out here where he'd been dumped out of the darkness of a boxcar. He stretched that long neck and sniffed at my shirt and I took hold of the halter and that was all there was to it. . . .

That was the beginning of my education. Yes, mister, it was me had to be taught, not that horse. The next lesson came the first time I tried to ride him. I was thinking what a big brute he was and what a lot of power was penned in him and I'd have to control all that so I used a Spanish spade bit that would be wicked if used rough. He didn't want to take it and I had to force it on him. The same with the saddle. I used a double-rig with a high-roll cantle and he snorted at it and kept sidling away and grunted all the time I was tightening the cinches. He stood steady enough when I swung aboard but when we started off nothing felt right. The saddle was too small for him and sat too high-arched over the backbone and those sloping withers. He kept wanting to drop his head and rub his mouth on his legs over that bit. At last he sort of sighed and eased out and went along without much fuss. He'd decided I was plain stupid on some things and he'd endure and play along for a while. At the time I thought he was accepting me as boss so I started him really stepping and the instant he understood I wanted him to move that was what he did. He moved. He went from a walk into a gallop in a single flowing rush and it was only that high cantle kept me from staying behind. I'm telling you, mister, that was something, the feel of those big muscles sliding smooth under me and distance dropping away under those hooves.

Then I realized he wasn't even working. I was traveling faster than I ever had on horseback and he was just loafing along without a sign of straining for speed. That horse just liked moving. I never knew another liked it as much. It could get to him the way liquor can a man and he'd keep reaching for more. That's what he was doing then. I could feel him notching it up the way an engine does when the engineer pushes forward on the throttle and I began to wonder how he'd be on stopping. I had an idea twelve hundred pounds of power moving like that would be a lot different from eight hundred pounds of bunchy little cow pony. I was right. I pulled in some and he slowed some but not much and I pulled harder and he tossed his head at the bit, biting, and I yanked in sharp and he stopped. Yes, mister, he stopped all right. But he didn't slap down on his haunches and slide to a stop on his rump the way a cow pony does. He took a series of jumps stiff-legged to brake and stopped short and sudden with his legs planted like trees and I went forward, bumping my belly on the horn and over his head and hanging there doubled down over his ears with my legs clamped around his neck. That Mark horse was surprised as I was but he took care of me. He kept his head up and stood steady as a rock while I climbed down his neck to the saddle. I was feeling foolish and mad at myself and him and I yanked mean on the reins and swung him hard to head for home and that did it. He'd had enough. He shucked me off his back the way someone might toss a beanbag. Don't ask me how. I'd ridden plenty horses and could make a fair showing even on the tough ones. But that Mark horse wanted me off so he put me off. And then he didn't bolt for the horizon. He stopped about twenty feet away and stood there watching me.

I sat on the ground and looked at him. I'd been stupid but I was beginning to learn. I remembered the feel of him under me, taking me with him not trying to get away from me. I remembered how he'd behaved all along and I studied on all that. There wasn't a trace of meanness in that horse. He didn't mind being handled and ridden. He'd been ready and willing for me to come up and take him in the station corral. But he wasn't going to have a rope

slapped at him and be yanked around. He was ready and willing
to let me ride him and show me how a real horse could travel. But
he wasn't going to do much of it with a punishing bit and a rig
he didn't like. He was a big batch of damned good horseflesh and
he knew that and was proud of it and he had a hell of a lot of self-
respect. He just plain wouldn't be pushed around and that was
that and I had to understand it. I claim it proud for myself that
I did. I went to him and he waited for me as I knew now he would.
I swung easy as I could up into the saddle and he stood steady with
his head turned a little so he could watch me. I let the lines stay
loose and guided him just by neck-reining and I walked him back
to the ranch. I slid down there and took off the western saddle and
the bridle with that spade bit. I hunted through the barn till I
found a light snaffle bit and cleaned it and put it in the bridle. I
held it up for him to see and he took it with no fuss at all. I routed
out the biggest of the three English saddles we had for eastern dudes
who wouldn't use anything else and that I'd always thought were
damned silly things. I showed it to him and he stood quiet while I
slapped it on and buckled the single leather cinch. "Mark," I said,
"I don't know how to sit one of these crazy postage stamps and I'm
bunged up some from that beating. Let's take it easy." Mister, that
horse knew what I'd said. He gave me the finest ride I ever had. . . .

See what I mean, the best damn horse either of us'll ever see? No,
I guess you can't. Not complete. You'd have to live with him day
after day and have the endless little things happening tally up in
your mind. After a while you'd understand as I did what a combination he was of a serious dependable gent and a mischievous
little kid. With a neat sense of timing on those things too. Take
him out for serious riding and he'd tend strict to his business, which
was covering any kind of ground for you at any kind of speed you
wanted. The roughest going made no difference to him. He was
built to go at any clip just about anywhere short of straight up a
cliff, and you'd get the feeling he'd try that if you really wanted
him to. But let him loaf around with nothing to do and he'd be
curious as a cat on the prowl, poking into every corner he could
find and seeing what devilment he could do. Nothing mean, just
playful. Maybe a nuisance if you were doing a job where he could
get at you and push his big carcass in the way whiffling at every-

thing or come up quiet behind and blow sudden down your shirt collar. Let him get hold of a bucket and you'd be buying a new one. There'd not be much left of the old one after he'd had his fun. He'd stick his nose in and flip the thing and do that over and over like he was trying for a distance record then start whamming it around with his hooves, tickled silly at the racket. And when there'd be no one else around to see how crazy you were acting he'd get you to playing games too. He liked to have you sneak off and hide and whistle low for him and he'd pad around stretching that long neck into the damndest places looking for you and blow triumphant when he found you. Yes, mister, that horse liked living and being around him'd help you do the same.

And work? That horse was a working fool. No. There was nothing foolish about it. The ranch was still in the beef business too in those days and he'd never had any experience with cattle before. He was way behind our knowing little cow ponies when it came to handling them and he knew it. So he tried to balance that by using those brains of his overtime and working harder than any of the others. He'd watch them and try to figure what they were doing and how they did it and then do it himself. He'd try so hard sometimes I'd ache inside, feeling that eagerness quivering under me. Of course he never could catch up to them on some things. Too big. Too eager. Needed too much room moving around. He couldn't slide into a tight bunch of cattle and cut out the right one, easing it out without disturbing the rest much. And he wasn't much good for roping even though he did let me use a western saddle for that soon as he saw the sense to it. Lunged too hard when I'd looped an animal and was ready to throw it. Maybe he'd have learned the right touch in time but he didn't get the chance. The foreman saw us damn near break a steer's neck and told us to quit. But on straight herding he couldn't be beat. He could head a runaway steer before it even stretched its legs. He could scour the brush for strays like a hound dog on a scent. He could step out and cover territory all day at a pace that'd kill off most horses and come in seeming damn near as fresh as when he started. I used to think I was tough and could take long hours but that horse could ride me right out of the saddle and act like he thought I was soft for calling a halt.

But I still haven't hit the real thing. That horse was just plain honest all through. No, that's not the exact word. Plenty of horses are that. He was something a bit more. Square. That's it. He was just plain square in everything he did and the way he looked at living. He liked to have things fair and even. He was my horse and he knew it. I claim it proud that for a time anyway he really was my horse and let me know it. But that meant too I was his man and I had my responsibilities. I wasn't a boss giving orders. I was his partner. He wasn't something I owned doing what I made him do. He was my partner doing his job because he wanted to and because he knew that was the way it ought to be with a man and a horse. A horse like him. Long as I treated him right he'd treat me right. If I'd get mean or stupid with him I'd be having trouble. I'd be taking another lesson. Like the time along about the second or third week when I was feeling safer on that English saddle and forgot he wasn't a hard-broke cow pony. I wanted a sudden burst of speed for one reason or another and I hit him with my spurs. I was so used to doing that with the other horses that I couldn't figure at first what had happened. I sat on the ground rubbing the side I'd lit on and stared at him watching me about twenty feet away. Then I had it. I unfastened those spurs and threw them away. I've never used the things again ever, anytime on any horse. . . .

Well, mister, there I was mighty proud to have a horse like that but still some stupid because I hadn't tumbled to what you might call his specialty. He had to show me. It was during the fall roundup. We had a bunch of steers in the home corral being culled for market and something spooked them and they started milling wild and pocketed me and Mark in a corner. They were slamming into the fence rails close on each side. I knew we'd have to do some fancy stepping to break through and get around them. I must have felt nervous on the reins because that Mark horse took charge himself. He swung away from those steers and leaped straight at the near fence and sailed over it. He swung in a short circle and stopped looking back at those steers jamming into the corner where we'd been and I sat the saddle catching the breath he'd jolted out of me. I should have known. He was a jumper. He was what people back east called a hunter. Maybe he'd been a timber horse, a steeplechaser. He'd cleared that four-foot fence with just about no take-off space like a kid skipping at hopscotch. I'm telling you, mister, I had me a time the next days jumping him over everything in sight. When I was sure of my seat I made him show me what he really could do and he played along with me for anything within reason, even stretching that reason considerable. The day I had nerve enough and he took me smack over an empty wagon I really began to strut. But there was one thing he wouldn't do. He wouldn't keep jumping the same thing over and over the same time out. Didn't see any sense in that. He'd clear whatever it was maybe twice, maybe three times, and if I tried to put him at it again he'd stop cold and swing his head to look at me and I'd shrivel down to size and feel ashamed. . . .

So I had something new in these parts then, a jumping horse bred to it and built for it with the big frame to take the jolts and the power to do it right. I had me a horse could bring me some real money at the rodeos. I wouldn't have to try for prize money. I could put on exhibition stunts. I got together with some of the old show hands and we worked up an act that pleased the crowds. They'd lead Mark out so the people could see the size of him and he'd plunge around at the end of the shank, rolling his eyes and tossing his head. He'd paw at the sky and lash out behind like he was the worst mean-tempered mankiller ever caught. It was all a joke because he was the safest horse any man ever handled and anyone who watched close could see those hooves never came near connecting with anything except air. But he knew what it was all about and he made it look good. The wranglers would get him over and into the outlaw chute with him pretending to fight all the way. They'd move around careful outside and reach through the bars to bridle and saddle him like they were scared green of him. I'd climb to the top rails and ease down on the saddle like I was scared too but determined to break my neck trying to ride one hell of a bucking brute. We'd burst out of the chute like a cannon going off and streak straight for the high fence on the opposite side of the arena. All the people who'd not seen it before would come up gasping on their seats expecting a collision that would shake the whole place. And at the last second that horse Mark would rise up and over the fence in a clean sweet jump and I'd be standing in the stirrups waving my hat and yelling and the crowd'd go wild.

After a time most people knew what to expect and the surprise part of that act was gone so we had to drop it. But we worked up another that got the crowds no matter how many times they saw it. I never liked it much but I blew too hard once how that horse would jump anything and someone suggested this and I was hot and said sure he'd do it and I was stuck with it. He never liked it much either but he did it for me. Maybe he knew I was getting expensive habits and needed the money coming in. Well, anyway, we did it and it took a lot of careful practice with a slow old steer before we tried the real thing. I'd be loafing around on Mark in the arena while the bull riding was on. I'd watch and pick a time when one of the bulls had thrown his rider and was hopping around in the clear or making a dash across the open. I'd nudge Mark with my heels and he'd be off in that forward flowing with full power in it. We'd streak for the bull angling in at the side and the last sliced second before a head-on smash we'd lift and go over in a clean sweep and swing to come up by the grandstand and take the applause.

Thinking of that since I've been plenty shamed. I've a notion the reason people kept wanting to see it wasn't just to watch a damned good horse do a damned difficult job. They were always hoping something would happen. Always a chance the bull might swerve and throw us off stride and make it a real smash. Always a chance the horns might toss too high and we'd tangle with them and come down in a messy scramble. But I didn't think about that then or how I was asking more than a man should except in a tight spot that can't be avoided from a horse that's always played square with him. I was thinking of the money and the cheers and the pats on the back. And then it happened. . . .

Not what maybe you're thinking, mister. Not that at all. That horse never failed in a jump and never would. We'd done our stint on the day, done it neat and clean, gone over a big head-tossing bull with space to spare and were just about ready to take the exit gate without bothering to open it. Another bull was in the arena, a mean tricky one that'd just thrown his rider after a tussle and was scattering dust real mad. The two tenders on their cagey little cow ponies had cut in to let the rider scramble to safety and were trying to hustle the bull into the closing out pen. They thought they had

him going in and were starting to relax in their saddles when that
brute broke away and tore out into the open again looking for someone on foot to take apart. While the tenders were still wheeling
to go after him he saw something over by the side fence and headed
toward it fast. I saw too and sudden I was cold all over. Some
damn fool woman had let a little boy get away from her, maybe
three-four years old, too young to have sense, and that kid had
crawled through the rails and was twenty-some feet out in the arena.
I heard people screaming at him and saw him standing there confused and the bull moving and the tenders too far away. I slammed
my heels into Mark and we were moving too the way only that
horse could move. I had to lunge forward along his neck or he'd
have been right out from under me. There wasn't time to head
the bull or try to pick up the kid. There wasn't time for anything
fancy at all. There was only one thing could be done. We swept
in angling straight to the big moving target of that bull and I
slammed down on the reins with all my strength so Mark couldn't
get his head up to jump and go over, and in the last split second all
I could think of was my leg maybe getting caught between when
they hit and I dove off Mark sidewise into the dust and he drove
on alone and smashed into that bull just back of the big sweeping
horns.

They picked me up half dazed with an aching head and assorted
bruises and put me on some straw bales in the stable till a doctor
could look me over. They led Mark into one of the stalls with a
big gash from one of the horns along his side and a swelling shoulder
so painful he dragged the leg without trying to step on it. They
put ropes on the bull where he lay quiet with the fight knocked out
of him and prodded him up and led him off. I never did know
just what happened to the kid except that he was safe enough. I
didn't care because when I pushed up off those bales without waiting
for the doctor and went into the stall that Mark horse wouldn't
look at me. . . .

So that's it, mister. That's what happened. But I won't have
you getting any wrong notions about it. I won't have you telling
me the way some people do that horse is through with me because
I made him smash into that bull. Nothing like that at all. He
doesn't blame me for the pulled tendon in his shoulder that'll bother

him long as he lives when the weather's bad. Not that horse. I've thought the whole business over again and again. I can remember every last detail of those hurrying seconds in the arena, things I wasn't even aware of at the time itself. That horse was flowing forward before I slammed my heels into him. There wasn't any attempt at lifting that big head or any gathering of those big muscles under me for a jump when I was slamming down on the reins. He'd seen. He knew. He knew what had to be done. That horse is through with me because at the last second I went yellow and I let him do it alone. He thinks I didn't measure up in the partnership. I pulled out and let him do it alone.

He'll let me ride him even now but I've quit that because it isn't the same. Even when he's really moving and the weather's warm and the shoulder feels good and he's reaching for distance and notching it up in the straight joy of eating the wind he's doing that alone too. I'm just something he carries on his back and he won't look at me. . . .

Ghost Town

Iowned a whole town once. What was left of it anyway. A ghost town. One of the mining camps back in the hills that must have been quite a place when the gold rush was on. Then the diggings there petered out and people began moving on and the flimsy houses started collapsing after everyone was gone.

You can find traces of plenty of those old towns scattered up the back creeks. But this one was better than most. Some of the men there knew how to build a kiln and fire it and there was a clay bank nearby. A half dozen buildings were made of brick and these stood solid enough through the years. The roofs had fallen in, and the windows and doors were missing, but the walls were still standing. You could even figure out what they had been: a general store; a post office and stage station; a blacksmith shop; a two-room jail; a small saloon; another saloon with space for dancing or gambling tables and some rooms on a second floor.

This old town of mine was up a narrow gulch that wasn't good for a thing once the gold was gone. But it was only about a half mile from a modern main highway and the old dirt road leading to it was still passable. I drove in there one day and was poking around when another car loaded with tourists pulled up and the people piled out and wandered around with the women oh-ing and ah-ing as if they were seeing something wonderful.

That's when I had my idea.

It took time but I ran that town down on the tax books and found out all about it. The county had taken title to the whole place for back taxes maybe fifty years before—so long before, it had been written off the accounts as a dead loss and just about forgotten.

When I offered to buy it the county officials thought I was crazy and jumped to make a deal. They hadn't expected ever to get another nickel out of the place. I paid $800 and I owned a town.

I cleaned out the old buildings enough so you could walk around inside them. I painted names on them telling what they had been. I fixed a few bad spots in the dirt road. I plastered signs along the highway for maybe five miles in each direction and a big one where the dirt road turned off. I roofed over one room of the old jail for my own quarters. I charged fifty cents a head for a look-see through the old place—and I was in business.

It was a good business. Not in the winter, of course, and slow in the spring and fall, but good all summer—enough to carry me comfortably all year. During the rough months I'd stay at a rooming house in the live town that was the county seat and as soon as the weather was right I'd move out and start collecting my half dollars.

Sometimes I'd have four or five cars at a time parked by the entrance and a dozen or more people listening to my talk. I'd check the license plates and temper the talk accordingly. If they were from the home state or one nearby, I'd go easy on the fancy trimmings. Those people might know too much real history. But if they were from far states, maybe eastern ones, I'd let loose and make it strong. I'd tell about fights in the saloons—shootings and knifings and big brawls with bottles flying. I'd tell about road agents stopping stages carrying gold and getting caught and being locked up in the jail and maybe a daring escape or two. I'd make it good and the eastern tourists lapped it up. What if all of it happened only in my head? Such things could of happened and maybe did. What if I did get a couple of complaints from the state historical society? There wasn't anything anyone could do so long as I made up the names too. The town belonged to me.

It was a good business. For three years. Then it collapsed just the way the old town itself did 'way back when. The state started straightening the highway and knocked off the loop that came near my ghost town. That put the main route about seven miles away. I slapped up more signs but not many people would bother to turn off onto the old route and try to find the place. My business started skidding. I tried to unload it on the historical society and they just laughed at me. They'd bought a ghost town of their own and were fixing it up. Soon as they had it open, they'd finish the job of killing my business.

I was stuck with that town. I'd put hard money into it and now I was stuck with it. The summer season started and I was lucky to average a single car a day. I was figuring I'd have to swallow the loss and move on when this pink-cheeked young fellow came along. It was late one afternoon and he was pink-cheeked like a boy with maybe a little fuzz on his chin that hadn't begun to be whiskers yet. He drove up in an old car that had lost its color in dust and he paid his fifty cents and started poking around. I was so lonesome for customers, or just anyone to talk to, that I stuck close and kept words bouncing back and forth with him. He looked so young and innocent I figured he was a college kid seeing some of the country on vacation time. But no. He said he'd had all the college he could absorb. He was a mining engineer by profession but there wasn't much professing to be done in that field about then, so he was knocking around looking over the old camps. He liked to see how they did things in the old days. Maybe he'd write a book on it some time.

"Mighty interesting town you have here," he said. "Those buildings. Brick. Don't see much brick in the old camps. They haul them in here?"

"Why no," I said. "They had a kiln right here—you can see where it was behind the blacksmith shop. They dug the clay out of the bank over there." And right away this young fellow had to see that too.

"Mighty interesting," he said. "Found the clay right here. Don't often come on good brick clay in these parts. But you can see they cleaned out this streak in the bank. They sure liked bricks. If they hadn't run out of the clay they might still be making them."

"That'd be a damn fool stunt," I said. "Who'd be wanting bricks around here now?"

"Yes," he said. "Yes, it would. A damn fool stunt." And he wandered on, me with him and him talking more about what sturdy buildings these bricks had made and other things like that.

"Mighty interesting business you're in," he said. "Playing nursemaid to an old town like this and having people pay to look it over. Must be kind of a nice life."

That's when I had another idea.

I took that pink-cheeked young fellow into my jail-room and persuaded him to stay for supper. I began coughing at strategic intervals during the meal and I told him my health was bad and the climate bothered me, otherwise I wouldn't even be thinking of maybe leaving such a nice life in such an interesting business. I played it clever with indirect questions and got out of him the fact he had a bit of cash to invest. Then I really went to work on him.

"Stay here tonight," I said, "and stick around tomorrow. You'll see what a good business this really is." He said he would and I worked on him some more and after a while I asked him to keep an eye on the place while I drove over to the county seat to tend to a few things.

I tended to the things all right but not at the county seat. I burned up the roads getting to various men I knew around about. Each stop I put the same proposition. "There's ten dollars in it for you," I said, "if you'll take time tomorrow to put the missus and anyone else handy in the car and drive over to the old town and make like a tourist gawking around some." I covered a lot of miles and I was turned down at a few stops, but at last I had eleven cars promised and with the extras that would run to about forty people.

When I got back my pink-cheeked baby was sleeping like one on the cot I'd fixed up for him. He woke long enough to grunt a greeting, then rolled over and went to sleep again. But I could tell he'd been snooping in the last summer's tally-book I'd left out on purpose where he would see it. The highway change hadn't been finished then and that had been a good summer.

Come morning everything clicked just right. My home-grown tourists started coming and kept coming at about the times I'd suggested all the way through the morning and early afternoon. I was worried that my young visitor might get to talking with them and sniff some suspicions but he didn't bother with them at all. He just watched what was going on and wandered around by himself and spent some time poking in what was left of the old kiln. I worked on him a bit during lunch and about the middle of the afternoon, when the last of the cars had left, I figured it was time to hook him.

"Not bad," I said. "Eleven cars and forty-one people. Twenty dollars and a fifty cent piece over. And all I did was just sit here and let them come."

"Mighty interesting," he said. "That's more people than I expected."

"That?" I said. "Just a low average. Good enough for a weekday but you should see the week ends. Saturdays double it. And Sundays? Why, Sundays triple it."

"You don't say?" he said. "Too bad about your health. Didn't you mention something about wanting to sell out?"

And right then I knew I had him.

It was just a matter of price after that and on price I always was a tough one. When I chucked my things in my car so I could turn the place over to him that same day and led the way to the county seat with him following so we could find a notary and sign the papers, I'd pushed him up to a thousand bucks. He looked so young and innocent tagging after me into the notary's that I was almost ashamed of myself . . .

Brother, let me tell you something. When a pink-cheeked young tenderfoot with maybe some fuzz on his chin that hasn't even begun to be real whiskers comes your way, just watch your step. Watch it close. That's the kind will take you for anything you've got worth taking—while you're still wondering whether he's been weaned. It wasn't a week later I saw this baby-faced sucker I thought I'd trimmed coming toward me along a street and I ducked quick into a bar. He followed me in and cornered me.

"How's business?" I said, hoping to get any unpleasantness over with fast.

"Business?" he said. "Now that's mighty interesting. Do you really think you fooled me with those fake tourists? The licence plates tipped me right away. All from this state. All from this county." He grinned—the same innocent grin he had the first time I saw him. "Let me buy you a drink. No hard feelings. Your so-called business didn't interest me at all. It was the buildings. I've a crew out there now tearing them down."

"Tearing them down?" I said.

"Certainly," he said. "Those bricks. That clay was the best pocket of pay dirt in the whole gulch—only those old-time miners didn't know it. There was gold dust in that clay and it's right there in the bricks. I'm having them crushed and washing the gold out. There's close to a hundred tons of those bricks and they're panning about eight hundred dollars to the ton."

Takes a Real Man

THAT'S FAIR cussing, gents. Stings the ears a bit. But it's mule-team cussing. Might do to make the rope tails move along. Wouldn't push a yoke of oxen ten feet on a downgrade. Now if you could hear Big Jake Bannack. . . .

Never drove an ox team did you? Slowest critters in harness ever grew hooves. Outpull anything else on four feet and do it on a little dry grass for fodder. But slow. I've seen a turtle come up behind a three-yoke freighting outfit and swing wide and go past without even hurrying. And they're stupid. And stubborn. And aggravating in endless ways. Maybe all that because, being oxen, riling folks to fury is about the only kick they can get out of life. Just one thing they understand. Strong language. Strong and stinging with smoke coming out of it. That'll make them move. Takes a real man to do it. . . .

Big Jake can do it. Big Jake can make the slowest oxen step along so fast for them they look almost alive. He's big with near the heft of an ox himself. Chest like a hogshead. Mouth like a megaphone. Mind made for cussing, chockfull of all the words plain and fancy any man ever knew and plenty more he's thought up for himself. When he rears back and uncoils his whip and sucks in air till that chest's ready to bust out the oversize shirt he's awearing, timid folks with tender ears run for cover. He starts easy, voice just arumbling in his throat, but all the same oxen that'll stand sleepy through the best cussing another man can do'll perk their ears and begin to blow a bit. They know. He's talking their language. In no time at all he's really aroaring and the echoes bounce through the hills and the air gets hot and a blue smoke rises and the oxen move. They move all right. They haul the heaviest wagon out of the deepest mudhole and plod up the road with the wickedest whip in the world picking flies off their rumps and the most sulphurous cussing this side the devil's fireplace roasting their hides every step. . . .

Yep. Big Jake can do it. Big Jake freights supplies from the railroad up the slopes to my town. Nothing's too big or too heavy for him to haul, not with those six big oxen of his and the two biggest under the lead yoke. Garfield and Hayes he calls those two. Big Jake's a Democrat. Gives his critters Republican names so his cussing can do double duty.

Once a month he makes the round trip up from the railroad. It's quite an event when he arrives. We know he's coming long before he's in sight. There's a bad stretch about half a mile out of town where the grade's particular steep and the road runs narrow between two cliffs. Springs from the rocks keep the ground soft. When he hits that stretch he lets out the last notches in his cussing and just about plain blasts those oxen through. We're doing this and doing that around town and we hear the first hot echoes hopping through the hills and the womenfolk close their windows and stuff cotton in their ears and the rest of us gather to watch the road. First thing we see is the blue smoke floating up over the cliffs. Then we see Garfield and Hayes heaving and straining to top the grade and behind them come the other two yokes on the chain and then the wagons, four of them, the big-bodied lead and the two trailers and the small camp outfit tagging on two wheels, and beside them Big Jake himself snaking out the whip and aroaring. His cussing comes straight at us along the road then and we listen close to catch what he's saying and any new brand of profanity he's invented. But when he reaches town we scatter quick. For the first five minutes the main street's his. He needs time to celebrate and simmer down. He plants his feet firm in the dust and sends his forty-foot whip lashing out in every direction and cracking like cannon on the Fourth. He looks around to see is anyone fool enough to be within range so he can nip a hat off a head or a button off a vest. His oxen stop and stand sleepy-eyed chewing their cuds and maybe a mite proud that he's cussed them into doing it again but, being oxen, too cantankerous ever to let that show. The cussing dwindles to a kind of purring and the whip-cracking fades in a last few tickling pops and when he starts coiling

the leather the rest of us come running out to see who'll be first to
buy Big Jake a big drink. . . .

Yep. That's the way he used to do it. That's the way he still does
it. But there's a difference nowadays. Echoes still bounce through
the hills when he starts aroaring. Smoke still rises and the oxen still
move. The tone's the same and the tune's the same. But the words
are different. . . .

The Right Reverend Pemberton Willoughby's responsible. It's
all his, the whole credit. He beats Big Jake at Big Jake's own game.
Beats him fair and square, and that changes the words and likely
the Right Reverend Pemberton Willoughby's the one man ever
could do it. . . .

Parson Pem we call him. The full name's too much in the mouth.
He's big too, almost of a size with Big Jake himself, though he doesn't
seem so at first in his pegleg pants and frock coat. Has a fine preaching voice too, deep and round and carrying far for outdoor services.
He comes to town one day riding on his old mule and slides off and
announces he's heard we need a church. He's decided our souls must
be sickly from sojourning in a churchless town and require weekly
applications of verbal mustard plasters in the form of sermons and
he's arrived to see we get the same. If there are any objections, will
the objectors please to step forward at once so he can take care of
them right away without wasting any time. None of us really object.
Anyone can come into my town any day and set up any kind of a
shop he wants long as he doesn't step on too many toes too hard.
But this gent wants objections and we're always obliging so a couple of the boys step forward to offer some and before they know
what's happening he has them both by their necks and pops their
heads together and there they are both sitting dazed on the ground
and he's looking around bright and cheerful for more. There aren't
any more. "Fine," he says. "Couldn't be better. This is Tuesday.
There's no reason why, come Sunday, with you all working the way
I'll show you, we shouldn't have a church built."

He's right. Come Sunday, he has his church up. No pews in it yet
and no pulpit, but the walls are solid and the roof's almost on and
there's the start of a little steeple sprouting in front. Everybody con-
tributes something, material or work, because he's that kind of a
man. Makes you want to contribute. By time the next Sunday rolls

around we're all convinced. He's our parson. Maybe we don't all expect to be too regular in attendance at his little church, but he's our parson and we're proud of him. His preaching's the right kind, simple and straight and scorching the sinners and short so the wooden seats don't get too hard. And he's the helpingest man ever lived. Let a neighbor be putting in some fence and Parson Pem is out there with his frock coat off adigging post holes. Let a woman have an extra heavy week's washing and like enough Parson Pem'll be coming along and rolling up his sleeves and plunging his hands into the soapsuds. Let a jam develop at the blacksmith shop with people waiting long for work and it's Parson Pem who'll be in there pumping the bellows and swinging the second hammer. Can't say he converts every one of us to every point in the dogma he likes to expound. Can say he converts plenty of people and some surprising at that to his way of being neighborly.

Yep. The Right Reverend Pemberton Willoughby's our preacher. I figure it's about the third week he's been with us and the tip's being put on the steeple and just about everybody in town is standing around watching, when we hear the first hot echoes hopping through the hills far down the road where it comes up between those two cliffs. Parson Pem hears them too but they're still too faint for him to make out the words. He stares in surprise at the womenfolk scattering to their houses and slamming doors and pulling down windows. He stares along the road with the rest of us and sees the blue smoke with sulphur edgings float up over the cliffs. He sees Garfield and Hayes come heaving and straining over the top of the grade and behind them the other two yokes and then the wagons and beside them Big Jake snaking out the whip and aroaring and filling the air with the smell of brimstone. The words come straight along the road now and Parson Pem can make them out. A look of horror settles over his face and he claps his hands to his ears. But that's not much protection against Big Jake's voice and brand of cussing and, anyway, the temptation's strong. He eases on the hands and then drops them and just stands there staring in a kind of unbelieving fascination at Big Jake acoming.

He's still standing there still staring when Big Jake hits main street and the rest of us skip for cover. The oxen stop and drop their eyelids and start chewing their cuds and Big Jake plants his feet firm in the road dust and starts cracking the whip. He sees Parson Pem standing there and out snakes the whip and off sails the parson's hat. Big Jake is some surprised when Parson Pem still stands there a-staring and out snakes the whip again and off comes the top button of the frock coat. Still the same. Out snakes the whip again, tip flicking neat and precise for the next button, and up comes one of Parson Pem's big hands and grabs the tip and yanks hard on it and forward and down into the dust goes Big Jake. He comes to his feet aroaring and arushing for the tussle and sudden he sees what he hasn't seen before, the hindside-foremost collar around Parson Pem's neck. He roars and he bellows and he simmers down to a gurgle. "A rev-rend," he says in disgust. "A big one and the best chance for a ground-thumping in a month of freighting and it's a rev'rend." Parson Pem looks at him in equal disgust. "A heathen," he says. "A foulmouthed and profane and benighted heathen." Big Jake lets loose again. Beats even his own best previous cussing. The oxen open their eyes and look startled and the blue smoke rises with fiery edgings and Big Jake finally gets it out. "Take off that collar," he roars. "I'll show you who's a heathen!" And Parson Pem reaches up and unhooks the collar in back and tosses it over on the board sidewalk.

They meet with a thump that shakes buildings both sides the street. They wrap their big arms around each other and butt with their chins and heave and grunt and heave again. Parson Pem's a tough one at this kind of tussling but Big Jake's a tougher. He's used to wrestling oxen in and out of yokes and hoisting freight in and out of wagons. He heaves extra hard and swings Parson Pem off his feet and lifts him and thumps him down on the ground so that the air goes out of him in a big whoosh and he can't move for a minute or two. Big Jake looks down at him and grins some. "You're a mealymouthed rev-rend," Big Jake says. "But you're quite a man too." Parson Pem looks up at him grim and determined and fights for breath and gets some. "You're a heathen," Parson Pem says. "A cursing profane heathen and an abomination to men's ears. But when I've knocked that out of you, you'll be a mighty man of the Lord." Big Jake plain can't believe what he's hearing from the man he's just beat and he shakes his head and snorts and stomps off into Willie Lord's saloon to clear the dust out of his throat. . . .

That's the way it goes. Every month the same. The echoes bounce through the hills and the blue smoke rises strong with sulphur and the smell of brimstone and Garfield and Hayes appear straining over the grade and Big Jake comes along the road snaking out his whip and aroaring and there in the middle of main street is Parson Pem reaching up to unhook that collar. Every month Parson Pem lands thumping on the ground and the air goes whoosh out of him and Big Jake stands looking down and shaking his big head in wonderment and stomps off for liquid comfort. Rest of us don't mix in. This is between those two big men and we let it be. That's how we do things in my town. Not saying we don't have bets running on the outcome. But Parson Pem is our preacher and Big Jake is our bullwhacker and we're proud of them both. Only interfering we'd do would be to stop any outsider from interfering with them.

Then the month comes when Big Jake can't take it any more. The blue smoke is sort of thin this time and Garfield and Hayes just about crawl over the top of the grade, maybe out of habit much as anything else, and Big Jake doesn't even let a little pop out of his whip when he reaches town. Coils it slow and careful and hangs it on the lead wagon and walks over where Parson Pem is standing collarless in the middle of the street. "Rev'rend," he says, almost plaintive, "ain't there anything'll stop you tackling me every time I get here?" Parson Pem beams at him bright and cheerful. "Certainly. When you stop poisoning the air with your profanity, why then I'll put my collar on and keep it there."

Big Jake shuffles his feet and runs a big hand across his forehead and down over his face, wiping off the dust. "Rev'rend," he says, "you just don't know. In your business freighting souls to where you think they ought to go, there's no call for strong language. Not that kind anyway. But a man who whacks bulls has just plain got to cuss them. I'll lay you a straight proposition. If you can drive those critters of mine five miles and up that last grade without cussing, I'll quit it and never cuss again."

Yep. That's what turns Parson Pem into a bullwhacker for the first and maybe the only time in his life. It's early evening when Big Jake puts that proposition. It's late evening by time the rules are ready. The two of them start discussing the whys and wherefores of this cussing-no-cussing contest right there in the middle of main street. Rest of us come out from cover and join in. Look at it first as kind of a joke but see how strict earnest those two are and soon we're all the same. We name old Sandburr Sam Claggett, our sheriff, to be judge of the proceeding. With him in charge we know it'll be run right. He sets eight o'clock the next morning for the start so the oxen'll have a chance to rest and not be asked to be hauling again after already doing a day's work. Big Jake allows that seems fair to him. Old Sandburr says next he thinks there ought to be a time limit. Parson Pem agrees that's only fair and suggests two hours and Old Sandburr looks sorrowful at him and announces firm he's making it four hours, which is still less than he'd want if he was trying this himself. There's to be only one wagon but a load on that to give it heft and they argue a bit over that. Not over the weight but over the cargo. Willie Lord offers ten barrels of whiskey but Parson Pem balks at that and they settle on ten barrels of flour. Near the end Parson Pem is squirming a little. Wrastles with his conscience and at last says he believes in doing the Lord's work by whatever means come to hand but still it only seems fair to him to let Big Jake know he's handled a whip some in his time and had experience making critters move. "What kind of critters?" Big Jake says. Parson Pem explains he's busted sod with a four-horse span when he was agrowing and he's been a helper on a mule train heading west after graduating from his preacher-school. "Horses," Big Jake says. "Mules. It's the same's before. You just don't know. . . ."

Come morning we're all out there to watch at the five-mile mark Old Sandburr's measured off, just about all of us including the women, who are set to do some yipping and huzzaing because they look on Parson Pem as their champion in this. He's wearing a pair of overalls borrowed from Big Jake because they're the only ones in town of a size to fit. He's bareheaded and his eyes are aglowing and the only thing preacher-like about him is that hindside-foremost collar he's kept on, maybe to remind him to watch his words if or when the going gets rough.

Wagon's there, ready loaded with ten barrels of flour from Jed Durkin's store. Oxen's there too. Been out there all night, pegged by good grass. They're rested and they've grazed and it's just another day to them. Big Jake's yoked them and Old Sandburr's inspected the yoking and they're standing there placid and quiet chewing their cuds and, being oxen, paying no more attention to all of us buzzing around than to a flock of flies.

Parson Pem takes the whip and uncoils it. "Got the time?" he says. Old Sandburr checks his stemwinder and nods. "Stand back," Parson Pem says. He snakes out the whip and he does know how to handle it. Gets some nice sharp cracks out of it near the oxen's ears. "Gee, Garfield!" he shouts. "Haw, Hayes!" he yells. They don't even know he's there. He chirrups at them. Clucks at them. Tries all the starting noises he's ever heard. He whistles. Shouts. Stomps his feet. Makes the whip hum and crackle mean. Those oxen chew their cuds sleepy-eyed and don't pay any mind to him at all. He stands looking at them and there's a faint pink flush coming up his neck above that collar of his.

He walks around front and puts a rope on the lead yoke to try leading them. Pulls. Pulls hard. Garfield and Hayes grunt a bit and go on chewing their cuds. He wraps his big hands tighter around the rope and digs in his heels and heaves. Garfield opens one eye a little wider and blows soft and Hayes knows the signal and sudden they both stretch their necks forward and the unexpected slack catches Parson Pem off balance and down he goes on his rump. He sits there staring at those oxen and the pink above his collar is darkening red and spreading on up over his face. Garfield and Hayes look at each other and to show what they think of his little annoyances they double under their front legs and plop down in the road dust to take a nap.

Up the slope where we're all standing awatching there's a snort and something like a mixed cackle and bellow. It's Big Jake near busting his ribs with the merriment inside pushing out. Old Sandburr fixes him with a cold eye. "Rules are," Old Sandburr says, "no outside meddling of any kind. That burbling of yours adds insult to the injury those critters are doing the parson." Big Jake pushes a big fist in his mouth and subsides sort of strangling, all the same enjoying himself more'n he has since the first time the parson shed his collar to tackle him.

Parson Pem gets to his feet. Sweat's showing on him and he's breathing deep and fast. He goes up to Garfield and Hayes and unfastens his rope and you can tell by the way his fingers fumble with the knot that already he's madder'n a man who can't let some out in cussing has a right to be. He squats down on his heels in front of them and stares at them two, maybe three minutes. Then he begins.

His voice is low at first, but it's his preaching voice, the one that can carry against any wind for outdoor service, and it grows and swells deep and round as he talks and he hits each word harder and harder. "You're naught but benighted heathen too," he says to those oxen. "Benighted heathen dwelling in the darkness of ignorance and your sins testify against you. But that's not your fault. Your education's been neglected something shameful. No one's told you and no one's taught you. But it's there in the Book for all to read and for all to know. Genesis One: Twenty-eight. *Subdue it,* the Lord said to man, meaning the earth and all things upon it. *Have dominion over the fish of the sea, and over the fowl of the air, and over every living thing that moveth upon the earth.* That means you too, you four-footed loafing benighted heathen beasts of the field. There's no escaping it for you. Stupid you are and stupider you'd like to pretend to be even than the Lord made you, but you can't mistake the meaning of those words." Parson Pem's voice is rolling out like a roaring thunder and righteous anger is putting wisps of smoke around the edges and Garfield and Hayes open their eyes and look at him. "No excuse for you now!" he roars. "I'm telling you and now you know! Dominion it is! Dominion it'll be! I'll smite ye in wrath with a continual stroke! I'll dominion ye if I have to kick each and every one of ye the whole five miles!"

Parson Pem stretches up straight and goes around and steps in by the chain behind Garfield and Hayes. He applies the toe of his right boot with plenty of power to Garfield and to Hayes in special tender spots and they both grunt surprised and lumber up to their feet. He goes back by the wagon and takes the whip and whirls it around his head and sends it out with a crack that near tears off the tip. "Dominion!" he roars and a puff of smoke floats upward. "Dominion over the beasts of the field! Get amoving, ye benighted bulls of Balaam afore I punish ye seven times seven for your sins!" And Garfield and Hayes heave reluctant into their yoke and the others follow their lead and the wagon moves and the women with us on the slope start yipping and Parson Pem throws back his head triumphant and strides forward and Big Jake pulls his fist out of his mouth. "Sounds suspicious like cussing to me," he says. But Old Sandburr fixes him again with a cold eye. "Kind of strong in spots," Old Sandburr says, "but I listened careful. Caught nary a cussword."

Yep. Parson Pem has those critters amoving. Keeps them moving without too much trouble. Not at first, that is. Load's light alongside what they're used to hauling and they're remembering the town's not far ahead and when they reach there they always get a grain feeding, so they plod along fair enough for them. He strides along beside, putting his feet down deliberate and matching pace to theirs, and he's recalling that the Book mentions oxen often and feeling good and sort of biblical himself because of that and cracking the whip and roaring "Dominion!" every now and then when he thinks they're hesitating some. He's so tickled with having them moving that it's quite a spell before he realizes that, being oxen, they're amoving almighty slow. Cocks an eye at the sun and does some figuring. It took him all of half an hour to get them started. He's been a full hour, maybe a mite more, on the way and he hasn't even reached the halfway mark. He notches up the whip-cracking and the roaring and tries to hurry the critters. That's when his troubles start again.

Making oxen move is one thing. Making them hurry is flour out of another barrel. One thing they don't take to, that's hurrying. They'll work when blasted into it, but they'll work in their own way and their own time. Parson Pem tries to hurry them and they won't hurry and the sweat starts dripping off him and he gets madder by the minute and the madder he gets the stubborner they get and they begin trying tricks on him. No sense telling all they try. Anyone's ever watched them knows the slow deliberate devilment they can do. Just a sample's the time they give him when he has to pull out so the morning mail coach with the right of way in the road ruts can go past and they pull out for him surprising willing and in doing it manage to tangle their feet over the chain and just stand there looking disgusted at a driver that'll let that happen to them. Takes him better'n fifteen minutes to straighten that out and another five to get them moving again. He's a patient man but by then all the patience he packs is worn out and when he dominions them on along the road his hair's waving wild and his face is dark red and he has to send out smoke puffs mighty frequent.

All the same he's moving them along. Doing it so well that Big Jake is getting worried. He takes Old Sandburr off to one side. "Sandburr," he says, "dry weather we been having. Ain't much mud on up that grade. Would you say there was anything in the rules to stop my hurrying ahead and toting some buckets and sloshing some water in a few places?" Old Sandburr just looks at him and Big Jake shuffles his big feet. "Ain't no harm," he says, "in a man asking, is there?" Still Old Sandburr just looks at him and Big Jake shuffles his feet some more. "Well, anyhow," he says, "you keep listening close. He's building up a head of steam that's plain got to bust out in cusswords."

Big Jake's not the only one thinking that. About all of us figure the same. Then we're certain because those oxen hit the beginning of the grade and start up and feel the wagon dragging hard and they stop. Stop dead. Hunch down and droop their heads and start chewing their cuds placid and determined showing they've stopped to stay. The dominioning they've been getting's enough to move them along the near level but it won't push them up that grade and they think they've got the measure of this man driving them and he hasn't got what it takes. For a while they're right.

Parson Pem works on them. Works hard. Tries what he's been doing right along only harder. Tries it with variations and new angles. Blasts at them. Blows at them. Sends up puffs of smoke that're acquiring a bluish tinge. They don't even twitch their ears. Tries the toe of his boot again and has to quit because he's only hurting himself. Lays the whip right onto their hides and they hunch their shoulders a bit and go on chewing. His face gets a bright purple and his neck is so fiery red you'd think that hindside-foremost celluloid collar'd bust into flames. He throws the whip to the ground and jumps on it with both feet and tears at his hair with his hands. He glares at those oxen and he rears back his head and draws in a mighty breath and opens his mouth to let the roaring out and Big Jake and Old Sandburr lean forward intent to listen and already there's a grin starting on Big Jake's face. But the words he hears ain't what he expects. Parson Pem's voice rolls out like a thunder. "Job Six: Two and Three. *Oh that my grief were thoroughly weighed, and my calamity laid in the balances together! For now it would be heavier than the sands of the sea!*" He stretches taller and his voice rolls even louder. "Job Seven: Eleven. *Therefore I will not refrain my mouth; I will speak in the anguish of my spirit; I will complain in the bitterness of my soul!*" He swoops down and grabs up the whip. His voice roars forth and the echoes begin to bounce through the hills. "Isaiah Twenty-nine: Six. *I shall visit ye with thunder, and with earthquake, and great noise, with storm and tempest, and the flame of devouring fire.*" He sends the whip humming and cracking at Garfield and Hayes and his voice roars up and a tinge of brimstone edges the air. "Jeremiah Seven: Twenty. *Behold, mine anger and my fury shall be poured forth upon this place!"* Garfield and Hayes lift their heads and their ears perk and Parson Pem's voice fills all the wide spaces with its roaring and the smoke comes not in puffs but in a steady cloud. "Chronicles One: One through Four," he roars. *"Adam, Sheth, Enosh! Kenan, Mahalaleel, Jered! Henoch, Methuselah, Lamech! Noah, Sham, Ham, and Japheth!"* And those oxen heave into the yokes and the wagon moves and they go almost jumping up that grade and Big Jake looks at Old Sandburr who shakes his head and Big Jake trudges after the wagon into town to shake Parson Pem's hand and admit he's beat. . . .

Yep. That's our preacher, the Right Reverend Pemberton Willoughby. But that's our bullwhacker too. Big Jake Bannack. Maybe you ought to know how he comes out on that proposition too. Not so good at first. We don't realize that till another month's gone by and it's time for him to be in with another load. We're waiting for it and Parson Pem in particular because a barrel organ's coming for his church. The day passes and Big Jake doesn't show. All the next morning and still he doesn't show. The mail coach driver says he saw Big Jake down the road a piece and thought he seemed to be having trouble. Old Sandburr saddles up. Rides out to see what's doing. Back in less than an hour looking thoughtful. "Jake's there," he says. "Bottom of that last grade. From the look of him he's just about been pulling those wagons himself. Says he's been subduing and dominioning those critters all the way and it's mighty slow going. Can't get them to budge up the grade. He's sitting on the ground turning pages in the Book he's bought and can't find the right place."

Old Sandburr looks around for Parson Pem but that's not needed. Parson Pem is already out climbing bareback on his mule. He goes down the road whacking it with his heels. Rest of us gather outside and watch him disappear between those two cliffs and go on down the grade. We wait. It's worth waiting for. First thing we hear is the echoes bouncing through the hills and the rumbling as they shake stones loose and start rockslides off in the distance. Then we see the smoke rising, thick and blue and floating up over the cliffs. And heaving forward in positive leaps come Garfield and Hayes over the grade and behind them the other oxen and the wagons with the organ lashed and swaying on top of the lead load and beside the wagons those two big men, with the mule tagging. They're striding along each with an arm over the other's shoulders and their heads are back and they're aroaring: *"Adam, Sheth! Kenan, Mahalaleel, Jered! Henoch, Methuselah, Lamech!"*

Out of the Past

THIS IS a story of revenge. But revenge is an ugly word. It carries suggestions of hatred and personalized viciousness that may or may not be involved. There are times when revenge is more accurately a plain balancing of accounts, an expression of one man's loyalty to another. It is a balancing of accounts, an expression of loyalty bridging many miles and many years, that is chronicled here.

This is a story, too, of three parts. Three happenings. Three individual bursts of violent action separated in time and place. I will not tell you whether these happenings were true in literal fact. That is no longer important at this date. But you should know that they could have been true. Such things happened in this America in the years of westward settlement. I will not even insist that you accept these three happenings as parts of the one same story. I am content to present them in the hope you will understand them. And I will present them as you might come upon them searching, as I have often done, through the records of that westward settlement, the old letters and books and newspapers that remain as a legacy to us out of the past.

First, a letter. A letter written from a military post in the parched badlands of southern New Mexico in 1885.

This letter was written by a soldier, a sergeant, a cavalryman, to his mother back home in Missouri. He wrote it lying on a cot in a curtained-off section of an adobe and log-walled barracks marked with a sign that said "Hospital." He was a badly wounded, badly shaken man, profoundly grateful that he was alive and that he would live. The tone of his letter and a few hints in the text suggest that he was young without being youthful, maybe in his middle twenties, reasonably well educated for the time and the territory, a serious, capable man and a good soldier. He wrote the letter in segments on several different days, probably because he was too weak to do it all at once. His narrative of what happened is rambling and understandably confused but the main outline is clear and direct.

Geronimo was off the reservation again, he and his renegade Apaches off on their last and bitterest raiding campaign. Troops were out after them and this soldier, this sergeant, was with those troops. The Apaches were up to the usual trick of scattering to strike in many places at the same time and the troops were spread thin in small detachments combing the territory. The detachment this sergeant was with had penetrated some rough country. The enemy smell was strong. The Indian scout leading the way slowed the pace till the horses were barely moving and said the signs spoke trouble. The lieutenant in command had the sense to figure that was warning enough and called a halt where rocks gave good cover in case of an attack. He sent the sergeant and the Indian scout on forward. There was no way of knowing whether the Apaches in the area had spotted the detachment yet. The plan was for those two to look over the ground ahead and try to locate the enemy, if possible without being seen. They were to go maybe three miles but no further. If nothing developed they were to look for another easily defended spot and one of them slip back to bring up the full detachment. The lieutenant was a cautious man, a good officer. He was going to move now only from strong position to strong position, not risking his whole command in a possible ambush.

That's the picture to hold in mind. Two men riding forward. Two men obeying orders and riding forward into rough country with the enemy smell in the air around. One of them is the sergeant, the letter writer, a good soldier who is serious about the Army as a career and has won his stripes early in his second enlistment. The other is an Indian, a Miniconjou Sioux from the northern plains, a man well into middle age who has fought the white men in the vigor of his youth and seen his tribe dwindle in defeat and has wandered far and has served now several years as a scout with the men he once fought. It is the letter writer who remains a shadowy figure, featureless, known only in character as revealed by his letter. It is the Indian who emerges in fairly clear focus, seen as the sergeant saw him, not to the sergeant just an Indian obscure in the anonymity of his race, in which all seem the same because of their very difference, but a man distinct and individual with the marks of a hard life upon him. He is a man of medium height, thick in the body with shoulders not wide but thick through and a heaviness around the hips. His eyes are small and black in a flat face pitted with old smallpox scars and he limps with his right leg from a stiffness in the knee joint and two fingers of his left hand are missing. He is a man hidden behind the blank wall of his flat expressionless face, nondescript in appearance in castoff Army-issue pants and shirt faded past color, yet a man on whose word an old-hand lieutenant would set the safety of his command and not think twice about it.

They rode forward. They went cautiously, holding to cover, working upward as the land rose toward a long ridge athwart their course. They stopped. Ahead and beyond the ridge they saw a thin streamer of smoke floating upward. A signal? A campfire? They moved forward again, even more slowly. They dropped into a hiding gully that led toward the ridge top. The Indian was in the lead, head up, eyes alert, nostrils wide in the slight wind. Suddenly he whirled his horse and waved to the sergeant to do the same and drove back down the gully at full gallop. As he passed the sergeant in the act of swinging his horse, the first shots came from up the gully among rocks along the sides. A bullet smashed through the sergeant's left leg above the knee and into his horse and the horse went down and he was thrown free and rolled headlong, striking against a stone that tore a jagged gash along his jaw, and as he rolled in the turning he saw the Indian scout diminishing into distance down the gully and then the Apaches scrambling out from among the rocks up the gully and starting toward him. He did not know where his rifle was. It had been jarred from his grasp and lay somewhere beyond the dying horse. He could not stand but he pushed up, leaning on his left arm, and clawed at his service revolver and had it in his right hand when another bullet smashed into his shoulder and he was flat and helpless on the ground.

Curiously he felt no pain in the shock of that moment. But everything about him was immeasurably clear and distinct, the hard ground beneath and the clear baked blue of the sky overhead and beyond and above all else the utter aloneness. He could hear the

shouts of the Apaches coming and somehow the sounds did not penetrate the silence that surrounded him. And into that silence and
that aloneness came another sound that could penetrate and that
hit him as even the bullets had not. It was the sound of hooves
and he could move and raise his head and twist it to look back
down the gully. The Indian scout had whirled his horse again and
was racing toward him, low-bent along the straining neck, reaching
with one arm to lash the frantic animal to greater speed. The Indian scout pulled the horse spinning on its hind legs to a stop by
the sergeant and leaped off and scooped up the sergeant like a limp
sack of grain and flung him over the horse's withers and leaped again
into the saddle and the heaving animal struggled into a gallop beneath the double burden.

How long they rode that way the sergeant could not know. The
pounding of the horse's foreshoulders under him was an unbear-
able torment. He had time only to think that it was hopeless, that
this horse was carrying double and the Apaches would have their
own horses hidden near and be after them and overtake them, and
then the jolting was too much and he dropped into darkness.

That was early afternoon. It was late afternoon when he regained
consciousness for a few moments. He was lying in a tight crevice
between two big rocks. All he could see was the sheer stone sides
rising and the patch of deepening blue of sky between. Then he was
aware that an Indian with a flat pitted face, naked to the waist, was
bandaging or rebandaging his shoulder with strips of a faded old
Army shirt. Again he had time for only one thought. He was thinking that this Indian was doing a good job considering the fact two
fingers of his left hand were missing, when the darkness rose and
overwhelmed him. Much later his mind flickered for a few seconds
out of that darkness into another, into the darkness of the moonless
star-pointed night, and he was aware that he was being carried, lying
limp and doubled down, not now over the withers of a horse, but
over the thick shoulder and tensed upper arm of a man. He could
hear the slow strained breathing of the man carrying him and then
he knew nothing and then drops of some raw stuff, rum or whiskey,
were raking his throat and he was lying on the ground about thirty
feet from a small fire and the lieutenant was kneeling beside him.
He tried to move and sit up, fighting the pain that streaked through
his stiffened body, and the lieutenant clamped him to the ground.

"Easy," the lieutenant said. "You're not going anywhere. There's
a lot of them out there. They've got us pinned down tight." And
still the sergeant tried to move, to turn his head and look about,
and the lieutenant understood. "He waited till dark to bring you
in. But he's gone now. He slipped out again to make a try for reinforcements."

There it is, all that is needed. The rest of the letter is unimportant. What it chronicles is, in a sense, anticlimax. Reinforcements
came and the Apaches sighted them and faded further into the badlands. The sergeant and two other wounded were sent back in a
quartermaster's wagon. He was out of the campaign, out of the
long later days of fighting and hard hectic riding and knew only by
heresay what those days brought. He was on a hospital cot with two
bullet wounds which the doctor said would heal nicely and with
a gash along the side of his jaw which the doctor said would leave
a neat scar to remind him of what he had been through.

Lying there, writing his letter, this sergeant had plenty of time to
think over what he could remember of what had happened and to
wonder what must have happened during the hours he was lost in
the darkness and an aging Indian with a limping leg got him away
from Geronimo's Apaches and took him through to the safety of
the detachment's rock barricade. That impressed him deeply and
he wrote about it at length. But what impressed him more was the
sudden shattering of his aloneness as he lay helpless on the ground
in the gully. His mind returned to that again and again. Three
times the same brief sentence leaps out of the letter. *He came back.*

Second, an account of a court trial cited in a paper-bound local
history of a Kansas town. The trial occurred in 1898. That is a jump
of thirteen years in time and several hundred miles northwestward
in place. But the mind can make it in an instant if interest holds.

This trial is cited in the town history as an example of lingering
frontier conditions, of the kind of excitement that could still break
forth in that part of Kansas near the turn of the century. The
historian himself offers no hint of his sympathies in the case. He
simply offers the facts established by the evidence and summarizes
the testimony taken. Out of these facts and the varied testimony
comes a plain picture of the event at issue and the reasons for the
verdict given.

Background is important here. The town was close to an Army post, a cavalry headquarters and supply depot. Some people liked that, those who made money out of the soldiers, especially during the first week after each payday. Other people didn't like it, those with short memories who could forget the time when the presence of troops was a reassurance for settlers and those afflicted with the urge to impose their brand of respectability on their fellows. There were periodic complaints about brawls and noisy disturbances in the saloons and disorderly houses supported chiefly by the soldiers and the inevitable collection of rough and often unsavory individuals who congregated in the neighborhood of an Army establishment. A particular annoyance to many people seems to have been a small batch of Indians, most of them well along in years, who lived, or in the usual local phrase, squatted near the post with the apparent permission of the commanding officer and loafed in and out of town with no visible means of livelihood.

That was the situation when a drastic change took place. Far off in Havana harbor the battleship *Maine* was sunk. The United States declared war on Spain. The troops at this Kansas post were ordered east en route to Cuba. Within ten days the post was deserted except for a small squad left to dismantle it. An unnatural quiet settled over the outlying section of the town that had annoyed so many respectable citizens. And out of that quiet came the sudden violence that precipitated the trial.

The key character was a bartender, a reckless, red-headed, ready-tongued man. He must have had a quick temper to go with the hair and a streak of cruelty in him, because his wife had left him and had been trying to divorce him on precisely those grounds. Yet he was well liked in the district, among the men at least, well enough for some of them to chip in a few dollars apiece and pay his lawyer when he was brought to trial. And apparently he was a good hand at his job. His employer had kept him on month after month even though he was constantly overdrawn on his pay. It was a better than average bartending job too. He worked at the one saloon that had rarely been a target for complaints, not so much a saloon as a semi-club, a place where sandwiches as well as liquor were available to order and where the officers of the post had been accustomed to gather when they came to town.

On this particular morning the bartender had much on his mind.

He was brooding over his family troubles—or so he said later. He was worrying about losing his job—which certainly could have been true. Business had all but died with the departure of the troops a few days before. These morning hours were dull. They edged toward noon and the only customers there were two beer drinkers fiddling with a deck of cards at a rear table. And an old Indian wrapped in a mangy old buffalo robe despite the warmth of the weather came in the door and sat down at one of the front tables near the bar.

The bartender knew this Indian, knew him by frequent sight and serving at least. It was unusual for an Indian to be in that saloon, but this Indian had been there often during the previous months, always with a group of middle-aged officers, had sat at that same table in that same chair, not exactly a part of the group yet with it, sitting silent there with the officers and drinking when they drank and sometimes nodding his head gravely at what was said. Now he was alone. The officers were hundreds of miles away, riding the rails toward the port from which they would embark for Cuba.

The old Indian sat stiff and still on the chair and the bartender watched him and a familiar anger began to burn in the bartender's mind.

That was one thing the bartender hated, serving drinks to a lousy Indian. What right did one of those smelly thieving old relics with his dirty coppery skin and ugly face have to come into a white man's place and drink a white man's liquor and expect a white man to serve it to him? The way to handle Indians was to throw them the stuff by the bottle, sell them the cheapest and make them pay plenty and go drink themselves into a stupor outside in some gutter.

The old Indian moved on the chair. He raised a hand to catch the bartender's attention as the officers had always done. "Whiskey," he said as the officers had always said. "The best."

For a moment the bartender fondled the thought of jumping over the bar and grabbing hold of the Indian and heaving him bodily out into the road. No. His employer was somewhere in the back room and would hear the noise and his employer was in no mood to tolerate the loss of a customer, any customer. The bartender took a whiskey glass and reached under the bar to the slopjar on the shelf there in which the dregs left in used glasses were dumped. It had not been emptied for several days. He dipped the whiskey glass in and brought it out dripping with the foul mixture. He walked around the end of the bar and to the table and set the glass on it. Fifty cents was the top price for a single drink. No one was ever expected to settle his score until ready to leave. But the bartender stood there looking down at the Indian. "One dollar," he said. "Now."

The old Indian looked up at him. Slowly he fumbled with one hand inside the discolored old buffalo robe. He took a long time finding what he sought. A slow satisfaction began to build in the bartender and then suddenly faded as the Indian laid a silver dollar on the table. The bartender reached for it and the anger rekindled in his mind made his hand shake and he fumbled the coin and it fell to the floor and rolled. He bent to pick it up and as he did so he heard a chuckle from back by the rear table and the sound fanned the fire in his mind. He grabbed the coin and went again behind the bar and leaned against it staring at the old Indian and the whiskey glass filled with the slopjar dregs.

The old Indian lifted the glass in his right hand. He looked around the empty table and raised the glass a little higher as if in salute. He put the glass to his lips and took a first swallow into his mouth and his head bobbed forward and he spat the stuff out and then was still, sitting quiet in the chair, staring at the glass in his hand. He rose, still holding the glass, and went straight to the bar and set the glass down and looked over it at the bartender. "Not good," he said.

Those were the last words the old Indian ever spoke for the anger in the bartender flamed upward and destroyed all restraint and he reached and took the revolver that lay on the shelf beneath the bar and brought it up for the purpose, he said later, of forcing the complaining old fool to drink the stuff anyway, but the Indian read more than that in his eyes and knew and dropped below the bar level clutching his old robe about him to escape and the bartender leaned and reached over and fired. The bullet drove angling downward through the Indian's neck into his body. He crumpled to the floor and rolled over and was still. He was dead before the two beer drinkers at the rear table had risen to their feet to come running forward.

There had to be a trial so there was a trial. A man had been killed and in the presence of two witnesses. But no one was very

enthusiastic about it. The prosecution was less than vigorous, simply
went through the formalities. The old Indian was as alone in death
as he had been those last moments in the saloon. His officer friends
were far away, traveling toward a new military frontier. Even those
of his own race quickly, and perhaps wisely, disappeared from the
neighborhood of the town when they heard what had happened.

It was a peculiar trial in one respect. The original charge was
murder. That was changed to manslaughter, then raised to murder
again—at the request, no less, of the bartender's lawyer himself. But
that lawyer knew what he was doing. He was aiming at a direct
acquittal. He pleaded self-defense for his client. He brushed aside
the fact that the old Indian was unarmed. How could his client
have been certain that the old scarecrow didn't have a gun or a
knife concealed under that buffalo robe and wasn't crouching down
to pull it and then come after him? The jurymen jumped at that
lead. They were out less than ten minutes. Not guilty. "There was
nothing to get excited about," one of them said later. "It was just
an Indian. What's another one of them more or less."

Just another Indian. The almost casual opening testimony establishing some identity for this Indian offered a few facts bearing on
that point. When he was younger he had served as an Army scout.
He walked with a stiffness in his right leg and two fingers of his left
hand were missing.

Third, an article in a small local weekly newspaper published in
a Montana mining camp in 1901. The jump this time is three years
and more than half a thousand miles. But again the mind can make
it if the will prompts.

The man who wrote the article, probably the editor of the local
weekly because the paper could scarcely have supported more than
a one-man staff, really cut loose in the writing. He filled nearly two
columns of the single-sheet issue with it, wordy, bombastic, strongly
personalized in the tradition of western journalism of the period,
well larded with high-flying phrases about the up-and-climbing quali-
ties of the enterprising settlement in glorious Montana in which he
was privileged to live and hold a position of civic responsibility in
the opening years of the bright new century called the twentieth. He
was variously shocked, amazed, disgusted, startled, outraged at what
had happened. He was thunderingly insistent that something should

be done about it but not quite certain what. It is quite possible that he wrote to some extent with his tongue in his cheek. That boom camp in Montana, even in 1901, was not exactly a quiet humdrum community.

A man had been killed.

Everyone knew him, so the writer said. Everyone knew everyone else in that tent-and-shack settlement so new that the census of the year before had passed it by. He was the man who tended the bar in the larger of the camp's two emporiums devoted to the dispensing of liquid refreshment. Breathed there a citizen of the camp who had not gone into that emporium tired and thirsty from grubbing gold or copper out of the stubborn unyielding rock and been grateful to see that redheaded talkative man waiting behind the bar to dispense that liquid refreshment? What if the name he used was likely not the name his parents had bequeathed him? He served good drinks. What if he had come up to Montana from down Kansas way with a somewhat vague reputation of being a dangerous man in anger? He served good drinks and with a flourish. He was free, white, and well past twenty-one, with the usual supposedly inalienable right to life, liberty, and the pursuit of happiness. And he was dead. Ah, the shifting fluctuations of fate.

So much for the journalistic rhetoric. What had happened was in itself short and simple. And deadly serious. This man, this bartender, had opened the place as usual about ten o'clock in the morning. Most of the men of the camp were out at the diggings and had been for hours. He was fussing behind the bar, wiping glasses and arranging them on a shelf. One customer was there, almost hidden in a corner, a miner whose wildcat claim had petered out and who was already starting the new day's drowning of his misfortune. And a man wearing an old slouch hat and a shapeless old overcoat came in and went straight to the bar and spoke to the bartender in a low voice. The bartender whirled from the shelf and stared at the man and dropped the glass he was holding and the man took a revolver from the right-hand pocket of the old overcoat and fired and drilled the bartender neatly through the heart. The man turned and saw the miner in the corner half out of his chair and staring. "Don't be in a hurry to follow me," the man said. The miner wasn't. The man went out the door and around the side of the shack and was gone. The only trace of him found afterwards was a neatly rolled bundle under a bush a half-mile away, the revolver and the hat tucked inside the rolled overcoat. They offered no identification. Hoofprints of a horse were found nearby, but the trail faded out in the rocky country.

There is only one more point important. That miner was the sole eyewitness. The killing had happened so quickly and the man's hat had shadowed his face so completely that the miner had difficulty trying to describe him. It seemed to him, the miner said, that the man walked and stood very erect like someone who had seen a lot of military service. And he thought, he wasn't certain, but he thought the man had a scar along the side of his jaw.

Of course that man had a scar. He had to have it. A scar made by a stone in a gully in New Mexico sixteen years before.

Hugo Kertchak, Builder

I N AMERICA, people said, there was work for anyone willing to work. A man with a trade could make his way there and freedom would be a real thing freshening the air he breathed.

Four years Hugo Kertchak saved for the passage money. He had the few coins that remained from his mother's burial fund and the small amount that had been left to him by his father. He had the smaller amount that had come to him with his wife. He had the gold piece given to him by his uncle at the birth of the first child because it was a son and would bear the uncle's name. He had these and he saved in many ways. He saved though he had work only about one week in three. He put away his pipe, out of sight and out of mind. He drank only one mug of beer and that only on Sunday and after a time none at all. He fed himself and his family on bread and potatoes and occasional green vegetables. The money that would have bought meat joined the rest in the old leather purse that had been his father's and that was kept behind a stone of the fireplace.

After four years and two months he had enough. He sold the few pieces of furniture that were his in the rented cottage. He led the way for his family. Under his left arm he carried the long narrow toolbox that had been his father's and his grandfather's. His right hand held the small hand of his seven-year-old son. Behind him came his wife. On her left shoulder she carried the bundle of extra clothing wrapped in a blanket with a strap around it. Her right hand held the small hand of their five-year-old daughter. They walked the nine miles to the station, where they waited for the train that took them west across Europe to the port and to the ship that took them west across the Atlantic.

Hugo Kertchak walked the streets of New York. He left his wife and children in the boardinghouse run by a man from the old country and walked the streets of the strange city. He knew fifty-three words of English, useful words learned the last days of the crossing from another steerage passenger on the ship. He could not learn them as fast as his wife, for she was quick at such things, but he was learning more each day, learning them slowly and thoroughly so that he would never lose them and so that he could pronounce them clearly, with only a small trace of accent. He walked the streets and times were hard. Even in America times could be hard. There was no work.

There was plenty of work in the new lands, people said, in the new settlements westward with the afternoon sun. A country was growing and a man could grow with it, even a man already in his middle thirties.

Hugo Kertchak talked to the boardinghouse man, who could speak to him in his native tongue. He talked to a patient man at the railroad station, using the words he had learned, and had difficulty arranging in right order. He counted what was left of the money. It was enough.

Hugo Kertchak and his wife and two children rode upright on stiff railroad coach cushions west to Chicago. All one day and one night they rode. They walked across the sprawling city to the other station. They carried the toolbox and the bundle and they walked asking directions. They rode upright on other slat-backed seats west across Iowa into Nebraska. They leaned against each other and slept in snatches as the train jolted through the darkness of night. The sun rose and they sat up straighter and divided and ate the last loaf of bread and the last piece of the cheese bought in Chicago. They looked out the train windows and saw the wide miles reach and run past them. It was a new and a strange and a big country. But in the side pocket of Hugo Kertchak's jacket was a letter from the boardinghouse man addressed to a friend out in this new and strange and big country.

The train stopped at the town. Hugo Kertchak and his wife and two children stepped down into the dust of the road that was the town's one street, flanked on one side by the single line of track, on the other by a brief row of false-fronted frame buildings. The wind that blew over the wide country, tireless and unending, swirled the dust stirred up around their legs and made the children cough. The train moved on and the sun beat down and the wind blew and they were alone in the road dust. The few sparse buildings of the town seemed lost in a circling immensity. Distance stretched outward and on and beyond grasp of the eyes in every direction. They walked through the swirling dust across the road and up the two steps to the platform along the front of the building whose sign said "Store & Post Office." Hugo Kertchak set the toolbox down on the platform and went into the building.

At the rear of the store two men sat hunched on stools playing checkers on the squared-off top of a barrel. They raised their heads and looked at him. Behind a counter at the right another man leaned back in an old chair with his feet up on the counter reading a newspaper. This one lowered the paper and looked over at him like the others. Hugo Kertchak took the letter from his pocket. He went to the counter and held the letter out so that the name on it could be seen. "You know?" he said.

The man behind the counter raised his feet and set them carefully down on the floor. He folded the newspaper and laid it carefully on the counter. He leaned forward and took the letter and held it at arm's length to read the name. He handed the letter back. "Sure I know," he said. "Or aiming it a mite better I'd offer I used to know. That there particular person ain't inhabiting these parts any more."

Hugo Kertchak frowned in the effort to understand. "You say what?"

The man behind the counter smacked a hand down upon it. "I say hightailed out of the county. Skedaddled. Vamoosed. To put it pretty, he ain't here any more. He's gone."

Hugo Kertchak understood the final words. "You say where?"

The man behind the counter shouted a question at the checker players. "Back east somewheres," one of them said. "Didn't name a place." The man behind the counter shrugged his shoulders and spread out his hands. "Reckon that's that. Anything else, stranger?"

Hugo Kertchak shook his head. He could think of nothing else, only the fact that confronted him. Slowly he turned and went out again to the front platform. He stood staring into the far reaches of distance. He tore the letter into many small pieces and let these fall fluttering around his feet. Slowly he sat down on the platform edge with his feet on the lower step and his head sank forward until it was almost between his knees. In the old leather purse in his pocket there was thirty-seven cents of the strange American money. And a woman and two children were staring at him in a stricken silence.

The tireless wind of the wide country blew upon him, hot and dry. The wind brought with it a sound, the sound of a hammer driving a nail.

Hugo Kertchak's head rose. He stood, erect on the step. He reached and took the toolbox. "Anna," he said to his wife, "here you wait."

Hugo Kertchak walked along the road through the swirling dust. The sound led him to the last building westward. Around the far side, out of sight before, a man was constructing a small shed. The framework was already up, the rafters for the flat, slightly sloping roof already in place. There was a pile of lumber on the ground with a small keg of nails beside it. The man had cut several side lengths of board and was nailing them to the corner posts. He stopped and turned to look at Hugo Kertchak. He seemed glad of an excuse to stop.

"Am carpenter," Hugo Kertchak said. That was wrong. He made the correction. "I am carpenter."

"Be damned if I am," the man said. "This beswoggled hammer has a mind of its own. Likes my thumb better'n the nails."

Hugo Kertchak was not certain what all the words meant. But here was work, the work he knew. "I show," he said. He laid down the toolbox and opened it. He took out the hammer with the new handle that he had whittled and sanded long hours on the journey until the balance was exactly right for his broad, square hand. He dropped some nails from the keg into his jacket pocket. He lifted the next side board and set it in position. He swung the hammer in smooth, steady strokes, short arcs with clean power in them. It was good to be using a good tool again. But the framework was not solid. The whole skeletal structure quivered under the strokes.

Hugo Kertchak forgot the man watching him. He was intent upon the problem before him. He walked around the framework, examining it from each side. The joints were not well fitted. They did not lap each other so that they would share and subdue the strains. The braces were in the wrong places. This America needed good workmen.

Hugo Kertchak took his wooden rule from the toolbox and unsnapped it to full length. He made his measurements. He selected several boards and marked them off, using a nail to scratch the lines. The saw was in his hands, the saw that had been his father's and that he had filed and refiled on the long journey until its teeth yearned for good wood to cut. It sliced through this wood swiftly and sweetly. Here were his braces. He nailed these into place. He put a shoulder against a corner post and heaved. The framework stood solid. It was not as firm as it would have been if it had been built right from the beginning, but it was much better. He reached for the next board and stopped. The man was making a noise.

"Hey!" the man was saying again and again, each time louder, trying to catch his attention. "Hey, carpenter. What'd you stick me to polish off this thing?"

"Stick?" Hugo Kertchak said. "Polish off?"

"How much to finish it?" the man said. "Do the job up right."

Hugo Kertchak looked at the framework again. The shed would have no windows. There would be only a door to make. This work was nothing, just nailing boards in place. He tried to estimate a price, one that would not be too low because this was America and yet would not be so high that the man would be unwilling to bargain. "Four dollar," he said.

"Well, now," the man said, rubbing a hand up and down along one side of his chin. "That's a reasonable fair price, I reckon. But cash is mighty scarce in these parts around about now. Tell you what. I'll make it two dollars cash and toss in whatever stuff's left, boards and nails and the like."

Hugo Kertchak's mind worked slowly over the words. "I can do," he said. "Done," the man said. "Reckon all else you'll need is some hinges and a latch for the door. I'll go rustle some." The man swung away and Hugo Kertchak stared after him in amazement. There was no arguing back and forth. There was no talk about how much wood he should use and how many nails. There was no talk about how good the work must be for the price or how long he must wait for the money. There was no writing about the business on

paper so that there could be no argument afterwards over what had
been said and promised. A man said "done" and it was settled.
Hugo Kertchak shed his jacket in the warm sun and began sawing
board lengths and the endless wind of the wide country sent the
sawdust swirling as he sawed.

The sun climbed high overhead and the shed sides climbed with
it. The man came back with a pair of big hinges and a latch and
screws to go with them. He set these down by the lumber. "Lunchtime," he said. "Better go wrastle yourself some food." He disappeared into the nearby building.

Lunchtime. Suddenly Hugo Kertchak remembered his wife and
two children alone on the store platform. Thirty-seven cents would
buy bread if bread could be found in this strange place. He started
toward the road. He had not gone ten steps when around the corner
of the last building came his wife. She walked proudly with her head
high. In one hand she carried two fat sandwiches made of thick
slices of bread with meat between them and in the other hand she
carried a tin pitcher of cool water. "The store man gives," she said
in English and then she began talking rapidly in their native tongue,
but she had no chance to say much because the store man himself
came around the corner close behind her and he was talking so
loudly that he almost shouted. He talked straight at Hugo Kertchak.
He was very angry. He thought that Hugo Kertchak was closely
related to an animal called a polecat with maybe a dose of rattle-
snake thrown in. What kind of a horned toad was Hugo Kertchak
anyway to leave a woman and two kids in the hot sun breathing
road dust when decent neighbors were around that would let them
come in and sit a spell and stay as long as they liked? Why hadn't
he spoken up like a man with a chunk of backbone and said he had
a family with him and was flat busted and didn't have a place to
stay? What brand of mangy miscreants did he think people in that
state were that they couldn't provide food and shelter for a family
that needed same till they could provide their own? He, the store
man, was going to tell this Hugo Kertchunk or whatever crazy name
he called himself what he, this Hugo Kertchunkhead, was going to do
and he'd better do it. This ringtailed baboon of a Hugo crazyname
was going to set himself and his family down in the extra room of
the living quarters back of the store and he was going to pay a stiff
price. How? He was supposed to be a carpenter, wasn't he? So his

wife said anyway. Well, he was going to prove that. He was going to slap some decent shelves in the store to take the place of the rickety ones there and they'd better be good shelves or he'd find himself with a sore backside from being kicked all over a quarter section. And maybe he wasn't such a hollow-head of a bohunk as he looked because he seemed to have rustled himself a hammer-and-saw job already but the shelf proposition still stood and was he man enough to rear up on his hind legs and say would he do it?

Hugo Kertchak understood only part of the words. But he understood that the store man's anger was a good anger and that there was more work for him to do. What exactly it was did not matter. It was carpenter's work. He was a good carpenter, almost as good a carpenter as his father had been. He looked straight at the store man. "Done," he said.

The store man was not angry any more. He chuckled. "Talking American already," he said. "When you're through here, come on down to my place." He turned abruptly and disappeared around the corner of the building.

Hugo Kertchak nailed the last roof board in position. He was worried about the roof. It should have some other covering to make it waterproof. He would talk to the man about that. He slid to the ground and cut and shaped the last side boards to fit up snugly under the eaves. He ran neat finishing strips down the corners. There was still a nice pile of wood left and the keg of nails was only half empty. It was not really fair. All this good wood and all these nails and two dollars too for a little sawing and hammering finished with the afternoon only half gone. There was still a door to make. It should be a good door.

He selected the wood carefully. The door grew under his hands. He cut and mortised the pieces for the outer rim. He planed and fitted the pieces to be set in these and give a paneled effect. The wind of the wide country set the shavings dancing. This was the kind of work that showed what a good carpenter could do. He was so intent on it that he did not hear the hooves approaching, the sound softened in the dust. He was startled when he looked up and saw a man, a new man, watching him about thirty feet away. It was a horseman and he had a pistol in a leather holder on his hip. Hugo Kertchak saw the horse and the pistol and was afraid. It was an instinctive fear out of old memories deep in his mind. Then he

saw the face of the horseman and he was no longer afraid. It was
a young face, serious and sunburned, with many small wrinkles
around the eyes from much squinting into the endless wind, and
the expression in the eyes and on the face was wide and open like
the country around.

"Man oh man," the horseman said. He pushed his hat up from
his forehead and wiped at the dust there. "You sure can wrangle
those tools." He turned his horse and went out of sight around the
building.

Hugo Kertchak fastened the hinges to the door. He set the door
in the doorway and slipped thin shavings under it for clearance and
fastened the hinges to the door frame. He pulled out the shavings
and tried the door. It hung true and swung easily out and back to
fit snug and flat in line with the frame. He began work on the latch.
This time he heard the hooves. The horseman appeared around the
building. A tied bundle of letters and newspapers hung from his
saddlehorn. He stopped his horse and leaned forward in the saddle
inspecting the shed. "Man oh man," he said. "That's what I call a
door. Kind of like a fancy beaver on a roadside bum but there ain't
no mistaking it's a door." He clucked to the horse and moved on,
straight on out into the wide country, riding easily and steadily into
the far distance.

Hugo Kertchak stood on the small rear platform or porch of the
store building and saw the last tinges of almost unbelievable color
fading out of the western horizon and the clear clean darkness claiming the land. There were two silver dollars with the thirty-seven
cents in the old leather purse in his pocket. Behind him in the
lamplit kitchen his wife and the store man's wife were clearing
dishes from the table and rattling them in a tin washbasin. The
two voices made a gentle humming. It was remarkable how women
did not need to know many of each other's words to talk so much
together. But there had been much talk too with the store man
himself, who was still sitting by the table reading his newspaper as
if he had to cover every word in it. This was only a small town, a
very small town, the store man said, but it would not always be
small. It would change, and quickly. Now there were only wide
stretches of land around where men raised cattle for meat and
leather and let them wander without fences to hold them. But soon

the government would open the land for farmers and their families. They would come. Whole trainloads of them would be coming. They would settle all around and the town would grow and business would be good and there would be more work than men to do it.

Hugo Kertchak could hardly believe that what was happening was true. In one day he had new money and some materials for his trade and a friend who could be angry at him for his own good. This was a strange country and the people were strange but theirs was not an alien strangeness. It was only a difference that a man could learn to understand.

His wife was on the porch beside him. "Hugo. Think of it. In the cold time, in the winter, they have a school. Free for all people's children." She put a hand on his arm. She had not complained very much through the four years of saving. She had followed where he led on the long journeying. "We stay here?" she said.

The tireless wind of the wide country blew full in Hugo Kertchak's face. It was still hot and it was still dry. But there was a freshness in it that was not just the beginning of the evening cool. Hugo Kertchak put an arm around his wife's shoulders. "We stay," he said.

Hugo Kertchak was the town carpenter. He helped the town get ready for the coming land boom. He built new shelves in the store and a long new counter and racks for farm tools. He built and polished to a shining finish a bar in the biggest of the buildings that was a saloon and would be a dance hall. He patched the blacksmith shop roof and extended it out to form a lean-to addition where wagons could be kept waiting repairs. He built stalls in the broad shedlike structure that would be a livery stable. These were honest jobs well done and he could pay the store man board money and even save a little for the house he would build for himself with the materials he was assembling. But they did not satisfy him. They seemed so small in the bigness of the land.

He sat on the front steps with the store man and watched the western color fading out of the sky. A man on a horse came along the road, hurrying, stirring the dust for the tireless wind to whirl. It was the young horseman. He stopped and looked down at the two on the steps.

"Howdy, Cal," the store man said. "Climb off that cayuse and sit a spell. Could be there's a bottle of beer hanging to cool in the well out back."

"Man oh man," the horseman said, "you would think of that when I ain't got the time." He looked straight at Hugo Kertchak. "Reckon me and the other hands ain't so hot with our hammers. Barn we built's in bad shape. Haymow's collapsed with hardly no hay in it at all. And everybody's pulling out early morning for fall roundup. So I tell the boss how you wrangle those tools. So he sends me to put a rope on you for repairs."

Hugo Kertchak picked out the important words here and there as he had learned to do with these Americans. "Done," he said. "Where is barn?"

It was a big barn, casting a long shadow in the morning sun. Hugo Kertchak drove toward it, perched on the seat of the store man's light wagon. All the last miles he could see the barn bumping up out of the wide flat land and he did not like what he saw. It was too high for its width. It leaned a little as if the bottom timbers on one side had not been set right on a firm foundation. There were no neat slatted windows high up under the pointed eaves to give proper ventilation. The doors sagged and could not be closed all the way. Hugo Kertchak shook his head and muttered to himself.

He stood inside the doors and saw the remains of the haymow and listened to the boss, the ranchman, speak many words about propping it up again and perhaps strengthening it some. He did not listen to catch the important words. He was looking up at the fine big timbers that should have been cut to lap each other and fastened with stout wooden pegs and instead were simply butted against each other and tortured with long spikes driven in at angles that had already started splittings in the good wood. He did not even wait for the ranchman to stop talking. "No," he said in a loud voice. "Sorry is it to me I said 'done.' This work no." He sought for the words that would say what he meant and found them and as always in excitement he forgot the pronouns. "Is America," he said. "Has freedom."

The ranchman's eyes narrowed. His voice was soft and gentle. "What in hell has freedom got to do with my barn?"

"Freedom," Hugo Kertchak said. "Freedom for work right." He waved his arms at the walls around. "You see? Bad work. Not strong. Cold weather come. Snow. On roof. All the time wind blow. One year. Two year. Not no more. Everything down." The ranchman's eyes were wide open again. He sucked in one end of his mustache and chewed on it. "That bad, eh? I know it was slapped together in a hell of a hurry. Couldn't you fix it up some?"

"Fix bad work," Hugo Kertchak said, "makes better. But all the time still bad."

The ranchman chewed more on his mustache. He remembered that the range would be shrinking as homesteaders came in and he would have to depend more and more on winter feeding. He couldn't take chances on a rickety barn. The old days were slipping away and he would have to plan closer for the future. "Maybe," he said, "maybe you could build me a good barn?" He saw Hugo Kertchak's eyes begin to shine. "Whoa, now," he said. "Take it slow. I don't mean the best damn barn in the country. And no fancy doors. Just a good solid dependable barn. Knocking this one apart and using as much of it as you can for the new one."

Hugo Kertchak no longer said "I am carpenter." He said "I am builder." The land boom arrived and the trainloads and wagon-loads of settlers and they fanned out over the wide land and with them for miles in all directions went word that when it came to building, Hugo Kertchak, builder, could do a job right. Most of the homesteaders threw up their own shacks. Many of them simply squatted on their claims in tents and flimsy tarpapered huts waiting to prove title and sell out for a quick profit. Many others were too shiftless even to do that and drifted away. But here and there were a few and their number gradually increased who had capital or the competence to acquire it and could meet the conditions of the new land. They looked forward and they built for the future and Hugo Kertchak built for them. They paid what and when they could and sometimes he waited months and a year or more and longer for the last of the money but that did not matter because there was work for every working day and he was building and he had enough.

He built toolsheds and wagonsheds, sturdy and unshakable. He built barns, strong and solid, that seemed to grow out of the earth itself and settled firmly to the long competition with wind and weather. He built houses, small ones at first and then larger when

times were flush and money plentiful and small ones again when
that was all people could afford. No roof on these houses sagged
when snow was heavy on it. The tireless wind found no chinks to
whip through and widen. Sometimes he hired a helper or even two,
but mostly he worked alone or when there was no school with his
growing son as helper because that was the way to be certain that
all work was done right.

The town grew and spread out on both sides of the railroad track
and other builders came, men who underbid each other on jobs and
hired many men and had the work done rapidly, sometimes good
and sometimes not good. They built a town hall and a hotel and
a jail and a railroad station and some store blocks and some fine-
looking houses and other things and how they built them was their
own business. Always there was someone out across the wide land
who needed a shed or a barn or a house built as Hugo Kertchak
could build it.

Hugo Kertchak's son was a good carpenter. He worked on Saturdays and during vacations with his father and was paid what a
helper would have been paid. Sometimes he seemed to think more
of the money to be earned than of the job to be done and he had
a tendency to hurry his work. But when his father was there to
watch he was a good carpenter. When he graduated from high
school, he did not work as a carpenter any more. He worked at
many jobs in the town, only a week or two at each. He was restless
and irritable in the home. He talked with his father. He wanted
to go to the state university and study to be an architect. "That is
right," Hugo Kertchak said. "In America the son should do more
and better than the father. Work with me until the school begins
and save the money." His son did and when the school began again
what he had with what Hugo Kertchak had in the town bank was
enough.

Hugo Kertchak's daughter was a good cook like her mother, fine-
colored and well-rounded as her mother had been at the same age.
She was quick with words, too, like her mother and did well in her
studies. She won a scholarship to go to the state normal school and
study to be a teacher. But in the first year at the school she met a
mining engineer who was leaving soon to work for a mining company in western Montana. She wanted to marry him and go with

him. Hugo Kertchak comforted his wife. "Is she different than you?" he said. "Is it not she should go where her man goes?" There was only a little money in the bank now but there was enough for a wedding.

Times were slack. The town was very quiet. The opening of new lands had long since moved far on farther westward. The population of the town dwindled and dropped to a stable level. There was no more building.

Hugo Kertchak became a maker of barrels. He made them of all sizes for many purposes, from small kegs to big hogsheads. He made them firm and tight. He shaped the staves and fitted them together as he had shaped and fitted the timbers of his barns and houses. On most of them he used iron hoops, but he liked to make some completely of wood with wooden hoops fitted and shrunk so that they held better than the iron itself. He made them outdoors in the back yard of his house, where his wife could see him from the window, working under the high sky while the endless wind blew through his graying hair and made the shavings dance around his feet. He had a broad shed there for a workshop but he worked in it only when the weather was bad. He was building outdoors in the open, using his tools on good wood with the skill he had brought with him to this new land. He was building good barrels. But he did not call himself Hugo Kertchak, builder, any more.

Hugo Kertchak's son was home for the summer vacation. After one more school year he would have the parchment that would say he was an architect. Now during the summer he worked with his father, making barrels. He talked as a young American talked, fast and with much enthusiasm, and his talk was big with his plans for his profession. Hugo Kertchak listened and thought of the time when men who worked with steel and stone and concrete as he worked with wood would build the fine structures his son would design for them. And Hugo Kertchak's wife sat on the small back porch in the summer sun and watched the father and the son making barrels together.

Hugo Kertchak's son went back to the university and the winter was long and hard and when the spring arrived Hugo Kertchak's son and other young men at the university were given their degrees early so that they could enlist and fight in the war with Spain. There would be time enough for him to be an architect when the war was finished. But there was no time. The telegram came telling that he died in Cuba of the yellow fever. Hugo Kertchak tried to comfort his wife and she tried to comfort him. He at least had his work, his barrels to make, and she had nothing. Even her daughter was far away to the west in Montana. She sat on the small back porch and watched him work where their son had worked with him. She sat there too often and too late in the endless wind with no shawl over her shoulders and no scarf around her head. It was pneumonia with complications, the doctor said. Four days after she took to her bed she died quietly in the night. Hugo Kertchak stood by the bed a long time in the early morning light. He cranked the handle on the telephone in the hall and called the undertaker and made the arrangements. He went out to the back yard to his tools, old and worn but still serviceable like himself. Only with them in his hands did he feel alive now.

Two days after the funeral the letter came from his daughter telling why she herself had not come. Her husband had been hurt in the mine. His left leg was crushed and he would not walk again. The company was paying for the doctor and the hospital but even so there was no extra money. Her husband would not be able to do mine work any more but in time perhaps with his training he could do office work of some kind. Meanwhile they thought of establishing a small store which she could run. The local bank might loan her the money she would need.

Hugo Kertchak sold his house. He kept the workshop and a small bit of land with it bordering on the rear alley and moved a bed and a table and some chairs and a bureau into the shop. It had a coal stove that gave good heat and on which he could do his small cooking. There was a mortgage on the house and the price he received was not high but when the mortgage was paid there was enough. He sent the money to his daughter and her crippled husband. He did not need it. He had a workshop and he had his tools.

Hugo Kertchak made barrels but they did not sell as they used to sell. They stood in rows and on top of each other along the side of the workshop and he had no orders for them. Tin and galvanized-iron containers were being used more and more. These were cheaper and more convenient and more easily handled. Hugo Kertchak became a maker of coffins.

The coffins Hugo Kerchak made were good coffins, built as the houses and the barns and the barrels had been built, shaped and fitted, firm and solid. Always, as he worked on them, he remembered that one he had made for his wife and worried about the one someone else had made for his son far off in Cuba. He did not make many, most of them only on order from the town undertaker, because good wood was becoming expensive and he could not have a big supply on hand and because working was harder now. He moved more slowly and there was a stiffness at times in the muscles. But the skill was unchanged, the sure strong touch with the tools.

People he had known in the first years died and were buried in Hugo Kertchak's coffins. People he did not know were buried in them too. The town was changing. New people and new generations walked the streets. Electric lights brightened many houses. Horseless carriages began to cough along the roads and their owners talked about the paving of streets. The new ways of the new century changed old habits. The undertaker came to see Hugo Kertchak. He could use no more of the coffins. People wanted the shiny decorated models that came from the manufacturing places in the cities. People wanted these and there was a nice profit in them. That was business.

Hugo Kertchak puttered around town with any little jobs he could find. Sometimes he built bookcases or pantry shelves or flower trellises when he found people who wanted these. Most of the jobs were tending people's yards, planting bulbs in the spring, cutting grass in the summer, raking leaves in the fall. His daughter wrote to him regularly, once a month. She sent him snapshots taken by a neighbor of the two grandchildren he had never seen. She wanted him to come and live with her. He could help in the store. There was not much money but it would be enough. But he could not do that. The thought of going so far now and of living in the mountains frightened him. He could not leave the town and the wide flat country that had welcomed him and the quiet grave in its half of the small plot in a corner of the town cemetery. Regularly he wrote back, laboring hours over his broad rounded script, careful of his spelling and to put in all the pronouns. He was well. There was plenty of work. Someday soon he would come on a visit, in the fall perhaps when the rush of summer work was done, or in the spring when the winter cold was past. And sometimes he managed to put several dollar bills in the envelope for the grandchildren. He did not need much for himself.

Days when there was no work and the weather was pleasant he liked to sit in the sun on one of the benches by the town hall and watch the two morning trains go past on the track across the way, the express that roared through without stopping and the local that puffed to a stop by the station for a flurry of activity there. Always people were arriving and people were leaving and new faces were around and things were changing and that was America. He could remember when a train could stop and only a single small family step down from it into a dusty little town that seemed deserted and yet they would find friendship springing up around them as if from the wide land itself. That too was America. He sat on the bench and remembered and people smiled at him as they passed and sometimes stopped to talk to him because he was a part of the town and of the past that had made the town and he did not know it but he was America too.

A woman from one of the county boards came to see Hugo Kertchak in his shop. She sat on the edge of one of his old chairs and talked in a self-consciously kind voice. She had a card in her hand that told her facts about him and she did not know these were not the important facts. He was an old man, living alone, with no regular work. The card told her that. It would be much better for him if he would turn over to the county any small property he still had and let the county take care of him. The county had a nice old folks' home where he would have companionship and would not have to worry about anything.

The woman saw the tightening of the old muscles of Hugo Kertchak's face and she hurried to say more. That would not be charity. Oh, good heavens, no. He had been one of the early settlers and he had helped the community grow. The county owed it to him to take care of him. "Wrong," Hugo Kertchak said. "All wrong. This America owes me nothing at all. It gave what a man needs. A home without fear. Good friends. A chance to work. Freedom to work right. If there is owing, it is for me. To take care of myself." He was indignant and this made his voice sharp and the woman flushed and stood up and turned to go. Hugo Kertchak was a little ashamed. "I have thanks that you think of me," he said. "It is good that you help people. But for me there is no need."

Hugo Kertchak sat on the bench by the town hall and the tireless wind of the plains country ruffled the dwindling gray hair on his bare head. People nodded at him as they passed but few people talked to him any more. That was his fault. He talked too much. He said the same things over and over. He wanted to talk about the weather or politics or prospects for the year's crops or anything else another person wanted to talk about. But inevitably his voice rose, shriller and more querulous, and he would be doing most of the talking, telling about the old days when a man got angry at another man for his own good and a man said "done" and a thing was settled and a young horseman remembered a man he saw doing good work and people appreciated work that was done right, not slipshod and in a hurry, but right with every beam and board shaped and fitted and fastened to join its strength with the strength of the others in the solid firmness of the whole structure.

Hugo Kertchak remembered. His old hands remembered the feel of his good tools. He began going home by different and roundabout routes, walking along the roads and alleys and looking for stray pieces of wood. He gathered what he could find, pieces of old shingles, broken boards, boxes and crates thrown away. He carried them to his workshop. Day after day he worked in the old shop. Two days a week he did gardening and that paid for his food. The rest of the time he stayed in the shop and worked. When the wife of the man who had bought the house went out to hang her wash in the back yard near the shop, she heard the sounds of old tools in use, the steady striking of a hammer, the soft swish of a plane, the rhythmic stroke of a saw.

The day came when she hung out her wash and heard no sounds in the shop. When she took down the dry clothes in late afternoon there was no sign of activity. In the evening, when she stood on the back porch and peered into the darkness, there was no lamplight showing through the shop window. Her husband refused to leave his newspaper. "So what?" he said. "The old windbag can take care of himself. He's been doing it for years, hasn't he?" But in the

morning, after a worrying night, she insisted and her husband went
out to investigate. He came in again quickly and to the telephone
and called the coroner's office.

The coroner and a deputy sheriff found the body of Hugo Kertchak on the floor where he had toppled from a chair in the last
struggle for breath as his heart failed. The old pen he had been
using was still tight in the fingers of his right hand. They picked
the body up and laid it on the old bed. "Sometime yesterday," the
coroner said. "That's the way it is with these old ones. One day
they're fussing around. Next day they're gone."

The deputy sheriff was looking around the shop. "What d'you
know," he said. "Take a look at these things." On a shelf above the
workbench was a row of little buildings, small birdhouses, each deli-
cately made yet sturdy with every piece of the old wood shaped and
fitted and fastened with skillful care. The deputy sheriff put his
hands on his hips and stared at the tiny buildings. "I'll be damned,"
he said. "You never know what these old bums'll be doing next, fussing around with things like that when anyone's a mind for one can
get it for a quarter or maybe fifty cents at a hardware store. Wasting
his time on those when likely he didn't have a nickel. Now the
town'll have to bury him."

"Shut up," the coroner said. He was holding the unfinished letter
that had been lying on the old table. He was reading the last words:
"The town people will sell my shop and the land that is left and
send the money to you. They are good people. It is for the boy. For
help with a school. To study it may be for an architect . . ." The
coroner folded the paper and put it in his pocket. He moved around
the foot of the bed and pulled an old blanket from what lay between the bed and the wall. It was a coffin, firm and strongly built,
the once rough planks cut and fitted and planed smooth and polished
to a good finish. On the top lay an old cigar box. In the box were a
title form for a small lot in the town cemetery and an old leather
purse. In the purse were some crumbled dollar bills and a handful
of coins. "No," the coroner said. "Not this one. He paid his score
to the end."

The man filling in the grave in a corner of the cemetery shivered
a bit in the chill sunny air. He finished the job, piling the dirt in
a mound so that when it settled it would be level with the ground
around. He leaned a moment on the shovel while he took a scrap

of paper from his pocket and looked at the name on it. "Kertchak," he muttered to himself. "Seems like I remember that. Made barrels when I was a kid." He lifted the shovel over one shoulder and went away.

An automobile approached and stopped by the cemetery and two men stepped from it. One was the editor of the local newspaper. The other was tall and erect with the heaviness of late middle-age beginning to show in a once lean body. He wore a wide-brimmed hat and under it his face with the many wrinkles about the eyes was windburned and wide and open like the country around. Under his arm he carried a cross made of two pieces of wood. "Man oh man," he said to the editor, "I'd never have known if it wasn't for that article in your paper. Started me remembering things." He went to the mound of dirt and stuck the wooden cross into the ground at the upper end. He stood silent a moment, staring at the wooden cross. The upright was a piece of new two-by-four. The crossbar was an old board found in the old shop that had once been nailed over the doorway of the house in front of the shop. Carved into it in square solid letters were the words: Hugo Kertchak, Builder.

The automobile moved away and silence settled over the cemetery. The endless wind blew and whipped some of the dried earth of the mound in tiny dust whirls around the base of the cross and blew in soft whispers on out over the wide land where they stood, strong against weather and time, the sheds and the barns and the houses Hugo Kertchak had built.

Prudence by Name

SOME FOLKS wonder why I've stayed on here at Cubb's Crossing all these years, deputy sheriff at the start and still the same, just handling the fussy little cases and the office routine and tending the jail. Some seem to figure that if I'd pushed myself at the right times I might have been sheriff. I know myself better'n they do. I'm not big enough for that and I don't mean in size because I'm close to six foot in my socks and not too long ago could still hoist one end of a solid wagon without grunting extra much. I'm not complaining. I've been a fair average deputy and I've kept a nice jail on the little tax money squeezed out for that and I've found the job a good spot to get to know people and what goes on around town and in the country hereabouts. Some of the best friends I've had have served time in my jail. People are what count anywhere and you might not believe it but in this work you get to know a few worth knowing. Like Amos Birdsall and his wife Prue.

They came to the Crossing on a Monday. They could have got here on Sunday but Prue wouldn't travel on the Lord's day so they camped out along the trace a ways and waited for the day to pass. They came on in Monday morning, the whole family, Amos and Prue on the front seat of their wagon and the two kids riding on the lowered tail gate beside the crate of chickens and their skimpy belongings piled between with a tattered old canvas pulled over and lashed down.

Quite a few people were coming in those days, off and on over a stretch of months. A parcel of sections west of town had been opened to homesteading and the people were coming to stake claims. The land wasn't much, middling fair for cattle grazing but not for quarter-section farming, but a promotion outfit had been sending out the usual fancy-talk fliers back through more settled areas and the people had been coming. Some stayed and stuck it and some didn't. My first bet was the Birdsalls wouldn't.

You could hardly blame me on that. They sure didn't show much when I first saw them. This was back in Sheriff Godbee's time and the two of us were sunning on the porch of the building where we had our office and my jail when the wagon came along and stopped smack in front of us. They were a queer pair sitting on the wagon seat, big rawboned knuckly Amos in faded old overalls and patched plaid flannel shirt and a straw hat pulled down over raggedy hair, and long thin wispy Prue, all stiffness and angles, in a bebuttoned back-east dress so long it came down and hid her feet and so high and tight up around her neck it made her chin jut out sharp and stern. She had that laced-in hardshell look a woman gets when she wears a whalebone or wire-rigged corset and she had a back-east hat on her head, round and lopsided with fake flowers and a birdwing sewed on it and two big hatpins stuck through it. I saw her and I saw the two kids peeking around the wagonload from the tail gate and I couldn't help wondering how a woman like that ever managed to have kids. She didn't see us, not so you'd notice. She sat there, prim and stiff, with her lips pulled in to a thin straight line and her eyes fixed straight ahead. It was Amos spoke to us, bobbing his head and grinning like he felt he had to be kind of apologetic and soothing or someone'd start snapping at him.

"The Birdsalls," he said. "That's us, whole kit and caboodle. Me here, called Amos, and my wife, Prudence by name, and a couple of sprouts, boy and girl." He pushed the straw hat back a bit and scratched through the raggedy hair around one ear. "This the sheriff's place, ain't it? Was thinking, I was, maybe you could tell me the way to the Jenkins claim. Bought it, we have, in hard cash and hopes." He pulled the hat down again, hard. "There's a claim locator back at the hotel, there is, but he wants ten dollars. I ain't got ten dollars." He shuffled some on the wagon seat and pushed the hat up again and leaned toward us. "You see, sheriff, we had some extra, cash I mean, and two days ago at evening camp and the dark coming down, it was, this gent rides along with those two guns showing on his hips and—"

Amos stopped talking. Prue had turned on the seat and was looking at him. He shrank about two sizes in two seconds. He grinned again in that apologetic way. "Forget it, sheriff," he said. "I was just blowing. Fact is we didn't have much left and I lost that, I did, back at Twin Forks bucking a faro bank. Can't figure what went wrong, I can't. My system ought—"

He stopped again. His wife, Prudence by name, was clearing her throat with a little rasping sound. She looked at us on the porch and away. "It was my fault," she said. "I let him go into that town by himself. The children were tired and I couldn't leave them and everything was so dirty we had to have some soap. So he did it again."

She sat still on the wagon seat looking straight ahead and Amos sat beside her bobbing his head and grinning in that apologetic way and Sheriff Godbee uncrossed his lean old right leg from over his left leg and crossed them again in reverse order and looked at me. "Howie," he said, "your jail's empty. Your desk's clear. Your middle's plumping. Saddle a horse and show these folks the way."

So there I was ambling along in the saddle beside the wagon and there Prue was jolting silent on the seat and there Amos was holding the reins in his big knuckly hands and squinting sideways at me and asking questions about the territory and telling me something about the two of them. They'd had several places, back in Iowa the last one and a mortgage on it and they kept missing payments, maybe bad luck, as he said flipping a quick glance at Prue, maybe faro as he didn't say, and they'd had to sell out and take whatever was left over and start again. They were heading west out our way when they met Jenkins heading east and they liked the notion of a claim with some buildings on it already and pulled him down on his price and paid him. "Too bad, it was," Amos said. "Him in poor health like that and having to leave. Good luck too. For us, that is."

"Poor health?" I said. "Jenkins? The only poor health he ever had came out of a bottle."

Prue turned on the seat and they both looked at me and the wagon jolted along and they both stared at me. "Buildings," Amos said. "There's buildings on it, there is. There's got to be."

I couldn't look at them. I watched the road ruts sliding past under the wheels. "Well, yes," I said. "Yes, there's buildings." I nudged my horse ahead and led the way off to the right down the wagon

trace along the section lines and across the creek branch and up over
the first rise beyond. I stopped and Amos brought the wagon along
beside me and they could see the buildings, all the ramshackle three
or really two and a half of them, the single-room tarpapered and slab-
roofed shack and the split-log pole-and-sod-roofed shed with the
open lean-to spreading out from one side.

They sat still and stared at the buildings. The two kids climbed
down off the tail gate and stared too. "Anyway," I said, "there's a
well. A good one."

Prue turned on the seat and looked at me and then at Amos.
"Men," she said. "Why did God have to make men." She climbed
down over the wheel on her side and marched straight to that ugly
rough shack and through the door hanging on one hinge and the
two kids looked accusing at me and Amos just as she had and followed her.

Amos bobbed his head at me but he didn't grin. "Edgy, she is,"
he said. "Been angry, she has, ever since out of blankets this morning
and all because I wouldn't put on my Sunday clothes, I wouldn't, for
coming into town. Knew I'd be unloading, I did, and starting work
right away. Wasn't going to be changing back and forth." He
pushed the straw hat back on his head and looked around. "Ain't
much. Ain't much at all." He climbed down his side of the wagon
and started toward the shack and Prue was in the doorway and her
voice was high and shrill. "There's no floor," she said. Her legs
seemed to crumple under her and she sat down on the big stone that
was the doorstep and bent her head and put her face in her hands.

Amos stopped still, rocking on his big clumsy feet. "That man
lied to me," he said. He raised one big knuckly hand and clenched
it into a fist and smacked it into the palm of the other hand. "There
ain't no floor," he said. "All right, there ain't. But there's a roof,
there is. We can rig a partition in that house. That shed'll make a
fine chickencoop, it will. That lean-to'll take care of the team.
We've got food in the wagon. Got our health too. We'll make out,
we will, till I get a crop in and some more building done."

For a moment he seemed big and almost impressive standing there
and then Prue raised her head and looked at him. "You promised
me a board floor," she said. "It isn't decent without a board floor.
Only the good Lord knows what it is to have to live with a man who
doesn't even care if things are decent." And the little girl in the

doorway behind her spoke up, with the boy trying to shush her, and her voice was an exact copy of her mother's. "He doesn't care. He just doesn't care." And Prue stood up, all stiff and angles, and marched past Amos standing there and past me still sitting quiet on the horse, and pulled a broom out of the wagon and marched back and into that house.

Amos sighed and came over by the wagon and began to unlash the load. I slipped down and helped. Together we hoisted everything out and piled it on the ground. The kids came running and scurried like packrats carrying small stuff and I helped Amos carry the heavy things into the house where Prue was bustling and raising dust. That was easy for her to do because the top layer of the packed dirt that was the floor was dry and crumbly. She didn't say another word but it wasn't long before I had the feeling too I ought to step careful and watch how I behaved or someone'd start snapping at me. I was glad when there wasn't much else I could do to help and I could head home to town and my jail.

That was late spring. By early summer the talk drifting around was that the Birdsalls were queer folk, unfriendly and plain peculiar. After a while I began to notice that when people talked like that they were really talking about Prue. Amos was just there, a hard worker when he worked, which was irregular, and a talker when anyone would listen, but just a man roundabout bobbing his head and being apologetic when people were near. Prue was the dominant one. She made the sharp impression. She made one plenty sharp on Sheriff Godbee's wife Martha.

It took a lot to rile Martha Godbee. She was just as broad and ample in spirit as she was in body, which was more'n enough for any one person, but she was riled when she drove back to town in the old buggy that day. The sheriff and I, up on the porch, saw her coming along the road at quite a clip. She pulled in close and climbed out before I could jump down to help her and she heaved up the two steps and pushed herself into the extra-wide chair we kept there for her. "That woman," she said and blew out her cheeks with a puffing noise.

We didn't say a thing. We knew we'd get it all and in a rush. "That Prudence Birdsall woman," she said. "And I was only trying to be neighborly. Things being said around town and by women I respect and I wondered were they true and went out to see and get acquainted, and they are. She can't even say hello like ordinary folks. Puts her nose up and says how do you do in that silly voice supposed to be refined and it's a pleasure meeting a person and she stands smack in the doorway blocking it and won't ask a person in. Oh she would she says but it wouldn't be decent not having a board floor but just plain dirt and she'd like a person to know she wasn't raised to walk around indoors on dirt and she wouldn't have to if she didn't have a man doesn't care one way or another about things being decent and is so shiftless and plain no-account he can't even put boards under the feet of his wife and children."

Martha Godbee puffed out her cheeks again and took in a big breath and started again. "Her talking like that and him standing right there and hearing it and the whole place looking so much better with the work he's done on it and him standing there trying to look friendly and like she's really only joking and her going on and on with more of the same talk in that silly voice that's not joking at all and sneaking looks at him to see him wince. And what she's doing to those children is a crying shame, with her letting them stand around hearing her and making nasty remarks too and referring to their father like he was a thing and call him 'he' and 'him' like he didn't even have a name and her not slapping them even once for it. Who does she think she is running down her man like that and with people listening and her putting on airs out here where we're all just folks and proud to be and don't care what kind of floor a person's got long as she's really folks too."

Martha Godbee took in another breath and jutted her chin at the sheriff. "What kind of floor did we have when we first came out here? Speak up now, Fred, and tell Howie here. What kind was it?"

Sheriff Godbee looked at her with his old eyes bright. "Dirt," he said. He chuckled. "Whole damn house was dirt. Sod walls. Sod roof. Dripped water two days after a rain." He jutted his own chin a bit. "But why ain't you peeved at him too? If he was the man he ought to be he'd shut her off soon enough. He'd whale her backside the way I'd've yours had you gone around nagging and complaining."

"Humph," Martha Godbee said, making her extra-size chair squeak. "It wasn't worrying over any whaling you'd do kept me from complaining."

"Well, now, Martha," Sheriff Godbee said and his old voice was soft and gentle. "You tell me what it was kept you from it."

"Because I'm not the complaining kind," Martha Godbee said and then she pulled in her chin till it was about lost in the folds of her ample neck and her voice was soft and gentle too. "And because I knew soon as we had a little over from things we needed more, getting started, you'd get me a better house."

"Well now, Martha," Sheriff Godbee said again, "maybe that's just the difference. Maybe that Prudence woman doesn't know what you knew."

I expect that was it. Prue couldn't know whether Amos ever would get her a floor or any of the other things she nagged about because there wasn't much he'd ever done to show he was the getting kind. He had good intentions maybe but he couldn't seem to follow through on them. He'd start something and then he'd want to finish it the easy way. He worked hard, irregular as I said before but hard when he did, and he put in a crop and didn't run too big a bill at Rudy Ferebee's store for seed and for food when what they'd bought ran out. The season was good that year and he had a fair crop and he sold his stuff, mostly corn and other truck, through Rudy to the Army post back near Twin Forks and he paid off his bill and laid in supplies right careful according to Prue's list and he had thirty-three dollars left. Prue was there with him when he got the money and bought the supplies. She was with him when they loaded the supplies and drove around to Luke Wagaman's place, where Luke did blacksmithing and handled what building materials were freighted into town. Amos climbed down and went inside the shop to talk to Luke about boards and he didn't come back out, and after a stretch Prue climbed down and went in after him and he wasn't there.

So there was the Birdsall wagon stopped again by our office-and-jail porch, only Prue was alone on the seat this time looking mad and worried all at once and talking but not in any high-toned voice. So the sheriff and I climbed up on the seat with her and I took the reins and we went around to see Luke and found out what happened.

Lumber was high around here in those days. The nearest timber and a sawmill were a long ways off and the railroad hadn't come through yet. Freighting costs pushed prices up. Amos didn't want rough boards either, green and likely to warp. He wanted finished boards seasoned right. He went in the shop and got to figuring with Luke what he'd need for a floor and even though their house was small it tallied eighty-seven dollars. Amos took out his money and counted it over again and it still was only thirty-three of those dollars and then while Luke was scratching around in his head what kind of a deal he might fix to help these new Birdsall folks Amos lit out the back door. "Didn't say another word," Luke told us, looking up at us on the wagon seat. "Jammed the money in his pocket and scatted out the back way."

Sheriff Godbee reached and took the reins out of my hands. "The lop-eared jackass," he said and he smacked the team on their rumps with the rein ends. I had to grab Prue and hold her from jouncing off as we swung in a half-circle. "Have to ask your pardon, ma'am," Sheriff Godbee said, slapping steady at the team to keep them stepping fast. "But it's the truth. Any man thinks he's got a faro system is a lop-eared jackass."

We pulled to a quick stop in front of Clem Rickey's saloon. The sheriff and I piled down and hurried in and straight through to the back room and there he was, chewing on a big knuckle and slumped in a chair across the table from the dealer with the box. He saw us and he knew what was doing right away. He bobbed his head and grinned in that apologetic way. "Lost again, I have," he said. "And it ain't right. Should have run it up to more'n enough. Played my system, I did, but something went wrong and—" His voice died away. I expect we looked peeved. At least the dealer thought so because he put in fast with his own words. "It was straight play, sheriff. I don't run it crooked." And Sheriff Godbee fixed the dealer with a cold look. "Ain't arguing that," he said. "You wouldn't be in my district did I think different." He swung to Amos again and I thought he might let loose with some chilling comments but he just looked at Amos a moment and sighed. "Better go on out. Prue's waiting for you to take her home." And Amos pushed up and walked out front slow and heavy on his feet and climbed up on the wagon seat beside her and took the reins. She didn't look at him, not once after she saw him coming. She didn't even speak to him. She didn't need to.

She knew. She just sat silent, jolting as the wagon moved, and stared straight ahead and they went on along the road growing smaller and smaller in the distance.

That was a tough winter, snow often and staying and choking the roads. We were busy in town what with people sort of jammed together, not able to get out and around much. Sheriff Godbee had to spend a lot of time at Clem Rickey's helping Clem keep the boys behaving right and heading off fights when nerves were jumpy and since he couldn't always head them off my jail had boarders fairly frequent. I couldn't know much what went on at the Birdsalls' except that they were making out with Amos hustling to keep the house warm and Prue teaching the kids out of some schoolbooks she'd brought in her trunk. I expect no matter how big a fire Amos had inside the house it was still cold in there for him because people who happened by when the going was passable said he always seemed to be outside even in the coldest weather, puttering and wandering around all bundled in an old overcoat.

Then it was spring and everyone was buzzing busy while the good weather held and of a sudden Amos was standing in the office where I was helping the sheriff catch up on paperwork. He hadn't driven in. He'd hiked it. He had a bundle under one arm and he was about busting with his plans. "Going to get her that floor," he said. "Got my crop in. Boy and the team can do the cultivating, they can. Me now, I'm heading for the railroad camp. Forty and found, they're paying grading crews. Two months'll about make it. Appreciate it, I will, if one of you'll stop off at my place now and again and see everything's all right."

Two months he said. Two months, add a few days, it was and he was back. He came back the way he went, hooking a ride on a freight wagon, and hiked straight on home and drove into town again with his own wagon and to Luke Wagaman's and paid cash for good lumber and loaded it and stopped to push his head in our door and thank us and drove home. There was something wrong about the whole business and that wasn't just the fact Prue wasn't with him when he came in for the lumber. It was the fact he wasn't the least bit happy about what he was doing. He'd gone off tickled silly and proud he'd figured a way to get Prue her floor. He came back tight-faced and quiet, hardly speaking to anyone, staring down at the ground in front of him when he walked along.

Maybe a week later, maybe longer but not much, I found Sheriff Godbee in his office chewing on a pencil and wanting to talk. "Howie," he said, "I never did like arithmetic and don't like the way things add up now. That Birdsall woman's invited Martha out to call tomorrow afternoon."

"Why not?" I said. "She's got her floor. But what's arithmetic got to do with that?"

"Not much," he said. "Not direct. But there's a couple other things. One's what Lewis told me when I was over at Twin Forks the other day. They had a little ruckus over there, a week, ten days ago. Man tried bucking a faro bank. Had a little luck and was winning. Began blowing what he'd do with it. Put a floor in his place, build it bigger, maybe ship in a piano. Luck turned and he lost, all he'd won and what he started with. Took it hard and had to be bounced into the road."

"I'll be damned," I said. "What's the other thing?"

"This in the mail today," he said, poking at a letter on his desk. "From Bowlus over at the junction on the freight route. Little trouble over there too. Figures about the day after the other. Somebody nipped a fistful of cash out of the drawer behind the bar in the saloon there. Probably did it while everybody was out watching a dogfight but wasn't noticed till a while later. Bowlus's been checking and can't find a trace. Now somebody's remembered seeing someone come out the door while the fight was on. Didn't know him but thinks he's seen him over this way sometime. Big man. Overalls and a straw hat."

"How much did he take?" I said.

Sheriff Godbee grunted. "What would you expect? They don't know exactly. Money hadn't been checked. But they figure it eighty-some dollars. I figure it eighty-seven."

I sat down in the other chair and stared at him and he stared back at me and after a while he sighed and pushed up. "Come on," he said. "Waiting never made any of these things any better. We'll go have a talk with Amos."

He wasn't in sight but Prue was when we stopped the buggy by the house. The door was open and she was standing in the doorway

with a broom in her hand and past her we could see the floor, good
boards well fitted together, smooth and already almost shining like it
had been swept and scrubbed half a dozen times a day. She didn't
act at all the way she had that first time. She looked right at us and
she almost smiled. "Oh, do come in," she said. "I can have coffee
ready in a minute."

"No, thank you, ma'am," Sheriff Godbee said. "We haven't time.
Just want to see Amos on a bit of business. Want to see him alone if
you don't mind."

She was so still she seemed almost to have stopped breathing and
her face began to change, getting pinched and tight again. "He's
around somewhere," she said. "He was cleaning the chicken shed."

We started toward the shed and Amos came around the side of it
and Sheriff Godbee took him by the arm and we went around the
side together out of sight of the house and Prue in the doorway, and
Sheriff Godbee started asking questions, making them more pointed
as he got a little peeved, and Amos just looked at the ground. "I
don't know what you're talking about," was all he would say and in
a voice we could hardly hear. And sudden another voice, high-
pitched and sharp, said the one word "Amos" and he jerked up
straighter and Prue came around the corner of the shed. She must
have been hiding there, listening to what went on.

"Amos Birdsall!" she said. "You can lie all you want to other people but you've never lied to me. Did you lose that money like all
the rest?"

He tried to look at her and couldn't and stared down at his big
knuckly hands. "Yes, Prue. I lost it, I did."

"And did you steal money from that saloon?"

"Yes, Prue. I took it, I did."

Prue turned to Sheriff Godbee. "All right," she said and her voice
was harsh and bitter. "That's what you wanted to know."

"No," Sheriff Godbee said. "I knew. But that's what I wanted
Amos to say."

There was a moment of quiet while we all were thinking our own
thoughts and the two kids came running from somewhere calling out
for their mother, and right away they sensed something was wrong
and they ducked quick toward her and stood beside her, clutching
at her skirt. The boy just scowled at Amos and scuffed the dirt but

the little girl began a sort of whimpering chant. "He's been bad
again. I just know it. He's been bad again." And Prue shushed her
by gathering her in closer with one arm and looked over her at Sheriff Godbee. "Well, anyway," she said, "you tell your wife to stay
home now and walk around on her own floor. But there's one thing
you'll have to let him do before you take him to jail."

Sheriff Godbee's old voice snapped. "Watch your words, woman.
In front of these children."

"I will not," she said. "If their father's a thief, they might as well
know it."

"All right," Sheriff Godbee said. "But there's thieving and there's
thieving and stealing a man's self-respect is a damn bad thing too.
Who but you's said anything about jail? It ain't our way to jail a
man's got family responsibilities if that can be helped. What we've
got to do now is figure a way for Amos to square this thing."

"I don't care what you do with him," Prue said. "But before you
do whatever you do with him you'll have to let him get things out of
the house for me. The children's cots and some blankets and the
stove and all the food there is. I want them in this chicken shed."

"Chicken shed?" Sheriff Godbee said and that was one of the few
times I ever saw him really surprised.

"That's where," Prue said. "You don't think I'm ever going to
set foot on that floor again. Not on a floor that's not really mine and
that's been paid for with thieving money. Not my children either."

Sheriff Godbee stared at her and started to speak and thought better of it. He turned to me and Amos. "A damn funny world," he
said. "Maybe there's something to that woman after all. Come
along. We'll tote those things out here and then see what can be
done in town."

Plenty could. Plenty always could be done when Sheriff Godbee
put his mind to it. He talked Luke Wagaman into handing back the
eighty-seven dollars Amos had paid for the lumber. More than that,
he talked Luke into letting Amos work out the price by helping at
the blacksmith shop. That wasn't too big a favor Luke was doing
because he had more work than he could handle fast as people
wanted at the shop, and finding a helper could swing a hefty hammer like Amos during the busy summer season wasn't easy. In a way

Luke wasn't really handing back the money. He was just paying that much in advance for work Amos would do. Then Sheriff Godbee took the eighty-seven dollars and put them in an envelope with a letter to Bowlus at the junction, and just what he wrote in that letter I never knew but it stopped any further action in the case. So after I posted the letter and came back by our office-and-jail building and went in to have supper with the Godbees at their house next door I was thinking this Birdsall business was working out all right. Amos would get his meals at Luke Wagaman's and sleep in the shop till his stint was done and if Prue wanted to be stubborn and live in that chicken shed till her floor was really paid for that was her lookout. She was about as much to blame as Amos. It was her nagging drove him to do what he did.

That's the way I was thinking at the supper table, so I was somewhat surprised when there was a knock and Sheriff Godbee called a come-in and it was Amos pushed in through the front door. I wasn't so much surprised at seeing him as at what he said. "Mr. Godbee," he said. "Sheriff, I mean. I want you to lock me up in your jail, I do."

"Well now, Amos," Sheriff Godbee said and he didn't seem to be much surprised. "That's an interesting idea. Why?"

"Seems to me, it does," Amos said, "I ought to do some time for what I did. Can't do it while working, I can't. But nights and Sundays I can."

"Amos," Sheriff Godbee said and his voice was a little stern, "have you been out home and got that idea from Prue?"

"I have not," Amos said. "But it's thinking of her in that shed's helped me think of it for myself, it has."

"Howie," Sheriff Godbee said, "lock this man up. Tight. Let him out breakfast time weekday mornings and lock him up again smack after supper. Sundays you'll have to feed him like you do other boarders. Any time he doesn't show when he should, you go after him."

So there I had Amos in my jail, off and on, nights and Sundays, most of the summer. That's when I got to know him, not just the way you know somebody who happens to live in your district and calls you by name and passes the time of day with you, but the way you know a man who sleeps under the same roof for a while and sees you close and gets to talking personal with you when a lantern's burning low. I'd come over after supper from the Godbees' and he'd be waiting on the porch and I'd take him in the building and lock him up, not in the waiting-for-trial quarters with bars all around but in the cooling-off quarters with the barred window and barred door and the old phonograph I had there to help boarders pass the hours.

He'd stretch out on one of the bunks and like as not, evenings when he had no company, not even a drunk sobering up, I'd bring a chair and set it by the barred door and we'd talk till time for me to head for the cot I kept in my office. Talking with him like that got to seeming quite natural but I never did get used to him saying, as he did last thing at night, "Appreciate it, I do, you locking me up like this."

Not many nights and he was telling me a lot about himself and his early days. He'd been a farm boy in eastern Iowa and after his mother died and he was growing some size he skipped for a couple years and was a cowhand on a middling big ranch. Trailing with the older hands he had his first taste of faro. He had luck that first time and ran up a roll that went soon enough with the other hands' help but the memory of it stuck. Then his father died and since he was the only child the farm was his and he went back there and tried working it. Along about then he got married and began having bigger ideas and he slapped a mortgage on the farm to stock it with purebred cattle and then when payments were coming due he never seemed to have quite enough and he took to remembering his faro luck. I could fill in the rest easy.

It was while he was talking that way I asked the question that was bothering me. "Amos," I said, "back east where you were women aren't so scarce. How'd you ever hook on to one like Prue?" He didn't get mad at me. I expect he knew what I meant, at least how it looked to me. He scratched around in his raggedy hair and tried to answer me straight. "She's from New England, she is," he said like he was proud of that. "Had to earn her living so she came out to teach school. Had a hard time, she did, book-taught woman like that. Big boys wouldn't behave in school. Made fun of her and her ways. I whopped a few and she called to thank me, she did. Come summer we called on the preacher." Amos looked at me, a little red in the face and defiant. "She was pretty then, she was. Kind of soft and—and womanlike." He rolled over on the bunk and wouldn't look at me any more and that was the only night he didn't thank me for locking him up.

A couple more weeks and I was beginning to nurse a worry. I was right fond of Amos by then and I could see this Birdsall business wasn't working out too well after all. There was Prue out in that chicken shed and there was Amos spending all his time working and being in jail and she hadn't come in once to see him. She knew what he was doing. Sheriff Godbee had been out special to tell her. But she'd been into town twice, driving their team, and got whatever she needed each time at Rudy Ferebee's store and gone right home again without stopping at the blacksmith shop and without even looking at my jail, when she went past on the road. And Amos was fretting about her. He wouldn't say anything more about her, but he was getting to look more like a big raggedy lonesome dog every day. I didn't know what to do about that but Sheriff Godbee did. He did it quick and direct and almost brutal the way he could be when he felt a need.

It was the next time Prue came to town, on a Saturday. She went to the store and would have gone on out of town again past our building but Sheriff Godbee stepped down into the road and grabbed the bridle of the near horse of the team and stopped the wagon. "Prue," he said, "you're a damn stupid woman. Why haven't you been in to see Amos?"

She reared up some on the seat. "Don't you dare talk to me like that!"

"I'll talk to you any way I've a mind to," he said. "You, a woman running out on her man a time like this."

"I'm not running out," she said. "I'm staying right there at that excuse of a home he's given me. Oh, I know what he's doing. He's trying to get back at me for nagging at him and now for living in that shed. Putting himself in jail. Working days and being locked up nights. Making himself look like—like a chain gang criminal."

"No," Sheriff Godbee said. "Like a man paying his debts. Working to pay for some boards for a silly woman. Serving time to pay the rest of us for breaking one of the rules of living we call laws." He let go the bridle and swung around and stomped up the steps and into his office.

Prue sat on the wagon seat staring after him. She saw me watching and jerked herself straighter and clucked to the team. But the next day, Sunday, she was back, all decked in her eastern dress and hat, bringing a clean pair of overalls and a clean shirt and some biscuits and a jar of her jelly in a basket. She waited in my office and I went and got Amos and pushed him in where she was and had enough sense to close the door quick.

That's how things went along until close to harvest time, Amos working and being locked up and Prue coming every Sunday, always with something tasty in her basket. She was just as prim and sharp-faced as ever and Amos acted some Sundays when she left like she had worked him over mighty thorough with her tongue but at least she was coming to see him and he didn't have that lonesome-dog look any more. Then, one day, midweek, Amos came along from the shop just after noon and up on the porch where the sheriff and I were soaking sun. "Paid up, I am," he said. "Every last cent. Own that floor now. Every last board. Got a new deal with Luke, I have, start-ing next week. Two days' work a week for ready cash. Now I'm go-ing home and move Prue back into the house and watch her walk around on those boards and feel good." He pushed his old straw hat up a bit and bobbed his head and grinned at us. "Ought to be some celebrating, there ought. Why'nt you two come along. Best friends we have around here, you are. Be the first visitors on Prue's floor."

Sheriff Godbee squinted at the sky, thinking his own thoughts. "Might be interesting," he said. "Howie, get the buggy out. Beats walking any day."

So there the three of us were bouncing along in the buggy follow-ing the road and then off to the right and down the wagon trace and across the creek branch and all the way Amos was talking and hum-ming and bobbing his head in anticipation. Right then that floor and going home to tell Prue she could walk on it now was the big-gest thing in the world to him.

The two kids saw us coming and ran out to see who it was and looked startled at his shouts and scurried back and around the house and when we swung in near the chicken shed there Prue was waiting and the two kids were behind her peering around at us. Amos jumped out and I started to follow and Sheriff Godbee stopped me. "No hurry," he said. "Maybe there's more to this thing."

There was. I don't know how he knew there would be but there

was. Amos hurried straight to Prue and she kind of backed away
and didn't seem happy to see him coming. He was too full of his
own feeling to notice and he grabbed her by the waist and picked her
up and whirled her around and set her down and she stood quiet
with a funny flat frightened look on her face. He still didn't notice.
He took her by the arm and hustled her toward the house, talking
steady how the floor was all paid for, every board, and how much
better things were going to be all around, and she just stumbled
along beside him with the two kids tagging and keeping her between them and Amos. He stopped by the doorstep and reached
and pushed the door open and she pulled back away from him.
"No," she said. "I can't. I just can't." The words faded away and
the silence was a strange feeling all about with Amos caught in it
and the two kids crouched by the house wall now afraid to move.

Amos seemed to sag all over. "Why, Prue. I don't understand, I
don't."

She just stood there, all stiffness and sharp angles, and she couldn't
look in through the doorway and she couldn't look at him. "Prue,"
he said, his voice getting an edge. "What's wrong with you?"

"I can't do it," she said. "All these weeks I've been out here knowing that floor was in there and how silly I've been. I can't go in
there. It wouldn't ever seem right."

Amos looked in through the doorway at that floor that represented
two months' railroad work and two more months' blacksmithing and
a lot of nights and Sundays in jail to him. He stood straighter and
he drew in a long breath that seemed to fill him out to full size.
"Prue, girl," he said, "would you feel better if that floor just wasn't
there?" She nodded, a bare little bobbing of her head, and he
marched over by the chicken shed and took the rusty old ax leaning
against it and marched back and in through the doorway and the
whole house seemed to shake with the sounds of splintering wood.
He came out and his arms were full of smashed pieces of those good
boards. He threw them on the ground and with the ax he sliced
shavings off one and huddled these in a little pile and put a match
to them and when they were blazing he began to lay the pieces of
board across the flames. And all the while Prue stood and watched
him and the two kids crept close to her and held to her skirt and
watched him too and she stood still and a flush of color climbed up
her cheeks.

Amos rose tall from squatting by the fire and looked across it at her and the silence was a taut tight feeling there between them and it broke with the sound of the little girl's whimpering voice. "He's being bad again, bad again, bad—" And Prue's hands moved sudden and sure and she had the girl by the shoulders and shook her. "Don't you ever," she said, "ever once again let me hear you speak about your father like that." She looked back across the fire at Amos and her face was all twisted and crinkled from the effort not to cry. "Amos," she said. "My Amos." She came around the fire reaching out toward him and he put out a big arm around her shoulders. She raised her head toward him and for a moment there in the line of her throat arching upwards and her face open and eager to him you could see it. It was there and it was gone but it had been there. She was almost pretty and she was kind of soft and womanlike.

"There now, Prue," Amos said. "No more worrying now. Not ever again." He looked over her head at the two kids standing sort of lost and alone on the other side of the fire. He left Prue and went around and he scooped the little girl up in the crook of one big arm and held her high so her head topped his own and you could see this was something that hadn't happened to her for a long time and she was frightened at first and then kind of excited and pleased and he reached with his other arm and took the boy by the hand. "Sprouts," he said, "we have work to do, we have. Your mother doesn't want that particular floor in her house and she's right about it. Let's get busy. I'll do the chopping and you do the carrying."

Sheriff Godbee and I sat in the buggy and watched the four of them working together. The ax was thumping in the house and the kids were scurrying in and out with pieces of board and Prue was chucking these one by one on the fire. "You know what I'm going to do?" I said. "I'm going to kick in some myself and take up a collection in town. I'm going to get them another board floor."

"No need to do that," Sheriff Godbee said. "Prue's all right now. They're both all right. She's got something better'n a board floor."

She had. She had all right. Because sudden she remembered us and noticed us swinging the buggy quiet as possible to slip away and she came hurrying to stop us a moment. "Mr. Godbee," she said, "I want you to tell your wife to come call on me again soon as convenient for her." And Sheriff Godbee looked at Prue with his face seeming stern but his old eyes shining. "Prudence Birdsall, ma'am," he said. "I ain't so sure I ought to let my wife call on people that've only got a dirt floor for her to walk on." And Prue gave him look for look with her own eyes snapping and she snorted just the way Martha Godbee would. "Humph," she said. "A lot of difference your letting or not letting would make. It was me and not any dirt floor made her mad when she was here before. We'll be having a board floor again and it won't be because I nagged about it and maybe that'll be soon and maybe it won't because there are other things we need more but that won't have anything to do with her coming to call. She knows a floor isn't nearly as important as the people who walk around on it." And then Prue said what knocked all words out of Sheriff Godbee and made him fumble for his old bandanna to blow his nose. "Maybe she was born knowing that the way I wasn't," Prue said, "or maybe she's just lived so many years with you she couldn't help learning it."

We were mighty quiet, me and the sheriff, all the way back to town. But it was a nice warm good-feeling quiet.

Harvey Kendall

MY FATHER had two pair of boots. He had a pair of shoes too but he wore those only when my mother made him, to church on Sundays and to funerals and the like. The boots were what you'd call his regular footwear. One pair was plain, just rough and ready old-style cowboy boots, nearly knee high, made of stiff cowhide with canvas pulling-straps we used to call mule ears that dangled and flapped on the outside when he walked along. He wore those at work on weekdays. He was cattle inspector at the local stockyards, where the ranchers for quite a stretch around brought their stuff to be checked and weighed before being shipped out. He'd pull out of bed in the morning and pad around the house in his socks, or when Mother got after him, in the slippers she'd bought for him, until after breakfast and then he'd squat on the edge of a chair and heave and yank at those boots till they were on and tuck his work pants down inside the tops and stand up and stretch and say, "Another day, another dollar," which was sort of silly because he earned more than a dollar a day, and out the door he'd go with those mule ears flapping.

We lived a short ways out of town and sometimes he'd walk in those boots down to where the stockyards spread out beside and behind the station about a half-mile away, and sometimes he'd saddle his old cow pony and ride down and maybe during the day circulate some through the pens helping the handlers move the stuff around, which he didn't need to do because he wasn't paid for that. "Can't let this Mark horse get too lazy and fat," he used to say but that was only an excuse. The truth was he plain liked the feel of that horse under him now and again and the tickle of dust rising up in a man's nose saddle high and the fun of shooing a few steers through some tricky gates. It reminded him of the old days when he was a free-roaming cowhand with a saddle roll for a home before my mother herded him into the same corral with a preacher and tied him down to family responsibilities.

Those cowhide boots were just everyday knockabout working boots. The others were something else again. They didn't reach quite as far up the legs but they had high narrow heels that curved under in back with a real swoop and they were made of soft calfskin that fitted like a glove over the feet and ankles and then opened out some to take care of the pants if those were folded over neat and tucked in careful. The tops were curved up on the sides with little leather pulling-straps that stayed out of sight inside and those tops were made of separate pieces of the calfskin darker brown in color than the bottoms and they had a clever design of a rope loop stitched into them. He wore those boots on Sundays after he came home from church and on special occasions like meetings of the stockmen's association and when he was riding old Mark near the front in the annual Fourth of July parade. They reminded him of the best part of the old days, the times he was representing whatever range outfit he was with that season in the early rodeos and showing the other cowhands from the whole country roundabout what a man could do with a good horse and a good rope.

When he wore those calfskin boots my father always wore the belt that went with them. It was made of calfskin too and it was so wide my mother had to fix new belt straps on every pair of new pants she bought for him. It had a big solid slide-through silver buckle that had three lines of printing engraved in the metal. The first line said "First Honors" and the second line said the one word "Roping" and the third line said "Cheyenne 1893." That belt and that buckle, tight around his waist above those calfskin boots, reminded him of the best thing of all about the old days, the time he set a record busting and hog-tying a steer, a record that stood seven years before anyone beat it and then it was beat only because they shortened the run some and changed the rules a bit and fast work was really easier to do.

Anyone knows anything about kids knows which pair of those boots I liked. Cleaning and polishing both pairs with good saddle soap to keep the leather in right condition was one of my regular chores every Sunday morning before church. I'd get out the soap and a moist rag and if my father wasn't around watching I'd give those old cowskin boots a lick and a promise and then I'd really go to work on those calfskins even though they didn't need much, not being worn often. Sometimes I wouldn't do more than just run the rag quick over the old cowskins and figure my father wouldn't notice I'd let them go because that old leather was rough and stiff all the time anyway and then like as not I'd be enjoying myself on the calfskins and sudden I'd look up and there my father would be watching me with his eyebrows pulled down till they about met over his nose. "Gee-rusalem, boy," he'd say. "One of these days you'll rub those boots clean through. It's the others need the limbering so my feet don't ache in them. Get busy on them now afore I sideswipe you one."

Mention of sideswiping points to maybe one reason I didn't like working on those old cowskins. Whenever I'd done something wrong, broke one of the rules my folks made for me or messed up some chore when I should've known better, my father would come after me from behind and hop on his left foot and turn his right foot toe outward and swing his right leg so that the side of his foot swiped me hard and hurting on my rump. He'd sideswipe me a good one or two or three according to how bad it was that I'd done and until I began to get some size there were times he raised me smack off the ground. Just about every time he did that he had those old cowskins on. But likely that didn't have too much to do with my feeling about them. I never was mad after a thumping or went around being sulky. My father sideswiped me only when I had it coming and he'd do it quick and thorough and tell me why, and then to show it was over and done and he was ready to forget about it he'd tell me to stick close around after supper and we'd saddle old Mark and he'd let me sit the saddle and get in some practice-throws roping a fence post before dark.

The truth was I didn't like working on those old cowskins because they were tough and hard to do anything with and old-fashioned and pretty well battered and they didn't mean a thing to me. Working on those others, those fine-looking calfskins, meant plenty. I'd rub away on that soft dark-shining leather and talk proud to myself inside. Not many boys had a father who had been a roping champion and in country where roping was real business and a man had to be good at it just to hold an ordinary ranch job. Not another boy anywhere had a father who had made a roping record that stood seven years and might still be standing if changes hadn't been made. I could work on that leather and see in my mind what I never saw with my eyes because all that was over and finished before I was born, my father on old Mark, young then, firm and straight in the saddle with the rope a living thing in his hands, my father and young Mark, working together, busting the meanest toughest trickiest steer with the hard-and-fast method he always said was the best. I could see every move, as he had told them to me over and over, young Mark reaching eager for speed to overtake the steer and knowing what to do every second without a word or a touch on the reins and my father riding easy and relaxed with the loop forming under his right hand and the loop going forward and opening and dropping over the wide horns and Mark slowing as my father took up the slack and pulled the loop tight and Mark speeding again to give him slack again enough so he could flip the rope over to the right side of the steer and then Mark swinging left in a burst of power and speed and the rope tightening along and down the steer's right side and pulling its head around in an outside arc and at the same time yanking its hind legs out from under it and making it flip in a complete side-winding somersault to lie with the wind knocked clean out of it and then all in the same motion Mark pivoting to face the steer and bracing to keep the rope taut and my father using that pivot-swing to lift and carry him right out of the saddle and land on his feet and run down the taut rope with his pigging string in his hand and wrap it quick around three of the steer's legs and draw it close and tie it and Mark watching and keeping the rope taut ready to yank and make that steer behave if it started causing trouble and then easing some slack at the right instant so my father could cast the loop loose and stand up to show the job was done and walk casual back to Mark without even looking at the steer again like he was saying in the very set of his head on his shoulders that's that and there's a steer hog-tied for branding or earmarking or anything anybody's a mind to do with it.

Well, what I'm telling about this time had a lot to do with those boots and that belt and my father and old Mark too but mostly my father. It began the night before the sort of combination fair and rodeo at our town that year. The committee running things had

some extra money available and they'd telegraphed and persuaded
Cal Bennett to agree to come for the price and they'd plastered the
town with bills saying the topnotch champion roper of the big-town
circuit would be on hand to give some fancy exhibitions and everybody'd been talking about that for days. We were finishing supper,
my father and my mother and me, and I notched up nerve enough
and finally I said it. "Father," I said, "can I wear your belt tomorrow? Just a little while anyway?"

My father settled back in his chair and looked at me. "What's on
your mind, boy? Must be something special."

"I'm sick of it," I said. "I'm sick of all the other kids talking
about that Cal Bennett all the time. There's a new kid too and I
was trying to tell him about you setting a record once and he won't
believe me."

My father kept on looking at me and his eyebrows pulled down
together. "Won't believe you, eh?"

"That's it," I said. "If I was to be wearing that belt and let him
see it then he'd know all right."

"Expect he would," my father said and he leaned back further in
his chair, feeling good the way he usually did with a good meal
inside him, and he said in a sort of half-joking voice, "Expect he
would even more if I was to get out there tomorrow and swing a
rope in the free-style steer busting and show everyone around here a
thing or two."

That was when my mother started laughing. She laughed so she
near choked on the last bite she was chewing and my father and I
stared at her. "Gee-rusalem," my father said. "What's so blamed
funny?"

My mother swallowed down the bite. "You are," she said. "Why
it's eleven years since you did anything like that. You sitting there
and getting to be middle-aged and getting thick around the middle
and talking about going up against young fellows that are doing it
all the time and could run circles around you nowadays."

"Oh, they could, could they?" my father said and his eyebrows
were really together over his nose.

"That horse of yours too," my mother said and to her it was still
just something to chuckle at. "He's the same. Getting old and fat
and lazy. He couldn't even do it any more."

"He couldn't, eh?" my father said. "I'll have you know being young and full of sass ain't so all-fired important as you seem to think. It's brains and know-how that count too and that's what that horse's got and that's what I've got and like riding a bicycle it's something you don't ever forget."

He was mighty serious and my mother realized that and was serious too. "Well, anyway," she said, "you're not going to try it and that's final."

"Gee-rusalem," my father said and he thumped a fist on the table so hard the dishes jumped. "Just like a woman. Giving orders. Tie a man down so he has to keep his nose to a grindstone getting the things they want and start giving orders the moment he even thinks a bit about maybe showing he still can do something."

"Harvey Kendall," my mother said, "you listen to me. I saw you near break your neck too many times in those shows before we were married. That's why I made you stop. I don't intend to have anything happen to you."

They were glaring at each other across the table and after a while my father sighed and looked down and began pushing at his coffee cup with one finger the way he always did when they'd been having an argument. "Expect you're right," he said and he sighed again and his voice was soft. "It was just an idea. No sense us flaring at each other over a little idea." He turned to me. "Wear the belt," he said. "All day if you've a mind to. If your feet were big enough you could wear the boots too."

In the morning my father didn't go to work because that day was a local holiday so we had a late breakfast and he sat around quiet like he was thinking things over in his mind the way he'd been all the evening before after supper. Then he pulled on the calfskin boots, looking a bit different in them without the belt on up above, and he went out and saddled old Mark and rode into town to help with the preparations there. I couldn't go along because just before he left he told me to stick close to my mother and watch out for her, which was a backhand style of putting it because she would really be watching out for me and that was just his usual little scheme to tie me to her so I wouldn't be roaming around and getting into any devilment. Soon as he was gone I got out the belt and put it on and it went around me almost twice but I could fix it so the buckle was in the middle in front as it should be and I stood on a chair to admire that part of myself in the little mirror my father used for shaving. I waited while my mother fussed with her good dress and the trimmings, doing the things women do to make themselves look what they call stylish, and then the two of us, my mother and me, walked the half-mile into town and the day's activities.

We stopped at all the exhibits and saw who had won the prizes for jams and jellies and raising vegetables and the like and we spent some time looking over the small pens where the prize-winning stock animals were. I stood on one foot and then the other and chewed molasses candy till my jaws were tired while my mother talked to women and then more women and I didn't get a chance to roam around much and show off that belt because she was watching out for me just about every minute. Three or four times we bumped into my father busy circulating all over the place as the cattle judge and one of the local greeters of out-of-town folks and he'd stop and talk to us some and hurry away. He was enjoying himself the way he always did at these affairs, joshing with all the men and tipping his hat to the women, and he was developing a sort of glow from a drink or two with the other greeters.

He joined us for a quick lunch at the hotel. He was feeling good again and he joked me over being about half hidden inside that belt and as soon as we were through eating he hustled us out and to the temporary grandstand along one side of the main stockyard pen so we all could have good seats for the rodeo doings. He picked a place in the third row where he always said you could see best and he sat in the middle with my mother on one side of him and me on the other and it wasn't till we had been there a little while and the two of them were talking hearty with other folks around that I had my chance to slip away by sliding through and under the grandstand and go find some of the other kids so I could strut and show off that belt. I went hunting them proud and happy as I'd ever been and I found them and in maybe five minutes I was running back under the grandstand as mad and near crying as I'd ever been too. I knew where to crawl up through by my father's boots and I did and he felt me squirming through against his legs because the stand was filled now and he took hold of me and pulled me up on the seat beside him. "Quiet now, boy," he said. "We wouldn't want your mother to know you've been slipping away like that." He swung his head to

look at her on the other side and saw she was busy talking to a
woman beyond and he swung back to me and saw my face. "Gee-
rusalem, boy," he said. "What's eating at you?"

"Father," I said, "he doesn't believe it about you."

"Who doesn't believe it?" he said.

"That new kid," I said.

"Did you show him that belt?" my father said.

"Yes," I said. "But he just laughed. He said it's a fake. He said if
it isn't you just found it somewhere or got it from some old pawnshop."

"Found it?" my father said. His eyebrows were starting to draw
down together but the people all around were starting to buzz
louder and things were beginning out in the big pen that was the
arena for the day. "All right, boy," my father said. "We'll do something about that when this shindig's over. Maybe a good sideswipe'd do that kid some good. Be quiet now, the bronc riding's
coming up." He didn't pay any more attention to me because he
was busy paying attention to what was happening in the arena but
not all his attention was out there because he kept fidgeting on the
plank seat and every now and then he was muttering to himself and
once he did it loud enough so I could hear. "Pawnshop," he said
and kept on fidgeting around and didn't seem even to know he was
doing that.

Plenty was happening out in the arena, the kind of things I always enjoyed and got excited about, but I wasn't in any mind to
enjoy much that day and then sudden there was an extra flurry of
activity and the main gates swung open and the people began to
shout and cheer. A man came riding through the gateway on a
beautiful big buckskin that was jouncing with each step like it had
springs in its feet and you could tell right away the man was Cal
Bennett. He was slim and tall and straight in the saddle and he was
mighty young-looking and mighty capable-looking all at the same
time. He had on boots just like my father's calfskins, maybe not
exactly the same but so close to it there wasn't much difference, and
a wide belt like the one I was wearing, and sitting there so easy on
that jouncing saddle like he was glued to it he was about the best-
looking figure of a man I ever saw. He had a coiled rope in his hand
and he shook out a loop as he came forward and began spinning it

and it grew bigger and bigger and sudden he flipped it up and over and it was spinning right around him and that buckskin and sudden he flipped it again and it was spinning big and wide in front of the horse and he gave a quick little wriggle with his heels and the horse jumped forward and he and that horse went right through the loop and it was spinning behind them and then the people really went wild. They shouted and clapped and stomped their feet. Cal Bennett let the loop fall slack on the ground and bowed all around and took off his big hat to the women and put it back on and coiled in his rope and rode over to the side of the arena where he'd wait for time to do his real roping stunts and still the people shouted and stomped. And my father sat there beside me and pulled up straight with his head high, looking around at the shouting people, and his face got tight and red and he shrank down till he was hunched low on the seat and he sat very still. He didn't fidget any more or mutter to himself. He just sat still, staring out at the arena and things happened out there, and then the announcer was shouting through his megaphone that the free-style steer busting for the local championship was next and sudden my father turned and grabbed me by the arm. "Hey, boy," he said, "take off that belt."

I fumbled with it and got it off and handed it to him and he stood up right there on the grandstand and yanked off the ordinary belt he was wearing and began slipping that big belt through the special pants straps my mother had sewed for him. She saw him looming up there beside her and what he was doing and she was startled. "Harvey Kendall," she said, "just what do you think you're going to do?"

"You keep out of this," my father said and the way he said it would have made anybody shy away. He pulled the belt tight through the buckle and started down toward the arena, pushing through the people in the two rows ahead. He stepped to the ground and turned to look back at my mother. "Just keep your eyes on that arena," he said, "and you'll see something."

He squeezed through the fence rails into the arena and went straight to the little bunch of men who were acting as judges for the rodeo events. He was reaching in his money pocket as he went and he took out two dollar bills. "I'm in this one," he said to the men. "Here's my entry fee."

They all turned and stared at him. "Lookahere, Harve," one of

them said. "You want to show us how you used to do it, that's fine.
That's wonderful. We'll be proud to have you. But don't you go
trying to do it racing against a stop watch."

"Shut up, Sam," my father said. "I know what I'm doing. You
just take this money." He pushed the bills into the man's hand and
swung away hurrying and by time the other entries were lined up he
was back leading old Mark and with a good rope he'd borrowed
somewheres in his hand. He took a place in the line and the judges
put all the names on slips of paper in a hat and pulled them out one
by one to get a running order and my father's name was one of the
last. He stood there among those younger men and their young
horses, quiet and waiting by old Mark, just running the rope
through his hands to see it had no kinks and coiling it careful and
exact, and all the while the excitement was building up in me, and
my mother sat still and silent on the plank seat with her hands tight
together in her lap.

One after another the others made their runs, flipping their steers
and dashing in to hog-tie them, and they used a lot of different
methods, some forefooting the steers and some going straight for the
heads and quick pull-arounds, some risking long throws to save time
and some playing it safer and chasing till they were close in, and
some of them were good and some maybe better than just good but
you could tell easy enough none of them were in the real champion
class, and then it was my father's turn. He led old Mark out and
walked around by old Mark's head and reached up a hand to scratch
around the ears and he whispered something to that old horse nobody could hear and he came back around and swung up to the
saddle. Seeing him there, straight and sturdy in the saddle, I
couldn't hold it in any longer. I jumped standing right up on the
seat. "Father!" I shouted. "Father! You show them! The whole
bunch of them!" My mother pulled me down quick but she was just
as excited because her hands trembled and out there in the arena
my father didn't pay any attention to anything around him. He sat
quiet on old Mark checking the rope again and a hush spread over
the whole place and off to the side Cal Bennett reined his big buckskin around so he could watch close and sudden my father let out a
whoop. "Turn that critter loose!" he yelled and the bars on the
chute were yanked away and a big rangy steer rushed out into the
arena and as it crossed the starting line the timer slammed down

with his hat and old Mark was leaping forward. Not three jumps and there wasn't a person watching didn't know that old horse knew what he was doing and maybe he was a mite slower than the young cow ponies that'd been performing but he was right up there in the champion class with the know-how. The steer was tricky and started twisting right away and old Mark was after it like a hound on a hot scent, keeping just the right distance to the left of it and closing in steady. My father was riding high in the stirrups and a loop was forming under his right hand and while he was still a ways back the loop whipped forward fast like a snake striking and opened out over the steer's head and the steer twisted and the loop struck on one horn tip and fell over the other horn and pulled off.

"Gee-rusalem!" My father's voice roared out over that whole arena. "Stick with him, Mark!" And old Mark was hard on that steer's tail with every twist and turn and my father yanked in the rope and whipped out another loop and it settled smack over the horns and head and he pulled it tight and flipped the rope over to the steer's right side and old Mark swung left, head low and plowing into the sudden strain coming, and that steer spun like a cartwheel somersaulting as it spun and was down flat and old Mark pivoted to face the steer and keep the rope taut and my father tried to use that pivot swing to lift him out of the saddle and his foot caught on the cantle going over and he went sprawling on his face in the dust. He scrambled up and scrabbled in the dust for the pigging string and started down the taut rope trying to run too fast and stumbled and went down again. He came up this time puffing with his face dark red and ran on and just about threw himself on that steer. He grabbed at the legs and got the string around three of them and tied it quick and jumped to the steer's head and old Mark eased some on the rope and he loosened the loop and threw it off and straightened up. He didn't even turn to look at the timekeeper. He didn't look around at all. He just looked down at the ground and walked slow toward old Mark. And while he was walking there, slow and heavy-footed, the one thing that could rule him out even if he'd made good time and was the worst thing that could happen happened. The steer had some breath back now and was struggling and the knot had been tied in such a hurry that it slipped and the steer got its feet free and pushed up hot and mad and started after my father. Maybe it was the shouts that warned him or maybe it was old Mark shying back and snorting but anyway he turned and saw and dodged quick and began to run and the steer was right after him and sudden a rope came fast and low to the ground and the loop in it whipped up and around that steer's hind legs and tightened and the steer hit the ground again with a thump and at the other end of that rope were Cal Bennett and his big buckskin.

The people went wild again and they had a right to because that was about as fast and tricky a job of roping as they'd ever seen anytime and it wasn't just a show-off stunt, it was serious business, but my father didn't pay any attention to the shouting or even to Cal Bennett. He just stopped running and looked around once and started walking again toward old Mark, slow and heavy-footed with those calfskin boots all dusty. He reached and took hold of the reins and went right on walking and old Mark followed him and he remembered the rope dragging from the saddle horn and stopped and unfastened it and coiled it in and went on walking and old Mark followed and together they went to the outside gate and someone opened it enough for them to go through and he left the rope hanging on a gatepost and they went outside and along around the fence toward the road, the two of them alone together, my father walking like an old man and sweaty old Mark tagging with his head low. I felt plain ashamed of being me, of being a boy with a father who'd made a fool of himself like he had, and I wanted to crawl away somewhere and hide but I couldn't do that because my mother was standing up and telling me to come along and starting down out of the grandstand right in front of all those people. She had her head high and she looked like she was just daring anyone to say anything to her. She marched along in front of the grandstand and around the side toward the road and I had to follow, trying not to look at anybody. She hurried a little and came alongside my father and he kept staring at the ground ahead of him and didn't seem to notice but all the same he knew she was there because he put out a hand and she took hold of it and they walked on along the road toward our house like that, neither one of them saying a word.

It was sad-feeling and mournful around our place the rest of that afternoon. My father was as silent as if he'd forgotten how to speak. After he took care of Mark he came in the house and pulled off those calfskin boots and tossed them in the hall closet with the other pair and put on his slippers and went out and sat on the back steps. My mother was just as silent. She hustled around in the kitchen and it looked like she was baking things but for once I wasn't interested in that. I didn't want to be anywhere close to my father so I took the front steps and I sat there whittling some and chewing on my knuckles and being miserable. I was mad at what he'd done to me, made me feel ashamed and fixed it so the other kids would have something to torment me about and so that new kid never would believe it about him. "He ain't so much," I said to myself. "He's just an old has-been, that's all he is."

Then we had supper and we were all just as silent as before and Mother had fixed the things my father liked best, which was kind of a waste because he only picked at the food and didn't seem to be tasting it. But he perked some and at last he looked up at her and grinned a sick little grin and looked down and began pushing at his coffee cup. "I told you you'd see something in that arena," he said. "Well, you did."

"Yes," my mother said. "I did." She hesitated a moment and then she found something to say. "And I've been to a lot of those shows and I never saw a steer slapped down as hard and thorough as that one."

"That wasn't me," my father said. "That was Mark." He pushed up and turned away quick and went out again to the back steps.

It was only a while later and I was on the front steps again when I saw something that made me jump up and my heart start to pound and what I saw was a big buckskin coming along the road and turning in at our place and sitting easy in the saddle was Cal Bennett.

"Howdy, bub," he said. "Is your father handy?"

"He's around back," I said. He nudged the buckskin and started around the house and all at once it came rushing up in me and I had to shout it at him. "Don't you dare make fun of him! He was better'n you once! He made a record nobody's ever really beat!"

Cal Bennett reined in his horse and leaned over toward me and his eyes were clear and bright looking down at me. "I know that," he said. "I wasn't much bigger'n you are now when I saw him make it. That's what started me practicing." He straightened in the saddle and went on around the house. I stood still in the surprise of his words and then I had to follow him and when I went around the rear corner of the house there was my father sitting on the steps looking up and there was Cal Bennett on that big buckskin looking down and they were holding a silence there between them for what seemed a long while.

My father shifted a little on the steps. "Nice of you to come around," he said. His voice was taut and careful. "I forgot to thank you for pulling that steer off me this afternoon."

"Shucks," Cal Bennett said. "That wasn't much. You've done it yourself many a time. There ain't a man ever worked cows ain't done it often for another man out on the range."

They kept looking at each other and the tightness that had been in my father's face all those last hours began to ease away and when he spoke again his voice was steady and friendly the way it usually was. "I sort of messed it up out there today, didn't I."

"Yes," Cal Bennett said. "You did kind of hooraw it some." He chuckled and sudden my father chuckled too and then they both grinned like a pair of kids.

"From what I hear," my father said, "you're good. You're damn good."

"Yes," Cal Bennett said and his voice was easy and natural and he wasn't boasting at all. "Yes, I am. I'm as good as a man named Harvey Kendall was some years back. Maybe even a mite better."

"Expect you are," my father said. "Yes, I expect you are." He leaned backward on his elbows on the steps. "But you didn't come here just to chew that kind of fat, pleasant as that can be as I used to know."

"No," Cal Bennett said. "I didn't. I've been figuring. This rodeo business is all right for a young fellow long as he's young but there ain't any future in it. It's getting to be more fancy show for the crowds and less real roping all the time anyway. I've been saving my money. With what I collected in town a while ago I've got the tally I was aiming at. Now I'm figuring to get me a nice little spread somewhere in this territory and put some good stock on it and try raising me some good beef."

"Keep talking," my father said. "There's a lot of sense in what you're saying."

"Well, now," Cal Bennett said. "I figured to ask you to help me some getting started."

My father straightened on the steps and he cocked his head to one side, looking up. "Tell me something, Bennett," he said. "There's a woman mixed up in this somewhere."

"Yes," Cal Bennett said. "There is."

"And she wants you to quit risking your fool young neck showing off with a rope in front of a lot of shouting people."

"Yes," Cal Bennett said. "She does."

"And she's right," my father said. "And now you tell me something else. Why did you come to me?"

"Simple," Cal Bennett said. "I been asking questions round about for some months. Found out a few things. Found out there's one name signed to a checklist on a cattle shipment that'll be accepted without question anywhere the rails run and that name's Harvey Kendall. Heard people say and for quite a ways around these parts that when you want good stock picked out and straight advice on how to handle them right you go find that same man. Heard them say that man never did another man dirt and never will. Heard them say—"

My father put up a hand to stop him. "Whoa, now," my father said. "No need to pile it on too thick. Of course I'll help you best I can. You knew that before you started all that palaver. Stop being so damn formal up there on that horse. Hop down and squat on these boards and tell me just what you have in mind."

And there the two of them were side by side on the steps talking quiet and friendly and the buckskin wandered off far enough to find a few grass tufts by our little pasture fence and whiffle some over the rails at old Mark and I was standing by the house corner with the strangest feeling in me. Somehow I didn't want to disturb them or even let them notice I was there and I stepped back soft and around the house again, wondering what was happening to me, and then I knew what I wanted to do. I went in through the front door and past my mother sitting quiet in the front room with our old photograph album in her lap and I went straight to the hall closet. I hardly even looked at those calfskin boots even though they were mighty dusty and could stand a cleaning. I took out the rough old cowskins and I got the saddle soap and a moist rag and I went over by the back door, where I could sit on a stool and hear them talking, and I really went to work on those old boots. I wanted to make that hard old leather comfortable as I could for his feet. I wanted to make those old boots shine.

Cat Nipped

CORPORAL CLINT BUCKNER ambled slowly across the flat baked surface of what would some day be the parade ground of Fort McKay. He carried a stubby cavalry carbine in the crook of his left elbow and patted the stock affectionately with his right hand as he walked. The hot Kansas sun beat full strength upon him and upon the double row of tents that flanked one side of the level space and upon the three sod-walled structures that stretched at a right angle to mark another side. The sun beat with equal untiring fervor upon the sweating bodies of Sergeant Peattie and a crew of half-naked privates piling strips of sod one on another for the walls of the first of the structures that would line the third side.

Corporal Clint ambled in a slow curve to pass near Sergeant Peattie and his sweating crew. He paused to yawn and wipe imaginary dust from the carbine and ambled on. The dripping privates stopped their work to watch him move past.

"Ain't he the brave hunter, toting that big gun."

"Takes nerve to go after those critters like he does."

"Yep. Turrible dangerous when wounded."

Chuckles and a climbing guffaw disturbed the afternoon quiet. Corporal Clint paid no attention to them. "Envy makes a mighty strong poison," he remarked to no one in particular. He ambled on and to the doorway of the middle of the three sod-walled structures and into the shaded interior.

Outside the sun beat down with steady glare. Inside Corporal Clint widened his eyes to look through the relatively cool dimness. He stood in a semblance of attention and raised his right hand in a limp salute. Angled across from him in a corner Lieutenant Henley, acting commissary officer, was perched on a stool using an upturned packing box as a desk. Lieutenant Henley waggled a hand in what could have been a languid salute or a mere greeting and returned to pencil-figuring on a piece of wrapping paper. Corporal Clint perched himself on another stool with his back to the wall where he could look along the rough ground-floored aisle between two long piles of grain in bags. He set the carbine across his knees.

Partway down the aisle between the grain bags a prairie mouse crept out and into the open and darted back and crept out again. Corporal Clint raised the carbine and aimed with casual ease and fired. There was a smudge on the ground where the mouse had been. Over in his corner Lieutenant Henley looked up. Corporal Clint nodded at him. Lieutenant Henley reached with his pencil and made a mark beside many other marks on a piece of paper tacked to the side of his box desk. He sighed and returned to his figuring. Corporal Clint took out of a pocket a linen cartridge holding its lead ball and powder and reloaded the carbine. He inspected the percussion cap. He set the carbine on his knees and watched the aisle in quiet content.

Outside the sun beat down upon the laboring soldiers. Inside was shaded silence punctured only by the occasional sharp blast of the carbine and the sighs and some soft new anguished grunts from Lieutenant Henley. Corporal Clint smiled drowsily to himself. A mouse slipped into view. Corporal Clint raised the carbine.

"Stop that infernal racket!"

Corporal Clint jumped to his feet. He snapped to attention. Off in his corner Lieutenant Henley did the same. Captain McKay stood in the doorway mopping his face and peering into the dimness.

"How's a man to get a report written or even take a nap wondering when that damn thing's going off again?" Captain McKay waved Corporal Clint aside and sat on the stool by the wall and stretched out his legs. "An infernal nuisance."

"You're right, sir." Lieutenant Henley came forward with his paper in his hand. "And useless, sir. Utterly and completely useless."

"Yes?"

"Well, sir, I've been doing some figuring." Lieutenant Henley's voice was weighty with overtones of awe. "According to that animal book these damn mice have four to ten young ones at a time and it only takes them six weeks to have them. Worse than that, they start breeding soon as they're six weeks old." Lieutenant Henley sighed and stared down in somber fascination at his paper. "Well, sir, you take a middle figure for that litter number to be on the safe side and you just say only half each litter is females and you say again only half those females live to breeding age and all the same starting with just one pair after ten generations you've got close to half a million of those damn mice ruining my commissary and all of them busy breeding when they're not eating and they're averaging about a bag of grain a day already and making holes in all the bags. They're multiplying fifty times faster than Buckner here could kill them if he was triplets and every one of him as good a shot."

Captain McKay mopped his face again. "A formidable enemy, the way you put it."

"Beg pardon, sir, but it's no joke." Lieutenant Henley waggled his piece of paper. "We'll run short of feed for the horses and they're getting into our own provisions. We could try wooden bins but we can't get any good wood out on this damned prairie and they'd gnaw through it anyway. I just don't know what to do."

"Cats," said Corporal Clint.

Captain McKay slumped in his chair and drummed fingers on the onetime kitchen table that was his desk. From behind the hanging canvas partition that marked off his one-room living quarters in the same sod-walled building came a soft melodic humming and other small bustlely noises as his wife moved about engaged in some incomprehensible feminine activity. The humming annoyed him. Two months they had been out here on the empty prairie creating an Army post out of next to nothing with supplies always short and no new appropriation to draw on for things needed and he didn't even have decent quarters for her yet because he was an old-line Army fool who believed in taking good care of his men first and still she was cheerful and could hum silly tunes and never once complain. By rights she ought to complain. And because she wouldn't, he couldn't, not even in the bosom, so to speak, of his own family and had to go on pretending to be a noble soul who enjoyed hardship for the sake of duty nobly done.

His fingers stopped drumming and he looked down again at the canceled requisition that had been returned in the fortnightly mail. Clipped to it was a note in vigorous handwriting: *Mac—Lucky I caught this before it went any higher. Cats! You're starting a post out there not a blooming menagerie. Next thing you'll be asking for slippers and dressing gowns and a squad of nursemaids.*

The chair squeaked as he shifted his weight. "Nursemaids," he muttered. "I'll nursemaid that jackass when I see him again. Even if he does outrank me."

The finger-drumming began again. It stopped short as Captain McKay realized he was keeping time with the humming from behind the partition. He stood up and strode to the doorway and looked out where his sweating sod crews were raising the walls of the second barracks. "Buckner!" he bellowed. He saw the solid chunky figure of Corporal Clint Buckner turn and start toward him and he swung back to his table desk.

The side edge of the canvas partition folded back and the cheerful face of Mrs. McKay appeared around it. "You be nice to that boy. He found me some more flowers this morning."

"Boy?" said Captain McKay. "He's seen thirty years if a day. Spent most of them doing things a boy wouldn't. Or shouldn't. I don't mean picking flowers."

Sweat gleamed on the broad face and dripped from the broad chin and rolled in little streams down the bare peeling chest of Corporal Clint as he came to attention before the table desk. Not even the heat had wilted the jaunty manner that often stirred in Captain McKay brief memories of his own cocksure youth. "Rest," said Captain McKay and Corporal Clint relaxed all over and began to appreciate the shaded interior of the room.

Captain McKay clasped his hands behind his head with his elbows flung wide. He noted that the canvas hung undisturbed but there was no humming behind it. He noted too the wary what's-coming-now look on Corporal Clint's face. "Buckner," he said. "How many times have you been busted and had to earn that stripe all over again?"

"Not so often, sir. Only about four times, sir."

"And how many times have you been in line for a sergeantcy and missed it for some damnfoolishness or other?"

Corporal Clint had the tone pegged now. His face exploded in a grin. "Reckon I've lost count on that, sir. But I'll make it yet."

"Maybe," said Captain McKay. "At least I'm giving you a chance. I'm giving you ten days and fifteen dollars and telling you to go find me some cats. Go easy on the money. It's coming out of my own pocket. My guess is there ain't a cat yet in the whole of Kansas Territory. But it was your notion and now you're stuck with it. You bring me some cats and the other stripe's yours."

Corporal Clint Buckner woke with the first light of dawn through the open doorway of the dugout. He lay on a thin matting of straw on the dirt floor of this one place that offered any accommodations at all for thirty miles in either direction along the wagon trace outside. He was not alone. His host, a beard-matted trader, was snoring two feet away. A pair of lank and odorous mule skinners lay like logs on the other side of the doorway. And the straw had a moving multitude of its own inhabitants.

Corporal Clint sat up and ruffled bits of straw out of his hair. Four of his ten days and a large part of the fifteen dollars were gone. It was time to start looking for cats in earnest. He had covered considerable territory already and made casual inquiries but there had been no pressure in the search. Two whole days he had wasted in the one settlement within a hundred miles of the post. Well, not exactly wasted. The settlement boasted no cat but it did boast a pert waitress at the false-fronted building called a hotel. She had slapped him the first time he kissed her. She had forgotten to slap the second time. He might have been there yet if her husband had not come home with a wagonload of potatoes and turnips and a positive itch to lambast anyone interested in her. Corporal Clint had no aversion to fighting, any place and any time, but it was against his principles to fight husbands.

Outside by the well he stripped himself bare and sloshed himself thoroughly with several buckets of water. While his skin dried in the early morning air he conducted a careful search through his clothes to eliminate any visitors from the straw. "Wouldn't want to kidnap any of these critters," he said. "Now if they were only cats. . . ."

Dressed again, he caught his horse in the small-pole corral by the dugout and saddled and started off. He was traveling light in boots and pants and shirt and hat. His saddleroll consisted of a blanket, a razor, and an empty grain bag with a few holes punched near the top. He had a vague notion of carrying any cats he might collect in the bag. His armament consisted of a standard cavalry pistol in a snap-shut holster on his left hip and the cherished carbine in a saddle scabbard. He had a long day's route mapped in his mind to cover the far-scattered squatters' roosts and ranch stations within a wide radius.

The welcome slight coolness of evening found Corporal Clint Buckner atop a long rolling ridge that gave him a view of several hundred square miles of catless Kansas. He was a tired and downcast man. As usual the more tired and downcast he was, the more determined he became. "Legwork won't do it," he said. "Like hunting a needle in a hell of a big haystack without even knowing a needle's there. This calls for heavy thinking."

He dismounted and let the horse graze while he studied the problem. There were several villages of friendly Indians within reaching distance but Indians didn't have cats. They likely wouldn't even know what a cat was. Only white settlers who might bring them from back east would ever have cats. At that only a few would do it. Cats weren't good travelers like dogs. They had to be carried in the wagons and were a nuisance. They wandered off and were left behind or got lost or some bigger animals made meals of them. But settlers offered the only possible chance. New settlers, those fresh out from back east a ways.

In the cool of the dark Corporal Clint dismounted and picketed his horse. He was ten miles farther south near the deepening road ruts of the main route of the emigrant wagon trains heading farther west to pick up the Santa Fe Trail. He lay quiet, rolled in his blankets, and watched the nearly full moon rise over the left-hand ridge. "Just one of the scratching little brutes," he said, "and I'll make the old man give me that stripe."

Refreshed and jaunty in the morning sun, Corporal Clint rode along beside the wagon ruts. As he rode he hummed a small wordless tune. He had breakfast with an emigrant family, exchanging advice on the best route ahead for his food and edging around at last to the subject in hand. "Cats?" said the man. "Why sure, we had one. Coyote got it two days back."

Corporal Clint rode on, jauntier than before. "On the right track now," he said. He began humming again and after a while his small tune had words.

> I'm hunting a feline critter
> Some people call a cat.
> To me any day it's a sergeant's pay—
> A new feather in my hat.

Ten hours, seventy miles, three wagon trains, and two ranch stations later, no longer jaunty, Corporal Clint dismounted by a small stream and unsaddled before he led the horse to the water. There were several hours of daylight left but the horse was done for the day. He could have pushed it farther but he had the true cavalryman's respect for his mount. He fastened the picket rope and sat on a slight rise near the stream and chewed on the sandwiches he had collected at his last stop. "There ain't a cat between here and Missouri," he said. "Wonder if a gelded skunk might do."

He finished the sandwiches and plucked a blade of grass and chewed this long and thoughtfully. Far to the east along the rutted trail a small dust cloud rose and grew and drifted in the freshening breeze. It came closer, always renewed, and beneath it and moving in it were men on horseback and oxteams straining into yokes to pull a motley collection of wagons. They came closer and swung past in an arc to line up and stop along the bank of the stream.

Corporal Clint chewed on his grass blade and watched the wagons swing past. The third wagon was driven by a faded woman in a faded sunbonnet and beside her on the seat sat a brighter, sharper-colored copy with no sunbonnet to cramp a tumbled glory of dark brown hair. Corporal Clint forgot to chew and stared at this second woman. "Man alive," he said, "that's a mighty attractive sight." He leaned forward and stared some more. "Yes, sir," he said. "Without any argufying or equivocating whatsomever that's the most attractive sight I ever sighted." The woman had seen him on his knoll and had turned to look at him as the wagon swung past. Curled in her lap was a cat.

*

Corporal Clint Buckner was helpful to have around. He helped the man unyoke the third wagon and water the oxen and picket them along with the man's horse by some good grass. He was expert at finding buffalo chips for the fire in places overlooked by previous overnight campers. And he was a contagious and shrewd talker. By time cooking smells were drifting around he had adequate information in hand. The man and the faded woman, his wife, were headed for California. The other woman was the wife's sister. Her name was Ellen. The cat belonged to her and it was a damn nuisance too. The man didn't think much of this sister business. She was too independent and she thought she knew all there was to know and she made too much fuss over animals and she was another mouth to feed, but his wife had nagged him into letting her come along.

Corporal Clint squatted on his heels and sniffed the cooking smells. "Why sure, ma'am," he said to the faded woman, "I've only had four meals so far today so of course I'll join you. Ain't often I get me real woman's cooking."

Corporal Clint squatted on his heels by the stream bank and watched the sister rinsing off the dishes. "Miss Ellen," he said, "that cat must be a trouble to you on a jaunt like this. If you're so minded I'd do you the favor of taking it off your hands. Give it a nice home at my quarters."

Corporal Clint leaned against a wagon wheel and looked down at Miss Ellen on a stool plying a needle with knowing skill. "Tell you what," he said, "I always was seven kinds a fool. I'll give you a dollar for that cat."

Corporal Clint stood straight and solid and indignant and glared at Miss Ellen shaking out blankets before making up beds under the wagon. He calculated what remained in his pocket. "Miss Ellen," he said, "you're the obstinatest female I ever met. That cat's just a scrawny, mangy, pie-bald sort of thing. But I'll give you four dollars and thirty-seven cents for it."

Miss Ellen faced him, not as solid but just as indignant. "Mr. Soldier. That's a good healthy cat and you're a mangy sort of thing to say it isn't. I've told you and told you it's not for sale. It's my cat. It stays with me. It goes where I go. Now you go do some soldiering and stop bothering me."

Corporal Clint lay sleepless in his blanket on his knoll and watched the almost full moon climb the sky. "Could sneak down there now they're asleep," he said. "Nab the critter, leave the money, make some tracks." The moon climbed higher. "No," he said. "Can't do that to a woman." He lay on one side for a while and then on the other and the ground seemed uncommonly hard. "If I'm going to get places in this damned army," he said, "I got to get started soon. I need that stripe." The moon arched overhead and started its downward sweep and still his eyes remained open. "So it goes where she goes," he said. "Got to keep that in mind." He squirmed on the ground and sat up and hunted under the blanket and removed a small stone and lay quiet again. "Awful lot to ask of a man," he said, "just to get hold of a cat." The moon dropped toward the horizon and he began figuring the time he had left. Four days. One would be needed for the return to the post. Three days. Nights too. It would work out about right. In that time, the way the train was headed, it would be close to a meeting with the regular mail wagon bound for the post. "Shucks," he said. "She's unattached and she's a woman. That's plenty of time. Even got me a full moon coming on schedule."

In the early light of morning Miss Ellen held fast to the handle of a bucket of water as Corporal Clint Buckner tried to take it from her. "I'm quite capable of carrying this myself. And if you say one word about my cat I'll dump this water right over your grinning head."

"Cat?" said Corporal Clint. "Oh, you mean that pet of yours. Shucks, ma'am, I was only pretending to be interested in that cat try-ing to please you, you're so fond of it. Took one look at you coming along in that wagon and haven't been able to think of a thing else ever since but trying to please you."

Corporal Clint Buckner was very helpful to have around. He was on hand wherever help was needed along the wagon line, particu-larly in the neighborhood of the third wagon. Neither heat nor dust dimmed his cheerfulness. He knew the best camping places. He knew every kink in the trail and a cutoff that saved ten miles. He rode away across the prairie and out of sight and Miss Ellen watched him go with a speculative look in her eyes. He rode back with the carcass of an antelope over the withers of his horse and Miss Ellen

watched him come back with a half-smile on her lips and found her
hands fussing with her hair. Corporal Clint knew his way around in
many ways. Walking with her in the moonlight he wasted no time
talking about cats.

In the relative cool of approaching evening Corporal Clint stood
by the unyoked wagon and watched Miss Ellen and her sister making antelope stew. He felt a familiar warning prickling on his skin
and looked down the arc of bedded wagons and saw two men coming toward him, the two men, youngish and healthy and hefty in the
shoulders, who herded the milk cows and spare oxen that tagged the
train. He had the notion from the way they had looked at him now
and again that their opinion of him was not flattering. They were
looking at him now and their forward tread was full of purpose.

"Soldier," said the first one, "me and Bert been talking about
you. We been watching you. We don't like it. We decided a couple
weeks back Miss Ellen was going to have one of us and she'd have to
pick which when we get where we're going. We decided now it's
time you—"

"Oh-h-h-h," said Miss Ellen. "I guess I have something to say
about that."

No one paid any attention to her, not even Corporal Clint. He
was inspecting the two men and his eyes were beginning to brighten.

"That's right," said Bert. "We just don't like it. Three days you
been hanging around Miss Ellen. Last night was my night and
night before was Jeb's but when we come looking she wasn't
around. She was gallivanting off with you somewheres. We decided
you better start traveling."

"Well, well," said Corporal Clint. "Ain't it too bad I don't feel
any traveling urge."

"We decided mebbe you wouldn't," said Bert. "We decided we'd
just have to give it to you."

They stepped forward. Corporal Clint stepped to meet them.
With a grin on his face and a gleam of joy in his eyes Corporal Clint
moved into battle. He bent low and drove his broad head like a
cannonball into Bert's middle and straightened and swung to work
on Jeb with experienced fists. Bert rolled on the ground and
groaned.

"Oh-h-h-h," said Miss Ellen and ran to bend over Bert, "you poor
man. Did he break your ribs?"

Corporal Clint heard. He saw. His blows began to go wild. They missed Jeb entirely or when they hit they no longer carried a powerful jolt. He winced when Jeb struck him and began to retreat. Jeb rushed at him, hot with encouragement, and Bert struggled to his feet and gulped in air and plunged to join Jeb. Together they battered Corporal Clint. The air hummed with sweeping fists. Corporal Clint went down. He groaned. He staggered to his feet. He went down again. His groan was a plaintive and appealing sound. His body twitched and was still.

"Oh-h-h-h-h," said Miss Ellen. She stood beside his prone body and smacked at Bert and Jeb with her words. "You cowards! Two of you beating him!"

Bert and Jeb stepped backward. "Why, Miss Ellen," said Jeb. "We just decided—"

"Who cares what you decided?" said Miss Ellen. "I hate the sight of both of you. You get away from here and back with those cows which is just about all you're fit to associate with." As Bert and Jeb retired in confusion she ran to the wagon and dipped a cloth in the water bucket and ran back to raise Corporal Clint's limp head with one hand and wipe off his bruised dusty face with the other. Corporal Clint opened his eyes. "You have such nice hands," he said and groaned again, a small satisfied groan, and closed his eyes.

Half an hour later, limping painfully, Corporal Clint edged around the wagon. Out of sight behind it, he strode off toward the rear of the line of wagons. The limp disappeared and he strode with purposeful stride. He found Bert and Jeb squatted by a fire downing third cups of coffee in sullen discouragement. "Stand up, boys," he said. "We'll take up now where we left off." With a grin on his bruised face and a gleam of joy in his half-closed eyes Corporal Clint moved into battle. Seven minutes later he looked down upon Bert and Jeb reclining dazed and much more discouraged on the ground. "Take a bit of advice," he said. "Don't go deciding to interfere with the Army again." He strode back the way he had come behind the line of wagons and as he went the limp began once more and became more pronounced with each step and as he limped he caroled his small tune to himself with new words.

I found me a feline critter—
A lady's personal pet.

Goes where she goes but I'm one knows
It won't be hard to get.

Walking with Miss Ellen in the moonlight he endured his limp
with gallant fortitude. It forced him to lean some on her for support and to put an arm over her shoulders.

The light mail wagon rolled steadily over the prairie. Fifty yards
ahead the escort, two privates and a lance corporal, trotted steadily
forward and with them, happy at freedom from constant sitting on a
board seat, trotted the regular driver astride Corporal Clint Buckner's horse. In the wagon, jaunty and cheerful with the reins in his
hands, sat Corporal Clint and behind him, between the mail bag
and a box, was a woman's trunk and beside him sat Miss Ellen and
curled in her lap was the cat.

The miles slipped away under the wheels. "Clint," said Miss Ellen, "my head's been in such a whirl I didn't think before. Is there a
preacher at the post?"

"Preacher?" said Corporal Clint. "Whatever for?"

"Why, to marry us, silly."

"Shucks," said Corporal Clint. "We don't need a preacher. The
old man, that's the captain, he's got authority to do the job tight
and even better."

"A military ceremony!" said Miss Ellen. "That'll be fun. Will
they cross swords for us?"

"Sabers," said Corporal Clint. "I ain't a commissioned officer so it
won't be too fancy."

More miles slipped away. "Clint," said Miss Ellen, "you're a sergeant, aren't you? You said so. But there's only one stripe on your
sleeve."

"Well, I am," said Corporal Clint, not quite as jaunty as before.
"In a manner of speaking I am. I mean I will be when I get back
there."

"Oh," said Miss Ellen. "You're being promoted you mean. I
knew you'd be the kind of man who gets promotions. What did you
do to get this one?"

"Shucks," said Corporal Clint, "nothing much. Just a little special duty." He began to notice that it was a hot and dusty day.

They stopped for a midday meal and to rest the horses. Corporal

Clint strutted some giving orders because he was the ranking man present but his voice lacked its usual confident clip. He chewed in a strange silence, very thoughtful. The cat wandered about forty feet away, intent on its own individual business. Corporal Clint leaped to his feet and raced to grab it and bring it back. He smiled weakly at Miss Ellen. "Dangerous country," he said. "Coyotes and things around."

They drove forward again and Corporal Clint was restless on the wagon seat. Miss Ellen did not notice. She had missed most of her sleep the night before and the slight swaying of the wagon as it rolled easily along the trace among the grass tufts made her drowsy. She pulled his right arm about her and snuggled close and rested her head, half dozing, on his shoulder. Corporal Clint could feel her hair blowing softly against his cheek in the breeze of their movement and his shirt suddenly felt too small around his chest and this was very nice hair brushing his cheek and he knew he should be pleased but he was too bothered by troublesome thoughts to appreciate the pleasure.

The miles dropped away beneath the hooves and the wheels and they came to a shallow stream and splashed into it. The front wheel on Corporal Clint's side hit a stone and rose up on it tilting the wagon. Miss Ellen slid on the seat squealing and clutching at him and the cat tumbled out of her lap into the water. Corporal Clint yanked on the reins and dropped them and scrambled past Miss Ellen to follow the cat. He landed on all fours in the eight inches of water and scrabbled about in it and rose drippnig with the cat in his arms.

"Good grief!" said Miss Ellen. "You didn't even bother about me but just that cat."

"Might have been a pool over on this side," said Corporal Clint, trying to smile at her and failing. "Might have been real deep water."

"Silly," said Miss Ellen. "Maybe cats don't like water but they can swim all right if they have to. Well, I suppose it's nice you worrying so about that cat just because I like it so. I hope you don't catch the sniffles now."

"It ain't sniffles I'm worried about catching," said Corporal Clint.

*

The afternoon sun was low on the left as the mail wagon topped the last swell of the prairie that gave a clear view of the beginnings of Fort McKay in the distance. "That's it," said Corporal Clint Buckner with little of a prospective bridegroom's joy in his voice. His eyes brightened. "Maybe I'd better get on my horse and hurry on in ahead to sort of prepare the way some."

"And leave me?" said Miss Ellen. "I think we should drive in together. I want to see how surprised everyone is, too. And don't worry what I'll think about how you behave. I know you have to salute and stand at attention and things like that."

The escort dropped respectfully to the rear to tail the wagon in. Corporal Clint's face grew pale as he saw they had been sighted coming and the entire personnel of the post was assembling for a good view. It grew paler as he saw that Captain McKay, contrary to custom at this hour, was not in his quarters but was standing outside with Mrs. McKay beside him. Corporal Clint sighed. Then he straightened on the seat and snapped back his shoulders and cocked his head at a jaunty angle. He urged the team into a faster trot. He pulled up close to Captain McKay with a flourish and jumped to the ground. His salute was a gesture of swift and precise perfection. "Reporting for duty, sir. Right on the tenth day, sir. Brought a young lady with me, sir, who was done me the honor of consenting to become my wife, sir. With your permission of course, sir. I'm asking for same now, sir. And to perform the ceremony yourself, sir. As soon as—"

"But—," said Captain McKay. "But—but—"

"Awfully sudden, sir," said Corporal Clint. "But it had to be that way. Begging your pardon, sir, but I can report later. Bring her around for official introduction later too, sir. Really ought to be fixing her some quarters right away, sir. It's been a long drive. And dusty. She'll want to rest first, sir, and clean up some before a formal meeting. If you'll just let me have a tent, sir, I can fix—"

"But—," said Captain McKay. "But—but I sent you out to get some cats."

"Oh-h-h-h-h-h," said Miss Ellen.

"I told you I'd report later, sir." Corporal Clint had taken another breath. "Explain everything then, sir. I've done my duty. Done the best I could, sir. Things kind of happened and turned out this way. All for the best all around, sir. If you'll just let me have a tent—"

"Shut up!" bellowed Captain McKay. "I don't know what particular breed of devilment you've pulled this time but I know it's all of a piece with past behavior. Send you out with orders to find some cats and you come back bringing another woman to this Godforsaken place that ain't fit—"

"But she's got a cat, sir," said Corporal Clint.

"Oh-h-h-h," said Miss Ellen. "So that's why you were so interested in my cat! And jumping after it all the time without caring what happened to me! Talking about marrying just to trick me into coming here so maybe you could steal it!"

"I did not," said Corporal Clint. "That's not right. That's—"

"I hate you," said Miss Ellen. "I just plain utterly despise you. Taking me away from the only folks I had and making it all sound so nice when it isn't at all. I wouldn't marry you now even if—well, I just wouldn't—I wouldn't—" Suddenly Miss Ellen was crying and she was ashamed to be crying in front of a group of startled and embarrassed men and she put her head down in her arms and the cat slipped out of her lap and retreated over the seat into the rear of the wagon and she was sitting there with her shoulders shaking.

"Humph!" snorted Mrs. McKay. "A fine mess you men've made now. But then you always do. Where a woman's concerned anyway. Yelling at each other. Blathering about cats. A nice lovely girl like that too." She marched to the wagon and cooed soft reassurances at Miss Ellen and helped her down from the seat. In a silence made ominous by the expression on Captain McKay's face she led Miss Ellen into the captain's quarters. They disappeared from sight.

"Buckner," said Captain McKay. His tone was mild and deadly. "You have committed so damn many offenses under the military code from the moment you started yapping at me before I gave you permission to speak that I won't even try to list them now. God only knows what devilish things you've been doing while you were gone but I intend to find out. You're under arrest. Go to your quarters and stay there till I decide what to do with you. While you're there improve your time taking that stripe off your sleeve."

Captain McKay wiped his forehead and turned to go inside and face Mrs. McKay and Miss Ellen. Surrounded by his fellows and a babble of jeering and commiserating and even envious voices, Corporal Clint moved toward the double row of tents. The mail escort rode forward and one of them dismounted and climbed to the wagon seat to drive it over by the stable. "Wait a moment," said Lieutenant Henley, pushing out from the shade of one of the sod-walled buildings. He leaned over the backboard of the wagon and reached inside and lifted out the cat.

Private Clint Buckner sat on a three-legged stool in the end tent of the front row facing the stretch of level ground that would some day be the parade ground and stared out into the morning sun. Somehow it was hotter under the canvas than it would have been outside under the open sun with a sod crew. The heat was personal, oppressive, made so by the silence, the solitude of that particular corner of the post, and his complete ignorance of what was happening in Captain McKay's quarters and adjacent areas.

He twisted on his stool to get a better view. Across the way there was a flurry of unusual activity. Sergeant Peattie appeared with a squad of fast-stepping privates carrying various things and walking beside him, pert and chipper with her dark brown hair a tumbled glory about her head, was Miss Ellen. Private Clint could see that Sergeant Peattie was unusually neat and natty and was strutting to good effect and barking orders with obvious relish. The squad stopped and began to erect a tent almost exactly opposite the one in which Private Clint sat in his solitude and close to the bend in the lazy almost-dried-up little river than ran alongside the post. The tent went up quickly and was pegged tight. Into it went a cot, a chair, a washstand made of a box set on end with a cloth covering the open side, and Miss Ellen's trunk.

The squad was gone. Even Sergeant Peattie, who had lingered long, was gone. The flaps of the newly erected tent were closed. "Can't any more than shoot me," said Private Clint. He crawled under the rear canvas of his tent and set off on a wide circuit, bent low and crawling at times, taking advantage of all possible cover. He came up behind Miss Ellen's tent. He lifted its rear canvas and poked his head under. "Good morning, ma'am."

Miss Ellen was busy at her trunk. She jumped around, startled.

She stared at the broad face peering up turtlewise. "Oh, it's you," she said.

"It's me all right," said Private Clint. He crawled the rest of the way under and perched himself on the chair. "I'm mighty peeved too. If you'd only had sense enough to keep your yap shut—"

"Mr. Buckner," said Miss Ellen, "all I have to do is yell and you'll be—"

"Go ahead and yell," said Private Clint. "Another charge or two won't mean much to me now. I want to know what the hell and-I-won't-ask-pardon-for-that-either is going on over here."

"Why, Mr. Buckner," said Miss Ellen, very sweetly. "I don't know as you have any right to know but I'll tell you. Everybody's being so nice to me. That Lieutenant Henley's taking good care of my cat and he says it's just a marvelous mouser. And this tent is all my own and I'm to have a better place soon as more buildings are up and it'll be fixed real nice and I'm to be the officers' laundress and have my meals with the McKays and get right good pay too."

Private Clint groaned. He tried to make his voice plaintive. "But what about me?"

"You?" said Miss Ellen. "I don't know as that's any concern of mine. I have myself to worry about, seeing as you got me in such a fix. I think I'm doing right well." Miss Ellen reached up and fluffed her hair. "Maybe you've not noticed, being a man, but that Sergeant Peattie is a fine-looking man himself."

"Peattie," moaned Private Clint. "You watch out for him. I've been on leaves with him and I'm telling you—"

"He's told me plenty about you," said Miss Ellen. "Now I remember what he's told me I think it's time you crawled out of here and stayed away."

"Shucks," said Private Clint. "Peattie always did stretch things too far. How about you remembering those nights when the moon—"

"I will not!" Miss Ellen stamped one foot and glared at him. "You get out of here now or I really will yell!"

"Damn woman," muttered Private Clint as he crawled under the canvas. "Always being so damn womanish." The last he saw before he let the canvas drop and departed on his return circuit was Miss Ellen standing straight and glaring at him and prettier than he'd remembered her all through the previous night. What he did not see and what Mrs. McKay did see five minutes later, as she pushed through the tent flaps with her arms laden with blankets and a mirror, was Miss Ellen slumped on the chair and crying.

Captain McKay stomped into his office hot and dusty from his afternoon jaunt to inspect his work crews at their labors. For an instant he thought he had been hearing voices from behind the canvas partition as he entered but now there was no sound. He listened. A soft melodic humming began and he relaxed. His wife indulged in that silly humming only when she was alone. He sat behind his table desk and wiped dust from his face. The canvas partition folded back at the front edge and Mrs. McKay's face appeared around it followed by the rest of her.

"Mac," she said, "you've left that Buckner boy sweating in that tent and wondering what you're going to do all last night and most of today. Don't you think it's time you had him over here to speak up for himself?"

"Speak up?" said Captain McKay. "He spoke up so damn much yesterday I've a mind to let him squat over there the rest of the summer. If we were back anywhere near civilization and he behaved like that and I didn't have his hide there's plenty other officers'd think I was losing my grip."

Mrs. McKay simply looked at her husband and smiled a small smile. "Oh, I know," he said. "We're way out here the end of nowhere and I'm top dog and I can do about anything I damn well please. So I'm just letting him sit there a while meditating on his sins. It'll do him good."

"Mac," said Mrs. McKay, "he's the only one out here, yourself included, ever thought to find me flowers. He's talked a girl you've been making sheep's eyes at yourself into coming here to marry him and now he's talked himself under arrest and into having her think mighty small of him. Sometimes I think you're not the same man I married twenty-too-many years ago." The canvas partition folded back again and Mrs. McKay disappeared behind it.

Captain McKay sat still, drumming his fingers and remembering many things. He rose and went to the doorway and out a short distance. "Buckner!" he bellowed across the level space and remembered bellowing that same name in that same voice when he and his command were pinned down in small scattered groups in a dry stream bed by many times their own number of hostile Indians and he needed a man who might be just reckless enough and tough enough to get through with a message for reinforcements. The thought flashed through his mind that likely he'd be bellowing that same name again when the settlers his post and others were supposed to protect began coming in real numbers to populate the Territory and the Indians got worried again about losing their lands and made trouble. He returned and sat again behind his table desk and made himself look stern and official.

Private Clint Buckner stood before him with that what's-coming-now look on his face.

"Buckner," said Captain McKay, "how much of my fifteen dollars have you got left?"

"Four dollars and thirty-seven cents, sir."

Captain McKay thumped a fist on the table. "Better'n ten dollars gone and you didn't spend a nickel on cats. I've heard the girl's story. By rights I ought to skin you alive and hang your hide out to dry. Maybe I will yet. First I want you to tell me how you got yourself in such a fool fix."

"Well, sir," said Private Clint, "you wanted cats. I couldn't find cats. Well, sir, I found one and it was attached to that Miss Ellen woman and she wouldn't sell it. I figured the only way to get it here was get her here. I figured the only way to get her here was to marry her. You're a man, sir. You know how it is. It seemed a kind of good idea at the time."

"Damned if I do know how it is," said Captain McKay. "It's never crossed my mind to marry a woman to get a cat."

"That's only how it started, sir. More I saw of her the more I figured it was a good idea all by itself. She's a mighty attractive woman, sir."

"In a sort of way," said Captain McKay, conscious of Mrs. McKay behind the partition. "But she says it's plain you've been interested mostly in that cat all the time. Says you paid more attention to it coming here than to her. Says you were willing to about knock her out of the wagon to save that cat from a little water."

"That's all backwards," said Private Clint. "That cat gives me a pain just thinking of it. You see, sir, when we headed here I got to thinking. I got to thinking what a real chunk of woman she is. Nerve enough to leave that wagon train and the only folks she knew and go to a place she didn't know a thing about and take a chance on a cross-branded Army mule like me. That's my kind of woman, sir. I got to thinking the only way I'd ever keep up with her and take care of her the way I ought was being a sergeant. That's the cat. I had to keep it safe. You promised me if I—"

"So-o-o-o," said Captain McKay. "A hell of a soldier you are. Conducted your campaign without thinking through to the finish. Forgot till too late how your fine talk would sound to her when she found out about the cat. Walked right into what I'd call a verbal ambush. Now you've lost out all around. Lost the girl. Lost the sergeantcy. I distinctly told you cats. Plural. You brought just one."

The partition folded back and around it came Mrs. McKay. Behind her and moving up beside her came Miss Ellen. Miss Ellen's head was held high and her eyes were bright. "Captain McKay," she said, "that cat is cats." Miss Ellen blushed very prettily and looked at Private Clint and looked away and blushed even more prettily. "That cat had an—well, an affair with another cat back in Springfield when we came through. It won't be long now. She always has four or five at a time."

Captain McKay looked at Miss Ellen blushing so prettily. He looked at Private Clint Buckner, who was looking at Miss Ellen with his head at a jaunty angle and a grin on his broad face. He looked at Mrs. McKay who was looking at him with that expectant expression that meant he had better do something and it had better be the right thing to do. He cleared his throat. "Sergeant Buckner, you will report back here directly after mess in the neatest uniform you can beg, borrow or steal around this post. You may regard the fifteen dollars as a wedding present. The ceremony will be at seven o'clock."

Stalemate

A STORY? Me? Expect there's plenty packed away in this head of mine. But my yap's been closed on them so long likely they're a mite mildewed. I been sitting here by the fire listening to you young ones tell yours. Been noticing how you blow considerable air into them. How the hunting you say you've done gets dangerouser and dangerouser. How the critters you say you've killed get bigger and bigger. That's plumb natural. Storytelling runs that way. Next story's always got to top the one afore or it aint worth the telling. All the same such talk puts me in mind of a man I used to know.

This was back down the years a good piece. Charlie Forespell was still around then, had a nice spread a couple miles out that level stretch west of town. Ranch buildings about where the railroad yard is now. Open country it was then with the fence lines just beginning to sneak in around the edges. Old Charlie'd been one of those hated even the thought of a fence but he'd learned a thing or two back in the winter of '86. He'd been near wiped out like the other cattlemen in these parts. Cattle on the open range couldn't take it that winter. Couldn't stand out the storms. Couldn't get through the snow to the dried bunch grass. Starved. Froze. Come spring maybe one in ten was still staggering around. Old Charlie never forgot that. Winters seemed to ease some after but Charlie never forgot. He ran some fence of his own. Built himself a winter feedlot, big one, must have been more'n a hundred acres. Kept his best stuff in there through the bad months. Couple of his boys would bring a wagon along the near fence every morning and fork the hay over.

This time I'm telling about the winter wasn't bad, not much snow and warmish spells. One morning the boys on the hay wagon came running to the house to get old Charlie and took him out to the feedlot and through the fence and showed him something on the ground inside. It was one of his best steers, a four-year-old, lying there with its neck broke and big chunks of the belly and haunch meat gone. Didn't need even an oldtimer like Charlie to know what'd happened. The tracks were plain. It was a grizzly'd done that trick, a granddaddy grizzly from the signs, big and knowing, that'd slipped down out of the mountains and right to that feedlot not much more'n a quarter mile from the barns and bunkhouse and over the fence and to dinner. Didn't stampede the rest of the steers or set them to bawling. Just nipped off that one over in a corner to windward. Surprised it, that steer, bedded down and it piled up and started running and this bear was alongside in about three jumps and smacked it on the head with one paw flip and broke its neck.

Charlie was plenty peeved. If this big old bear was having a restless winter because of the warmish spells and couldn't sleep through and took to roaming some and couldn't find ready meals and had to knock over one of his cheap-grade range steers, why Charlie wouldn't have minded too much. That was part of the cattle game in those days. Course he'd have had his boys packing rifles when they were out and on the prod for anything in fur, but he wouldn't have taken it so personal and peevish. This blamed bear hadn't bothered with any of the scrub stuff roaming loose. It'd come straight to headquarters and picked one of his prize stock.

Charlie whistled in all hands and they saddled and took out on the trail. Tracking was easy because there was snow in patches and this bear hadn't tried to skirt them, had gone straight ahead like it didn't care what followed, leaving its sign big and bold. Charlie and the boys found where it'd snugged down for a nap and had roused and started on not too far ahead now. They rode hard and they rode long and they climbed into rough country and wore out the horses and then the tracks just faded. Seemed like this bear'd figured to give them a workout and final decided to shake them and did. They beat the brush some but not too thorough where it was thick because they'd seen the size of those tracks. They rode home about dark, tired and disgusted and jumping at shadows.

Well, now, that was only the beginning. Four nights later this bear was back. Nipped off another steer in the far corner of the feedlot and made a meal and departed. This time Charlie sent a couple of hands out with supplies on a packhorse to stick to the trail and scour the country where it led. Three days and they were back, ready to draw their time rather'n do any more of that kind of work. The blamed bear'd been running them out of their saddles and about out of their boots too. Seemed to them like it knew what they were doing and wanted to wear them down. They'd find tracks and follow and these'd take them over country that'd worry a mountain goat into places they'd have to go on foot worrying about the critter jumping them any minute. They'd lose the tracks and spend hours searching around and be about wore down to quitting and there'd be more tracks, fresh-made like just done for their benefit and the whole thing'd start all over again. Nights they were certain sure the critter was somewhere close, maybe arguing with itself whether to try a new kind of meat, and that didn't encourage sound sleeping. Two days and two nights and the closest they came to catching sight of this bear was spotting a little snarl of silver-tip hair on a bramble bush. Third morning they found a nice set of tracks new-made close by and figured to try once more. They followed a quarter mile, maybe a mite more, when they heard a racket back by their camp. Scurried there, rifles ready, and this bear'd been and gone. The packhorse'd snapped his picket rope and likely was halfway to the Missouri already and their camp stuff was smashed and scattered over half an acre. They looked around careful but they knew they'd never get a sight down on a critter that smart. Started talking together and in a matter of minutes talked themselves into heading for the ranch. Old Charlie cussed those two some but not too much. He'd seen some of those tracks himself and had a taste how this bear could operate. He simmered down enough to lay out a schedule of night work, two men a night to be patrolling the feedlot from dark to sunup.

That was one way to do it. Keep the steers safe, that is, not get this bear. Likely it slipped close and figured what was doing because long as there was night guarding things were quiet. But there was a catch. Man who's been out all night in the shivery, moving to cover territory and keep warm, ain't in shape or mind to do much the next day. Charlie had to let his night men lay off days and being as he was close-handed already that meant getting behind on regular work. About a week and he stopped the night guarding to catch up and this bear was back for another meal off another steer.

Charlie was more'n peeved now. Went around muttering to himself and swearing he'd have this bear's hide for a rug so he could tromp on it. Tried everything he could think up. Hid traps along the fence lines and caught only a lonesome old coyote and one of his own horses that got out of the corral and went wandering. Horse had to be shot after what the trap did to a leg. That didn't improve Charlie's feeling much of anything. He left the latest steer carcass lying in the feedlot dosed heavy with poison figuring this bear might try a second helping the way most of them will but the critter knew about such or just plain didn't like its meat cold and nipped off a fresh supply. He got Cal Whipman out from town who had a pack of dogs he boasted about and they spent a long day on the trail and pulled in late and lame without once sighting this bear but the dogs must of because two of them never came home at all and the rest dragged in, tails on the ground and acting like they wouldn't tackle even a rabbit any more.

Charlie began taking all this mighty personal. Seemed to him like this bear had a grouch against him alone. A couple of other ranchers were within riding distance, easy range for a bear like this one, but they didn't lose any stock. Course Charlie could of looked at that as another proof he raised the best beef around but he was raising that beef for cash-money not bear food. He took to prowling at night himself, night after night, old as he was, wearing himself ragged what with the cold and the lack of sleep until final, at the doc's say so, the boys had to put him to bed and tie him down.

Next morning they came in to tell him another steer was nipped, seventh it was since the whole business began, and old Charlie was licked. He'd had a stiff neck always and he'd taken care of things himself or with his own outfit never asking for help but this blamed bear had him licked. He lay on the bed and chewed his old mustache. "Unwind this rope," he said, "and don't fret over me cutting any capers. I ain't playing it young any more." So the boys unwound him off the mattress and he had himself heaved on a horse and rode into town to see Cal Graham who used to put out a little weekly sheet between more pressing duties tending his bar. "Five hundred dollars," old Charlie said. "Spread that big in your paper.

I'm paying five hundred good American dollars to the man that brings me the hide of that grizzle-hair that's raiding my place."

Well, now, that stirred quite a fluttering. Charlie had to clamp hard on his own hands or they'd have been out most of the time whacking the brush and he wouldn't have got any work done. People packing rifles were thicker'n bugs in a bun for a while up in the hills where this bear hid out. Plenty ammunition was wasted by jackasses blazing away into thickets on the off chance of flushing the critter. Only thing accomplished that way was when one fool firing into a big patch winged another who was around the other side preparing to do the same. A few others claimed they sighted this bear with each swearing it was bigger'n the one afore but talk like that don't cost much. Likely this bear, being what it was, knew the first day what was doing and passed the light hours off somewhere high up where it could see the fun, slipping down during the dark to leave more tracks and keep the pot boiling. Anyways nothing real much happened and after a time people began thinking they didn't need five hundred dollars that bad or if they did maybe they'd find easier ways of getting same. Course soon as they'd all been gone a day or two this bear ambled down to headquarters again and nipped another steer. But old Charlie was clean beat by then. "Guess I'll have to figure it something like taxes," he said and took to moping in the house.

That was when this man came along. Came jogging along late one afternoon on a mean-looking knotty buckskin shy an ear leading a scrub-haired packhorse weighted with his gear. Stepped right to the ranchhouse and in the door. Saw Charlie doing his moping in a rocker. "Still offering five hundred?" this man said. "Yes," Charlie said. "Get it out of the bank," this man said. "I'll be coming for it soon." He turned and went right out again and stripped down his animals and shooed them into the corral and headed for the bunkhouse where the boys were slicking some for supper. Went straight in, blankets under one arm, rifle hooked with the other. Tossed the blanket on an empty bunk and set the rifle careful against the wall and it was a .303 Savage and a mighty powerful and efficient-looking weapon. "Howdy and greetings and all such palaver," he said while the boys were reading his sign and seeing it meant he was one of them, half horse and half human and gristle all through. "Have a good look," he said and gave out his name and smacked himself on the chest. "I'm the one," he said. "I been hearing how you lost souls let yourselves get buffaloed by a bear. Me, I eat bears for breakfast when there ain't anything more substantial to work on. I'm the one going to get that hide just so you bangtails won't be afraid to go out in the dark."

That was a bad jump-off but the boys knew the name he'd given and they figured it was worth a fair bit of brag. He wasn't so old, this man, not more'n in his middle thirties then, but he was a hangover from the old days when a man could make a living with a rifle and traps collecting bounty on wolves and a bear or two and once in a long moon a mountain cat. He was good and no mistake because he was still making a living at it though the critters were getting scarce and scary and a man had to follow them into country where the odds came close to even. The boys didn't bristle too much. They let him brag and he talked through supper doing the impossible which was eating more'n his share with his tongue still wagging and he kept on talking back at the bunkhouse spinning his tales with each one getting taller and the critters bigger and his talk was so plumb full of the little one-letter word "I" and the little two-letter word "me" that final somebody had to call him. It was Long Bullard did the job.

"Lookahere," Long said. "You been blowing about doing this and doing that and killing this-here whale that wore panther skin and that-there elephant that had bear fur and I'm atelling you that's mostly wind. To hear you tell a man'd think you chewed or clawed those critters personal to death all by your lonesome. I'm atelling you it ain't you, it ain't the skin and bones and maybe some stringy muscle and a thimble of brains that's you asquatting on a bunk there, that did all that. I'm atelling you," Long Bullard said pointing at the .303 Savage against the wall, "it's that gun did it. A passel of mighty smart men who could put more brains into a sneeze'n you could into ten years living did a lot of inventing over a lot of years to make that gun which you couldn't make in a whole hatful of lifetimes. Those men made you bullets that'll carry straight and pack the kick of a thundering old he-buffalo and then you take those bullets and put them in that gun and go point same at a critter and squeeze the trigger and keep squeezing if there's need and that gun does the killing and you go strutting around saying you did it. You helped some and that's all. Take that gun away, you'd be as harmless to those critters and special to this bear that's bothering us as a squeaking little field mouse."

This man sat there on the bunk with his lower jaw sprung. He wasn't as stupid as Long said. He'd just never thought along such lines afore. But his temper was up and he didn't take to being dressed down that way. "You think," he said, "you think I couldn't get this bear's got you bluffed without a gun?" "Think?" Long Bullard said. "I know." "You'll know different," this man said, "when I bring in the hide. Find a bullet hole in it and you can kick me from here to Christmas."

Well, now, that was a fool way to talk. But this man said it and the boys heard him say it and he was stuck with it. He pulled out early next morning, him and that knotty buckskin and his old pack-horse with what of his gear he figured he'd need. Went straight up into the hills where this bear had its private range. Lonesome country that was, lonesome and rough, the kind that can make a man feel mighty single and small if he lets himself get low in his mind. First time this man came on some of the tracks he stopped and studied them and he whistled soft under his breath and maybe a first bit of real worry began to creep into him. But he didn't make camp, not then, not there. He knew bears. Not just the blacks and the cinnamons but the big gray-tips too. Matter of fact, some folks back then said he was part critter himself and that was why he could still get skins. Anyways, he didn't spend much time fussing around about tracks. He just took to studying the country higher up. Began to figure what he'd do was he an old maverick he-bear boss of the whole range with an itch for privacy when tired of having fun. Picked the likely territory, up where the rock ledges climbed and the slide-rock gave bad footing, and went towards it, close but not too close, and had to go afoot leading the horse part of the way and found a level piece with good windbreaks and some graze free of snow and made camp.

Early next morning he was out of blankets and had breakfast and was scouting the ground. Found a rubbing tree with some tufts of hair clinging to the bark and knew he was right. Found another tree with gashes in the bark way up, high as he could reach standing on tippytoe, and stepped back and measured the distance from the dirt up to those jaw marks with his eye and maybe a bit more of the worry crawled inside him but all the same he left that .303 Savage where it was, wrapped in a piece of old canvas at his camp, and went about his business packing only an ax and his side Colt which he'd have felt undressed without anyways. He spent all that day combing the slopes for a mile each way, picking his places. Spent all the next day placing and hiding his traps, heavy steel ones that'd caught him many a critter. Baited for those traps with some jerked beef he'd brought along. Went back to camp hungry and hopeful. Come morning he found this bear'd made the circuit, sprung the traps one way or another, taken the beef, left a few calling cards as a kind of insult, and moved on.

That was when this man began to have real respect for this bear and the worry began to take on some real size in him. Three days he'd been on this bear's range and likely it'd known he was there from the first hour or two and maybe'd been keeping tally on him and he hadn't so much as seen a bush move the whole time. Course he hadn't been trying to spot the critter the way he would of if he'd been packing that Savage and looking for a shot. But all the same the only way he knew this bear was there was from the feel of it in the air which he could tell, being as people said half critter himself in those days, and from what it'd done to his traps. A bear like this one could be mighty tricky if it had a hankering for his hide like he had for its hide. Only thing that kept the worry from getting too big and sending him scurrying for the Savage was that he was about certain it had plenty of respect for him too. It stayed out of sight and didn't come near his camp and was careful not to leave tracks for him to follow.

Well, now, that got to be quite a game up there in those rocky hills. Between times this bear slipped down to the ranch again and nipped another steer but this man didn't know that then. He was busy hatching his schemes. Seemed to him like the critter thought about him the same way Long Bullard did and he was bound determined to have its hide and without a bullet hole too. Got so, by instinct more'n anything else, he felt he knew more about this bear without ever seeing it than he'd ever known about another critter. Knew where its trails were, the regulars it used when not scouring for food, always on the hard rock and slides and ledges where no tracks'd show. Got so he thought he knew how it felt day to day according to the weather and why some days there was more hair on the rubbing trees and others there was new gashes on the biting tree. He put all he'd ever learned about such things into trying to get it without gunning. Tried every kind of trap he'd ever rigged before or ever heard tell of and some he thought of new. Tried rope traps and spring tree traps. Spent two days rigging a heavy deadfall, triggered neat. Spent four days building a stout box trap. He was wasting time and just providing little between-meal snacks for this bear and after a time he knew that and wouldn't let the knowing sink in. Three weeks he'd been up there and he didn't have anything left for bait and nothing for his own food but some flour and raisins and he was using old coffee grounds third and fourth rounds. Day came he squatted an hour or two staring at that piece of canvas with that .303 Savage in it with anger a bitterness in his belly and getting bigger and he took that gun and slapped shells into it and started out. Covered miles, combing the likely places. Thought once he saw it, shadowy and moving away through a thicket, and poured lead through that bush and found himself yelling while the echoes died but when he pushed in watching careful there was nothing. Maybe this bear'd been there, maybe not. But when he headed for camp just afore dark he met the buckskin wandering with a snapped picket rope and near the camp itself he found the old packhorse down with a twisted neck and the claw marks plain in the torn hide.

Anyone wants to can figure that any way suits him. This man figured it his way. Maybe you'll say he was sliding off to one side in his mind. Anyways he looked at the carcass of that old packhorse and he began thinking. Wasn't much used to thinking in those days and it took him time. "The critter knows," he said smack out loud like someone could hear him. "I broke the rules. I didn't play it square." He looked at the carcass of that old packhorse and did some more thinking. "Here's bait," he said smack out loud again. "I'll try it another last time."

Not much sleep for him that night. He was going over the country in his head, picking his spot. In the morning he saddled the buckskin and put a rope on what was left of the packhorse and dragged the carcass to the place. This was a kind of pocket like a good-sized hiding place at the bottom of a rock cliff that rose straight up behind some thirty foot or more. He brought his steel traps there and hid them careful all around. Course he didn't have the littlest notion of catching this bear with those. Idea was to fool this bear into thinking he did. He was about certain it'd come see what he'd been doing, locate those traps, spring them one way or another or just plain work around them, and maybe then make a meal. Soon as the traps were hid right he took a wide circuit up and around and came out on the cliff top. This was just the way he wanted it which was why he'd picked the spot, sloping down to the edge and the straight drop below. Direct above the packhorse carcass he set his key rock. Piled others behind it and fanning out some, big ones, big as he could lug, each set careful and leaning on the one ahead, till he had a heap there that'd crush anything in its way if it ever got moving. Only thing holding it was that key rock and if that was pried loose the whole heap'd start plunging down and over the cliff edge. Got himself a stout pole and trimmed it and wedged one end in behind that key rock. He'd trigger that trap himself. He'd be up there and when the right time came he'd heave on that pole and those rocks'd cut loose.

Well, now, this man had himself a trap, a big one, maybe about the biggest any lone man ever made, baited with other traps and some horsemeat that'd begun to get a mite ripe around the edges under that afternoon sun the way some bears like their meals. He scurried to camp and made his own meal with the flour and raisins and old coffee, hurrying to use the last of the light, and by full dark he was back on his cliff top, stretched out flat by the outer end of his lever pole where he could just lift his head and stretch his neck a bit to peer over the edge. It being nighttime didn't bother him much. Never gets so dark up in the hills under the starlight except where trees're thick that a man can't make out shapes and any movings and there was a late moon coming to help and anyways this man had half-critter eyes in those days. Snugged himself down comfortable as he could on the rock and waited.

Moon came on schedule and sometimes the wind sighed mournful overhead and the dwindling cold of winter's last days soaked into him and he lay there waiting. Passed the time tightening and loosening the muscles of one leg then the other then his arms then his back then his belly to keep the circulation good without him moving around on that cliff top and the moon climbed mighty high and nothing happened. Found his mind wandering and thinking of this bear like it was a person that could get mad and take to hunting him like he was hunting it and was afraid and shook that off. Lay quiet there and got drowsy and maybe closed his eyes a time or two and sudden was awake, every last little twitch of him, with sweat starting on his skin spite of the cold. He just plain knew, that critter instinct was telling him, this bear was near. He stretched his neck, peered out, studied the whole ground far as he could see below. Nothing moved, not anything anywhere, and the only sound was the wind passing with a sigh and his nerve ends shook him with little jerks. Pressed himself hard against the rock and the shaking went away and the prickling on his skin faded and he knew, certain as before, this bear was gone, had been somewhere below and was gone. He lay quiet, arguing with himself whether to wait longer, and sudden the knowing had him again, strong and shaking, and his breath dragged unwilling in his throat and he rolled over and up to sitting position in one motion and his muscles froze stiff and rigid because it was there, not more'n fifteen feet away, there on the cliff top facing him. It was big, up against the skyline from where he was low sitting, bigger'n any bear he'd ever seen, bigger'n any critter in any of the stretching tales he'd ever told. He could see the moonlight faint on the silver tips of its winter coat and gleaming low on the long claws of those forepaws that could snap the neck of a grown steer with a single stroke. He could see the bulk of it, shaggy with the long hair of winter, blocking out half the whole sky, and all the power and strength of the whole wide wild of the mountain in it. And there he was squatted low on the rock with the cliff edge right behind him and that .303 Savage far away at his camp and only his side Colt handy which wouldn't be more'n a kid's popgun to this bear and he couldn't use anyway because if he moved to pull it this bear could be on him afore he even cleared the holster.

There they were, this bear standing still watching this man and this man sitting still watching this bear, and time just plain stopped being at all and there wasn't anything only the dark stillness of fifteen feet of space between them. This man wasn't afraid, not any more after the first shock of seeing. He was past being afraid. He felt empty and like he'd been pushed past some limit inside his own mind. Felt there was nothing he could do or not do that would change things at all. Felt this bear had him and the whole world right where a crunch of big jaws or a flick of a forepaw could wipe everything away into a nothingness and he watched it standing there big and still and it made him feel small and smaller and not just in size. He saw a thin vapor float up in the cold from its muzzle and heard his own breath, held back till now, empty from his own lungs and he saw it move, not hurrying, steady, turning and swinging and drifting, quiet as it'd come, out of sight back over and beyond and below the skyline.

Well, now, this man eased down till he was lying flat again, on his back now. Lay there staring up, not thinking because he didn't need to be thinking. He knew right down in the marrow of his bones what he had to do. He just lay there staring up and not even noticing the cold till the first streaks of light showed off to the east. He pushed up then, stiff and creaking some in the joints. Pulled his trigger pole out from behind the key rock and tossed it aside. Climbed around and down and hunted out his traps from around the carcass of that packhorse and slung them together so he could carry them. Went straight to his camp and dumped them and ate some of the raisins and crammed the rest in his pocket. Picked up that .303 Savage and checked to see the magazine was full and started off again.

He went back the way he'd come and circled wide around where he'd fixed that biggest trap of all and climbed on up and up the next hogback ridge rising maybe two hundred yards beyond and found a perch, a flat ledge wide enough to lie on and settled down there flat on his belly with the Savage beside him. Across and down he could see the cliff top where he'd spent the night and below in the kind of pocket place the packhorse carcass and all the pathways up to and around for quite a stretch. He lay quiet again, not watching sharp yet because now in this hunting he was all critter only with his man's mind there and in charge and he knew this bear'd be holed somewheres sleeping and likely wouldn't show for a while. Knew too it'd be hungry not having much food, this being the bad time of year, and likely would wake with a gnawing belly and get to remembering that horsemeat ripening there that hadn't been touched yet. Was so certain he'd figured it right and the sun was so warm on his back that he drowsed some himself and then the sun was sliding below the peaks behind him and the shadow chill was on him and he was full awake and watching.

Moving an arm cautious, he eased some raisins out of his pocket and to his mouth and chewed slow and steady. Moving the same, he eased the Savage closer alongside so he could check the sights for the distance. Maybe he smiled a bit to himself under the whisker grizzle of three weeks without shaving because he knew what he could do with that gun at even two or three times the distance. He lay quiet and sudden he had that prickling on his skin and it was there, out and down by the packhorse carcass, and he hadn't even seen it come and it was there, nosing into the pocket place and testing where the traps had been. It was small across the two hundred yards slanting down and he felt a little jolt of disappointment and then he saw the bulk of it against the measuring size of the old packhorse and he saw it lower its head and take hold of the packhorse carcass and lift this till only the legs were dragging and back off carrying that eight hundred and maybe more pounds of dead weight like a cat with a little gopher and he knew he was looking at the great granddaddy of all the grizzle-hairs that ever lived. He saw it take the carcass twenty feet out from under that cliff trap and drop it and raise its head to test the wind in all directions and lower its head to feed and then inch by inch he began to ease that .303 Savage forward.

Cautious, by slow stages, this man got the gun in position, stock snug against his right shoulder, barrel out and resting in his left hand with the left elbow braced on the rock and the forearm straight up and down. Measuring careful in his mind, he drew his lines crossed for the spot that'd drive the bullet direct forward from behind and a bit under the big shoulder to the heart. The sights steadied on the crossing spot and he drew a deep breath as he always did and let it half out and held it so the barrel wouldn't waver from any tiny movement of his chest and shoulder and his right forefinger tightened on the trigger like for the final squeezing only it didn't squeeze and he let the rest of that held breath out in what could of been a chuckle only it was mighty grim and he stood up and started off without once looking back.

Well, now, that's what this man did. Made a wide swing around and went to his camp and saddled the buckskin and draped his gear over it best he could. Headed straight for old Charlie's ranch. Took considerable joshing from the boys for coming in empty-handed and minus a horse without saying much in return. Gathered the rest of his stuff and went into town and sold all his hunting gear. Got himself a job horse-wrangling at a ranch further out on the flat and I expect that's about all there is to tell.

Oh, you're wondering about the bear? Well, now, I don't rightly know. Spring was coming which always brings plenty natural bear food of one kind and another and old Charlie's steers weren't bothered any more so likely this bear felt he didn't need prime beef or else just moved on deeper and higher into the hills. Couple of line riders bumped into a bear along in summer, a grizzly too, not far from where this one'd been playing its games, and had themselves a time afore they killed it. Claimed it was the one but Charlie wasn't paying by then and anyways it wasn't. Good-sized skin all right. But not big enough.

And what's that? How do I know so damn much about what this man did and what this man felt up there alone in the hills? Well, he didn't tell me. Didn't need to. You just figure that out for yourself. I'm through talking for one night.

Nate Bartlett's Store

SOUTH LICKS was a nice town in those days. It couldn't compete with the boom cattle-towns along the railroads, not in bustle and noise and general human devilment, so it didn't even try. It made out fair enough as supply and market center for a rising number of homesteads and small ranches round about and picked up extra business feeding folks passing through on the stageline. It was a nice town, not wide open and roaring like some but all the same not fussy about folks having their fun as they saw fit, and it had Nate Bartlett's store.

Nate was New England Yankee stock seasoned by a lot of grown-up years out in the new States and territories where there was plenty of room for the spirit in a man to stretch and grow some and that was a combination hard to beat. He'd turned his hand to many a thing in his time and he'd made his pile, staked a claim on a rich ledge and sold out to a mining syndicate for a fine price, and he'd looked around and settled on South Licks as the place to do what he'd always wanted to do and that was run a store. All those years he'd remembered the one his grandfather had back east when he was a kid and he'd remembered the tangy smells and the neighborly feel and he'd never got over the notion that running a good store right was a pleasant way for a man to spend his slow-down days. He put up a solid frame building fronting on the main street with living quarters for himself at the rear. He stocked that building with anything and everything he could think of in the general merchandise line. He sent away to have a sign made and he hung that sign on a pole sticking out from the roof of the building and that was some sign.

NATHANIEL P. BARTLETT
Dealer in
EVERYTHING
Wholesale & Retail   Satisfaction Guaranteed
"If we haven't got it we'll get it."

A sign like that was certain to make comment and liven a town's temper. It wasn't long before the South Licksians were proud of Nate and his store. They noticed it had special tangy smells and a special neighborly feel and they enjoyed themselves testing Nate's service. They'd stroll in chuckling and ask for some odd thing or other. More than likely Nate'd have it somewheres in his stock. Even if he didn't he'd never bat an eye but just remark he was fresh out of that particular item and would have it ready in a day or two. Smack after closing he'd be over at the stage office confabbing with the telegraph operator there and right enough, in a matter of days, he'd have that item ready and at a fair price, the straight cost plus his usual percentage. Like the time Al Foster who ran the Good Licks Restaurant came in and asked for a pair of red-white-and-blue suspenders. Nate looked up from the mail-order catalogue he was scanning for more things to put on his shelves. He never even cracked a smile. "Any particular design?" he said. "Why, certain," Al Foster said. "Red straps, white hooks, blue cross-hatches." Nate tapped his forehead thoughtful like he was studying over what he had. "Seems to me I had some like that," he said, "but I'm fresh out as of now. Come around next week." And right enough, when Al was passing the store one day next week, Nate hailed him from the door and Nate had those suspenders, just as ordered. He'd sent to the factory and had them made special. Al was so tickled with them and the talk they stirred he was down a while with pneumonia in the fall waiting too long to start wearing a coat over them.

It was about two-three months after Nate arrived in South Licks and opened his store that Kemp Ackley first saw that sign.

Kemp was a Texan-born-and-raised who'd been away from his home state long enough to have the usual brag and horny layer rubbed off exposing the real man underneath and that was a hard combination to beat too. He was somewheres in his early thirties, a hard-riding, hard-working, hard-playing man who'd filled his pockets one night bucking a faro game and right away put the cash into good cows and started building himself a herd. He had a ranch about eight miles out of South Licks, the biggest spread in those parts. He worked the place himself, along with four-five riders who could keep pace with him at whatever he might be doing whether that was working or playing or just plain yipping at the moon. The scale he operated, he didn't try to market through South Licks. Roundup time he'd cut out his beef stuff and drive cross-country to one of the railroad towns. He'd collect his money there but he wouldn't spend it there even though he and his riders'd be ripe for a pay-off spree. He had local pride, Kemp Ackley had. He figured that South Licks was his town. He figured that if he and those who sided him were going to take any town apart and fill the evening air with the clink of glasses and the clatter of chips and the melody of song and gunshots, why then South Licks ought to be so favored. He'd head up there from the railroad and coming near he'd collect dry-throated gents from the smaller ranches along the way till there was quite a crowd of them raising dust on the road and they'd come whooping into South Licks with him to help him spend a fair share of the beef money and whatever they could scrape out of their own pockets.

This time Kemp came whooping along in the lead and when he swung into Main Street the first thing he saw was that sign hanging bright and brave overhead. He pulled his horse back on its rump and the others did the same and he looked that sign over. "Well, now," he said. "Here's something new to add to the merriment of men and nations and such. Ain't that a pretty target!" He pulled a gun and spun it fancy on a finger through the trigger guard and clamped his hand on the butt and was raising his arm to fire when out of the corner of one eye he caught sight of old Nate standing in the store door. Nate was leaning easy against one doorjamb and he was holding a double-barreled shotgun hip-high with both hammers cocked and both barrels bearing on Kemp. "I wouldn't do that was I you," Nate said.

Kemp stayed still, just as he was. "Is that thing loaded?" he said.

"I wouldn't take a chance on it was I you," Nate said. "I heard you coming the whole last mile."

"Well, then," Kemp said. "I expect you're right. You've got two mighty powerful arguments there." Kemp let his arm down slow, careful where his gun pointed, and slid that gun back into its holster. "Shucks," he said. "You ought to know popping signs is all part of the game. Likely you've peppered a few in your own time."

"Likely I have," Nate said. "But I've learned different too in my time. I'm learning you different right now."

"Well, now," Kemp said, "it kind of looks like you are at that." Something about that old rooster of a Nate leaning there quiet and easy and maybe deadly too seemed to tickle him. "Boys," he said. "This is one sign we leave strict alone." He slapped spurs to his horse and led the way on along the street to swing in by Ed Lafferty's Licks-That-Thirst saloon.

It was six-seven-maybe-eight drinks later, near the time Kemp and his crew'd be heading to feed at Al Foster's place and get up strength for a full evening's fun, that Kemp got to realizing he couldn't keep that sign out of his head. "Cocky old bird," he said to himself. " 'Dealer in EVERYTHING.' Puts that in capitals too. I expect we ought to give him a whirl." He downed the last in his glass and called out, "Come along, boys. We've got to find out does everything mean anything." Nate was tidying up his store for closing when the crowd came in. He set his broom aside and took his usual spot behind his main counter.

"No hard feelings on what was previous," Kemp said. "I was just wondering do you really stand by that sign outside?"

"Certain as sunrise," Nate said. "Each and every word."

Kemp chuckled low in his throat and tipped a wink around at his crew. "Well, then," he said, "me and the boys here have a hankering for some genuine one-dollar-per-each seegars."

Nate tapped his forehead thoughtful. "I'm fresh out of any at that precise figure," he said, "but maybe these might do." He rummaged under his counter and came up with a fancy box and slit the seal and lifted the lid and inside were fat cigars each wrapped separate and that lid said in curlycue letters they were super-extra-panatelas-de-luxe costing one dollar and twenty-five cents per each.

"I'm a flop-eared jack rabbit," somebody in the crowd said. "He's topped you, Kemp. You'll have to pay."

Kemp paid. He had to shuck his roll plenty to spread those cigars all around but he paid. He didn't mind that much. What he minded was being capped so neat by Nate. He lit his cigar and looked around and tipped another wink at his crew. "Well, now," he said, "you met me on that and I've paid. But now me and the

boys are thinking it would be nice to top off eating this evening with
some of that stuff they call cavvy-yar."

"Are you certain you want some of that?" Nate said. "That's
powerful stuff for simple stomachs." There was a twinkle deep in
Nate's eyes but he was speaking slow and hesitating like he was worried some.

"Certain I'm certain," Kemp said. "I want all you've got—if
you've got any."

Nate turned and went to pushing things aside on his shelves and
pulled out a flattish wooden box and pried off the top. Inside were
twenty-four flattish round cans. "That'll be seventy-two dollars," he
said.

"Yippee for Nate!" someone shouted. That was Al Foster standing in the doorway and snapping his red-white-and-blue suspenders.
"He'll match you every time, Kemp my boy. You'd better quit."

"Quit?" Kemp Ackley said. "I'm just beginning." He stood there
scratching the slight stubble along one side his chin. He leveled a
finger at Nate like it was a gun. "I'm telling you what I want now,"
he said. "I'm wanting me a pair of those fancy striped pants dudes
wear back east when they go strutting up the avenue showing off for
the ladies. I'm wanting me a forked-tail coat to go with those pants.
And some pearl-buttoned spats and a—a—"

"Top hat?" Nate said.

"Certain a top hat," Kemp said. "And a gold-headed cane and—"

"And I'm telling you," Nate said in a voice that showed he'd been
a lot of things in his time and had stood on his own two feet wherever he was. "I'm telling you I've got all those items right here in
my stock and more of the trimmings than you'd ever think of. And
I'm telling you I'm not going to sell them to you. Fun's fun. But
you don't need those things and you'd look like a misplaced jackass
in them and it's closing time for this store anyway. And now," Nate
said with the twinkle in his eyes shining plain, "I'm telling you too,
son, there's a few aspects of your so-called disposition that remind
me of the kind of fool I was at about your age. If you'll let me pay
the tariff on food for the crowd, by which I mean up to and including that caviar, and then soak in some liquid refreshment to sort of
catch up, why then I'll show you how we used to outhowl the coyotes
on payday when I was a cowhand down on the Cimarron."

South Licks rocked some on its foundations those evening hours.

There were folks used to date things before and after by that night.
But the chief thing to be dated from it was the game played by those
two, Nathaniel P. Bartlett and Kemp Ackley. Just about everybody
else knew better than to keep betting against Nate about that sign
but Kemp couldn't quit. Every time he came to town he'd try
again. It got so he'd be out with his riders working his cattle and
sudden he'd swing his horse and head for town and they'd know
he'd hit another notion. He'd step into the store and say, "Still
standing by that sign?" and Nate'd say, "Certain as sunrise," and
Kemp'd spring his new one and sometimes Nate'd have it already
and sometimes Nate wouldn't but he'd take the order without bat-
ting an eye and come through on it surprising quick. One time it
was a genuine imported Swiss cuckoo clock. Nate located one in
Chicago and had it out by special express and a pony rider in five
days. Another time it was a live monkey with coconuts for feeding.
Nate spent plenty of telegrams over that but all the same he had one
there in a cage with a crate of coconuts too in a day over three
weeks. Kemp was about sure he had Nate stopped the time he
stepped in and said he wanted an engine, a locomotive like they
used on the railroad. Nate just looked at him and said, "Eight-
wheeler or ten-wheeler?" and Kemp had to say something and said,
"Ten-wheeler, of course!" and Nate said he was fresh out of that
particular kind but he'd have one soon and in five weeks there it
was, standing solid on all ten wheels back of the store. He'd bought
it from the railroad by offering more than they'd paid themselves
and had it taken apart and carted up to South Licks in freight wagons and put together again. Kemp had to put his ranch in hock to
meet the bill that time. He managed to sell the thing back to the
railroad at a fair figure but even so he was hit with quite a loss plus
the cartage.

That should have slowed Kemp down. It only made him more
determined. He thought and thought and took to moping around
in his bachelor ranchhouse thinking. He knew he'd have to get
something mighty tricky and special and at last he had it. The more
he thought about it and from fresh angles the more tickled he was.
He slapped his thighs and laughed smack out loud. He saddled up
and rode into town. He looked at that sign and read it over again
and laughed some more. He stepped into the store and grinned at
Nate. He waved a hand back out towards the sign.

"Everything?" he said.

"Everything," Nate said.

"Well, then," Kemp said, fighting to hold back the chuckles. "I'm here to order me a wife."

For a full moment, maybe two, old Nate really was stopped. He stared at Kemp and his mouth dropped open a little. Then that twinkle started deep in his eyes but his face stayed solemn. He waggled his head sorrowful and started to talk. "I've been here and I've been there," he said, "and I've been about everywhere in between. I've seen strange things and some stranger yet only a fool'd believe. But I never thought to see the day a white man of the male sex and cattle-handling persuasion would regard a woman of the female sex, a wife-to-be of his board and bosom, as a merchandisable item to be talked of as such across a storekeeper's counter. True, I've heard tell that in biblical times . . ." Nate kept on talking and Kemp kept on grinning, certain he had Nate licked at last and Nate was just stalling to avoid admitting he was licked.

". . . and I've bumped into an Indian tribe or two," Nate said, "that some folks might claim put a price tag on a squaw. But you ain't an Indian and I expect it ain't a squaw you have in mind." Kemp shook his head, still fighting the chuckles, and sudden Nate reached a pencil and order pad and popped quick words: "Any particular specifications?"

Kemp was startled some. He hadn't thought much past just putting his joke. Then he chuckled out loud. Old Nate was trying to run a bluff on him. "Why, sure," he said. "I like me a woman that has good meat on her bones. Nice curves in the right places, up and down. Face that won't stampede a steer and—and—"

"Reddish hair?" Nate said.

"Why, yes, if you say so," Kemp said, near to busting inside at the way his joke was growing. "I'm kind of partial to reddish hair. And I like me a woman old enough to know better but—"

"Know better'n what?" Nate said.

"Better'n to marry a maverick like me," Kemp said, "but still young and giddy enough to take a chance." He couldn't hold the laughing in any more and he let it out in bursts between his words. "Oh, I know—you're fresh out—that particular item—but if I'll come around—next week—next month maybe—next lifetime'd be more like it. Shucks, you're licked—backed right off the board—just too ornery to say so." Kemp was staggering around, slapping his arms and weak with the laughing. He plain had to share his joke with others who'd appreciate it the way his boys would and he staggered out the door and climbed aboard his horse and went skittering towards his ranch.

For quite a stretch, maybe four-five miles, that was about the most enjoyable ride Kemp Ackley'd ever had. He was rolling in the saddle, figuring to get his boys and swing back for some real celebrating, tasting already how he'd tell his tale, about Nate's jaw dropping and Nate's long-winded stalling and Nate's trying to run a bluff and how he'd called it. Then sudden, for some reason, the whole business didn't seem so funny to him. He began remembering. He remembered things like one-dollar-and-a-quarter cigars and a cuckoo clock and a monkey and a locomotive. He yanked his horse around and headed larruping back to town. He pulled to a stop in front of the store. The door was closed tight and padlocked. He saw Al Foster coming along the sidewalk.

"Nate?" Al Foster said, snapping his red-white-and-blue suspenders in a way that seemed mighty suggestive to Kemp. "Nate's closed down for a few days. Caught the afternoon stage out of town."

There was a lot of talk around South Licks all the next weeks. People knew Nate had gone off to get something Kemp had ordered and since he'd gone off personal they figured it must be a tough one and they began laying bets would he get it. At the same time there was a lot of silence out at Kemp Ackley's ranch. Kemp sat around in his ranchhouse chewing his fingernails. Every now and then he'd stand up and try to kick himself clear across the room. He sent one of his riders into town each day in turn to loaf about and keep an eye open for Nate's coming back. He got so he shivered like he had the ague just at the sight of the day's rider coming home along the road. He thought some of selling out, maybe just leaving without bothering to sell out, fading away into the hills so he wouldn't have to face the town, but he'd never dodged off yet on a bet or a debt and he knew he'd have to play this through. Then it was late one afternoon and the one of his boys they called Skimpy because he couldn't raise much hair was fogging home in a hurry. Kemp made it to the porch and wilted there waiting.

"Nate's back," Skimpy said.

Kemp groaned. "Alone?" he said.

"Not exactly," Skimpy said. "There's something with him."

"Something?" Kemp said. "Is it alive?"

"Seems like," Skimpy said. "Leastways it was moving under its own power."

Kemp groaned again. "Female?" he said.

"More'n likely," Skimpy said. "But I couldn't be sure. Nate had it wearing his long coat and his hat with a veil down hiding the evidence."

Kemp was getting expert with all his practice and he managed to kick himself clear across the porch.

"My oh me oh my," Skimpy said, grinning wide. "That's some fancy acrobatics. But you'd best save your strength. Nate says he believes in prompt closing of important deals so he'll be open this evening waiting for you."

Kemp Ackley came into South Licks that evening like he was coming to an execution for which he was slated principal performer. He kept thinking of the happy free-roaming days likely he was leaving behind. He kept seeing horrible visions in the air around him of the frightening things unfeeling folk might regard as marriageable critters of the female sex. His boys had the good sense to tag back a bit where their grins and undertone joshing were out of range. In town, he climbed off his horse and looked up at that sign shining in the light from the store window and he shuddered all over. It didn't help his spirit any when he went inside and found near all the inhabitants of South Licks perched at vantage points on counters and boxes about. He looked around, mighty fearful. There wasn't a woman in sight he didn't already know as the nailed-down wife of some South Licks man. He saw Nate sitting quiet and easy on the usual high stool behind the main counter. He sighed.

"All right," he said. "I'm here."

"So you are," Nate said. Nate's face was solemn as ever but that twinkle was showing deep in his eyes. "Seems to me though," Nate said, "you're a mite pale as a man ought not be on a happy occasion such as this. Now before I produce the merchandise you saw fit to order through me and my store I want to tell you that so as to be able to produce same I've had to talk myself into a sore throat two weeks running and prognosticate things about you as an upstanding gentleman and citizen of this community that your own mother'd blush to believe. Be all that on my own head, but you came blowing in here with what you maybe thought was a good joke but nothing about this store of mine is a joke to me and I took what you said straight and I'm making good on it. I've got the merchandise and to be certain the service along with same is right I've had myself made a justice of the peace so as I can do the ceremony myself."

Nate stepped back to the door that led to his living quarters and opened it. "South Licks in general and Mister Ackley in particular," he said, "I'm making you acquainted with my ward and niece, Miss Barbara Bartlett, late of St. Louis and points east." And out through the doorway, stepping dainty as primed in advance by old Nate, with color high in her cheeks and the lamplight shining on reddish hair, came as fresh and shapely and hearty-looking a young woman as any South Licksian'd ever seen. There were clucklings from the other women present and foot-shufflings and a few whistles from the men. Kemp Ackley stepped back like someone had hit him. He reached up hesitating and took off his hat and a sort of sick grin spread over his face. He pulled himself together and stiffened some. "Howdy, ma'am," he said.

"Whoa, now," Nate said. "I intend to do this proper." He motioned Kemp to come closer and all the while this Barbara niece stood still as a statue with a twinkle like old Nate's deep in her own eyes. "I ain't forgot those specifications," Nate said. "I ain't going to have you claiming misrepresentation any time later. You said good meat on her bones. Any objections to the meat on these bones? Step up and feel it if you've a mind to."

Kemp jumped back like someone had kicked him. "Oh no," he said, quick. "Looks all right from here where I am."

"Nice curves too," Nate said, "and in the right places. So you specified. Find anything wrong with these curves?"

"Now, lookahere, Nate," Kemp said. "You've got no call to—"

"My oh me oh my," someone said in the background and it was Skimpy, grinning wide again. "If you're scared out, Kemp, step aside and I'll take over."

"And give yourself a real good look," Nate went right on. "Do you have any lingering suspicion that face might stampede a steer?"

"Shucks," Kemp said. "Ain't you through riding me yet? How'd you expect me to have any objections anyway with the woman herself standing right there listening? There ain't any need for all this talk. I'm caught on my own fool play and—"

"Humph," this Barbara niece said. "So he feels caught, does he? Well, this specifying business goes two ways." She stepped out and around Kemp while he stood stock-still like he was fastened to the floor, only swiveling at the waist to keep an eye on her. "Uncle Nate," she said. "You claimed he was handsome. Well, maybe he is in a coarse, unwashed sort of way. You said he has a good ranch and is the kind of man could give a good home. I can't say I see much evidence of that in his present appearance looking like a sick calf that's afraid someone'll say boo."

Kemp jerked up straight. His color was high now too. He was getting his hell-raising legs back under him the way they hadn't been ever since Nate left town.

"Sick is it," he said, "and a calf? You just try saying boo and I'll—"

"Boo!" this Barbara niece said.

Kemp tossed his hat to one side and started for her and old Nate jumped between them. "Whoa, now," he said. "Don't you two go messing up this deal just because one's stiff-necked and the other's got reddish hair. This is a business proposition and for and as of now it's to be regarded as such. It's considerable irregular because in this case the merchandise can talk back so it's only fair it be a two-way deal. Barbara," old Nate said, "seeing him now and remembering the things I've told you, are you still willing?"

"Humph," this Barbara niece said. "Marrying a man who seems to think a wife is something you can pick up at a store like a barrel of flour is likely a poor risk." She was looking at Kemp mighty intent and speculative and seemed to enjoy watching him squirm. "But seeing as how the honor of our family seems to have got involved through that sign of yours, Uncle Nate, why maybe I can take a chance." "Well, then, Kemp," Nate said. "Here's your merchandise as per order. How do you stand?"

"What's the price?" Kemp said. He was looking at this Barbara niece just as intent and speculative as she was at him and he seemed to enjoy watching her wince at that question of his.

"No price," Nate said. "Except your present freedom as a bachelor."

"All right," Kemp said. He wasn't going to let himself be outdone by any woman. "Seeing as how my own honor's got involved here too, why I'll just pay that price."

It was on that basis those two let old Nate marry them. It was on the same basis those two behaved, free and easy with everybody else except each other, all through the evening at Al Foster's restaurant where the South Licksians cleared away the tables for a noisy dancing jamboree. It was on the same basis they departed for the ranch about sunup in a buckboard from the livery stable with this Barbara niece sitting way over on one side of the seat and Kemp sitting way over on the other side and her trunk behind them in the wagon and Kemp's boys riding well out of earshot range.

Old Nate stood under his sign and watched them go. "Maybe I've pushed it too far this time," he said to himself, "but it still seems like a good notion to me. Once they're alone together they'll work it out. If I was either one I'd want me another one just about like the other."

But Nate had his doubts when he went out to call two days later and found those two acting like a brace of gamecocks walking around wary and ready to start clashing spurs over any little thing. Neither one could say much at all without the other snapping to twist it into something mean. Nate didn't stay long because he was too uncomfortable. Any way he looked at it, he knew he was really responsible for bringing them together and maybe, because of the way he'd handled it at the store, for setting them to striking sparks. He felt he ought to do something but he couldn't figure what.

Nate's doubts didn't improve with the rumors that began reaching town the following days. Kemp was said to be staying in the bunkhouse with his boys. This Barbara niece was said to be holed up in the ranchhouse. Nate was worried plenty when he heard that. He was just tidying things to go on out there and see what he might be able to do when this Barbara niece came walking in the store door. She was mussed and dusty and right ready to cry any minute. She'd waited till Kemp and his boys were off somewheres out of sight and she'd wangled a horse out of the corral and made it to town.

"Uncle Nate," she said. "I'd hate to have that long-legged excuse for a husband you wished on me think I'd run away from anything but it can't go on like this."

Nate was mighty sorry for her but he remembered she was good Bartlett stock and he figured he could be brief and blunt.

"So maybe you'd like to get free of him, eh?" he said.

"Well, I don't know," she said and she was so close to crying that a couple of tears leaked out and started down through the dust on her cheeks. "Out there bossing around that ranch which is where a man like him belongs I can see maybe he's some of those things you said he is. But he isn't a real man. He's just a big chunk of wood. He's got about as much sentiment in him as one of those big steers of his. Every time he gets near me he can't seem to get past thinking of all that silly specification business and how he was caught and just had to marry me."

"I wonder now do you give him much chance to—" Nate started to say and had to stop quick because he saw something outside. He managed to push this Barbara niece into his living quarters and close the door and be back at his main counter when Kemp Ackley came in, walking slow and sorrowful and looking back at that sign outside.

"Nate," Kemp said. "When I think of that wife you pushed off on me holed up in the ranchhouse and me slipping off in the other direction and circling around to come here so she won't know what I'm doing, well, Nate, I feel plumb bad. Things can't go on like this. You take that sign of yours now. You still stand by it?"

"Certain I do," Nate said, stiffening some.

"Well, it says something I never paid much notice before," Kemp said. "It says 'Satisfaction Guaranteed.' "

"Soo-o," Nate said. "So you ain't satisfied with this last transaction." He felt a mite sorry for this Kemp too but he remembered Kemp was stock he'd thought could match the Bartlett and he figured he could be brief and blunt this time too.

"You want to turn the merchandise back?" he said.

"Don't be so allfired hasty," Kemp said. "I ain't exactly complaining about the merchandise as such. It meets those specifications right enough and now I've seen it close maybe some we didn't even mention. But it acts most of the time something like a snapping turtle that tolerates living in the same country with me only because of that silly family-honor business. I ain't so cocky as I used to be. I'm not demanding a thing. I'm just wondering is there any way you could go about guaranteeing some of that satisfaction."

Nate looked at Kemp a long minute or two. Then that twinkle began to show in his eye. "Kemp," he said. "If you acquired a windmill or a hay cutter or some such piece of machinery from me, there'd be instructions how to operate same and keep it operating along with it. You'd pay smart attention to those instructions, wouldn't you?"

"Of course I would," Kemp said. "That's simple sense."

"Precisely and exact," Nate said. "Well, you acquired a wife from me. There was some instructions supposed to go along with her that I forgot to give you. Wait a spell and I'll see can I remember what they were." And old Nate took a piece of paper and his old quill pen. He chewed the top end of the pen a while and then he dipped it in ink and started scratching with it. He finished and reached the paper across the counter to Kemp.

INSTRUCTIONS
to keep a wife happy
and derive satisfaction from same

Rule 1. Tell her you love her.
Rule 2. Tell her how pretty she is.
Rule 3. Think up three new ways each day
for following rule 1.
Rule 4. Think up three new ways each day
for following rule 2.
Rule 5. Mean what you say each time.

"And now," Nate said. "You just keep that paper out of sight but not out of mind. And start following those rules right away." He took Kemp by the arm and back to the door of his living quarters and pushed Kemp through and closed the door again. He stood there listening a moment and then he nodded his head. He returned to his main counter and perched himself on a stool behind it and began looking through catalogues for new things he might put on his shelves. He raised his head and looked out the window at that sign and the twinkle in his eyes was blazing bright. It wouldn't be too long now before he'd be having some grandnieces and grandnephews and they'd be in and out of his store and maybe in later years they'd remember the tangy smells and the neighborly feel of the place.

Salt of the Earth

OLD CLYDE FOSKINS finished milking the one old cow and turned her out into the poled pasture behind the barn where a few clumps of winter-cured grass remained. He tilted the milk from the pail through a strainer into another pail. He carried this out and to the well and pulled on a cord hanging down into the shadowy depth until a large glass mason jar rose dripping from the water. Carefully he unscrewed the top and filled the jar from the pail. Carefully he screwed the top tight again and lowered the jar into the water. He stared down after it, sniffling some through his limp mustache. "Beats any icebox," he said. "Keeps it cold in summer. Keeps it from freezing in winter."

He picked up the pail and went to the pigpen beside the barn and poured the rest of the milk into the tin-lined trough there. He watched the old boar and two unwieldy sows jostle each other for position. "Funny way of doing," he said. "Take it out of one critter and put it right back into some others." He carried the empty pail into the barn and hung it with the other on their regular nails in an overhead beam. He stood peering about the dim interior wrinkling his nose. "Kind of sour. Needs an airing." He pushed and heaved at the wide old main doors and the hangers squealed on the track above and the doors moved and the morning sunlight streamed through the opening.

Old Clyde Foskins stood in the wide doorway and looked across the rutted barnyard at the brown field beyond long since stripped of the last grass tufts and at the horse close behind the rails, still, motionless, a part of the brown country stretching on to the broken gullies that led to the far hills. Gaunt with age, big bones pushing against shrunken hide, the horse stood as if propped on four stiff legs and the big head hung low with its weight, almost touching the ground. Old Clyde whistled through his mustache, sharp and shrill. The big ears of the horse twitched and the head rose a few inches and stopped and sank slowly again. He turned back into the barn and reached with a folk to pull hay from the low loft. He gathered an armful and went out and across the barnyard and dropped it over the rails close by the big head. "Cri-ma-nently!" he said. "Get some interest in life. At least you can still eat." The head moved and the neck stretched and the horse took a mouthful of hay, not in hunger but in old instinctive obedience to do what was wanted. The big jaws ground in slow rhythm working the hay back over worn gums and the nubs of the few remaining teeth.

Old Clyde slapped his hands on the top rail and surveyed the horse from scraggly burr-locked tail to graying bearded muzzle. "You certainly ain't very pretty," he said. "Crowbait, that's about all. Maybe even they'd pass you by." The horse rolled its eyes towards him till the white of the near one showed plain and he slapped his hands on the top rail again. "Don't go getting worried. It's near to plowing time, certain enough, but I'll not be making you do that. I'll be getting me another one. Maybe two. It'll take two to match what you were." He rubbed his hands along the rail and stared at them and for a moment had trouble seeing them through the mistiness clouding his eyes. "You've done enough for a dozen," he said. He pushed against the rail and straightened his old shoulders. "Company. That'll perk you some." He snorted at himself and at the horse in exasperation. "No. You don't need company. Not at your age." He turned and started across the barnyard ruts towards the small back porch of the silent three-room house. "Like me," he said.

Sunlight through the kitchen window had reached the crack in the floorboards that meant the general neighborhood of two o'clock. Old Clyde sat at the kitchen table turning and returning the pages of last week's newspaper and worked with slow sips at the last cup of coffee, reheated, half milk the way he liked it, from the pot made for lunch. Old dishes on the shelf above the corner cupboard rattled gently and he looked up and out the window and heard the hoofs first then saw the team of small quick-stepping trotters and then the buggy sagging with the weight of his two stout sons as it slid to a stop in the lane beside the house. He started up in sudden eagerness and put his face close to the glass and dropped back into the chair. "Cri-ma-nently," he said. "Both at once. That means something." He pushed up again, slowly, and went to the door and opened it for them. "Afternoon, Ed. Same, Mert. Find yourselves chairs. Won't take a moment for a fresh pot of coffee."

"Not now, Father." Ed Foskins, owner of the trotters, owner of a smooth fresh face, ruddy with good living, watched his younger brother hurry to the nearest chair and sink his wide shape on it with a sigh. "What's the matter, Mert? That road get you? You're softer than me already." He closed the door and stood with his back against it facing old Clyde. "No time for coffee, Father. I have to be back at the bank by closing. Mert here oughtn't be away from the store. But Lord knows when we'd have another chance to get out here. We want to talk to you."

Old Clyde backed across the room until he felt the sustaining solidity of the table behind him. He was painfully aware of his unshaven face, of his crusted heavy work shoes and stained dungarees and patched flannel shirt. He looked from one to the other of his sons, neat and respectable in their town clothes, and as always pride and regret matched themselves in him. "Go ahead, talk," he said.

Mert shifted for more comfort on his chair. "Ed'll do it. But I agree with him. Absolutely. It's logical. It's right."

"Well, now." Ed Foskins, the glib one, the good talker, swung into stride. "We didn't want to rush you right after the funeral and all. But it's been six months now since Mother was buried—"

"Six months," old Clyde said. "And four days."

"Right. And four days. But you can't go on living way out here alone. It isn't natural. It doesn't make sense. On an old rundown farm that—"

"It ain't rundown!" Old Clyde's voice shook with indignation. "I had a good corn crop last year, didn't I? Wheat did good too. Paid off my seed loan and some over. You ought to know, you being in the bank."

"Well, yes, sure you did. But you don't need to. That's it. That's the point. No sense a man working when he doesn't need to. You've done your share. All Mert and me can remember when we were boys is you working. All the time. Never any end to it. And you don't need to any more. I checked your account again this morning. You've got better than two thousand. With what you can get for this place, which won't be too much but I can help you get what it's worth, you'd have enough to take it easy in town for—well, for—for as long as—"

"Go ahead, say it!" Old Clyde's voice shook again. "For the little time I've got left you mean. I know that ain't much. I'm your father but I'm old enough to be your grandfather, I got married so damn late." The words were coming and he could not stop them. "Maybe that's why we didn't get along so good, you had to hurry out of here into town soon as you could. Both of you. Maybe I was too old already to be the kind of father you wanted. Well, you wasn't exactly the kind of sons I wanted either. Had to keep after you getting things done around here. Had to do most of it myself. Well, I did it, didn't I? And, well, I'm older now. But I ain't afraid of it." He shifted along the table and around the corner and sank into the chair there and pushed with a shaking finger at his half-empty coffee cup. "Cri-ma-nently! I ain't meaning to get mad. What d'you have to keep worrying about me now for? Whyn't you just let me worry about myself?"

Mert Foskins teetered his bulk forward on his chair. "See, Ed? Still the old rooster. That's what I keep telling Flossie. I want him to move in with us. Pay a little board to help out but that's all. Be good for the kids, the way she keeps spoiling—"

"Shut up, Mert." Ed Foskins, the elder, the leader from boyhood, was in command. He took a deep breath. "Father, you don't understand. We aren't trying to push you into anything. We're just thinking what's good for you. These days people take things easier. There's no sense doing the way you do, rest some in winter and then be at it every daylight hour soon as the ground is soft enough for plowing. Maybe that made sense when it was the only way to get along. These days things are different. How do you think you make Mert and me feel, us doing well in town and you living out here like you didn't have a nickel?" Ed Foskins saw the muscles of old Clyde's face tightening. "Now wait a minute, Father. This is hard to say, to you anyway, but I'm saying it. Maybe now Mert and me are older too and we're realizing a few things we didn't before. We wouldn't be where we are now if you hadn't worked like that. Not many men could do what you did, past fifty already and with a wife and two little kids and having to start all over again with nothing on a piece of poor government land. You raised us and you squawked when we pulled out but all the same you helped us get started in town with what you could and, well, your job's done and it's about time you quit working and took life easy. Mert and me, we—"

Old Clyde was no longer listening. His head was high. He was thinking back twenty-some years. "I had a horse," he said.

He looked out the window past the buggy and the shining young trotters, beyond the fence, at the big gaunt figure propped on four stiff legs, head low, motionless. "I've still got him."

Mert's chair squealed as he straightened on it. "You mean that rack of bones out there is old Mark? I thought he was gone years ago. Must be more'n thirty."

"Twenty-eight," old Clyde said. "Twenty-five years I've had him and twenty-five years he's been doing anything I ever asked of him." Old Clyde's head dropped and he stared down at his coffee cup. "Nearly twenty-five anyway."

"You mean," Ed Foskins was surprised, "you mean you've been thinking of going right on farming and with that old horse?"

"No!" Old Clyde pushed his coffee cup clattering on its saucer. He looked up at Ed half apologetic, half defiant. "Not that horse. He's done his share. Gave out on me one day last fall and more'n about time the way I see it. I been figuring to get another one. Maybe a team. Herb Calloway towards town has a few for sale." He grabbed the cup and gulped the cold remainder of his coffee and wiped his mustache. "No siree bob, that horse ain't going to do another day's work. He's earned his rest. He's going to get plenty to eat and loaf around and take it easy and—" Old Clyde stopped, startled at his own words.

"That's right!" Ed Foskins jumped at the chance. "That's exactly what we mean. You've earned your rest too. You're going to loaf around and take it easy and let somebody else, me and Marilyn or Mert and Flossie or likely both of us in turn, take care of you and see you get decent meals. You're going to quit working and do just what you feel like doing and not a damn thing else. You said it yourself. You've earned it."

Old Clyde felt trapped and by his own reasoning and this time he felt no answering urge to pull free. He was suddenly aware of what he had kept hidden, even from himself, the tiredness deep in him, the desire to be still, like the big gaunt figure out by the fence, head low, doing nothing. "I don't know," he said. "I been getting muddled, off and on, lately. Never could figure things quick like you, Ed." He slumped lower on the chair and felt the tiredness taking him. "But I'd just be a nuisance around."

"Sure you would. But so what?" Ed Foskins, the first rebel, the sound at heart, grinned in remembrance. "Me and Mert were nuisances to you. Turn-about's fair enough."

"No," old Clyde said. "I can't do it. There's that horse—"

Mert's chair squealed again. "Old Mark? Him too. There's a field back of my place. Won't cost much to rent it."

"Well, then," Ed said, quickly. "That's settled. That's the way to do things, make up your mind and do them. Suppose you move in with Mert first. My new place isn't finished yet and he has more room right now. You'll be wanting a little time to get used to the idea. Suppose we make it week after next. Monday. I'll send a wagon . . ."

Old Clyde Foskins stood on his little back porch and watched the buggy back and swing and move out of the lane into the road. There was an ache in his throat, a tightness no gulping could ease. "I didn't know they felt that way," he said. He watched the buggy dwindle into the distance and drop out of sight beyond the first rolling ridge. "Maybe Ed's right. Maybe Ed's been right all along. Certainly doing well." He saw the buggy, small, a moving dot in the distance, top the second and higher rolling ridge and disappear beyond towards town. He turned slowly and looked at his old outbuildings and the leaning fences in ragged lines between his fields. "It is kind of rundown. Needs a lot of fixing. No sense doing that now."

The water was hot on the stove, steaming in the bucket and making it wobble on the rusty burner. Old Clyde sloshed some into the dishpan and did up his breakfast dishes with a minimum of soap and effort. He rubbed one hand around his chin and felt the stubble there. "Cri-ma-nently," he said. "Must be a week, ten days, since I shaved last. Time's coming and they'll be wanting to slick me some. Might as well get in practice." He sloshed more water into a basin and set this on the chest-high shelf by the window. He rooted around in the corner cupboard until he found his nubbin of a brush and his old straight-edge. He put these with a small square mirror on the shelf beside the basin and went to work on his whiskers. He pulled at the loose skin under his chin to stretch out the wrinkles and let the blade catch the bristles. "Kind of a silly business," he said. "Most natural thing in the world for a man to have hair on his face. Wouldn't feel a man without it. Yet right away they have to come off." He rooted in the cupboard again and found a pair of old scissors and went back by the shelf and started trimming his mustache. "Got to be more particular. Bird could build a nest in this thing." Suddenly he pulled back and stared at himself hard in the mirror. "Talking to myself. How long've I been doing that?" He shrugged his old shoulders and grabbed the flour sacking that served for a towel and rubbed his face vigorously. "Ain't nobody's business but my own anyway." He tossed the flour sacking on the table. "But it will be. Have to quit it come next Monday."

He was reaching to gather the things on the shelf when he caught a glimpse of movement through the window. He shifted to see more clearly. Out in the field, just beyond the fence, the big gaunt figure was moving. Head up, sniffing the air, stiff and awkward with age, the old horse was walking along the fence line. It reached the gate opposite the barn and stopped and looked over. It turned and came back to the familiar resting spot opposite the house and turned and started up along the fence line again.

Old Clyde watched, his eyebrows twitching upward. "Well, now," he said, "look at him perking some. Must be a touch of spring." He went out on his little back porch and sniffed the air himself. The unending wind was strong and chill but faint along its edges was the old eternal promise. He drew in a deep breath. "It's there. Snow's been gone about three weeks. Dampness going. A man figuring on some planting would be getting the ground ready." He sighed softly. "Not me. Mighty nice not to have that hanging over me any more. Sit all day if I feel like it."

Inside, by the stove, old Clyde soaked up warmth and began to leaf through his pile of farm journals for the articles he had always intended to read but never got around to. He read slowly, sometimes following the lines with a blunt forefinger, mumbling the words to himself, agreeing and disagreeing with what he read. The sun inched across the kitchen floor and he hitched his chair along to follow it. And outside the wind blew and carried its ancient message and the sun shone and the old horse stood in its resting place opposite the house, head low, motionless, and now and again raised its head and sniffed and walked, slow and ungainly with the wind ruffling its long winter hair, up along the fence line to look over the gate opposite the barn and swing around and return.

Old Clyde fidgeted on his chair. Suddenly he dropped the journal he was holding. "Got things to do. Might as well get at them." He went to the dusty telephone on the front room wall and took down the earpiece and cranked the handle on the side. He gave his number and waited a moment and then, as always, put his mouth close and shouted. "Mrs. Calloway? Clyde Foskins down the road. You tell Herb I've got a cow and some pigs to sell him. You tell him to be here right after lunch or I'll sell 'em to somebody else."

Herb Calloway finished fastening the tail gate of his big stock wagon. He climbed to the driving seat and waved a cheery farewell. He clucked to his team of plump young workhorses and they surged willingly into the traces. Old Clyde watched the wagon turn into the road and start its steady rolling into the distance. The sun was so warm on his bare head and old jacket that he settled himself on the edge of the back porch to enjoy it. He chuckled softly to himself. "These younger ones don't know how to bargain any more. Got eleven dollars more'n the top I figured on getting."

Out in the field, just beyond the fence, the old horse had turned, head up, to watch the young team go past. It swung around and started up along the fence line and broke into a lumbering trot. It stopped by the gate opposite the barn and looked over. Old Clyde studied it, eyebrows twitching. "What you so all-fired interested in that barn for? There's hay out there if you want it." He moved a bit to look at the old barn straight on and saw that the wind was swaying one of the big main doors and that the wood at the top was rotten and the hangers were tearing loose. "Well, now, ain't that too bad," he said. "Can't argue I'll be sorry to leave this rundown old place, everything falling apart." He let his breath out in a long sigh. "Mighty nice not to have to be doing things all the time. Just what I feel like doing. Right now I feel like sitting."

He sat in the sun and watched the old horse go back down the fence line, wait a moment, turn and go up again and stop by the

gate, and swing yet again and repeat the maneuver, over and over.
"Cri-ma-nently!" He stood up. "If you want some exercise, why
keep following that fence? You've got a whole damn field to move
around in." He walked towards the barn and stood staring up at
the creaking door. "Shucks. Might as well fix that anyway. Can't
get a good price, things falling apart."

The wind blew, steady and chill but with a softness blunting its
bite, and fiddled with the edges of the loosened worn shingles old
Clyde was renailing on the barn roof. The morning sun was warm
on his back. He fastened the last shingle and inched, crablike, down
the slope to the ladder. Rung by rung he descended, moving slowly,
calculating each step like a man who knows his muscles have lost
their snap and he must use what strength he has carefully, spread
out over a job. On the ground, he straightened himself, wincing a
little at the twinges in his back. He looked up the ladder. "Well,
now," he said, "that ought to be worth fifty dollars more on the
price."

He went around and through the wide open doorway and hung
his old hammer on the wall between its two nails. He stood in the
doorway and saw the big gaunt figure in the field moving, moving,
slowly, steadily, up the fence line and stop and down and return,
wearing ever deeper into the pathway already worn. Suddenly an
anger, out of nowhere, forced his voice into a shout. "Stop it!
What's got into you?"

The old horse had reached the gate opposite the barn again. It
looked over and across the barnyard at him. One big forefoot rose
and pawed at the lowest rail. There was a small crackling sound
and little splinters broke from the wood. Old Clyde stared and as he
stared the anger dwindled in him.

He went towards the gate and the old horse raised its head higher
and whiffled softly at him and pressed its chest forward against the
top rail. "Mark," he said. "Mark boy. You want out? What in hell
for?" He felt a strange lightheadedness, a deliberate emptiness of
thought. He stepped forward, hardly aware what he was doing, and
the horse stepped back and he tugged at the rails till they fell at his
feet. Head high, breathing deeply, the old horse stepped over them
and past him. Straight to the barn it went and in through the wide
doorway. He followed. He stood in the doorway and saw it stand-

ing, waiting, motionless, patient, by the harness rack, and seeing he felt the anger flare and fill him, strong and bitter. "So you think you've still got it in you! I'll show you! You couldn't drag it ten feet!" With trembling, hurrying fingers he snatched the old bridle with its long driving reins from its peg and jammed the rusty bit between the big old waiting jaws. He grabbed the harness and threw it over the big bony frame. He fought with the buckles to fasten them and cursed at the clumsiness of haste. He took the reins and slapped with the loose ends hard at the horse's rump and swung it around and backed it to where the old plow lay on the barn floor. He fastened the tugs with sharp jerks, muttering steadily under his breath. He took the reins again and slapped again with the loose ends. "All right, get moving! I'll show you! I'll show you good!"

Head high, ears forward, the old horse moved and the old plow clattered on its side along the rough floor planks and old Clyde walked beside it. Out of the barn, around the pigpen, past the empty back pasture, to the wide spreading rear field where the corn stubble marked its old rows with withered tufted weeds and grass between. Old Clyde's voice rose, still in anger but with a note of frantic appeal. "Cri-ma-nently Ain't I been telling you? You're too old! There ain't any sense to it! Wait'll you hit the dirt! Wait'll the 'share digs in! That'll show you!"

He yanked on the reins and the old horse stopped, leaning its weight slightly forward into the harness to hold the tugs tight. Quickly, with the sureness of old habit, he knotted the rein ends together and flipped the loop over his head and around his shoulders. He leaned and took hold of the plow handles and struggled with them until the plow was upright, ready. "Giddap!" he yelled. "Yank your goddamn heart out! That'll learn you!" The old horse surged forward and as it moved old Clyde heaved up on the handles so that the blade pointed into the ground. Smoothly, surely, the blade sank in and leveled for the straight pull and stopped against the hard mass of the subsoil. He heard the breath of the old horse wheeze in its throat and saw the ribs straining through the shaggy hide and the old cracked hoofs digging into the dirt—and the plow moved, slow, hesitating, forward and stop and forward again and not stopping and the clean earth rolled from the moldboard and lay in a darkened ribbon by the fresh furrow beside his plodding feet.

Slowly, unsteadily, but always forward, concentrating with an intense earnestness, the horse and the man with the plow biting into the earth between them crawled along the length of the wide spreading field.

They stopped at the far end and old Clyde turned his head to look back along the furrow. "Cri-ma-nently," he said softly. "Straight as a string." He jerked his head around and pulled quickly on the plow to free the blade from the ground, for the old horse, breathing heavily, was moving again, was starting to swing in the arc that would bring them around for the return trip back along the field. He fought with the plow to get it turned in time and pulled it upright and heaved quickly on the handles so they would not lose the forward momentum and the blade sank into the ground and leveled and the new furrow began to unroll. And suddenly he was no longer an old man plodding along, plowing often-plowed ground behind an old gaunt horse that struggled with each forward step, whose big old bones thrust out against shrunken hide. He was a man with a snap still in his knees, striding along, striding behind a huge young horse, filled out, great-muscled, sleek with sweat, big head slogging forward into the terrific strain as the plow sliced deep through the tangled matted roots of virgin prairie sod. "Yippee!" he yelled. "Smash into it, Mark boy! I know what people are saying. That Foskins is a damn fool. He'll never make it. Have to have oxen or a four-horse span to break that ground. I ain't got those. But I've got you, boy! We'll show 'em!" He was striding along, feet striking firm beside the furrow, striding along behind huge young Mark, the tireless, the indomitable, great heart driving great muscles, plowing forward through unending resistant sod, through the days and the weeks and the months, and the sweat of their work salted the earth of the years.

Old Clyde Foskins realized he was standing still, gripping the plow handles so hard that his fingers hurt. The plow had stopped. Ahead of him the old horse wavered on four stiff legs and shudders ran through its body and its breath whistled shrill in its throat. The big head sank lower and lower and the big gaunt frame crumpled and toppled forward and sideways and to the ground and the weight dragging on the harness pulled the plow over on its side.

Carefully old Clyde lifted the knotted reins over his head and dropped them. He went around by the still figure and looked down.

The eyes were open, staring, and there was no life in them. He stood quietly, looking down, for a long time. "It'll take a mighty big hole," he said. He raised his head and looked out along the fresh furrows. "I expect a corner of this field'll be about right. It's as much his as mine." He stood quietly, staring into the distance. He raised one calloused old hand and brushed it across his eyes to clear the mistiness from them. "Yes," he said. "Yes. He was right. That's the way to do it."

He walked, slowly and steadily, out of the field, past the empty back pasture, around the empty pigpen, across the barnyard, up on his little back porch and into the house. He went straight to the dusty telephone on the front room wall and took down the earpiece and cranked the handle. He gave his number and waited. He put his mouth close and shouted. "Marilyn? You tell Ed when he gets home I don't want any wagon on Monday. Or any time." Quickly he pushed down the receiver hook with a finger and waited again. After a moment he released the hook and cranked the handle once more and gave his number. He put his mouth close and shouted. "Mrs. Calloway? You tell Herb I'll be there to see him shortly. Want to dicker for a couple of horses."

He pulled his old jacket closer about him and went out on his little back porch. He heard the telephone ringing behind him, three rings, his call. "Let 'em keep that thing buzzing all day," he said. "I ain't got time to argue. Got my spring plowing to do." He went around the house and along the lane. "That team Herb had here yesterday. The two of them together might do. Maybe buy back that cow too. She always gave down good for me." Walking slowly and steadily, he headed up the road.

One Man's Honor

THIS HAPPENED out where distance ran past vision and only clumped silver-green of sagebrush and blunt bare rising ridges of rock broke the red-brown reaches of sand and sun-baked silt. No highways or railroads sliced it into measurable stretches. Only a lone rutted trace snaked through, following the lower levels, worn by freighters who crawled at long intervals with their clumsy wagons from the last meager town far southward on the river to the rolling cattle ranges far northward on the more fertile uplands. Yet here and there, off the trace, widely separated and hidden between the ridges where slow short-season streams made narrow areas of green before dying in the sand, the first settlers had come. They would increase and windmills would rise to draw upon the subsurface water and in time a network of roads would fan out and wheels would grind dust for hot winds to whirl. Now they were few and far, lost in the immensity of distance and red-brown desolation under the limitless depth of sky.

Late afternoon sun slanted over one of the higher ridges and shone on the sparse beginnings of a homestead claim. Clear and hot in the clean air, it shone on a long strip of shallow-plowed ground that followed the gradual curve of an almost-dry stream bed where a few brackish pools lingered and on a sagging pole corral where an old milk cow and two stocky ungainly draft horses drooped in motionless rest and beside this on the shelter, half dugout cut into the rise of a small ground swell, half timbered with scrub logs from the stunted cottonwoods that straggled along the other side of the stream bed. Trimmed branches corded together and plastered over with clay formed the roof and a rusting stovepipe rose from it. On the split-log doorstep sat a little girl. Her short scratched sunburned legs barely reached the ground. Her light brown hair, sun-bleached in lighter streaks, curled softly down to frame a round stub-nosed face whose dark eyes, unmasked by the light lashes, were wide and bright. A twenty-foot length of rope was tied around her waist and fastened to a staple driven into the doorjamb. She was small and serious and very quiet and she smoothed the skirt of her small flour-sacking dress down over her bare knees and poked, earnest and intent, one small moccasined foot at an ant scurrying in the dooryard dust.

Behind her, in the dim recess of the one-windowed shelter, a tall flat-bodied man stooped over a rumpled bed against the rear wall and laid a moistened cloth across the forehead of a woman lying there. His voice was low and harsh with irritation but the touch of his hand was gentle. "What's got into ye?" he said.

The woman stared up at him, apology plain on her thin flushed face. "I don't know," she whispered. "It just came on me sudden-like." Her thin body under the patched gingham of dress shook with slight tremors as with a chill yet drops of sweat streaked her cheeks. Her voice came faint and wavering. "You'll have to do the food. There's soup in the kettle."

The man brushed one hand impatiently at the flies hovering over the bed. "Ye'll be better in the morning," he said. Abruptly he turned and went to the stove set against the right wall. The woman watched him. She tried to speak and could not. She lay still a moment and summoned strength to rise on her elbows and send her voice across the room to him. "Wait," she said. "Wait. You'll have to do the game with her. It's her fun. It helps her learn."

The man swung his head to look at the doorway. The little girl sat still, her back to him, her head bent forward as she peered at something by her feet. The last sun slanting over the ridge filtered through the tangled curls along her neck. Slowly the lines of worry and irritation faded from the man's face and the tightness around his mouth eased. He went to the doorway and leaned low to untie the rope around her waist. She stood up, small and soft beside his hard height, and stretched back her head to look up at him. She

raised one small hand and reached to put it in one of his big calloused hands. Together they went along the front of the shelter
towards the corral.

Near the corner the man stopped. He slapped his free hand on
the side of the shelter. "This," he said.

Gravely the little girl regarded the shelter. A triumphant smile
crinkled her small face. "Hello, house," she said.

"Right," the man said. They moved on and stopped by an old
wagon pulled in close alongside the shelter. The man reached under and pulled out an empty milk pail and held it up. Gravely the
little girl regarded it. Her small eyebrows drew down in a frown.
She looked up at the man in doubt and back at the object in his
hand. "Hello," she said slowly, "hello, buck-et."

"That's it!" The man grinned down at her and reached to put
the pail back under the wagon. They moved on to the sagging poles
of the corral. The man pointed over the poles at the cow and the
little girl peered through them beside him. She spoke at once, quick
and proud. "Hello, cow."

"What's the cow's name?"

"Bess-ie."

"Mighty smart ye're getting to be," the man said. He pointed
over the poles at the draft horses standing together in a corner.

The little girl tossed her head. "Hello, horse."

"No," the man said. "There's two of them. More than one. Horses."

The little girl looked up at him, small and earnest and intent.
She looked back through the poles across the corral. "Hello, horses."

Forty-three miles to the south and five miles west of the meager
town on the river, where the ground dipped in a hollow some ten
feet below the level expanse around, a saddled horse stood alone,
ground-reined, patiently waiting. A wide-brimmed weather-worn
hat hung on the saddle horn. Several hundred yards away the river
road followed the bank, a dust track running west into fading distance and east towards the low hills hiding the town. Close by the
roadside two small rocks jutted out of the ground, butted against
each other. Together they were little more than three feet wide,
irregular in shape, no more than eighteen inches high at the highest

point. The late afternoon sun slanted down on them and they made a small lengthening patch of shade. Beside them, stretched out, head and shoulders into the shade, a man lay flat, belly down, pressed against the ground. Beside him lay a rifle. Its barrel had been rubbed with dirt to remove all shine. He was a short man, short and thick, with a head that seemed small, out of proportion to the thick body, set too close into the hunched shoulders. His hair was a dirty black, close-cropped with the rough scissor slashes of his own cutting plainly marked, and it merged with no visible break into the dark unshaven stubble down his cheeks and around his narrow tight-lipped mouth.

He raised his head higher to sight along the road to the west through the cleft where the tops of the two rocks joined. Pushing with his toes in beaten scarred old knee-length boots, he hitched his body a few inches to the left so that it lay almost exactly parallel to the road, invisible to anyone approaching in the distance from the west. As he moved, the hammer of the revolver in a holster at his side made a tiny groove in the ground and he reached to test the firmness of its seat in the holster and free it of any clinging dirt. His voice was a low murmur lost in the vast empty reaches of space, the flat inflectionless voice of a man accustomed to being alone and to talking to himself. "Last place they'd be expecting trouble," he said.

He lay flat, his head relaxed on its side with one ear against the ground, and the sun dropped slowly down the sky and the patch of shade of the rocks spread down his back and reached the brass-studded cartridge belt around his waist and far out along the road to the west a tiny puff of dust appeared and crept closer, barely seeming to move only to grow imperceptibly larger in the angled foreshortening of distance. Faint tremors in the ground came to the man's ear. He raised his head and sighted through the rock cleft. He rolled on his side and pulled the tattered old bandanna tied loosely around his neck up over his face, up to the bridge of his nose so that only his eyes and forehead showed over it. He rolled back into position and took the rifle and eased the barrel forward through the cleft. Propped on his elbows with the curved butt of the rifle against his right shoulder and his right cheek under the bandanna against the stock, he watched the puff of dust far out along the road.

It was no longer just a puff of dust. Emerging from it yet never escaping and always emerging as the dust rose under the hoofs was a light fast freight wagon drawn by two stout horses at a steady trot. Two men sat on the board-backed seat, the driver and another man with a shotgun between his knees, the butt on the floorboard, the barrel pointing at the sky.

The man behind the rocks waited. He waited until the wagon was little more than one hundred feet away and in a few seconds he would begin to be visible over the top of the rocks and his finger tightened on the trigger of the rifle and with the crash of the shot the man with the shotgun jolted hard against the back of the wagon seat and the horses reared, beating upward with their front hoofs and trying to swing away, and the man with the shotgun dropped it clattering on the floorboard and struggled to stand on the swaying platform and toppled sideways into the road dust and lay still.

The man behind the rocks let the rifle stock fall to the ground and leaped up and in the leaping took the revolver from the holster at his side. He moved out and around the rocks and closer to the wagon and watched the driver fighting with the horses to quiet them. He watched the driver pull them to quivering stillness and become aware of him and the gun in his hand and stiffen in a tight silence. "That's right," he said. "Keep your hands on those reins where I can see them." He moved closer and to the right side of the wagon and with his left hand took the shotgun from the floorboard and tossed it back from the road. He moved out and around the horses to the left side of the wagon and took the driver's revolver from its holster and threw it towards the river. He stepped back, away from the wagon. "Now," he said. "Take it slow. Wrap the reins around that brake. Put your hands up behind your head." The driver hesitated. His lips were pale, pressed tight together, and a slow flush crept up his cheeks. He reached slowly and looped the reins over the brake handle and raised his hands and clasped them together at the back of his head.

The man with the gun stepped up by the body of the wagon. He was careful to stand facing part way forward so that the driver was always within his angle of vision. With his left hand he unfastened the rope lashed over the wagon and pulled away the light canvas dust cover. Four square boxes and several small crates and a half-dozen sacks of potatoes were exposed to view. He chuckled, a strange harsh sound in the wide silence. "Mighty little load to be packing a guard," he said. He swung his head for a quick check of the load and back to look straight at the driver. His voice was suddenly sharp and biting. "Where is it? I know you're carrying it." The driver had pivoted his body at the hips to watch him and stared at him and said nothing.

The man with the gun grunted and reached with his left hand to yank aside one of the sacks of potatoes. He reached again and heaved to move aside the one that had been beneath the first. He plunged the hand into the hole opened to the bed of the wagon and felt around and pulled out a small metal box. He stepped back and again his strange harsh chuckle sounded in the silence.

The voice of the driver broke through the tight line of his lips. "You'll never get away with it, Kemp. I'd know that gunbelt anywhere."

The man with the gun let the metal box fall from his left hand and lifted the hand and pulled the bandanna down from his face. "Too bad," he said. He raised his right hand and the gun in it bucked with the shot and the driver rose upright off the seat arching his back in sudden agony and fell sideways over the footboard to strike on the wagon tongue and bounce to the ground between the harness tugs and with the roar of the shot the horses were rearing and they plunged ahead and the wheels crunched over the driver's body as they rolled forward along the road.

The man with the gun took one leap after the wagon and stopped. He raised the gun again and in almost aimless haste fired the four remaining bullets in it at the plunging horses. The horses drove forward, goaded by several flesh wounds, and the reins ripped off the brake handle and the wagon careened after them and swerved to the left and the left front wheel struck against the rocks behind which the man had been hiding. The wagon bounced upward as the wheel cracked and the harness tugs snapped and the horses, freed of the weight, surged in frantic gallop along the road.

The man threw the empty revolver to the ground. He raced to the wagon and around it to the rocks and leaped over them and grabbed the rifle. He dropped to his right knee and braced his left elbow on his left knee to steady his aim and fired and one of the horses staggered and fell and the other, pulled sideways by the falling weight, lashed frantically with its hoofs and the harness parted and the horse galloped ahead alone along the road. Already it was a far shape, dwindling into distance, and the man fired again and again until the magazine of the rifle was emptied and the bullets kicked small spurts of dust and the horse galloped on unhit into the low hills. The man threw down the rifle and stood erect. He was shaking with a tense fury. He stood still, forcing himself to quiet, driving the shaking out of his body. He drew a long breath. "That'll tell 'em too damn soon," he said. Quickly he took up the rifle and opened the breech and blew through the barrel and loaded the magazine with bullets from the pocket of his faded old shirt. He hurried back where he had dropped the metal box. The two bodies lay near in the road dust and already the flies were gathering and he paid no attention to them. He picked up the revolver and loaded it with bullets from the brass-studded belt around his waist. He reached down and blasted the lock of the metal box with a single shot and ripped the top open and took out two small plump leather bags and a sheaf of bills and jammed these into the pockets of his old patched pants. At a steady run he moved away from the road, across the level expanse, to the hollow several hundreds yards away and the waiting horse. With swift sure gestures he slapped the hat on his head and pushed the rifle into its saddle scabbard and transferred the two small bags and the bills to the saddlebag. He swung up and yanked the horse around, lifting it into a fast lope, and headed north through the red-brown reaches of distance.

Early morning sun slanted in from the east on the homestead shelter. It made a narrow triangular patch of brightness on the packed dirt floor through the open doorway and pushed a soft glow further into the room. On the edge of a low short trundle cot against the back wall by the foot of the big bed the little girl sat, her body bent forward, her small face puckered in a frown as she concentrated on the problem of putting the right little moccasin on the right foot. On the bed itself the woman lay thin and motionless. Her eyes were closed. At intervals the eyelids twitched and flickered and were still. Her mouth was partly open and her breath drew through it in long slow straining gasps. On the floor beside the bed, stretched on an old quilt folded over, the man lay asleep, fully dressed except for his short thick boots.

The little girl finished with the moccasins. She slid to the floor

and turned and tried to smooth the old blanket on her cot. She took
hold of the cot and tugged at it to pull it a few inches out from the
wall. She went to the end of it away from the bed and turned her
small back to it and against it and pushed with her feet to move it
along the floor and slide it under the bed.

The scratching sound of the cot runners scraping on the hard dirt
floor roused the man. He bent his body at the waist to sit up and
wavered and fell back. He pushed against the floor with both hands
and was up to sitting position. He looked around, his eyes glassy
and staring, and saw the boots and his attention focused on them
and he reached for them and struggled to get them on. He heaved
himself over on one hip and pushed against the floor and stood
swaying on his feet. Sweat streamed down his face and his body
shook as with a chill. He took a step and staggered and fell towards
the wall and clutched at it for support. He moved along it to the
head of the bed. Leaning his weight on one hand on the bed, he
reached with the other to the woman's shoulder and gently shook
her. Her head wobbled limply at the pressure and her eyes remained closed. He straightened against the wall. Slowly he wiped
one hand down over his damp face and let it fall to his side.

The little girl stood by the foot of the bed and looked up at him.
Slowly his attention focused on her. He stared at her for a long
moment and she looked up at him and a small smile of greeting
touched her face and was gone. He drew a long slow sobbing breath
and by sheer effort of will pushed out from the wall. His feet
dragged and he moved in a strange lurching walk. He took the old
quilt from the floor and reached under the bed to take the old
blanket from the cot and pulled a pile of empty flour sacks down
from a shelf. With these in his arms he staggered to the doorway
and out and along the front of the shelter to the old wagon beside
it. He heaved his load into the body of the wagon and leaned panting on the side to reach in and spread out the sacks and put the
blanket and quilt over them. Weakness took him and he swayed
against one of the wagon wheels and hung over it while sweat
dripped in tiny glistening beads from his chin to the ground below.
He pushed out from the wheel and veered to the shelter wall and
hitched his way along towards the door. The little girl was in the
doorway and she backed away inside and he held to the doorjamb
and pulled himself around and in and a short way along the inside

wall and reached for the team harness hanging on two wooden pegs and in the reaching suddenly sagged in a limp helplessness and collapsed doubling forward to bump against the wall and slide to the floor. His body stretched out and rolled over and his unseeing eyes stared upward a few seconds and the lids dropped and no motion stirred in him except the long slow heaving of his chest.

The little girl stared at the man lying still and silent and her eyebrows drew together in a frown. She looked at the woman on the bed and back at the man on the floor. She turned away and went to the table under the one window in the right wall and climbed on the chair beside it and then onto the table. Standing on tiptoe and leaning out she reached one hand into an earthenware jar on the shelf by the window and took it out with a cracker clutched in her fingers. She climbed down to the chair and sat on it with her short sunburned legs swinging over the edge. Gravely she regarded the object in her hand. "Hello, crack-er," she said in a soft hushed voice. Gravely she bit off a corner and began to chew it.

A mile and a half to the southeast the early morning sun sent long shadows streaming out from a man and a horse climbing the rough slope of a twisting boulder-strewn ridge. The man rode with his short thick body hunched forward and the sun glinted on the brass studdings of the cartridge belt around his waist. The horse was sweat-streaked, tired, taking the slope in short spurts as the man kicked it forward.

They topped the ridge and dropped a short way down the near side and stopped. The man swung to the ground. He took off his weather-worn hat and slapped at himself with it to knock some of the dust off his clothes and hung it on the saddle horn. He turned back to the top of the ridge and lay flat on the blunt bare rock to peer over. No motion anywhere disturbed the empty distance. He turned his head to look at the horse standing with braced legs apart, head hanging, grateful for the rest. He settled himself more comfortably on the rock and watched over the ridge top. The shadows of the boulders down the slope shrank slightly as the sun crept upward and far out along his back trail around a swelling shoulder of wind-piled sand a straggling line of seven tiny figures crawled into view. "Damn funny," he said in a flat inflectionless voice. "Can't shake 'em."

The seven tiny figures crawled closer, increasing in size, seeming to increase in pace as the distance dwindled, and they were seven men on horseback, six in a ragged relatively compact group and one alone in the lead.

The man on the ridge top shaded his eyes against the slant sun and studied the figure in the lead, distinguishable now across the dwindling distance, a lean long-armed figure wearing a buckskin shirt, slim and straight in the saddle on a tall gray horse. He wore no hat and his hair, iron-gray and long, caught the sun clearly in the bobbing rhythm of riding. He rode at a fast trot and at intervals pulled his horse to a brief walk and leaned in the saddle to check the ground beside and ahead.

The man on the ridge top smacked a clenched fist on the rock. "That's it," he said. "Thought he'd left for the mines." He licked his dry lips and spat out the dust-dirty saliva. "Can't just keep running," he said. "Not with him after." He crawled down from the ridge top a few feet and turned squatting on his heels to look down the near slope. Down where it slipped into level expanse of red-brown ground and sparse silver-green of sagebrush, a few-score feet out from the base, a stony dry stream bed followed the twisting formation of the ridge. To the right, swinging in along the level from around a curving twist of the ridge and cutting across the dry stream bed to push in a long arc towards a far break in the next ridge, ran the wagon trace. Plain in the sand dust of the trace, visible from the height, were the day-old unending ribbon ruts of wheel tracks and the hoofprints of many horses heading north.

The man's eyes brightened. He leaped down the slope to his horse and took the rifle from the saddle scabbard and was back on his belly at the ridge top. The seven figures, suddenly larger, made grotesque in the clear clean brightness of sun by the long shadows streaming sideways from them, were little more than half a mile away. Deliberately, in slow succession, careless of exact aim at the range, he fired once at the figure in the lead and twice at the group behind and a strange harsh chuckle came from him as he saw them scatter and swing their horses and gallop back and cluster again in a jumble around the lean man on the gray horse. "That'll do it," he said. "They'll take time working up this hill." He pulled back from the ridge top and ran to the horse and jammed the rifle into the scabbard and slammed the hat on his head and swung into the saddle. At a hard run he drove the horse angling down the slope, across the first few-score feet of level stretch, across the dry stream bed and angling on across the level to the wagon trace.

He rode along the trace thirty feet, forty, and eased the horse to a slow stop. Holding it steady, headed north, he backed it along the trace, back to where he had angled in and past, back to the crossing of the dry stream bed. Gripping the reins short and pulling up hard on the horse's head so that it rose on its hind legs, front hoofs pawing the air, he yanked its head savagely to the left and slammed the heels of his heavy old boots into its flanks and it leaped, twisting sideways, and was off the trace on the dry stones of the stream bed and he clamped down hard on the reins to hold it from breaking into a surging gallop. Head bent to one side, peering down in steady concentration, he walked the horse along the stream bed, picking his way, holding to the side where the rolled loose stone lay thickest.

He turned his head to look back and up at the ridge top where he had been. Faintly, over the high rock, came the sound of a shot and then another. He looked ahead where the stream bed, following the ridge, curved left with it and disappeared from sight. He urged the horse into a trot and he was around the bend, out of sight of the wagon trace behind. He pulled the horse to the right and out of the stream bed and on the easier sand-silt ground he pushed it into a lope, moving west as the ground rose and swinging northwestward as it dropped again.

The morning sun, higher now, shone clear and hot on the homestead shelter and beat slanting against the high ridge behind and beyond. A quarter of a mile away, up past the long shallow-plowed strip by the almost dry stream bed, close in by the base of the ridge, a man sat, short and thick and hunched in the saddle, on a tired sweat-streaked horse. He held the wide brim of his weather-worn hat low over his eyes with one hand as he studied the whole scene before him. Not a sound that he could hear disturbed the empty silence. Not a living thing moved anywhere in sight except the two horses and the old cow in the corral twitching in patient endurance at the flies. He dropped the hand from his hat and reached to take the rifle from its scabbard and hold it ready across the saddle in front of him. He urged the horse into a slow walk, along the base of the ridge and swinging to come to the shelter from the rear.

Fifty feet from the low blank rear wall of the shelter he stopped the horse and dismounted. Quietly he slipped the rifle back into the scabbard and took off his hat and hung it on the saddle horn and in the same gesture flowing onward took the revolver from the holster at his side. Quietly he walked to the rear wall of the shelter. He moved along the rear wall to the right corner and leaned to peer around and then to look across the short space at the corral. He saw that the horses were heavy draft animals and he shook his head in disgust and he saw the swelling udders of the cow, and a puzzled frown showed through the dark stubble on his face and the cow, sighting him, pressed against the poles of the corral and lowed with a soft sighing moan. At the sound he leaped back, close against the rear wall, and the empty silence regained and held and he relaxed and moved again, forward and around the corner.

He was moving past the wagon drawn in by the side of the shelter when he stopped and dropped below the wagon level and listened. Faint, from inside the shelter, he heard a slow creaking sound, then again and yet again and continuing in slow steady rhythm. He waited. The sound stopped and in the silence there was another sound, not heard, below hearing, sensed or felt, and the slow creaking began again and continued, deliberate, unhurried. Cautiously he moved, forward, around the front corner, along the blank wall towards the open doorway. Half crouched, gun raised and ready, he swung swiftly around the doorjamb and into the doorway and there, halfway across the room and confronting him, perched on the seat edge of an old rocking chair and swinging her small body to make the chair roll on its rockers, was a little girl. Caught, rigid in a kind of frantic immobility, he stared at her and her eyes widened at the sight of him and her small body stiffened, swaying gently to the dying motion of the chair. Gravely she regarded him. Her lips lifted slightly in a suggestion of a smile. "Hello, man," she said.

Slowly he straightened. He turned his head and saw the woman motionless on the bed and the man limp on the floor and heard the other sound, audible now inside the room, the long slow unconscious gaspings for breath. He looked back at the little girl and suddenly he was aware of the gun in his hand and he turned his body sidewise to her and as he turned, his head remained towards her swiveling on his short thick neck, and with a quick furtive motion he slid the gun into its holster. He stood still a long moment, his head fixed in its sidelong tipped slant over his shoulder, and looked down at her and gravely she watched him and he seemed unable to look away. Abruptly he jerked his head around straight, swinging his eyes to inspect the room. He went to the shelf by the one window and took a nearly empty flour sack from the floor beneath and laid this on the table. He reached to the shelf and snatched the few cans there and dropped them into the sack.

He stopped, silent and tense, his jaws clenched together, the cords in his neck standing out in strain. He swung around and leaned against the table and jutted his head forward and down at her. His voice struck at her with an angry intensity. "There'll be people coming! They'll untangle my trail! They'll get here sometime!" She stared at him, understanding or not understanding unknown on her face, and he pulled himself around and scooped the bag off the table. He strode to the doorway and out and along the front wall of the shelter and around and back to his horse. He jammed the old hat on his head and fumbled in the saddlebag until he found a short piece of cord and with this tied the flour sack close up to the saddle horn. He mounted and the horse, stronger for the rest, responded as he pulled it around and headed off northwestward, angling towards the high ridge.

He rode slowly, head down, hunched in the saddle, letting the horse find its own pace. There was no urging along the reins, no drumming of heels on its flanks, and the horse stopped. The man sat still in the saddle. He drew a long breath and let it out with a sighing sound. His voice came, flat, inflectionless. "Maybe they won't," he said. Suddenly an explosive fury seemed to burst inside him and strike outward into action. Viciously he yanked the horse around to the right and kicked it into headlong gallop, heading northeastward towards a far lowering of the ridge.

The fury in him dwindled with the wind of movement and a quietness came over him. He was aware of the horse straining under him, of its heavy breathing. He pulled it to a steady jogging.

He rode on, a short thick man on a tired horse, dirty, unshaven, dingy in old stained clothes except for the glintings of brass on the cartridge belt around his waist. He rode on, a small moving blot in the vast red-brown reaches of distance, and he passed over the far lowering of the ridge and down the long gradual slope beyond and up a wide ground swell of shifting sand and before him, stretching out of distance into distance, was the wagon trace and a third of a mile away, headed north along it, moving away from him, were seven men on horseback. The lean man on the gray horse and another man were in the lead, one on each side of the trace, bent in their saddles, studying the ground as they moved ahead, and the other five followed.

The man on the ground swell of shifting sand stopped his horse and took the rifle from its scabbard. A strange harsh chuckle sounded in the sun-hot silence and was cut short by the shot and he saw the spurt of dust beside the lean man's horse and all of them halt with sudden startled jerks and swing in their saddles to look towards him. He jammed the rifle back into its scabbard and lifted his horse rearing to wheel it around and drove it at a fast gallop back down the ground swell of sand the way he had come. He was well up the long gradual slope towards the lowering of the ridge when he looked back and saw them coming over the ground swell and lining out in full gallop behind him. Savagely he beat at the horse and it surged up and over the lowering of the ridge and as it raced down the other side towards the long level stretch to the homestead shelter he felt the first falterings in its stride, the slight warning stumblings and recoveries, and he took hold of the sack tied to the saddle horn and snapped the cord with a lurch of his weight in the saddle and let the sack fall. The horse drove on, frantic in lessening rushes of strength, and again he looked back. They were coming steadily, no closer than before, coming with steady intensity of purpose. He saw them pull sliding to a bunched brief stop by the sack and one swing down and grab it and shake out the contents in a flurry of flour and in the stopping he increased his lead. The shelter was just ahead now and he yanked the horse to a skidding stop in front of it and whipped the revolver from the holster at his side and fired two shots towards the doorway, low, into the doorstep. He caught a flashing glimpse of the little girl inside shrinking back from the roar of the shots and he was beating the horse forward again, past the corral, across the shallow-plowed strip, angling back towards the high ridge.

He reached the base and started up and the horse, faltering often now, labored into the climb. It stopped, legs braced and quivering, ribs heaving, a bloody froth bubbling in its nostrils. He pivoted to the right in the saddle and looked back. Riderless horses stood in front of the shelter and the lean man in the buckskin shirt near them directing the others. One man ran towards the closest brackish pool in the almost dry stream bed with a bucket in his hand. Another strode towards the corral with the team harness over his shoulder. Another heaved at the tongue of the old wagon to swing it out from the side wall of the shelter. And yet another mounted one of the saddled horses and swung off southeastward.

The man on the ridge slope checked each in the one swift sliding glance and stared intently at the blank walls of the shelter as if trying to force vision through them. Suddenly, as thought and bodily awareness coincided, he pivoted around and to the left in the saddle. Two of them had not stopped by the shelter, had galloped on past and swept in a wide arc towards him. They were little more than three hundred yards away. One of them was still approaching and the other had stopped and was raising a rifle to his shoulder. The man on the ridge yanked upward on his reins trying to lift the horse into motion and even before he heard the shot he felt the horse leap shuddering and its forelegs doubled under and he jumped free as it collapsed forward and sideways on the slope. He leaned down and jerked the rifle free and crouched behind the still quivering body of the horse and sent a single shot crashing down towards the level and saw the two men circle back to a safer distance and turn their horses sideways towards him and dismount to stand behind them with the barrels of rifles resting over the saddles.

He reached with one hand into the pocket of his old shirt and with fumbling fingers counted the rifle bullets there. He turned his head to study the slope rising behind him. Bare rock climbed with scant crevices and small pockets of dirt where a few scraggly bushes clung. Fifty feet higher the slope leveled in a small ledge that had caught several large stones in age-gone descent. At intervals above were other small ledges. He looked back over the body of the horse and sent another shot crashing down and leaped up crouching and scrambled towards the first ledge above and a barrage of shots battered from the two men below and out and a bullet smashed into his left shoulder and spun him falling and he rolled back behind the body of the horse and hitched himself around to hold the rifle with his right hand over it. The sun beat clean and hot upon him and the two men below and out watched over their saddles and he lay quiet watching them.

Down and across the level expanse the lean man in the buckskin shirt stepped out from the doorway of the shelter and around the corner for a clear view of the ridge and the body of the horse, small at the distance yet distinct against the rock. His eyes narrowed as he peered intently and he made out the dull dirtied deadliness of the rifle barrel pointing over the body. He walked to the tall gray horse ground-reined in front of the shelter and took his rifle from its saddle scabbard. Quietly, paying no attention to the harnessing of the draft horses to the old wagon, he walked around the other side of the shelter and started back towards the ridge directly behind. He came on tracks, hoofprints in the loose dirt heading southwestward into distance towards the far lowering of the ridge. He stopped and looked down at these a long moment and moved on and came to the base of the ridge and climbed until he was almost parallel on it to the man behind the body of the horse not quite a half mile away. He lay flat on a slight leveling of the slope and adjusted the sights on his rifle and pushed the barrel out in front of him and settled into position and waited. Several shots came from the two men out on the level expanse and the man behind the body of the horse hunched himself forward and up to reply to them and the man in the buckskin shirt tightened his finger on his trigger in a slow steady squeeze. He saw the man behind the body of the horse jerk convulsively and try to rise and fall forward over the body of the horse and lie still. He saw the two men out on the level mount and start towards the ridge. Quietly he stood up and walked back towards the shelter.

The wagon was ready. Two of the saddled horses were tied behind it and a blanket had been rigged over the wagon body for shade. Under it lay the still forms of the man and the woman from inside the shelter. The little girl, small and shrinking and silent, sat on the seat between two of the other men.

"Take it easy but aimin' for time," the man in the buckskin shirt said. "Hit for the trace then towards town. Maybe the doc'll meet you part way."

The draft team, fresh and strong, leaned into the harness and the tugs tightened and the wagon moved away. The man in the buckskin shirt turned to watch the two men who had ridden to the ridge approach leading their horses. An old battered saddle and a bridle hung bouncing from the saddle horn of one of the horses. The body of a man, short and thick with a brass-studded cartridge belt around its waist, hung limply over the saddle of the other horse.

"Did you get it?" said the man in the buckskin shirt.

"Yes," said one of the men. "In the saddle bag there."

The man in the buckskin shirt stepped forward and bent to slip a shoulder close against the saddle up under the body of the man in the brass-studded belt and lifted it away and went and heaved it over the saddle of the tall gray horse. He stepped into the shelter and came out carrying a spade in one hand. He took the reins of the tall gray horse with the other hand and led it away. Head low, staring at the ground before him, he led it, past the corral, across the almost dry stream bed, and stopped at last by the straggling row of stunted cottonwoods. He looked up. The other men had followed him.

"Don't be a fool," one of the other men said. "Drag him out somewheres and let the buzzards and coyotes have him. He wasn't no more'n an animal himself."

"No," the man in the buckskin shirt said. He looked back past the shelter, on into the vast empty distance where the trail of a tired horse led northeastward towards the far lowering of the ridge and returned. "He was a murderin' thievin' son-of-a-bitch. But he was a man." Quietly, bending to the hot task in the clean sun, the man in the buckskin shirt struck the spade into the red-brown earth.

The Old Man

ERRY LINTON was ten the year the old man came to live with them in the still-new house his parents had built the year before. He knew the old man was coming, knew it the day the letter came and his mother read it with her lips folding in to a tight line and put it up on the mantel-piece and in the evening he sat cross-legged in his flannel nightshirt on the floor of the dark upstairs hall behind the top newel post of the still shiny front stairs and heard his parents discussing it downstairs in the parlor. He could even hear the faint rustling of paper as his father refolded the letter.

"Frozen his feet," said his father, dry-voiced and precise, nailing down the essential fact in invariable precise manner. "Well, something was bound to happen to the old fool sometime. I suppose this means we'll have to take him in."

"Trapped," said his mother. "That's how it makes me feel. Just plain trapped. If we don't, you know what they'll all say. We have the room. We're about the only ones can afford it right now. But if we do—well, you know what he is."

"Yes," his father said. "I know. But he's your kin and that's that."

So that was that as it always was when his father spoke and Jerry Linton knew the old man was coming, the not even imaginable old man who lived alone off up somewhere in the far mountains, whom he had never seen and never dared ask questions about because his parents and all the relatives, the few times the old man was ever mentioned, looked at each other as if even thinking about him was a mistake and hurried on to talk of almost anything else. But Jerry Linton did not know what to expect and the excitement in him that he kept hidden because his mother did not believe in noise and disturbance about the house reached a high pitch that Saturday morning as he and his mother stood on the front porch and watched his father, coming back from the station, drive their new Ford with its gleaming brass oil lamps into their alleyway and stop it and get out of it all alone and come towards them and shrug his shoulders in an exasperated way and say: "He wouldn't come in the machine. I've got him coming in a carriage from the livery stable."

Then the carriage came and stopped out front and the driver swung down and opened the door and Jerry Linton was disappointed at first because what climbed out, slow and awkward, backing out and down and leaning against the side of the carriage to turn around, was just an ordinary old man, thin and stooped in wrinkled and dirty clothes. The driver took him by one arm to help him up the front walk and he snapped out something in a sharp peevish old voice and shook the driver's hand from his arm and turned back again to reach inside the carriage and lift out a battered old carpetbag with something long strapped to one side and sticking out at both ends. He held the bag with one hand and leaned away from it to balance the weight and hobbled up the walk, taking slow short steps and easing down carefully on each foot in turn as if it hurt him to step on it. He hobbled up the walk without a look back at the carriage pulling away and he was a very old man with skin drawn tight over high cheekbones and a scraggly gray tobacco-stained mustache hanging down over his mouth and bright old eyes deep sunk below heavy brows. He stopped by the porch steps and set the old carpetbag down and what was strapped along its side was an old heavy-barreled rifle. He straightened and peered up at the three of them on the porch, at Jerry Linton and his mother and father.

"Made it," he said. "Bet ye thought I wouldn't. Mebbe hoped so. Ain't nothin' wrong with me 'cept these gol-damned feet." He poked his head forward a bit at Jerry's mother. "Mary, ain't ye? Young Tom's girl."

"That's right, Grandpa Jonas," said Jerry's mother in her careful company-manners voice. "It's so nice seeing you again. It'll be so nice having you with us."

"Will it now?" said the old man and he peered straight up at her and there was a short embarrassing silence and Jerry's mother broke it by turning to him. "Gerald. This is Jonas Brandt, your great-grandfather."

The old man turned his head a little and his bright old eyes peered at Jerry. "Looks like his father," the old man said and leaned and picked up the carpetbag and hobbled up the steps. "Where'll ye be puttin' me?"

But Jerry's mother had noticed the rifle. Her voice was normal again, with an extra little thin cutting edge. "Grandpa Jonas. We might as well get some things straight. One is I won't have any firearms in my house."

The old man stood still, caught, motionless, frozen in the midst of easing forward from one sore old foot to the other, penned between Jerry Linton on one side and Jerry's mother and father on the other. He looked at Jerry's mother and she looked right back at him and he lowered his head and looked down at the porch floor. "Ain't no hurt in it," he said. "It's broke. Won't work no more." He turned his head sideways towards Jerry Linton and put up his free hand as if to rub his cheek but the hand was there just to hide his face from the other side and far back in Jerry Linton's consciousness a slight tremor of shock and a kind of savage joy shook him because the old man was winking at him, the heavy old brow coming down and the high skin-stretched cheekbone seeming to rise to meet it until the bright old eye was lost between them, and then his father was making it that's that again by saying: "Well, then, Mary, there's no real harm in it. Just so he keeps it where the boy can't get at it."

So the old man was living with them and at first it was difficult because Jerry's parents didn't know what to do with him, what he could or would do to pass the long hours of just being alive. That was really Jerry's mother's problem alone most of the time, except on Sunday, because every other day in the week his father left the house right after breakfast exactly at half past seven to go to work at the bank and was away all day until the clock on the mantelpiece was striking six and he was opening the front door and coming in to hang his hat and coat in the front hall closet. But the old man solved that problem himself. At the supper table, after only a few days, he suddenly put down his knife, which he always held in his right hand all through the meal while he used his fork with his left hand, and poked his old head forward a bit diagonally across the table corner at Jerry's father and said: "Ye payin' that coalman much a anythin'?" He meant the man who stopped by three times a day to tend the big round furnace in the basement that sent hot air up through tin ducts and out through square registers into all the first and second floor rooms.

Jerry's father started a little in surprise. He pursed his lips together in a small frown because he disapproved of discussing financial matters at the table. "I'm paying him enough," he said. "Probably more than the job is worth."

"Get rid a him," said the old man.

"Now, Grandpa Jonas—" began Jerry's mother.

"These goldamned feet ain't that bad," said the old man. He picked up his knife again in his right hand and let the fork drop from his left hand and reached with it and took a slice of bread from the dish in the center of the table and began mopping at the gravy on his plate. Jerry's mother watched him shove the dripping bread through his drooping old mustache into his mouth and take half of the slice in one bite and chew it briefly and shove the rest of the slice in. She turned her head and saw Jerry staring in fascination as the old man pushed out his tongue and pulled it back in through the mustache hairs with a tiny sucking noise to get the traces of gravy there. She looked straight across the table at Jerry's father and raised her eyebrows and sighed.

"Bein' fancy ain't never made food taste better," said the old man and reached for another slice of bread and bent his head over his plate to concentrate on the last of the gravy and an almost imperceptible little shivery tingle ran down Jerry Linton's spine because he saw, just as the old head bent down, the glint, the unholy fleeting sparkle in the old eyes under the heavy brows.

So tending the furnace kept the old man busy much of the time. He was always up at the first light of dawn and this filled the early morning for him, hobbling his slow way down to the basement, shaking out the night's ashes, shoveling in the coal and fussing with the dampers until the fire was burning right for the kind of weather outside. After breakfast there was the job of taking the ashes and clinkers out to the growing pile behind the garage that would be hauled away in late spring. Then there was only an hour or two to sit smoking one of his stubby old pipes, in good weather when the sun was bright on the front porch steps, in bad weather in the parlor by the front window looking out on the street, before it was lunchtime and the furnace to be tended again and only a few hours more of sitting and smoking before it was suppertime and the furnace to be tended yet again. And when the warm weather really arrived there would be the other chores the coalman had done, cutting the grass of the neat rectangle around the house which was the yard, trimming the hedge along the side opposite the alleyway, cleaning out the basement and getting rid of accumulated trash. For an old man with frozen feet these things could consume many hours.

That left the evenings and at first these were particularly difficult because Jerry's parents tried to be polite and include the old man in at least some of whatever talk there was and he just couldn't or wouldn't fit into their kind of talk and almost always said things that seemed to irritate or embarrass them. But the old man solved that problem too. There was the evening they were all in the parlor, Jerry's mother with her sewing in her platform rocker under the overhead electric light and Jerry's father with his newspaper in his easy chair by the red-tasseled electric lamp and Jerry with his arithmetic homework on the high-backed sofa and the old man with his pipe on the straight ladder-back chair by the front window, and Jerry's mother looked up from her sewing and said in her half-joking voice that meant she was trying to make a point without any fuss about it: "Grandpa Jonas, don't you think it would be nice if you trimmed your mustache more often?"

The old man looked at her what seemed a long time. He looked at Jerry's father who was being very quiet behind the paper. He turned his head to look out the window where one of the town's carbon arc lights on its high pole cast a wide yellow circle along the street. "Mebbe so," he said and Jerry's mother took up her sewing again with a triumphant little half-smile curving her lips. And suddenly the old man turned his head back again and said right out into the middle of the room, his old voice cracking some: "Don't ye folks ever do anythin' diff'rent? Allus the same doin's the same time. Like a bunch a goldamned clocks."

Jerry's mother stopped sewing. She stared at the old man and two spots of color began to show on her cheeks. Jerry's father lowered the paper and looked over it at first one of them then the other. "Regularity," he said. "That's the secret of success." But for once

Jerry's mother paid no attention to his father. She had her hands folded in her lap over the sewing and she stared at the old man. Her voice was prim and sharp. "Grandpa Jonas. We are decent, respectable people. The least you can do is try to understand that. You, of all people, trying to tell us how to live."

The old man pushed up from his chair and balanced himself on his sore old feet. "Wasn't tryin' to tell ye a goldamned thing," he said. "Was just wonderin' why." He hobbled across the room and into the front hall and they could hear him making his slow way upstairs.

And the very next day his deafness began to develop. It came on fast and within a few days he couldn't hear a thing that was said to him unless a person was close and shouted. That was peculiar because the way his eyes moved and the look in them changed off and on when there was talking going on around him made it seem as if he knew who was speaking and maybe even what was being said. But he kept quiet and when anyone spoke directly to him he poked his old head forward and cupped one hand by an ear and the remark or question had to be repeated in a loud voice before he would understand it.

So his being deaf made the evenings easier because there wasn't much sense in trying to talk to a person who couldn't hear. It wasn't long before none of them ever said much of anything at all to him except to shout things absolutely necessary. It wasn't long before his evening routine was settled too. After supper he hobbled down to the basement and took a time tending the furnace for the night and hobbled back up and sat by the parlor window and waited for Jerry's father to finish reading the paper. When the reading was done and the paper refolded and placed on the parlor table, he pushed up from his chair and hobbled over and took it and hobbled out into the hall and on up the stairs to his own room.

All the first weeks he was something new and strange to Jerry Linton and the boy couldn't help staring at him and watching him. Jerry's mother worried about that and had one of her talks with him about it. "Gerald," she said, "you're still a child and children are very impressionable. I don't want you ever to forget that you are a Linton and I intend you to grow up to be a gentleman like your father." That was a word his mother used often in these talks.

Sometimes it seemed that she thought there was nothing worse than not being a gentleman. But this time she was not talking about how a gentleman behaved and what a gentleman did or did not do. She was talking about the old man. "Jonas Brandt," she said—she usually spoke of him not as if he were her grandfather, Jerry's great-grandfather, but someone removed who had no real connection with them—"well, Jonas Brandt is, well, he is just not a very nice person. That may not be altogether his fault because he didn't have a very good upbringing and, well, he just couldn't be after what he did. I don't want you watching him all the time and maybe learning bad habits—"

"But, Mother, what was it that was so bad that he did?"

"Gerald. It's not nice to interrupt. Jonas Brandt just wouldn't ever settle down and take care of his family the way a decent man would. Expecting a woman and with children to go off into wild country and not live decent when there was nice work he could do at home. He was always going off by himself and doing what he wanted and not even thinking of them and getting just cruder and coarser all the time. And then he—well, I'm sorry, Gerald, but you're not old enough yet to know about that. You just have to take my word about him. After all, I'm your mother. He has to stay with us because there's no place else for him to go and after all he is related. The least you can do for my sake is just not pay much attention to him at all."

And after the first weeks that was not hard to do. The newness of the old man was gone. He was there, but he was less and less there in actual seeing and noticing, somehow quietly slipping or being pushed ever further into the background of household affairs. He never ate with them when they had company and used the dining room and Jerry's mother had out a linen tablecloth and linen napkins in honor of people from the bank or members of her Book and Thimble Club. He took to using the back stairs all the time, the narrow enclosed flight of steps that led from the rear of the upstairs hall down to the kitchen. He was no longer sleeping in the other back bedroom across the hall from Jerry's room. When Aunt Ella came to stay a few days he moved up into the little finished room in the attic so she could have his room and after she left he stayed on up there where he didn't have to bother so much about Jerry's mother wanting things neat and tidy even though being there meant another flight of narrow steps to climb.

He was no longer on the front porch steps when Jerry came home from school, just before lunch and again in midafternoon. Jerry's mother worried about him sitting there, what people would think, seeing him dirty and disreputable sitting there, drawing on his bubbly old pipe and spitting sideways into the shrubbery. She bought him a nice new suit that first Easter, one with matching coat and pants and vest, and he grumbled some and at last began to wear it but within a week it seemed as wrinkled and dirty as his old clothes had been. She must have said something then because he shifted around to the back steps and, later, to a bench he built behind the garage.

He was no longer even in the parlor, even in bad weather, except the brief silent time each evening when he waited for the paper. There was the rainy afternoon Jerry's mother was upset because Jerry had tracked mud into the front hall and the old man was sitting by the parlor window with his pipe in his hand and his old head cocked a bit to one side as if he could really hear what she was saying to Jerry and she caught a glimpse of him and swung around and marched into the parlor and said in a sharp voice: "Grandpa Jonas. Do you have to smoke that horrible pipe in my house? It's ruining my curtains." She didn't wait to see if he heard her. She swung around again and marched out to get a broom and dustpan and sweep up the drying mud. But the old man must have heard because after a few minutes he pushed up and hobbled off and down into the basement and after that, in bad weather when he couldn't be on his bench behind the garage, he stayed down there, sitting and smoking on an old kitchen chair with an old cushion pad on it in the recess between the coalbin and the basement stairs where a window up behind him just above the ground level gave some light.

So he was just there, something familiar now and receding ever further into the taken-for-granted background of daily living. Jerry Linton hardly ever even thought or wondered about him any more. Every morning, for some reason, lying in his bed in the second-story back room, the boy would suddenly be awake and the first light of dawn would be creeping in his window and he would hear, overhead, slow hobbling footsteps, quiet and muffled, that would fade away then be heard again coming down the narrow attic stairway and going past his door and fading out again down the back stairway to the kitchen. But even then he would not think of the old man, not as another living person separate and discernible apart from all the ordinary almost unquestioned everyday surroundings. The hobbling steps were simply another sound out of the familiar round that measured existence and they simply meant there would be time for more sleep and somehow the best sleep before his mother would be calling to him to get dressed and come down to breakfast.

Jerry Linton was two weeks past his fourteenth birthday when the man from the historical society came to call. He came on a Saturday afternoon in a dust-covered green Maxwell that he had driven all the way from the state capital. Jerry answered the door because he was in the stage of being taught how a gentleman greeted strangers and he did very well, inviting the man in and showing him into the parlor before running to get his mother.

The man sat in the platform rocker facing Jerry and his mother on the high-backed sofa. He introduced himself as a Mr. Finley, as the secretary of the state historical society, and said he was assembling information for an article he was writing for the society's quarterly publication. Jerry's mother sat up straighter with a proud little smile on her face and then suddenly she looked as astonished as Jerry felt because Mr. Finley was saying that he wanted to talk to a Jonas Brandt.

Jonas Brandt?

Why certainly. Of course, what was happening nowadays in the state, the tremendous strides forward of economic and social progress, was what was really important. But still it was interesting to get down facts about the past and the time to do that was now while some of the oldtime settlers and pioneers were still alive. Of course, their memories were not always to be trusted but the scholarly approach, checking this against that, sifting out the probable truth, often yielded excellent results.

Mr. Finley was somewhat self-important as he explained his work. Jerry's mother listened and seemed a bit worried as she listened and she gave a soft little sigh of relief when Mr. Finley said his article was about the Sioux outbreak of 1862, about one aspect of it, one incident, that had been generally overlooked in the wealth of material available. He had his article well in hand. In fact, he was quite satisfied with it. But his scholar's conscience told him he should check his facts with every source and, after all, he liked traveling about and so where was Jonas Brandt?

He was out on his bench behind the garage but Jerry's mother did not tell that. She simply excused herself and went out to get him and in a few minutes he had hobbled in after her and was sitting, of all places, in the big easy chair by the red-tasseled lamp. He sat on the edge of it, hunched forward in his wrinkled and dirty clothes, his old hands on his old knees, peering at Mr. Finley from under his heavy old brows.

"Mr. Brandt—" began Mr. Finley.

"You'll have to speak up," said Jerry's mother. "He doesn't hear. very well."

"Mr. Brandt—" began Mr. Finley again in almost a shout.

"What ye shoutin' fer?" said the old man.

"Well," said Jerry's mother quickly. "This must be one of his good days."

"Mr. Brandt," began Mr. Finley again. He spoke slowly, separating the words, almost as if he were speaking to a child. "In August of 1862 you were living in a little crossroads settlement about ten miles from the town of New Ulm."

"Nope," said the old man. "Just passin' through. Freightin'."

Mr. Finley cleared his throat. "In any event, you were there when the Santee Sioux under Little Crow went on the warpath and began massacring defenseless women and children."

"Men too," said the old man. "Fightin' men." His old eyes were beginning to brighten.

"Well, yes," said Mr. Finley. "In any event, you were one of the party, all the people there, who set out to slip through those massacring Indians and get to Fort Ridgely."

"Yep," said the old man.

"Thirteen of you, including the children."

"Sixteen," said the old man.

"Very good, Mr. Brandt. I was just testing your memory. And who was in charge?"

"Feller named Schultz. Marty Schultz."

"Splendid, Mr. Brandt. And this Martin Schultz was an excellent leader, was he not? Took charge and—"

"Nope. Seven kinds of fool. Didn't know much. About Injuns anyway."

"Now, Mr. Brandt." Mr. Finley seemed somewhat irritated. "Let's not permit personal feelings or perhaps even jealousy to creep in here. The facts prove otherwise. There were only five of you men and the rest were women and children and Martin Schultz was in charge and you were three days getting to the fort with just about no food at all and unable to make a fire with murdering Indians all about—and yet you all got through safely. Now, didn't you?"

"Yep."

"And on the last day you wouldn't have. You were hiding in a ravine and an Indian way off on a hilltop sighted you and if he had got word to the rest of his band or been able to signal them you would all have been slaughtered. But he didn't because—"

"Ye're goldamned right he didn't!"

Mr. Finley was excited now. He jumped up from the platform rocker and began pacing back and forth in front of it. "There you are, Mrs. Linton. That is my article. With full details added of course. I got it first from Martin Schultz himself. And two of the women are still living. They check it on most points. Can you see it? Of course you can. What a climax. That murdering Indian off on the hilltop and sixteen innocent white people hiding in that ravine. And Martin Schultz takes his rifle and steadies it on a rock and takes his aim. It was all of nine hundred yards, Schultz claims, but of course that's exaggerated. Those old guns you know. But it was quite a distance anyway. And sixteen lives dependent on that one shot. And Martin Schultz knows that and maybe offers up a little prayer and—"

"Quit yappin'," said the old man. "Marty allus was one to hog it. Never made that shot." The old man raised his old hands and slapped them down on his old knees. "I did."

Mr. Finley stopped pacing. He raised one hand and looked down at it and turned it over and studied his neat fingernails. He cleared his throat. "Yes, yes, of course, Mr. Brandt. After all these years and thinking about it so much, perhaps it seems—"

"It was better'n a thousand yards too!"

Mr. Finley looked at Jerry's mother and raised his eyebrows and shrugged his shoulders. He cleared his throat again and followed this with a little cough and turned towards the old man. "Well, thank you, Mr. Brandt. You have been most helpful. At least I'm sure you meant to be. Perhaps sometime I will want to consult you about some of your other—"

The old man was not even trying to hear him. The old man was pushing up from the easy chair and hobbling towards the hall. "Thought ye wanted facts," he said and disappeared towards the back of the house.

So Jerry's mother was out in the front hall with Mr. Finley by the front door and she was saying apologetic things to him and Mr. Finley was saying polite things to reassure her and alone in the parlor, tense upright on the high-backed sofa, was Jerry Linton, shaking, shaking far down inside with a kind of savage joy and a desire for knowing, knowing, knowing—

"Mother. What was that other thing he did?"

"Oh, Gerald. I don't want you thinking about such things. We're civilized now. I don't see why, even if it is history, people have to go raking up all those horrible old things and making people remember them. People ought just try to forget things ever weren't as decent and quiet as they are now. I wish that Mr. Finley, even if he is a gentleman—"

"Mother. What did he do?"

"Well . . . I suppose you do have to know sometime, Gerald. He, well, after his wife died—worried her into her grave, I'm sure that's what happened—he took up with, well, with an Indian woman. And he, well, he never even married her. There. I've told you. Now I want you to just put it out of your mind and not go around thinking about it . . ."

Out of mind?

So Jerry Linton had to wait until his mother was busy again picking up and tidying about upstairs then go find the old man. He was not out behind the garage. He was in the basement, on his old chair in the recess by the coal-bin. Jerry Linton, stretching and gangling into his fifteenth year, almost as tall already as his father, stood on the basement steps near the bottom and saw the old man sitting there sucking on a bubbly old pipe and was afraid, afraid of this suddenly strange-again old man, thinner and more stooped than when he first came, with old eyes dulled now, somehow even in his dwindling meager smallness looming tremendous and blotting out the whole neat horizon of accepted living.

Jerry Linton could barely get the word out. "Grandpa."

It was really one of the old man's good days. He did not turn his head but he heard. "Eh, boy?"

"Did you . . . did you really shoot that Indian?"

Long seconds of waiting then the old man's head turned slowly towards Jerry and nodded. "With that rifle a mine. That's a Sharps, boy."

"They . . . they don't believe you."

"That don't mean nothin'. How'd they know? Thing is, I know."

It was peculiar. Grown folks couldn't talk to the old man. But a boy could. Jerry Linton sat down on the second step from the bottom. His chin fitted into the notch between his knees poking up with his arms around his legs holding them together and by twisting his head just a bit he could look at the old man.

"That Indian woman . . . Why didn't you ever marry her?"

"Yer mother's been talkin'." The old man chuckled. "Fact is, I did. Injun style. Good enough fer her so good enough fer me. Stuck with me till she finished." He chuckled again. "Tell ye somethin', boy. She was more woman 'n the first one . . ."

And after that Saturdays were special because in the mornings when Jerry's mother was uptown doing her household shopping and picking out the groceries that would be delivered in the afternoon he was with the old man, in the basement or out behind the garage, and there was no end to the questions that kept coming.

"Grandpa. Did you ever shoot a buffalo?"

"Buffler, boy? That's fer sure. Partner'n me worked hides two-three years. Toted in more'n 'leven hundred once. Worked out a Bismarck up in Dakoty . . ."

That was the way it was, simply the plain unslicked statements somehow more real and exciting because of their very matter-of-fact plainness, to be expanded in imagination and given meaning in the thinking over afterwards.

"But why won't you ever ride in the car?"

"Goldamned machine. Legs or a hoss's the way to get around. What good'd that thing be fer rough goin'? Up in the mount'ns? Ain't worth a buffler chip off a road. Me, I ain't never stuck to roads . . ."

"Did you ever see Jesse James?"

"Nope. Didn't miss much nuther. Saw Boone Helm once. Knife man, he was. Killed a lot a people. Folks got together an' used a rope up in Montanny. Used to see the place freightin' into Virginny City . . ."

"But, Grandpa, weren't you ever scared? Indians and wild animals and things like that?"

"Why, fer sure, boy. Lots a times. Bein' scared's all right. Backin' away ain't. I'd start shiverin' an' I'd say, Jonas, ye goldamned mule, ye got yerself into this here fix an' so what comes ye can just take—an' after that it wouldn't be so goldamned bad . . ."

So Jerry Linton, in a sense, was living two lives, one neat and orderly, cushioned by security and the polite courtesies of respectability, bounded by school and family meals and the rules and almost unvarying routine of his parents' household, the other unruly and exciting, pushing haphazard into the long echoing past of an old man who had never stuck to roads, pushing in imagination outward into the open spaces of new land and of wild land and of land not yet tamed but only being tamed where distance pulled at the mind and danger could be a frequent companion and a man could look along the barrel of a Sharps rifle and aim true. After a while the two lives began to merge in almost unnoticed small ways, unnoticed even by Jerry Linton himself. But one day in history class a picture of Andrew Jackson came alive on the page and he suddenly knew that the names in the book were not just names but people and not people apart and different but ordinary everyday-seeming people who ate meals and dressed and undressed and sometimes were tired and sick and just went ahead and did things and lived and in time grew thin and stooped and old.

Walking to school he saw the other houses in their neat rectangles of yards, the squared corners of the streets laid out in regular blocks, and he knew that almost everywhere out beyond the town were the neat sectioned farms with their neat cultivated fields and pastures, almost everything here and out there neat and decent and respectable. It was not always like that. Indians once roamed even this tamed land at will. And buffalo. Men had made it the way it was, men like his father, steady and dependable, careful with figures, planning ahead. And suddenly he knew, knew in real knowing not just as an idea taught in class, that other men had come first, men who didn't stick to roads and who knew Indians and fought them and sometimes even lived with them and could bring in eleven hundred buffalo hides in a single season. The wind drifting in from the west was not just the wind any more. Maybe that blowing against his cheek came from way off, beyond this Minnesota, from beyond the far Black Hills near the Devil's Tower where the old man had killed a mountain lion once or even from on up in the real mountains themselves where Boone Helm lay buried with a rope-broken neck.

In small ways. Even in games. When he was in grammar school he never played much with the older boys, except sometimes with the two younger ones who lived next door. The older boys stayed around after school and played on the grounds and on the athletic field beside the big building. His mother wanted him to come straight home, to play around the house and yard. She couldn't see why boys always liked to play such rough games anyway. There were so many ways they could be hurt, like the boy in the next block who broke an arm playing football. Now Jerry was in high school, even just the first year, it was different. His mother had one of her talks with him and told him he could stay around after school two or three days a week if he really wanted to because she was sure she could trust him not to be wild and rough like some of the boys. He stayed around and it was early fall and they were playing football and at first, for quite a few days, he just stood and watched. He wanted to play too but he couldn't help thinking about getting hurt. And one day he pushed in with the others and he was let be on one side just to fill in and then he was out on the field more frightened than he had ever been before and ready to run away. And suddenly he was telling himself without thinking how or why that he'd gotten himself into this fix so he'd just have to take what came and in a kind of savage joy almost as if he hoped to be hurt so he could show he could take it he plunged into the game and it wasn't so bad after all. In a little while it was even fun, to be run-

ning and yelling and bumping into other boys trying to block them
and gasping for breath with the blood in him pounding strong.

It was spring and Jerry Linton was past the halfway mark of his
fifteenth year when his mother came home one Saturday morning
from her household shopping and called and called to him and at
last he answered from behind the garage and then he forgot and she
had to call him again.

"Gerald," she said. "I do wish you would come when I call. Now
carry these parcels upstairs. The least you can do is help with all the
running up and down stairs that has to be done in this house." And
when he had put the parcels in the upstairs hall and was back down
and starting out the kitchen door she stopped him. "Gerald. It
seems to me you're spending entirely too much time with Jonas
Brandt. It's beginning to show in your talk. And you're becoming
entirely too loud and noisy lately."

Jerry Linton stood in the doorway shifting from one foot to the
other and his mother said: "Sit down, Gerald. I want to have a talk
with you. I don't see how it can do you any good to have a man like
Jonas Brandt filling your head with wild notions and horrible old
stories that very likely aren't the least bit true anyway. I'm sure
most of the time he's just trying to justify himself and make you
think that after all he really was something. You know how old
people are, getting things mixed up and getting to think maybe
things are true that really weren't true at all. I'm sure you remember what happened when that Mr. Finley—"

"Oh-h-h, mother. He really did shoot that Indian!"

So Jerry Linton had spoken back to his mother and spoken
sharply too and his father had to have a talk with him, dry-voiced
and precise, reasoning it out. "Jerry. I know you didn't mean to
upset your mother but you did and that's that. I know when we're
through here you will go and tell her you are sorry. What you have
to realize is that she is right. No doubt there is some truth in the
things your great-grandfather has been telling you. But he is nearly
ninety years old and they happened a long time ago. Most people's
memories, especially old people's, are very faulty as we keep finding
out at the bank. Trying to straighten out wills and property deeds
and things like that. Your great-grandfather has not given much
evidence in his life that he has much sense of responsibility. And,

after all, what happened so long ago is not nearly as important to a growing boy as what is happening right now. This is a practical world we live in these days and it is run on business principles. What you should be doing is tending to your lessons and learning how best to get along in it."

So Jerry Linton told his mother he was sorry. But his parents saw the stubborn look on his face and worried about it and only a few days later his father brought home a copy of the historical society's quarterly and showed him Mr. Finley's article.

There it was, in the cold clear neat precise not-to-be-questioned authority of printed words, the whole story, very well told and with impressive footnotes, of sixteen people fleeing for their lives under the leadership of a Martin Schultz and evading the bloody-handed Sioux for three days and on the third day sighted by an Indian scout who never got word back to his band because of the cool courage and unerring marksmanship of Martin Schultz. The only mention of Jonas Brandt was in a footnote: *The fifth man was a freighter named Jonas Brandt, who joined the group for added safety in reaching the fort.*

So his parents were right. There were no more Saturday mornings behind the garage for Jerry Linton. He was too busy playing with the other boys. It wouldn't be exciting listening to the old man anyway. Jerry Linton saw him in sensible perspective now and realized that for quite a while his memory had been getting bad after all. He contradicted himself sometimes and when he tried to pin down a date he kept getting mixed up. He was just an old relic out of another time who didn't fit in the modern practical world.

Jerry Linton was fifteen, in his sophomore year at high school, when he woke one spring morning in his second floor bedroom soon after the first light of dawn with a strange feeling that something was wrong. He found himself listening and not sure for what. Then he knew. There were no slow hobbling footsteps overhead. He lay quiet wondering about that and after a while slipped back into sleep and when his mother called him and he dressed and went downstairs there was a slight chill in the house and his father was in the basement rattling and banging at the furnace. While they were eating breakfast the doctor came and Jerry's father went off with him upstairs. In a few moments they were back down, the doctor bustling and good-natured, rubbing his hands together and saying: "Nothing to get too much upset about, Mrs. Linton. He's a bit feverish but that's to be expected. He's had some kind of a light stroke. A remarkably tough old constitution, I'd say. Wouldn't surprise me to see him up and about again in a few days."

But it was not a few days. It was the very next day, early in the morning with the first light of dawn. Jerry Linton woke and heard slow hobbling steps overhead, quiet and muffled, that faded away and then were heard again coming down the narrow attic stairway and going past his door and fading out again down the back stairway to the kitchen. A kind of warm feeling drifted through him and he slipped back into sleep and suddenly he was awake again. Wide awake. The footsteps were returning past his door and on up the attic steps, not slow and hobbling, but quicker, lighter, hurrying. Jerry Linton lay still and listened and they came down the attic stairs again and were going past his door again. He eased quietly out of bed and tiptoed to the door and opened it a crack. The old man was just disappearing into the back stairway and he was carrying his old rifle.

Jerry Linton couldn't move at first. He was still, motionless, with his face pressed close against the door crack. Then he opened the door and went, soft and quick, along the hall towards the front of the house and stopped by the closed door of his parents' bedroom. He stared at the door almost a full minute. And suddenly he turned and hurried back to his own room and dressed as fast as he could and pulled on a sweater and went out and down the back stairs.

The old man wasn't in the basement. He wasn't on the back porch or anywhere in sight in the yard. He was behind the garage and he was standing straight, hardly stooped at all, with the heavy old rifle firm in one hand, and his old eyes were brighter, brighter than they had ever been, when he looked at Jerry coming around the corner of the garage.

"Time ye were out a blankets," he said. "There's things doin'." He looked at Jerry in a strange way, not the way he ever had before, in a strange and straight and piercing way almost as if Jerry were someone else who should have been out of blankets before this. "What's got into ye, Jed?" he said. "Can't ye sniff it? Injun smell."

He pointed with his free hand off across the vacant lot behind theirs and the fields beyond to the slight rise that hid the town dump. In the growing light of dawn Jerry saw it, a last thin wisp of smoke floating upward and dissolving away. "That's just a fire over in—" he started to say but the old man was poking his old head at him and saying in a fierce whisper: "Tell me I don't know Injun sign! Someun's got to do some scoutin' or they'll be on us afore we know it!"

The old man started off, striding fast, across the vacant lot, and Jerry Linton wavered and turned to hurry back to the house and stopped. Slowly he turned around again and saw the old man striding away, head forward and intent, striding fast on old feet that must hurt him but he didn't seem to notice that, striding ahead with his heavy old rifle in his right hand, and far down in Jerry Linton a tingling started and shook him and would not stop and he was running to catch up.

The old man flicked one sideways glance at him as he came alongside. "Right, Jed," the old man said. "Two's got more chance 'n one."

They were across the vacant lot and they struck straight across the fields beyond, climbing fences as they came to them. Once a dog ran up barking at their heels and the old man swung around and down and snarled something at it that didn't seem to be words and it stopped barking and put its tail between its legs and dropped behind and away. They went over the rise that hid the dump and on past the dump itself where some fire still smoldered which the old man didn't even notice and he stopped and raised his left hand to shield his eyes against the sun just beginning to show over the horizon and peered all around, studying the countryside. "They'll come snakin' down that draw," he said and struck off again towards the only rough land, the only untamed-to-farming land, anywhere around, towards the far base of the huge wide slow-sloping hill that rose west of town with its near slope torn and eroded by an ancient dry boulder-strewn stream bed. They reached the base of the hill and Jerry Linton's legs were tiring from the pace but he couldn't have stopped if he had wanted to. It was impossible how the old man kept going on his old frozen feet, striding forward, head swinging from side to side, old eyes bright and intent under their heavy brows. He struck straight up along the upper left side of the dry stream bed that widened upward like a vast shallow funnel and Jerry Linton followed and followed and his legs were aching and the old man stopped. "Can't figger it," he said. "Sioux ain't been liftin' hair lately." He started on and they were near the top of the hill and Jerry Linton's legs were aching and suddenly the old man clapped him on the shoulder so hard he went forward on his knees. "Down," said the old man in a fierce whisper, dropping to the ground and scrambling over behind a boulder. "Over here."

So there they were, Jerry Linton and the old man, behind a boulder on the edge of a wide gully, really just a wide stretch of rough eroded hillside, and far off down the slope and across the level, like a neat picture in the midst of neat surrounding farms, was the neat town with its square-blocked streets where decent and respectable people were still sleeping with maybe some of them already beginning to stir in their neat houses. And the old man raised and peered over the boulder, intent old eyes studying the wide gully. "Take a peek, Jed," he said. "See 'im? Ahind that rock looks like a keg. Straight across an' down some."

Jerry Linton, aching and scratched but with a tingling inside that wouldn't stop, peered over the boulder too and at last he saw the rock that looked like a keg, way off across and up the other side of the wide gully. But it was only a rock and that was all.

"Got it," said the old man. "Pawnee. Sneakin' devils they are. Paint up like that." And then Jerry Linton, squeezing his eyes to sharp focus, saw showing above the rock in a small patch an outcropping of red sandstone in the ground beyond, bright and shimmering a little in the early morning sun.

"Likely a passel a bucks over the ridge," said the old man. He turned towards Jerry. His old voice was an urgent hoarse whisper. "Git amovin', Jed, an' rouse the folks. I'll slow 'm here while ye get help."

It was the tingling in Jerry Linton that pushed him up and started him a few steps away. Then he felt foolish and he stopped and looked around. The old man was beside the boulder, flat on his stomach, and he was shoving the old rifle forward and muttering to himself. He put a finger in his mouth and licked it and stuck it up to test the air. "Wind about ten mile," he muttered. "Figger the

drop across there maybe thirty feet." His left arm was out, resting
on its elbow, and his left hand held and steadied the heavy old rifle
barrel and the stock was snuggled up against his right shoulder and
he squinted through the strange old double sights and suddenly the
old Sharps roared like a Fourth of July cannon and the recoil
smacked shaking through the old man's body. He rolled over and
behind the boulder again and sat up with the rifle still in his hands
and yanked down on the trigger guard and the breech opened and
he clawed in a pocket and took out a funny old linen cartridge and
started reloading and his fingers fumbled and dropped it and the
old gun fell too, down and across his legs, and his whole body
seemed to stiffen into a kind of rigidness. Slowly his old head came
up and his eyes, dulling rapidly, looked around and stopped on
Jerry Linton.

"What ye doin' up here, boy?" he said and his whole body sagged
out of the rigidness into a kind of limpness and relaxed back against
the boulder and slipped down sidewise to the ground.

Jerry Linton knew. He had never seen this before but he knew.
He looked down at the crumpled still body a long time. He looked
up and across the wide gully where a patch of red sandstone showed
above a keg-shaped rock. Slowly he started down the rough eroded
near side of the gully and then he was walking faster and then he
was running, down and across the center dip and up the other side
and then slowing, almost afraid to look.

There was the rock. There behind it, farther behind than it
seemed from the other side, was the patch of red sandstone. And
there, near the top of the patch where it would show over the rock,
close to the edge but there, was the fresh, chipped, the shining gouge
in the stone.

Jerry Linton stood with his back to the patch of sandstone. He
started again across the gully, taking long steps, stretching them to
what he judged the right length. Down and across and up. One
thousand and twenty-seven. Taking into account the slope down
and up that was still close enough.

Jerry Linton picked up the old rifle and looked at it. There was
not a spot of rust on the metal. The old stock was sound. "Yes," he
said. "Yes. I'm a Linton. But I'm a Brandt too." He said it to the
body of an old man who had given him what no one else could,

what no one could ever take away from him because always, simply by closing his eyes, he would be able to see, across a thousand yards of untamed land, a patch of red chipped sandstone.

He turned and went down the slope towards the town to get his father, who, in his own precise way, steady and dependable, would make arrangements to take care of what was left of the old man.

The Coup of Long Lance

T HIS WAS a large camp, a late-spring hunting camp, more than forty lodges, set in a broad bottom by a river. The lodges stood in a wide circle with a gap, an entranceway into the central open area, at the east to face the rising sun. They were arranged, clockwise around the circle from the entranceway, in the customary order of the ten divisions or clans of the tribe. Always a Cheyenne camp of any size was made thus, even the great bustling camp of the midsummer Medicine Lodge ceremony when all the people of all the villages and camps within traveling distance gathered for eight days of feasting and dancing and careful ritual in honor of the annual rebirth of the spring now accomplished again, the re-creation of the earth and of life upon it.

This was a large camp. It slept, close to the earth in its hollow, under the moonless star-touched night of the high plains of the heartland of North America. And out across the rolling plains, scattered in small herds across the endless plains, the buffalo too were bedded down for the night in their own vast slow migration northwestward into the late-spring winds bringing their subtle sensed message of the renewing grasses.

The first faint glow of dawn crept up the eastern sky. Across from it, in the western arc of the camp circle where stood the lodges of the *Hev-a-tan-iu*, the Rope Men who used ropes of twisted hair instead of the usual rawhide, the aging warrior Strong Left Hand stirred on his couch. He turned his head. The door flap of the lodge had been swung wide, letting in the rising light. In the center of the lodge by the hollowed-out fireplace his wife, Straight Willow, knelt by a small pile of twigs with her fire sticks in her hands. There was a woman.

A true Cheyenne woman. The mother of tall grown sons, with work-gnarled hands and deepening lines in her face, yet still strong and supple and independent, firm mistress of the lodge and its place in the camp. Always he woke with the first light of dawn and always she was awake before him, tending to her woman's duty, her woman's privilege, of lighting the lodge fire. It was no longer crowded in the lodge now that the three sons, the two real sons and the foster son, were married and living with their wives' clans as was proper, because descent and clan always passed to children through the mothers. But it was never lonely, would never be lonely, in a lodge shared with Straight Willow.

He spoke to her, using one of the silly names out of their long-ago early years together, and without looking up she called him a lazy lie-abed as she always did. He chuckled, filling the lodge with good feeling, and rose with the couch robe held about him and stepped past her and out into the morning air. Ah, it was good, fresh and clean the air, and rich color was climbing the eastern sky. Already smoke was coming from other lodges too. Men and boys were emerging from them and heading for the river for the morning plunge that all male Cheyennes took when near water, the hardiest all through the year, even when thick ice had to be broken.

Behind him Straight Willow put larger twigs on the fire and picked up her two buckets of bullhide. She brushed past him and joined other women on their way upstream, above the swimmers, where they would dip fresh water. No Cheyenne woman, when she could avoid it, used dead water, water that had stood all night.

That was Bull Hump beckoning to him, a wide grin on his face. Bull Hump's middle daughter had been married yesterday. He was coming from her new husband's new lodge and she was in front of it, waving him on. Bull Hump spoke quickly. The young men who had visited his new son-in-law last night and feasted late and stayed in the lodge all night, according to custom, to be there to eat the new bride's first breakfast as a wife, were still asleep. They were true lazy lie-abeds. Here was a chance for some sport in the old way. But it must be a man who had counted many coups. A man like Strong Left Hand.

Strong Left Hand stepped into his lodge and dropped the robe on his couch. He came out, clad only in his manhood string around his waist with the breechclout suspended from it. He hurried towards the new lodge of Bull Hump's new son-in-law, picking up a long stout stick. He stood just outside the entrance and his voice rolled out, deep and strong, telling a coup, short and quick so the young men would not have time to get past him.

"It is Strong Left Hand who speaks. Traveling by the yellow river I met a man of the Crows on a good horse. He fled. I came up by him and pushed aside his lance and knocked him to the ground and took his horse."

The young men were awake now. They knew what to expect. Like rabbits out of a burrow they ran headlong through the entrance and Strong Left Hand thwacked each a stinging blow with the stick. They ran, scattering, towards the river and he ran after them, thwacking those he could reach until they plunged into the water, shouting and pretending to be hurt mightily. Strong Left Hand stood on the bank laughing. It was not all pretending on their part. He was not so old after all. He had given them some good thwacks and kept up with them in the running. He tossed the stick aside and waded into the water and dived under and came up spouting. The young men splashed water at him and called out cheerful morning greetings to him and moved out of the way in the instinctive Cheyenne custom, invincible through life, of deference to one older.

When he returned to his lodge to put on his leggings and shirt and get fresh pine gum to hold his hair in a dozen bunches hanging down his back, Straight Willow had food cooking over the fire. There was no need to tell her of the thwacking. He knew by the way she looked up at him sidewise, her eyes bright, that she knew. It was amazing how every woman in the camp always seemed to know almost everything as soon as it happened. And he knew she liked him to be doing things like that. She was strong on the old customs, stronger on them, as women usually were, than he was. She was of the *Suhtai* clan and even now she wore her dress longer than most women and dipping on the right side and still wore her hair in braids with little deerskin and sweet sage ornaments bunched on the back of her head, not in the new fashion of doubling them up in two humps, one on each side.

He left her with her cooking and went out beyond the camp circle where the other men were gathering, waiting for the boys who had gone to round up the horses. Only a few horses, the most valuable, were kept in the camp at night, tied by their owners' lodges. The rest were out over the rolling ridges where the grass was good.

The horses came trotting over the last rise before the camp, the boys behind them. Strong Left Hand's eyes swept over them with the keen almost unthinking glance of the Plains Indian who, once having seen a horse clearly, could know it unerringly any time, any place. There were his six horses. Yesterday morning he had had eight horses. But Bull Hump was his cousin and yesterday Bull Hump's daughter had been married and it had simply been right that Strong Left Hand should add two horses to the presents Bull Hump was giving to the bridegroom's family. There too were his wife's twelve horses. She was very proud of them, perhaps too proud. She was the richest woman in horses in the camp. She was also the best robe maker. But that was different. She made them to give as presents. She liked to think that newly married couples slept under her robes. She was not like that with her horses.

Strong Left Hand caught the horses with the one glance but he did not say so to the boy coming towards him, his nephew, the son of his brother, Owl Friend. This was the boy who herded for him now that his own sons were grown. It was good for the boy to feel important.

"Are they all here, little one?"

"Every one, my uncle."

"Is any one of them lame?"

"The black one with the two white spots limped a little. It was only a stone in the hoof. I took it out."

"You took it out? He stood for you?"

"Yes, my uncle."

"You will be a brave man with horses, little stone picker."

A meadow lark, startled by the many hoofs disturbing the grasses, rose out of them to the left and swooped, trilling, up into the glowing color of the rising sun, and the heart of Strong Left Hand leaped within him. So it had been long ago, in his youth, in the time of his starving on a hill for his dreaming, and in the dawn of the third day a meadow lark had risen trilling into the rising sun and he had a vision, a vision of himself with hair thin and gray, and he had known that he would live to be an old man and count many coups. And always, after that, when a meadow lark had risen thus from near his feet, trilling for him and the morning, the day had been a good day for him. The clean sweet air of this morning was like a strong drink.

"Little lifter of horses' feet, listen to your uncle. You will tie the gray horse that is quick and fast and the spotted one that is thick and strong by my lodge. We hunt today. The others go back with the herd. You will take good care of the black one because from this moment forward he is yours. Remember what I say. You will do with him as your father tells you. Now run."

The boy ran, leaping like a grasshopper, frantic in his hurry to tell the other boys, and Strong Left Hand turned back towards his lodge remembering when his uncle, who had given him his name, had also given him his first horse and he, too, had run leaping like a grasshopper. And now he was a man and a warrior with tall grown sons and he was a giver of horses to eager young nephews and the life cycle, endlessly repeating, moved on and it was all good, all of it, the youngness and the manhood and the drawing on towards old age, for still the meadow lark rose trilling into the sun of the morning to tell him it was good.

Back at the lodge the food was ready. Straight Willow took a small piece from the kettle of boiled Indian turnips and a small piece from the other kettle of stewed meat and each in turn she held high towards the sky, an offering to *Heammawihio,* the Wise One Above, then laid it on the ground by the fire. There the pieces would remain until she swept out the lodge. Once offered, they were as consumed, no longer really there. She scooped more of the food into two wooden bowls. She and Strong Left Hand sat cross-legged by the fire, eating with the ornamented spoons he had made of the horns of the first buffalo he had killed after their marriage. They talked quietly and between talkings they listened. The old crier was making his round, riding along the inside of the camp circle, calling out the news.

The chiefs (one of the tribe's four head chiefs and three of the forty council chiefs, four from each of the ten clans, were with this hunting camp) had said the camp would not be moved for many days . . . The Kit Fox Soldiers would have a social dance that night . . . All men should remember what had been told yesterday, that there would be a hunt today . . . Word had come from Yellow Moon's camp, two days eastward, that Big Knee, chief of the Red Shields, the Bull Soldiers, had pledged to be this year's Medicine

Lodge maker and the celebration would be in the first days of the *Hivi-uts-i-i-shi* moon (July, the buffalo bull rutting month) when the grasses would be long and the leaves of the cottonwoods in full growth . . .

Big Knee? Ah, there was a man. He and Strong Left Hand had been boys together. They were both Bull Soldiers now, Red Shield carriers. Not many men could say that. A man could not just join the Bull Soldier band; he had to be mature and seasoned and be chosen for it. Strong Left Hand had helped persuade Big Knee to take the present term of leadership. Did Straight Willow recall the time that he and Big Knee . . .

What was the old crier saying? The Dog Soldiers in the camp had challenged the Bull Soldiers to a coup-telling competition that night. They were foolish; good young men, but foolish. Perhaps they thought they could win because there were more of them in the camp. They would find out. The Bull Soldiers were fewer but they were real warriors, with age and experience on them. Anyone could know that from the many red coup stripes on their wives' arms at the ceremonial dances.

Ah, this competition would be a fine thing. Strong Left Hand was full of talk. Their youngest son, Long Lance, would have a chance to tell his first coup. He was a Dog Soldier. Four days ago he had returned with the others who had gone with Many Feathers, chief of the Dog Soldiers, raiding the Crows to the north. They had gone on foot, as they had pledged to do, and they returned on horses herding others, and they carried two scalps—but there had been no scalp dance and telling of coups, because one of them had been killed by the Crows. Long Lance could claim a coup, but he had not spoken of it, because a true Cheyenne did not go about speaking big words about his deeds; only in telling a coup did he speak of them and then he simply stated the facts. It was for others to tell what he had done in many fine words. And the others had told what Long Lance had done.

They had found a Crow camp. In the first light of morning they had crept close and started the herd of Crow horses moving away and each caught a horse and mounted and they were slipping away fast when someone, perhaps a guard hidden where they had not seen, gave an alarm and many Crow warriors, on horses kept in the camp, came after them. The chase was long and the Crows were gaining and the young Cheyennes turned, few against many and proud it was so, and charged in the swift sweeping charge their enemies knew so well, and the Crows, close now, slowed and wavered, and the Cheyennes were among them, striking and scattering them. Many Feathers was in the lead, as was right, and an arrow struck him in the shoulder and he fell from his horse, and a Crow, a brave one that Crow, swung down from his own horse and ran towards Many Feathers swinging his war club. And Long Lance, rushing up from behind Many Feathers in the charge, almost past, too far past to turn his horse in time, leaped from its back and struck bodily against the Crow and sent him sprawling. The Crow scrambled to his feet and ran and another Crow swung back and took him up behind on his horse and all the Crows were scattering and riding off except two who would ride no more. Many Feathers, not minding his wound, was on his feet and shouting to his men to come back from the chasing because the horses were stampeding. It was when the horses, most of them, were gathered and quieted and moving along together again that they saw that one of their own men was missing. Many Feathers chose Long Lance to ride back with him and they found the body. They laid it in a low hidden place with head towards the east so that the spirit, hovering near, would find the spirit trail where all footprints point the same way. They left it there because it was right that the body of a man killed in battle far from his home village should become food for the birds and the animals of the plains who would scatter his bones across the earth from which all that he now was, with the spirit gone, had originally come. Then they saw the Crows, gathered together again, coming again, and they hurried to join the others and all chose fresh horses from the herd and pushed on fast. The Crows, with no fresh horses, not eager for another Cheyenne charge, followed until late afternoon, dropping back more all the time, and then were seen no more.

Strong Left Hand was full of words, talking about their son. Straight Willow said little and then she stopped him, raising her hand. "We are happy for him. Why is he not happy too? Look."

Strong Left Hand looked out through the lodge doorway. Over in the eastern arc of the camp circle where were the lodges of the *O-missis,* the Eaters, so known because they were always good hunters and well supplied with food, his youngest son sat on the ground before his still new lodge. His hunting weapons were beside him

and his hunting horses were close by and he sat with his arms resting
on his knees and his head sunk low. A sadness was on him.

Strong Left Hand set aside his bowl and rose. At sight of his son
in sadness a shadow seemed to be over him fighting with the clean
light of the morning. He spoke to Straight Willow. "Perhaps there
is trouble with him and his wife. They are still new together. Perhaps you can be close to her today and she will speak to you." He
drove the shadowing away from his mind. It was time for the hunting. He took his stout bow made of the horns of the mountain
sheep, the bow that few other men could bend, and his quiver with
twenty good arrows, arrows he had made from well-grained red willow shoots tipped with edged bone heads and firmly feathered. He
took his hair-rope hackamore and the single pad he used for a hunting saddle and went out to his horses.

The whole camp was abustle now. The hunters were gathering.
Women and older girls were starting off with digging sticks to find
the white potato roots that grew on some of the slopesides. Other
women were following the path downstream where a stand of cottonwoods beckoned them to gather wood. Already small children
were assembling around two of the old men who would teach them
stories of the old days and of the old ways of the tribe. Older boys
were splashing across the river at the ford, holding their small bows
above the water, bound for the marshy land beyond where they
would practice shooting wild fowl and perhaps bring in food.

Straight Willow came out of the lodge, her sewing things in her
hand, the bone awl for punching holes in tanned hides and a handful of threads, separate strands plucked from the big sinew that follows along the spine of the buffalo. Her sewing guild was meeting to
help one of the women make a new lodge. She saw Strong Left
Hand swinging up on the spotted horse in the Indian way, from the
off side. "Perhaps you will bring me an untorn bull's hide. It is in
my mind to make a heavy robe." He looked at her and he knew that
she meant that his arrows should sing true and that he should come
back to her unharmed, and in his mind he pledged to her the biggest bull of the day's hunting. He rode off, leading the gray horse,
and was one with the hunters, all the able-bodied men of the camp,
moving out across the plains.

They talked and laughed as they rode, for they were Cheyennes, a

gay and talkative people, but not too much now because this was
not sport, like fighting, this was the most important work of men,
the obtaining of food and of materials for clothes and lodges and the
necessary articles of daily life. On the success of the hunting during
these good days would depend the welfare of the tribe during the
long snowbound months of winter.

Strong Left Hand rode up close by his youngest son, should he
wish to speak. He would not press him, for a grown Cheyenne did
not interfere with the thoughts and visions of another. He spoke of
such things only when that other wished to speak of them and seek
counsel. But now his son rode straight ahead, silent and stern.

The hunters rode on, far out across the plains, and then Many
Feathers, in charge for this day, stopped and gave his orders. Scouts
had reported a herd of buffalo over the next rolling rise. Quietly
they changed to their hunting horses and left the heavier burden
bearers in the keeping of a young man. In small groups, as Many
Feathers directed, they slipped away to come on the herd from all
sides.

Silence held over the plain under the climbing sun and the endlessly moving wind, broken only by the rustling of the buffalo in the
grasses and their occasional small snorts and belchings. Suddenly
from the far side a shouting rose and Many Feathers and his group
rushed over the last rise between them and the buffalo, and the
buffalo snorted loud, facing towards this disturbance, heads up, and
then they turned and ran, slow at first, then galloping in their seem-
ingly awkward gait that could outdistance all but the best horses.
Ahead of them, shouting and waving, rose another group of
mounted men, pounding towards them, and they swerved to the
side, and ahead was another group. The buffalo snorted and galloped, tails stiffening upright in terror, and always a group of shouting men on horses was in front of them. And now they were running in a big circle, milling around it in the frantic feeling that
because they were running they were escaping.

Many Feathers raised his bow high and waved it and the hunters
began swooping in close to the milling buffalo, superb horsemen the
equal of any the world had known, and their arrows sang death and
mortal-wound songs in the dust-driven air. Buffalo staggered and
fell and others stumbled over them and now and again a stricken

animal would dash outward from the milling circle at the pounding horses, and the horses, quick and fast, would dodge and twist until an arrow struck true and the buffalo went down.

Strong Left Hand swept in close, wasting no arrows, searching always for the biggest bull. He would like to kill that one himself. Two cows and a young bull had gone down under his arrows, stopped almost in their tracks by the power of the big horn bow that few men could bend. Ah, there was strength still in his left arm, his bow-string arm, that had given him his name.

Ahead of him, hazy through the dust, he saw a horse step into an animal ground hole and its rider thrown towards the milling buffalo, and a huge old bull, bloody-frothed at the nostrils, come charging out towards the man. Another horse swooped in, its rider leaning down to pick up the fallen man, and the bull swerved and its great head drove under this horse's belly and its short thick horns ripped upward and its great neck strained and horse and rider rose into the air, the horse screaming, its legs flailing, and now two men were scrambling on the ground. Other men came swooping in, Strong Left Hand foremost among them. There was no time for full bow-draw and certain aim. His arrow struck too far forward, close by the shaggy neck, and drove in only a short way, slowed by the matted hair and thicker hide there. Yet it stopped the bull, made it pause, pawing the ground, shaking its great head. But the circle of hunters was now broken. The bull rushed through the opening, bellowing, and other buffalo followed, streaming across the plain.

Now it was the chase, the hard riding, the pounding after the fleeing buffalo, the riding alongside them and in among them. But the chase did not go far because the hunters had killed enough for one day's hunting and their arrows were nearly all gone. And back along the trail of the chase lay the huge old bull with another of Strong Left Hand's arrows driven deep into its side.

Now there was no more wild excitement, only hard drudgery, bloody work that would take much of the next day too, skinning and butchering and loading the meat on the slower, stronger horses, and the patient searching for arrows to use again. Only once was there an interruption when a warrior gave warning that he had seen a man peering over a neaby rise and Many Feathers sent two men to circle around while the rest stood ready by their horses, weapons in hand. Then the two men came back, straight over the rise, and a boy was with them leading a black horse with two white spots.

Strong Left Hand smiled to himself when he saw his nephew approaching. But Owl Friend, his brother, father of the boy, stepped forward, stern of face. "What are you doing here?"

"To see the hunt, my father."

"And to ride your new horse. I did not say you could come."

The boy looked down at the ground and suddenly Owl Friend smiled at him. "You are not much bigger than a badger, but you will be a brave hunter one day." He took the boy by the hand and led him to Many Feathers. "Here is a small man who thinks he is a hunter."

Many Feathers, too, was stern. "Is this the first hunt you have seen?"

"Yes, my chief."

"Do you know what must happen the first time?"

The boy stared at him and then Many Feathers smiled. He bent down by the carcass of a buffalo and dipped his right hand in a pool of blood there and lifted it, dripping, and smeared the blood over the boy's face. "Now you know how it feels, still warm from the life that was in it, how it smells, how it tastes. You must not wipe it from your face until you are home. Now the time is for work. Take this knife that is yours from this day forward and do as I show you, freeing the hide from the good meat."

The sun was low in the west, sending long shadows into the hollows, when the hunters returned to the camp, leading the loaded horses. As they neared it they passed many boys out on the plain playing games with sliding sticks and hoops and the boys, seeing them, ran up to race about and follow them. As they came nearer a group of older girls too was approaching the camp. They had been out digging bear roots and turnips and they carried tied bunches of them. They shouted at the hunters and raised the war cry, daring the young men to try to take their roots. Some of the young men called to boys to hold their horses and they ran towards the girls and the girls quickly dropped their roots and began gathering sticks and buffalo chips and clumps of sod and one of them took her root digger and drew a line in the ground all around them. Such a line was their fort and it could be passed only by a man who had counted a coup within enemy breastworks. The young men dashed around the line-circle, leaping and laughing and teasing and dodging the missiles thrown at them. One stepped inside and told his coup and the girls had to stand aside and let him take what roots he wanted. He scooped up several bunches and tossed them to the other young men and they all went towards their horses munching on the roots and throwing back teasing remarks at the girls. They were good young men, not too tired after the day's work for leaping and laughing. But Long Lance was not with them. He sat on his horse, stern and silent, and his head drooped.

Inside the camp circle the hunters separated to their lodges. Strong Left Hand stood his tired horses in front of his lodge and went down to the river for a thorough washing. Straight Willow came hurrying from woman-talk with a neighbor and unloaded the spotted horse. Most of the meat she put away under covering. She would be busy now, beginning tomorrow, for many weeks, cutting this meat and that from other huntings into strips and flaking it into chips to be sun-dried and smoke-cured for winter saving and the other women would be doing the same and all of them gossiping endlessly around the drying racks. Three hides were there too, Strong Left Hand's share of the day's taking, and she put these where she would peg them on the ground for scraping. Then she led the spotted horse to the river to wash away the buffalo blood and fat clinging to its short hair. She rolled up her skirt and waded into the water with the horse and then, only then, her work well in hand, she looked over the horse's back at Strong Left Hand, who was sitting for a few moments' quiet and rest in the late sun.

"It is a good, big, very big bull's hide," she said and he knew she was saying more than that. The meadow lark had trilled true, for it was a good day. And then the shadow was over him again, for he saw his youngest son, Long Lance, walking on down by the lower river, slow and with a sadness on him.

Straight Willow saw too. "His wife does not know. He has been like that since they came back with the horses. But she does not know."

Strong Left Hand went back to the lodge and took a bunch of his stored willow shoots and sat on the edge of his couch and began smoothing and shaping them for arrows while Straight Willow rebuilt the fire and began her cooking. This was one of the times he liked, the two of them together in the quiet companionship built through the long years, the good years and the bad years and all part of living. This would be one of the best of days but for that shadow in his mind.

It was a fine meal as the evening meal of a successful hunting day should be. There was much meat, and there was feasting all around the camp. Soon darkness dropped over the land and the mystic living light of the many fires lit the camp. A huge fire began to glow out in the circle where the Kit Fox Soldiers would soon be having their social dance.

Strong Left Hand took out his pipe and filled it with tobacco mixed with dried bark of the red willow. He held it by the bowl and pointed with the stem to the sky and to the earth, making his offering to the father spirit above and to the mother earth below. He pointed the stem to the four cardinal points of the compass around, making his offering to the spirits that dwell in those quarters. He took a burning stick from the fire and lit the pipe and drew in the smoke with slow satisfaction. Straight Willow sat by the fire and watched him in quiet content, for no one should move about in a lodge when the pipe was being smoked.

Music began to sound through the camp. Drumming and songs were beginning by the dance-fire. The quick lively beat of a gambling song came from a nearby lodge where some were playing the hand-hiding game. Strong Left Hand put aside his pipe and took his big red shield, his Bull Soldier shield with the buffalo head painted on it, made of the thickest bullhide with deerskin stretched over it and raven feathers around the edge. He went out and as he moved away he saw several women coming towards his lodge. He smiled to himself. Straight Willow would be having company. He went on to the big temporary lodge that had been put up during the day well out into the camp circle by the wives of the Dog Soldiers. Most of the other men were already there.

To the left inside, in a line, were the Dog Soldiers, his son, Long Lance, among them. They would give a brave account of themselves this night. There were staunch old veterans among them and two of them were men who wore black-dog ropes into battle, leather loops that passed over their shoulders and under their other arms and had ropes fastened to them with picket pins at the ends. Such a man, dismounting to fight the enemy hand to hand, must stick his pin into the ground and in the doing pledge himself not to retreat from that spot. He himself, no matter how hard-pressed, must not pull the pin loose or be dishonored forever after. Only another of his band could free him by pulling up the pin and striking him to drive him back. Such a man counted coups or died on the spot.

To the right were the Bull Soldiers, fewer in number but the same as many in experience and honors. And at the back of the lodge, behind the central fire, sat the man who would preside, as always an old man belonging to neither of the two competing bands. He was well chosen. He was Standing Elk, twice chief of the Elk Soldiers in his younger years, now one of the most honored men of the tribe. He was wise and just and he knew well how to keep a competition close and exciting in his calling for coups. And he wore the scalp shirt.

Only three men in the entire tribe wore scalp shirts. Such a shirt could be made only by a man who had worn one. It could be worn only by a very brave man, a man who dedicated himself to his people. When he wore it, he must be the first to advance in battle, the last to retreat. If a comrade were dismounted or fell, he must dare all dangers to pick him up. He must act always as a chief should act, be above personal angers and quarrelings, not become angry even if his wife should run away or be carried away or his horses be stolen, never seek a personal vengeance. He must take care of widows and orphans, feed the hungry, help the helpless. Some men had worn the scalp shirt and given it up. Standing Elk had worn it many years and always with honor.

Strong Left Hand waited according to custom until Standing Elk pointed to the place kept for him. He went to it, passing behind the others, careful not to be so discourteous as to pass between anyone and the fire. He placed his big shield against the lodge wall behind his place and sat down before it. Two more men arrived and they were ready to begin. Standing Elk asked one of the young men to close off the entrance. He had beside him a pile of small sharpened sticks. His pipe lay on the ground before him with the bowl towards the south, the symbol of truth-telling. No true Cheyenne would speak false in its presence.

Standing Elk passed one of the pointed sticks to the first of the Dog Soldiers. "Which one of you has counted a coup on foot against an enemy on horseback?" The Dog Soldier passed the stick to the next man and it went down the line until it reached a man who could claim it. He told his coup. The stick went back to Standing Elk and he stuck it in the ground on the Dog Soldiers' side. He started another stick down the Dog Soldier line and it came back unclaimed. He passed it to the Bull Soldiers and he passed yet another before they were through with that question and they had two sticks in the ground on their side.

Standing Elk asked his questions. He was a wise old man. He knew the history of every man there and he framed his questions to give everyone a chance to speak and to keep the score close. Good feelings and memories of brave deeds done, always good in the retelling, filled the big lodge. And yet young Long Lance, in his place in the Dog Soldier line, sat silent, his head sinking lower and lower. Now everyone else had spoken at least once and much time had passed and the sticks were even on the two sides. Standing Elk looked at young Long Lance and then he looked at Strong Left Hand and his old eyes twinkled in the firelight. He looked straight ahead. "This is the last. Which one of you has leaped from a horse to count a coup against a Crow warrior by striking him with your whole body to save the life of your soldier chief?"

There was a stirring among the Dog Soldiers and a chuckling and they passed the stick quickly and the one beside Long Lance thrust it into his hand. Long Lance held it, but he could not speak. And suddenly he raised his head high and spoke with the strongest truth-telling pledge a Cheyenne could give. "I say this to the Medicine Arrows. I did not do it. I did not know Many Feathers was down. I did not see the Crow warrior. The thong in my horse's mouth had broken and I was leaning forward to grasp his nose and guide him. He stumbled and threw me and I struck against the Crow. It was not my doing." And Long Lance tossed the stick into the fire and his head dropped again.

The heart of Strong Left Hand was big within him. There was no shadow over him even in the dim darkness of the big lodge above him. His son was a brave man, brave enough not to grasp a false bravery. But it was not for him to speak. That was for Standing Elk. The silence in the lodge held, waiting.

And Standing Elk, his old eyes twinkling even more than before, picked up another stick. "Which one of you has counted a coup because he had a horse that knew when to stumble and throw him against an enemy?" And the laughter in the lodge, the good feeling sweeping through it, seemed enough to lift it into the air. The stick passed down the line and young Long Lance held it and he raised his head, his face shining in the firelight, and spoke: "I claim it as a coup only for this night so that the Red Shields must provide a feast for my brother soldiers. From this time forward I give it to Many Feathers as a laughing story to tell."

The camp was quieting, most of the lodges were dark, only embers remained of the dance-fire, when Strong Left Hand entered his own lodge again. In the dark he heard the soft regular breathing of Straight Willow on her couch. He put away his shield and squatted on his heels by her couch to tell her of their son, and because he wanted to and she wanted him to, he told it to her again.

He rose and stood tall. There was no sleeping in him yet a while. Quietly he left the lodge and walked through the outer star-touched darkness, out of the camp circle, up to the top of the first rolling rise. Behind him, in the camp, the only firelight remaining shone faintly through the entrance of the lodge where the gambling game was still being played. Always there were a few men who would keep at that until they had nothing left to stake on the next chance. They played with whispers now that would not disturb other lodges. The only sound drifting to him from the camp except the occasional muffled shifting of horses' hoofs or stirring of a dog in its sleep was the faint trembling flute song of a lover serenading his sweetheart somewhere on the far side of the circle. And even this was not a real sound but a sweet lingering pulsing of the silence.

He stood on the rise and stretched his arms upward and from him flowed a wordless prayer of thanking to the meadow lark of the morning of a good day and through this to the Great Mystery of which it was for him his personal symbol. He sat on the ground and the small night breezes moved through the grasses and the clean sweet dark was around him and in him and he was a part of the earth beneath and the sky above and the web of life they nurtured and it was good.

Why should the thought of old Standing Elk come into his mind at this moment? Ah, there was a man. A tribe needed men like that. They were an example to the young men, even to older men who had grown sons. Strong Left Hand rose and walked quietly back to his lodge. He took off his shirt and leggings and moccasins and lay on his couch. He spoke softly: "O my wife."

He heard her shift a little on her couch. "What is it, my husband?"

"In the morning I will carry the pipe to Standing Elk. I will keep my gray horse and my spotted horse for the hunting and take my other three horses and a quiver of arrows to him as an offering. I will ask him to make me a scalp shirt."

There was silence in the lodge. Strong Left Hand sighed gently to himself. It would be hard on her, it would mean more work and a harder time for her, too, when he wore the shirt. He heard her shifting on her couch again. "O my husband. Standing Elk is a great one of the tribe. There should be more. You will take half of my horses too. We will have need of the others when you wear the shirt."

Strong Left Hand breathed in so deeply that he felt as if his lungs would burst. A meadow lark sang in his heart. "O my wife. You are far away from me there on your couch. I feel young again tonight."

He heard her moving to throw off her robe covering and come to him. Her voice was low with a small chuckle in it. "When her man feels young towards her, a woman is young again too."

Enos Carr

H E WAS touched in the head all right.

Myers sent a man to meet us and we worked winding up the long snowy slopes in a jeep and pulled in by the log ranchhouse with its string of sleeping units beside it. The driver took our bags and Peyton and I were easing out the guncases from the gunnysack padding around them, when this character came along leading two tired horses down towards the barn. He had a long thin spraddle-legged carcass topped by a face like a blunted ax blade, the whole wrapped in a wide-brimmed hopeless old hat, a decrepit thick old jacket hunched high around his shoulders and neck, pipestem dungarees long ago shrunk to highwater mark, and heavy old boots. He stopped and looked us over. He turned away and couldn't have been talking to anyone but those two horses.

"Another batch of predators," he said. He patted the near horse on the neck. "Don't worry any, boy. They're not after your kind." He started on.

Peyton couldn't take that. "Hey, you!" he said. "What the devil do you mean?"

This character stopped again, looking back. "Up here after deer, aren't you?" he said. His voice was mild, even friendly. "Never shy away from the truth, boy." He moved on, setting down those boots in easy spraddled stride.

Myers himself was coming out to greet us. Peyton wasn't waiting for any greeting. He pointed a finger down-slope. "Who or maybe what is that?"

Myers turned it on, a grin, the one developed through years of operating the place in the hunting season, keeping everyone happy, smoothing away frictions. "That's old Enos Carr," he said. "Didn't you run into him when you were up here last year? No, maybe not. Has a ranch over beyond that first high ridge."

"What the devil," Peyton said, responding to the grin, trying to keep this light. "What the devil is he doing here?"

"Shucks, man," Myers said. "When we're full up like now, have to borrow some of his horses. Damn good horses. He won't let anyone else take care of them. We have his horses, we have him too."

"He called us a couple of predators."

Myers put more power into the grin. "One thing you learn up here is not to let old Enos bother you any. He's touched a bit in the head." Then Myers was himself, serious, the man you got to know behind the grin. "But don't go getting old Enos wrong. A damn good rancher. A damn good neighbor too." Myers grinned again, hearty, strong. "Shucks, man, the thing to do is take him as part of the natural scenery around. Kind of interesting, viewed that way."

A lot of things happened while we were up there. But I'm not writing about them now. Peyton got his deer, a fine buck. I was his partner this trip so he was out another day with me till I got mine. Peyton's a good man. Matter of fact, about the best I know. He writes about guns for the sports magazines and what he knows about guns, what he can do with a gun, any gun, makes you proud to know him. He's a real sportsman. Clean. Decent. He writes about that too and always acts straight on what he writes. It wouldn't even cross his mind to take a shot at anything out of season or bag a single bird above the limit. He tosses a coin with his partner for first try at whatever they're after and sticks to that toss no matter what. He never pulls trigger till he knows absolutely what he has sights on. I've know him to pass up a fine elk because he'd got separated from his partner and wasn't certain that partner wasn't somewhere between him and that elk. I've known him to push on alone in nasty weather and be out all night in bitter cold tracking down a wounded deer to put it out of its misery. But I'm not writing this about him. I'm writing about this Enos Carr character. Not a story, not anything like that, because it doesn't have any form and hasn't any action and doesn't get anywhere. Just an account of what we saw of him and learned about him. I'm writing it because I collect odd characters, like to get them down on paper. They're quaint, interesting. They're not important because a world made up of odd characters would be a weird one to live in and probably couldn't even function at all. Matter of fact, studying odd characters can help you appreciate the normal everyday capable people who keep the world wagging on a fairly even keel, a place where most of us can earn a decent living and get some enjoyment out of life.

And I'm writing this because this Carr character was one of the oddest I've encountered, because Peyton can get along with anybody and most people naturally take to him and this character is still the only one I know anything about he couldn't get along with. No trouble, no real arguing, nothing like that. But this Enos Carr rubbed him the wrong way, seemed to irritate him by just being around. I guess Peyton just couldn't take him the way I could, the way Myers said, as an interesting local oddity.

It was late afternoon when we arrived and we'd be out riding higher in those mountains before daylight next morning so we stayed in and after an early dinner were in the big main room cozy and comfortable by the big stone fireplace. Quite a few there, more arrivals and others who had already been around a day or two. We were feeling good, all of us, passing a couple of flasks around and staking out in talk the general territories each pair or more of us would be trying next morning so we wouldn't be getting in each other's way and run much risk of a shooting accident. It was pleasant in that room. Heat and light mean a lot when you're way up in the cold and the mountains. The fire in that big fireplace that could take four-foot logs without crowding was mighty reassuring. And from a shed outside you could hear the steady chugging of the mounted truck motor that ran the generator supplying electric current.

The outside door opened and in came this Carr character, stomping snow off those heavy old boots, lugging another big chunk of log. He went over to the fireplace and reached in with one of those boots and kicked a place for that log and dropped it in and hopped back from the bouncing sparks and then squatted off to one side on the raised stone hearth. He was limp and relaxed there, that long thin carcass doubled up, and he took off that hopeless old hat and set it on one bent-up knee and he was about bald, just a fringe of scraggly hair over his ears and dipping in back. That slant-sided head beveled smooth on top looked even more like a blunted ax blade than before. He was in shadow to the side there, just a queer-shaped bump against the fireplace stones, and quiet, and it was easy to forget he was there at all.

Peyton couldn't forget. He kept looking at the old character and looking away. Finally he gave up looking away and when there was a break in the talk spoke right at him. He was just trying to get something straight, friendly, just one man by a fire talking friendly to another. "Carr," he said. "You called me a predator this afternoon."

That was Peyton. He tied that remark strictly to himself. He left me out of it. If he was going to raise an issue that might lead to a little arguing, he wasn't going to presume on friendship and pull anyone else into it.

This Carr character didn't even move. He just said, mild: "Likely I did."

"Yes, siree, you certainly did," Peyton said. "And that makes me curious. People I pal around with generally reserve that particular label for things like wolves and mountain lions. Just how do you mean it?"

This Carr uncoupled a bit. It was like Peyton had pulled a cork out of him and a big supply of words had just been waiting to pop out, not fast, just steady, in that mild voice of his, patient, like he was explaining a lesson to some kid. "I'm a dictionary man," he said. "There's more real sense in a dictionary, providing you read it right and fit things together, than in about all other books boggled into one big heap. I read my dictionary the way some folks read— well, read sports magazines. It says a predator is an animal that preys on other animals. That's prey spelled with an e not an a and a mighty lot of difference that one letter makes. Now a man is an animal. Maybe something more too, but an animal all the same. Mammal variety. You're a man. You prey on other animals. That makes you a predator."

"Because I shoot deer?" Peyton said. He had a good hold on himself. You had to know him as well as I did to sort of feel the little sharp underneath edge to his tone.

"That's part of it," Carr said. "But you have to look at—" He stopped talking because someone else was talking. That was one thing about him, he was willing to let another man, any other man, have his own say too. That someone else this time was a youngish fellow up there for his first hunting season and all excited about it. "Fooey!" he said, sudden and sharp. He seemed surprised at himself for being so sharp but went right on anyway. "That's no way to talk. That type of thinking puts men right beside wolves and coyotes and cougars and such and anybody with any sense knows those are slinky sneaky cowardly things."

"Well, now, yes," this Carr character said. "They do slink around and they do sneak around, especially when after a meal off a fat deer, and they are cowardly in the meaning that a man comes along, especially a man with a gun, they scat out of his way fast as possible. But when you get out in these hills tomorrow hunting your deer too, you'll be slinking along and sneaking along just the same as they do and after a deer or two's got away from you you'll be wishing you could slink and sneak as efficient as they can. And anybody has a mind to bet'd have a certain thing betting if you were out there without a gun and some other man with a gun was roaming around right ready to pot you first chance you'd be scatting out of his way fast as you could. There's a point you missed too some folks make which is they say critters like wolves are cowards because sometimes they hunt in packs. Look at it right that's not being cowards. That's being efficient. Take any batch of men and let them get hungry enough and let game be the only food around and mighty scarce at that and they'd be pack-hunting too. I've read somewheres that's how they did it back before they had things like guns and hunting was a serious food-getting business not just a pleasuring. Fact is, they still do it anyway, even nowadays, like over at Skinner's place up the north creek where they're so all-fired anxious to guarantee a man his deer they put him in a good spot and some of the hands swing out around driving game his way. That's pack-hunting any way you look at it."

Old Carr had that young fellow stopped. It was Peyton who went after him again.

"I suppose you don't hunt deer?" Peyton said.

"That's right," Carr said. "Nor elk or turkey either. But I don't claim any special credit on that. I'm a predator too. I belong to the race of man and that's a race of predators. Always has been. Always will be. I don't shoot deer. But I raise cattle for market. That's the same thing only better organized. I eat beef mighty regular. Enjoy it too. When it comes to deer, though, I kind of figure—"

"Whoa, now," Myers said. I guess Myers had seen something like this happen before and was stepping in to shoo old Carr down a side track. "That's a new one, Enos. Never heard you spring that 'better organized' business before. Raising cattle the same as hunting deer, only better organized. What kind of addled egg you been hatching this time?"

"Certain they're the same," Carr said. "There's a lot of differences, but there's plenty of sameness too. What's raising cattle at bottom? Letting some critters breed and multiply and graze and put on weight. What for? So they can be killed and butchered and the meat tucked away in folks's bellies. What's this state government we're living under do with deer? Sets up laws to keep some deer around to breed and multiply and graze and put on weight. And what for? So hunters can go out kill and butcher them and bring in the meat to be tucked away in bellies. The pattern's the same. But look at it right the deer doing is kind of sloppy. Hit-or-miss all through. Breeding's not controlled. Slaughtering is just chance, which hunter stumbles into which deer and can he shoot straight. And he has to do his own messy butchering of the carcass. That's plain poor organization. The cattle business is almighty neat against it. Breeding's controlled for the best stock. The right animals, by age and weight, culled out for killing. Sent off to a place set up to do the killing and butchering quick and efficient. Look at it right that's plenty more civilized. My dictionary says civilization is a state of being well organized and refined. I notice one thing civilization tries to do is cover things up for people. Shut off things that aren't refined and maybe aren't pleasant to see or know. Like the fact some critter had to be killed and butchered for there to be meat to eat. Man goes into a store buys a piece of meat and that's all it is to him, a piece of something good to eat and he doesn't even think about the killing and butchering and pulling out of guts had to be done for that meat to be there. Civilization, being organized, shuts that off for him. Hunting, being sloppy, just plain rubs his nose in the messy part."

This Carr character had everybody stopped. Nobody was going to talk to an old head-touched oddity who rambled on like that, miss-

ing most of what hunting is all about. And he was stretching up to
his feet anyway. I guess he always shut himself off in time and
Myers knew that which was why Myers had been letting him run on.
His voice got almost plaintive. "You boys," he said. "You ought to
know better'n get me to talking. I don't want to spoil your fun any.
Just talking for myself. Maybe civilization shuts off too blamed
much. Maybe rubbing noses in the messy part of living is a good
thing now and again."

He jammed that hopeless old hat on that bald beveled head and
went spraddle-stride to the door and on out.

It was morning. I mean it would be morning soon. There was the
first faint graying of light creeping up behind the mountains. We'd
had breakfast, Peyton and I, and shrugged into our coats and caps
and picked up our packed lunches and got our gear and when we
went down towards the barn there were our horses saddled and
waiting. Not just the horses. Old Carr was there too. He had his
back to us and didn't see us coming. He was talking. To those
horses.

Peyton took me by the arm and stopped me. We stood there,
listening.

"No tricks now," old Carr was saying. "Not a one. Understand?
Especially you, Joe. This is business. For your own good. Understand? You're earning money and we'll be needing that money to
buy feed for your greedy belly before the winter's done. You know
well as I do it's going to be a tough one. What'd you grow that
longer thicker coat for if it isn't? No tricks. Your men get lost today
you bring them back. Not to our place. Back right here. Understand?"

I guess he noticed the horses looking past him at us because he
turned around.

"Quit worrying, Carr," Peyton said. "Predators like me don't get
lost."

"Don't talk foolish, boy," Carr said. "No skin off a man's pride to
get lost. You know well as I do any man can do it. Especially in
winter. Snow changes things plenty. You get caught in a bad storm,
can't see ten feet, then what? Your horse brings you in. Man's way
ahead of a horse on a lot of things. Not on that."

Peyton wasn't wanting any long palaver. Peyton was starting

on a hunt, already getting the way I knew he would be as soon as we were really out, keen, alert, concentrating on the job in hand. We just swung into the saddles and started off. But as I said old Carr seemed to irritate Peyton just by being around. We hadn't gone more than about twenty feet when Peyton reined back. "Carr," he said. "Why the devil do you talk to your horses like that?" He changed his voice, giving it that mild drony tone Carr used. "You know well as I do they don't understand you."

This Carr character hesitated, the one time I saw him seem to search around for what to say. "Maybe they don't exactly understand the words I use," he said. "But they understand me. Maybe better'n I understand them. And they like it. Folks like Myers here wonder why my horses are always good horses. Just scrub mountain ponies like the others around. But good horses. Well, I give them something. They work for me so I try to give something back more'n just feed."

Peyton was reining away again and rightly too. We had more important things to do than stall around listening to odd talk like that.

Old Carr raised his voice a bit. "And it's not just for them I do it. For myself too."

Peyton was the one who was right on that as I knew he would be. We didn't get lost. We didn't have to depend on those horses to bring us in. We worked all the way up Hart Mountain and along the top ridge some and even down the rough breaks on the other side and tied the horses and went plenty more miles in and about on foot and we knew where we were every minute. We made it straight back to the horses without any wandering around. It was working back down Hart that Peyton got his buck, a shot from the saddle off through thick timber that dropped that deer after one jump. Peyton dressed it out quick and neat and not the least bit messy. Then we didn't just hang it and ride on in and send someone the long way out with a packhorse for that deer. We tied it tight over the saddle on my horse and we took turns the long way in, one hiking and one riding Peyton's horse and switch about. I'll say this: those were good horses. We didn't have any trouble with them at all.

Peyton felt good that evening and rightly too. This Carr character was in his place on the hearth, just a quiet odd-shaped and odd-thinking bump there, and I guess Peyton couldn't help going after him again.

"Carr," Peyton said. "Speaking as one kind of predator by your definition which I'm not sure I accept to another kind of predator which you admit being, I'm curious. Last night you started to tell how you figure about deer and I take it about elk and turkey and no doubt any other kind of game and then you got steered off sideways. I'm curious about that figuring."

"Nothing much," old Carr said. Maybe Myers had got hold of him and told him to take these things easy. "I just don't figure on adding to the general competition is all."

"Competition?" Peyton said. "Do you mean competition with hunters like me? Do you mean you've kidded yourself into thinking you ought to be what you regard as noble enough to stand aside so there'll be more chance for me and other hunters? That's ridiculous. The law allows you one deer. One deer isn't going to make much difference."

"It makes one deer difference," old Carr said.

"So it does," Peyton said. I could feel that little underneath edge slipping into his tone and I knew by the way his eyes tightened a bit at the corners he was trying to hold it down. "But don't expect me to be grateful. A dyed-in-the-wool predator like me, again by your definition which I don't accept, is ready to take his chance in any competition. He's not asking for any nobility from you."

That did it. That pulled out the cork again. "Being noble," old Carr said, mild, patient, explaining a lesson again. "That's your word. I didn't use it. Just being a bit fair is all I mean. Fair from my way of thinking. I said general competition and I meant general. Including other predators like wolves and coyotes and mountain lions and such, in this country mostly lions I expect, who don't have much else of anything to turn to the way men have when deer and other game get scarce. Look at it from their side they've been pushed around plenty. Men get so blamed greedy, want all the deer for themselves, they hire rangers and such to go around shooting lions to cut down the competition. Get to talking like those lions, just because they want to keep on eating and living, are mean slinking cruel sneaking cowardly critters for doing only what those men are doing too. Men make laws about hunting. What for? To protect deer and other game, so they say. Protect them enough so they can keep on making a few more to be killed. And protect them against what? Mostly against men themselves. Lions been killing deer a long time and always more deer around. Men get to killing them and without those laws a year or two and there'd be no more deer. Lions been in these mountains long before any men. Look at it right you can call deer their cattle. They don't organize their cattle business because they don't need to. Don't put up fences, go around knocking off competition, making laws how many deer can be killed and such. Don't need to. Nature keeps a balance and they leave it at that. Along come men strutting and thinking the whole dadburned universe was made just for them to kick around. Times are I get to kind of dozing and thinking and half dreaming, silly maybe but some sense in it, and I see those lions up on a mountain top somewhere holding a meeting. Those dadburned two-legged predators, they say, are getting too thick around here with their slinky sneaky cowardly ways, killing off our cattle. Don't even go up and wrassle the things down and do nice clean brave killing. Have some kind of cowardly contraption that messes up a deer while still a long ways off. So they, that's those lions, pick a few of themselves that have good claws and husky jaws and say to those, we'll keep you supplied with meat which'd be their way of giving pay and you put in all your time hunting down and knocking off all you can find of those dadburned two-legged predators that are killing our cattle. Don't go getting queasy about it, they say. Those things are out-laws, taking what's ours and been ours long as there's been any of our race around, and being hoggish about it too, wanting to take all."

This Carr character had Peyton stopped. Peyton's eye corners were mighty tight and I knew there were plenty of things he wanted to say. A man like Peyton could see right away talk like that was just silly sentimental at bottom and about so full of holes a sieve would be watertight by comparison. I guess Peyton was realizing there was no sense trying to get anywhere with an old oddity like that.

Carr was stretching up to his feet anyway. "They don't do that, of course," he said. "Those lions. They don't think that way. Can't think that way. Not civilized enough. But I get to thinking that way for them and got plenty beef in my belly I just figure I'll stay away from the competition."

He jammed that hopeless old hat on his head and the only way you could tell he had worked himself up some was that he jammed it on backwards and he went spraddle-toed to the door and on out. But he left a funny feeling in the air. Nothing definite, just a little uncomfortableness around the edges of the big room. I guess Myers felt that. He grinned. "Old Enos tells that one mighty well," he said. "But there's a wrinkle that occurs to me he ought to add. Ought to have those lions of his round up a passel of wolves or coyotes to use as a hunting pack getting after the two-legged predators. Reckon I'll have to try that on Enos next time."

There were chuckles around the room and I guess it was worth listening to an old oddity ramble on just to have the following, a chance to see a man like Myers operating, big and solid and sensible, big enough and not just in size to tolerate and joke along with and even stand up for a touched-head old neighbor like that.

Next morning when we went out the horses were there and this Carr with them. But he saw us coming and he just waved at us and pointed to the horses and went off towards the barn. I got my deer that day and we packed it in the same as before. And that evening he wasn't squatting there on the hearth and didn't come in to squat there. Peyton kept looking at the spot and finally Myers said: "Enos went back over to his place for the night. Likes to check every few days to see everything's all right."

The talk drifted around the way it does and then Peyton said: "What's the story, Myers? Did he just grow that way or did something happen?"

Myers knew who he meant all right. Myers settled back some and stretched out his legs and put one booted foot on top the other, heel on toe, and looked at the top toe-point. "Both," he said. "Enos grew that way though I don't know too much about that and then something happened. Leastways I think what happened had plenty to do with it. He was already up in these hills when my dad came in here homesteading. Already known as a character when I was a sprout and first noticing things. Couldn't have been much more'n in his thirties then but looked about exact as now. He'd had a wife though likely that's hard to believe and maybe her dying with a still birth did something to him. Talks plenty about damn near anything but not a word all the years about that which likely means it cut clear down to the quick. Took to making pets of all kinds of animals. You can figure how that'd appeal to a kid so I was over at his place a lot. Got to know him mighty well. Best man with a gun I ever knew though mostly just peppering at marks. I wouldn't be surprised, Peyton, if he could still take that old Enfield hanging over his fireplace and get you mighty worried slapping slugs right along-side yours from the fanciest latest custom-made you have. But even then he was just hunting in the lean years when he really needed the meat. Said he didn't see much sense in showing anybody even him-self what he could do when he knew already damn well what he could do. But that's getting off the mark. It was those pets, one of them, that made what happened happen. And damn it, I've never quit damning it, it was me had to be the one to do it. Had my size then and my dad was dead and I was running this ranch and likely biggity about it and we had sheep as well as cattle up in here in those days and we formed a sort of stockmen's association and I was a big talker forming it and the neighbors made me president of it that year."

Myers raised his top foot carefully and set it down beside the other. He wouldn't look at anybody, just into the fire. "Well," he said, "it was a coyote. A damned little coyote. Enos got it when a squirming little pup, I never knew just how, and a part-collie sheep-dog bitch he had suckled it for him. Cute little critter, no doubt about that. And smart. Got to be fair-sized, big as any collie, and with the good food he was giving it regular furred out mighty nice. Yes, as nice-looking a doglike critter as you could find anywhere. Trouble was Enos treated it like one. Like a dog. Trained it like one. Gave it the run of his place like that collie. Maybe you think I'm stretching this but wasn't long before he had that coyote bring-ing in his one old milk cow morning and evening. You'll be think-ing I'm stretching it more when I say he had that coyote helping him handle his sheep. It had that collie to kind of copy but it caught on fast and before long that collie was loafing with that damn coyote doing the work."

Myers was quiet a minute or two, looking at the fire. Nobody else said a word. That's one thing about sitting around a fire up in the mountains in hunting season. A man starts telling a story, you let him tell it and in his own way.

"Well, now," Myers said, "there's no need explaining what came of that. Coyote's a coyote, not a dog. Even at that there's dogs get to acting like coyotes now and again. First notice was when deSilva down the valley, he's not around any more, lost some chickens. Coyote sign around. Then Skinner found a dead lamb and a few days later another. Things like that scattered along over a month or two and talk was passing around. Folks came to me because I was president of the association. Knew how they felt because I'd lost a calf myself. Weren't thinking much of Enos's pet at first because it was so damned doglike and there were still wild ones roaming through here. Still a few even now. Maybe always will be. Anyhow, folks were saying I ought to be doing something, putting out poison, getting a ranger up in here, something like that. Then deSilva, he was raising some turkeys, tipped it. Was worried about those turkeys. Put some traps about. Came to me one morning collecting neighbors along the way. Had found a trap sprung and a couple of toes, claw pads that is, in it. Coyote. Had followed the trail a ways by blood drips and seen where it was heading."

Myers lifted the same foot again and set it on top the other and looked down along his legs at it. "No need explaining what had to be done. Three of us went over to Enos's place. Told him we figured his coyote was one of them, maybe the one. He wouldn't believe it. Hard as hell for a man, any man, to believe that about one of his own. Asked him had that pet come home limping, shy a couple of toes. Not that he knew of. Where was it? He whistled and called and there was a shuffling under the porch on his place and that damned coyote crawled out, limping. It was like someone had hit old Enos on the head with a club. He knew, just like that. And that damned coyote knew too. It slunk right back, snaking on its belly under that porch again. No sense letting a situation like that go on getting sour and bitter so I asked Enos was he going to shoot it or did he want us to do that for him. He just looked at me kind of blank and went inside his place and came out with the old snap-top purse he kept hid in there somewhere. Wanted to know what damage we figured had been done so he could make it good."

Myers reached up one hand and ran it fingers-spread through the thick shock of hair he had and let it drop. He still wouldn't look at any of us, just at that boot toe. "No need explaining why that wouldn't do," he said. "Money damages don't come into a thing like that. Not with neighbors that know each other and pull each other out of holes now and again when pulling's needed. Wasn't a one of us would've touched a cent of old Enos's money on a thing like that. But when a dog takes to killing stock there's only one recipe for it and that's killing the dog. That's been the rule long as men have had dogs which I expect goes way back to when they were living in caves and first learning to fuss some with sheep and cattle. And this thing wasn't even a dog. Just a damned coyote he'd been trying to make act like a dog. Tried to make him see it that way. And that's when he got excited. Hard to believe now I expect but Enos could get excited in those days. Not just talk but get going like a blamed preacher at a revival. Kept saying that damned coyote wasn't to blame, it was all his fault. Kept saying he'd taught it not to touch anything around his place but'd been too stupid to realize it wouldn't know that applied to other people's places too. Kept saying it oughtn't have to pay for his stupidity."

Myers raised his head a bit and looked around at all of us, then back at that boot toe. "Yes," he said. "You all know how it is. A man has to do something he has to do it. Letting that thing live wouldn't be fair to the association I was president of. Wouldn't be fair to old Enos himself. People'd be getting bitter about him. Anybody lose anything and right or wrong he'd be getting the blame. Way he was carrying on I wasn't sure what he might do so I motioned the other two with me to grab hold. Which they did, one on each arm. I took my rifle out of the saddle scabbard and looked under that porch. Couldn't see much except the eyes and the teeth showing in a kind of snarl. Aimed smack between those eyes and that was that."

Myers stopped talking. Nobody said anything. It was Peyton who finally spoke, just two words. "And Carr?" he said.

"Oh, he didn't do anything," Myers said. "When the others let go just stood there a while. Acted like we weren't even around. Went over to a shed he had and got a shovel. He was digging a hole out in the little orchard he had when we rode off. I hung on the ridge top a while where I could see his place. When he finished his burying he just went inside and shut the door. That was the last I saw of him, anybody saw of him, for quite a stretch. Just stayed to himself and nobody figured on pushing in. Then we had a big rain on up in the hills and the creek rose clean up in my meadows out the side here and carried away some fence and some of my best steers I was grain feeding took off. Figured to fix that fence before I went scouting. Was working on it when along came Enos on one of those ponies of his bringing in my stock. Swung down and helped finish that fence. Same old Enos. Only quiet, talking the way he has ever since, you know how, mild, kind of patient, like a teacher explaining things to kids. Aggravating, I expect, till you get used to it. Never said a word about what happened. Never has."

Myers straightened up some and looked around. "I've shot that damned coyote a hundred times," he said. "Lying awake at night and thinking. I did right. I'd do it again today. And tomorrow. And the day after. All the same, anytime old Enos gets to blowing his offside notions around my place he's going to blow and nobody's going to stop him. Except maybe me. And I don't have to. He stops himself."

Next morning Peyton and I were pulling out. Myers let us have the jeep to take our deer down to the little town where we'd left our car. We could tote them on the fenders from there. He had someone coming in later who would bring the jeep back. We were packed and ready to leave when we saw this Carr character back again and down by the barn. He could stay there as far as I was concerned. We had heard him talk and odd as it was once you caught the hang of it, if you wanted, you could spin out that kind of stuff by the yard yourself. We had his story, what there was of it, and it was interesting enough as stories about oddities can be but it was also really about Myers as much as old Carr and Myers had put a nice finish to it and there wasn't much sense in adding any more. But Peyton wasn't satisfied. That character rubbed him wrong just by being in sight. Peyton was driving and he swung the jeep down by the barn and stopped it.

"Carr," he said. "What the devil are you aiming at in your talk? Where the devil does that cockeyed thinking of yours lead you?" He was keeping this light the way he would, even taking Carr's own label for him to hold it friendly. "To the notion that all we two-legged predators ought to resign from the competition and let the lions take over?"

You couldn't catch this character off balance. He always had words ready. I guess he spent his time at his own place, when he wasn't reading his dictionary, just sitting around thinking up answers to anything anyone might ask him. "No," he said, mild, patient, aggravating the way Myers had mentioned. "I don't go laying down rules for other people. Just for myself. Anyway, men and lions been competing as long as both have been around this old world. Just plain natural for both." He stopped, hunching that decrepit old jacket up around his neck against the morning cold.

"Go on," Peyton said. "I know damn well you don't stop there."

"Well," this Carr said. "Look at it this way. We're men. Me, you, everybody. All tarred with the same stick. It's our brand and we wear it. Mighty nice too, in a way, being men. Top dogs of creation or so it seems. Being predators is our nature just like with about all living things. It's the way things are. Even deer eat grass and leaves and such and those have life too. It's the way things are. No sense trying not to be predators because that'd be unnatural and about impossible anyway. We're animals like I say. But we're thinking animals and that makes a mite of difference. We can think about what we do. Don't often, but can. Lions and the others can't. Not in the same way. And that kind of puts an obligation on us. Seems to me we, all of us, myself anyway, ought to realize other animals have living problems too, have their places too in the over-all mixed-up scheme of things we're sitting on top of. Seems to me it makes things a mite better if we just mix a little something more than just being proud to be men and taking for granted the whole dadburned universe is made special for us in with our thinking."

He stopped again. I could see Peyton's eye corners tightening and I was hoping Peyton would slip the clutch and we'd be rolling.

"Go on," Peyton said. "What the devil would you want to mix in?"

"That's hard to put," Carr said. "Maybe the right word's not been thought up yet. I've looked through my dictionary plenty times and can't find it. Best one there comes close but still misses some."

"All right," Peyton said but I knew by his tone this wasn't right with him at all. "What's that word?"

"Humility," Carr said. "Seems to me it makes things better to put a bit of that in with being a man."

I was afraid there for a moment that Peyton was going to let his irritation at a sermonizing platitude like that bust right out. But he didn't. Not Peyton. He just let the clutch out with a snap and swung the wheel and we sliced around and over to the road. We headed down the long curving slopes with the jeep slugging hard in low in the deeper snow ruts and I noticed he was gripping the wheel hard and his eye corners were crinkled tight. I tried a couple of times to start him talking and he wouldn't say a word. I was beginning to get peeved at this Carr character for irritating a man like Peyton and maybe spoiling the finish of our hunting trip together.

We worked on down. Then Peyton kind of shook himself. "There's plenty of time," he said. "After we get the car let's swing around by the turnpike. There's a fellow along there I know who has a new rifle Fanzoi made for him over in Austria he wants me to see."

He sat up straighter behind the wheel. "There's a man for you. Josef Fanzoi. Lives in a little village called Ferlach. Did you ever hear about that place? More gunsmiths and the best there are than any place else in the world. They start them in as kids. Even have a damn fine school just for that . . ."

I sat back listening to Peyton talk about what he knew as well as any man alive, about guns and those who make them, and watching him drive that jeep the way he did whatever he ever tackled, easy and sure and efficient. Everything was all right again.

The Fifth Man

I S NOT all matter composed of atoms, themselves of whirling mites of energy, and some simple in organization, as hydrogen, and others complex, as uranium, with all shadings from simple to complex between? Do not these atoms, restless as in gases, more serene as in solids, impinge upon one another, touch and meet and often mingle, all through any cluster of matter, star or planet or moon or meteorite, out to the edges where what is discoverable, verifiable, merges into the mystery of space? And does not a movement, a convulsion, among these atoms anywhere send impulse radiating outward, producing effects according to the character of the ever adjoining atoms? What was it Carlyle said? "It is a mathematical fact that the casting of this pebble from my hand alters the centre of gravity of the Universe."

Just so perhaps with people, individual atoms of humanity, ranging from simple to complex, restless to serene, impinging upon one another in the cluster called society, civilization. What one, or a group of ones does, sends impulse radiating out, communicating atom to atom, person to person, in the wondrous involved web of existence. And who can know how many atoms it reaches before it fades into the mystery of surrounding space?

That is a kind of nonsense, of course. You do not understand what I am saying. Who among us ever truly understands another, what another says or does, in full impact of meaning? I do not understand it myself. I simply see glimmers of a possible pattern, impulse communicating person to person, and am trying to pin down a manifestation of it in these words. A story perhaps, yet not really a story, simply an account and a wondering.

Various people in the little southwestern town told me he was crazy. He lived some twenty miles out, in a lonely arid region, at a long-ago-abandoned stage stop. Squatted rather, because he did not own the place, did not need to. No one else wanted it, had wanted it for the thirty years or more since the new road had by-passed it by many miles. He ran a few bony cows and now and again butchered one and jerked the meat in the sun in the old almost forgotten manner and raised a few beans and chiles and other things and at long intervals appeared in town, walking in moccasins of his own make, to count out a few coins for a few necessities.

Yes, they said, old Cal Kinney was crazy, in a harmless sort of way. Crazy to be living out there alone with nothing but horned toads and coyotes and a sidewinder or two and a few bony cows for company. Crazy in the way he didn't talk or, when he did talk, didn't make sense. But he never bothered anybody so why should anybody bother him? And he did keep the tiny spring out there cleaned and flowing its small trickle which was sometimes a good thing when some fool took to wandering that dry region without an extra canteen.

You never know exactly what you will turn up in a case like that, not in this Southwest where time is an almost tangible dimension of all things and the past is part of the present and the dust your toe stirs in the emptiness of apparent nowhere may have crumbled from Spanish adobe puddled before the Pilgrims set sail or from Indian masonry worked a thousand years before Columbus. Sometimes a tale of treasure, a legend of buried gold or silver, and a secretive man poring over an ancient map always obtained at third or fourth or fifth hand in some mysterious way and digging, digging, digging, here and there and everywhere as his taut obsessed mind extracts new interpretations from his ancient map.

There was no tinge of treasure this time. Not a whisper of legend in the region. I packed some supplies with the sleeping bag in my car and drove out.

Maybe a truck or two had been over that old stage route within the last ten-twenty years. You couldn't tell. But the old trace was plain enough, passable if you didn't mind scraping cactus, dragging bottom once in a while, taking small arroyos with a rush through the sand. I knew I was there when I saw the cottonwood, the only tree other than a few scrubby junipers in the twenty miles, big, big as a barrel at the base, but more than half dead, broken off jagged among the top branches, kind of a half-skeleton of a tree. It must have had a tremendous root system to suck moisture out of that dry basin. Maybe, back along the years, the spring about a hundred yards up the side slope at the base of a rough outcropping of red rock had trickled on down here and given it a start. Maybe the water was once even piped down, because the stage station had been close beside that tree. The building, probably just a stable for change of horses or mules, was gone, not even a weathered board left, but the lines of the stone foundation still showed.

I left the car by the tree and walked up the slow slope. The spring seeped out of the rock at the base through clean sand and trickled into a small catch basin inside a three-sided pen out from the rock made of old boards, probably from the onetime stable. A small wooden sluice led the overflow outside the pen into an old tin bathtub sunk into sand for a water trough. Off to the right, out a bit from the abrupt rock behind, was the garden, enclosed by a fence that must have been made of every odd piece of anything accumulated around the place in the active years, chunks of old pipe and beams for posts, snarls of rusty barbed wire, a stretch of mangled chicken wire, several old doors propped lengthwise, glassless window frames, a crooked old bedspring, even an old stove. Inside that parody of a fence the garden itself was neat and practical, leveled, laid out in humped rows separated by little irrigation ditches. A length of one-inch old pipe poked out the side embankment of the catch basin, through that fence, ending in a small faucet at the lead ditch along the end of that garden.

Over beyond the garden was the cabin, shack, hut, whatever you might want to call it. A haphazard squarish crazy-quilt thing, covered around with odd-sized old boards fastened this way and that and some places two and three over each other to close off cracks. My guess was it was the tender's cabin, once well built, that had weathered weak and started to collapse then been patched up again. I walked over. The door was open and I looked in. The walls and roof were as makeshift as that fence, but they were tight enough. The interior was as neat and practical as that garden. Two windows, one with glass panes intact, the other covered with chicken wire and with a hinged wooden shutter that could be closed over it. A homemade wooden cot with several old blankets spread, a table, a chair, a bench along one wall, a couple of long shelves, supplies on one, a few books and some old dishes and a kerosene lamp on the other. In the back corner a small old woodstove with two boxes beside it, one filled with dry cow chips, the other with pieces of dry juniper.

I stepped back out of the doorway and looked around. There were two small sheds beyond that cabin, low, solid, doors closed and fastened with rusty clasp hatches. Toolshed, I figured, and storehouse. Angled back a ways behind them was another small square structure. Outhouse. I looked on around. Not a movement anywhere. There was a biggish box upturned like a bench along the shady side of one of the sheds. I sat there studying the whole layout.

A clinky sound started, faint at first then clearer. A gaunt old cow with a tarnished dull-clappered bell on a leather thong around her neck came stepping slow, stiff-legged, down from where the outcropping of red rock shaded off into sandy slopeside. Two others followed. A half-grown calf, late, tagged them, coming with a little scrambling rush, then slowing into place in the plodding procession. They moved straight to the old bathtub.

I remember I was sitting on that upturned box wondering how he ever managed to get a cow bred in that empty arid loneliness when I realized I was looking at him. He was down by that tree, suddenly there out of nowhere, standing quiet, motionless, as if he had always been there, staring at my car. He was about as ordinary-seeming a man as I ever saw, except that perhaps ordinary men don't often live to be as old, age showing in the shape and sagging outline even at that distance and yet with it a kind of indestructible ageless spry endurance. He wore the moccasins I had heard about, faded shrunk levis with a piece of rope for a belt, a faded patched denim shirt, a frayed-edge battered Mexican-style straw hat. I've seen men dressed about like that by the dozen all through the out-of-the-way little settlements of the Southwest. In a way he was just a natural part of the country.

All the same I remember thinking there was some little thing wrong, not quite right. He was clean-shaven. Usually, in these cases, there are whiskers, maybe a sign, a gesture, of independence, maybe just that a man living out alone doesn't see much sense in shaving, in doing more than a bit of trimming now and again. He was clean-shaven.

He turned and came up the slope towards the cabin. He was spry enough in those moccasins all right, not hurrying, but moving along as if he were quite aware of what he was doing every moment and quite capable of doing it. I didn't see him look at me but he knew I was there and I knew he knew. He went into the cabin.

I sat quiet. The beginning is the most important time in these things. You try to shove in, push yourself forward, and like as not you run head-on into stubbornness, irritation, maybe rejection. So you sit quiet and let the situation drift and the other man make any move.

He appeared in the doorway, stepped out, sat down on the big chunk of red rock that was the doorstep. He stared down-slope at my car. He seemed more interested in that car than in me, that my being there or not being there barely brushed against an indifference in him.

I sat quiet. At last he turned his head and looked at me.

"I'm writing a story," I said, "that takes place in country like this. I thought maybe you wouldn't mind my staying around a few days."

He looked back again at the car. I was about ready to give up hope of an answer when he spoke. "We don't mind," he said.

I sat quiet, studying on that. Did he mean himself and those old cows?

He stood up. "You'll have to move that vehicle," he said. "He might not like it there." He disappeared into the cabin.

I sat quiet, listening to sounds from inside of the old stove being rattled. I had the tingle. There was something around. I could wait. I could let it drift. I went down to the car, started it, drove it up past the two sheds, began to pull out a few things for my own camp.

Two days and I knew that the days didn't matter. It was the nights.

He was regular in his habits, punctual as a still-sound old clock. He slept late in the morning, or at least he lay in there on that cot until late. He had to, I expect, because he didn't sleep much during the night. And he could be comfortable until along towards forenoon before sun beating on the flimsy roof would heat up that cabin because the sun rose behind the rock outcropping and had to be well up before it could find the cabin in the rock shadow. He fixed himself a good breakfast, in quantity anyway, because he didn't bother with a midday meal. The rest of the morning he puttered around, checking over his entire layout, fiddling with anything that seemed to him to need fixing or cleaning or setting straight. Along in early afternoon he set out somewhere and was gone about three hours. He didn't go like a man going any particular place with any particular purpose. He just walked off. He took nothing with him. He brought nothing back. He was just passing time.

When he came back he fussed around his garden. He didn't that first late afternoon because my being there, my car being there, threw him off stride some. After that he was in routine again. He alternated his work on that garden, weeding and a little cultivating one afternoon, watering the next. Then he retired to the cabin and took his time with his evening meal and afterwards, in the deepening dusk, lit his old lamp and settled beside it with one of his old books. The day was done, passed. There wasn't a clock in that cabin and he had no watch, but he had clocked off the hours as if he had a timepiece tucked away in his head.

As I say, two days and I had that straight. I was getting hold of the nights too.

That first night, along about full dark, when I was deciding whether to sleep on or inside my sleeping bag, I heard him moving in the cabin. He blew out the lamp and came to the doorway and stepped out and sat down on the doorstep. The moon, nearly rounded, was beginning to show over the rock outcropping behind but he was in the shadow of both rock and cabin and I couldn't make out what he was doing. I watched and listened. Not a movement, not a sound. He was just sitting there. At last I drifted into sleep. I woke up suddenly a few hours later by my watch and he was still there. The moon was high now and I could see him plain. He was just sitting there, staring down towards that old tree. I drifted into sleep again and when I woke up several hours later, maybe waked by sense of the movement, he was stretching up and going into the cabin.

The next night, after the first full day of watching him, I was certain he would be right on schedule. He wasn't. The lamp went on burning and he went on reading. I lay quiet and time passed and the lamp was blown out and he came to the doorway and sat on the doorstep. I looked at my watch. Something past nine, about an hour later than the night before. I lay awake quite a while before I had an answer that could fit.

The next night, after two full days of watching, I knew I was right. He would blow out the lamp and take position on the doorstep soon after ten. He did. The moon, almost completely rounded now, was beginning to show over the rock behind, sending its soft shimmer down-slope towards that tree.

All this time he paid about as much attention to me as to those old cows which wasn't any more that you could notice than a look morning and evening to see if they were still alive and around. His indifference seemed to be complete. He gave the impression that there could have been dozens of me, all kinds of people, cluttering the immediate neighborhood and he would still have been alone, going his way, following his routine, wrapped inviolable in his own existence. I couldn't figure how I might get in to him or get him to come out to me.

It was late afternoon of the second full day that I caught a glimmer. People are people. A man is a man. There is always some residue of recognition of the existence of others, of another, an instinctive perhaps unthinking reaching out. It is the ineradicable call of kind. He was at the end of his garden by the pipe from the catch basin and had just opened the small faucet to let water run into the lead ditch. He saw me sitting on the upturned box by one of the sheds. He saw me look at him. He raised a hand to focus my attention. He turned away and straddled over a low part of that parody of a fence and stepped up by one of the posts of the pen around the catch basin and reached and lifted off a nail something I had not noticed before. An old tin dipper. He held this up. He hung it again on the nail and straddled back over the garden fence and went on with his watering.

I studied on that. He was not only aware of my presence but aware enough to notice what I did. And he did not resent me. He might even feel some small tinge of companionship because I was there. He had seen me going on my frequent jaunts to that catch basin for a drink of the water trickling fresh and cool out of the rock. He had seen me carrying my tin cup over and carrying it back again to my camp.

In the morning I made my own move. I remembered something I had seen that first day when I checked the cabin. On the supply shelf a small bucket half filled with used coffee grounds. There is only one reason anyone saves used coffee grounds. To use them again. I waited until sounds from inside the cabin told me he was starting the day and until he had come out with his big bucket and started towards the spring for his morning supply of fresh water. I slipped into the cabin. I set on the table a fresh unopened one-pound can of coffee and slipped out again and sat on the upturned box by one of the sheds.

He came back, leaning to the weight of the bucket, apparently not even noticing me, and went inside. I waited. The can of coffee came out the doorway, turning over and over in the air, and hit in the dirt and rolled a short way down-slope. I waited. He stood in the doorway, not looking at me, staring down at the can in the dirt. Time passed. He walked down and picked up the can and returned to the cabin and went in. More time passed. He stood in the doorway. He looked directly at me. "There's two cups on the table," he said.

That was a beginning. I sat on the bench inside drinking coffee and he sat on the chair eating his morning meal. Crazy? Not in any way you could notice. Individual, eccentric, opinionated, yes. If you said something that failed to interest him, to touch him, he simply ignored you. It hadn't been said. If he felt like being silent, he was silent. If he felt like talking, he talked, and in a steady unhurried flow that gave the impression nothing less than a sudden cataclysm could stop it. I touched off one of those flowings when I reached and pulled the book lying on the table a bit closer so I could see the title. It was an old geology text. He started talking and for the next ten to fifteen minutes without a break gave me a lecture on the geologic history of the Southwest in general and of that specific area in particular. He talked about that outcropping of red rock behind the cabin as if it had life of its own, placing its birth, its formation, in such and such an age, tracing its long burial under the sediments of inland seas, its rise again with shiftings of the earth's crust and exposure after millennia of erosion.

He stopped, looking at me as if I might be some sort of geologic specimen myself. "If you're prospecting around here for some kind of mineral strike," he said, "you're a fool."

I took a chance. "The only strike I'm after," I said, "is the kind you can put into words. In a story."

He pushed up from his chair. I watched him gather the few dishes and rinse them in his bucket. I wasn't there any more. He walked past me and out of the cabin and started on his morning round.

Early afternoon and I made another move. I waited where the rock faded off into sandy hillside and along he came, on schedule, for his afternoon walk. I swung into stride beside him. He didn't stop or slow or pay any attention to me. Then suddenly he did stop. He looked at me. As far as I could make out any expression on that ordinary old clean-shaven face, he was amused. "Do you think," he said, "I've got a lost mine or anything like that hidden in these hills? Or if I did, I'd lead you to it?"

"No," I said. "I think you're just passing time."

He nodded a bit, at least I thought he did, and he started on and I went with him. One of those subtle inexplicable shiftings had taken place. I was not just walking alongside him. I was going with him.

He took me quite a few miles. There was plenty of spry vigor left in his old legs. We went wandering, what would have looked like wandering to anyone watching, but I could make out traces of trail, probably worn by successive pairs of his own-make moccasins. He had something of a routine out there too. In and about, following the low levels, working on a wide circuit into hills that were not really hills but the remaining twisted fingers of what had once been the general land level now standing strange and misshapen between sharply eroded arroyos and miniature canyons. The Southwest has many of those stripped eroded badlands where color and barrenness and the bare bones of earth breed beauty and a haunting sense of penetration towards the source of ultimate secrets. He had his own private preserve, not his and yet his because there was nothing tangible of commercial value there to bring people and the blight of settlement and exploitation.

He slowed once to point out some pieces of what I thought were a peculiar rock. "Petrified wood," he said. "Triassic." And he was off on another lecture, not so much a lecture this time as a speculation whether the region had once, millions of years ago, been truly tropical, under heavy rainfall, or simply well supplied with water in the low places by long run-off from other areas. He slowed again to point out a jack rabbit scudding around a turn in the arroyo ahead. And he was off again, this time on a monologue about jack rabbits as the perfect adaptation of life to conditions in that particular region in this particular geologic age.

I was with him, yes, but I was stopped. I didn't dare push much, try to lead his talk, because the few times I tried I simply hadn't spoken. All I could get was his brand of scientific information and I knew enough myself to recognize that his brand was that of a man who reads some in the scant outdated books he has and applies that to what he sees wandering around.

His circuit brought us back on schedule, about the time the old cows and the calf came in for water. He puttered at his garden and I stood watching, certain that if I tried anything I would merely touch off a lecture on plants and the arid-adaptability of the pinto beans that comprised about half that garden. At last I went over and sat on that upturned box. At last he came towards the cabin and went in. I thought of getting a few things from my car and suggesting we share supper but decided no. He wasn't deliberately forgetting me and my can of coffee, deliberately pushing me aside. He was isolated in his own existence again. The shadows were sliding towards night.

And that night he broke his routine. Not a break really but a fulfillment. It only seemed like a break to me at the time.

I was ready, watching, quiet on my sleeping bag, at the right time. A little past eleven. That timepiece in his head clicked or nudged or prodded or whatever it did and he blew out the lamp and came to the doorway and sat on the doorstep. The moon, nicely rounded, was rising clear with only a thin tracery of light clouds floating across the sky. He was in the rock and cabin shadow but I knew what he was doing. He was sitting there staring down towards that old tree.

I remember thinking that maybe I didn't have a timepiece in my own head but I did have an awareness now that could tell me what he would be doing any hour out of the twenty-four. I had his routine fixed, filled in. What was needed was what was behind it, what went on in that old head when he sat on that doorstep. I drifted into sleep wondering what move to make the next day and time passed and I was awake and aware that something had changed.

The moon was high now and the doorstep was plain in the soft light. He wasn't there. I pushed to my feet, careful, quiet, and eased along by the first shed. He was out in the open, moving down towards that old tree. He moved slowly, cautiously, like a man stalking something either very shy or very dangerous. I looked on ahead of him. There was nothing to be seen, nothing anywhere about. That is a point I want to make very clear. There was nothing in sight. Absolutely nothing. Only that gaunt old half-skeleton of a tree standing still and silent on down the slope.

He began to move faster, hurrying. Then he was running. Suddenly he stopped, close by the tree, peering up through the gaunt branches then all around the immediate area. His head drooped and he stood still, as still as the tree itself, and it seemed to me that as he stood there, unmoving, he shrank some, the old outline of him growing older. At last he turned and came up towards the cabin, slow, tired, just a little old man lost and alone in his own private existence. I had the plain impression that I could have stepped out into the open and he could have looked full at me without seeing me. He went slowly into the cabin and I heard his old cot creak a bit as he lay down on it.

In the morning, as far as anyone watching the two of us could have told, nothing had changed, the night had not been. He was the same as before, right in his routine, moving through it with that same seeming indestructible spry vigor. I was part of it now, taken in on the basis of the previous day. I sat on the bench inside and drank coffee while he ate his morning meal and I listened to another lecture, this one on the probable history of an Indian pueblo whose mounded remains he said were still partially decipherable back in the hills. In the afternoon we went off on his circuit again and I listened to a monologue on some fossils from the Pliocene and another on the silliness of the fable of prairie dogs and prairie owls and rattlesnakes living in the same burrows.

It was the day before repeated. But I could sense the difference. There was a tension in him, a tiny beat of anxiety or apprehension under that ordinary old enduring time-passing exterior. And he was reaching out a bit more towards me, was willing to let a little more information slip out. I learned that he was Missouri-bred and had once attended some small jerkwater college planning to be a preacher and had originally come west for his health. I learned too that it was only seven years since he had come into the region and patched up that old cabin and squatted there. I was disappointed at that. It didn't fit into my thinking. I had been figuring that he had been there from way back in the stage days. I was fool enough for a while to feel that maybe I was wasting my time.

It was that feeling which made me try to push him. We had just come back to the place. "That story you're writing," he said. "Are you making it all up?"

"Yes," I said. "Not because I want to but because I have to. This is the kind of place where things should have happened. But apparently nothing ever did." Then I pushed direct. "Or did it?" I said.

He looked straight at me. I could see it. Something. Something hidden in that old mind behind that ordinary old face. He turned away and went to his watering as if I no longer existed. But I knew. He was about ready to talk. All I had to do was wait and let the situation drift some more. What I didn't know was how soon and how completely it would break for me.

If I were reading this, not writing it, I'd say it was too pat, too neat, too tailored to old-fashioned tale traditions. Midnight, in such tales, is the witching hour, the hovering hesitant pause between one full day and the next when anything that is eerie, weird, mystic, is supposed to come to a climax. That is nonsense, of course. Midnight is only a man-marked moment, a notch in the twenty-four hour convention man has established for his own parceling out of the passage of time. And it is not a universal moment; it varies by approximately an hour every thousand miles around the girdle of the globe. To the universe in which man is an infinitesimal flicker, midnight has no significance beyond that of any other moment through the period of dark that itself is only the turning of a portion of the earth's surface away from the sun.

Why cannot fact plagiarize fiction? The fact in this case was the result of an orderly sequence of events. His nightly vigil was determined by the moon. The moon, in its current phase, was rising approximately an hour later each night. A little past eight the first night I was there. Then nine . . . ten . . . eleven. Now twelve. Midnight. A moon beginning to be flattened a bit on the edge now, into the waning.

If you have been patient and have followed me this far, you have the setting, the situation, in mind. A lonely spot in a lonely arid land where once were brief little spurts of once-familiar activity when stages arrived and teams were changed, the place and its type of activity now long since by-passed and all but forgotten in the forward push of what is called progress. An old man living there, existing through routined days aimed at the nights. And myself, edging in, meddling, prying, and justifying my meddling and prying as a search for story material, for more understanding of the endlessly varied ways in which we humans, we midges infesting, in Cabell's phrase, the epidermis of one of the lesser planets, confront the inevitable dilemma of living.

Midnight. Midnight in that particular time-belt, attested to by my watch and by the moon rising behind that outcropping of ancient rock. He blew out his lamp and came to the doorway and sat on the doorstep. I lay quiet on my sleeping bag and that awareness nudged and I pushed up and eased along by the first shed. He was out in the open, in the moonlight, beyond the rock-and-cabin shadow, moving down towards that old tree. There was no need to look on ahead of him but I did. Nothing was there. Absolutely nothing.

He moved faster, hurrying. Then he was running. His old voice rose, quivering through the almost still air, urgent. "Johnny!" he called. "Wait! Wait!" He stumbled and fell forward, almost at the base of the tree. I saw one old hand, clenched, beat on the ground and then he was still.

I moved into the open, down towards him. As I came near, he rolled over and hunched up to sitting position. He looked at me but I don't think he saw me. He tried to stand up and made it and started towards the cabin, limping on his right foot. I moved in close and put out an arm to steady him and he relaxed his old weight some against me, aware of me, I'd say, in his muscles but not yet in his mind. Together we went to the cabin and in and I helped him slump down on the edge of his cot and I stepped over and sat on the bench along the opposite wall. There was enough soft light from the moon through the windows for me to make him out there on the cot edge.

We were quiet, both of us. But I could feel it. He knew I was there. He was grateful that someone was there with sense enough to be quiet and just be there.

I heard him draw in a deep breath and let it out slowly. "Something did happen here," he said.

"Yes," I said. "There were people here. So something had to happen."

"Not many," he said. "Just two. Usually one and sometimes two. And one night more."

I waited. At last he told me, not like one of his lectures, but slow, careful, completely objective, simply stating the facts.

There was a man named Johnny Yeager, a breed, a half-Cherokee, who drifted into the Southwest out of the Indian Territory as a freighter with his own small outfit. He was a quiet capable man with no itch to make money, just to live and enjoy life in his own way. When he worked, he worked hard, picking up jobs with his mules and two wagons freighting supplies to some of the more isolated Army posts. Between trips, when he had money in his pocket and could pay his way with no need for more, he liked to go on pack trips into the lonely distances or loaf around some place where he had a friend or two and soak up southwestern sun. He spent considerable time, off and on, at the stage station by the old cottonwood, then a flourishing tree and landmark. He knew the station tender, the agent as the company obligingly let the tender call himself, and the two of them got along well together. Johnny Yeager would hang around the station, making it his headquarters for long rides round about, pitching in with a will to help with change of horses when a stage came through. He was a good man with anything on hoofs. He liked to sleep in the open. He liked best to sleep on the flat roof

of the stable where he said the sky seemed spread out best for him
and the air moved friendly all around him.

There was a man too named Mills, another freighter, but down
on his luck, or maybe it was his irritableness that was his bad luck,
losing him business until he lost his outfit too. Johnny Yeager took
him on as a driver on one of his trips. Johnny already had a second
driver at the time but Mills pestered him for a job and Johnny took
him on. Out along the lonely way Mills began making trouble. He
had his own ideas about handling mules. He didn't like taking orders from an Indian, even a half-Indian. Maybe he was brooding
over his bad luck too. Somewhere along the trail he worked himself
into a rage and pulled his belt gun and began shooting at Johnny.
That was a mistake for him with a man like Johnny, who jumped
in by the second wagon, yanked the rifle there from under the lash
rope and drilled Mills through the forehead. The other driver had
seen it all and at the inquest he testified straight and Johnny was
exonerated.

But there was another man too named Mills, a brother, and he
came up from his place further south. He talked around that white
men ought to be ashamed letting a goddamned thieving Indian get
away with murder. One night he and three other men rode out and
around into the badlands and staked their horses and slipped down
to the station. The first the agent knew anything was happening
was when they were in the cabin and one of them woke him with a
gun barrel in his ribs and said: "Where's Yeager?" The agent was
fuddled with sleep and all he could focus on at the moment was that
gun barrel in his ribs. "Sleeping on top the stable," he said.

They made the agent get up and go with them, soft, silent, slipping down by the stable. One of them held a gun jammed against
his back every step. They hugged in close against the stable wall,
under the jutting roof. "All right," this Mills whispered. "Call him
down. Try to warn him any and you're done."

The agent didn't have a chance. That gun barrel was hard
against his back. He tried to make his voice sound natural.
"Johnny," he called.

They could hear the man on the roof rousing some, probably sitting up. "Johnny," the agent said. "Come on down here a minute."

Johnny came to the roof edge and sat down, legs hanging over, and pushed out and as he landed the other three of them jumped him. They all rolled over scrambling and then they had him and they jerked him to his feet still struggling and he saw the agent standing there with another man behind and he stopped struggling and stared at the agent and looked away and let those three take him, not struggling any more, down the slope towards the tree. Two of them had him tight by the arms and the third went into the stable and came out with a rope. Down by the tree they fixed a noose and put it around his neck and were ready to throw the other end over the first big limb about eleven or twelve feet up and that was when Johnny spoke.

"I'm not afraid to die," he said. "I'll show you how a man does it." He pulled loose from the two holding him, who let him go but stood and watched close, and he stepped to the trunk of the tree and climbed up by the rough bark and a few old branch stubs with the rope dragging from his neck and hitched himself out on that big limb. He passed the rope end around it and pulled it taut from his neck and knotted it. "Just remember this," he said. "I know you. Each one of you. If there's such a thing as a spirit staying here on earth, I'll do it. I'll make life a hell for each of you as long as you live." And he pushed out from the tree limb, dropping straight to the sharp snapping jerk of the rope.

The agent did what he could. He took Johnny's body into town and arranged for decent burial. He knew that Johnny had a sister in the Indian Territory and he sold out Johnny's outfit and sent her the money. He went to the sheriff and tried to have warrants sworn out. The sheriff made a few gestures at investigating but the four men alibied each other and rang in testimony from accommodating friends and the inquest verdict was death at the hands of persons unknown. The agent made a nuisance of himself trying to stir some action until people were telling him to shut up and why make a fuss over the killing of an Indian anyway. He quit his job and drifted away.

We sat in that patched-together old cabin and he was quiet again. I waited. I knew what he would say, what he would have to say. I expect you do too.

He stirred on the cot edge and raised his head a bit higher. "I was that agent," he said.

I waited. I knew that all he had told me was only the beginning, the background, that he was over the hump now.

"My mistake," he said, "was telling them he was on that roof. The moment I did that it was all inevitable. It had to be."

I waited. "Johnny wouldn't have made that mistake," he said. "Johnny would have been all awake at once and aware. He would have handled it somehow. He doesn't know how it happened, but even if he did, he wouldn't blame me. He knows I slept hard in those days and took a time to come really awake. He knows I don't think fast. He knows I'm not a brave man. He knew all that from the beginning and still he was my friend."

I waited. He was started on this and he would do it in his own way.

"People think I'm crazy," he said. "Maybe I am. Or maybe they're the ones who're crazy. I don't know and I don't care about that. I just know what I know. It took me a long time to believe it and to have it straight in my mind."

He put his thin old arms behind him and leaned back on them on the cot. "That Mills," he said. "The brother. He was first. Only three years later. He was on a prospecting trip. In the Sacramento Mountains. His packhorse came in without him. A search party found him, what was left of him, at the bottom of a forty-foot cliff. There hadn't been any rain and the tracks were still there. He'd camped several hundred feet away, on the upper level. Sometime, probably in the night, he'd roused and started running. Why would a man do that unless he was running after something or away from something? But there wasn't another track except those of the pack-horse where it'd been tied and finally broke loose and wandered home. He was running, in the dark, and he went over. . . .

"Then the one named Skinner. Five years later. He knew something about pharmacy and he'd started a drugstore along with a trading post in town. He began having headaches, mostly at night, that wouldn't let him sleep well. He'd been a big man and he got thinner and thinner and more stooped and worried-looking. He took to dosing himself with all kinds of pills and powders for those headaches. One night, so his wife told, he got up and stumbled around and went into the store to fix himself something and he took hold of the wrong bottle or can or other kind of container. Suicide, some people said. Accident was the official verdict . . .

"All right. That was two. Coincidence, you might say. The fact is, that's what I did say to myself when I heard about it. Or tried to say . . .

"Then there was Cramer. He had a saloon in town but he sold that and moved on. I heard about him once in a while. I don't know what he was before but he was a restless man now, always trying it some new place, always moving on. He'd settle some place and seem to be doing well, then he'd start drinking and getting careless with money, and then one day he'd just sell out whatever he had for any price and move on. Nine more years it was and I hadn't heard anything about him for a long time and I was handyman for a couple of geologists studying strata over in the Caballo Mountains and I was gathering wood for the cookfire and a magazine some hunter or somebody had left up there caught my eye. There wasn't any breeze blowing that I could feel and yet some of the pages were fluttering so I couldn't miss it. I picked it up and turned a few pages and there he was. Cramer. In a picture with some other men. I checked what it said under the picture and the name was right. There was an article too. It didn't have much about him but it had enough. He'd been up in Montana for a few years guiding hunting parties. The party he was with this time got caught in an early blizzard. It couldn't have been too bad because the rest of the party, who didn't even know the country, pulled out all right. But Cramer got separated from them somehow and never showed again. They found him later, froze stiff, nearly buried in snow where he'd hunched down between some rocks like he'd been hiding from something . . .

"All right. That was three. By that time I knew I had to know about Nordyke. I couldn't find any trace of him. He'd run a kind of overnight and eating place in town but sometime back he'd sold out and just disappeared. I'd work a while and get some money together and then move on trying to find him or something about him. I'd tell myself that was silly but all the same I knew, I just felt, I'd get track of him. It was just a matter of time. About five, close to six years it was and I noticed I was moving north and east. Every time I'd have a new stake and start out again a kind of hunch would set the direction for me. I was up in Nebraska, eastern Nebraska, in a little town there, and I'd checked for the name and I was about broke again and I was sitting on a bench in a little park like a plaza there and a piece of newspaper kept blowing around and finally caught in a bush right beside me. I took hold of it. The edges were all ragged and it was only a little piece but there was one article complete. Some politician was demanding an investigation of certain institutions. He claimed they were poorly run. He referred to what he called the Nordyke case . . .

"All right. I had the name. It was a Lincoln paper. I went to Lincoln and to the public library and looked through back issues of that paper. I found it. All of it or anyway enough. It had happened a few weeks before. This Nordyke, and the first name and initial were right, had been committed to an insane asylum on evidence given by his wife and relatives. He'd been subject to bad nightmares for quite a while and they got worse and he took to sleeping or trying to sleep in a room alone with the door and windows locked and then he even boarded up those windows and then he began having fits in the daytime too. He'd hide somewhere around the house and jump anyone who happened to come near and start shouting for someone to bring a rope. So he was committed to that asylum. They had to take him in a strait-jacket. He wasn't there two days before he got hold of a sheet and tore it into strips and knotted those together and hung himself . . ."

We sat quiet again. I waited.

"All right," he said. "I knew what I had to do. I had to tell him. I wandered around kind of aimless for a while, just working some and waiting, before I understood he wouldn't come to me. Not in any way I could know him. So I came here."

He was silent. He was silent so long I had to speak. "And he was here," I said.

"Of course he was here," he said. "Where else would he be? It isn't finished. There wasn't just four men he saw that night. There was five. But he was always straight and he was my friend and he won't bother me. I have to tell him. And he won't let me. He stays away from me. He shuts me out the way he did that night when he just looked at me once and that was all. The only time I can even try to catch him is when he comes and sits for a while on the branch of that tree. I think he has to do that. It's a kind of ritual he has to go through. And he only does it when everything is just right, the way it was, in a summer month when the moon is about full."

It was so dark in the cabin I could barely make him out now. He was just a shape in the dimness. But I could hear him ease out breath in a sigh. "It'll be about another month now," he said, "before I can try again."

He was silent. I had to push a bit. "Do you really see him?" I said.

"I'm not positive," he said. "Sometimes I do and then again I'm not sure. That's unimportant. I know when he's there. I can feel it, the same as it was that night, that exact moment when he was up on that tree branch. But when I go down there he fades away. He just goes. He shuts me out . . ."

He stopped. He was not just silent. He had stopped. He thought he had told it all and perhaps he had. All the pieces were plain and I could fit them together. But I wanted to be certain. "What is it," I said, "that you have to tell him?"

I could sense him peering at me in the dimness, a bit exasperated, a bit sorry for my stupidity. "I have to tell him," he said, "that they had a gun in my back."

I lay outside on my sleeping bag in the thin grayness before dawn, aware of him inside that old patchwork cabin stretched on his old cot, and I could see the whole thing complete. Nothing more would happen for another swing of the moon in its ancient cycle and what would happen then would be only a repetition of what had happened. There was nothing to hold me now and I had already spent more time than I really had available on this side trip. I would be leaving in a few hours.

I could see it all complete. I thought I could see something of a pattern in it, of the way things happen to and by us midges infesting the epidermis of a lesser planet. For a beginning there was a movement, a convulsion, involving two individual atoms of humanity, a Johnny Yeager and a man named Mills. Not really a beginning, as no movement is ever a beginning only a becoming in an infinite webbed process, because that movement was the result of all those before that had made those two atoms what they were and to behave as they did. But a beginning at least in the sense of a happening isolated, selected, as a starting point. That movement, that impulse, radiating outward, was communicated to the brother, the second

Mills, and through him to three more men, Skinner and Cramer and Nordyke, and the reaction of those four took in another, the agent, Cal Kinney, then a youngish man, now an old man lying in there on that cot. The initial movement and its result, the shooting of the first Mills and the hanging of Yeager, were long since over, done, finished as discernible movements. But the impulse, reinforced, had remained in the minds of four men and a fifth. It held, certainly the evidence suggested that it held, as a strong influence through the years and the lives of those four. It was still strong in the mind of the fifth, influencing him, determining his very existence.

I fell asleep in the satisfaction that sometimes comes when, in the very process of drifting into sleep, you feel that you have really grasped something, have caught hold of something vital that will expand into something valuable when you get to work on it.

And in the late morning light, when I was stowing my things in the car, I didn't think about it because I knew from experience that such notions, such graspings, are elusive and rarely stand practical examination in the wide-awake daytime arena. You have to let them simmer and season in the background of your mind that the psychologists are exploring nowadays and then come forward when they have taken on shape and substance.

He was up and puttering on his morning round, apparently indifferent to me again. He acted as if he had told me nothing, as if the night had not been. Perhaps he regretted telling me; he made no move to share coffee with me. Or perhaps he had seen me packing and had just not bothered. He was crazy, yes, in a harmless way. But I wanted to shake his old hand. He had given me what I had come to find and I wanted to give him something in return.

I went over and stepped in front of him. He stopped and looked at me. I put out my right hand. He put out his and I could feel that spry enduring vigor in the brief clasp. "Could he read?" I said.

He hesitated. I could see the recognition and the reluctant acceptance of a sharing in his old eyes. "Of course he could read," he said.

"He won't wait for you," I said. "You can't tell him. But you can write a note and fasten it to that tree."

He stared at me. At last he nodded a bit. At least I think he nodded. I turned and went to my car. He was still staring after me as I drove away.

So there it is, the account. There remains only the wondering. That remains because of what I did not realize at the time, that the impulse launched by the initial movement, the killing of a man named Mills by a Johnny Yeager, was still radiating outward, still producing effects according to the character of the adjoining atoms.

I say that because it had been communicated to me and it had produced an effect according to the composition of the individual atom that bears my name . . .

I couldn't write that story. It simmered and seasoned in the background of my mind and never came forward in shape and substance. At last I thought I knew why. I did not have it all. It was not finished. There had been and there still was a fifth man.

Eventually I was back in the little southwestern town. I heard what might seem to be a finish. About a month after I left that first time he appeared in town and found a buyer for his old cows and the calf and went out with the buyer and helped bring in the stock and he brought along the few personal things he had and settled in an abandoned shack on the edge of town. He wasn't crazy any more, not in any way that showed. He wasn't anything, except perhaps a nuisance, just another old character who wandered around doing nothing except drink himself into a kind of silly grinning stupor and talk endlessly about the old days with anyone he could get to listen and, when his money gave out, cadge drinks and enough food to stay alive from people in the local cafés and, when the proprietors finally kept him out, panhandle tourists for whatever he could inveigle out of them. It was only about six months later that he went stumbling after a quarter some tourist gave him that fell out of his hand and rolled into the road and he tripped over his own feet and fell right in front of a fast-moving big interstate bus.

So the story of Johnny Yeager and a man named Mills and four more men and a fifth was finished, is finished. But the impulse launched by that movement, that happening isolated, selected, as a starting point, is not finished. It goes on, still radiating outward. It exists in me, in my mind, as a wondering. I reacted to it, I interfered, I nudged old Cal Kinney with the notion that led to his finish. I know, as surely as if I had been there, that about a month after I left, a piece of paper or cardboard or maybe a board was tacked or fastened somehow to that old tree and old Cal Kinney blew out his lamp and got up from his book and went out and sat on the doorstep of that old patchwork cabin. And I know, as surely as if he had told me, that as he watched that tree in the moonlight his old mind solved for itself the problem it had created for itself. Whatever my motive, the result, I can see now, was as inevitable as the result of his mistake, his telling that Johnny Yeager was sleeping on the stable roof.

There was an old man living alone yet not alone at an old aban-doned stage station out in the arid hauntingly beautiful badlands of this southwest where time is an almost tangible dimension of all things and the past is part of the present and life has worked through the dust of millennia. He was crazy, yes, if you see any meaning in that word. But he was a distinct independent individ-ual, a character complete within himself, a whole man, an atom of humanity with a purpose, a meaning, that gave direction to his ex-istence. Does it alter the essential balance that can be seen in that existence of his that its purpose, its meaning, would have seemed ridiculous, unreal, a delusion, to most other people? I interfered. The effect of my interference took that purpose, that meaning, from him. He became just another of those aimless drifting old nuisances who are barely tolerated and whose final passings, usually by one kind of accident or another, are regarded with suppressed relief by those about them.

Was my interference a mistake too? Should I have calculated the possible result instead of simply reacting according to the emotional and thinking-I-was-thinking composition of the individual atom that bears my name? Can the ancient problem of good and evil, of rightness and wrongness, be applied to my interference? I do not know, not with any certainty. But I do know that the impulse launched long ago by Johnny Yeager and a man named Mills still exists, communicated to me, and that it colors, if ever so slightly, my attitude towards and my relationship with all other atoms of hu-manity around me.

And it still radiates outward. If you have followed me this far, it has been communicated, if only in another brief wondering, a brief pondering, to you.

Stubby Pringle's Christmas

HIGH ON THE mountainside by the little line cabin in the crisp clean dusk of evening Stubby Pringle swings into saddle. He has shape of bear in the dimness, bundled thick against cold. Double socks crowd scarred boots. Leather chaps with hair out cover patched corduroy pants. Fleece-lined jacket with wear of winters on it bulges body and heavy gloves blunt fingers. Two gay red bandannas folded together fatten throat under chin. Battered hat is pulled down to sit on ears and in side pocket of jacket are rabbit-skin earmuffs he can put to use if he needs them.

Stubby Pringle swings up into saddle. He looks out and down over worlds of snow and ice and tree and rock. He spreads arms wide and they embrace whole ranges of hills. He stretches tall and hat brushes stars in sky. He is Stubby Pringle, cowhand of the Triple X, and this is his night to howl. He is Stubby Pringle, son of the wild jackass, and he is heading for the Christmas dance at the schoolhouse in the valley.

Stubby Pringle swings up and his horse stands like rock. This is the pride of his string, flop-eared ewe-necked cat-hipped strawberry roan that looks like it should have died weeks ago but has iron rods for bones and nitroglycerin for blood and can go from here to doomsday with nothing more than mouthfuls of snow for water and tufts of winter-cured bunch-grass snatched between drifts for food. It stands like rock. It knows the folly of trying to unseat Stubby. It wastes no energy in futile explosions. It knows that twenty-seven miles of hard winter going are foreordained for this evening and twenty-seven more of harder uphill return by morning. It has done this before. It is saving the dynamite under its hide for the destiny

of a true cowpony which is to take its rider where he wants to go—
and bring him back again.

Stubby Pringle sits his saddle and he grins into cold and distance
and future full of festivity. Join me in a look at what can be seen of
him despite the bundling and frosty breath vapor that soon will
hang icicles on his nose. Those are careless haphazard scrambled
features under the low hatbrim, about as handsome as a blue boar's
snout. Not much fuzz yet on his chin. Why, shucks, is he just a boy?
Don't make that mistake, though his twentieth birthday is still six
weeks away. Don't make the mistake Hutch Handley made last
summer when he thought this was young unseasoned stuff and took
to ragging Stubby and wound up with ears pinned back and upper
lip split and nose mashed flat and the whole of him dumped in a
rainbarrel. Stubby has been taking care of himself since he was or-
phaned at thirteen. Stubby has been doing man's work since he was
fifteen. Do you think Hardrock Harper of the Triple X would have
anything but an all-around hard-proved hand up here at his farthest
winter line camp siding Old Jake Hanlon, toughest hard-bitten old
cowman ever to ride range?

Stubby Pringle slips gloved hand under rump to wipe frost off the
saddle. No sense letting it melt into patches of corduroy pants. He
slaps rightside saddlebag. It contains a burlap bag wrapped around
a two-pound box of candy, of fancy chocolates with variegated interiors he acquired two months ago and has kept hidden from Old
Jake. He slaps leftside saddlebag. It holds a burlap bag wrapped
around a paper parcel that contains a close-folded piece of dress
goods and a roll of pink ribbon. Interesting items, yes. They are
ammunition for the campaign he has in mind to soften the affec-
tions of whichever female of the right vintage among those at the
schoolhouse appeals to him most and seems most susceptible.

Stubby Pringle settles himself firmly into the saddle. He is just
another of far-scattered poorly-paid patched-clothes cowhands that
inhabit these parts and likely marks and smells of his calling have
not all been scrubbed away. He knows that. But this is his night to
howl. He is Stubby Pringle, true-begotten son of the wildest jackass,
and he has been riding line through hell and highwater and winter
storms for two months without a break and he has done his share of
the work and more than his share because Old Jake is getting along
and slowing some and this is his night to stomp floorboards till

schoolhouse shakes and kick heels up to lanterns above and whirl a willing female till she is dizzy enough to see past patched clothes to the man inside them. He wriggles toes deep into stirrups and settles himself firmly in the saddle.

"I could of et them choc'lates," says Old Jake from the cabin doorway. "They wasn't hid good," he says. "No good at all."

"An' be beat like a drum," says Stubby. "An' wrung out like a dirty dishrag."

"By who?" says Old Jake. "By a young un like you? Why, I'd of tied you in knots afore you knew what's what iffen you tried it. You're a dang-blatted young fool," he says. "A ding-busted dang-blatted fool. Riding out a night like this iffen it is Chris'mas eve. A dong-bonging ding-busted dang-blatted fool," he says. "But iffen I was your age agin, I reckon I'd be doing it too." He cackles like an old rooster. "Squeeze one of 'em for me," he says and he steps back inside and he closes the door.

Stubby Pringle is alone out there in the darkening dusk, alone with flop-eared ewe-necked cat-hipped roan that can go to the last trumpet call under him and with cold of wicked winter wind around him and with twenty-seven miles of snow-dumped distance ahead of him. "Wahoo!" he yells. "Skip to my Loo!" he shouts. "Do-si-do and round about!"

He lifts reins and the roan sighs and lifts feet. At easy warming-up amble they drop over the edge of benchland where the cabin snugs into tall pines and on down the great bleak expanse of mountainside.

Stubby Pringle, spurs a jingle, jogs upslope through crusted snow. The roan, warmed through, moves strong and steady under him. Line cabin and line work are far forgotten things back and back and up and up the mighty mass of mountain. He is Stubby Pringle, rooting tooting hard-working hard-playing cowhand of the Triple X, heading for the Christmas dance at the schoolhouse in the valley.

He tops out on one of the lower ridges. He pulls rein to give the roan a breather. He brushes an icicle off his nose. He leans forward and reaches to brush several more off sidebars of old bit in the bridle. He straightens tall. Far ahead, over top of last and lowest ridge, on into the valley, he can see tiny specks of glowing allure that are schoolhouse windows. Light and gaiety and good liquor and fluttering skirts are there. "Wahoo!" he yells. "Gals an' women an' grandmothers!" he shouts. "Raise your skirts and start askipping! I'm acoming!"

He slaps spurs to roan. It leaps like mountain lion, out and down, full into hard gallop downslope, rushing, reckless of crusted drifts and ice-coated bush-branches slapping at them. He is Stubby Pringle, born with spurs on, nursed on tarantula juice, weaned on rawhide, at home in the saddle of a hurricane in shape of horse that can race to outer edge of eternity and back, heading now for high-jinks two months overdue. He is ten feet tall and the horse is gigantic, with wings, iron-boned and dynamite-fueled, soaring in forty-foot leaps down the flank of the whitened wonder of a winter world.

They slow at the bottom. They stop. They look up the rise of the last low ridge ahead. The roan paws frozen ground and snorts twin plumes of frosty vapor. Stubby reaches around to pull down fleece-lined jacket that has worked a bit up back. He pats rightside saddlebag. He pats leftside saddlebag. He lifts reins to soar up and over last low ridge.

Hold it, Stubby. What is that? Off to the right.

He listens. He has ears that can catch snitch of mouse chewing on chunk of bacon rind beyond the log wall by his bunk. He hears. Sound of ax striking wood.

What kind of dong-bonging ding-busted dang-blatted fool would be chopping wood on a night like this and on Christmas Eve and with a dance underway at the schoolhouse in the valley? What kind of chopping is this anyway? Uneven in rhythm, feeble in stroke. Trust Stubby Pringle, who has chopped wood enough for cookstove and fireplace to fill a long freight train, to know how an ax should be handled.

There. That does it. That whopping sound can only mean that the blade has hit at an angle and bounced away without biting. Some dong-bonged ding-busted dang-blatted fool is going to be cutting off some of his own toes.

He pulls the roan around to the right. He is Stubby Pringle, born to tune of bawling bulls and blatting calves, branded at birth, cow-man raised and cowman to the marrow, and no true cowman rides on without stopping to check anything strange on range. Roan chomps on bit, annoyed at interruption. It remembers who is in saddle. It sighs and obeys. They move quietly in dark of night past boles of trees jet black against dim greyness of crusted snow on ground. Light shows faintly ahead. Lantern light through a small oiled-paper window.

Yes. Of course. Just where it has been for eight months now. The Henderson place. Man and woman and small girl and waist-high boy. Homesteaders. Not even fools, homesteaders. Worse than that. Out of their minds altogether. All of them. Out here anyway. Betting the government they can stave off starving for five years in exchange for one hundred sixty acres of land. Land that just might be able to support seven jack-rabbits and two coyotes and nine rattlesnakes and maybe all of four thin steers to a whole section. In a good year. Homesteaders. Always out of almost everything, money and food and tools and smiles and joy of living. Everything. Except maybe hope and stubborn endurance.

Stubby Pringle nudges the reluctant roan along. In patch-light from the window by a tangled pile of dead tree branches he sees a woman. Her face is grey and pinched and tired. An old stocking-cap is pulled down on her head. Ragged man's jacket bumps over long woolsey dress and clogs arms as she tries to swing an ax into a good-sized branch on the ground.

Whopping sound and ax bounces and barely misses an ankle.

"Quit that!" says Stubby, sharp. He swings the roan in close. He looks down at her. She drops ax and backs away, frightened. She is ready to bolt into two-room bark-slab shack. She looks up. She sees that haphazard scrambled features under low hatbrim are crinkled in what could be a grin. She relaxes some, hand on door latch.

"Ma'am," says Stubby. "You trying to cripple yourself?" She just stares at him. "Man's work," he says. "Where's your man?"

"Inside," she says; then, quick, "He's sick."

"Bad?" says Stubby.

"Was," she says. "Doctor that was here this morning thinks he'll be all right now. Only he's almighty weak. All wobbly. Sleeps most of the time."

"Sleeps," says Stubby, indignant. "When there's wood to be chopped."

"He's been almighty tired," she says, quick, defensive. "Even afore he was took sick. Wore out." She is rubbing cold hands together, trying to warm them. "He tried," she says, proud. "Only a while ago. Couldn't even get his pants on. Just fell flat on the floor."

Stubby looks down at her. "An' you ain't tired?" he says.

"I ain't got time to be tired," she says. "Not with all I got to do."

Stubby Pringle looks off past dark boles of trees at last row ridgetop that hides valley and schoolhouse. "I reckon I could spare a bit of time," he says. "Likely they ain't much more'n started yet," he says. He looks again at the woman. He sees grey pinched face. He sees cold-shivering under bumpy jacket. "Ma'am," he says. "Get on in there an' warm your gizzard some. I'll just chop you a bit of wood."

Roan stands with dropping reins, ground-tied, disgusted. It shakes head to send icicles tinkling from bit and bridle. Stopped in midst of epic run, wind-eating, mile-gobbling, iron-boned and dynamite-fueled, and for what? For silly chore of chopping.

Fifteen feet away Stubby Pringle chops wood. Moon is rising over last low ridgetop and its light, filtered through trees, shines on leaping blade. He is Stubby Pringle, moonstruck maverick of the Triple X, born with ax in hands, with strength of stroke in muscles, weaned on whetstone, fed on cordwood, raised to fell whole forests. He is ten feet tall and ax is enormous in moonlight and chips fly like stormflakes of snow and blade slices through branches thick as his arm, through logs thick as his thigh.

He leans ax against a stump and he spreads arms wide and he scoops up whole cords at a time and strides to door and kicks it open . . .

Both corners of front room by fireplace are piled full now, floor to ceiling, good wood, stout wood, seasoned wood, wood enough for a whole wicked winter week. Chore done and done right, Stubby looks around him. Fire is burning bright and well-fed, working on warmth. Man lies on big old bed along opposite wall, blanket over, eyes closed, face grey-pale, snoring long and slow. Woman fusses with something at old woodstove. Stubby steps to doorway to backroom. He pulls aside hanging cloth. Faint in dimness inside he sees two low bunks and in one, under an old quilt, a curly-headed small girl and in the other, under other old quilt, a boy who would be

waist-high awake and standing. He sees them still and quiet, sleeping sound. "Cute little devils," he says.

He turns back and the woman is coming toward him, cup of coffee
in hand, strong and hot and steaming. Coffee the kind to warm the
throat and gizzard of chore-doing hard-chopping cowhand on a cold
cold night. He takes the cup and raises it to his lips. Drains it in
two gulps. "Thank you, ma'am," he says. "That was right kindly of
you." He sets cup on table. "I got to be getting along," he says. He
starts toward outer door.

He stops, hand on door latch. Something is missing in two-room
shack. Trust Stubby Pringle to know what. "Where's your tree?" he
says. "Kids got to have a Christmas tree."

He sees the woman sink down on chair. He hears a sigh come
from her. "I ain't had time to cut one," she says.

"I reckon not," says Stubby. "Man's job anyway," he says. "I'll
get it for you. Won't take a minute. Then I got to be going."

He strides out. He scoops up ax and strides off, upslope some
where small pines climb. He stretches tall and his legs lengthen and
he towers huge among trees swinging with ten-foot steps. He is
Stubby Pringle, born an expert on Christmas trees, nursed on pine
needles, weaned on pine cones, raised with an eye for size and shape
and symmetry. There. A beauty. Perfect. Grown for this and for
nothing else. Ax blade slices keen and swift. Tree topples. He
strides back with tree on shoulder. He rips leather whangs from his
saddle and lashes two pieces of wood to tree bottom, crosswise, so
tree can stand upright again.

Stubby Pringle strides into shack, carrying tree. He sets it up,
center of front-room floor, and it stands straight, trim and straight,
perky and proud and pointed. "There you are, ma'am," he says.
"Get your things out an' start decorating. I got to be going." He
moves toward outer door.

He stops in outer doorway. He hears the sigh behind him. "We
got no things," she says. "I was figuring to buy some but sickness
took the money."

Stubby Pringle looks off at last low ridgetop hiding valley and
schoolhouse. "Reckon I still got a bit of time," he says. "They'll be
whooping it mighty late." He turns back, closing door. He sheds
hat and gloves and bandannas and jacket. He moves about checking everything in the sparse front room. He asks for things and the

woman jumps to get those few of them she has. He tells her what to do and she does. He does plenty himself. With this and with that magic wonders arrive. He is Stubby Pringle, born to poverty and hard work, weaned on nothing, fed on less, raised to make do with least possible and make the most of that. Pinto beans strung on thread brighten tree in firelight and lantern light like strings of store-bought beads. Strips of one bandanna, cut with shears from sewing-box, bob in bows on branch-ends like gay red flowers. Snippets of fleece from jacket-lining sprinkled over tree glisten like fresh fall of snow. Miracles flow from strong blunt fingers through bits of old paper-bags and dabs of flour paste into link chains and twisted small streamers and two jaunty little hats and two smart little boats with sails.

"Got to finish it right," says Stubby Pringle. From strong blunt fingers comes five-pointed star, triple-thickness to make it stiff, twisted bit of old wire to hold it upright. He fastens this to topmost tip of topmost bough. He wraps lone bandanna left around throat and jams battered hat on head and shrugs into now-skimpy-lined jacket. "A right nice little tree," he says. "All you got to do now is get out what you got for the kids and put it under. I really got to be going." He starts toward outer door.

He stops in open doorway. He hears the sigh behind him. He knows without looking around the woman has slumped into old rocking chair. "We ain't got anything for them," she says. "Only now this tree. Which I don't mean it isn't a fine grand tree. It's more'n we'd of had 'cept for you."

Stubby Pringle stands in open doorway looking out into cold clean moonlit night. Somehow he knows without turning head two tears are sliding down thin pinched cheeks. "You go on along," she says. "They're good young uns. They know how it is. They ain't expecting a thing."

Stubby Pringle stands in open doorway looking out at last ridge-top that hides valley and schoolhouse. "All the more reason," he says soft to himself. "All the more reason something should be there when they wake." He sighs too. "I'm a dong-bonging ding-busted dang-blatted fool," he says. "But I reckon I still got a mite more time. Likely they'll be sashaying around till it's most morning."

Stubby Pringle strides on out, leaving door open. He strides back, closing door with heel behind him. In one hand he has burlap bag wrapped around paper parcel. In other hand he has squarish chunk of good pine wood. He tosses bag-parcel into lap-folds of woman's apron.

"Unwrap it," he says. "There's the makings for a right cute dress for the girl. Needle-and-threader like you can whip it up in no time. I'll just whittle me out a little something for the boy."

Moon is high in cold cold sky. Frosty clouds drift up there with it. Tiny flakes of snow float through upper air. Down below by a two-room shack droops a disgusted cowpony roan, ground-tied, drooping like statue snow-crusted. It is accepting the inescapable destiny of its kind which is to wait for its rider, to conserve deep-bottomed dynamite energy, to be ready to race to the last margin of motion when waiting is done.

Inside the shack fire in fireplace cheerily gobbles wood, good wood, stout wood, seasoned wood, warming two-rooms well. Man lies on bed, turned on side, curled up some, snoring slow and steady. Woman sits in rocking chair, sewing. Her head nods slow and drowsy and her eyelids sag weary but her fingers fly, stitch-stitch-stitch. A dress has shaped under her hands, small and flounced and with little puff-sleeves, fine dress, fancy dress, dress for smiles and joy of living. She is sewing pink ribbon around collar and down front and into fluffy bow on back.

On a stool nearby sits Stubby Pringle, piece of good pine wood in one hand, knife in other hand, fine knife, splendid knife, all-around-accomplished knife, knife he always has with him, seven-bladed knife with four for cutting from little to big and corkscrew and can opener and screwdriver. Big cutting blade has done its work. Little cutting blade is in use now. He is Stubby Pringle, born with feel for knives in hand, weaned on emery wheel, fed on shavings, raised to whittle his way through the world. Tiny chips fly and shavings flutter. There in his hands, out of good pine wood, something is shaping. A horse. Yes. Flop-eared ewe-necked cat-hipped horse. Flop-eared head is high on ewe neck, stretched out, sniffing wind, snorting into distance. Cat-hips are hunched forward, caught in crouch for forward leap. It is a horse fit to carry a waist-high boy to uttermost edge of eternity and back.

Stubby Pringle carves swift and sure. Little cutting blade makes final little cutting snitches. Yes. Tiny mottlings and markings make no mistaking. It is a strawberry roan. He closes knife and puts it in pocket. He looks up. Dress is finished in woman's lap. But woman's head has dropped down in exhaustion. She sits slumped deep in rocking chair and she too snores slow and steady.

Stubby Pringle stands up. He takes dress and puts it under tree, fine dress, fancy dress, dress waiting now for small girl to wake and wear it with smiles and joy of living. He sets wooden horse beside it, fine horse, proud horse, snorting-into-distance horse, cat-hips crouched, waiting now for waist-high boy to wake and ride it around the world.

Quietly he piles wood on fire and banks ashes around to hold it for morning. Quietly he pulls on hat and wraps bandanna around and shrugs into skimpy-lined jacket. He looks at old rocking chair and tired woman slumped in it. He strides to outer door and out, leaving door open. He strides back, closing door with heel behind. He carries other burlap bag wrapped around box of candy, of fine chocolates, fancy chocolates with variegated interiors. Gently he lays this in lap of woman. Gently he takes big old shawl from wall nail and lays this over her. He stands by big old bed and looks down at snoring man. "Poor devil," he says. "Ain't fair to forget him." He takes knife from pocket, fine knife, seven-bladed knife, and lays this on blanket on bed. He picks up gloves and blows out lantern and swift as sliding moon shadow he is gone.

High high up frosty clouds scuttle across face of moon. Wind whips through topmost tips of tall pines. What is it that hurtles like hurricane far down there on upslope of last low ridge, scattering drifts, smashing through brush, snorting defiance at distance? It is flop-eared ewe-necked cat-hipped roan, iron boned and dynamite fueled, ramming full gallop through the dark of night. Firm in saddle is Stubby Pringle, spurs ajingle, toes atingle, out on prowl, ready to howl, heading for the dance at the schoolhouse in the valley. He is ten feet tall, great as a grizzly, and the roan is gigantic, with wings, soaring upward in thirty-foot leaps. They top out and roan rears high, pawing stars out of sky, and drops down, cat-hips hunched for fresh leap out and down.

Hold it, Stubby. Hold hard on reins. Do you see what is happening on out there in the valley?

Tiny lights that are schoolhouse windows are winking out. Tiny dark shapes moving about are horsemen riding off, are wagons pulling away.

Moon is dropping down the sky, haloed in frosty mist. Dark grey clouds dip and swoop around sweep of horizon. Cold winds weave rustling through ice-coated bushes and trees. What is that moving slow and lonesome up snow-covered mountainside? It is a flop-eared ewe-necked cat-hipped roan, just that, nothing more, small cowpony, worn and weary, taking its rider back to clammy bunk in cold line cabin. Slumped in saddle is Stubby Pringle, head down, shoulders sagged. He is just another of far-scattered poorly-paid patched-clothes cowhands who inhabit these parts. Just that. And something more. He is the biggest thing there is in the whole wide roster of the human race. He is a man who has given of himself, of what little he has and is, to bring smiles and joy of living to others along his way.

He jogs along, slump-sagged in saddle, thinking of none of this. He is thinking of dances undanced, of floorboards unstomped, of willing women left unwhirled.

He jogs along, half-asleep in saddle, and he is thinking now of bygone Christmas seasons and of a boy born to poverty and hard work and make-do poring in flicker of firelight over ragged old Christmas picturebook. And suddenly he hears something. The tinkle of sleigh bells.

Sleigh bells?

Yes. I am telling this straight. He and roan are weaving through thick-clumped brush. Winds are sighing high overhead and on up the mountainside and lower down here they are whipping mists and snow flurries all around him. He can see nothing in mystic moving dimness. But he can hear. The tinkle of sleigh bells, faint but clear, ghostly but unmistakable. And suddenly he sees something. Movement off to the left. Swift as wind, glimmers only through brush and mist and whirling snow, but unmistakable again. Antlered heads high, frosty breath streaming, bodies rushing swift and silent, floating in flash of movement past, seeming to leap in air alone needing no touch of ground beneath. Reindeer? Yes. Reindeer strong and silent and fleet out of some far frozen northland marked on no map.

Reindeer swooping down and leaping past and rising again and away, strong and effortless and fleeting. And with them, hard on their heels, almost lost in swirling snow mist of their passing, vague and formless but there, something big and bulky with runners like sleigh and flash of white beard whipping in wind and crack of long whip snapping.

Startled roan has seen something too. It stands rigid, head up, staring left and forward. Stubby Pringle, body atingle, stares too. Out of dark of night ahead, mingled with moan of wind, comes a long-drawn chuckle, deep deep chuckle, jolly and cheery and full of smiles and joy of living. And with it long-drawn words.

We-e-e-l-l-l do-o-o-ne . . . pa-a-a-artner!

Stubby Pringle shakes his head. He brushes an icicle from his nose. "An' I didn't have a single drink," he says. "Only coffee an' can't count that. Reckon I'm getting soft in the head." But he is cowman through and through, cowman through to the marrow. He can't ride on without stopping to check anything strange on his range. He swings down and leads off to the left. He fumbles in jacket pocket and finds a match. Strikes it. Holds it cupped and bends down. There they are. Unmistakable. Reindeer tracks.

Stubby Pringle stretches up tall. Stubby Pringle swings into saddle. Roan needs no slap of spurs to unleash strength in upward surge, up up up steep mountainside. It knows. There in saddle once more is Stubby Pringle, moonstruck maverick of the Triple X, all-around hard-proved hard-honed cowhand, ten feet tall, needing horse gigantic, with wings, iron-boned and dynamite-fueled, to take him home to little line cabin and some few winks of sleep before another day's hard work . . .

Stubby Pringle slips into cold clammy bunk. He wriggles vigorous to warm blanket under and blanket over.

"Was it worth all that riding?" comes voice of Old Jake Hanlon from other bunk on other wall.

"Why, sure," says Stubby. "I had me a right good time."

All right, now. Say anything you want. I know, you know, any dong-bonged ding-busted dang-blatted fool ought to know, that icicles breaking off branches can sound to drowsy ears something like sleigh bells. That blurry eyes half-asleep can see strange things.

That deer and elk make tracks like those of reindeer. That wind sighing and soughing and moaning and maundering down mountains and through piny treetops can sound like someone shaping words. But we could talk and talk and it would mean nothing to Stubby Pringle.

Stubby is wiser than we are. He knows, he will always know, who it was, plump and jolly and belly-bouncing, that spoke to him that night out on wind-whipped winter-worn mountainside.

We-e-e-l-l-l do-o-o-ne . . . pa-a-a-rt-ner!